P9-DVQ-345

LONG-TIME LISTENER, FIRST-TIME WEREWOLF

LONG-TIME LISTENER, FIRST-TIME WEREWOLF

KITTY AND THE MIDNIGHT HOUR
KITTY GOES TO WASHINGTON
KITTY TAKES A HOLIDAY

CARRIE VAUGHN

FANTASY

The characters and events in this book are fictitious. Any similarity to real persons, living or dead, is coincidental and not intended by the author.

KITTY AND THE MIDNIGHT HOUR Copyright © 2005 by Carrie Vaughn
    Publication History: Warner Books paperback, November 2005
KITTY GOES TO WASHINGTON Copyright © 2006 by Carrie Vaughn
    Publication History: Warner Books paperback, July 2006
"Kitty Meets the Band" Copyright © 2006 by Carrie Vaughn
    Publication History: first appeared in KITTY GOES TO WASHINGTON
KITTY TAKES A HOLIDAY Copyright © 2007 by Carrie Vaughn
    Publication History: Warner Books paperback, April 2007

First SFBC Science Fiction Printing: April 2007

All rights reserved. Except as permitted under the U.S. Copyright Act of 1976, no part of this publication may be reproduced, or transmitted in any form or by any means, or stored in a database or retrieval system, without the prior written permission of the publisher.

Published by arrangement with:
Warner Books
Hachette Book Group USA
1271 Avenue of the Americas
New York, NY 10020

Visit the SFBC online at http://www.sfbc.com

ISBN 978-0-7394-8276-6

Printed in the United States of America.

Contents

Kitty and the
Midnight
Hour

The first one's for Mom and Dad.
Thanks for all the stamps.

Acknowledgments

Many thanks to Paula Balafas of the Wheatridge Police Department, for checking the police stuff, and for being a stalwart literary partner in crime at CU.

Thanks to my housemates when I was writing this: Joe "Max" Campanella, for the radio and music insights, the advice, the high fives, and the shoulder; and Yaz Ostrowski for beta testing, and for the immortal words, "Don't make me hungry. You won't like me when I'm hungry."

Thanks to the Odfellows, Odyssey Fantasy Writing Workshop graduates, especially the Naked Squirrels, and to the WACO writing group (Michael Bateman, Barry Fishler, Karen Fishler, Brian Hiebert, and James Van Pelt), most of whom have had to deal with Kitty in her various incarnations. I'd especially like to thank Jeanne Cavelos for her always enthusiastic support.

I could keep thanking people for pages, but let's just add a few more: to Thomas Seay for his giddy anticipation; to George Scithers, Darrell Schweitzer, and the staff at *Weird Tales*, who gave Kitty her first home; to Dan Hooker, who called the day after I almost decided to quit; to Jaime Levine, for "getting it" in ways that exceeded my wildest expectations.

And finally, to Robbie, my biggest fan, and to Debbie, for humoring us.

A portion of Chapter 5 appeared in *Weird Tales* #324 (Summer 2001) as "Doctor Kitty Solves All Your Love Problems."

A portion of Chapter 8 appeared in *Weird Tales* #333 (Fall 2003) as "Kitty Loses Her Faith."

THE PLAYLIST

When I finished the first draft of *Kitty and the Midnight Hour*, I burned a CD of some of the music I listened to while writing it. Here's that impromptu sound track:

Creedence Clearwater Revival, "Bad Moon Rising"
Concrete Blonde, "Bloodletting"
Siouxsie and the Banshees, "Peek-a-Boo"
No Doubt, "Just a Girl"
Garbage, "When I Grow Up"
David Bowie, "Let's Dance"
They Might Be Giants, "Man, It's So Loud In Here"
Oingo Boingo, "Skin"
Creedence Clearwater Revival, "Long as I Can See the Light"
The Sisters of Mercy, "Lucretia My Reflection"
Rasputina, "Olde Headboard"
Depeche Mode, "Halo"
The Canadian Brass, Bach's "Sheep May Safely Graze"
The Clash, "Train in Vain"
Peter Murphy, "I'll Fall With Your Knife"

I tossed my backpack in a corner of the studio and high-fived Rodney on his way out.

"Hey, Kitty, thanks again for taking the midnight shift," he said. He'd started playing some third-generation grunge band that made my hackles rise, but I smiled anyway.

"Happy to."

"I noticed. You didn't used to like the late shift."

He was right. I'd gone positively nocturnal the last few months. I shrugged. "Things change."

"Well, take it easy."

Finally, I had the place to myself. I dimmed the lights so the control board glowed, the dials and switches futuristic and sinister. I pulled my blond hair into a ponytail. I was wearing jeans and an oversized sweatshirt that had been through the wash too many times. One of the nice things about the late shift at a radio station was that I didn't have to look good for anybody.

I put on the headphones and sat back in the chair with its squeaky wheels and torn upholstery. As soon as I could, I put on *my* music. Bauhaus straight into the Pogues. That'd wake 'em up. To be a DJ was to be God. I controlled the airwaves. To be a DJ at an alternative public radio station? That was being God with a mission. It was thinking you were the first person to discover The Clash and you had to spread the word.

My illusions about the true power of being a radio DJ had pretty much been shattered by this time. I'd started out on the college radio station, graduated a couple of years ago, and got the gig at KNOB after interning here. I might have had a brain full of philosophical tenets, high ideals, and opinions I couldn't wait to vocalize. But off-campus, no one cared. The world was a bigger place than that, and I was adrift. College was supposed to fix that, wasn't it?

I switched on the mike.

"Good evening to you, Denver. This is Kitty on K-Nob. It's twelve-oh-twelve in the wee hours and I'm bored, which means I'm going to regale you with inanities until somebody calls and requests a song recorded before 1990.

"I have the new issue of *Wide World of News* here. Picked it up when I got my frozen burrito for dinner. Headline says: 'Bat Boy Attacks Convent.' Now, this is like the tenth Bat Boy story they've done this year. That kid really gets around—though as long as they've been doing stories on him he's got to be what, fifty? Anyway, as visible as this guy is, at least according to the intrepid staff of *Wide World of News*, I figure somebody out there has seen him. Have any of you seen the Bat Boy? I want to hear about it. The line is open."

Amazingly, I got a call right off. I wouldn't have to beg.

"Hello!"

"Uh, yeah, dude. Hey. Uh, can you play some Pearl Jam?"

"What did I say? Did you hear me? Nothing after '89. Bye."

Another call was waiting. Double cool. "Hi there."

"Do you believe in vampires?"

I paused. Any other DJ would have tossed off a glib response without thinking—just another midnight weirdo looking for attention. But I knew better.

"If I say yes, will you tell me a good story?"

"So, do you?" The speaker was male. His voice was clear and steady.

I put my smile into my voice. "Yes."

"The Bat Boy stories, I think they're a cover-up. All those tabloid stories, and the TV shows like *Uncharted World*?"

"Yeah?"

"Everybody treats them like they're a joke. Too far out, too crazy. Just mindless trash. So if everybody thinks that stuff is a joke, if there really is something out there—no one would believe it."

"Kind of like hiding in plain sight, is that what you're saying? Talk about weird supernatural things just enough to make them look ridiculous and you deflect attention from the truth."

"Yes, that's it."

"So, who exactly is covering up what?"

"*They* are. The vampires. They're covering up, well, everything. Vampires, werewolves, magic, crop circles—"

"Slow down there, Van Helsing."

"Don't call me that!" He sounded genuinely angry.

"Why not?"

"It's—I'm not anything like him. He was a murderer."

The hairs on my arms stood on end. I leaned into the mike. "And what are you?"

He let out a breath that echoed over the phone. "Never mind. I called about the tabloid."

"Yes, Bat Boy. You think Bat Boy is a vampire?"

"Maybe not specifically. But before you brush it off, think about what may really be out there."

Actually, I didn't have to. I already knew.

"Thanks for the tip."

He hung up.

"What an intriguing call," I said, half to myself, almost forgetting I was on the air.

The world he talked about—vampires, werewolves, things that go bump—was a secret one, even to the people who inadvertently found their way there. People fell into it by accident and were left to sink or swim. Usually sink. Once inside, you especially didn't talk about it to outsiders because, well, who would believe you?

But we weren't really *talking* here, were we? It was late-night radio. It was a joke.

I squared my shoulders, putting my thoughts back in order. "Right. This raises all sorts of possibilities. I have to know—did I just get a call from some wacko? Or is something really out there? Do you have a story to tell about something that isn't supposed to exist? Call me." I put on Concrete Blonde while I waited.

The light on the phone showing an incoming call flashed before the song's first bass chord sounded. I wasn't sure I wanted anyone to call. If I could keep making jokes, I could pretend that everything was normal.

I picked up the phone. "Hold, please," I said and waited for the song to end. I took a few deep breaths, half-hoping that maybe the caller just wanted to hear some Pearl Jam.

"All right. Kitty here."

"Hi—I think I know what that guy's talking about. You know how they say that wolves have been extinct around here for over fifty years? Well—my folks have a cabin up in Nederland, and I swear I've heard wolves howling around there. Every summer I've heard them. I called the wildlife people about it once, but they just told me the same thing. They're extinct. But I don't believe them."

"Are you sure they're wolves? Maybe they're coyotes." That was me trying to act normal. Playing the skeptic. But I'd been to those woods, and I knew she was right. Well, half-right.

"I know what coyotes sound like, and it's not anything like that. Maybe—maybe they're something else. Werewolves or something, you know?"

"Have you ever seen them?"

"No. I'm kind of afraid to go out there at night."

"That's probably just as well. Thanks for calling."

As soon as I hung up, the next call was waiting. "Hello?"

"Hi—do you think that guy was really a vampire?"

"I don't know. Do you think he was?"

"Maybe. I mean—I go to nightclubs a lot, and sometimes people show up there, and they just don't fit. They're, like, way too cool for the place, you know? Like, scary cool, like they should be in Hollywood or something and what the hell are they doing *here*—"

"Grocery shopping?"

"Yeah, exactly!"

"Imagination is a wonderful thing. I'm going to go to the next call now—hello?"

"Hi. I gotta say—if there really were vampires, don't you think someone would have noticed by now? Bodies with bite marks dumped in alleys—"

"Unless the coroner reports cover up cause of death—"

The calls kept coming.

"Just because someone's allergic to garlic doesn't mean—"

"What is it with blood anyway—"

"If a girl who's a werewolf got pregnant, what would happen to the baby when she changed into a wolf? Would it change into a wolf cub?"

"Flea collars. And rabies shots. Do werewolves need rabies shots?"

Then came the Call. Everything changed. I'd been toeing the line, keeping things light. Keeping them unreal. I was trying to be normal, really I was. I worked hard to keep my real life—my day job, so to speak—away from the rest. I'd been trying to keep this from slipping all the way into that other world I still hadn't learned to live in very well.

Lately, it had felt like a losing battle.

"Hi, Kitty." His voice was tired, flat. "I'm a vampire. I know you believe me." My belief must have showed through in my voice all night. That must have been why he called me.

"Okay," I said.

"Can—can I talk to you about something?"

"Sure."

"I'm a vampire. I was attacked and turned involuntarily about five years ago. I'm also—at least I used to be—a devout Catholic. It's been really . . . hard. All the jokes about blood and the Eucharist aside—I can't walk into a church anymore. I can't go to Mass. And I can't kill myself because *that's* wrong. Catholic doctrine teaches that my soul is lost, that I'm a blot on God's creation. But Kitty—that's not what I feel. Just because my heart has stopped beating doesn't mean I've lost my soul, does it?"

I wasn't a minister; I wasn't a psychologist. I'd majored in English, for crying out loud. I wasn't qualified to counsel anyone on his spiritual life. But my heart went out to him, because he sounded so sad. All I could do was try.

"You can't exactly go to your local priest to hash this out, can you?"

"No," he said, chuckling a little.

"Right. Have you ever read *Paradise Lost*?"

"Uh, no."

"Of course not, no one reads anymore. *Paradise Lost* is Milton's great epic poem about the war in heaven, the rebellion of the angels, the fall of Lucifer, and the expulsion of Adam and Eve from the Garden of Eden. As an aside, some people believe this was the time when vampires and lycanthropes came into existence—Satan's mockery of God's greatest creation. Whatever. At any rate, in the first few chapters, Satan is the hero. He speaks long monologues what he's thinking, his soul-searching. He's debating about whether or not to take revenge on God for exiling him from heaven. After reading this for a while, you realize that Satan's greatest sin, his greatest mistake, wasn't pride or rebelling against God. His greatest mistake was believing that God would not forgive him if he asked for forgiveness. His sin wasn't just pride—it was self-pity. I think in some ways every single person, human, vampire, whatever, has a choice to make: to be full of rage about what happens to you or to reconcile with it, to strive for the most honorable existence you can despite the odds. Do you believe in a God who understands and forgives or one who doesn't? What it comes down to is, this is between you and God, and you'll have to work that out for yourself."

"That—that sounds okay. Thanks. Thanks for talking to me."

"You're welcome."

At 4:00 A.M., the next shift came on. I didn't go straight home and to bed, even though I was shaking. All the talking had taken a lot out of me. After a late shift I always met T.J. for coffee at the diner down the street. He'd be waiting for me.

He wasn't, but I ordered coffee and when it arrived, so did he. Slouching in an army surplus coat, glancing around to take note of every person in the place, he didn't look at me until he slid into the booth.

"Hey, Kitty." He flagged the waitress for a cup of coffee. The sky outside was gray, paling with the sunrise. "How'd your shift go?"

"You didn't listen to it?" I tried not to sound disappointed, but I'd been hoping to talk to him about it.

"No, sorry. I was out."

I closed my eyes and took a deep, quiet breath. Grease, cigarette smoke, bad breath, and tired nerves. My senses took it all in, every little odor. But strongest, right across the booth from me, was the earthy smell of forest, damp night air, and fur. The faintest touch of blood set my hair on end.

"You went running. You turned wolf," I said, frowning. He looked away, ducking his gaze. "Geez, if you keep doing that, you're going to lose it completely—"

"I know, I know. I'm halfway there already. I just—it feels *so good*." His look grew distant, vacant. Part of him was still in that forest, running wild in the body of his wolf.

The only time we had to Change was on full moon nights. But we could Change whenever we wanted. Some did as often as they could, all the time. And the more they did, the less human they became. They went in packs even as people, living together, shapeshifting and hunting together, cutting all ties to the human world. The more they Changed, the harder it was not to.

"Come with me next time. Tomorrow."

"Full moon's not for another week," I said. "I'm trying my damnedest to keep it together. I like being human."

He looked away, tapping his fork on the table. "You really aren't cut out for this life, you know."

"I do okay."

That was me patting myself on the back for not going stark raving mad these last couple of years, since the attack that changed me. Or not getting myself ripped limb from limb by other werewolves who saw a cute young thing like me as easy prey. All that, and I maintained a semblance of normal human life as well.

Not much of a human life, all things considered. I had a rapidly aging bachelor's degree from CU, a run-down studio apartment, a two-bit DJ gig that barely paid rent, and no prospects. Sometimes, running off to the woods and never coming back sounded pretty good.

Three months ago, I missed my mother's birthday party because it fell on the night of the full moon. I couldn't be there, smiling and sociable in my folks' suburban home in Aurora while the wolf part of me was on the verge of tearing herself free, gnawing through the last fringes of my self-control. I made some excuse, and Mom said she understood. But it showed so clearly how, in an argument between the two halves, the wolf usually won. Since then, maintaining enthusiasm for the human life had been difficult. Useless, even. I slept through the day, worked nights, and thought more and more about those times I ran in the forest as a wolf, with the rest of the pack surrounding me. I was on the verge of trading one family for the other.

I went home, slept, and rolled back to KNOB toward evening. Ozzie, the station manager, an aging hippie type who wore his thinning hair in a ponytail, handed me a stack of papers. Phone messages, every one of them.

"What's this?"

"I was going to ask you the same thing. What the hell happened on your shift last night? We've been getting calls all day. The line was busy all night. And the messages—six people claiming to be vampires, two say they're werewolves, and one wants to know if you can recommend a good exorcist."

"Really?" I said, sorting through the messages.

"Yeah. Really. But what I *really* want to know—" He paused, and I wondered how much trouble I was in. I was supposed to run a late-night variety music format, the kind of show where Velvet Underground followed Ella Fitzgerald. Thinking back on it, I'd talked the entire time, hadn't I? I'd turned it into a talk show. I was going to lose my job, and I didn't think I'd have the initiative to get another one. I could run to the woods and let the Wolf take over.

Then Ozzie said, "Whatever you did last night—can you do it again?"

The second episode of the show that came to be called *The Midnight Hour* (I would always consider that first surprising night to be the first episode) aired a week later. That gave me time to do some research. I dug up half a dozen articles published in second-string medical journals and one surprisingly high-level government research project, a kind of medical Project Blue Book. It was a study on "paranatural biology" sponsored by the National Institutes of Health and the Centers for Disease Control and Prevention. Researchers attempted to document empirical evidence of the existence of creatures such as vampires, lycanthropes, etcetera. They more than attempted it—they *did* document it: photos, charts, case histories, statistics. They concluded that these phenomena were not widespread enough to warrant government attention.

The documentation didn't surprise me—there wasn't anything there I hadn't seen before, in one form or another. It surprised me that anyone from the supernatural underworld would have participated in such a study. Where had they gotten test subjects? The study didn't say much about those subjects, seemingly regarding them in the same way one would disposable lab rats. This raised a whole other set of issues, which gave me lots to talk about.

Pulling all this together, at least part of the medical community was admitting to the existence of people like me. I started the show by laying out all this information. Then I opened the line for calls.

"It's a government conspiracy . . ."

". . . because the Senate is run by bloodsucking fiends!"

"Which doesn't in fact mean they're vampires, but still . . ."

"So when is the NIH going to go public . . ."

". . . medical schools running secret programs . . ."

"Is the public really ready for . . ."

"... a more enlightened time, surely we wouldn't be hunted down like animals ..."

"Would lycanthropy victims be included in the Americans with Disabilities Act?"

My time slot flew by. The week after that, my callers and I speculated about which historical figures had been secret vampires or werewolves. My favorite, suggested by an intrepid caller: General William T. Sherman was a werewolf. I looked him up, and seeing his photo, I could believe it. All the other Civil War generals were straitlaced, with buttoned collars and trimmed beards, but Sherman had an open collar, scruffy hair, five-o'clock shadow, and a screw-you expression. Oh yeah. The week after that I handled a half-dozen calls on how to tell your family you were a vampire or a werewolf. I didn't have any good answers on that one—I hadn't told my family. Being a radio DJ was already a little too weird for them.

And so on. I'd been doing the show for two months when Ozzie called me at home.

"Kitty, you gotta get down here."

"Why?"

"Just get down here."

I pondered a half-dozen nightmare scenarios. I was being sued for something I'd said on the air. The Baptist Church had announced a boycott. Well, that could be a good thing. Free publicity and all. Or someone had gone and got themselves or someone else killed because of the show.

It took half an hour to get there, riding the bus. I hadn't showered and was feeling grouchy. Whatever it was Ozzie was going to throw at me, I just wanted to get it over with.

The door to his office was open. I shoved my hands into the pockets of my jacket and slouched. "Ozzie?"

He didn't look up from the mountains of paper, books, and newspapers spread over his desk. A radio in the corner was tuned to KNOB. A news broadcast mumbled at low volume. "Come in, shut the door."

I did. "What's wrong?"

He looked up. "Wrong? Nothing's wrong. Here, take a look at this." He offered a packet of papers.

The pages were dense with print and legalese. These were contracts. I only caught one word before my eyes fogged over.

Syndication.

When I looked at Ozzie again, his hands were folded on the desk and he was grinning. That was a pretty big canary he'd just eaten. "What do you think? I've had calls from a dozen stations wanting to run your show. I'll sign on as producer. You'll get a raise for every new market we pick up. Are you in?"

This was big. This was going national, at least on a limited scale. I tried to read the proposal. L.A. They wanted me in L.A.? This was . . . unbelievable. I sat against the table and started giggling. Wow. Wow wow wow wow. There was no way I could do this. That would require responsibility, commitment—things I'd shied away from like the plague since . . . since I'd started hanging out with people like T.J.

But if I didn't, someone else would, now that the radio community had gotten the idea. And dammit, this was my baby.

I said, "I'm going to need a website."

That night I went to T.J.'s place, a shack he rented behind an auto garage out toward Arvada. T.J. didn't have a regular job. He fixed motorcycles for cash and didn't sweat the human world most of the time. I came over for supper a couple of times a week. He was an okay cook. More important than his cooking ability, he was able to indulge the appetite for barely cooked steaks.

I'd known T.J. forever, it seemed like. He helped me out when I was new to things, more than anyone else in the local pack. He'd become a friend. He wasn't a bully—a lot of people used being a werewolf as an excuse for behaving badly. I felt more comfortable around him than just about anyone. I didn't have to pretend to be human around him.

I found him in the shed outside. He was working on his bike, a fifteen-year-old Yamaha that was his pride and joy and required constant nursing. He tossed the wrench into the toolbox and reached to give me a hug, greasy hands and all.

"You're perky," he said. "You're practically glowing."

"We're syndicating the show. They're going to broadcast it in L.A. Can you believe that? I'm syndicated!"

He smiled. "Good for you."

"I want to celebrate," I said. "I want to go out. I found this all-ages hole-in-the-wall. The vampires don't go there. Will you come with me?"

"I thought you didn't like going out. You don't like it when we go out with Carl and the pack."

Carl was the alpha male of our pack, god and father by any other name. He was the glue that held the local werewolves together. He protected us, and we were loyal to him.

When Carl went out with his pack, he did it to mark territory, metaphorically speaking. Show off the strength of the pack in front of the local vampire Family. Pissing contests and dominance games.

"That's not any fun. I want to have *fun*."

"You know you ought to tell Carl, if you want to go out."

I frowned. "He'll tell me not to." A pack of wolves was a show of strength. One or two wolves alone were vulnerable. But I wanted this to be *my* celebration, a human celebration, not the pack's.

But the thing about being part of a pack was needing a friend at your back. It wouldn't have felt right for me to go alone. I needed T.J. And maybe T.J. needed Carl.

I tried one more time, shameless begging, but I had no dignity. "Come on, what could possibly happen? Just a couple of hours. Please?"

T.J. picked up a rag off the handlebars and wiped his hands. He smirked at me like the indulgent older brother he'd become. If I'd been a wolf, my tail would have been wagging hopefully.

"Okay. I'll go with you. Just for a couple of hours."

I sighed, relieved.

The club, Livewire, got a deal on the back rooms of a converted warehouse at the edge of Lodo, just a few blocks from Coors Field, when the downtown district was at the start of its "revitalization" phase. It didn't have a flashy marquee. The entrance was around the corner from the main drag, a garage-type rolling door that used to be part of a loading dock. Inside, the girders and venting were kept exposed. Techno and industrial pouring through the woofers rumbled the walls, audible outside as a vibration. That was the only sign there was anything here. Vampires liked to gather at places that had lines out front—trendy, flashy places that attracted the kind of trendy, flashy people they could impress and seduce with their excessive sense of style.

I didn't have to dress up. I wore grubby, faded jeans, a black tank top, and had my hair in two braids. I planned on dancing till my bones hurt.

Unfortunately, T.J. was acting like a bodyguard. His expression was relaxed enough, and he walked with his hands in his jacket pockets like nothing was wrong, but he was looking all around and his nostrils flared, taking in scents.

"This is it," I said, guiding him to the door of the club. He stepped around me so he could enter first.

There was always—would always be—a part of me that walked into a crowded room and immediately thought, *sheep*. Prey. A hundred bodies pressed together, young hearts beating, filled with blood, running hot. I squeezed my hands into fists. I could rip into any of them. I could. I took a deep breath and let that knowledge fade.

I smelled sweat, perfume, alcohol, cigarettes. Some darker things: Someone nearby had recently shot up on heroin. I felt the tremor in his heartbeat, smelled the poison on his skin. If I concentrated, I could hear individual conversations happening in the bar, ten paces away. The music flowed through my shoes. Sisters of Mercy was playing.

"I'm going to go dance," I said to T.J., who was still surveying the room.

"I'm going to go check out the cute boys in the corner." He nodded to where a couple of guys in tight leather pants were talking.

It was a pity about T.J., really. But the cutest, nicest guys were always gay, weren't they?

I was a radio DJ before I became a werewolf. I'd always loved dancing, sweating out the beat of the music. I joined the press of bodies pulsing on the dance floor, not as a monster with thoughts of slaughter, but as me. I hadn't been really dancing in a club like this since the attack, when I became what I am. Years. Crowds were hard to handle sometimes. But when the music was loud, when I was anonymous in a group, I stopped worrying, stopped caring, lived in the moment.

Letting the music guide me, I closed my eyes. I sensed every body around me, every beating heart. I took it all in, joy filling me.

In the midst of the sweat and heat, I smelled something cold. A dark point cut through the crowd like a ship through water, and people—warm, living bodies—fell away like waves in its wake.

Werewolves, even in human form, retain some of the abilities of their alter egos. Smell, hearing, strength, agility. We can smell well enough to identify an individual across a room, in a crowd.

Before I could turn and run, the vampire stood before me, blocking my path. When I tried to duck away, he was in front of me, moving quickly, gracefully, without a sign of effort.

My breaths came fast as he pushed me to the edge of panic.

He was part of the local vampire Family, I assumed. He seemed young, cocky, his red silk shirt open at the collar, his smirk unwavering. He opened his lips just enough to show the points of his fangs.

"We don't want your kind here." Wiry and feral, he had a manic, *Clockwork Orange* feel to him.

I looked across the room to find T.J. Two more of them, impeccably dressed in silk shirts and tailored slacks and oozing cold, blocked him in the corner. T.J.'s fists were clenched. He caught my gaze and set his jaw in grim reassurance. I had to trust him to get me out of this, but he was too far away to help me.

"I thought you guys didn't like this place," I said.

"We changed our minds. And you're trespassing."

"No." I whined a little under my breath. I had wanted to leave this behind for a few hours.

I glared, shaking. A predator had me in his sights, and I wanted to flee, a primal instinct. I didn't dare look away from the vampire, but another scent caught my attention. Something animal, a hint of fur and musk underneath normal human smells. Werewolf.

Carl didn't hesitate. He just stepped into the place the vampire had been occupying, neatly displacing him before the vampire knew what had happened.

Our slight commotion made the vampires blocking T.J. turn. T.J., who could hold his own in a straight fight, elbowed his way between them and strode toward us.

Carl grabbed my shoulder. "Let's go outside."

He was about six-four and had the build to match. He towered over my slim, five-six self. He had rough brown hair and a beard, and glared constantly. Even if I didn't know what he was, I'd have picked him out of a lineup as most likely to be a werewolf. He had this *look*.

I squeaked as he wrenched me toward the door. I scurried to stay on my feet, but I had trouble keeping up. It looked like he dragged me, but I hardly noticed, I was so numb with relief that the vampire was gone and we were leaving.

A bouncer blocked our way at the passage leading from the dance floor to the main entrance. He wasn't as tall as Carl, but he was just as wide. And he had no idea that Carl could rip his face off if he decided to.

"This guy bothering you?" the bouncer said to me.

Carl's hand tensed on my shoulder. "It's none of your business."

Frowning, the bouncer looked at me for confirmation. He was judging this based on human sensibilities. He saw a girl get dragged off the dance floor, it probably meant trouble. But this was different. Sort of.

I squared my shoulders and settled my breathing. "Everything's fine. Thanks."

The bouncer stepped aside.

Joining us, T.J. followed us down the passage and out the door.

Outside, we walked down a side street, around the corner and into an alley, out of sight of the people who were getting air outside the club.

There, Carl pinned me against the brick wall, hands planted on either side of my head.

"What the hell are you doing out where they could find you?"

I assumed he meant the vampires. My heart pounded, my voice was tight, and with Carl looming over me I couldn't calm down. My breaths came out as gasps. He was so close, the heat of him pressed against me, and I was on the verge of losing it. I wanted to hug him, cling to him until he wasn't angry at me anymore.

"It was just for a little while. I just wanted to go out. They weren't supposed to be here." I looked away, brushing a tear off my cheek. "T.J. was with me. And they weren't supposed to be here."

"Don't argue with me."

"I'm sorry, Carl. I'm sorry." It was so hard groveling upright, without a tail to stick between my legs.

T.J. stood a couple of feet away, leaning back against the wall, his arms crossed and shoulders hunched.

"It's my fault," he said. "I told her it was okay."

"When did you start handing out permission?"

T.J. looked away. Carl was the only person who could make him look sheepish. "Sorry."

"You should have called me."

I was still trying to catch my breath. "How—how did you know where to find us?"

He looked at T.J., who was scuffing his boot on the asphalt. T.J. said, "I left him a note."

I closed my eyes, defeated. "Can't we do anything without telling Carl?"

Carl growled. Human vocal cords could growl. The guys in pro wrestling did it all the time. But they didn't mean it like Carl meant it. When he growled, it was like his wolf was trying to climb out of his throat to bite my face off.

"Nope," T.J. said.

"T.J., go home. Kitty and I are going to have a little talk. I'll take care of you later."

"Yes, sir."

T.J. caught my gaze for a moment, gave me a "buck-up" expression, nodded at Carl, and walked down the street. Carl put his hand behind my neck and steered me in the opposite direction.

This was supposed to be *my* night.

Usually, I melted around Carl. His personality was such that it subsumed everyone around him—at least everyone in the pack. All I ever wanted to do was make him happy, so that he'd love me. But right now, I was angry.

I couldn't remember when I'd ever been more angry than scared. It was an odd feeling, a battle of emotions and animal instinct that expressed itself in action: fight or flight. I'd always run, hid, groveled. The hair on my arms, the back of my neck, prickled, and a deep memory of thick fur awakened.

His truck was parked around the corner. He guided me to the passenger seat. Then, he drove.

"I had a visit from Arturo."

Arturo was Master of the local vampire Family. He kept the vampires in line like Carl kept the werewolves in line, and as long as the two groups stayed in their territories and didn't harass each other, they existed peacefully, mostly. If Arturo had approached Carl, it meant he had a complaint.

"What's wrong?"

"He wants you to quit your show." He glared straight ahead.

I flushed. I should have known something like this would happen. Things were going so well.

"I can't quit the show. We're expanding. Syndication. It's a huge opportunity, I can't pass it up—"

"You can if I tell you to."

I tiredly rubbed my face, unable to think of any solution that would let us both have our way. I willed my eyes to clear and made sure my voice sounded steady.

"Then you think I should quit, too."

"He says that some of his people have been calling you for advice instead of going to him. It's a challenge to his authority. He has a point."

Wow, Carl and Arturo agreed on something. It was a great day for supernatural diplomacy.

"Then he should tell off his people and not blame it on me—"

"Kitty—"

I slouched in the seat and pouted like a little kid.

"He's also worried about exposure. He thinks you're bringing too much attention to us. All it takes is one televangelist or right-wing senator calling a witch hunt, and people will come looking for us."

"Come on, 90 percent of the people out there think the show's a joke."

He spared a moment out of his driving to glare at me. "We've kept to ourselves and kept the secret for a long time. Arturo longer than most. You can't expect him to think your show is a good idea."

"Why did he talk to you and not me?"

"'Cause it's my job to keep you on your leash."

"Leash or choke collar? Sorry." I apologized before he even had a chance to glare at me.

"You need to quit the show," he said. His hands clenched the steering wheel.

"You always do what Arturo tells you to?"

Sad, that this was the best argument I could think of. Carl wouldn't want to think he was making Arturo happy.

"It's too dangerous."

"For whom? For Arturo? For you? For the pack?"

"Is it so unbelievable that I might have your best interests in mind? Arturo may be overreacting, but you are bringing a hell of a lot of exposure on yourself. If a fanatic out there decides you're a minion of evil, walks into your studio with a gun—"

"He'd need silver bullets."

"If he thinks the show is for real, he just might have them."

"It won't happen, Carl. I'm not telling anyone what I am."

"And how long will that last?"

Carl didn't like the show because he didn't have any control over it. It was all mine. I was supposed to be all his. I'd never argued with him like this before.

I looked out the window. "I get a raise for every new market that picks up the show. It's not much right now, but if this takes off, it could be a lot. Half of it's yours."

The engine hummed; the night rolled by the windows, detail lost in darkness. I didn't even have to think about how much I'd give to keep doing the show. The realization came like something of an epiphany. I'd give Carl *all* the syndication bonus to keep doing the show. I'd grovel at his feet every day if he wanted me to.

I had to hold on to the show. It was *mine*. I was proud of it. It was important. I'd never done anything important before.

He took a long time to answer. Each moment, hope made the knot in my throat tighter. Surely if he was going to say no, he wouldn't have to think this hard.

"Okay," he said at last. "But I might still change my mind."

"That's fair." I felt like I'd just run a race, I was so wrung out.

He drove us twenty minutes out of town, to the open space and private acreage that skirted the foothills along Highway 93 to the west. This was the heart of the pack's territory. Some of the wolves in the pack owned houses out here. The land was isolated and safe for us to run through. There weren't any streetlights. The sky was overcast. Carl parked on a dead-end dirt road. We walked into the first of the hills, away from the road and residences.

If I thought our discussion was over, I was wrong. We'd only hashed out half of the issue. The human half.

"Change," he said.

The full moon was still a couple of weeks away. I didn't like shape-shifting voluntarily at other times. I didn't like giving in to the urge. I hesitated, but Carl was stripping, already shifting as he did, his back bowed, limbs stretching, fur rippling.

Why couldn't he just let it go? My anger grew when it should have subsided and given way to terror. Carl would assert his dominance, and I was probably going to get hurt.

But for the first time, I was angry enough that I didn't care.

I couldn't fight him. I was half his size. Even if I knew what I was doing, I'd lose. So, I ran. I pulled off my shirt and bra as I did, paused to shove my jeans and panties to my feet, jumped out of them, and Changed, stretching so I'd be running before the fur had stopped growing.

If I didn't think about it too much, it didn't hurt that badly.

Hands thicken, claws sprout, think about flowing water so she doesn't feel bones slide under skin, joints and muscles molding themselves into something else. She crouches, breathing deep through bared teeth. Teeth and face growing longer, and the hair,

*and the eyes. The night becomes so clear, seen through the Wolf's
eyes.*

*Then she leaps, the Wolf is formed and running, four legs feel so
natural, so splendid, pads barely touching soft earth before they fly
again. Wind rushes through her fur like fingers, scent pours into
her nose: trees, earth, decay, life, water, day-old tracks, hour-old
tracks, spent rifle cartridges from last season, blood, pain, her
pack. Pack's territory. And the One. The Leader. Right behind her,
chasing.*

*Wrong, fleeing him. But fleeing is better than fighting, and the
urge to fight is strong. Kill her if she doesn't say she's sorry. But
she is sorry; she'd do anything for him.*

*Run, but he's bigger, faster. He catches her. She tumbles and
struggles, fear spurring her on, but he holds her fast with teeth.
Fangs dig into her shoulder and she yelps. Using the grip as purchase, he claws his way to her throat, and she's on her back, belly
exposed. His control ensures that he never breaks her skin.*

*She falls still, whining with every breath. Stretches her head
back, exposing her throat. He could kill her now. His jaw closes
around her neck and stays there.*

*Slowly, only after she has stayed frozen for ages, he lets her
loose. She stays still, except to lick his chin over and over. "You are
God," the action says. She crawls on her belly after him, because
she loves him.*

*They hunt, and she shows him he is God by waiting to feed on
the rabbit until he gives her permission. He leaves her skin and
bones to lick and suck, but she is satisfied.*

I awoke human in the gray of dawn. The Wolf lingered, bleeding
into my awareness, and I let her fill my mind because her instincts
were better than mine, especially where the One was concerned.

*She lies naked in the den, a covered hillock that is his place when
he sleeps off his Wolf. He is there, too, also naked, and aroused. He
nibbles her ear, licks her jaw, sucks her throat, and pulls himself on
top of her, leveraging her legs apart with his weight. She moans
and lets him in; he pushes slowly, gently. This is what she lives
for—his attention, his adoration.*

Speaking in her ear he says, "I'll take care of you, and you don't ever need to grow up. Understand?"

"Yes. Oh, yes."

He comes, forcing her against the earth, and she clings to him and slips away, and I am me again.

Alpha's prerogative: He fucks whomever he wants in the pack, whenever he wants. One of the perks of the position. It was also one of the reasons I melted around him. He just had to walk into a room and I'd be hot and bothered, ready to do anything for him, if he would just touch me. With the scent of him and the wolves all around us, I felt wild.

I curled against his body, and he held me close, my protector.

I needed the pack, because I couldn't protect myself. In the wild, wolf cubs had to be taught how to hunt, how to fight. No one had taught me. Carl wanted me to be dependent. I wasn't expected to hunt for myself, or help defend the pack. I had no responsibilities, as long as I deferred to Carl. As long as I stayed a cub, he would look after me.

The next afternoon at the studio, I jumped at every shadow. Every noise that cracked made me flinch and turn to look. Broad daylight, and I still expected vampires to crawl through windows, coming after me.

I really didn't think anyone took the show that seriously. *I* didn't take it that seriously half the time.

If Arturo really wanted me to quit the show, and I didn't, there'd be trouble. I didn't know what kind of trouble, but one way or another it would filter back to me. Next time, he and his cronies might not bother going through Carl as intermediary. He'd take his complaint straight to me. I walked around wishing I had eyes on the back of my head. And the sides. I contemplated the fine line between caution and paranoia.

Carl might not always be there to look after me. He couldn't come to work with me.

I found Matt, the show's sound engineer, as he came back from supper. One of the benefits of my newfound success: Someone else could pay attention to make sure the right public service announcement played at the right time. He was laid-back, another intern turned full-timer, and always seemed to have a friend who could do exactly the job you needed doing.

"Hey, Matt—do you know anyone who teaches a good self-defense class?"

I'm Kitty Norville and you're listening to *The Midnight Hour,* the show that isn't afraid of the dark or the creatures who live there. Our first call tonight comes from Oakland. Marie, hello."

"Hi, Kitty. Thank you for taking my call."

"You're welcome. You have a question?"

"Well, it's a problem, really."

"All right. Shoot."

"It's about my Master. I mean, for the most part I have no complaints. He's *really* sexy, and rich, you know? I get lots of perks like nice clothes and jewelry and stuff. But—there are a couple of things that make me uncomfortable."

I winced. "Marie, just so we're clear: You're human?"

"Yeah."

"And you willingly enslaved yourself to a vampire, as his human servant?"

"Well, yeah."

She certainly wasn't the first. "And now you're unhappy because—"

"It isn't how I thought it would be." And Marie certainly wasn't the first to discover this.

"Let me guess: There's a lot more blood involved than you thought there would be. He makes you clean up after feeding orgies, doesn't he?"

"Oh, no, the blood doesn't bother me at all. It's just that, well— he doesn't drink from my neck. He prefers drinking from my thigh."

"And you're quibbling? You must have lovely thighs."

"It's supposed to be the neck. In all the stories it's the neck."

"There are some vampire legends where the vampire tears out

the heart and laps up the blood. Be happy you didn't hook up with one of those."

"And he doesn't wear silk."

What could I say? The poor girl had had her illusions shattered. "Does he make you eat houseflies?"

"No—"

"Marie, if you present your desires as a request, not a demand— make it sound as attractive as you think it is—your Master may surprise you. Buy him a silk shirt for his birthday. Hm?"

"Okay. I'll try. Thanks, Kitty."

"Good luck, Marie. Next caller, Pete, you're on the air."

"I'm a werewolf trapped in a human body."

"Well, yeah, that's kind of the definition."

"No, really. I'm *trapped.*"

"Oh? When was the last time you shape-shifted?"

"That's just it—I've never shape-shifted."

"So you're not really a werewolf."

"Not yet. But I was meant to be one, I just know it. How do I get a werewolf to attack me?"

"Stand in the middle of a forest under a full moon with a raw steak tied to your face, holding a sign that says, 'Eat me; I'm stupid'?"

"No, I'm *serious.*"

"So am I! Listen, you do not want to be attacked by a werewolf. You do not want to *be* a werewolf. You may think you do, but let me explain this one more time: Lycanthropy is a disease. It's a chronic, life-altering disease that has no cure. Its victims may learn to live with it—some of them better than others—but it prevents them from living a normal life ever again. It greatly increases your odds of dying prematurely and horribly."

"But I want fangs and claws. I want to hunt deer with my bare hands. That would be so cool!"

I rubbed my forehead and sighed. I got at least one of these calls every show. If I could convince just one of these jokers that being a werewolf was not all that cool, I'd consider the show a success.

"It's a lot different when you hunt deer not because you want to but because you have to, because of your innate bloodlust, and because if you didn't hunt deer you'd be hunting people, and that would get you in trouble. How do you feel about hunting people, Pete? How about *eating* people?"

"Um, I would get used to it?"

"You'd get people with silver bullets gunning for you. For the last time, I do not advocate lycanthropy as a lifestyle choice. Next caller, please."

"Um, yeah. Hi."

"Hello."

"I have a question for you. Werewolves and vampires—we're stronger than humans. What's to stop us from, oh, I don't know . . . robbing banks? The police can't stop us. Regular bullets don't work. So why aren't more of us out there wreaking havoc?"

"Human decency," I said without thinking.

"But we're not—"

"—human? Do you really believe that you're not human?"

"Well, no. How can I be?"

I crossed my arms and sighed. "The thing I keep hearing from all the people I talk to is that despite what they are and what they can do, they still want to be a part of human society. Society has benefits, even for them. So they take part in the social contract. They agree to live by human rules. Which means they don't go around 'wreaking havoc.' And that's why, ultimately, I think we can all find a way to live together."

Wow. I shocked myself sometimes with how reasonable I made all this sound. I might even have believed it. No, I *had* to believe it, or I wouldn't be doing the show.

The caller hesitated before saying, "So I tell you I'm a werewolf, and you'll tell me that you think I'm human?"

He couldn't know that he was asking me to label myself. "Yes. And if you live in the human world, you have to live by human laws."

The trick with this show was confidence. I only had to *sound* like I knew what I was talking about.

"Yeah, well, thanks."

"Thanks for calling. Hello, James, you're on the air."

"I have a question, Kitty." His voice came low and muffled, like he was speaking too close to the handset.

"Okay."

"Does a werewolf need to be in a pack? Can't he just be on his own?" A sense of longing tainted the question.

"I suppose, theoretically, a werewolf doesn't need a pack. Why do you ask?"

"Curious. Just curious. It seems like no one on your show ever talks about being a werewolf without a pack. Do they?"

"You're right, I don't hear much about werewolves without hearing about packs. I think—" This was where the show got tricky:

How much could I talk about without bringing up personal experience, without giving something away? "I think packs are important to werewolves. They offer safety, protection, a social group. Also control. They're not going to want a rogue wolf running around making a mess of things and drawing attention to the rest of them. A pack is a way to keep tabs on all the lycanthropes in an area. Same thing for vampire Families."

"But just because a werewolf is on his own doesn't mean he's automatically going to go out and start killing people. Does it?" The guy was tense. Even over the phone I could hear an edge to his voice.

"What do you think, James?"

"I don't know. That's why I called you. You're always talking about how anybody, even monsters, can choose what they do, can choose whether or not they're going to let their natures control them, or rise above all that. But can we really? Maybe—maybe if I don't have a pack . . . if I don't want to have anything to do with a pack . . . maybe that's my own way of taking control. I'm not giving in. I don't have to be like that. I can survive on my own. Can't I? Can't I?"

I couldn't do it. From the night I was attacked until now, someone—T.J., Carl, or somebody—had been there to tell me I was going to be okay, that I had friends. They helped me keep control. They gave me a place to go when I felt like losing it. I didn't have to worry about hurting them. If I didn't have that, what would I do? I'd be alone. How many people were there—people like James, who didn't have packs or Families or anything—how many of them were listening to my show and thinking I had all the answers? That wasn't what I'd planned when I started this.

Had there *been* a plan when I started this?

Who was I to think I could actually help some of these people? I couldn't get along without my pack. Maybe James was different.

"I don't know, James. I don't know anything about your life. If you want me to sit here and validate you, tell you that yeah, you're right, you don't need a pack and everything's going to be okay, I can't do that. I don't have the answers. I can only go by what I hear and think. Look at your life and decide if you're happy with it. If you can live with it and the people around you can live with it, fine, great, you don't need a pack. If you're not happy, decide why that is and do something about it. Maybe a pack would help, maybe not. This is a strange, strange world we're talking about. It'd be stupid to think that one rule applies to everyone." I waited a couple of heartbeats. I could hear his breathing over the line. "James, you okay?"

Another heartbeat of a pause. "Yeah."

"I'm going to the next call now. Keep your chin up and take it one day at a time."

"Okay, Kitty. Thanks."

Please, please, please let the next call be an easy one. I hit the phone line.

"You're on the air."

"Hi, Kitty. So, I've been a lycanthrope for about six years now, and I think I've adjusted pretty well. I get along with my pack and all."

"Good, good."

"But I don't know if I can talk to them about this. See, I've got this rash—"

I had an office. Not a big office. More like a closet with a desk. But I had my own telephone. I had business cards. *Kitty Norville, The Midnight Hour, KNOB.* There was a time just a few months ago when I'd assumed I would never have a real job. Now I did. Business cards. Who'd have guessed?

The show aired once a week, but I worked almost every day. Afternoons and evenings, mostly, in keeping with the nocturnal schedule I'd adopted. I spent an unbelievable amount of time dealing with organizational crap: setting up guest interviews, running damage control, doing research. I didn't mind. It made me feel like a real journalist, like my NPR heroes. I even got calls from the media. The show was fringe, it was wacky, and it was starting to attract attention from people who monitored pop-culture weirdness. A lot of people thought it was a gimmick appealing to the goth crowd. I had developed a set of canned answers for just about every question.

I got asked a lot if I was a vampire/lycanthrope/witch/whatever; from the skeptics the question was if I *thought* I was a vampire/lycanthrope/witch/whatever. I always said I was human. Not a lie, exactly. What else could I say?

I liked the research. I had a clipping service that delivered articles from all walks of media about anything pertaining to vampires, lycanthropes, magic, witchcraft, ghosts, psychic research, crop circles, telepathy, divining, lost cities—*anything*. Lots of grist for the mill.

A producer from *Uncharted World* called to see if I wanted to be on the show. I said no. I wasn't ready for television. I was never going to be ready for television. No need to expose myself any more than necessary.

I got fan mail. Well, some of it was fan mail. Some of it was more along the lines of "Die, you satanic bitch from hell." I had a folder that I kept those in and gave to the police every week. If I ever got assassinated, they'd have a nice, juicy suspect list. Right.

Werewolves really are immune to regular bullets. I've seen it.

Six months. I'd done the show once a week for six months. Twenty-four episodes. I was broadcast on sixty-two stations, nationwide. Small potatoes in the world of syndicated talk radio. But I thought it was huge. I thought I would have gotten tired of it by now. But I always seemed to have more to talk about.

One evening, seven or eight o'clock, I was in my office—my office!—reading the local newspaper. The downtown mauling death of a prostitute made it to page three. I hadn't gotten past the first paragraph when my phone—my phone!—rang.

"Hello, this is Kitty."

"You're Kitty Norville?"

"Yes."

"I'd like to talk to you."

"Who is this?"

He hesitated a beat before continuing. "These people who call you—the ones who say they're psychic, or vampires and werewolves—do you believe them? Do you believe it's real?"

I suddenly felt like I was doing the show, on the phone, confronting the bizarreness that was my life head-on. But it was just me and the guy on the phone. He sounded . . . ordinary.

When I did the show, I had to draw people out. I had to answer them in a way that made them comfortable enough to keep talking. I wanted to draw this guy out.

"Yes, I do."

"Do they scare you?"

My brow puckered. I couldn't guess where this was going. "No. They're people. Vampirism, the rest of it—they're diseases, not a mark of evil. It's unfortunate that some people use them as a license to be evil. But you can't condemn all of them because of that."

"That's an unusually rational attitude, Ms. Norville." The voice took on an edge. Authoritative. Decisive, like he knew where he stood now.

"Who are you?"

"I'm attached to a government agency—"

"Which one?"

"Never mind that. I shouldn't even be talking to you like this—"

"Oh, give me a break!"

"I've wondered for some time now what your motivations are in doing your show."

"Let me at least take a guess. Are you with the NIH?"

"I'm not sure the idea would have occurred to someone who didn't have a . . . personal . . . interest."

A chill made my hair stand on end. This was getting too close. I said, "So, are you with the CDC?"

A pause, then, "Don't misunderstand me, I admire the work you're doing. But you've piqued my curiosity. Ms. Norville—what are you?"

Okay, this was just weird. I had to talk fast to fend off panic. "What do you mean, 'what am I?' "

"I think we can help each other. An exchange of information, perhaps."

Feeling a bit like the miller's daughter in *Rumpelstiltskin*, I took a wild stab. "Are you with the CIA?"

He said, "See what you can find on the Center for the Study of Paranatural Biology." Then he hung up.

Great, I had my own personal Deep Throat.

Hard to focus on work after that. I kept turning the conversation over in my mind, wondering what I'd missed and what someone like that could accomplish by calling me.

I couldn't have been brooding for more than five minutes when the phone rang again. I flinched, startled, and tried to get my heart to stop racing before I answered. I was sure the caller would be able to hear it over the phone.

I answered warily. "Hello?"

"Kitty? It's your mother." Mom, sounding as cheerful and normal as ever. I closed my eyes and sighed.

"Hi, Mom. What's up?"

"You never told me if you were going to be able to make it to your cousin Amanda's wedding. I need to let them know."

I had completely forgotten. Mostly because I didn't, under any circumstances, want to go. Weddings meant crowds. I didn't like

crowds. And questions. Like, "So when is it going to be *your* turn?"
Or, "Do *you* have anyone *special*?"

I mean, define *special*.

I tried to be a little more polite. Mom didn't deserve aimless
venting. I pulled out my organizer.

"I don't know, when is it again?" She gave me the date, I flipped
ahead to next month and looked. The day after the full moon. There
was no way I'd be in any kind of decent shape to meet the family
the day after the full moon. I couldn't handle being nice to that
many people the day after the full moon.

Now if only I could think of an excuse I could tell my mother.

"I'm sorry, I've got something else going on. I'll have to miss it."

"I think Amanda would really like you to be there."

"I know, I know. I'm really sorry. I'll send her a card." I even
wrote myself a note to send her a card, then and there. To tell the
truth, I didn't think Amanda would miss me all that much. But
there were other forces at work here. Mom didn't want to have to
explain to everyone why I was absent, any more than I wanted to
tell her why I was going to be absent.

"You know, Kitty, you've missed the last few big family get-
togethers. If you're busy I understand, but it would be nice if you
could make an appearance once in a while."

It was her birthday all over again. That subtle, insipid guilt trip
that only mothers are capable of delivering. It wasn't like I was
avoiding the family simply for the sake of avoiding them.

"I'll try next time." I said that every time.

She wouldn't let up. "I know you don't like me worrying about
you. But you used to be so outgoing, and now—" I could picture
her shrugging in lieu of cohesive thought. "Is everything okay?"

Sometimes I wished I could tell her I was a lesbian or something. "Everything's fine, Mom. I'm just busy. Don't worry."

"Are you sure, because if you ever need to talk—"

I couldn't tell her. I couldn't imagine what sort of nightmare scenarios she'd developed about what I was doing when I said I was
busy. But I couldn't tell her the truth. She was nice. *Normal.* She
wore pantsuits and sold real estate. Played tennis with my dad. Try
explaining werewolves to that.

"Mom, I really need to get back to work. I know you're worried,
I appreciate it, but everything's fine, I promise." Lying through my
teeth, actually, but what else could I say?

"All right, then." She didn't sound convinced. "Call me if you
change your mind about the wedding."

"Okay. I'll talk to you later."

The sound of the phone clicking off was like a weight lifting from my shoulders.

A telephone. Business cards. Next, I needed a secretary to screen my calls.

When a knock on my door frame sounded a few minutes later, I just about hit the ceiling. I dropped the newspaper I'd been reading and looked up to see a man standing in the doorway. My office had a door, but I rarely closed it. He'd arrived without my noticing.

He was of average height and build, with dark hair brushing his shoulders and refined features. Unassuming in most respects, except that he smelled like a corpse. A well-preserved corpse, granted. He didn't smell rotten. But he smelled of cold blood instead of hot blood, and he didn't have a heartbeat.

Vampires had this way of sneaking around without anyone noticing them. He'd probably walked right past the security guy in the lobby of the building.

I recognized this vampire: Rick.

I'd met him a couple of times when Carl and Arturo got together to resolve squabbles. He was a strange one. He was part of Arturo's Family, but he didn't seem much interested in the politics of it; he always lingered at the edges of the Family, never close to Arturo himself. He didn't cultivate the demeanor of ennui that was ubiquitous among vampires. He could actually laugh at someone else's jokes. When I asked nicely he told stories about the Old West. The *real* Old West—he'd been there.

Sighing, my hair and blood prickling with anxiety, I slumped back in my chair. I tried to act casual, as if his presence didn't bother me.

"Hi, Rick."

His lips turned in a half-smile. When he spoke, he showed fangs, slender, needle-sharp teeth where canines should have been. "Sorry if I startled you."

"No you aren't. You enjoyed it."

"I'd hate to lose my knack for it."

"I thought you couldn't come in here unless I invited you."

"That doesn't apply to commercial property."

"So. What brings you here?" The question came out tense. He could only be here because I hadn't quit doing the show and Arturo wasn't happy about it.

His expression didn't waver. "What do you think I'm here for?"

I glared, in no mood for any more mind games tonight. "Arturo

told Carl to make me quit the show. I haven't quit. I assume His
Mighty Undeadness is going to start harassing me directly to try
and get me off the air. He sent you to deliver some sort of threat."

"That's a little paranoid, isn't it?"

I pointed. "Not if they're really out to get me."

"Arturo didn't send me."

I narrowed my gaze, suspicious. "He didn't?"

"He doesn't know I'm here."

Which changed everything. Assuming Rick was telling the truth,
but he had no reason not to. If he was seeing me behind Arturo's
back, he must have a good reason.

"Then why are you here?"

"I'm trying to find some information. I wondered if you could
help me." He pulled a folded piece of paper from his pocket,
smoothed it out, and handed it to me. "What do you make of this?"

It was a flyer printed on goldenrod-colored paper. The produc-
tion value was low. It might even have been typewritten, then pho-
tocopied at a supermarket. It read,

*Do you need help? Have you been cursed? Vampires, lycan-
thropes, there is hope for you! There is a cure! The Reverend Elijah Smith and his Church of the Pure Faith want to save you. Pure
Faith Will Set You Free.*

The bottom of the flyer listed a date a few weeks old. The site
was an old ranch thirty miles north of town, near Brighton.

Reading it over again, my brow wrinkled. It sounded laughable.
I conjured an image of a stereotypical southern preacher laying
hands on, oh, someone like Carl. Banishing the demons, amen and
hallelujah. Carl would bite his head off—for real.

"A cure? Through faith healing? Is this a joke?"

"No, unfortunately. One of Arturo's followers left to join them.
We haven't seen her since. Personally, I smell a rat and I'm worried."

"Yeah, no kidding. Arturo must be pissed off."

"Yes. But it's been next to impossible to learn anything about
this Smith and his church. Arturo's too proud to ask for help. I'm
not. You have contacts. I wondered if you'd heard anything."

"No." I flipped the page over, as if it would reveal more secrets,
but the back was blank. "A cure, huh? Does it work?"

Every hint of a cure I'd ever tracked down had turned out to be
myth. Smoke and folklore. I could be forgiven for showing skepticism.

"I don't know," he said simply.

"I've never heard of a cure actually working."

"Neither have I."

"Arturo's follower thought it was for real. And she never came back. So—it worked?"

"Some might be attracted by such a possibility. Enticing bait, if someone wanted to lure people like us."

"Lure why?"

He shrugged. "To trap them, kill them. Enslave them. Such things have happened before."

The possibilities he suggested were downright ominous. They incited a nebulous fear of purposes I couldn't imagine. Witch hunts, pogroms. Reality TV.

He was only trying to scare me so I'd get righteously indignant enough to do something about this. It worked.

"I'll see what I can find out." Grist for the mill. I wondered if Smith would come on the show for an interview.

"Thank you."

"Thanks for the tip." I pursed my lips, suppressing a grin. "It's a good thing the humble subordinates keep running around their leaders' backs, or nothing would get done around here."

Rick gazed innocently at the ceiling. "Well, I wouldn't say anything like that to Arturo's face. Or Carl's."

Things always came back to them, didn't they? The Master, the alpha. We were hardwired to be followers. I supposed it kept our communities from degenerating into chaos.

More somber, I said, "Do you think Arturo's going to do anything about the show?"

"That depends on what Carl does."

As in, if Carl did nothing, Arturo might. I winced. "Right."

"I should be going."

"Yeah. Take it easy."

He nodded, almost a small bow that reminded me that Rick was old. He came from a time when gentlemen bowed to ladies. Then he was gone, as quietly as he'd arrived.

Phone. Business cards. Secretary. Maybe I also needed a receptionist. And a bodyguard.

Dressed in sweatpants, sports bra, and tank top, I stood on the mat, and at the instructor's signal, kicked at dust motes. Craig, an impossibly fit and enthusiastic college student who looked like he'd walked straight out of an MTV reality show, shouted "Go!" and the dozen of us in the class—all of us women in our twenties and thirties—kicked.

Rather than teaching a specific martial art, the class took bits and pieces from several disciplines and combined them in a technique designed to incapacitate an assailant long enough for us to run like hell. We didn't get points for style; we didn't spend a lot of time in mystical meditation. Instead, we drilled moves over and over again so that in a moment of panic, in the heat of an attack, we could move by instinct and defend ourselves.

It was pretty good exercise as well. Breathing hard, sweating, I could forget about the world outside the gym and let my brain go numb for an hour.

We switched sides and kicked with the other leg a dozen or so times. Then Craig put his hands on his hips.

"All right. Line up so we can do some sparring."

I hated sparring. We'd started with a punching bag the first few sessions. Where most of the women hit the bag and barely budged it, I set it swinging. I got many admiring compliments regarding my upper-body strength. But it had nothing to do with upper-body strength. Something about werewolves made them more powerful than normal humans. Without any training at all, by just being myself and what I was, I could outfight all my classmates, and probably Craig as well.

That wouldn't help me with vampires.

What the episode with the punching bag taught me was that I had to be very careful sparring against humans. I didn't know how strong I was or what I was capable of. I had to pull every punch. I didn't want to hurt anyone by mistake.

I didn't want to hurt anyone at all. The Wolf part of me groveled and whined at the thought of fighting, because she knew Carl wouldn't like it. Wolf, ha. I was supposed to be a monster. Ferocious, bloodthirsty. But a monster at the bottom of the pack's pecking order might as well be as ferocious as a newborn puppy.

Dutifully, I lined up with the others and gritted my teeth.

We practiced delivering and taking falls. Tripping, tackling, dropping, rolling, getting back up and doing it all over again. I fell more often than not, smacking on the mat until my teeth rattled. I didn't mind. My sparring partner was Patricia, a single mom on the plump side who'd never even thought about sports until it looked like her eight-year-old son, a Tae Kwon Do whiz, was going to be able to beat up Jackie Chan soon (she claimed), and she wanted to keep up with him. Patricia seemed gleeful at the idea that she could topple a full-grown adult with a couple of quick moves. A lot of these women had to overcome cultural conditioning against hurting other people, or even confronting anyone physically. I was happy to contribute to Patricia's education in this regard.

"You're holding back, Kitty."

I was flat on my back again. I opened my eyes to find Craig, six feet of blond zeal, staring down at me, weirdly foreshortened at this angle. He was all leg.

"Yeah," I said with a sigh.

"Come on, get up." He offered his hand and helped me to my feet. "Now I want you knock me all the way across the gym."

He had the gall to put a twinkle in his eyes.

The rest of the class formed a circle around us, an audience that I didn't want and that made me bristle. Wolf hated fighting. She was better at cowering. Inside, I was whining.

Craig bent his arms and hunched like he was getting ready to charge me. If he charged, I was supposed to drop, letting him trip over me, and shove, making sure he lost his footing. Sure enough, he ran at me. I dropped. Instead of tripping, though, he sidestepped. If I'd shoved like I was supposed to, he would have lost his balance. But I just sat there, allowing him to jump behind me and lock his arm around my neck.

"I *know* you can do better than that. Come on, let's try it again."

I could fight, I was strong enough. But I had no will for it. Too used to being picked on, a victim by habit. I closed my eyes, feeling like a kid who'd flunked yet another test. Slowly, I got to my feet.

Craig faced me again. "Okay, let's try something. This time, imagine I'm your worst ex-boyfriend, and this is your chance to get even."

Oh, that was easy. That would be Bill. All Craig had to do was say it, and I saw Bill there, and all that anger came back. I clenched my fists.

Being angry meant not holding back, of course. I wasn't sure I could have pulled the next punch if I'd wanted to, once I had Bill on the brain.

Craig charged. I ducked. Then I *shoved*, leading with my shoulder and putting my whole body behind it. I connected with his side. He made a noise, a grunt of air, and flew. Both his feet left the mat. Women squealed and dodged out of his way as he crashed to the floor, bouncing twice. He lay on his back and didn't move.

The bottom dropped out of my stomach and I nearly fainted. I'd killed him. I'd killed my self-defense instructor. *Shit.*

I ran to where he lay and stumbled to a crouch at his side, touching his shoulder. "Craig?"

His eyelids fluttered. A few panicked heartbeats later, he opened them. Then he grinned.

"Yeah, that's what I'm talking about! You gotta learn to *hit* people." He was breathing hard. He had to gasp the words out. I'd probably knocked the wind out of him. "Now, never do that to me again."

I gave him a hand up. He was rubbing his head. I bet he would hurt in the morning. How embarrassing.

"Wow," Patricia, coming to stand next to me, said. "Your ex must have been a real winner."

"You have no idea."

Between my mystery phone call and Rick's visit, I had my research assignments for the next week set. I worked on my mystery caller first.

The Center for the Study of Paranatural Biology was the government agency that had conducted the study on lycanthropy and vampirism overseen by the CDC and NIH. It was relegated to footnotes in the back pages of the obscure report that had been all but buried in the CDC archives. I couldn't find any names of people there I could contact. No one wanted to be associated with it. The people I called at the CDC hadn't heard of it. The NIH referred me to the CDC. It probably wasn't a real agency, but some kind of think tank. Or smoke screen.

I didn't usually buy into conspiracy theories. At least not where the government was concerned. After all, when Congress had trouble voting itself enough money to continue operating, how was I supposed to believe that this same government was behind a finely tuned clandestine organization bent on obfuscating the truth and manipulating world events according to some arcane plan for the domination of the minds and souls of all free people?

Unless vampires were involved. If vampires were involved, all bets were off.

I worked on Rick's flyer next.

As much as I hated to admit it, I started with the website for *Uncharted World*. The Internet had a thriving community that dealt in supernatural news. The trouble was separating the hoaxes and fanatics from the real deal. Most of what *Uncharted World* posted was sensationalist and inaccurate. But they had a search engine that filtered for "news of the weird," and with enough patience and by following enough links, I could trace the Web to good sources and cross-check the information to verify it.

I hit pay dirt when I found a collection of bulletin board postings and some missing persons reports filed with various local police departments. It seemed that about four months ago, an old revival-style tent had sprung up in the middle of the night on the outskirts of Omaha, Nebraska. Posters appeared all over the bad parts of town, the likely haunts of lycanthropes and vampires, advertising a cure based solely on faith and the intercession of a self-proclaimed holy man, Elijah Smith. I couldn't find any documentation of what happened during that meeting. The tent had disappeared by the next morning and a week later showed up in Wichita, Kansas. Then Pueblo, Colorado. Stories began circulating: The cure worked, this guy was for real, and the people he healed were so grateful, they didn't want to leave. A caravan of followers sprang up around that single tent.

Smith's congregation was known as the Church of the Pure Faith, with "Pure faith will set you free" as its motto. I couldn't find any photos, any accounts of what went on inside the caravan or what the meetings were like. I couldn't find any specifics about the cure itself. No one who wasn't earnestly seeking a cure could get close to Smith or his followers. People who came looking for their friends, packmates, or Family members who had disappeared into that tent were threatened. Interventions were forcibly turned back.

I came across a couple of websites warning people away from Smith. Some people screamed cult. After reading what I could find, I was inclined to as well.

Vampirism and lycanthropy were not medical conditions, so to speak. People had studied us, scanned us, dissected us, and while they found definite characteristics distinguishing us from *Homo sapiens*, they hadn't found their sources. They weren't genetic, viral, bacterial, or even biological. That was part of what made us so frightening. Our origins were what science had been trying to deny for hundreds of years: the supernatural. If there were a way to cure vampirism and lycanthropy, it would probably come from the supernatural, the CDC and Center for the Study of Paranatural Biology notwithstanding. In the case of a vampire, how else could one restore the bloodless undead to full-blooded life? Faith healing just might be the answer. That was the problem with trying to expose Smith as a fraud and his church as a cult.

I didn't believe there was a cure. Someone would have found it by now.

Welcome to *The Midnight Hour*. I'm Kitty Norville. Tonight I have a very special guest with me. Veronica Sevilla is the author of *The Bledsoe Chronicles, The Book of Rites,* and a half-dozen other best-selling novels that follow the trials and tribulations of a clan of vampires through the centuries. Her newest novel, *The Sun Never Rises*, has just been released. Ms. Sevilla, thank you for being on the show."

"Please, my dear, call me Veronica."

Veronica Sevilla, whose birth name was Martha Perkins, wore a straight, black knit dress, black stockings, black patent-leather heels, and a black fur stole. Her dark hair—dyed, I was sure—framed her pale face in tight curls. Diamond studs glittered on her earlobes. She sat back in the guest chair, hugging herself, hands splayed across opposite shoulders. It wasn't because she was cold or nervous—it was a pose. Her official biography gave no age or date of birth. I couldn't tell how old she was by looking at her. Her face was lined, but not old. She might have been anywhere from forty to sixty. There might have been surgery involved.

She wasn't a vampire. She smelled warm and I could hear her heart beat. But she sure was trying to act like one. I couldn't stop staring at her, like, *Are you for real?*

"All right, Veronica. You write about vampires in a way that makes them particularly vivid. Some critics have commented on your ability to take them out of the realm of standard horror fare and turn them into richly realized characters. They're the heroes of your stories."

"Yes, of course, why shouldn't they be? It's all a matter of perspective."

"You've gathered a following of admirers who seem to identify strongly with your vampire protagonists. Quite a few of them insist that your novels aren't fiction, but factual accounts of real vampires. What do you say to this?"

She waved her hand in a dismissive gesture that was totally lost on the radio.

"I wouldn't know where to find a real vampire. Vampires are a product of the human imagination. My books are all products of my own imagination."

I had my doubts. Putting Sevilla's rabid fans and her florid overwriting aside, she got too many details right. The way vampire Families worked, the things they said to one another, the dominance and posturing games that went on among them the same way they went on among werewolves—details that an outsider wouldn't be able to make up. So, she either did a great job on her research, in which case I wanted to know what her sources of information on vampire culture were, or she had connections. Before meeting her, I half-expected her to be a vampire, or a human servant of one, or something.

"Why do you think your fans are so attracted to your characters and stories? Why do people want to believe in vampires?"

"My books create a world that is enticing. My world, the Bledsoe Family, vampires in general—these are all metaphors for the power these poor children wish they could have in life but can't because they are so . . . so . . ."

"Insecure?"

"Outcast. Misfit. Badly adjusted."

"Are you saying your fans are social misfits?"

She touched a bitten-down fingernail to her lip. "Hm, that is imprecise."

"You have fans who come to you wanting to learn about vampires, wanting to become vampires. They see you as an authority on the subject. What do you tell them?"

"I tell them it's fiction. Everything I have to say is there in the books. What do *you* tell them, when people ask you such questions?"

"I tell them that maybe being a vampire isn't all it's cracked up to be."

"Have you ever met a vampire, Kitty?"

I paused, a smile tugging at my lips. "Yeah, I have. And frankly, I find that your novels are pretty accurate."

"Well. What am I supposed to say to that? Perhaps you could introduce me to one."

I thought about it and decided that Arturo would love to have her for lunch—but he had better taste.

"Why vampires? You write centuries-long family sagas—why not write historical epics without any hint of the supernatural?"

"Well, that would be boring, wouldn't it?"

"Yeah, God only knows what Tolstoy was thinking. Seriously, though, what's your inspiration? Where do you get your ideas?"

"Writers *hate* that question."

"I think writers only say they hate it to avoid answering it."

"Is that any way to speak to a guest?"

I sighed. She was used to being pampered. Dressing room and a bowl of peanut M&Ms with the green ones taken out, that sort of thing.

"I apologize, Veronica. I tend to be a bit on the blunt side."

She looked me up and down, nodding slightly, agreeing.

The interview wasn't one of my best. We got off on the wrong foot, and she was entirely too closemouthed to make it work. She didn't want to be here. Her publicist had set up the interview as part of the promotional tour for the new book. She'd probably done a dozen of these appearances already.

I took some calls and got the expected round of gushing, ebullient fans. Veronica handled them better than I did, but she'd had lots of practice.

At last, like the door of a prison cell slamming open, the show ended and we were done. I pulled off the headphones and regarded Veronica Sevilla.

"Thanks again for being on the show. I know my listeners got a kick out of it."

I expected her to humph at me, make a dismissive gesture, and stalk out leaving a trail of haughty slime behind her. Instead, she licked her lips. Her lipstick needed touching up. Her gaze downcast, she straightened and took a deep breath before speaking.

"I owe you an apology, Ms. Norville." Oh? "I was not entirely truthful with you. I have met a vampire. My son is one."

I had no response to that. I tried to look sympathetic and waited for more.

"I don't want that information made public. With a little imagination I think you can understand why. My fans are forward enough as it is. But I wanted you to know the truth. I hope I can trust you to keep this secret."

I nodded. "I'm good at keeping secrets. I've got a few of my own. How—I mean, if it isn't too brazen of me to ask—how did you find out?"

"He's been a youthful eighteen for twenty years now. I got suspicious. I asked for his secret, and he told me. My stories—they're about him. My son will not have the life I envisioned for him, and these novels are my way of reconciling myself to the life he does have. If one can call it life."

I saw her to the door, where she adjusted the mink stole around her shoulders and walked out, chin up, the epitome of dignity.

Full moon night. Time to run.

T.J. picked me up on his bike, which was behaving itself, rumbling smooth and steady like a grizzly bear. He drove fast and took the turns tight. I didn't wear a helmet so I could taste the air whipping by. I tipped back my head and drank it in, as the city scents of asphalt and exhaust gave way to the countryside, dry grass, earth, and distant pines. The sun was setting, the moon hadn't yet risen, but I could feel it, a silver breath that tugged the tides and my heart. A howl tickled the back of my throat—the pack was near. I clung to T.J., smiling.

The pack gathered at Carl and Meg's house, at the edge of the national forest. It might have been just another party, the dozen or so cars parked on the street, the collection of people congregating in the living room. But tension gripped the room, anticipation and nerves. The veil to that other world we lived in was drawn halfway. We could see through, but had to wait to enter. Carl wasn't here yet.

Twenty-two wolves made up the local pack. They came from an area of a couple-hundred-mile radius, drawing from the urban areas up and down the Front Range, from Colorado Springs to Fort Collins. Most of them I only ever saw on full moon nights. We knew our places. I slunk around the edges of the room, trying to be innocuous.

My skin itched. I hugged myself, trying to stay anchored. So close. She, the Wolf, was waiting, staring out of my eyes. Her claws scraped at the inside of my skin, wanting to push through the tips of my fingers. She wanted fur instead of skin. Her blood flowed hot.

I flinched when the presence of another entered my awareness, like a force pressing through a membrane that surrounded me. I felt Zan before I saw him move to block my path.

He was young, my age, but he'd been a wolf since he was a teenager. He had pale skin, unkempt dark hair, and an animal stared out of his eyes.

I hated him. His scent tinged my nightmares. He was the one who'd attacked me and made me this thing.

He followed me around sometimes, like he was waiting for a chance to finish what he'd started. Like he could still smell blood on me. Or like he thought I owed him something. I stayed away from him as much as I could. T.J., Carl, and Meg backed him off the rest of the time. He wasn't that tough.

T.J. was in the kitchen. I'd have to cross the entire room to get to him. Zan cornered me.

"What do you want?"

"You." He leaned close. I was already backed against the wall and couldn't move away when he brought his lips close to my ear. "Run with me tonight."

That was a euphemism among werewolves. Zan went through this whenever Carl wasn't around. I usually cowered and slunk away to hide behind T.J. Zan could take me, but he couldn't take T.J. That was how the dominance thing worked.

I was so not in the mood for this shit.

"No," I said, not realizing what I was saying until the word was out of my mouth.

"No? What do you mean, no?"

I straightened from the wall, squaring my shoulders and glaring at him. My vision wavered to gray. Wolf wanted a piece of him.

"I mean no. I mean get out of my face."

His shoulders bunched. An annoyed rumble sounded in his throat.

Shit. I'd just challenged him. I'd questioned his dominance, and he couldn't let it pass without severely beating me up. Carl and T.J. wouldn't save me because I'd gotten into it all by myself.

The room went quiet. The others were watching with a little too much interest. This wasn't the usual squabble—people were always duking it out, jockeying for positions in the middle of the pack. But this was me. I didn't fight. At best, as the pack's baby I was subject to good-natured teasing. At worst, I ended up on the wrong end of roughhousing. I always cowered, giving up status in exchange for safety. Not this time.

I couldn't break eye contact with Zan. I'd gotten myself into this. Let's see what I had to do to get out.

Those tricks I'd been learning in the self-defense class depended on the opponent's making the first move. It was supposed to be self-defense, not kick-ass. And here I was thinking a few cute punches made me tough. I'd made the challenge; Zan waited for me to start.

I feinted down, like I was going to tackle him in the middle. He reached to swipe at me, and I sidestepped, shoving into his back to topple him. He rolled, smacking into the back of the sofa. I rushed him again, not sure what I thought I was doing. But the Wolf knew. Before he could find his feet, I jumped on his back, hands around his throat, digging my nails into him.

He roared, grabbing my arms and rolling back and forth to dislodge me. My back hit the corner of the sofa, stinging my spine. But I held on, gripping with arms and legs. I wanted to use my teeth as well. At his next lunge, a floor lamp tipped.

Then Meg was there. Meg was Carl's mate, the alpha female of the pack. She was tall and lean, her straight black hair giving her an indefinable ethnic look. She wore a tank top and sweats, and would have looked at home on an exercise bike at the gym, except she vibrated. That was the only way to describe it. She vibrated with power, strength, and dominance. I could feel it across the room, usually. But I was so angry at Zan I didn't notice her until she grabbed my hair and pulled back. Her other hand held a chunk of Zan's hair.

She regarded me, brow lined with confusion. "Are you sure you want to do this?" She was giving me an out; protecting me from my own stupidity.

My blood was rushing. I wanted to rip out a piece of Zan so bad it hurt. I nodded quickly.

"Then take it outside," she said, pushing us away. Someone opened the kitchen door that led to the backyard.

I backed toward the door, holding his gaze. He followed, pressing me. I could hear his heart pounding. His sweat smelled like fire. He clenched his hands into fists. When his muscles tensed, I knew he was going to rush me the last couple of feet to the door.

I ducked, letting him trip over me. He flew headfirst, ungracefully, out the door to the concrete pad outside. I didn't wait; I jumped, landing on top of him as hard as I could. His head cracked on the concrete. Effortlessly, he spun me over, turning the tables so he pinned me to the ground. He backhanded me—I saw stars, my ears rang. He hit me twice more, wrenching my head back and forth while his other hand held my throat. I couldn't breathe.

He was going to kill me.

I'd wanted to learn to fight to defend myself against enemies, not engage in pack power struggles. What was I *doing*?

Anger and fear. That was what this whole life was about, anger vying with fear, and whichever won out determined whether you led or followed. I had spent almost three years being afraid, and I was sick of it.

I kneed him in the crotch.

He gasped, and while he didn't release me, his grip slackened. Grabbing his wrist, I squirmed out from under him. I kept hold of his arm as I slid onto his back, wrenching the limb around. Something popped and he cried out. I twisted it harder. With my other hand I grabbed his hair and pulled as hard as I could, tilting his head almost all the way back. It took all my weight pressing down on him to keep him at this angle, which made moving too painful for him. I didn't have the luxury of being able to let go to smack him around. So I bit him. Right at the corner of his jaw, taking in a mouthful of his cheek. I bit until I tasted blood, and he whimpered.

Finally, he went slack. I let go of his face, licking my lips, sucking the blood off my teeth. I'd taken a chunk out of his flesh—a bite-sized flap of it was hanging loose.

I leaned close to his ear. "I don't like you. I still hold a grudge against you and I always will, so stay out of my way or I'll rip you apart."

I meant it, too. He knew it, because as soon as I eased my weight off him, he scrambled away, cowering on all fours—submissive.

I crouched and stared at him. The blood was clouding my mind. I saw him, smelled his fear, and wanted to tear into him again. But I couldn't, because he was pack, and he was apologizing. I walked to where he was crouched, curling in on himself like he might disappear. This fight could have gone so differently—I didn't see fear in his eyes so much as surprise. I'd won this not because I was stronger, but because he hadn't expected me to fight back. I'd never have a fight this easy again.

He rolled onto his back. His breaths came in soft whines. I stood over him. Then I turned my back on him and walked away.

A part of me was nauseated, but no way would the Wolf let me go puke in the corner. She was hungry.

I swayed a little. I had a raging headache. I wiped my face; my hands came away bloody. My nose was bleeding. I tried to soak it up with my sleeve, then gave up. I healed fast, right?

The thing was, Zan hadn't been bottom of the pack. Now, others would challenge me in order to keep their places in the pecking order.

Carl stood at the kitchen door, arms crossed.

"He pissed me off," I said, answering the silent question.

"You don't get pissed off."

My first thought was, how the hell would he know? But the last thing I needed tonight was to challenge Carl. Carl wouldn't waste any time in knocking the snot out of me.

I dropped my gaze and meekly stood before him.

He said, "You may have a big-time radio show, but that doesn't make you anything here."

That reminded me. I groped in my jeans pocket and pulled out the envelope I'd shoved there before leaving home. It was filled with this month's payoff, in cash. I gave it to him. The blood I inadvertently smeared on it glared starkly.

He opened the flap and flipped through the stack of fifties. He glanced at me, glaring. It might not have made everything all better, but it distracted him. He handed the envelope to Meg.

If Carl was the bad cop, Meg was the good cop. The first year, I'd come to cry on her shoulder when this life got to me. She taught me the rules: Obey the alphas; keep your place in the pack.

I didn't want to make her angry. Inside, Wolf was groveling. I couldn't do anything but stand there.

Giving me her own stare, she crossed her arms. "You're getting stronger," she said. "Growing up, maybe."

"I'm just angry at Zan. He wouldn't leave me alone. That's all."

"Next time, try asking for help." She prowled off to stash the money.

T.J., beta male, Carl's lieutenant, had been standing behind her.

I forgot sometimes that within pack law he had as much right to beat up on me as Carl did. I preferred having him as a friend.

I leaned into T.J., hugging him. Among the pack, touch meant comfort, and I wanted to feel safe. I—the part of me I thought of as human—was slipping away.

"What was that all about?" T.J. said, his voice wary.

"I don't know," I said, but I—she—knew, really. I felt strong. I wasn't afraid. "I'm tired of getting picked on, I guess."

"You'd better be careful—you might turn alpha on us." He smiled, but I couldn't tell if he was joking.

Because the pack hunts together this night, she feeds on deer. An injured buck, rich with flesh and blood. Because she is no longer lowest among them, she gets to taste some of the meat instead of being left with bones and offal.

Others prick their ears and bare their teeth at her in challenge, but the leaders keep them apart. No more fighting this night.

She runs wild and revels in her strength, chasing with the others, all of them singing for joy. Exhausted, she settles, warm and safe, already dreaming of the next moon, when she may once again break free and taste blood.

I woke up at dawn in a dog-pile with half a dozen of the others. This usually happened. We ran, hunted, ate, found a den and settled in to sleep, curled around one another, faces buried in fur, tails tucked in. We were bigger than regular wolves—conservation of mass, a two-hundred-pound man becomes a two-hundred-pound wolf, when a full-grown *Canis lupus* doesn't get much bigger than a hundred pounds or so. Nothing messed with us.

We always lost consciousness when we Changed back to human.

We woke up naked, cradled in the shelter of our pack. Becky, a thin woman with a crew cut who was a couple of years older than me, lay curled in the crook of my legs. Dav's back was pressed against mine. I was spooned against T.J.'s back, my face pressed to his shoulder. I lay still, absorbing the warmth, the smell, the contentedness. This was one of the good things.

T.J. must have felt me wake up. Heard the change in my breathing or something. He rolled over so we faced each other. He put his arms around me.

"I'm worried about you," he said softly. "Why did you challenge Zan?"

I squirmed. I didn't want to talk about this now, in front of the others. But the breathing around us was steady; they were still asleep.

"I didn't challenge him. I had to defend myself." After a moment I added, "I was angry."

"That's dangerous."

"I know. But I couldn't get away. I couldn't take it anymore."

"You've been teaching yourself how to fight."

"Yeah."

"Carl won't like that."

"I won't do it again." I cringed at the whine creeping into my voice. I hated being so pathetic.

"Yeah, right. I think it's the show. You're getting cocky."

"What?"

"The show is making you cocky. You think you have an answer for everything."

I didn't know what to say to that. The observation caught me off guard. He might have been right. The show was mine; it gave me purpose, something to care about. Something to fight for.

Then he said, "I think Carl's right. I think you should quit."

Not this, not from T.J.

"Carl put you up to this."

"No. I just don't want to see you get hurt. You've got a following. I can see Carl thinking that you're stepping on his toes. I can see this breaking up the pack."

"I would never hurt the pack—"

"Not on purpose."

I snuggled deeper into his embrace. I didn't *want* to be cocky. I wanted to be safe.

chapter 5

Next caller, hello. You're on the air."

"It—it's my girlfriend. She won't bite me."

Bobby from St. Louis sounded about twenty, boyish and nervous, a gawky postadolescent with bigger fantasies than he knew what to do with. He probably wore a black leather jacket and had at least one tattoo in a place he could cover with a shirt.

"Okay, Bobby, let's back up a little. Your girlfriend."

"Yeah?"

"Your girlfriend is a werewolf."

"Yeah," he said in a voice gone slightly dreamy.

"And you want her to bite you and infect you with lycanthropy."

"Uh, yeah. She says I don't know what I'd be getting into."

"Do you think that she may be right?"

"Well, it's my decision—"

"Would you force her to have sex with you, Bobby?"

"No! That'd be rape."

"Then don't force her to do this. Just imagine how guilty she'd feel if she did it and you changed your mind afterward. This isn't a tattoo you can have lasered off. We're talking about an entire lifestyle change here. Turning into a bloodthirsty animal once a month, hiding that fact from everyone around you, trying to lead a normal life when you're not fully human. Have you met her pack?"

"Uh, no."

"Then you really don't know what you're talking about when you say you want to be a werewolf."

"Uh, no."

"Bobby, I usually make suggestions rather than tell people flat out what to do, but I'm making an exception in your case. Listen to your girlfriend. She knows a heck of a lot more about it than you do, okay?"

"Uh, okay. Thanks, Kitty."

"Good luck to you, Bobby," I said and clicked Bobby off. "And good luck to Bobby's girlfriend. My advice to her is dump the guy; she doesn't need that kind of stress in her life. You're listening to *The Midnight Hour* with me, Kitty Norville. The last hour we've been discussing relationships with lycanthropes, bones to pick and beef to grind. Let's break now for station ID and when we come back, more calls."

I waved to Matt through the booth window. He hit the switch. The On-Air sign dimmed and the show's theme song, CCR's "Bad Moon Rising," played. Not the usual synthesized goth fare one might expect with a show like this. I picked the song for its grittiness, and the joy with which it seemed to face impending doom.

I pulled off my headphones and pushed the microphone away. If I'd gotten tired of this, as I expected I would during the first six months, quitting would be easy. But I liked it. I still liked it. I hated making T.J. angry, though. Not in the same way I hated making Carl angry. But still. If they were both pissed off at me, what could I do? I didn't want to give up something that I was proud of, like I was proud of the show. I hated them for making me this stressed out about it.

A werewolf pack was the most codependent group of beings in existence.

"You okay in there?" Matt said. His dark hair was just long enough to tie in a ponytail, and he was a few days late shaving. Anywhere but here he'd have looked disreputable. Behind the control board, he looked right at home.

I had my elbows propped on the desk and was rubbing my temples. I'd been losing sleep. My head hurt. Whine.

"Yeah," I said, straightening and taking a big swallow of coffee. I'd have time enough to stress myself into an ulcer later.

Could werewolves get ulcers?

The two-minute break ended. Matt counted fingers down through the window. The On-Air sign lit, the lights on my caller board lit. Headphones on, phone line punched.

"Welcome back to *The Midnight Hour.* We have Sarah from Sioux City on the line."

The woman was in tears. She fought not to cry, a losing battle. "Kitty?"

"Hi, Sarah," I said soothingly, bracing myself for the onslaught. "What do you need to talk about?"

"My husband," she said after a shuddering breath. "I caught him last week. I mean, I spied on him." She paused, and I let her collect herself before prompting her.

"What happened, Sarah?"

"He—he turned . . . into . . . into a wolf. In the woods . . . behind our house. After he thought I'd gone to bed."

"And you had no idea he's a lycanthrope."

"No! I mean, I suspected. The business trips once a month during the full moon, eating his steaks rare. How could he keep something like this from me? I'm his wife! How could he do it?" The woman's voice quavered until she was nearly screeching.

"Did you confront him? Talk to him about it?"

"Yes, yes. I mean, I asked him about it. He just said he was sorry. He won't look me in the eye anymore!"

"Sarah, take a breath. That's a girl. I know this is a blow, but let's look at it together. How long have you been married?"

"Six—six years."

"And did your husband tell you how long he's been a werewolf?"

"Two years."

"Now, Sarah, I'm going to ask you to look at the situation from his point of view. It was probably pretty traumatic for him becoming a lycanthrope, right?"

"Yes. He was working the night shift alone, locking up the store, when it happened. He—he said he was lucky he got away. Why didn't he ever tell me?"

"Do you think maybe he was trying to protect you? You had a good marriage and he didn't want to mess things up, right? Now I'm not saying what he did was right. In a great marriage he would have told you from the start. But he's having to keep this secret from a lot of people. Maybe he didn't know how to tell you. Maybe he was afraid you'd leave him if he told you."

"I wouldn't leave him! I love him!"

"But people do leave their partners when something like this happens. He's probably scared, Sarah. Listen, does he still love you?"

"He says he does."

"You know what I'd do? Sit down with him. Tell him that you're hurt, but you want to support him if he'll be honest with you from here on out. Before you do that, though, you have to decide whether or not you can stay married to a werewolf. You have to be just as honest with yourself as you want him to be with you."

Sarah was calm now. She hiccuped a little from the crying, but her voice was steady. "Okay, Kitty. I understand. Thank you."

"Good luck, Sarah. Let me know how it turns out. All right, I've got lots of calls waiting, so let's move right along. Cormac from Longmont, hello."

"I know what you are."

"Excuse me?"

"I know what you are, and I'm coming to kill you."

According to Matt's screening, this guy had said he had a question about lycanthropy and STDs.

I should have cut off the call right there. But the strange ones always interested me.

"Cormac? You want to tell me what you're talking about?"

"I'm an assassin. I specialize in lycanthropes." His voice hissed and faded for a moment.

"Are you on a cell phone?"

"Yeah. I'm in the lobby of the building, and I'm coming to kill you."

Good Matt, he was already on the phone with security. I watched him on the phone, just standing there. Not talking. What was wrong?

Matt slammed the phone into the cradle. "No one's answering," he said loud enough to sound through the glass of the booth.

"I rigged a little distraction outside," Cormac said. "Building security is out of the building." At that, Matt picked up the phone and dialed, just three numbers after punching the outside line. Calling the cavalry.

Then he dialed again. And again. His face went pale. "Line's busy," he mouthed.

"Did you manage to tie up 911?" I said to the caller.

"I'm a professional," Cormac replied.

Damn, this was for real. I could see Carl standing there saying, *I told you so*. I hoped he wasn't listening. Then again, if he was, maybe he could come rescue me.

Over the line I heard the ping of the elevator on the ground floor, the slide of the doors. It was a scare tactic, calling me on the phone and walking me through my own assassination. It was a *good* scare tactic.

"Okay, you're coming to kill me while you warn me on the phone."

"It's part of the contract," he said in a strained way that made me think he was grimacing as he spoke.

"What is?"

"I have to do it on the air."

Matt made a slicing motion across his neck with a questioning look. Cut the show? I shook my head. Maybe I could talk my way out of this.

"What makes you think I'm a lycanthrope, Cormac the Assassin Who Specializes in Lycanthropes?"

"My client has proof."

"What proof?"

"Pictures. Video."

"Yes, I'm sure, video taken in the dark with lots of blurry movement. I've seen those kinds of TV shows. Would it hold up in court?"

"It convinced me."

"And you're obviously deranged," I said, flustered. "Have you considered, Cormac, that you're the patsy in a publicity stunt to get me off the air? Certain factions have been trying to push me off for months."

This time of night, Matt and I had the studio to ourselves. Even if some sharp listener called the police, Cormac would be at the booth before they arrived. He'd counted on it, I was sure.

Matt came into the booth and hissed at me in a stage whisper. "We can leave by the emergency stairs before he gets here."

I covered the mike with my hands. "I can't leave the show."

"Kitty, he's going to kill you!"

"It's a stunt. Some righteous zealot trying to scare me off the air."

"Kitty—"

"I'm not leaving. You get out if you want."

He scowled, but returned to his board.

"And grab one of the remote headsets out of the cupboard for me."

Matt brought me the headset and transferred the broadcast to it. I left the booth, removing myself from direct line of sight of the door. The next room, Matt's control room, had a window looking into the hallway. I moved to the floor, under the window, near the door. If anyone came in, I'd see him first.

Cormac would need maybe five minutes to ride the elevator and get from there to here. So—I had to talk fast.

"Okay, Cormac, let me ask you this. Who hired you?"

"I can't say."

"Is that in the contract?"

He hesitated. I wondered if he wasn't used to talking and resented that part of the job he'd taken on. I didn't doubt he really was what he said he was. He sounded too controlled, too steady.

"Professional policy," he said finally.

"Is this one of those deals where I can offer you more money to not finish me off?"

"Nope. Ruins the reputation."

Not that I had that kind of money anyway. "Just how much is my life worth?"

A pause. "That's confidential."

"No, really, I'm curious. I think I have a right to know. I mean, if it's a really exorbitant amount, can I judge my life a success that I pissed someone off that much? That means I made an impact, right, and that's all any of us can really hope to accomplish—"

"Jesus, you talk too much."

I couldn't help it; I grinned. Matt sat against the wall, shaking his head in a gesture of long-suffering forbearance. Getting pinned down by an assassin definitely wasn't in the job description. I was glad he hadn't left.

Thinking of everyone who had it in for me was an exercise in futility—so many did, after all: the Witchhunters League, the Right Reverend Deke Torquemada of the New Inquisition, the Christian Coalition . . .

The elevator pinged, one, two . . . two more to go. "So let's back up a bit, Cormac. Most of your jobs aren't like this, are they? You go after rogue wolves. The ones who've attacked people, the ones whose packs can't control them. Law-abiding werewolves are pretty tough to identify and aren't worth going after. Am I right?"

"That's right."

"You have any idea of how few wolves actually cause trouble?"

"Not too many."

Cormac's assertion about my identity, on the air, demanded some response. Denial. Claims of innocence, wrongful accusations—until he shot and killed me. Or until he tried to shoot me and I defended myself. I hoped it wouldn't come to that.

He probably expected me to make denials—you can't shoot me, I'm not a werewolf. But it was a little late for that. Denials now would sound a bit lame. And if he really did have photographs—where could he have picked up photos? Only thing left was to brazen it out. So this was it. The big revelation show. My ratings had better pay off for this.

"So here I am, a perfectly respectable law-abiding werewolf—must be kind of strange for you, tracking down a monster who isn't going to lift a claw against you."

"Come on, Norville. Go ahead and lift a claw. I'd like the challenge."

There it was. I'd said it on national radio. I'm a werewolf. Didn't feel any different—Cormac was still riding the elevator to my floor. But my mother didn't even know. I heard a series of metallic clicks over the headphones. Guns, big guns, being drawn and readied.

"Is this really sporting, Cormac? You know I'm unarmed. I'm a sitting duck in the booth here, and I have half a million witnesses on the air."

"You think I haven't had to deal with that kind of shit before?"

Okay, wrong tack. I tried again. "If I shut down the broadcast, would that void the clause in your contract saying this has to be on the air?"

"My client believes you'll stay on the air as long as possible. That you'll take advantage of the ratings this would garner."

Damn, who was this client? Whoever it was knew me too well. Maybe it wasn't the usual list of fanatics. Somebody local who had a grudge.

Arturo.

Carl hadn't made me quit the show. Maybe Arturo decided to take care of me himself. He couldn't do it directly. A vampire attacking a werewolf like that would be an act of war between the two groups. Carl and the pack would take it as a breach of territory at the very least. Then Arturo would have to deal with them.

But Arturo could hire someone. He wouldn't even have to do it himself. He'd work through an intermediary and Cormac would never know he was working for the vampire. Arturo had the means to get photos of me during full moon nights. He knew where the pack ran.

I heard elevator doors hiss open. Boot steps on linoleum.

"I can see the window of your booth, Norville."

"Hey, Cormac, do you know Arturo?"

"Yeah. He's in charge of the local vampires."

"Did he hire you?"

"Hell no. What do you think I hunt when I'm not after werewolves?"

So he hunted lycanthropes and vampires. I really wanted to get on this guy's good side, as impossible as that seemed at the moment.

I had to figure out how I could prove that Arturo had hired Cormac through an intermediary. Maybe that would get the bounty hunter to back off.

Then I heard the sirens. A window looked from my studio to the street outside. I didn't have to move to see the red and blue lights flashing. The police. The last few minutes had dragged, but even if an intrepid listener had called the cops as soon as Cormac announced his intentions, they couldn't have gotten here this quickly.

"You hear that, Cormac?"

"Shit," he muttered. "That's too quick."

Hey, we agreed on something. "It's almost like someone called ahead of time, that they knew you were going to be here. Are you sure you don't want to rethink my patsy theory?"

Arturo could get me via Cormac, and with the cops downstairs he could get Cormac, too, if he had it in for the bounty hunter. The cops wouldn't buy the werewolf story. They'd get him for murder.

"You can't be serious."

"Arturo, the local vampire Master, wants me off the air. Can I assume you've pissed him off recently?"

"Um, yeah, you could say that."

There was a story behind that. I'd have to wait until later to pry it out of him. "Let's pretend he hires you through a third party, calls the cops as you're doing the job, so there's no way you have time for an escape. You may have it in for werewolves on principle, but you can't justify killing me. The minute you pull that trigger, the cops bring you down. How does that sound for a theory?"

A pause, long enough for my palpitating heart to beat a half-dozen times. "You're insane."

I couldn't hear footsteps, couldn't hear weapons. He'd stopped moving. Was I nervous? I hadn't seen those guns yet. I didn't have to; I could smell Cormac's body odor, taut nerves with a spicy underlay of aftershave. I could smell the gun oil. I could smell—silver. He had silver bullets. Any doubts about the truth of his claims and intentions vanished. He hunted lycanthropes and vampires, and if he was alive enough to use the plural on that, he knew what he was doing.

I was still on the air. I was getting the show to end all shows, interviewing my own potential killer live on nationally syndicated radio. So was I nervous? I talked faster. Words were my weapons, like Cormac's guns were for him. I could only hope my aim was as deadly.

"Hey, Cormac. You ever have to deal with a PMSing werewolf?"

"No."

"Well, it's a real bitch."

He was right outside the door. All he had to do was lean in and shoot. My fingers itched; my bones itched. I wanted to Change; I wanted to run. I could feel the Wolf clawing at my rigidly held control, in self-defense, self-preservation. I could fight—but I wouldn't. Squeezing my trembling hands into fists, I held my breath. Matt crouched in a corner, his eyes wide. He was staring at me. Not at the door or at Cormac, but at me. The werewolf.

Cormac chuckled. The sound was soft, almost indiscernible even to my sensitive hearing. The next sound I heard was a click—the safety of a handgun snapping back into place.

"Can I ask you a question?"

Was I going to live? Die? What? "Sure."

"What the hell kind of name is Kitty for a werewolf?"

My breath hissed. "Gimme a break; the name came first."

"I have a deal for you, Norville. I call off the contract, and you don't press charges."

"All right," I said quickly. I was more interested in keeping my skin intact than pressing charges.

Cormac continued. "I'm going to do some checking. If you're wrong, I'll come back for you."

I swallowed. "That seems fair."

"If you're right, we can both rub Arturo's face in it. Now, I suggest we wait here for the cops to find us, then we can all explain things like reasonable people."

"Um, can I finish the show?"

"I suppose."

Matt scrambled to the board. "Forty seconds left," he said, a little breathlessly.

Perfect timing. "Hey, listeners, I haven't forgotten about you. Seems this was all a misunderstanding. I think Cormac the Assassin and I have worked things out. The police are coming up the stairs as I speak. If this were a movie, the credits would be rolling. So that's it for *The Midnight Hour.* Next week I have as my guest Senator Joseph Duke, sponsor of a bill in Congress that would grant federal marshal status to licensed exorcists. Is he a crackpot, or is the country really under threat from hordes of communist demons? I can't promise that it'll be nearly as exciting as it was tonight, but you never know. I'll do my best. Until then, this is Kitty Norville, Voice of the Night."

Matt started the closing credits, featuring a long, clear wolf howl rich with the full moon. It was my own howl, recorded for the show at the start.

I pulled off the headset and rubbed my eyes. Maybe Carl was right and I should quit doing this. So much trouble. Was it worth my life? I should just quit. Nah . . .

The hair on my neck tingled; I turned to see a man standing in the doorway, leaning on the frame. Even without the revolver in the holster strapped to his thigh, gunslinger style, he was scary: tall, six feet, and slim, dressed in a black leather jacket, black T-shirt, worn jeans, and thick, steel-toed biker boots. His mouth smirked under a trimmed mustache. He held a rifle tucked under his arm.

"That you?" he asked, indicating the last fading note of the wolf howl. He looked to be in his early thirties. His eyes glinted, matching the humor of his suppressed grin.

I nodded, climbing to my feet, propping myself against the wall. Big, dangerous werewolf—yeah, that was me. I wanted a hot shower and a nap.

Cops were pounding down the hallway now, shouting something about weapons down and hands up. Cormac followed instructions, gun down and hands up, as if he'd done this before.

I had a thousand questions for him. How did someone get into the business of hunting werewolves and vampires? What kind of adventures had he had? Could I get him on the show as a guest? What did I do now? Introduce myself? Shake his hand?

"Norville, don't ever give me a reason to come after you," he said, before the police flooded the floor.

My smile was frozen and my knees were weak as the uniformed men arrived, surrounded him, and led him away.

The cop in charge, Detective Jessi Hardin, escorted me down the emergency stairway herself. She explained how I'd have to go to the police station, make a statement, sign the report, and so on. The long night was going to get even longer.

I wanted to say something. Like, *I'm a werewolf.* I wondered if it would change anything. No, not if. *How* it would change everything. I'd told the world. I felt like I had to keep saying it, to believe it had happened.

For once I kept my mouth shut.

"By the way, there's a guy downstairs looking for you. Name of Carl? I told him he can talk to you after you go to the station. This might take awhile, though."

Carl. Carl, that bastard. Took him long enough to figure out I was in trouble. And he called himself an alpha.

"That's fine. Take as long as you like. Carl can wait."

chapter 6

The cops kept me for two hours. They were nice. Very polite. Hardin put me in a bland holding room with off-white carpet and walls and plastic chairs, got me coffee, and patted me kindly on the shoulder. Most of the others gave me a wide berth, staring at me as I walked past. Rumor traveled quickly. The whispers started as soon as we arrived at the station. *That's her. The werewolf. Yeah, right.*

Hardin didn't seem to notice.

I gave her my rundown of what had happened. Just a formality—we recorded the whole show. It was all there on tape. But Hardin kept me around, trying to talk sense into me.

"You sure you don't want to press charges? We can pin felony stalking on this guy. Criminal mischief, attempted murder—"

I'd made a deal with Cormac. I'd stick by it, and despite everything I trusted him to stick by it, too. I'd been so used to running under the law's radar—we made our own rules, us and people like Cormac. But if I told Hardin, "We take care of our own," she probably wouldn't appreciate it.

Ouch. What was I thinking? Cormac probably *belonged* in jail.

"Don't tell me this really was just a publicity stunt," she said finally. If possible, her frown grew even more irate.

"No." It might turn out that way. I might have to thank Cormac. "I think I just want to go home, if that's okay." I tried to smile like a demure little victim.

"It'll be a lot easier to prosecute this guy with your cooperation. I can hold him overnight, but not any longer than that without pressing charges."

"No one got hurt. It's okay, really."

She put her hand on the table next to me and leaned close. "Attitudes like that get girls like you killed."

I blinked, cringing back. She straightened and marched out of the room. I got to leave ten minutes later.

Outside the door of the police station, Carl and T.J. were waiting for me. T.J. put his arm around me; Carl took firm hold of my elbow.

I thought I would have argued with them. I thought I would have gotten huffy and shrugged away, asserting my independence. Instead, I nearly collapsed.

I leaned against T.J., hugging him tight and speaking into his shoulder in a wavering voice, "I want to go home." Carl stayed close, his body like a shield at my back, and kept watch. He guided us to his truck, and they took me home.

They just held me, and that was enough. I didn't want to be alone. I didn't want to be independent. I could say to Carl, "Take care of me," and he would. Part of me wanted nothing more than to curl up at his feet and feel protected. That was the Wolf talking.

I had a studio apartment, decent if small, with a kitchen on one side, a bathroom on the other, and everything else in the middle. I usually didn't bother turning the futon back into a sofa.

T.J. sat on the futon, his back to the wall, and I curled up on his lap like a puppy. Carl stalked back and forth between the apartment's window and door. He was convinced someone was going to come after me—Cormac wanting to finish the job; some other bozo who had it in for me on principle. I barely noticed—if T.J. was here, I didn't have to worry.

"What am I going to do?" I sighed. "They're going to can me. It's all going to blow up. God, it's going to be all over the *Enquirer*."

"You might make *Newsweek* with this one, babe," T.J. said, patting my shoulder.

I groaned.

The phone rang. Carl nearly hit the ceiling before springing for the bedside phone. I got to it first. "Hello?"

"Kitty. It's your mother. Are—are you okay?"

I had almost forgotten. How could I have forgotten? I was only *beginning* to deal with this.

I should have called her first.

"Hi, Mom."

"Cheryl called; she was listening to your show and she said . . . she said that you almost got killed and that you said . . . you said . . ."

Cheryl was my older sister. I barely registered how the rest of the call went. Mom couldn't bring herself to say the word "werewolf." I said a lot of "Yes, Mom. It's true, Mom. I'm sorry . . . no, I'm not crazy. I don't think, anyway. No, I couldn't tell you . . . it's hard to explain. No, I'm not going to die, at least not right now. About three years now, I guess. Yes, that long." Mom started crying.

"Yeah, I'll talk to Dad. Yeah . . . Hi, Dad."

"Hi, Kitty. How are you?" And he sounded sensible, like he always had, like I might have just been calling from college to tell him I'd wrecked the car, and he was assuring me everything was going to be okay.

I wiped away tears. "Shell-shocked. But I'll recover."

"I know you will. You're a good kid. I know that, and so does Mom. She's just a little off-balance right now."

"Thanks—that means a lot. Is she going to be okay?"

"Yeah, I think so. I bet if you call back this evening she'll be better."

"Okay."

"Are you alone? Is there someone you can stay with? Do you want me to come up there?"

That was all I needed, for Dad to come and find me tangled up in bed with the pack. "I've got friends here. They're looking after me."

After demanding about three more times that I call back tonight, he hung up.

T.J. smiled. "I could hear him on the phone. He sounds great. You're real lucky."

He hadn't let go of me all morning. No matter what happened, he'd be right there. He was pack, and he cared.

"Yeah," I said to him. "I am."

Carl crossed his arms. "That's it," he said. "You'll quit the show now."

I pressed my face to T.J.'s leg. I didn't answer; I didn't argue. In the face of all the evidence, he was right. I should quit. I didn't know how to explain to him that I couldn't. So I didn't. T.J. tensed, like he knew what I was thinking.

"He's right, Kitty," he whispered.

I covered my ears. I didn't want to hear this. I sat up and scooted away from T.J. until I was in the middle of the bed, and hugged my knees.

"Aren't you even the least bit upset at Arturo for hiring that guy in the first place?" If it was even Arturo. I was going to have to find out. Maybe Rick knew something.

Carl bristled, his shoulders twitching, his mouth turning in a snarl. "This isn't about Arturo. This is about you putting yourself in danger."

"I have to find out if Arturo was behind this. You could talk to him. Will you help me?"

Carl didn't answer. He just glared at me. T.J. looked back and forth between us, waiting for some cue.

T.J. settled his gaze on me and said, "If you quit the show, I'll call out Arturo for you."

Carl jumped onto the bed. I yelped; T.J. scrambled away, slipping off the bed and crashing to the floor. He rolled onto all fours in a heartbeat, but kept his distance. Carl pinned me, trapping me with his hands propped on the bed on either side of my head, his weight on my body. Trembling, I tried to pull away.

I wasn't ready to take on Carl.

"I don't bargain," he said, his voice low. He glanced sideways at T.J., who looked away, submissive. "You will do as I say. *I'll* take care of Arturo."

I didn't believe him.

I squeezed my eyes shut against tears, looking away even as I felt his breath on my cheek. He was close enough to bite. I nodded, wanting only for him to leave me alone, wanting only for it to stop. If we were human, and this was a human relationship, I'd have been expected to leave him. This was abuse.

After a moment, he wrapped himself around me, holding me tight. He only wanted to take care of me. The Wolf loved him so much.

It took until noon to convince them I was all right. I told them I needed to rest. I needed to go back to KNOB, if only to tell them I was finished. When I told them this, I believed it myself.

But by evening, all I felt was angry.

Everyone—receptionist, assistants, techies—stared at me as I walked through the reception area at the station that afternoon. No one said a word. It felt like one of those naked dreams. The Wolf—she loved it. All those chunks of living meat, quivering like prey. But I kept it together. I'd had lots of practice keeping it together.

I didn't know what they were all thinking, how many of them thought it was for real, how many thought I was crazy. Some fear misted the air. Also curiosity.

I hadn't had a chance to talk to Matt last night. The police dragged us to separate rooms for our statements. I didn't know what he thought about me now. He'd worked on the show long enough, I was pretty sure he believed.

He met me in the hallway. Grinning, he handed over a shoebox full of messages. I took it, studied him. A little bit of fear tensed the edges of his jaw. His shoulders were tight, his heartbeat thudded a little too loud. But he kept cool, managing to stand there like nothing was wrong. I loved him for it.

"You okay?" I said.

"Yeah. You?"

I shrugged. "It's weird. Everything's different now. Like I sprouted a second head."

"Or a tail and claws—sorry. But—you're for real, aren't you?" I nodded, and he shook his head. "You're right. It's weird. That guy was right. Kitty's a pretty funny name for a werewolf."

"I'm never going to live it down."

"Ozzie's in his office. He wants to see you."

Oh, great. I smiled grimly in thanks and continued down the hall.

Ozzie stood when I opened the door. He was definitely nervous. So was I, for that matter. I tucked the box under my arm and cringed against the doorjamb. What the hell was I going to tell him?

Then I realized—I'd gone submissive, but he couldn't read the cues. He was my boss; it made sense, but still . . . I made a conscious effort to stand straight.

"Hi, Ozzie."

"Kitty. This is—" I waited for him to speak, ducking my gaze, apologetic, not sure why I felt like I had to apologize. Then he melted, pleading with his hands. "Aw, Kitty, why couldn't you tell me? You didn't have to keep it secret."

"I kind of did, Ozzie. There are people out there who don't really like people like me. It may be tough to deal with after this."

"Do you need more security? We'll get you security—"

And what would Carl and T.J. say about that? I was supposed to be quitting. I glanced at some of the messages. Some I expected—reporters from *National Enquirer, Wide World of News, Uncharted World.* Some I didn't—CNN? *Newsweek?* Geez, why did T.J. always have to be right?

I shook my head. "No, I've got friends. It's okay. Any word yet on how this is playing out?"

He handed me a paper marked "Preliminary Ratings." The numbers were . . . big. This couldn't be right.

"We're flooded with requests to replay the show. An instant poll suggests the show's credibility shot through the roof last night. At least among the people who believe all this shit. Before, you were just easy to talk to. Now, you know what you're talking about. The people who don't believe it think it's a publicity stunt to garner ratings, and they're dying to see how you're going to keep it going. This is gold, Kitty. Can you keep it going?"

Carl would just have to deal. I'd show him his half of the money when the next expansion went through. *Then* he could deal, I was sure. "Absolutely."

"Right . . . look for the message from Howard Stern. He wants to do a joint show, kind of a double interview with both of you taking calls. Cross-pollination of audiences, I think it sounds great. I talked to Barbara Walters—"

"I'm not going on TV. I think you know why." My website didn't even have a photo of me.

"Yeah, yeah I do. Even so—you're going to be the country's first werewolf celebrity."

I had suspicions. "Only the first one to admit it. Thanks, Ozzie. Thanks for being nice to me."

"You're still Kitty after all, right? Hey, you look like you didn't get any sleep last night. Why don't you take the rest of the day off? *After* you call Howard Stern back."

I called T.J. as soon as I got home. The phone rang five times. I thought he'd gone out. Then he answered.

I said, "It's me. I'm going to Arturo's. Will you come with me?"

This was stupid, calling him. He'd tell Carl. There was no way he wouldn't tell Carl. Then I'd be in serious trouble. But I had to call. Who else *could* I call?

Maybe I was hoping he'd help me without any arguing.

"Have you quit the show?" I didn't answer. I think I even whined. He sighed. "You can't just pay Carl off, you know. This isn't about the money."

"No, it's not. You don't think that's why I keep doing it, do you?"

"No. I know how much it means to you."

"Then how can you ask me to quit?"

"Because it's changing you. You never would have argued with me like this six months ago. You've been picking fights, for Christ's sake."

I shut my eyes. My voice was hushed. "Is change all bad?"

"You're going to get yourself killed. And not because of people like that assassin."

"I'm an adult. I can take care of myself."

"No, you can't."

And that's what this was all about, wasn't it? Which one of us was right?

"Well, I guess we're going to find out."

I hung up.

I made it as far as the alley behind Obsidian.

Obsidian was a stylish art gallery that specialized in antiques and imports. The whole place was a front. Arturo lived in the lower levels below the basement. Under the posh downtown façade, the place was a vault where the city's vampires slept out their days.

Six months ago, the idea of going to Arturo's den by myself would have made me catatonic with fear. Now, at least, I could entertain the idea. But I couldn't walk those last few steps that would take me to the stairs leading to the basement door. I stood in the alley, my hands shoved into the pockets of my jacket. It was midnight, full dark. At any moment, a swarm of vampires would come crawling up those stairs. They'd take my being here as a territorial infraction and defend themselves accordingly. I could see the headline now: "Radio Show Host Murdered in Gang Dispute."

If I were lucky, if I stood here long enough, maybe Rick would show up and I could get his advice. Or get him to talk to Arturo. He owed me a favor for working on the Elijah Smith thing, didn't he?

In the end, fear won out over anger. I only stood there a minute before turning and walking away. I was still just a cub.

When I got to the corner, hands grabbed me. No, claws. Hands turning into claws. My vision flashed with stars as I was slammed against the wall, my head cracking on the brick. Someone held my shoulders in a viselike grip, pinning me to the wall, and the claws of his thumbs dug into my throat.

It was T.J.

His fingers were shortening, his hands thickening as his wolf came to the fore. He was strangling me. His face was inches from mine, his eyes flecked with gold. His teeth were bared, filtering a growl so low it rumbled through his limbs.

I stared wide-eyed, gasping for breath. Wasn't a whole lot else I could do.

He said, jaw taut, "You disobeyed. Every instinct I have is telling me to beat the fucking shit out of you. Why don't I?"

I swallowed. He could rip me apart, though he hadn't yet broken skin. I could fight him. I knew I could—Wolf was writhing, screaming for a chance to escape or fight. I couldn't beat him in a fight. But that almost didn't matter. I wasn't whining. I wasn't going to just roll over for him.

That scared me. I didn't want to fight T.J. I had to concentrate to keep my own hands away from him. I managed to draw enough breath to speak.

"Because sometimes we have to listen to the human side."

He was shaking. His hands trembled on my shoulders. I didn't move. I held his gaze, saw the creases in his brow and at the corners of his eyes, like he was too angry to keep it in, but he was trying. *Please, please.* I hoped he saw the pleading in my eyes, that he was still human enough to read the human expression.

Then he let me go. I sagged against the wall. He stared at me, a snarl pulling at his lips. Sweat matted his dark hair to his brow. I tried to say something, but I didn't know what I *could* say, and my throat was tight.

He turned and ran. He pulled off his shirt and threw it away as he rounded the corner. A sheen of slate-gray fur had sprouted on his back. He was gone.

I sat hard and pressed my face to my knees. Fuck fuck fuck. How had I gotten myself into this?

So. I didn't talk to the vampires, and I didn't quit the show.

". . . all I'm saying is that if this is a cry for attention, you should maybe talk to someone, a therapist or something, about your need to act out your aggressions . . ."

I leaned into the mike. "Hey, who's the pop-psychologist hack here? Frankly, I host a popular radio show. You think I want *more* attention? Next caller, please."

My stomach had been turning cartwheels all evening. Before the broadcast, I was scared to death. Not of Carl or T.J., though I hadn't seen either of them all week. Full moon was coming up. I didn't know what I was going to do. Go to the pack and get my ass kicked. Or spend it by myself.

No, it was because I had absolutely no idea what was going to happen during the show. I got Ozzie to postpone the guest who was previously scheduled. I wanted the full two hours to deal with cleanup. I was going to open the line to calls, anything and everything. I was going to have to explain myself—over and over again.

It wasn't so bad. It never is, I suppose. Anticipation is always the worst. Half the calls so far had been supportive, the rallying cries of devoted fans: "We're behind you all the way." I spent a lot of airtime saying thanks. Some disbelief, some threats, and some of the usual advice calls. Lots of questions.

"Have you ever killed anyone?"

Three different callers had asked that one. "No. I'm strictly a venison kind of girl."

"How did you become a werewolf?"

"I was attacked. Beyond that, I prefer not to talk about it."

"So it was, like, traumatic?"

"Yeah, it was."

One girl came on the line crying. "I don't understand how you do it. How can you talk about this stuff and sound so calm? There are days I just want to rip my own skin off!"

I made my voice as soothing as I could. "Take it easy there, Claire. I know how you feel. I have those days, too. I count to ten a lot. And I think talking about it helps. I'm not as scared when I talk about it. Tell me something: What do you hate most about being a werewolf?"

Her breathing had slowed; her voice was more steady. "Not remembering. Sometimes when I wake up, I don't remember what I did. I'm scared that I've done something horrible."

"Why is that?"

"I remember how I feel. I remember how the blood tastes. And—and I remember that I like it. When I'm human, it makes me want to throw up."

I didn't have to mince words anymore. I could answer her from experience now, which I couldn't have done before last week. She probably wouldn't have called me before last week.

"I think when we Change, a lot of human is still there. If we want to be a part of civilization, it stays with us. It keeps us from doing some of the things we're capable of. I guess that's part of the reason I'm here, doing the show and trying to lead a relatively normal life. I'm trying to civilize the Wolf part of me."

"Is it working?"

Good question. "So far so good."

"Thanks, Kitty."

"One day at a time, Claire. Next caller, hello."

"I knew it. I knew you were one." I recognized the voice—a repeat caller. I glanced at the monitor, and sure enough.

"How are you, James?"

"I'm still alone." The declaration was simple and stark.

"I'm almost afraid to ask, but how did you know?"

"I don't know," he said, and I could picture him shrugging. "You know what you're talking about. It's the only way you could know." Eager as a puppy, he continued. "So what's it like for you? Do you have a pack?"

Gosh, did I? I wasn't sure anymore. I'd been beaten up by T.J., I'd disobeyed Carl—when I showed up for the next full moon, I wasn't sure they'd have me. I took a chance. "Yes, I do."

"What's it like? What're *they* like?"

Occasionally, a werewolf attacked someone and there wasn't a pack to take care of the victim, to show him what had happened, to teach him how to live with it. James must have been one of those. I couldn't imagine that. T.J. held me my first full moon, the first time I shifted. It made it easier, at least a little.

I tried to be honest. Or honest for that particular moment in time. "Well. Can't live with 'em, can't live without 'em."

"What's that supposed to mean?"

So much for a sense of humor. "I value my pack a whole lot. It's been there for me when I needed it. But it can be frustrating. There isn't a whole lot of room for argument." I wondered if Carl or T.J. were listening.

"But you think werewolves need to be in a pack."

"I think packs serve a good purpose. They keep werewolves under some sort of control, so they don't go hunting sheep. Or small children—that was a joke, by the way."

"You don't think a werewolf can make it on his own, then?"

"I didn't say that. It's just that in my experience, it would be hard."

"Oh."

"You said you're alone, James. How do you handle it?"

"I—I don't." He hung up, the line clicking off. Great. I felt queasy about that one.

"Right. Thanks for calling, James."

Matt was waving through the window, pointing at the door to the booth. Rick was standing there. I hadn't noticed him come in. He was lounging against the doorjamb like he'd been there for hours. He waved his hand in a blasé greeting.

I turned back to the mike. "Okay, we're going to break for station ID. More calls when we get back. This is *The Midnight Hour.*"

Matt made the cutting motion that signaled we were off the air. This gave the local stations a few minutes for commercials and promotions. I pulled off my headphones and went to the door.

"Hey, Rick." I tried to sound casual. Either he was going to deliver a scathing message from Arturo or he wanted to know what I'd found out about the Church of the Pure Faith. I still hadn't learned much.

"Hello. So, this is the famous studio."

"Yeah. Not to be rude, but I'm going to have to get back to it in a minute. What can I do for you?"

"I thought we might trade information. What have you found out about Elijah Smith?"

There it was. I shrugged. "Not much. Nobody who knows him is talking. A couple of reporters tried to sneak into his caravan once and got thrown out. I'm going to keep at it. I've still got a couple of leads to try. I'm sorry I can't give you more."

He pursed his lips, masking disappointment. "Well, maybe your persistence will pay off. In the meantime . . ."

He offered me a manila envelope. "I heard your show last week. I thought you might be interested in this."

"What is it?"

"Evidence," he said. "Now you have no reason to go poking around Obsidian by yourself again."

I looked up. My throat got tight. "You know about that?"

He nodded. "So does Arturo. He's disappointed you didn't give him a chance to act against you directly."

"Yeah. I bet he is." How stupid could I have been? Of course Arturo had guards posted. Of course they spotted me. Score another point for cowardly self-preservation.

I took the envelope and scooped inside for the contents. There were a few photos, weirdly lit in black and white, like they had been taken with some kind of night vision camera. There was a forested area. I recognized the slope of hill behind Carl and Meg's house. A couple of people were running with a couple of wolves. One of the faces was circled. Mine, of course. A couple of photos later in the sequence, I was ripping off my clothes and my body was changing shape. These were copies of the photos that set Cormac on me. I put them back.

The rest of the envelope held a half-dozen pages of information. Some phone records, a terse written agreement—someone putting a contract on you didn't mean it was actually a *contract*. I didn't think hit men gave out receipts.

Rick explained. "Those show phone calls between Arturo and his go-between, and the go-between and Cormac. The go-between is a woman with ties to the local militia movement. Cormac has a background with them. She's been discussing with Arturo the possibility of, ah, signing up, as it were. She'd do anything for him."

"What else do you know about Cormac?"

"He doesn't work cheap. There are some figures listed." He showed me the appropriate piece of paper. I blinked.

"That's a lot of zeros."

"Indeed."

"Arturo wants me dead that badly?"

"Oh, I don't know. He had backing. There's a whole conglomerate that's unhappy with you."

"Who else?"

"That I'm afraid I don't know. Sorry."

"No, don't apologize. This is great." In fact, I was choked up. I'd been feeling friendless lately, and here came help from such an unexpected quarter. "Why help me like this? If Arturo finds out you did this—"

He made a dismissive gesture, as if he'd just loaned me five bucks and not saved my ass.

"Don't worry about that. He doesn't have to know. You may not believe it, but there are some of us who think you're doing good work."

There was always the possibility that Arturo had put him up to this, that this was all part of some nefarious plot to . . . to do *something*.

Rick deserved better than that kind of attitude. I sighed, humbled. "Thanks. Could you get a copy of all this to Cormac?"

"Already done."

"Thanks, Rick. I owe you one."

He tilted his head, regarding the ceiling for a moment. "You know, I could also be helping you because it would make Arturo crazy."

He winked, grinned, and slipped out as quietly as he'd arrived.

He melted into the shadows at the other end of the corridor. Like a vampire or something.

Matt was staring. "Was that . . . was that a . . ." He made a gesture, two fingers pointing down from his mouth like fangs.

"Yeah. So, Matt, how do you feel about this job now?"

He shook his head, whistling through his teeth. "Never a dull moment."

The next day at work, I had a list of phone numbers sitting on top of the pile of crap spread all over my desk—ratings projections, transcripts, unanswered mail, phone messages, newspapers and magazines that I used as fodder. The headline on *Wide World of News* this week was "Following Kitty Norville's Lead, Dozens of Vampire and Werewolf Celebrities Confess!" They had pictures of Quentin Tarantino, David Bowie, Britney Spears (huh?), and . . . Bill Clinton? Yeah, right.

I'd made it to the cover of *Wide World of News*. I must have really hit the big time. Or something.

I crossed off phone numbers as I made calls. Reporters, police departments, people who knew people who'd disappeared into Elijah Smith's caravan. I'd already talked to the reporters from *Uncharted World* who'd tried to break into the caravan. One of them had a theory that Smith was actually a front for government researchers who needed vampire and werewolf test subjects. The other one sounded a bit more sane, thinking that some sort of cult of personality had formed around Elijah Smith. Neither one of them believed he was really curing anyone. We couldn't know, because we couldn't talk to any of his people.

No one left him. The caravan was growing. What if it worked?

I tracked the latest piece of the puzzle to Modesto, California, where the caravan had parked two nights ago. The police there had tried to issue Smith citations for trespassing and causing a disturbance. The two officers who'd been sent to issue the tickets woke up in their patrol car the next morning with no memory of what had happened over the last eight hours. The caravan was gone. I tried to talk to the officers in question, but apparently they were still in the hospital, for observation. I spent two hours on the phone, but no one would tell me what was wrong with them, or where they thought the caravan would appear next.

As I hung up the phone, one of the KNOB interns brought me a letter. She bopped into the room, handed it to me, and bopped out again. It didn't have a stamp or return address—it had been hand-delivered. I should have been suspicious. But I had a feeling. It smelled okay. I opened it and drew out a card, blank except for a handwritten line, *You were right. I owe you one*, and a phone number.

chapter 7

Hello, you're on *The Midnight Hour.*"

"I want to know about the orgies."

"The orgies?"

"Yeah, the vampire orgies. How do I find out where they are? How do I get in on one of them?"

"Hm . . . let's see. Are you a vampire?"

"Yeah."

"Then you usually get invited. Are you part of an organized Family, or are you on your own?"

"I have a Family." He sounded indignant, like how dare I suggest he wasn't sufficiently pedigreed.

"Not all Families have orgies. I mean—what kind of orgy are you looking for?"

"You know . . . orgies. An *orgy* orgy." I could almost see the vague hand gestures accompanying his speech. The alarm bells started going off—that little twitching in my mind when I suspected I was being had.

I said, "*Orgy*, orgy. Right. How long have you been a vampire?"

"Uh . . . not *too* long."

"No, really. How long specifically? Because you realize that 'not long' has an entirely different scope to some vampires. If you've been around since the Roman Empire, 'not long' might be a couple of centuries, you know? How long is 'not long'?"

"Um . . . a year?" He was fishing for the right answer, the one that would get him on my good side.

"Okay, what's your name . . . Dave. Right. You're not a vampire."

"But—"

"You know why you're not? Because vampires don't have *orgy* orgies. You're looking for lots of hot sex with nubile vampire babes, and you're thinking a vampire orgy is the place to get it because you've heard all these stories. Right?"

"But . . . but . . . I mean . . ."

"But you know what? Sex is different for vampires. When a vampire says sex and a normal human says sex, they're talking about two different things. Because vampires don't have sex without sucking blood. Sex is almost synonymous with feeding for them. Are you getting this, Dave? If you feel like being the main course, by all means, go find yourself a vampire orgy, because I can tell you exactly what those nubile vampire babes are going to do to you."

"But . . . I mean . . . the stories . . . I've heard . . ."

Gullible *and* inarticulate. Gotta love it. "Next caller, you're on the air. Bruce?"

"Um, hi, yeah. I wanted to know, could I get the phone number for that assassin who was on the show last month?"

"You mean Cormac? You want Cormac's phone number?" I couldn't keep the tone of annoyance out of my voice. "The same Cormac who tried to kill me?"

"Yeah."

"May I ask *why* you want Cormac's phone number?"

"Well, you know. I kind of wanted to ask if he needs an assistant, or an apprentice or something."

"So, Bruce, you want to be a werewolf hunter?"

"Yeah."

"It's a dangerous line of work. You ever see a werewolf in action?"

"Um . . . on TV. You know—on *Uncharted World* and stuff."

"Oh, my God, the videos on that show are *so* doctored. Let me tell you what it really looks like. The average werewolf has four sets of claws as long as your fingers. Two-inch-long canines. Jaw pressure five times that of a human. And werewolves are fast. I'm talking a two-minute mile. Can you run that fast, Bruce?"

"Uh—"

"Can you shoot straight?"

"Uh—"

"Do you know how long it takes the average werewolf to tear apart a full-grown deer?"

"No—"

I smiled sweetly. The expression was lost on the radio, but the tone would carry through my voice. "The last time I did it, it took about five minutes. And I'm just an average werewolf."

I swore I heard Bruce gulp over the line.

"Whoa."

"Sorry, Bruce, it's kind of against my own personal self-interest to do free advertising for werewolf hunters. You know what I mean? Thanks for calling."

I did an inward shudder. People would *not* shut up about Cormac, and it was starting to get on my nerves.

"Next caller. Betty, you're on the air. What's your question?"

"Hi, Kitty. I just wanted to know, are you going out with that Cormac guy from last month?"

My jaw dropped. I took a full five seconds to recover and say, "What?"

"Are you going out with that Cormac guy?"

"We are talking about the same Cormac who tried to kill me on the air, yes? The guy who hunts werewolves for a living?"

"Uh-huh."

"And you want to know if I'm *dating* him? Why on earth do you think that's a good idea?"

"Well, I sort of sensed something between you two when he was on the show."

"You sensed something. Are you psychic?"

"I don't think so."

"Empathic?"

"No."

"Clairvoyant?"

"No."

"Then why the hell do you think we would go out? Of *course* you sensed something! He hunts werewolves. I'm a werewolf. There's this whole hunter-prey dynamic that happens. He wanted to kill me. I was ready to defend myself, claws and bullets on the verge of flying everywhere—things were tense. *That* was what you were sensing."

"But he *didn't* kill you. You worked it out. He sounded kind of nice. His voice sounded really cute. Was he cute?"

"Well, yeah, sort of. If you like guys who wear revolvers in hip holsters."

"It's just that you sound kind of anxious whenever anyone brings up Cormac, and I thought there might be unresolved tension there."

"He tried to kill me! What other explanation do you need? Moving on to the next call. Hello!"

"Um, hi, Kitty. I sort of forgot my question. But that last caller's idea—about you going out with Cormac and stuff. That would be kind of interesting, don't you think?"

"No. No, I don't think it would be interesting at all."

"Well, it's just that you're always talking about cross-supernatural racial understanding, and that would, you know, make a bridge. It would be diplomatic."

Diplomatic. Yeah. I thought real hard about being diplomatic before I answered. "Just a reminder: This is *my* show. *I'm* the one who's supposed to give out lousy advice."

I searched the monitor for a call that couldn't possibly have anything to do with werewolf hunters.

"Hello, Ingrid from Minneapolis."

"Hi, Kitty. I just wanted to tell you that I'm a werewolf, I've been one for about ten years now, and I'm married to the most wonderful man in the world. *And* he's a wildlife control officer. We get along fine; we're just careful to keep the lines of communication open."

The studio was getting stuffy. I fanned myself with my cue sheet.

"Wow, Ingrid. That's really interesting. Can I ask how you two met?"

"Well, it was a full moon night—"

I read between the lines of the story and was willing to bet that Mr. Ingrid had a fur fetish. It happened sometimes. But they sounded happy and that was what mattered, right?

"—so I wouldn't let your prejudice against bounty hunters interfere with what might turn out to be something wonderful."

Keeping my voice as even as possible, I said, "I don't have a prejudice against bounty hunters. I have a prejudice against people who are trying to kill me."

Matt started waving frantically at me through the booth window. "Kitty, you gotta take line two."

"What? Why?" I checked the monitor. "There's no name. Didn't you screen it?"

"Just take the call."

I punched the line. "Yes? What?"

"Norville. It's Cormac. If you don't change the subject right now, I'm going to have to go over there and have a word with you."

Cormac. Geez. I was strangely flattered that he even listened to the show.

"I've been *trying* to change the subject." Not that he'd know it from the last fifteen minutes. I wondered what would happen if I called his bluff. "But hey, thanks for calling. So, you did get out of jail."

"DA didn't want to prosecute without your testimony. Got off scot-free."

"And have you ever dated a werewolf?"

There was a pause of a couple of beats. "That is none of your business."

He didn't flat-out deny it. Oh, how interesting.

"What if someone you were dating was attacked and infected with lycanthropy and became a werewolf? Would you dump her? Would you feel a deep instinctual desire to kill her?"

"Change the topic. I mean it."

"Cormac, when was the last time you went on a date?"

One of the challenges of doing a radio show was judging everything by people's voices. I couldn't see their faces and expressions. I had to gauge the inflections of their voices to judge their moods and reactions.

So while I couldn't see Cormac's face, I could tell by the lightness in his voice that he was grinning. "Norville, when was the last time *you* went on a date?"

The phone line clicked off.

Bastard.

"That, my friend, is none of your business," I said at the microphone. I straightened, donned a smile, and thought happy thoughts. My claws around Cormac's throat. My hands itched.

A couple of days later I was still trying to clean up that same pile of crap on my desk when I got a phone call.

"Hello. How are you, Ms. Norville?"

It was the CDC guy, Paranatural Biology, whatever flavor of government spook he was. I should have expected him to call again.

"Hello, Mr. Throat."

"Excuse me?"

"Never mind. What can I do for you?"

"Nothing out of the ordinary. I'd just like to talk."

"The last time you called to have a chat, you hung up on me."

"I have to be careful. I don't think you quite understand my position—"

I huffed, exasperated. "Of course not; you haven't told me what your position is!" At this point, I was betting he was a wacko with delusions of grandeur trying to incorporate me into his paranoid fantasy. Then again, he might have been that *and* some kind of government spook.

He made an annoyed sigh. "I wanted to talk to you about your revelation. I'd wondered, of course. About your identity. This is a very brave move you've made."

"How so?"

"You've exposed yourself. But you've also created an opportunity. You might be making my job easier."

"You still haven't told me what your job is."

"I think you know more than you're letting on."

He'd mentioned the Center for the Study of Paranatural Biology. He must have been involved with that project, involved with reporting the findings to the government.

"Let's check that," I said. "The publicity my show is generating in some way lends weight to the research that's going on. You're trying to bring attention to that study, and my show is opening the door to that. Doing the legwork for you. Before too long, people will be demanding that the study be exposed."

"That's a distinct possibility." He sounded like he was smiling, like he was pleased.

"Can I ask a couple of questions?"

"I reserve the right not to answer."

"Oh, always. Why wasn't that study given more publicity to begin with? It's over a year old. It wasn't classified, but it was just . . . ignored."

"Ironically, classifying it would have drawn more attention to it, and some people don't want that. As for publicizing it—secrecy is a powerful tool among some communities."

Like vampires. I had my own streak of paranoia in that regard. "Next question. How did you get your test subjects to participate? Based on that secrecy you just mentioned, why would they submit to examination?"

"May I ask you a question?"

"Sure."

"If there were a cure, would you take it?"

A couple of months after the attack, when I'd gotten over the shock and started finding my feet again, I did a lot of research. I read about wolves. I read all the folklore I could get my hands on. A lot of stories talked about cures. Kill the wolf that made the werewolf. I couldn't try that one. Drink a tea made of wolfsbane under a new moon. That one just made me sick.

Then I gave up. Because it wasn't so bad, really.

"I don't know," I said finally. "Does the name Elijah Smith ring a bell with you?"

"No. Should it?"

"You might want to look it up. Is that what you guys are doing? Looking for a cure?"

"Tell me—who do you talk to when you need advice?"

What was this, a game of questions? "Are you offering to be my bartender?"

"No. I just—I respect you. Good-bye, Ms. Norville."

"Wait—" But he'd already hung up.

I needed a drink. I needed a bodyguard.

The phone rang again, and I nearly jumped out of my chair. I swear to God, if I wasn't doing a call-in radio show, I'd get an unlisted number.

"Hello?"

"Ms. Norville?"

"Hello, Detective Hardin."

"You remember me. Good."

"I'm not likely to forget that night." Probably the second-most-fear-intensive night of my life.

"No, I guess not. I wondered if I could get you to do a little consulting on a case."

"What about?"

She paused; I could hear her drawing a deep breath over the phone, like she was steeling herself. "It's a crime scene. A murder."

I closed my eyes. "And you think something supernatural did it."

"I'm pretty sure. But I want a second opinion before I start making noise. It could get ugly."

She was telling me? All it would take was one rogue vampire sucking dry an adorable preteen girl. "You know I don't have any sort of training in this, no forensics or even first aid."

"I know. But you're the only person I know who has any familiarity with this subject."

"Except for Cormac, eh?"

"I don't trust him."

That was something, anyway, getting a cop to trust a monster more than a monster killer. Maybe the show was doing some good after all. Maybe my being exposed would do some good.

"I'll need a ride."

"I'm on my way."

Hardin picked me up in an unmarked police sedan. As soon as she pulled away from the curb she started a rambling monologue. It sounded casual, but her knuckles were white and her brow was furrowed. She was also smoking, sucking on her cigarette like it was her first all day, tapping the ashes out the cracked window.

"I started listening to your show. That night we got called to your studio was so weird—I was curious. I still am. I'm learning more all the time. I've been going over all our mauling death cases from the last few years. Most of them are too old to have any evidence to follow up on, or we caught the animal that did it. But now—I don't think I can ever write off one of these to wild dogs again. You convinced me. You guys are known for ripping people's throats out."

She looked at me sideways, smiling grimly. She had dark hair tied in a short ponytail. Hazel eyes. Didn't wear makeup. Her clothes were functional—shirt, trousers, and blazer. Nothing glamorous about her. She was intensely straightforward.

I slumped against the passenger-side door. "We don't *all* rip people's throats out."

"Fair enough. Anyway, a year ago I would have been looking for a pack of wild dingoes escaped from the zoo on a case like this. But now—"

"You're stalling. How bad is it?"

She gripped the steering wheel. "I don't know. How strong is your stomach?"

I hesitated. I ate raw meat on a regular basis, but not by preference. "It depends on what I'm doing," I said, dodging.

"What do you mean, what you're doing?"

How did I explain that it depended on how many legs I was walking on at the time? I couldn't guess if that would freak her out. She might try to arrest me. Best to let it go. "Never mind."

"She was a prostitute, eighteen years old. The body is in three separate pieces. Not counting fragments. Jagged wounds consistent with the bite and claw marks of a large predator. The . . . mass of the remains does not initially appear to equal the original mass of the victim."

"Shit," I muttered, rubbing my forehead. She'd been eaten. Maybe I wasn't ready for this after all.

"It wasn't a full moon last night," she said. "Could it still be a werewolf that did it?"

"Werewolves can shape-shift any time they want. Full moon nights are the only time they have to."

"How do I tell if this is a lycanthrope and not a big, angry dog?"

"Smell," I said without thinking.

"What?"

"Smell. A lycanthrope smells different. At least to another lycanthrope."

"Okay," she drawled. "And if you aren't around to use as a bloodhound?"

I sighed. "If you can find DNA samples of the attacker, there are markers. There's an obscure CDC report about lycanthrope DNA markers. I'll get you the reference. Are you sure it wasn't just a big dog?"

If the attacker were a werewolf, it would just about have to be one of Carl's pack. But I didn't think any of them were capable of hunting in the city, of going rogue like that. They'd have to answer to Carl. If there were a strange werewolf in town, Carl would confront him for invading his territory.

I dreaded what I was going to find. If I smelled the pack at this place, if I could tell who did it—did I tell Hardin, or did I make excuses until I talked to Carl? Nervously, I tapped my foot on the floorboard. Hardin glanced at it, so I stopped.

We drove to Capitol Hill, the bad part of town even for people like me. Lots of old-fashioned, one-story houses gone to ruin, overgrown yards, gangbanger cars cruising the intersections in daylight. The whole street was cordoned off by police cruisers and yellow tape. A uniformed officer waved Hardin through. She parked on the curb near an alley. An ambulance was parked there, and the place crawled with people wearing uniforms and plastic gloves.

In addition, vans from three different local news stations were parked at the end of the street. Cameramen hefted video cameras; a few well-dressed people who must have been reporters lurked nearby. The police were keeping them back, but the cameramen had their equipment aimed like the film was rolling.

I kept Hardin between me and the cameras as we walked to the crime scene.

She spoke to a guy in a suit, then turned to make introductions. "Kitty Norville, Detective Salazar."

The detective's eyes got wide, and he smirked. "The werewolf celebrity?"

"Yeah," I said, an edge of challenge in my voice. I offered my hand. For a minute I didn't think he was going to shake it, but he did. He stood six inches taller than me, and I didn't look that scary. And I had a winning smile.

Salazar said to Hardin, "You sure this is a good idea? If those guys find out she's here, they're going to have a field day." He pointed his thumb over his shoulder at the news vans.

That was all I needed, my face all over the nightly news: "Werewolves Loose Downtown."

"I'll keep an eye on them. She's a consultant, that's all."

Too late. We were already attracting attention. One of the cameras pointed at us. A woman reporter in a tailored skirt suit glanced at the camera, then at us. As soon as their attention was on us, the other news teams looked to see what they'd found. In my jeans and sweater, I was obviously a civilian in a place where the cops didn't normally allow civilians. The media would ask questions. I turned my back to the newspeople.

"I don't like cameras," I said. "I'd rather people don't know what I look like."

"Okay." Hardin shifted, blocking the cameras' view of me. "Salazar, get people into those buildings to make sure they don't try filming down from the windows."

"Already done."

"Good. This shouldn't take too long."

"Let's just get it over with," I said. Salazar led us both to the mouth of the alley.

I'd seen what werewolves and vampires could do when they really lost it, when all they knew was blood and slaughter. Shredded venison. Deer guts everywhere, with a half-dozen wolves swimming in the carcass. I thought I knew what to expect. This was nothing like it.

Her eyes were open. Blood caked her dark hair, splattered her slack face, but I saw the eyes first, frozen and glistening. The head was about four feet away from the rest of the remains. My vision gave out for a moment, turning splotchy. There were pieces. Legs twisted one way, naked arms and torso twisted another way, clothing torn right along with them. A spill of organs—shining, dark lumps—lay between them. Like rejects from a butcher's shop, not something that belonged out in the street, in the open.

The worst part was, I could work out how the attacker had done it. Claws together in the belly, ripped outward in opposite directions, jaws on the throat—

I was human. I couldn't do that. I couldn't *think* it. But the Wolf could. Did. For a second, I didn't know which I was, because I was stuck between them. I had to remind myself who I was. I covered my mouth and turned away.

Some joker in a uniform laughed. "And you call yourself a monster."

I glared—another wolf would have taken it as a challenge. But this clown couldn't read the sign.

"I've never ripped anyone's throat out," I said. Though I got close with Zan . . .

Hardin stood at my shoulder. "She's the third one to match this MO in the last two months. The first two were written off as wild animal mauling deaths. Coyotes, maybe. Then I started asking questions. We found that the saliva on the bite wounds is human. Mostly human, anyway."

I turned the corner out of the alley and leaned against the wall. So. Could werewolves really overcome their natures to be productive members of society, or was I just blowing smoke? I wanted to believe a lycanthrope hadn't done this. Hardin was wrong; this was some animal—

I closed my eyes and took a deep breath.

The smell of blood and decay was overpowering. The victim had been lying here since the previous night. Carrion, my other self hinted, salivating. *Stop it.* I went further, to the little smells that fringed my senses, like the flash of sunlight on rippling water.

Tar and asphalt. Car exhaust. Hardin had brushed her teeth recently. Mint and tobacco. Rats. And . . . there it was. A wild smell, incongruous with the city's signature scents. Musky and fierce. And human, under it all. Male. He smelled of skin and fur.

I didn't recognize the individual scent mark. Nor did it smell like my pack—Carl's group. I was almost relieved. Except that it meant we had a rogue wolf running around.

"It's a werewolf," I said, opening my eyes.

Hardin was watching me, her gaze narrowed. "Friend of yours?"

I glared. "No. Look, you asked for my help, but if you're going to go all suspicious on me, I'm going to leave."

"Sorry," she said, holding up her hands in a defensive gesture. "But if I understand it correctly, if I was listening close enough to your show, you have packs, right? Can I assume that you know other werewolves in the city?"

She'd done some homework, for which I had to give grudging admiration. She stood close—but not so close she couldn't duck out of arm's reach in a second—one arm propped on the wall. Her expression wasn't inquisitive anymore. She wasn't looking to me for an answer. Suspicion radiated off her.

"You didn't bring me here as a consultant," I said. "You think I can tell you who did this. You want me for questioning."

She bowed her head for a moment; when she returned her gaze to me, her determined expression confirmed it. "You said you could smell it. If you know who did this, I really need you to tell me."

"I don't know who did this. You have to believe me."

"I could take you in as a material witness."

"*Witness?* I didn't see anything!"

"You're in possession of a piece of evidence our forensics people don't have. That makes you a witness."

My head was spinning. She'd drawn me straight into the middle of this, but there was no way she could hold me there. Precedents, legal precedents—I was going to need a research assistant before too long. Was I out of my mind? There weren't going to be any legal precedents.

Hardin continued. "Would you recognize the wolf that did this if you ran into him?"

"Yeah. I think I would."

"Then keep in touch. Let me know if you find out anything. That's all I want."

She wanted me to be a freakin' witness for a crime I had nothing to do with and was nowhere near. The manipulative bitch.

"There's no way in hell an after-the-fact witness by smell would be admissible in court. The courts aren't going to know what to do with that kind of testimony."

"Not yet," she said with a wry smile. "Give me another minute and I'll drive you back."

One of the reporters, the woman in the suit, was waiting for us at Hardin's car. A man held a camera pointed at us, over her shoulder.

"Shit," I muttered.

Hardin frowned. "Ignore them. Walk by like they're not even there."

"They can't air pictures of me without my permission, right?"

"They can. Sorry."

I hunched my shoulders and ducked my head, unwilling to lose my dignity to the point of covering my face. Besides, it was too late.

The reporter dodged Hardin and came straight toward me, wielding a microphone. "Angela Bryant, KTNC. You're Kitty Norville, the radio show host, right? What is your involvement with this case, Ms. Norville? *Are* you a witness? *Is* there a supernatural element to these deaths?"

For once, I kept my mouth shut. I let Hardin open the car door and close it when I'd climbed inside. Calmly, she made her way around to the driver's side. I propped my elbow on the inside door and shielded my face with my hand.

We drove away.

Hardin said, "For a celebrity, you're a shy one."

"I've always liked radio for its anonymity."

We stopped in front of the KNOB studio. I was about to get out of the car—slink out of the car as innocently as I could—when Hardin stopped me.

"One more question." I braced. She reached into her coat pocket. "I felt stupid when I went looking for these. But they were easier to find than I thought they'd be. I guess there really is a market for this kind of thing. I have to know, though—will they work?"

She opened her hand, revealing a trio of nine-millimeter bullets, shiny and silver. I stared at them like she was holding a poisonous snake at me.

"Yeah," I said. "They'll work."

"Thanks." She pocketed the bullets. "Maybe I should invest in a couple of crosses, too."

"Don't forget the wooden stakes."

Waving a half-assed good-bye, I fled before the conversation could go any further.

chapter

The phone rang eight times. Didn't the guy have voice mail? I was about to give up when he finally answered.

"Yeah."

"Cormac? Is this Cormac?"

There was a long pause. Then, "Norville?"

"Yeah. It's me."

"So." Another long pause. Laconic, that was the word. "Why are you calling me?"

"I just talked to the cops. That spate of mauling deaths downtown? A werewolf did it. I didn't recognize the scent. It's a rogue."

"What do you want me to do about it?"

I'd seen his rates. Despite the show's success, I couldn't exactly hire him to hunt the rogue. Did I think he'd do it out of the kindness of his heart?

"I don't know. Just keep your eyes open. Maybe I didn't want you to think it was me."

"How do I know you're not lying to me about it now?"

I winced. "You don't."

"Don't worry. You said it yourself. You're harmless, right?"

"Yeah," I said weakly. "That's me."

"Thanks for the tip." He hung up.

What was it with everyone thinking they could just hang up on me? *I* never hung up on anybody. At least not outside the show. Well, not often.

Then I realized—I'd talked to the werewolf hunter about this before talking to Carl.

I was going to have to talk to Carl soon anyway. Until now, I'd been avoiding him, but the full moon was tomorrow, and I didn't want to go through it alone. He wasn't going to let the fact that I was still doing the show pass without comment. I'd sort of hoped I could just show up and slink along with the pack without any of them noticing. That was about as likely as me turning up my nose at one of T.J.'s barely cooked steaks. It was really a matter of deciding in which situation—just showing up, or facing him beforehand—I was least likely to get the shit beat out of me. Or in which situation I would get the least amount of shit beat out of me.

Maybe it would have been easier if Cormac had just shot me.

I called T.J. first. My stomach was in knots. I thought I was going to be sick, waiting for him to pick up the phone. I hadn't talked to him since the night outside Obsidian.

He answered. My gut clenched. But it was still good to hear his voice.

"It's me. I need to talk to you. And Carl and Meg."

For a long time, he didn't say anything. I listened hard—was he beating his head against the wall? Growling?

Then he said, "I'll pick you up."

I rode behind him on his motorcycle, holding on just enough to keep from falling off. We hadn't spoken yet. I'd waited on the curb for him, shoulders bunched up and slouching. He'd pulled up, and I didn't meet his gaze. I'd climbed on the bike, cowering behind him. He'd turned around and ruffled my hair, a quick pass of his hand over my scalp. I'm not sure what this said. I was sorry that he was angry at me, but I wasn't sorry for anything I'd said or done. I didn't want to fight him, and I didn't want to be submissive. That would be admitting he was right. So I wallowed in doubt. He'd touched me, which meant—which meant that maybe things weren't so bad.

We pulled up in front of Meg and Carl's house. He got off. I stayed on. I didn't want to do this.

T.J. crossed his arms. "This was your idea, remember?"

"He's gonna kill me."

"Come on." He grabbed me behind the neck and pulled. I stumbled off the bike and let him guide me up the driveway, like I was some kind of truant.

He opened the front door and maneuvered me inside.

Carl and Meg were in the kitchen, parked at the breakfast bar like they'd been waiting for us. T.J. had probably called ahead.

Meg had been leaning with her elbows on the countertop; Carl had his back to the counter. Both of them straightened. With them in front of me and T.J. behind me, I suddenly felt like I was at a tribunal. I shrugged away from T.J.'s hand. The least I could do was stand on my own feet.

Carl stood before me with his arms crossed, glaring down at me. "You haven't quit the show. What do you have to say for yourself?"

I thought I'd finished with that when I moved out of my parents' house. I shrugged. "I got a raise."

He cocked his hand back to strike, and I ducked. We both froze midmotion. He stood with his fist in the air, and I bowed my back, my knees ready to give, cowering. Then he relaxed, and I did the same, straightening slowly, waiting for him to change his mind and hit me anyway.

This was so fucked up. But all Wolf wanted to do was put her tail between her legs and whine until he told us he loved us again.

His hands opened and closed into fists at his side. "Can't you say anything without trying to get a rise out of people?"

"No."

Carl moved away to stalk up and down the length of the kitchen. Meg, arms crossed, glared at me. I cringed and tried to look contrite, but she wasn't having it.

Nothing to do but plow ahead, now that I was here. What was it some weird philosophy professor had said to me once? *What's the worst thing that can happen? You'll die. And we don't know that's bad . . .*

Ah, so that was why I'd changed my major to English.

I wasn't here to talk about me. "The police came to talk to me—"

"*What?*" T.J. said, gripping my shoulder. Carl and Meg both moved toward me.

I ducked and turned, getting away from T.J.'s grasp and fleeing to the living room, putting the sofa between them and me.

"Just listen. You have to listen to me, dammit!" The sofa wasn't discouraging them. T.J. was coming around it from one side, Meg from the other. Carl looked like he was planning on going straight over. I backed against the wall, wondering if I could jump over him.

I had to talk fast. "A detective called me. They've got a serial killer—mauling deaths. At first they thought it was an animal, a feral dog or something. But now they think it's one of us. They asked me for help. They—they took me to a crime scene today." My breathing came fast. Talking about it, I remembered the scene, what it looked like, the way it smelled. The memory was doing something to me, waking that other part of me. My skin was hot; I rubbed my face. "I saw the body. I smelled it . . . I know . . . they're right. It's a werewolf, but I didn't recognize him. There's—it's a rogue, in our . . . in your territory."

Pressed against the wall, I slid to the floor, holding my face in my hands. I couldn't talk anymore. I remembered the smell, and it was making me sick. Wolf remembered, and it woke her up. Made her hungry. I held on to the feeling of my limbs, my human limbs and the shape of my body.

Then T.J. was kneeling beside me, putting his arms around me, lending me his strength. "Keep it together," he whispered into my hair. "That's a girl."

I hugged him as hard as I could. I settled down somehow, until I was calm enough to breathe normally, and I didn't feel like I was going to burst my skin anymore.

T.J. let me pull away from him. I huddled miserably on the floor. Carl looked like he was going to march over to me. Meg held him back, touching his arm. She stared at me, like she'd never seen me before.

"Why did you agree to talk to them?" she said.

"Don't you think it would have looked a little suspicious if I'd told them to fuck off?"

"What could they have done about it if you had?"

"I couldn't do that. I've got a reputation—"

"*That's* your problem."

I ran a hand over my hair, which was coming out of its braid and needed washing. This wasn't getting anywhere. How did I word this without seeming like I was questioning them, or ordering them around? "The pack should take care of this, shouldn't it?"

Carl glared. "If there was a rogue in town, don't you think I'd know about it?"

"I don't know. Maybe he's got a good hiding place. I mean, if you knew about him, he wouldn't be a rogue."

Meg blocked my exit around that end of the sofa. "You told them it was a werewolf that did this? You told them that was what you smelled?"

"Yeah."

Her shoulders were bunched, like hackles rising. She wasn't being the good cop anymore. "You should have lied. You should have told them you didn't know what it was."

Easy for her to say. I didn't lie well. Especially to cops. "They have tests for that kind of thing now. They would have found out eventually. I'm lucky they're not assuming that I did it."

"You're an easy target," Carl said, turning on me. "How many times do I have to tell you to quit the show?"

"Two hundred markets," I countered, raising an eyebrow. I could almost see him working out the math of how much money that was.

T.J. said to Carl, "If there's a rogue in town killing people, the cops can't handle it. We have to. If we don't want them paying more attention to us, we have to make the problem go away."

That was exactly what I'd been trying to say. I owed *him* a steak dinner.

I said, "This detective knows just enough to identify the problem, but not enough to do anything about it. T.J.'s right."

Carl paced, back and forth, back and forth, like he was caged. His jaw was tight. "Do you know anything else about this rogue besides how he smells?"

"No," I said.

T.J. said, "We could go looking. Find out where these deaths have happened. If he's marking a territory, we'll find him. I could do it on my own if you want—"

Meg said, "You're wrong. There's no rogue."

Of course she'd side with Carl. She kept glaring at me, and I didn't like the look in her eyes: cold, predatory.

"We have to do *something*," I said, ignoring Meg at my peril.

"Nobody's going to do anything until I say so," Carl said.

"When is that going to be?" T.J. crouched like he was getting ready to pounce.

Carl glared. "When I say so."

"And in the meantime he kills again."

Glaring down at him, Carl stepped close to T.J. His fists tightened. "Are you challenging me?"

For a minute I thought it was going to happen, right then and there. It wouldn't take much for an argument between an alpha male and his second to degenerate into an all-out fight. That was part of why T.J. sided with Carl most of the time. The least little dissension could be misinterpreted.

When T.J. didn't back down, but met Carl's gaze without flinching, I thought they would fight. Then T.J. slumped, his back bowing and his head drooping.

"No," he said.

Carl tipped his chin up with the victory. "Then it's settled. We wait. This is my pack, my territory. I'll take care of it." He grabbed my shirt and hauled me to my feet. "And you will not talk to the police again."

"Yeah, just wait until they come knocking on *your* door." I bit my lip. That came out more sarcastic than I'd intended.

Carl pursed his lips. "I think we need to have a little talk."

Oh, great. This was when he would put me in my place. His hand shifted to grip the back of my neck and he pushed me ahead of him, toward the hallway that led to the bedrooms.

Meg stepped in front of him, stopping him. "Let me talk to her."

Carl stared at her like she'd turned green. Meg had never had one of these "little talks" with me. She'd always left it to Carl. Even knowing that our "talks" often ended up with him screwing me, she left him to it. It was part of being with the pack, of being wolf. Maybe she'd finally had enough.

She glared at me like she wanted to bite a piece out of me. I concentrated on cowering. I didn't want to be an alpha; I didn't want to challenge anybody. I could feel the Wolf shrinking inside me, ready to whine. I never thought I'd prefer getting dressed down by Carl. I leaned back so I was touching his body, sheltered by him.

Then Carl and Meg were the ones trading glares. A good old-fashioned staring contest. What would happen if they got into a knock-down, drag-out fight? That wasn't supposed to happen.

"Not today," Carl said and marched past her, pulling me along with him. I scrambled to keep up, dizzy with fear and the irony that at the moment I actually felt safer with him.

When we got to the bedroom at the end of the hall, he pulled me inside and closed the door. He trapped me, hands spread on the wall on either side of my head, his usual stance. He glared at me for what seemed like a long time. My heart raced; I kept my gaze lowered, waiting.

Then he went for my neck.

I might have thought he'd turned vampire, if I didn't know better. He nuzzled my hairline, and his mouth opened over my skin, kissing me. I tipped my head back, giving him access. His tongue licked, he caught my earlobe in his teeth, released a hot breath against my cheek. He used the full length of his body to press me to the wall. I could feel him, aroused like he'd been let out of a monastery and into cheerleading practice.

Despite my confusion, I melted in his arms. I clung to him, not wanting to lose contact with a single inch of him. There was more than one way to win submission from an underling.

"You're not angry?" I murmured.

"I'm reminding you of your place."

Carl's toy. I'd almost forgotten. I moaned a little, both turned on and frustrated that he was completely avoiding the issue.

His hands kneaded my back, working through my shirt, then slipping under my shirt and digging into bare skin. I arched my back, leaning into him.

"I can't go back to what I was." I gripped his hair in my fists, holding his head to me while he traced my throat with his tongue.

"I know," he said, his voice low. "You've gotten strong. You could move up."

Inside, I froze. Carl didn't notice. His hands were working their way to my front, to my breasts. I gasped a breath and tried to think straight. "Move up?"

"You could challenge Meg. You could take her place."

Then it was like he was necking and groping someone else. I was still clinging to him, but I gazed over his shoulder and my mind was detached. Suddenly professional.

"You're not getting along with Meg, are you?"

He went still. His hands stopped groping in favor of simple holding, and he pressed his face to my shoulder. He didn't say anything. He just held me.

I smiled a little. It was such a revelation, the idea that Carl was having relationship problems. Idly, I scratched his hair until he let me go.

He moved to the nightstand, opened a drawer, and took out a business-sized envelope. He handed it to me, only then raising his gaze to mine.

Inside, I found photos. Blurry photos taken on a full moon night, people and wolves running together. One of them was me. These were copies of the photos Rick had given me. The ones Arturo had used to hire Cormac.

"You?" My voice was tight with hurt. Whoever had given these photos to Arturo had probably also put up funds to pay Cormac. Whoever had done that wanted me dead, but wanted to keep their hands, and maybe their teeth and claws, spotless. If it had been Carl, it had probably been the money I'd been giving him that had gone to pay Cormac. That was too terrible to think about.

"Meg," he said. He stood close to me, speaking low, but sex was gone from his manner. "She said she gave them to Arturo because she was jealous of you."

"Jealous, of *me*?" She was Meg. She was beautiful and strong.

"Of the success of the show. The attention. The attention from me." He looked away at that, probably the most human gesture I'd ever seen Carl make. Like he was admitting that he'd been using pack dynamics as an excuse to sleep around. Like for once he realized how odd it was, this in-between world we inhabited.

"You know what this means?" I said. "She sold me down the river. She practically gave me to Arturo on a silver platter—"

And it suddenly occurred to me that maybe Carl told me it was Meg so that I'd get angry enough at her to challenge her. That he was manipulating both of us, so he could get her out of the way without getting his own paws dirty. This was assuming I'd actually win if I challenged her. I didn't want to think about that.

But Carl's brown eyes were so hurt, so lost, and I didn't think he could fake that. He'd never been able to disguise his anger or lust. He wasn't good at masking his feelings, or faking them. He was a brute-force kind of guy.

"What did you do when you found out?"

"We had a talk." That was a euphemism. So, had they had the usual kind of ass-kicking talk, or had they had the kind of talk that Carl and I had been having a minute ago?

"What did she say?"

"She said she was sorry. She'll back off."

"That's it? Just like that, she'll back off?" I didn't know who to be angry at. Was she really sorry or was Carl making excuses for her? Why didn't he do anything to her for this? "Maybe I should have a talk with her."

"Maybe you should," Carl said. Slowly, he leaned in, his lips brushing my cheek, moving to my mouth.

I turned my face away. I shoved the photos back into the envelope and gave it to him, then left the room before he could throw a tantrum.

For a heartening moment, I thought I was going to reach the front door and escape without anyone stopping me. I touched the doorknob.

Meg put her hand on the door, in front of my face.

I didn't have to look. I felt her glare, the heat radiating off her body. Her breath feathered against my cheek. She knew I knew. Things would never be the same with us.

If I didn't react, she could stand there forever. She wanted me to react. She wanted to scare me. Where was T.J.? I didn't dare turn to look to see if he was still in the living room.

For a split second I thought that maybe T.J. was in on all this as well, though on which side I couldn't say. He wouldn't stand up for me in a fight. Suddenly, the whole world was against me.

Meg spoke, her voice low. "If he ever has to choose between me and you, don't think for a minute that he'll pick you." She meant Carl. She could have him.

"He won't fight for you," she continued. She grimaced, an expression of distaste. "He's spineless."

She may have been right. He was still in the bedroom, and if I screamed, I wasn't sure he'd come to help me.

Whispering, I said, "I don't want to fight you, Meg. I don't want anything."

"Nothing? Nothing at all?"

That wasn't true. Gritting my teeth, I braced for her to hit me. "I want to keep the show."

Her hand moved. I flinched, gasping. But she only touched my chin, then brushed her finger along my jaw before closing her fist and drawing away.

She opened the door for me and let me go.

T.J. was waiting at his bike, fiddling with some arcane bit of engineering.

"Can we go now?" I said, hugging myself.

"You okay? You're shaking." He wiped his hands on his jeans and mounted the bike. I crawled up behind him.

"Did you know Carl and Meg are fighting?"

"They're always fighting."

Not like this. I choked on the words. Closing my eyes, I hugged him tight.

I never watched the local TV news, so I didn't have to work too hard to avoid watching it tonight, to see if Angela Bryant had filmed my better side or not.

But at 6:15 P.M. exactly, Ozzie called.

"Kitty. Did you know you're on the news?"

Morbidly, I sort of hoped there'd be a plane crash or something that would bump a prostitute's murder off the news entirely.

"I had a feeling," I said tiredly.

"What's up with that?"

"Didn't the TV say anything?"

"They just said, and I quote, 'Well-known radio personality Kitty

Norville is involved with the investigation.' That doesn't sound too great. You didn't—I mean, you're not *really* involved, are you?"

"Geez, Ozzie, you really think I could do something like that?"

"I know *you* wouldn't. But there's that whole werewolf thing . . ."

I sighed. I couldn't win. "I'm an unofficial consultant. That's it."

"So there *are* werewolves involved."

"I don't want to talk about it."

He grumbled like he wanted to keep arguing. Then he said, "You couldn't have worked in a little free publicity for the show?"

"Good-bye, Ozzie." I hung up.

The phone blinked at me that there was a message waiting. Someone had called while I was talking to Ozzie. I checked.

It was Mom. "Hi, Kitty, this is Mom. We just saw you on the news, and I wanted to make sure everything is okay. Do you need a lawyer? We have a friend who's a lawyer, so please call—"

Again, I hung up.

Yet again, full moon night. My thirty-seventh. How many more would there be? For the rest of my life, full moon nights were planned and predetermined. How much longer could I keep this up? Some nights, the light of it, the wind in the trees, the rush of my blood made me shout with joy, a howl lurking at the back of my throat.

Some nights, I thought surely this time my body would burst and break, my skin split apart and not be able to come back together again.

I waited outside the house until the pack spilled out the back door and into the scrub-filled backyard, and the trees and hills beyond. Like a hiking club going for a midnight stroll. Some of them started Changing as soon as their feet hit the dirt. They trotted, then ran to the trees, melting into their other forms. Where people had gone, wolves circled back, urging their friends to hurry.

I stayed at the corner of the house, hugging myself, hearing their call. T.J., naked, silvery in the moonlight, looked back, saw me, and smiled. I didn't smile back, but I pulled myself from the wall and moved forward, toward him. Like my Wolf was dragging me by her leash.

Someone grabbed me from behind.

Meg squeezed my arm and came close, speaking into my ear.

"You've gotten too big for your skin. You're arrogant. And

you're in danger of splitting this pack apart. I won't let that happen. You think you're pretty hot right now, but I'll remind you where your place really is." Her hand pinched my arm. A growl was starting in my chest. I swallowed it back.

She didn't want to be the one to start the fight. She was alpha, and she wasn't going to stoop. She could chastise, dominate, threaten, but she wouldn't start the knock-down, drag-out stuff. I had to be stupid enough to challenge her. She talked like she thought I'd be stupid enough to challenge her. Like she wanted me to, so she'd have a chance to take me down.

I looked away, wondering how I could get away from her. Wolf was ready to fight to get away. Once, Meg's fingers digging into me would have had me cowering.

"I'm not trying to split up the pack. I just—I just need space." Like I was some kind of rebellious teenager.

"I know what you want. I know how this works, a young thing like you moving up in the world. And if you think you can have Carl, if you think you can have the pack, you have to talk to me about it. I'm still tougher than you."

I shook my head. "I don't want to fight you. I won't."

And I held it together. I didn't move. I kept still. *Just let me run.* I'd leave her alone if she'd let me. Almost unconsciously, I leaned away, toward the pack, the wolves, my family, where I could Change and be anonymous.

Her hands were shifting, claws growing. She didn't loosen her grip, so the claws broke my skin, blood trickling down my arm. I looked at her, but still I didn't move. Our gazes met again. I held my breath so I wouldn't growl.

A few of the others, wolves now, watched us, ears pricked forward, aware that something was happening. They trotted over, freeflowing animals burst loose from their prisons for this one night. We had an audience.

I caught the scent of my own blood. Wolf kicked and writhed; the smell made her crazy. But if I didn't react, Meg would leave me alone.

She let go of my arm. Halfway through my not-very-well-suppressed sigh, she slapped me across the face—openhanded, claws extended. My cheek lit with pain, so much pain I couldn't feel the individual cuts. Three, I thought, based on how she'd been holding her hand. A quick swipe. Probably felt worse than it was. Blood gathered in a rivulet trickling down my jaw.

I didn't fight. But I also didn't cower.

Finally, she turned away.

My body was fire. My skin was burning away, my breath coming in quiet sobs.

The wolves surrounded us. The whole pack had joined us. Wolves nudged us, bumping our hips with their shoulders. Pale, cream, slate, silver, and black fur moved in a sea around us. My vision went white and helpless.

I let Wolf rip out of me with a howl.

Like shaking off dead fur, shedding out last year's coat, she convulses, then runs free.

She follows his scent. Him, the One. Running, she can reach him at the head of the pack. He is pale, coppery, wondrous in the moonlight. She runs into him, knocking him. She bows, playing; yips, trying to get him to chase her. She licks his face and cowers before him, tail low to show him he is stronger, he can do what he likes with her. In the other life she can't say these things to him, but here she can, here she knows the language.

That other part of her is too proud. But Wolf knows better.

The One's mate snaps at her—not playful but angry. Keeps her away from the One—and the One doesn't protect her. He growls, snarls, dives at her. Whining, she runs away, tail tight between her legs. Then he leaves her. Trots away like she is nothing. She is left alone. The others snap and tease her for this rejection, but she doesn't feel like playing anymore.

That other part of her knows the heartbreak for what it is.

By the time I shifted back to human the next morning, the wounds had healed. At least, the cuts Meg gave me had healed.

Nights passed.

I didn't know where to find Rick. He'd always come to me. I knew where I might start looking, and if he wasn't there I could probably find someone who did know where he was. Assuming I didn't get beaten up first.

The nightclub Psalm 23 was a favorite vampire hunting ground. Despite what a lot of the legends said, vampires didn't have to kill their prey when they fed. They usually didn't, because littering the surroundings with bodies attracted too much attention. They could seduce a young thing with nice fresh blood, drink enough to sustain them but not enough to kill, let the victim go, and the poor kid might not have any idea what had happened. Supernatural Rohypnol. The process didn't turn the victim into a vampire.

In the right subculture, a vampire could find willing-enough volunteers to play blue-plate special. Psalm 23 was dark, stylish, played edgy music, and Arturo was a silent partner.

I had to dress up; they'd have turned me away at the door if I'd shown up in jeans. I wore black slacks, a black vest, and a choker. Understated. I didn't want to draw attention to myself.

Outside, I could hear the music, something retro and easy to slink to. The doorman let me in without a problem, but I hadn't gotten three feet inside when an incredibly svelte woman with skin so pale her diamond pendant looked colorful fell into step behind me.

I stopped. So did she, close enough that her breath brushed my neck when she spoke.

"I know you," she said. "You're not welcome here."

"Then you should have stopped me at the door," I said without turning around. "I already paid my cover."

"You're here without invitation. You're trespassing."

I stopped myself before saying something stupid. Like fuck territory. Any territory marking that was done was done by Carl, and I was on the outs with him right now. I didn't want to go so far as to say that.

I turned. "Look, I'm not interested in facing off with anybody. I need to find Rick; is he here?"

Her gaze narrowed; her lips parted, showing the tips of fangs. "I might ask for an additional cover charge from you." She ran her tongue along her teeth, between the fangs.

"You won't get it." Werewolf blood was apparently some kind of delicacy among vampires. Like thirty-year-old scotch or something.

"You're in our territory now. If you want to stay, you will follow our rules."

I backed away, bracing to run. I didn't want to fight. Maybe it had been a mistake coming here. Maybe I thought I could handle it on my own, and maybe I was wrong. I kept testing those boundaries and I kept falling on my ass, didn't I?

I'd never meant to cause trouble with any of this.

Someone stepped beside me, interposing himself between me and the woman. It was Rick. "Stella, Ms. Norville is my guest this evening and is under my protection."

She stepped back from him, gaping like a fish. "When Arturo finds out she was here—"

"I'll tell him myself and take responsibility for the consequences. I'll also make sure she doesn't cause trouble. Like start a fight with an aggressive hostess." He touched my arm and gestured me to a quiet section of the bar. The woman, Stella, stalked off with a huff. I let out the breath I'd been holding.

"Thanks for the save," I said as we took seats.

"You're welcome. Drink?" he said as the bartender drifted over. Tequila, straight up? "Club soda. Thanks."

"The question remains—what are you doing here? It's not exactly safe for you."

"I wanted to let you know, I got a tip that Elijah Smith is coming back to this area in a week or so, probably out toward Limon. I found that on the Web so take it with a grain of salt. But it's the best I've got right now."

"It's more than I have. Thanks."

"I'll tell you when I get more. Maybe you could leave me a phone number for next time?"

He had the gall to laugh.

"I take it you don't like phones," I said.

"Why don't I come see you at your office in a week instead?"

"Damned inconvenient," I muttered. It would have been nice to have someone agree with my suggestion for once.

He looked thoughtfully at me. "No one gets that put out over not getting a phone number."

A seething pit of frustrated intentions, that was me. I frowned. "Could you give me some advice?"

He blinked, surprised. "Well. I thought *you* had all the answers."

I ignored that, glancing back at where the monochrome Stella had gone to harass someone else. "You must be in pretty tight with Arturo, to toss around his name like that."

"Don't tell anyone, but I'm nearly as old as he is. Nearly as powerful. The only difference is I don't want to be Master of a Family. I don't want that kind of . . . responsibility. He knows this, knows I'm not a rival. We have an understanding about other things."

"Ah. Why are you even here at all? Why even follow him?" This was touching on what I wanted to talk to him about. He'd been around for a long time—he'd just admitted as much. He had answers I didn't.

He sat back, smiling like he knew what I was *really* asking and why I was asking. "Being part of a Family has its advantages. Finding sustenance is easier. There's protection. A guarded place to sleep out the days. These things are harder to find alone."

Dejected, I propped an elbow on the bar. Those were all the things I needed Carl for. What was I supposed to do if I couldn't stand him anymore?

Rick continued. "I spent about fifty years on my own, around the end of the nineteenth century. I . . . angered a few dangerous elements, so I set up a place in one of the Nevada boomtowns during the Comstock Lode silver rush. You wouldn't believe how well the mining operations in a place like Virginia City kept away a certain kind of riffraff."

I grinned, drawn into the story in spite of myself. "You pissed off a pack of werewolves."

"You didn't come to hear stories. You mentioned advice. Though this seems a strange place to find it."

"I'm running out of friends."

"Nonsense. You have half a million listeners who adore you."

I shot him a glare. "Someone asked me recently who I went to when I needed advice. And I couldn't answer. I didn't know."

"You still haven't told me what you need advice about."

I asked him because he was old and presumably experienced. And, ironically, he'd never given me a reason to be afraid of him.

"I don't understand what's happening. I don't know why Carl and Meg are acting the way they are. I don't know why I can't make them understand why I feel the way I do. I wish—I wish they'd leave me alone, but then I'm not sure I want them to. Especially Carl." There, I thought I'd gotten it all out.

"You're not looking for advice. You're looking for affirmation."

And I wasn't getting it from the people I most wanted it from. God, he made it sound so obvious. If someone had called in with this problem, I'd have been able to rattle off that answer.

I rubbed my face. I felt like I was five years old again. *See, Daddy, look at the pretty picture I made,* and what is that kid supposed to do when Daddy tears it to shreds? I didn't want to think about Carl as a father figure. More like . . . the tyrant in his harem. Or something.

Rick turned a wry smile. "It's growing pains. I've seen it before. It happens in a werewolf pack any time a formerly submissive member starts to assert herself. You're coming into your own, and Carl doesn't know what to do with you anymore."

"How do I make everything okay again?"

He leaned back. "If life were that easy, you'd be out of a job."

Right. Time to change the subject. I wanted to hear about the silver rush and Virginia City during the frontier days. I couldn't picture Rick in a cowboy hat.

"So, you want to be a guest on the show and tell some stories about the Old West?"

He smirked. "Arturo would kill me."

The trouble with this crowd was, you didn't know when that was a joke.

About a week later I came home from work and found Cormac leaning against the outside wall of my apartment building. It was well after dark. He had his arms crossed and stood at the edge of the glow cast by the light over the door. I stared for a good minute before I could say anything.

"You know where I live."

"Wasn't hard to find out," he said.

"Am I going to have to move now?"

He shrugged. "The place is kind of a dump. I thought you'd be making better money than this."

He didn't have to know about Carl's payoff. "Maybe I like it here. What do you want?"

My neck was tingling. I needed to get the hell out of here. But he wasn't armed tonight. At least not that I could see. Without all the guns he looked less like a hit man and more like a good-guy biker.

"You remember that cop? Hardin? She got in touch with me about those murders."

Just like that, the anxiety went away. The big picture took over. Being pissed off that someone was going behind my back took over. "Really? She told me she didn't trust you enough to talk to you about it."

"She seems to have the idea that you're too loyal to your 'kind' to be any help."

"Just because I wouldn't name names."

"Do you have a name?"

"No. Geez, it's like thinking that because someone's—I don't know, an auto mechanic—that they know every other auto mechanic in town."

"Werewolves are a little less common than mechanics."

I changed the subject. "Why are you helping her? Last time I talked to her, she wanted to prosecute you for stalking and attempted murder."

"She offered to keep off my back if I helped catch this guy."

Hardin knew how to be everyone's friend. "Convenient."

"I thought so." He paced a couple of steps toward me. "Listen. You have information about this killer that I can't get—the scent. Is there something you're not telling the cops?"

I huffed. "I didn't recognize the scent. It's not one of ours. At least, I don't think it is."

"Okay. I'm not the cops. I'm not territorial about information. We can get closer to catching this guy if we pool what we know."

"What do you know?"

"How to kill werewolves."

"Is that supposed to make me feel better?"

"No."

Defeated, I let out a sigh. "What do you want me to do?"

"If you see this guy, give me a call. You go places I don't, meet people I can't. You have contacts."

"You don't agree with Hardin? You don't think I'll protect him just because he's a werewolf?"

"I think you'll do the right thing. You have my number." He turned to walk away.

"Who owes who a favor now?"

He glanced over his shoulder. "Don't worry, I'm keeping track."

Matt leaned against the doorjamb between the sound booth and studio. "Kitty? There's a live one on line three. Might be a crank, but she sounds like she's really in trouble. You want it?"

I could say no. This was my show, after all. It would be a lot easier and better for everyone if I transferred her to a hotline. Too bad there wasn't a hotline for troubled vampires and werewolves.

I nodded, listening to my current caller's ornate commentary about miscegenation and purity of the species. Standard canned reactionary rhetoric.

"Uh-huh, thank you," I said. "Have you considered a career as a speechwriter for the Klan? Next caller, please."

"Oh, thank you! Thank you!" The woman was sobbing, her words unintelligible around the hysterics.

"Whoa, slow down there. Take a breath. Slow breaths. That's a girl. Estelle? Is this Estelle?"

She stopped hyperventilating somewhat, matching her breathing to my calm words. "Y-yes."

"Good. Estelle, can you tell me what's wrong?"

"They're after me. I'm hurt. They're coming after me. I need help." Her words came faster and faster. My heartbeat sped up along with them. Her voice lisped, like she held her mouth too close to the phone.

"Wait a minute. Explain your situation. Who's after you?"

She swallowed, loud enough to carry over the line. "Have you heard of Elijah Smith? The Church of the Pure Faith?"

I stood and started pacing. More than heard of him, I was almost ready to show up at his door and let him have at me just to learn something new. I so wanted to expose him for a charlatan. Right now, the church caravan was parked some sixty miles away from the studio.

"Yes, I've heard of them."

"I left. I mean—I want to leave. I'm trying to leave."

"Oh. I mean—oh." I, who made my living by my voice, was speechless. No one had ever left the Church of the Pure Faith. None of Smith's followers had ever been willing to talk about him.

I had so many questions: What was she? Had she gone looking for a cure? Did it work? What was Smith like? This was the interview I'd been waiting for.

"Okay, Estelle. Let me make sure I'm clear on this. You are—what, vampire? Lycanthrope?"

"Vampire."

"Right. And you went to the Church of the Pure Faith seeking a cure for vampirism. You met Elijah Smith. You—were you cured? Were you really cured?" What would I do if she said yes?

"I—I thought so. I mean, I thought I was. But not anymore."

"I'm confused."

"Yeah," she said, laughing weakly. "Me, too."

Estelle sounded exhausted. How long had she been running? The night was half over. Did she have a safe place to spend the day? And why had she called *me*?

Witnesses. We were live on the air. Thousands of witnesses would hear her story. Smart. Now if only I could live up to her faith in me.

"Are you safe for the moment? Are you in a safe place or do you need to get out of there right now? Where are you?"

"I lost them, for now. I'm in a gas station; it's closed for the night. I'll be all right until dawn."

"Where, Estelle? I want to send you help if I have to."

"I don't think I want to say where. They might be listening. They might follow you here."

This was going to be tough. One step at a time, though. I covered my mouthpiece with a hand and called to Matt. "Check caller ID, find out where she's calling from." Through the booth window I saw him nod. I went back to Estelle. "When you say they're after you, do you mean Smith? Do you mean his people? Do they want to hurt you?"

"Yes. Yes!"

"Huh. Some church. Why don't people leave him?"

"They—they can't, Kitty. It's complicated. We're not supposed to talk about it."

Matt pressed a piece of paper against the booth window. PAY PHONE—UNKNOWN, it read.

"Estelle? Walk me through the cure. You saw a poster announcing a church meeting. You showed up at the tent. How long ago was this?"

She was breathing more calmly, but her voice still sounded tight, hushed, like she was afraid of being overheard. "Four months."

"What happened when you got there?"

"I arrived just after dark. There was a group of tents, some RVs, campers and things. They were circled and roped off. There were guards. About eight of us gathered at a gate. There was a screening process. They patted us down for weapons, made sure none of us were reporters. Only the truly faithful ever get to see Smith. And— I wanted to believe. I really wanted to believe. One of the people they searched, I think he was a werewolf—they found a microphone or something on him, and they threw him out."

They threw out a werewolf. That took some doing. "People who've tried to break into the Church have met up with considerable force. Who works on the security detail?"

"His followers—everyone who lives and works in that caravan is a believer."

"But they've gotta be tough. Whole werewolf packs have gone after him—"

"And they're going up against werewolves. And weretigers, and vampires—everything. It's fighting fire with fire, Kitty."

"So they're not really cured."

"Oh, but they are. I never saw them shape-shift, not even during the full moon. The vampires—they walked in daylight!"

"But they retained their strength? They were still able to deal

with a werewolf on equal terms?" Lose the weaknesses without losing the strengths of those conditions? Some might call that better than a cure.

"I suppose so."

Interesting. "Go on."

"I was brought inside the main tent. It looked like a church service, an old-fashioned revival, with the congregation gathered before a stage. A man on the stage called to me."

"This was Smith? What's he like?"

"He—he looks very normal." Of course. She probably wouldn't even be able to pick him out of a lineup. "I expected to be preached at, lectured with all the usual biblical quotes about witches and evildoers. I didn't care; I would have sat through anything if it meant being cured. But he didn't. He spoke about the will to change. He asked me if I wanted to change, if I had the will to help him reach into my soul and retrieve my mortality, my life. Oh, yes, I said. His words were so powerful. Then he set his hands on my head.

"It was real, Kitty. Oh, it was real! He touched my face, and a light filled me. Every sunrise I'd missed filled me. And the hunger—it faded. I didn't want blood anymore. My whole body surged, like my own blood returned. My skin flushed. I was mortal again, alive and breathing, like Lazarus. I really was! He showed me a cross and I touched it—and nothing happened. I didn't burn. He made me believe I could walk in the sun."

When Estelle first started talking, I thought I'd gotten someone who'd been disillusioned, who'd be ready to expose Smith's secrets and tell me exactly why he was a fake. But Estelle didn't talk like a disillusioned ex-follower. She still believed. She spoke like a believer who had lost her faith, or lost her belief in her own right to salvation.

I had to ask: "Could you, Estelle? Could you walk in the sun?"

"Yes," she said, her voice a whisper.

Goddamn it. A cure. I felt a tickle in my stomach, a piece of hope that felt a little like heartburn. A choice, an escape. I could have my old life back. If I wanted it.

There had to be a catch.

I kept my voice steady, attempting journalistic impartiality. "You stayed with him for four months. What did you do?"

"I traveled with the caravan. I appeared onstage and witnessed. I watched sunrises. Smith took care of me. He takes care of all of us."

"So you're cured. That's great. Why not leave? Why don't those who are cured ever go away and start a new life for themselves?"

"He's our leader. We're devoted to him. He saves us and we would die for him."

She was so earnest, it made me wonder if I was being set up. But I was close to something. Questions, more questions. "But you want to leave him now. Why?"

"It—it's so stifling. I could see the sun. But I couldn't leave him."

"Couldn't?"

"No—I couldn't. All I was, my new self, it was because of him. It was like . . . he made me."

Oh, my. "It sounds a little like a vampire Family. Devoted followers serving a Master who created them." For that matter it sounded like a werewolf pack, but I didn't want to go there.

"What?"

"I have a couple of questions for you, Estelle. Were you made a vampire against your will or were you turned voluntarily?"

"It—it wasn't against my will. I wanted it. It was 1936, Kitty. I was seventeen. I contracted polio. I was dead anyway, or horribly crippled at best, do you understand? My Master offered an escape. A cure. He said I was too charming to waste."

I developed a mental picture of her. She'd look young, painfully innocent even, with the clean looks and aura of allure that most vampires cultivated.

"When did you decide you didn't want to be a vampire anymore? What made you seek out Elijah Smith?"

"I had no freedom. Everything revolved around the Master. I couldn't do anything without him. What kind of life is that?"

"Unlife?" Ooh, remember the *inside* voice.

"I had to get away."

If I were going to do the pop-psychology bit on Estelle, I'd tell her she had a problem with commitment and accepting the consequences of her decisions. Always running away to look for a cure, and now she'd run to me.

"Tell me what happened."

"I was mortal now—I could do whatever I wanted, right? I could walk in broad daylight. I was assigned screening duty at the front gate two nights ago. I lost myself in the crowd and never went back. I found a hiding place, an old barn I think. In the morning, I walked past the open door, through the sunlight—and I burned.

The hunger returned. He—he withdrew his cure, his blessing. His grace."

"The cure didn't work."

"It did! But I had lost my faith."

"You burned. How badly are you hurt, Estelle?"

"I—I only lost half my face."

I closed my eyes. That pretty picture of Estelle I had made disintegrated, porcelain skin bubbling, blackening, turning to ash until bone could be seen underneath. She ducked back into shade, and because she was still a vampire, immortal, she survived.

"Estelle, one of the theories about Smith says that he has some sort of psychic power. It isn't a cure, but it shields people from some of the side effects of their natures—vulnerability to sunlight and the need for blood in the case of vampires, the need to shapeshift in the case of lycanthropes. His followers must stay with him so he can maintain it. It's a kind of symbiotic relationship—he controls their violent natures and feeds off their power and attention. What do you think?"

"I don't know. I don't know anymore." She sniffed. Her voice was tight, and I understood now where her hushed lisp was coming from.

Matt came into the studio. "Kitty, there's a call for you on line four."

Four was my emergency line. Only a couple of people had the number. Carl had it. I bet it was him, still trying to be protective.

"Can't it wait?"

"No. The guy threatened me pretty soundly." Matt shrugged unapologetically. He'd let me mess with the threats from the supernatural world. One of these days he was going to quit this gig, and I wouldn't be able to blame him. I needed to get Ozzie to give him a raise.

"Estelle, hang on for just a minute. I'm still with you, but I have to take a break." I put her on hold, punched the line, and made sure it wasn't set to broadcast. The last thing I needed was Carl lecturing me on the air. "What?"

"Hello, Katherine," said an aristocratic male voice.

It wasn't Carl. Oh, no. Only one other person besides my grandmother ever called me Katherine. I'd met him only a couple of times in person, during territorial face-offs with Carl and the pack. But I knew that voice. That voice made my bone marrow twinge.

"Arturo. How the hell did you get this number?"

"I have ways."

Oh, please. On the phone, behind the microphone, I had the power. I switched the line over to live. "Hello, Arturo. You're on the air."

"Katherine," he said tightly. "I wish to speak to you privately."

"You call me during the show, you talk to my listeners. That's the deal." Maybe if I was brazen enough, I'd forget that he'd tried to have me killed.

"I do not appreciate being treated like your rabble—"

"What do you want, Arturo?"

He took a deep breath. "I want to talk to Estelle."

"Why?"

"She's one of mine."

Great. This was getting complicated. I covered the mike with my hand. "Matt, how does three-way calling work again?"

A few seconds later, I had Estelle back on the line. "Estelle? You still there?"

"Yes." Her voice was trembling. She swallowed.

"Okay—I have Arturo on the other line—"

She groaned like I'd just staked her. "He'll kill me. He'll kill me for leaving him—"

"On the contrary, my dear. I want to take you home. You're hurt and need help. Tell me where you are."

Her breath hiccuped. She was crying. "I'm sorry, I'm so sorry—"

"It's far too late for that," he said, sounding tired.

I couldn't believe what I was about to say. "Estelle, I think you should listen to him. I don't know what I can do for you. Arturo can get you to a safe place."

"I don't believe him. I can't go back, I can't ever go back!"

"Estelle, please, tell me where you are," Arturo said.

"Kitty?" Estelle said, her voice small.

"Arturo—you promise you aren't going to hurt her?"

"Katherine, you're being harsh."

"Promise."

"Katherine. Estelle is mine. She is part of me. If she is destroyed, part of me is destroyed as well. I have an interest in protecting her. I promise."

Drama, tension, excitement! What a great setup for a show! But at the moment I would have given my pelt to have the whiny goth chicks back.

"I'm going to break for station identification. When we return, I hope I'll have a wrap-up for you on our sudden special broadcast

KITTY AND THE MIDNIGHT HOUR

of 'Elijah Smith: Exposed.'" I switched the phone lines off the air and said, "All right, Estelle. It's up to you."

"Okay. Okay. Arturo, come get me. I'm at the Speedy Mart on Seventy-fifth."

Arturo's line clicked off.

"You okay, Estelle?" I asked.

"Yeah. Yes, I'm all right." She had stopped crying and seemed almost calm. The decision had been made. She could stop running, for a little while at least.

I had one more call to make—to the cavalry, just in case. I should have called the police. Hardin—she'd help Estelle. Yeah, she'd take Estelle to a hospital. And they wouldn't know what to do with her. They wouldn't understand, and it would take too long to explain.

A normal person would have called the police. But I pulled a scrap of paper out of my contact book, got an outside line, and dialed. After six rings, I almost hung up. Then, "Yeah." Mobile phone static underlaid the voice.

"Cormac? Have you been listening to the show tonight?"

"Norville? Why would I be listening to your show?"

Oh, yeah, he could pretend, but I knew the truth. He'd listened once, it could happen again. "One of my callers is in trouble. Arturo says he'll help her, but I don't trust him. I want to make sure she doesn't get caught in a cross fire. Can you go help? Make sure nobody dies and stuff?"

"Arturo? Arturo is helping? She's a vampire, isn't she." It might have been a question, but he didn't make it sound like one.

"Yeah, actually."

"You're out of your mind."

"Yup. Look, chances are Arturo will get to Estelle first and the Church people won't even find her. But if the Church people do show up, they'll have some pretty hard-hitting supernaturals with them. You might get to shoot one."

"Whoa, slow down. Church?"

"Church of the Pure Faith."

"Hm. A buddy of mine was hired to go in there and never got through. I've been wanting to get a look at them."

"Here's your chance," I said brightly.

"Right. I'll check it out, but no promises."

"Good enough. Thanks, Cormac." I gave him the address. He grunted something resembling a sign-off.

Matt was signaling through the window. Time up. On-air light on. Okay. "We're back to *The Midnight Hour.* Estelle?"

"Kitty! A car just pulled up. It's not Arturo; I think it's people from the Church. They'll kill me, Kitty. We're not supposed to leave; they'll take me back and then—I've told you everything and now everybody knows—"

"Okay, Estelle. Stay down. Help's on the way."

Matt leaned in and didn't bother to muffle his voice for the mike this time. His expression was taut and anxious. He actually looked harried. "Line four again."

Maybe it was Arturo checking in. Maybe I could warn him. He was Estelle's only chance to get out of there. "Yeah?"

"Kitty, do you need help?" said a gruff, accusatory voice.

Not Arturo. Carl. Why was he worried about whether I needed help *now* of all times?

"I can't talk now, Carl." I hung up on him. I'd catch hell for that later.

Carl and I were going to kill each other one of these days.

Switched lines again, had to double-check to make sure it was the right one. "Estelle? What's happening? Estelle?" A sound rustled over the mouthpiece, then a banging noise like something falling. My heart dropped. "Estelle?"

"Yes. I'm hiding, but the phone cord won't go any farther. I don't want to hang up, Kitty."

I didn't want her to hang up. A nasty little voice in my head whispered *ratings*. But the only way I was going to find out what happened was if she stayed on the line.

"Estelle, if you have to hang up, hang up, okay? The important thing is to get out of there in one piece."

"Thank you, Kitty," she said, her face wet with tears. "Thank you for listening to me. No one's ever really listened to me before."

I hadn't done anything. I couldn't do anything. I was trapped behind the mike.

After that, I had to piece together events from what I was hearing. It was like listening to a badly directed radio drama. Tires squealed on asphalt. A car door slammed. Distant voices shouted. The phone slammed against something again: Estelle had dropped the handset. Running footsteps.

I paced, my hands itching to turn into claws and my legs itching to run. That happened when I got stressed. I wanted to Change and run. Run far, run fast, like Estelle had tried to do.

I called Cormac back.

"Yeah?"

"It's me. Are you there? What's happening?"

"Give me a break, it's only been a minute. Give me another five."
He hung up.

Then on the other line, bells jingled as the door opened and
closed. Footsteps moved slowly across a linoleum floor. I heard a
scream. Then sobbing.

What was it about Elijah Smith that could make a vampire afraid
of him?

"Estelle. Won't you return to me? You can regain what you have
lost. I'll even forgive this betrayal." A calm, reasonable voice
echoed like it came from a TV in the next room. It sounded like a
high-school social studies teacher explaining a lurid rite-of-pas-
sage ritual as if it were a recipe for mashed potatoes. A smooth
voice, comforting, chilling. This voice spoke truth. Even over the
phone, it was persuasive.

Elijah Smith, in his first public appearance.

"What are you?" Estelle said, as loud as she'd yet spoken, but the
words were still muffled, filled with tears. "What are you really?"

"Oh, Estelle. Is it so hard for you to believe? Your struggle is
most difficult of all. The ones who hate themselves, their monsters—their belief comes easy. But you, those like you—you love
the monsters you have become, and that love is what you fear and
hate. Your belief comes with great difficulty, because you don't
really want to believe."

I sat down so heavily my chair rolled back a foot. The words tingled on my skin. He might have been talking to me, and he might
have been right: I didn't believe in a cure. Was it because I didn't
want to?

"A cure is supposed to be forever! Why can't I leave you?"

"Because I would hate to lose you. I love all my people. I need
you, Estelle."

What was it Arturo had said: *She is part of me. If she is destroyed, part of me is destroyed as well.* Could Elijah Smith be
some sort of vampire feeding on need, on his followers' powers?

If only I could get *him* to pick up the phone.

Yet again, I called Cormac.

"Yeah?"

"Has it been five minutes? At least keep the line open so I know
what's happening."

"Jesus, Norville. Hang on. There's an SUV parked here. Three
guys are standing guard in front of the building. I don't see weap-

ons. They might be lycanthropes. They've got that animal pacing thing going, you know? Arturo's limo is parked around the corner. Lights off. Wait, here he comes. He's trying to get in. I gotta go." I heard the safety on a gun click, then rapid footsteps.

I hated this. Everything was happening off my stage. I was blind and ignorant. For the first time, I hated the safety and anonymity of my studio.

Then Cormac said, "Don't move. These are loaded with silver."

"You!" That was Arturo. "Why on earth—"

"It's Norville's idea. Get your girl and get out of here before I change my mind. You, step aside. Let him through."

I had two lines open on a conference call. Two feeds of information culled from static and noise, all of it broadcasting. Outside, nothing. Cormac must have had something big trained on Smith's goons, because I didn't hear a grumble from them.

Then, from inside—

"Estelle? Time to come home. Walk with me." This voice was edgy, alluring. Arturo.

"Estelle—," Smith said.

"No. No no no!" Estelle's denial became shrill.

"Estelle." Two voices, ice and fire, equally compelling.

"Estelle, pick up the phone! Pick up the phone and talk to me, dammit!" I shouted futilely.

I wished I could talk to her. What would my voice do to the mix? What could I possibly say to her except: Ignore them! Ignore us all! Follow what heart you have left, if any, and leave them.

She gave one more scream, different from the previous shrill scream of fear. This was defiant. Final. There was a crash. Something broke, maybe a set of shelves falling to the floor.

A pause grew, as painful and definitive as a blank page. Then, "This is your fault," said Arturo, his voice rigid with anger. "You will pay."

"You are as much to blame," said Elijah Smith. "She killed herself. Anyone would agree with me. Her own hands are wrapped around that stake."

For a moment, I could feel the blood vessels in my ears, my lips, my cheeks. I felt hot enough to explode.

I could piece together the bits of sound I'd heard and guess what had happened. A piece of split wooden shelf, maybe a broken broom handle. Then it was just a matter of aiming, falling on top of it.

Goddamn it. My show had never gotten anyone killed before.

Arturo said, "What are you?"

"If you come to me as a supplicant, I will answer all your questions."

"How dare you—"

"Everyone get out before I start shooting." That was Cormac, showing admirable restraint.

Quick, angry footsteps left the room, growing distant. Calm, slow footsteps followed. Then, nothing.

Cormac's voice burst through my silence, in stereo, coming through both lines now.

"Norville? Are you there? Talk to me, Norville."

My hands dug into the edge of the table. The plastic laminate surface cracked; the sound of it startled me. When I looked, my fingers were thickening, claws growing. I hadn't even felt it. My arms were so tense, my hands gripping the table so hard, I hadn't felt the shift start.

I pushed away from the chair and shook my hands, then crossed my arms, pressing my fists under my elbows. Human now. Stay human, just a little longer.

"Norville!"

"Yes. I'm here."

"Did you get all that?"

"Yes. I got it all."

I hadn't even said thank you to her. Thanks for the interview. I knew better than anyone how much courage it sometimes took just to open your mouth and talk.

"There's a body here. A girl. It's already going to dust. You know how they do."

"I should have done more for her."

"You did what you could."

A new sound in the background: police sirens.

Without a closing word, Cormac hung up, and I heard silence. Silence inside, silence out.

Silence on the radio meant death.

Matt said, "Kitty? Time's up. You can go thirty over if I cut out the public service announcements."

I gave a painful, silent chuckle. Public service, my ass. I sat here every week pretending I was helping people, but when it came to *really* helping someone—

I took a deep breath. I'd never left a show unfinished. All I had to do was open my mouth and talk. "Kitty here, trying to wrap up. Estelle found her last cure. It's not one I recommend.

"Vampires don't talk about their weaknesses as weaknesses. They talk about the price. Their vulnerability to sunlight, wooden stakes, and crosses—it's the price they pay for their beauty, their immortality. The thing about prices, some people always seem willing to pay, no matter how high. And some people are always trying to get out of paying at all. Thanks to Estelle, you now know what Elijah Smith and his Church offer, and you know the price. At least I could do that much for her. As little as it is. Until next week, this is Kitty Norville, Voice of the Night."

The police couldn't go after Smith for anything. There wasn't a body. The only crime they had evidence of was breaking and entering at the convenience store, and the suspect, Estelle, was gone. The Church caravan had pulled up stakes and left town by the next morning. If I hadn't had the recording of the show proving otherwise, I could have believed that none of it had happened. Nothing had changed.

The next day, another mauling death downtown, the fourth this year, made the front page of the newspaper. A sidebar article detailing the police investigation included an interview with Hardin's colleague, Detective Salazar, who happened to mention that one of the detectives on the case had consulted with Kitty Norville, the freaky talk show host. Did that mean the police were seriously considering a supernatural element to these deaths? Were they part of some ritualistic serial killing? Or did they think a werewolf was on the loose downtown? The police made no official comment at this time. That didn't stop the newspaper from speculating. Wildly. The press was calling him "Jack Junior," as in Jack the Ripper.

Sheer, pigheaded determination got me through the day. Putting one foot in front of the other, thinking about things one step at a time, and not considering the big picture. The life-and-death questions. I stopped answering my phone altogether, letting voice mail screen calls. At least the CDC/CIA/FDA government spook didn't leave any messages.

Jessi Hardin left three messages in the space of an hour. Then she showed up at my office. She crossed her arms and frowned. She looked like she needed a cigarette.

"I need you to take a look at the latest scene."

I sat back in my chair. "Why not get that hit man, what was his name . . . oh, yeah, Cormac? He knows his stuff."

"We got paw prints from three of the crime scenes. I took them to the university. Their wolf expert said it's the biggest print he's ever seen. It would have to be a 250-pound wolf. He says nature doesn't make them that big. The precinct is actually starting to listen to me."

"Oh, that's right. You said you didn't trust Cormac."

"If you could come to the scene, identify any smells, or whatever it is you do, that would at least tell me that I'm dealing with the same killer."

"Why don't you just hire a professional?"

She unfolded her arms and started pacing. "Okay. Fine. How did you find out that I talked to the bounty hunter?"

"He told me."

"Great," she muttered.

"He wants to pool information. He has a point."

"Look, at this stage I'm talking to everyone I can think of. I'm even consulting with someone from the FBI Behavioral Analysis Unit."

I tilted my head. "You're treating this like a serial killer case? Not an out-of-control monster?"

"Serial killers *are* monsters. This guy may be a werewolf, but he's acting like a human, not a wolf. His victims aren't random. They're well-chosen: young, vulnerable women. I'm betting he picks them, stalks them, and kills them because they're easy prey." Oh, *that* was a choice phrase. "His MO is a serial killer's MO, not a wolf's. Or even a werewolf's. Yeah, I've been doing some of that reading you gave me. The wolves usually seem smart enough to stay away from people."

"Yeah. Usually. Look, Detective." I fidgeted, forcing myself to look at her only at the last minute. "I don't think I can go through that again. The last time really bothered me."

"What, did it look tasty to you?"

"Can't I be shocked and traumatized like anyone else?"

Arching an eyebrow skeptically, she said with a heavy dose of sarcasm, "Sorry."

I looked away, my jaw tightening. "I suppose I should feel lucky you aren't treating me like a suspect."

"I'm not being nice. It's a matter of statistics—serial killers rarely turn out to be women."

Saved by statistics. "I may know what he smells like, but I don't know how to find this guy."

She closed her eyes and took a deep breath, like she was counting to ten or organizing an argument. Then she looked at me and said, "You don't have to see the body. Just come to the site, tell me anything you can about it. You have to help me, before more women die."

If this conversation had happened at any time other than the day after the show with Estelle, I could have said no. If she hadn't said that particular phrase in that particular way, I might have been able to refuse.

I stood and grabbed my jacket off the back of my chair.

The site of this killing wasn't far from the other, but the street was retail rather than residential. The victim was a late-night convenience store clerk walking home after her shift.

The media vans were there again, thicker than ever. The city had a serial killer, and they were all over it.

"How do they know where to go?" I said. "They must have gotten here the same time your people did."

Hardin scowled. Not at me this time, but at the reporters drifting toward us as she parked. "They listen to police band radio."

The shouting started before I opened the car door.

"Ms. Norville! Kitty Norville! What do you think is behind these killings? What are you talking to the police about? Do you have any statement you can give us?"

On Hardin's recommendation, I ignored them. She formed a barricade between me and the cameras and guided me to the corner.

She showed me the first splatter of blood at the end of the alley behind the row of shops. It looked wrong in the daylight. Too bright, too fake. Half a bloody paw print streaked the concrete nearby. The whole paw would be as big as my head.

The blood started a trail that led into the alley, where a half-dozen investigators worked intently. They blocked my view of anything else. My stomach clenched and I turned away.

Hardin crossed her arms. "Well?"

I smelled it, the same wolf, along with the blood and decay. Those smells were connected to him. Like he didn't bathe, like he wallowed in death.

My nose wrinkled. "He smells . . . damp. Sick. I don't know."

"Is it the same guy?"

"Yeah." I still didn't want to look at the body. I couldn't. "This is worse than the last one, isn't it? He's getting more violent."

"Yeah. Come on. I'll drive you back."

She'd parked around the corner. I stood at the car door for a moment, breathing clean air before I got in.

I caught Hardin watching me.

"Thanks," I said. "Thanks for not making me see it."

"It really gets to you, doesn't it?"

We got in the car finally, and she pulled away from the curb.

I said, "With the last one, the one that I saw, I could work out how he had done it. He wasn't shifted all the way to wolf. He could get the leverage to knock her over at the same time he ripped into her. I don't like knowing that I could do something like that."

"Being physically able to do it and being inclined to do it are two different things. You don't seem like the type."

"You only say that because you haven't met Ms. Hyde."

She eyed me with a mix of curiosity and skepticism at that, her brow furrowed and her smile uncertain. She dropped me off with the usual message: Call me if you find out anything. I promised I would.

I worked late. The building was dark and quiet when I left. Once again, it was just me, the late-night DJ, and the security guard. I hadn't slept well last night, and tonight wasn't looking any better. I didn't really want to go home, where I'd worry myself into a bout of insomnia.

I planned on walking back. It would make me tired and maybe numb my brain enough to sleep.

When I stepped out of the elevator and into the lobby of the building, I smelled something wrong. Something that didn't belong. I looked—a half-dozen people were waiting there, some standing, some sitting on the sofas pushed against the wall.

They smelled cold. They smelled like the clean, well-preserved corpses they were.

The elevator door closed behind me, trapping me.

Pete, the night watchman, was sitting at his desk in the back of the lobby. Just sitting there, hands folded calmly in front of him, staring straight ahead, not blinking, not noticing anything. The vampires had done something to him, put him in some kind of trance.

"Katherine."

I flinched, startled at the sound of his voice. Arturo stepped to the center of the lobby, into the spot of illumination formed by the security light. It was like he'd designed this stage himself and timed his entrance perfectly.

Arturo appeared to be in his late twenties, handsome and assured, with shining blond hair swept back from a square face. He wore a black evening coat, open to show the dinner jacket and band-collar dress shirt underneath. He looked like he'd stepped out of an Oscar Wilde play, except that he moved too confidently in the modern era, looked too comfortable in the office lobby setting.

His entourage, three men and two women, moved from the sofa and the shadows to fan out around him, lending their own intimidating presences to his authority.

If vampires ever spend less time playing theatrics and living down to their stereotypes, they might actually take over the world someday.

One of the women was Stella, from the nightclub. She stood a little behind Arturo, frowning imperiously, like a statue. The other woman held Arturo's arm and leaned on his shoulder. She was lithe and pretty, dressed in a corset and a long, chiffony skirt, an image plucked from another century. She touched him like she couldn't bear to be parted from him.

The men stood on the fringes like bodyguards. Rick was among them. When I caught his gaze, he flashed a smile, seeming terribly amused by it all.

They all remained still, staring at me with detached ennui. That didn't mean they weren't paying attention.

"What do you want?" I tried not to sound scared, but my heart was racing and my gaze kept shifting to the glass doors and the street beyond. I tensed my feet, wondering if I could make a run for it.

"To thank you."

I blinked. "Why?"

"For helping Estelle. And for helping me. At least, for trying to." He smiled thinly and tipped his head in a small bow.

His words brought it all back, and I felt drained all over again. I rubbed my face and looked away. "I'm sorry. I don't know what else I could have done. I didn't want it to turn out like that."

"I know," he said, his voice soft. Without the pompous edge, he sounded almost kind. He straightened, discarding that hint of another self, and smoothed the lapel of his coat. "You might also like to know that any grudges toward you I may have acted on in the past are no longer a consideration to me."

I had to think about that for a minute. "You're not going to try and have me killed? No more threats?"

"For the time being. I do reserve the right to change my mind should your behavior warrant it. Good evening, Katherine."

He started to turn. I took a hesitating step after him. He paused and regarded me with a questioning tilt to his head.

It couldn't hurt to ask. Especially when he was being so nice—for him. I plunged ahead. "Did Meg back you in hiring Cormac to come after me?"

He narrowed his gaze, studying me. I glanced away, not wanting to get caught in his stare.

"Yes," he said finally.

I hadn't expected a straight answer. My stomach knotted. Somehow, I still wanted to think there'd just been a misunderstanding. That I'd wake up tomorrow and we'd all be friends again. "Could—could you tell Carl that?"

He chuckled without sound, showing the tips of fangs. "My dear, he already knows. If he hasn't acted on that knowledge, there's nothing I can do about it."

He strolled out the front doors, trailing vampires behind him. Rick was the last to leave. Before passing through the doors, he looked over his shoulder at me and pressed his lips together in a sympathetic smile. Weakly, I waved a farewell.

"What the hell was that all about?" I muttered. I was just filling space, breaking the intense silence, by saying it. By leaving his lair and going through the trouble of coming to see me, risking a potential breach of territory, Arturo had paid me one hell of a compliment. It was unexpected, to say the least.

I was still staring at the door when a voice said, "Kitty, you okay?"

Pete was standing behind his desk, looking like he was getting ready to come over to me and take my temperature. He seemed fine, mildly concerned—and seemed to have no memory of the six vampires who had just occupied his lobby.

"I'm okay," I said, taking a breath to bring me back to earth. "How do you feel, Pete?"

He shrugged. "Fine."

"Good," I said, forcing a smile. "That's good. See you later."

I left the building. My arms were covered with goose bumps.

I'd walked home at midnight, and later, plenty of times. I'd never thought twice about it. Most mundane threats I was likely to meet couldn't hurt me. So I wasn't paying as much attention as I probably should have. The breeze was blowing toward my apartment building. I was walking downwind. I would have smelled the wolf, otherwise.

He ran around the corner of the building full-tilt, his legs pumping, his body streamlined. A flash of fur and bronze eyes streaked at me, and a second later he knocked me over. I sprawled flat on my back, my arms guarding my face.

I thought I'd found the rogue. Vaguely, I reminded myself to call Hardin about it as soon as I could. I would have thought a rogue wolf would recognize what I was and know better than to attack me. But as soon as he breathed on me, I knew him. He smelled like pack. Not the rogue.

I shouted, "Zan, get the fuck off me, you asshole!"

Zan straddled me, his jaw clamped on my forearm. He shook his head, ripping into flesh. When I shouted, he hesitated, but didn't let go of my arm. If I tried to pull away, he'd tear it off.

At least he couldn't infect me with lycanthropy again.

With my free hand, I grabbed his muzzle and squeezed, trying to pry his head away from me. I wasn't strong enough to do that. But I squeezed *hard*. Cartilage popped under my hand. I twisted my grip, pulling his lips away from his teeth. He coughed, choking, unable to breathe through his nose. He let go.

I shoved away. When I turned, I landed on the injured arm, which gave out. Somehow, I got to my feet. Zan was right there, though, claws out and jaw open. This time when he tackled me, I rolled with him.

I pushed him to the ground and landed on top of him. He was a squirming bundle of muscle. His gray and black fur was slippery. I kicked him under the ribs. He yelped and burst away, all that strength flinging me like I was a feather.

From within me, from a space inside my ribs and heart, my Wolf responded, her own strength surging to break free. She was in danger, and she was going to do something about it.

I clenched my teeth and fought it. I hated losing control. But my bones were melting, my skin was sliding. Right now, it would be a better use of my energy to run like hell than to shape-shift. But she wasn't having it.

I screamed, hunching over myself with the pain of it, angry at Zan for making me do this. The puncture wounds on my arm stretched and seared. While I was huddled and immobile with the Change, Zan attacked me again.

His paws landed on my shoulders; his jaw closed around my neck. I elbowed him, wriggling out of his grasp. His claws dug into me, but his teeth didn't catch. By this time, I had claws as well. I sat on my knees, raised my forelimbs, now stout and ending in thick, razor-tipped fingers, and raked them down his exposed belly.

They snagged and caught with a satisfying rip. I grunted as I put more effort behind it. Six lines of blood welled and matted with his fur. Elation, glee, and joy surged through me—through her. This was her. This power, this joy, this *blood*. My mouth watered. Her mouth. I had thick canines. Fangs. She wanted a piece of him.

She could have him. He backed off, meeting my gaze. My vision had gone soft and glaring. The lights were too bright and the shadows too clear, but I saw him. We growled, lips curled back from angry teeth. An official challenge between us. I was halfway there, to her, my Wolf. Just let it go—

Like a cannonball, another wolf crashed into Zan. They tumbled, a mess of fur, claws, and furious snarls. I backed away, gagging, hugging myself, trying to hold on to myself.

Cold water. Ice. Clothing. Broccoli. Pull it in. I'd never been so far gone and pulled her back before. I had the list of words, things I thought of that made her go away, at least a little. Sprouts. Green. Daylight. Calm. Music. Bach, "Sheep May Safely Graze." Ha.

And she went away, but it hurt, like my guts were being dragged over razors, like teeth were chewing me from the inside. Bile rose in my throat, sank back, and my stomach churned.

The fight between Zan and the other wolf was over.

Where I had struggled for my life, fought for every inch of ground and barely held my own, the newcomer swatted him once and that was that. Zan whined, tail between his legs, crawling on his belly, smearing blood on the sidewalk as he went. His attacker snarled and bit his face. Zan rolled onto his back and stayed there. The dominant wolf stood over him, growling low.

The attacker was T.J.

As a wolf, he was slate gray, with silver hair like frosting on his muzzle, chest, and belly. His eyes were soft amber. He was big and scary as hell.

He was always saving my ass.

When one wolf showed submission to another, that usually meant they were done. The dominant wolf accepted the other's deference, order in the pack was restored, and they both went their separate ways.

T.J. didn't stop growling.

Jaws open, he dived at Zan. I flinched at the ferocity of the action. The dominant wolf tore into Zan's throat, gnawing without mercy. Zan twisted and yelped, screaming almost, as if his human side was trying to get out. His hind legs pumped the air, looking for purchase to claw into T.J. and failing. T.J. was too fast and ruthless. Arterial blood flowed and pooled on the ground.

With the other's neck fully in the grasp of his teeth, T.J. shook his head until Zan flopped in his grip like a rag. A dozen times he jerked his victim back and forth. Finally, he dropped Zan and backed away.

I fell on my backside, jarring my spine.

My shirt was so ripped up it was falling off. My left side, where Zan had clawed my shoulder, bitten my neck, and torn into my arm, was covered in blood. I cradled my arm to my chest. I couldn't feel it.

T.J.'s face and chest were bloody. Zan's body started shifting to human, slipping back to its original state in death. He lay sprawled, covered in his own blood. The claw wounds that I had given him showed as stripes all the way down his naked torso. His head was almost separated from his body.

He looked a little like Hardin's mauling victim.

T.J. gazed at me like nothing was wrong.

I tried to think of what he was thinking. Besides thinking of the taste of blood filling his mouth. He was tired of Zan, who had caused trouble too many times. He wanted to be finished with Zan once and for all. At least that was what I was thinking. Zan had been stupid coming after me like this. I embarrassed him in front of the pack, and he wanted revenge. So why didn't he challenge me in front of the pack?

I stared at the wolf sitting a few feet away from me. Smug. He looked smug.

"You jerk, I could have taken him! I was doing okay! You *still* don't think I can take care of myself!"

He probably understood me. He probably didn't care.

"How do you think this is going to look when the cops find a chewed-up body outside my apartment? Huh? Did you think of that? How am I going to explain this? 'Sorry, Officer, he just needed killing.' How is *that* going to sound?"

He looked at me, not twitching, not growling. Just watching me with utter calm and patience. Like, *Are you finished? Ready to come home like a good cub?*

"Yeah, well fuck you, too!"

This was pretty funny, me yelling obscenities at an oversized wolf.

I gasped a sob and pushed myself to my feet. I swayed, caught in a dizzy spell. How much blood had I lost? A lot. My arm was slick with it. I stumbled toward the door of my apartment building. I wanted a shower.

"Stop staring at me. I don't want to talk to you." I turned away from him.

He ran off. Gliding like a missile over the concrete, he disappeared into the dark.

Too late, I realized I'd told off my best friend. I needed him. How was I going to get through the night by myself? I hadn't been this hurt since the first night Zan attacked me and brought me into the pack.

Zan wasn't any older than I was. His hair splayed around his head like a crown, soaked with the blood that was pooling on the street. His mouth was open. His eyes were closed. He still smelled like the pack, a familiar, warm scent that jarred with the overwhelming wash of blood. Wrong, wrong. I gagged, but didn't vomit.

I managed to stumble to my apartment. I sat in a kitchen chair and tried to think. I was cold, shivering. Werewolves had rapid healing. I just had to wait for the healing to start. And go into shock in the meantime.

I was more hurt than I wanted to admit. I needed help.

I considered who I could call. No one from my pack. One of my pack had done this to me, and I'd just driven T.J. away. Not too many others would know what to do with me. I thought of Rick, then thought of what he might do when he saw this much blood drenched over everything. He might not have my well-being immediately in mind.

I called Cormac. Again, I called Cormac when any normal, sane person would have called the police. And for the same reason: How would I explain this to the police? To a hospital staff, as the nurses watched my wounds heal themselves? I wouldn't have to explain any of this to Cormac.

I dialed the number, and as usual he didn't answer until after half a dozen or so rings.

"Yeah."

"It's Kitty. I need help."

"Where are you?"

"Home." I dropped the phone into its cradle.

I made my way to the kitchen sink and ran water over my arm. I watched the patterns, water turning the blood pink, the holes in my skin that were revealed when the blood washed away. If I stood quietly, I could watch them heal, like time-lapse photography; watch the scabs form and the edges of the holes come together, like dirt filling in a grave. Fascinating.

The next thing I knew, he was standing there. Cormac. I squinted at him. He might have been standing there for hours, watching me.

"How'd you get in?" I said.

"You left your front door open."

"Shit."

"What happened to you?"

"Sibling rivalry. Never mind."

He was as cool as ice. Never once broke his tough-guy tone. He searched the kitchen cupboards until he found a glass. He leaned over the sink, turned the faucet away from my arm, filled the glass with water, and handed it to me. I drank and felt better. A drink of water. I should have thought of that.

"You look like hell," he said.

"I feel worse."

"You're not hurt that bad. Looks like you're healing pretty quick."

"It's not that." Wolf was still gnawing at my insides for putting her on the leash.

"Have anything to do with the mangled body in the driveway?"

Shit. Had he called the police? "Yeah."

"Did you do it?"

"No," I said harshly.

"Anyone you know do it? Was it the rogue?"

"He—the guy outside—was a werewolf, too. Pack squabble."

He watched me, frowning, his eyes unreadable. Like a cop at an interrogation, waiting for the suspect to crack. My throat felt dry. "Do you believe me?"

He said, "Why'd you call me for help?"

"I can't trust anyone, and you said you owed me. Didn't you?"

"Don't move." He went to the dresser on the other side of the room and opened drawers, looking for something. I stayed where I was, leaning on the counter until he came back. He had a towel over his shoulder and held a shirt out to me.

He turned away, staring at the opposite wall as I removed the shredded T-shirt and pulled on the tank top.

"I'm done," I said when I was finished changing.

He returned to the sink, wet the towel, and turned off the water. The place seemed quiet without the running faucet. He handed me the towel.

I sat in a chair and started cleaning the blood off while Cormac watched.

"Is Cormac your real name?"

"It seems to work all right."

The blood wouldn't come off. I just kept smearing it around.

Sighing, he took the towel from me. "Here. Let me." He held my wrist, straightened my arm, and started wiping off blood with much more focus and vigor than I'd given the task.

My arm had been numb. Now, it started to sting. Weakly, I tried to pull away. "Aren't you afraid of catching it? All the blood—"

"Lycanthropy isn't that contagious. Mostly through open wounds, and even then mostly when you're a wolf. I don't think I've ever heard of anyone catching it from a werewolf in human form."

"How did you learn so much about werewolves? How did you get into this line of work?"

He shrugged. "Runs in the family." Efficiently, as if he'd had lots of practice cleaning up blood, he washed my arm, shoulder, and neck. He even cleaned the blood out from under my fingernails. On both hands. Zan's blood, that time. "Don't you have a pack? Shouldn't one of your buddies be doing this?"

"I'm kind of on the outs with them right now." Feeling was coming back to the arm, which was bad, because it hurt, throbbing from neck to fingers. I started shaking.

"Jesus, I didn't think werewolves went into shock." He threw the towel into the sink, stomped to the bed and grabbed the blanket off it. He draped it over my shoulders, moving to my front to bring the edges close together, tugging me into a warm cocoon. I snuggled into the shelter of the blanket, sighing deeply, finally letting go of the tension.

Just how long had it been since I'd felt warm and safe? And how ironic, that I should feel like that now, with him. The werewolf hunter. He was right; I must have been in shock.

Before he could draw his hand away from the blanket, I reached for it. I was fast and gentle; he didn't even flinch when I pressed his hand against my shoulder. The pressure was there before he realized that I'd moved.

Members of a pack feel safer in groups. Touch holds them together. Two members of a pack can rarely be in the same room without touching every now and then, sometimes nothing more than the backs of their hands brushing together, or the furred shoulders of wolves bumping. Touch meant everything was going to be okay. For that moment, for a split second, I wanted Cormac to be pack.

Then the human voice came to the fore and noticed how freaking odd this must have looked to him. I pulled my hand away and looked down, shaking my head. "Sorry. I—"

He took my hand back. My eyes widened. He curled my fingers into his grip and squeezed. His skin was warm, still a little damp from the wet towel. The touch rooted me, brought me away from the pain. Everything was going to be okay.

He was still kneeling by my chair, which meant his head was a little lower than mine. I looked down on him, slightly. He was in the perfect place for me to kiss him.

I touched his cheek with my free hand and brushed my lips against his, lightly, just to see what he would do. He hesitated, but he didn't pull away.

Then he kissed back, and he was hungry. His mouth was warm, his lips active, grasping. I tried to match his energy, move my lips with his, letting the heat of attraction burn through my body, through my muscles. I wrapped my uninjured arm around his neck and slid off the chair, pressing myself to him. He held me there, his hands against my back. He moved his kisses from my lips to my chin, up my jaw, to my ear. Clinging to him, I stifled a gasp.

I hadn't been with a normal, nonlycanthropic human since I'd become a werewolf. I'd been afraid to be with a normal human. Afraid of what I might do if I lost it. But Cormac could take care of himself. Being with him was different from being with a lycanthrope. I hadn't realized it would be different. I was stronger than he was. I could feel the strength in my muscles pressing against him. I could hold him away or squeeze him until he cried out. It made me feel powerful, more in control than I ever had been in my life. I wanted to take him in, all of him. I could hear the blood rushing through his body, sense the strain of desire in his tendons. He smelled different from lycanthropes. More . . . civilized, like soap and cars and houses. He didn't smell like pack, and that made him new. Exciting. I decided I liked the way he smelled.

I buried my face in his hair and took a deep breath. I squirmed out of his grip so that I could work my way down his whole body, tracing the whole scent of him, down his neck, along the collar of his shirt, down his torso and the hint of chest hair through the fabric, across his chest to his armpit, which burst with his smell. I lingered there, then nuzzled my way down to the waistband of his jeans, and oh, I couldn't wait to find out how he smelled down there . . .

Grabbing my shoulders, Cormac pushed me away and held me at arm's length.

"What are you doing?"

"You smell fresh." I strained toward him, my eyes half-closed, wanting to plunge back into the scent of him.

He stood, putting space between us. "You're not human." He marched away.

I knelt on the kitchen floor, my knees digging into the tile, my heart pounding, reaching for the body that wasn't there.

After a moment, I wandered to the other half of the apartment. He leaned against the opposite wall, his arms crossed, defensive, staring at the door like he couldn't understand why he didn't just leave.

"I'm sorry," I said. I wasn't sure what I was apologizing for. For being what I was, maybe. I couldn't help that, though, so I didn't want to apologize for it. So I was apologizing for this. For calling him. For kissing him. For not guessing how he would react.

He started to say one thing, then shook his head. He looked at the floor, then looked at me.

"How did you get like this? You're not the kind that goes asking for it."

I sat at the edge of the bed and hugged my knees. My arm was getting better by the minute. The punctures were closed, covered with red scabs, fading to pink. The pain was turning to an itch.

What had that government spook asked me? Who did I go to when I needed advice, when I needed to talk? What would I say if someone called the show and told me my story? Tough break, kid. Deal with it. But that didn't assuage the anger I still felt. The anger I still hadn't dealt with. I'd never told anyone the whole story, not even T.J. or anyone else in the pack.

I wasn't sure Cormac was the right person to tell, but I didn't know when I'd get another chance to talk.

"Wrong place at the wrong time," I said, and told him the story.

Bill was cute. I'd give him that much. Sandy brown hair, square jaw, winning smile. But he was only interested in one thing from me. He was a frat boy type, and I was . . . well, I was confused. He impressed me because he was cute and arrogant.

We were at a Fourth of July party in Estes Park, in the mountains, where they launched fireworks into the valley and the noise echoed back and forth between the hills. He'd spent the whole time talking smack with his friends, while gripping me around the waist like I was some kind of accessory. That was what I got for being blond and looking good in a miniskirt. My face hurt from forcing it to smile at everyone. I didn't have a good time, and I was ready for the night to be over.

He spent the car ride back to town crawling his hand up my leg, trying to get under my skirt.

"I just want to go home," I said for the fifth time, pushing his hand away.

"But it's still early."

"Please."

"Whatever."

So he drove, and I stared out the window. When he turned onto a side road, it was in the middle of nowhere and there wasn't much I could do about it.

"Where are we going?" Scrub oak and pine trees lined the narrow road. It led to a trailhead near a river. "Turn around."

The place was popular with hikers and mountain bikers during the day. But this was midnight. Bill shut off the headlights and pulled to a corner of the parking lot shaded by overhanging branches.

I grabbed the door handle, but he pushed the automatic lock as he stopped the engine.

He moved so fast, I bet he'd done this before.

He held my arms, pinning them, and clambered to my side of the car, pressing me to the bucket seat. Two hundred pounds of Bill weighed on me, and no matter how much I squirmed, I couldn't get away. I started hyperventilating.

"Relax, baby. Just relax."

I kept saying, *No, stop, no, please,* the whole time. I'd never been so scared and angry. When he brought his face close, I bit him. He slapped me and pounded into me that much harder.

I tasted blood. I'd bitten my cheek, and my nose was bleeding.

With a sigh, he rolled away finally. It still hurt.

I scrabbled at the lock until it clicked, then I opened the door and tumbled out.

Bill shouted after me. "Don't you want a ride back? Christ!" He started up his car and pulled away.

I ran. Legs weak, breath heaving, I ran away. I only wanted to get away.

A full moon shone that night. Weird shadows lit the grass and scrub. This was stupid; I had no idea where I was, no idea how I was going to get home. I slid into the grass and sobbed. Stupid, Kitty. This whole night was stupid and look where it got me.

A picnic area lay a little ways from the parking lot. Shelters covered some of the tables. I sat down at one, pulling my knees to my chin and hugging myself. My panties were still in Bill's car. I figured I'd sit here until some jogger found me in the morning and called the cops. I could do that. Hug myself to stop shivering, maybe go to sleep.

In the distance, a wolf howled. Far away. Nothing to do with me.

Maybe I dozed. Maybe I thought it was a nightmare at first when the shrubs nearby rustled. A shadow moved. Its fur was like shadow, silvery and brindled. It turned bronze eyes on me. Canine nostrils quivered.

It stepped closer, head low, sniffing, never turning from me. The wolf was as big as a Great Dane, with bulky shoulders and a thick ruff of fur. Even with me sitting on the table, it could reach me without trying.

Later, I learned that the wolf could smell the blood from my injuries, and instinct had told it a wounded animal was near. Easy prey.

I trembled like a rabbit, and like a rabbit, the minute I thought of running, it pounced.

I screamed as its claws raked my leg and I lurched away, falling off the table. I kept screaming when its jaw clamped on my hip. Using that as purchase, it climbed up my body, scratching the whole way. My flesh gave way like butter, pieces of it flaying with every touch.

Panic, panic, panic. I kicked its face. Startled, it backed off for a moment. In an adrenaline haze, I jumped and grabbed hold of the edge of the shelter's roof. Gasping, clutching, gritting my teeth, I swung one leg up. The wolf jumped, scraped claws down the other leg. I screamed, falling—but no, I clutched the edge, the wolf lost its grip, and I caught one leg over the edge, then the other. Lying there, spent, I dared to look down.

The wolf looked back at me, but it couldn't reach me. It turned and ran.

I didn't have the energy to move another muscle, so I fell unconscious, one arm hanging over the edge of the shelter.

Something squeezed my hand. The sky was light, pale with dawn. With a shriek, I pulled my hands close and started shaking.

Blood caked my legs, my skirt, my shirt. Blood had pooled on the roof of the shelter, but it was dried. I wasn't bleeding anymore. Carefully, I inched closer to the edge.

Hands gripped there, and a woman hoisted herself up. I scrambled crablike away from her, all the way to the other edge. I looked down to where a couple of men stood, watching me with cold eyes. The woman knelt at the edge of the roof. She had long black hair, brown eyes, and moved with a dancer's grace, settling to a seated position without taking her gaze off me.

"What's your name?" she said.

I looked around. A half-dozen of them surrounded the shelter, men in various states of scruffiness, unshaven and uncombed, wearing leather or denim jackets, T-shirts, and jeans. All of them were barefoot. The woman also wore jeans and a T-shirt without much thought to style. Still, they all managed to intimidate, radiating strength just in the way they stood.

I didn't answer.

"The bites, the scratches—do they hurt?"

I had to think about it, which meant they didn't hurt. I touched my hip. It was tender, but not painful.

"Look at the wounds," she said. "What do you see?"

I pulled up my shirt, exposing where the wolf had taken a bite. A scar, red and healing, maybe a week old, puckered the skin. The gouges on my legs were pink lines, closed and healing.

I started hyperventilating again. I managed to gasp, "How do you know what happened?"

She said, "One of our people attacked you. We're here to take responsibility for his actions."

"But you're—"

She crept toward me, her eyes focused on me, her nostrils quivering. I flinched, but if I backed away any farther, I'd fall off.

"I won't hurt you. None of us will hurt you. Please, tell me your name."

All I wanted to do in that moment was fall into her arms, because I believed that she wouldn't hurt me. "Kitty," I said in a small voice.

For a moment, she looked disbelieving. Then, she smiled. "Oh, that's rich. You're way too nice for this life, kid."

"I don't understand."

"You will. You'll have to. I'll help. T.J.?"

Hands appeared on the edge of the roof behind me. One of the men pulled himself up easily, like he was hopping onto a tabletop and not climbing up a seven-foot-high shelter. He crouched at the edge, one hand resting on the roof to steady himself. He was—God, he was gorgeous. Tanned, well-built, biceps straining at the sleeves of his white T-shirt, dark hair flopped around an intense face.

He radiated energy and scared the daylights out of me. I backed away, scraping my knees on the roof's asphalt shingles. But then she was there, just as intense, trapping me. I curled in on myself, on the edge of screaming. Something inside me started to rip.

"Who are you people?"

The man, T.J., said, "We're the pack."

A convulsion wrenched me, and I blacked out.

I fell in and out of consciousness for the next three days. I remembered a little—the smell of the park that morning, pine trees and dew. Someone carried me. Someone else—her, the woman—kept a hand on my shoulder. Voices, which I couldn't keep straight.

"She smells like sex."

"Sex and fear."

"There's blood. Not from the bites and cuts. Meg, look."

I shook my head and tried to struggle, but I was like a baby, arms flailing without gaining purchase, too weak to pull away. "No, stop, don't touch, don't touch . . ." I gasped.

"She was raped," the woman said.

"You don't suppose Zan—"

"It doesn't smell like Zan."

"Someone else, then. Might explain how she ended up out here."

"Wish she'd talk."

"She will later. She's got a couple of days of this yet." I groaned. I had homework, I couldn't—

I opened my eyes.

I lay on a bed. A sheet was tangled around me, like I'd been thrashing in my sleep. I wore a T-shirt—nothing else—and I was clean. I was cold, and sweat matted my hair. I took a deep breath—I didn't know how long I'd been sleeping, but I felt exhausted, like I'd been running. I didn't want to move.

The bronzed idol from the park was sitting in a chair by the bed, watching me. The woman moved from another chair to sit at the foot of the bed. I looked back at them, waiting to feel panic. I'd been kidnapped. Some cult thing. Did Bill put them up to this? None of that seemed right, and I didn't feel afraid at all. Somehow, I felt safe. Like I knew they were here to watch over me, to take care of me. I was sick. Very sick.

"How do you feel?" he said.

"Not good. Tired. Wrung out."

He nodded like he understood. "Your metabolism's all fucked up. It'll work itself out in a few days. Are you hungry?"

I hadn't thought so, but as soon as he said it, my belly felt hollow and I was starving.

"Yeah, I guess I am." I sat up.

He left through a door in what appeared to be a well-lit bedroom. Meg studied me. I looked away, feeling suddenly shy. T.J. returned carrying a platter with a steak, like he'd had it waiting. I looked skeptically at it. I wasn't much of a steak eater.

He set it on the bedstand and handed me a knife. Reluctant, I sliced into it. It bled. Profusely.

I dropped the knife. "I don't like them rare."

"You do now."

I thought I was going to cry. Glaring at him, my voice barely a whisper, I said, "What's happening to me? Why aren't I afraid of you?"

He knelt beside the bed. I looked down on him now, which was comforting. Meg came around to the other side and sat next to me, so close I could feel her body heat. I was trapped, and my heart started racing.

She took my hand, then raised both our hands to my face. "What do you smell?"

Was she nuts? But with our hands right in front of my nose, I couldn't help but smell as I breathed. I expected to smell skin. Maybe soap. Normal people smells. But—there was more. I closed my eyes and breathed deep. Something rich and vibrant, like earth and mountain air. It wasn't soap or new-age deodorant or anything like that. It was her. I calmed down.

Before I knew it, T.J. was sitting beside me, an arm around my shoulder, pressing his body close to me and breathing into my hair. It wasn't sexual; there wasn't anything sexual about it—that was so hard to explain to people who didn't know.

"This is our pack," Meg said, holding me from the other side. "You're safe here."

I believed her.

By now, Cormac was sitting on the floor. He seemed more relaxed. He didn't have that look on his face that he'd had when he left me, like he'd eaten something sour.

"That's shitty luck," he said finally.

I shook my head, smiling wryly. I'd made my peace with it. Telling the story, I realized who I'd been most angry at all this time.

I said, "Now ask me which one I think is the real monster. Zan—he was following instinct. He couldn't control it. But Bill—he knew exactly what he was doing. And he wasn't sorry." After a pause I added, "That's Zan, out in the street."

When I leaned back, I could see out the window. From the second floor, I could see the street, but not the spot where Zan was. I said, "You think anyone's called the cops yet?"

"Depends," he said. "How much noise did you all make?"

I couldn't remember. To the casual listener, it might have sounded like stray dogs fighting. I'd have to call Carl, to find out what I should do about Zan. I couldn't just leave him out there.

"You should get some rest. You may heal quick, but you still lost a lot of blood. You going to be okay on your own?"

I thought about it a minute, and thought I would be okay. Maybe I'd go to T.J.'s and see if he'd made it home yet.

"Yeah, I think so." I smiled crookedly. "I'm glad you're not the type to shoot all werewolves on principle."

He may have actually smiled at that, but it was thin-lipped and fleeting. "Just give me an excuse, Norville." He made a haphazard salute and left the apartment.

Man, that guy scared me. He also made my knees weak, and I wasn't sure if the two were related.

He was right, I was tired, but before I could sleep I had to call Carl. I was reaching for the phone when the door opened and Cormac returned.

Following him were Detective Hardin and three uniformed cops.

chapter **10**

Cormac, arms crossed and expression a mask, took his spot holding up the wall. One of the cops stayed with him. The officer didn't have his gun out, but he kept his hand at his belt. The other two began a search of the apartment, looking in closets, drawers, and behind doors.

Hardin came straight to me.

I'd expected lights, sirens, mayhem. Plenty of warning to maybe duck out the back. But Hardin probably wasn't going to advertise her presence when she was looking for a killer.

I should have had Carl come pick up the body before the cops showed up. Then again, that would have been just what we needed, someone watching us loading a body into his truck, writing down the license plate number, *then* calling the police. Werewolf battles usually happened in the wilderness, where bodies could just disappear.

This way, at least only I got bagged.

God, what was I *thinking*. This whole thing was a mess. Zan was *dead*.

She said, "You want to tell me about the ripped-up body we found downstairs?"

I glanced at Cormac, who didn't move a muscle, damn him.

"No," I said, which was probably stupider than not saying anything at all.

"Did you do it?"

I'd already been through this once tonight. "No."

"Ms. Norville, I think I'd like to take you down to the station and ask you a few questions."

Hardly surprising, but my stomach still did a flip-flop. I may have been a werewolf, but I'd never even gotten a parking ticket, much less been arrested for anything. Then again, I'd never owned a car.

But I wasn't being arrested. This was just questioning.

"Let me get a jacket," I said, my voice a whisper. When I stood, my injured side turned toward her. Hardin tilted her head, glancing at the red slashes and puckered skin on my arm.

"When did that happen?"

"Tonight."

"Impossible. Those have been healing for weeks."

"You need to do more reading. Did you get those articles I sent you?"

"Yeah." She stared, like she was trying to read my mind. "Who did this to you?" She said it like she actually cared about me or something.

I glared. "The ripped-up body downstairs."

She waited a beat, then, "Are you telling me that guy was a werewolf?"

I finished shrugging on the jacket and grabbed the key to the apartment. "Should I call a lawyer or something?"

Outside, there must have been a half-dozen cop cars, along with the coroner's van. They had the whole street blocked off. Yellow tape fluttered everywhere. A swarm of people wearing plastic gloves huddled around Zan, swabbing things and sticking them into baggies. Evidence. All the evidence they needed.

Too much exposure. Carl had always warned me this might happen. He really was going to kill me this time.

Cormac and I got a ride in the nice police car. He'd already called his lawyer, who he thought would represent me as well, if I asked him.

I shuddered to think of the kind of experience a lawyer got working for Cormac. But hey, the bounty hunter wasn't in jail.

They put Cormac and me in separate rooms. Mine was similar to the interview room I'd been in before, the size of a small bedroom, institutional and without character. I didn't get coffee this time.

It must have been four in the morning. I hadn't slept, and I was feeling light-headed. I wanted to ask someone for a glass of water. The door wasn't locked. I opened it, looked in the hall outside, and didn't see anyone. I had a feeling that if I tried to sneak out, a swarm of cops would suddenly appear. I went back inside.

I laid my head on the table, thinking about how much this week had sucked, and dozed. When the door opened, I jerked awake, startled, and shivered inside my coat. I felt worse for the few moments' worth of napping.

The man who entered was in his early thirties. He was rumpled, with swept-back, mousy blond hair that needed trimming, a stubbled jaw, a gray suit jacket that fit but still managed to seem too big, and an uninspiring brown tie. He slouched and carried his briefcase under one arm.

He strode to the desk, switching the briefcase out from under his arm so he could extend his hand for me to shake.

"Hi, Kitty Norville? I'm Ben O'Farrell. Cormac says you need a lawyer." He had an average voice, but spoke with confidence and met my gaze.

"Hi." Tentatively, I shook his hand. I tried to get more of a sense of him. He smelled average. Normal. The jacket maybe needed washing. "I don't know if I do or not."

He shrugged. "Never hurts when the cops are around. Here's my card, my rates." He pulled a card out of one pocket, a pen out of another, tried juggling them and the briefcase, then set the briefcase down so he could write on the card, which he handed to me when he was finished.

That was a big number. It was a per-hour number.

"You any good?" I said.

"Cormac isn't in jail."

I smiled in spite of myself. "Should he be?"

When O'Farrell matched the smile, he looked like a hawk. It made me feel better; at least, it would so long as he was on my side. It made me glad I hadn't pressed charges against Cormac that night he barged in on the show.

"Can you stick around for tonight? Hopefully I won't need you any longer."

He nodded and went to the door.

"Wait." I winced, only starting to realize the kind of trouble I was in. He was letting the cops in. I wanted to run. Wolf started itching, and I didn't need that now. "I don't want to tell them what happened."

He looked thoughtful a moment, then said, "Okay." He glanced out the still-open door and gestured someone inside. Detective Hardin.

O'Farrell took a seat at the table and looked busy with his briefcase. Hardin closed the door and remained standing by the wall, arms crossed, grouchy.

She said, "What was that hit man doing in your apartment?"

That wasn't a good place to start the conversation. *Was* there a good place to start this conversation?

I glanced at O'Farrell. He shrugged, noncommittal, and continued shuffling papers. Did that mean it was okay to talk or not? I could refuse to answer. Mainly because I didn't know what to say, and not because I was hiding anything.

"I called him. I was pretty beat up earlier, and I needed help. We've been in touch. Professional consulting."

"No hard feelings over what happened last month, then?"

"I guess not."

"What was the dead guy doing at your apartment?"

I swallowed, my throat dry. O'Farrell said, "Could we get some water in here? Thanks."

With an even more surly frown, Hardin leaned out and called to someone. A moment later a couple of cups of water arrived.

This all just wasted time.

"You going to answer me?" Hardin said. Her hair was sticking out in all directions, and her eyes were shadowed. She hadn't gotten any sleep either.

"He—he was waiting," I said, stammering. "For me. He wanted to hurt me." I took another drink of water and ducked my gaze. I was having trouble talking.

"Why?"

I couldn't answer that. I couldn't say it. It would take too long to explain.

"Then can you tell me who else was there?"

I couldn't answer that either. Once again, I looked at O'Farrell for help. Hardin looked at him, too.

He said to Hardin, "I'm assuming she hasn't been Mirandized? She doesn't have to answer any question she doesn't want to. She's here as a voluntary witness." Voluntary? *Nominally.*

"At this stage," Hardin said. She turned back to me. "It wasn't a wild dog that bit that guy's head off, and I'm pretty sure it wasn't you. They found blood under the victim's fingernails and in his mouth. I'm willing to believe that it's yours and that part of your story checks out. If it does, it means you were there and you probably know who did it. Was it that rogue werewolf you've been telling me about? The one we've been looking for in the mauling deaths?"

"No," I said, forgetting myself. "This doesn't have anything to do with the rogue." This was all inside the pack and none of her business.

Hardin started pacing. "Ms. Norville. Kitty. Right now you're a witness, not an accessory to murder. Don't make me have to change that assessment."

"What?"

"If you know who did it and you don't tell me, I can charge you with being an accessory to murder."

"That's a bluff," O'Farrell said. "The most you could charge without more evidence is obstruction of justice."

What the hell were they talking about?

Hardin plowed on, ignoring him. "If you're trying to protect whoever did this, you're guilty of a crime."

"It wasn't . . . like that. Zan made the challenge; he was asking for it—this isn't . . . this isn't . . . criminal."

"Ms. Norville." O'Farrell made a calming gesture. I sat back.

Hardin said, "A man has been murdered and you're saying there's nothing wrong with that?"

"No, it's just—" It's just that yeah, within the law of the pack, it was all right. T.J. was the dominant wolf and Zan had overstepped his bounds. I wanted the double standard, now that it would bene-fit me. "He did it to protect me. Zan attacked me first, and—"

"Ms. Norville." O'Farrell's tone was cautioning.

I was doing everything I could to not say the name. And really, it wasn't defensive. Zan had backed off. T.J. killed him anyway. In the eyes of human law, T.J. was a murderer.

I curled up in the chair and pressed my face to my knees.

O'Farrell stood up. "Detective Hardin, could I have a word with you?"

The lawyer and detective moved to the opposite corner of the room and spoke in low whispers. They didn't seem to know I could still hear them.

"Ms. Norville is cooperating to the fullest extent of her current ability. She's been injured, hasn't had any sleep, and is in no state to answer your questions at this time. Let her go home and get some rest. You can talk to her later. She'll probably be more help-ful then."

"Let her go so she can get together with this other guy and straighten out their stories?"

"Look at her record—she's not even a flight risk. Clean as a whistle."

"Except for being a werewolf."

He shrugged. "Not her fault."

Hardin looked away with a huff. She pulled a cigarette out of her trousers pocket, patted the other pocket for a lighter, but didn't find one. She pointed at O'Farrell with the unlit cigarette. "If I let her go, promise me you'll talk some sense into her. I don't want to have to arrest her for anything."

"I'll do my best, Detective."

I had to talk to T.J. That was all I wanted right now.

O'Farrell stood next to my chair. "Ms. Norville? Come on, let's go."

Hardin stopped me before opening the door. "Don't leave town."

My throat was still dry. This place tasted dry and cold. All I could do was press my lips together and nod, my eyes downcast.

Outside, the sky was gray with dawn. Almost too bright. My exhausted eyes stung with the faint light. The air was biting, reaching into my bones.

The lawyer and I stood for a moment on the sidewalk outside the police station.

I said, "Me being a werewolf. Does it bother you? Are you an antimonster crusader like Cormac?"

He smiled as if I'd said something funny, an expression reminiscent of one of Cormac's smirks. "If Cormac were a crusader, he'd have shot you the first time he met you, no matter what the circumstances were."

"Then what is he?"

"He just likes seeing how close to the edge he can get without falling off."

Somehow, Cormac as mercenary-with-a-death-wish was a scarier proposition than Cormac as mercenary-with-convictions.

"What are you?"

He shrugged. "Equal opportunity attorney-at-law."

"Yeah, I guess. Thanks for getting me out of there."

"It was easy. Hardin likes you. Can I give you a ride someplace?"

"No thanks."

"A word of advice, Ms. Norville. You should tell the cops his name. That way, only one of you goes down. If he's your friend, he'll understand." He was a good fit for Cormac, as lawyers went. I could picture him in a gangster movie, finding loopholes and talking tough at the judge.

"I'll think about it."

"At the very least, don't talk to this guy. If you go to him, you'll make it real hard for me to prove you're not trying to cover anything up."

"I'm—we're not used to human law. We're usually a lot better about cleaning up our bodies."

He didn't say anything. I got tired of waiting for him to speak, so I shoved my hands into the pockets of my coat and walked away. I could sense him staring after me.

I went to T.J.'s.

If Hardin sent someone to follow me, I didn't know about it. It wouldn't have surprised me if she had. It was stupid to go, to possibly lead her right to him. But I wasn't thinking straight by then.

I had a little bit of sense and took side streets and footpaths where cars couldn't follow. I ran, and I could run fast, even injured, like any werewolf worth her salt.

The front door of his house was unlocked. I slipped in, closed the door quietly, and locked it. He had two rooms, a living room with a hide-a-bed and a kitchen/utility room. The bathroom was in back.

He was lying asleep on the living room floor, naked and tangled in a blanket. He must have been out all night, too. He had a great body, muscled arms flowing into well-defined shoulders and back. He was curled in a ball, tense, like he was having a nightmare. His hair was damp with sweat. He hugged a pillow to his chest.

I took off my jacket and shoes and knelt beside him. I touched his cheek, holding my hand near his nose so he could smell me. He shifted, moaning a little. I lay next to him and snuggled close as he woke up, slipping into his arms.

He didn't open his eyes, but I could tell he was awake because his embrace tightened around me.

"I'm sorry I yelled at you," I whispered.

He smiled and kissed my forehead. "Hm. Are you okay?"

"Yeah." Now, I was. At least for a little while. "Why'd he do it, T.J.? I didn't think he was that dumb. If he'd wanted to challenge me, why didn't he do it in front of the pack? This wasn't going to win him back his standing."

He waited so long to answer I thought he'd fallen asleep again. The question was half-rhetorical anyway. I'd never understood why Zan did things.

Then T.J. said, "Someone put him up to it. Someone wanted him to kill you without the pack watching."

So it wasn't Zan's idea. That almost made sense. "How do you know?"

"Because I told him if he ever went after you again, I'd kill him." My eyes stung, tears slipping down, because I had to tell him about the police. I had to ask him to tell me what to do. He couldn't go to jail. What would they do with him during full moon nights? I nestled closer, resting my head on his chest. "Who put him up to it?"

"Someone who outranks me. He'd only listen to someone who scared him more than I did. That leaves Carl or Meg."

Time passed, and sunlight began to trace the window shades when I said, "I think it was Meg."

"I think it was Carl." Then, very softly, "I used to be in love with Carl."

In so many ways, the alpha of the pack was god to us. I remembered my first few months with them. I trembled whenever Carl came near. I cowered at his feet, worshiping him, adoring him. When had that gone away?

"Me, too," I said.

We slept for a time. I was only half-awake when he stretched his back and sat up. He paused, took several deep breaths, then brought his face close to me, smelling my hair, moving down to sniff my neck and shirt.

He said, his tone doubtful, "You smell like a police station."

I told him everything while he made bacon and eggs for breakfast. Even the smell of frying meat filling the kitchen couldn't make me hungry. We sat at his Formica table, plates of food in front of us, and neither one of us ate.

He picked at his for a while, breaking the yolks of his fried eggs and stirring them with bacon. He looked at me, and I stared at my plate.

Finally, he said, "This is what you get for going to the cops in the first place."

"It's because I went to the cops and got on their good side that I'm not in jail now." There I was, arguing again.

"I can't go to jail," he said. "Neither can you. You'll tell them I did it. That'll get you off the hook. And I'll run. I'll go into the hills, maybe go wolf for a while. That way I can hide."

I didn't like the sound of that. It wouldn't get *him* off the hook. We had no idea how long he'd have to hide. I wanted some solution that would let everyone believe T.J. was innocent. But he wasn't, really. That was the problem.

Any way we looked at it, I was in danger of losing him.

My voice cracked when I said, "Have you ever heard of someone Changing and not being able to shift back?"

"I've heard stories. It hasn't happened to anyone I know."

"I don't want you to go wolf. You're not a wolf."

"It can be a strength, Kitty. If it can help, I'd be stupid not to use it. That's something you've never learned—how to use the wolf as a strength."

"I'll miss you. Who'll look out for me if you go?"

He smiled. "I thought you said you could take care of yourself."

I wanted to say something rude, but I started crying.

"You can always come visit," he said.

I went home. The police cars, coroner's van, swarms of people, and Zan's body were gone. A few scraps of yellow crime-scene tape fluttered, caught in the shrubs outside the building. A guy sat in a sedan parked across the street, sipping coffee. Watching. I ignored him.

I threw away the bloody towel and shirt that were still lying in the kitchen sink. I opened a window and let in some air, because the place felt like Cormac, Hardin, and the cops were still trooping through, making the room stuffy. I pulled O'Farrell's card out of my pocket and left it on the kitchen counter. I washed my face and brushed my teeth, looked at myself in the mirror. Red, puffy eyes. Greasy, tired hair. I looked pale.

I started to tell myself that I just had to wait for everything to get back to normal. Take it one step at a time, things would settle down, and I'd feel better. But I stopped, because I tried to think of what was normal, and I couldn't remember.

Shape-shifting once a month, waking up tangled with a half-dozen other naked bodies, sniffing armpits as foreplay. Was that normal? Letting Carl beat up on me, fuck me, tell me what to do, just because it felt right to the wolf half? Was *that* normal? Did I want to go back to that?

Normal without the Wolf was so long ago I couldn't remember what it was like anymore.

I had two choices regarding Carl. I could leave him, or challenge him. Leaving him meant leaving the pack. That made it hard. Too hard to think about.

Could I make it on my own?

Could I fight him and win?

Six months ago, I would have said no to both those questions. Now, I wasn't sure. I had to be able to answer yes to one of those, if I couldn't go back to being what I was six months ago.

Now all I had to do was decide which one I could answer yes to.

". . . be kinda cool to look through a bunch of autopsy reports and find out how many of those people were shot with silver bullets."

"I'm going to add that to my list," I said into the microphone. "Do the police check bullets for silver content?"

"They ought to," the caller said with a humph. "Seems kind of obvious, doesn't it?"

"Indeed. Thanks for calling. This is Kitty, and in case you've just tuned in, I'm putting together a list of questions that law enforcement officials might want to start asking about certain crimes. Our topic tonight is law enforcement and the supernatural. I've got some national crime statistics here, a breakdown of murders that happened all over the U.S. last year—murder weapons, causes of death, that sort of thing. It says here that police reported that fourteen people died with stakes through their hearts last year. Of those fourteen, eight were also decapitated, and three were found draped with crosses. All were reported as, quote, ritualistic slayings, unquote. I should think so. My question is, did they check to see if those murder victims really were vampires? Could they check? Probably not. Some varieties of vampire disintegrate upon death. Though there exists a CDC report describing tests for identifying lycanthropes and vampires. Let's take a call. Hello, Ray, you're on the air."

"Hi, Kitty. I just want to bring up a point you seem to be missing: If those fourteen 'murder victims,' as you call them, really were vampires, is it really murder?"

Ooh, controversy. "What do you think?"

"Well, I'd call it self-defense. Vampires are predators, and their only prey is humanity. Humanity has a vested interest in getting rid of them whenever they can." Sounded like a rancher talking about wolves.

"Gee, Ray. Some of my best friends are vampires. What if the vampire in question has never killed anyone? Let's say she only takes blood from voluntary donors, keeps to herself, never causes trouble. Then one day some crusading vampire hunter comes along and stakes her just because she's a vampire."

"That's been going on for hundreds of years. I think you're the first person to call it *murder*."

"Actually, I'm not. And at the risk of offending lots of people out there in lots of different ways, the Nazis didn't call it murder either." I clicked him off the line before he could say anything indignant. "Let me present another thought experiment. We've got a werewolf, vampire, whatever. He's killed someone for no good reason. What should happen? If it were a normal person, he'd get arrested, go on trial, and probably go to jail for a really long time. Maybe be sentenced to death if the situation warranted. Now, let's take the werewolf. Can we put a werewolf in jail for a really long time? What are they going to do with him when the full moon comes along? Or the vampire—do you realize how impractical it would be to sentence a vampire to life in prison? I've got Timothy on the line. Hello."

The caller said in a low, smooth voice, "Of course it's impractical sentencing a vampire to life in prison. I think there'd be no other choice but to have a vampire hunter take care of the problem. That's what they're for."

"So you're saying law enforcement should stay completely out of it. Just let the vampire hunters loose willy-nilly."

"Of course not. Unless the vampires are allowed to hunt the hunters, willy-nilly, as you say."

I was guessing he was a vampire. He had that arrogant tone, and that clipped diction that usually meant someone had learned to speak in a culture that valued refined grammar, which meant not recent culture.

"Which is still outside mundane law enforcement. The supernatural underground should take care of its own, is that what you're saying?"

"I believe it is. If a werewolf kills another werewolf in the course of a pack dominance challenge, do you really want the police to become involved?"

Ouch. Double ouch. But I'd asked for it. That'd teach me to do a show on a personal topic I was worried about. Unfortunately, I wasn't the type to backpedal. I read a quote by Churchill once: *If you're going through hell, keep going.*

"Let me turn that question back on you: What would you recommend to a police officer who did get involved in an internecine squabble? Let's say a mauled body shows up. The cop looks into it, and in a particular show of brilliance and open-mindedness decides that the attacker couldn't have been an animal and thinks *werewolf*. What's more, he runs a couple of tests and discovers that hey, the victim was a werewolf, too." Maybe Hardin was listening. Maybe we'd both learn something. "What should he do next?"

"Buy lots of silver bullets," Timothy answered without hesitation.

"That is *so* not helpful." Yikes, I'd said that out loud. I hung up on him. "Okay, moving on. Are you a lycanthrope or a vampire or the like who has had an encounter with the law? What did you do? What's your advice? And as always, any comments on the issues we've been discussing throughout the hour are welcome. Next caller, you're on the air."

"Hi, Kitty. The best and only advice I can give when the cops are after you is to run like hell. There's no way the cops can keep up. That's the beauty of it . . ."

". . . if you're going to put vampires and werewolves under the jurisdiction of human law enforcement, then you absolutely need to put vampires and werewolves on the police force . . ."

Vampire cops? Was she serious? Then again, they'd always have somebody to take the graveyard shift.

The calls kept coming.

". . . the same laws don't apply. They never can, they never will. Death and murder don't mean the same thing to people who are immortal and nearly indestructible . . ."

My head hurt. My callers were making me feel stupid. They kept taking me to the same place, that T.J. was right and I shouldn't talk to the cops anymore. Supernatural *glasnost* was impossible. I was the stuff that nightmare stories were made of and I should learn to live with it. Or shoot myself with silver.

I wondered what the statistics were on suicide among lycanthropes.

For the last few days, Hardin had people watching me. I did nothing but travel between work and home. I didn't call anyone. I didn't tell Hardin anything.

I said, "True confession time. You know that I do it occasionally, take these questions out of the abstract and talk about how they apply to my own life. And what I'm thinking right now is, what's the point? If these two worlds, the supernatural and human worlds, are destined to be at each other's throats; if there's no way to compromise about things like who has the right to govern whom, then what am I doing here? Why should I even bother doing the show?

I'm feeling an impulse to run to the hills and forget I was ever human. But you know what? I would miss chocolate. And movies. And the next album by my favorite band. And I'm wondering if this is where the problem is, that lycanthropes and vampires might not technically be fully human, but they used to be, and they can't ever forget it. Or more to the point, they *shouldn't* ever forget it. When they do is when the problems happen."

The monitor was full of calls. I looked at Matt through the window, wanting some kind of guidance, not wanting to choose. I didn't want to hear about anyone's problems. I didn't want to hear any more righteous rhetoric from either camp. I just wanted . . . I didn't know. Maybe to play some music, like in the old days. Maybe I could do that for the next show, get a band on and talk about music for a couple of hours. Yeah, that was a plan.

Matt was leaning back in his chair, smiling at me. He'd stuck it out with me during the whole run of the show. That smile said he was happy to be here. I couldn't help but smile back.

He was my friend, and he was human. That said something.

I straightened and took a breath, making my voice lighter, to drag the show from its depressing low. "All right, it looks like I have a repeat caller on the line. I always appreciate the people who come back for more. James, hello."

"Kitty, I just want to tell you how much your show means to me. It's—you're this voice of reason, you know? You actually think these things through. It helps, it really helps. I hope you don't ever stop doing this." His voice sounded even more strained than it had the last time. If the show was helping him, I'd hate to think of what he'd sound like without it.

"Thanks. That means a lot. How are you doing?"

"I've been thinking about it. I think I'm okay. I think I'm doing what I was meant to do. Why else would this have happened to me, if not to be this way and be able to do these things?"

My stomach froze. "Do what things, James?"

"I have a confession, Kitty. I didn't much like being human, when I was human. So being a werewolf isn't much different, except I'm strong now. I'm—I know what to do. When I can't decide what to do, the wolf tells me what to do."

James was psychotic. He'd probably been that way before he became a lycanthrope. So, what happened when a self-loathing, misanthropic psychotic became a werewolf?

Blood pounded in my ears when I double-checked the monitor.

We collected first names and hometowns from the callers. I couldn't remember where he was from. I squinted to read the monitor.

Oh, my God. Denver. He'd been under my nose the whole time. I covered the mike and hissed at Matt, mouthing, "Caller ID. Get his number. Now!"

Leaning into the mike, I tried to keep my voice steady. "What does your wolf tell you to do, James?"

"You know, Kitty. You know. What does *your* wolf tell you to do? *You* understand."

Use claws. Teeth. Get blood. Run. Yeah, I understood. But I'd won that battle.

"Do you ever stop to think that your wolf may be wrong?"

"But the wolf is so much stronger than I am." He said this admiringly.

"Might doesn't make right. That's the whole point of civilization. You called me a voice of reason, James. Where does reason come into all this?"

"I *told* you. If there's a reason that this happened, then this is it. For me to be strong."

I checked the clock. I still had fifteen minutes to go. I'd never let a show go unfinished. I'd never had a better reason to. But I didn't. I finished. I tried to sound normal, because I didn't want James to think anything was wrong. "Okay, we're going to break for station ID. We'll be right back with *The Midnight Hour.*"

I switched off the mike and called to the booth, "Did you get the number?"

"Yeah," Matt said, walking through the door with a piece of paper in his hand. "And an address. Kitty, you've gone white. What is it?"

My mouth was dry, and my heart was beating so fast I was shaking. "I don't know yet. Just—let's just finish this up. I have to make a call before we go back on."

Call the police! That was the right thing to do. Except it wasn't, because all this shit, the supernatural, the claws and fangs and stuff that made us different, made *right* different. Maybe that would change someday.

James as a wolf wouldn't be a wolf. He wouldn't even be a psychotic human in the shape of a wolf. He'd be a little of both, and while I liked to pretend I had the best of both worlds, James seemed to have the worst. A wolf would run away when Hardin faced him down with a gun. James would attack. I couldn't call

Hardin. She'd be killed. Or infected. I wasn't going to put her in
that situation.

Once again, I called Cormac instead of the cops. The shadow
law.

"Yeah."

"It's Kitty. Feel like going hunting tonight?"

He hesitated for a beat. "I don't know. What've you got?"

"I think I've got the rogue who's behind the maulings."

"You call Hardin with this?"

"No. This guy—he called into the show. He's local. He was talking insane. Hardin wouldn't know what to do with him. She'd try
to arrest him, and he'd claw her to pieces."

"You don't mind if I get clawed to pieces, then?"

"I know you can handle it."

"Thanks, I think."

"I want to go with you."

"Are you sure?"

"I'll know his scent from the crime scenes. It's the only way I
can tell if this is the guy."

"Fine. You at work now?"

"Yeah."

"I'll pick you up there." The phone clicked off.

Matt was standing in the doorway between the booth and the
studio. "Kitty. Are you serious?"

"Yeah. You heard the guy. He wasn't talking like he was *going*
to do something. He's already done it. How much time do we have
left?"

"I don't know." He had to look back at his board. "Ten minutes?"

I took a couple more calls and spent all my effort trying to sound
normal. I couldn't remember what they were about, or what I said.
I hoped I sounded normal.

"This is Kitty Norville, Voice of the Night." I signed off with a
sigh and listened to my recorded howl.

"Be careful!" Matt called as I started out of the booth. I grimaced, the best kind of reassuring smile I could manage at the moment. He didn't look reassured. He gripped the doorway, white-
knuckled. Wasn't anything I could do about it.

Cormac pulled up to the curb as I left the front door of the station. He drove a Jeep. Not an SUV, but a real Jeep with mud cak-
ing the wheel wells. I got in the passenger side and told him the address. Thank God for the online reverse directory.

We'd driven for about five blocks when he said, "You understand that we have to kill this guy. By not calling the police, by going outside the law, that's the only thing we can do. Not arrest him, not talk reason into him, but kill him."

"You were listening to the show." I probably had double the number of listeners the ratings said I had, since no one seemed to want to admit they were listeners.

"You ever kill anyone?"

"No."

"Just stay out of the way so I can get a clean shot."

I leaned on the door, holding my forehead in my hand. Vigilantism, that was the word for what we were doing. But the niceties of legal technicalities were slipping away. Four women had been murdered. A werewolf had done it. Someone had to stop him.

Cormac's cell phone beeped. It was jammed into the ashtray, near the stick shift. He grabbed the hands-free wire dangling from it and stuck the earpiece into his ear. It took about six rings. So *that* was why he always took so long to answer.

"Yeah." He waited a minute, then said, "Just a minute." He covered the mouthpiece part of the wire with his hand. "It's Hardin. She wants to know if I know how to get hold of you. She wants to talk to you about tonight's show. I guess she was listening."

"Should I tell her?"

"What's the saying? It's easier to ask for forgiveness than permission."

He was right. She'd just get in the way. "I'll call her back when it's all over."

Cormac uncovered the wire. "Detective? I'll have to get back to you on that . . . What am I doing? Driving . . . Yeah, I'll keep in touch." He pulled the wire out of his ear, smirking. "She's an optimist," he said. "That's her problem."

The address was northeast, in a neighborhood of dilapidated houses on the edge of a region of industrial warehouses, oil refineries, and train tracks. It might have been a nice place once, maybe fifty years ago. A few big, old trees lurked in many of the yards. But they were dead, their branches broken, and the yards themselves were overgrown with weeds. The streetlights were all out, but the wash of the sodium floodlights from the warehouses reached here, sickly and orange.

As we pulled onto the street, Cormac turned off the Jeep's headlights and crawled ahead.

"There it is," he said, pointing to a bungalow set back from the road. A fifty-year-old house, maybe three or four rooms. It used to be white, but the paint was peeling, chipping, streaking; the wood of the siding was split and falling apart. Half the shingles were gone.

I rolled down the window. The air smelled of tar, gasoline, concrete. There was some wildness, even here: rats, raccoons, feral cats. This was a dried-up, unpleasant place. The pack never came here. Why would we, when we had hills and forest, true wilderness, so close by? That was one of the things I liked about Denver: It had all the benefits of a city, but forest and mountains were a short drive away. Why would any wolf—were- or otherwise—want to stay in this desolation? If he didn't have any place else to go, I supposed.

Then how had he gotten here in the first place? Werewolves weren't born, they were made. Someone had made him, then left him to fend for himself, and he came here.

Or someone put him here to keep him out of the way, where he wouldn't be found, because the pack never came here. That meant . . . *did* Carl know about this guy? If not Carl, then who?

"You okay?" Cormac said. "You look like you just ate a lemon."

"I don't like the way this place smells."

He smiled, but the expression was wry, unfriendly. "Neither do I."

We stepped out of the Jeep. Cormac reached into the back and pulled out a belt holster with his handgun. He strapped it on, then retrieved a rifle. He slung another belt, this one with a heavy pouch attached to it, over his shoulder. I didn't want to know what was in there. We closed the doors quietly and approached the house.

I whispered, "Let me go first. Get the scent, make sure he's the same guy. He might freak out if he sees you first."

"All right," he said, but sounded skeptical. "Just give the word, and I'll come in shooting."

Why didn't that make me feel better?

I walked a little faster, moving ahead. A light shone in horizontal lines through the blinds over the front window of the house. I tilted my head, listening. A voice sounded inside, low and scratchy—a radio, tuned to KNOB. The show had been over only a half an hour or so. I reached the walkway and followed it to the front door. Cormac was a couple of steps behind me. I tried to look through the front window, but the slatted blinds were mostly closed.

I put my hand on the knob, turned it. It was unlocked. I took my hand away. I didn't want to surprise anyone inside. So I knocked. Cormac stepped off the walkway and stood against the wall of the house, out of sight of the door. And, by chance, downwind of the door. Or maybe not by chance.

I waited forever. Well, for a long time. I didn't want to go into that house. But no one answered. Maybe he'd left. Maybe he was out killing someone. If I went in, at least I would get a scent. I'd know if it was the same guy I'd smelled at the murder sites.

I opened the door and went inside.

The hardwood floor of the front room was scarred and pitted, like a dozen generations of furniture had been moved back and forth across it, and several swarms of children had been raised on it. But that was long ago, in someone else's life. An old TV sat on the floor in one corner. The radio was on top of it. It might have been Rodney, the night DJ, calling the last set. A sofa that would have looked at home on the porch of a frat house sat in the middle of the floor. Wasn't much else there. A box overflowing with trash occupied another corner. The walls were bare of decoration, stained splotchy brown and yellow. I wondered what this guy did for a living. If anything. There was no evidence of a life here. Just a place, sad, decayed, and temporary.

I took a deep breath through my nose.

I didn't identify the smell so much as I flashed on the scene. The blood. The victim's body, splayed across the alley. People say scent is tied to memory. What does that mean for a werewolf, whose sense of smell is so acute? The memory sparked vividly, all the sights and sounds and other smells that I'd imprinted along with the scent of the werewolf, the murderer. My stomach turned with the same nausea.

Straight ahead, a hall led to the rest of the house, probably kitchen, bedroom, bathroom. A sudden gush of water ran through the house's pipes. A toilet flushing. A door opened and closed. A man emerged into the hallway and walked toward me.

He wore a plain white T-shirt and faded jeans. He was tall, built like a construction worker, thick arms, broad chest. He had a crew cut that was growing out, a beard that was a couple of days unshaven. He was barefoot. He smelled the same as the room, close and ripe.

He stopped when he saw me. His nostrils flared, taking in scent like a werewolf would. His hands clenched. Glaring, he moved toward me, stalking like a predator.

I stood straight, careful not to flinch, not to show any weakness that his wolf would take as an invitation to attack.

I said, "Are you James?"

Again he stopped, as if he'd hit a wall. His brow furrowed, his face showing confusion. "What did you say?"

It was him. That voice, low and strained, close to breaking. "James. Are you James?"

He squinted harder, like he was trying to bring me into focus. Then his eyes grew wide.

"You're *her*. Kitty." He closed the distance between us, and I thought he was going to pounce on me with a bear hug, but he halted a step away—I didn't quite flinch. He was gesturing with his hands like he was pleading. "I'm such a big fan!"

"Thanks," I said weakly. I should have yelled. Just yelled and ducked as Cormac came storming through the door, guns blazing. But James had stunned me.

James didn't ask the questions I would have asked a celebrity who happened to show up at my house, like how did you find me, why are you here. He acted like he didn't find this strange at all, like this sort of occurrence was a natural part of the life he'd made for himself. The kind of life where he constantly made calls to late-night talk radio shows.

He slouched, ducking in front of me like he was bowing. He had to stoop to make himself shorter than I. That was what he was doing, showing submission, one wolf to another. He kept turning his gaze away. His instincts were taking over.

I stared. Not a dominant, I'm-a-bigger-wolf-than-you stare. More like a bewildered, disturbed stare. What was I supposed to do with him? I didn't want him touching me, but he was inching closer, like he was going to start pawing me, rubbing me, the way a subordinate wolf would to the one he'd identified as the alpha. I stepped back.

He cringed, pulling his arms close to his body, his eyes sad and hurt. "You don't understand," he said. "This . . . this is great. It's what I've always wanted. You can help me. You're the only other one—one of us, one like us, I mean—I've ever met besides—" He stopped, swallowing. His breathing came fast.

"Besides who, James?" My voice caught.

"Besides the one who made me. She's been helping me. She said I could have a pack, if I killed this other werewolf and took his. She said she would show me. I—I can do that. I know I can do that. I've been practicing. But she won't tell me where to go. She—she hasn't been to see me in a while. But you'll help me, won't you? You help so many people."

I felt sick. James needed help, but I couldn't give it to him. Who could? What hospital could hold him? What could anyone do? That was the human talking, of course. I remembered Cormac's words: *You understand that we have to kill this guy.* As a wolf, he'd overstepped his bounds. Like Zan. But what did that mean if there'd been no one to teach him the rules?

James looked up, over my shoulder. Cormac stood in the doorway.

"Norville, is he the one?"

All I could do was nod.

Cormac raised his arm, fired his handgun.

I ducked out of the way. James was already running. I thought he would turn around, try to make for the back of the house. That was what I would have done. But he dived forward, under the range of the gun, past Cormac, shouldering him aside, and out the door.

Cormac struck the door frame, but recovered in a heartbeat, turned outside, and fired twice more. His arm remained steady, his sight aimed at his target, tracking smoothly like he was mounted on a tripod.

"Shit!" He pointed the gun up when James disappeared around the corner of the house.

I ran after him, aware that he might have been waiting on the other side of the house to ambush whoever followed him. I didn't want to lose sight of him. Cormac was right behind me.

In the strip of yard between the two houses a trail of clothing led away: jeans, briefs, and a white T-shirt, torn to shreds. There was a dark, wild odor—the musk, fur, and sweat of a recently shifted lycanthrope.

I unzipped my jeans and shoved them to the ground.

"What are you doing?" said Cormac, stopping in his tracks.

I paused. I didn't know if I could do this. I didn't have a choice.

"I can move faster if I Change. It's the only way I'll keep up." It can be a strength, T.J. had said. We'd see.

He opened his mouth, starting to argue. But he didn't say anything. His shoulders slumped, and he looked away. I took off my shirt, my bra. The air was cold, sending pimples crawling across my shoulders. Inside, I felt warm. My muscles tensed, already preparing to run, because I knew what this meant; Wolf knew what this meant. I wanted to hunt, and I needed her. I was ready. She crouched inside, filling me with anticipation.

Cormac started to walk away.

"Wait," I said. "I want you to watch."

"Why?" he said, his voice rough.

"I want you to see what I look like, so you don't shoot me by accident."

"If I ever shoot you, it won't be by accident."

I walked up to him, naked, unself-conscious. I was on the edge of my other world, human mores falling away. I didn't know how else to be, like this, with Wolf looking out of my eyes.

I stood a step away, holding his gaze.

"Here's your chance. If that's what you're planning, get it over with now so I don't have to keep looking over my shoulder."

I didn't know how long I planned on waiting for him to raise that gun and shoot me in the head. I stood, arms spread, offering myself to him. My glare didn't match my vulnerability. But once and for all, I had to know what he wanted to do.

Finally he said, "Be careful."

"Yeah. You, too." I turned away, walking to the back of the alley.

"Don't try to fight him, Kitty. He's bigger than you. Just find him, and I'll take care of it."

I nodded.

Holding her back felt a little like holding my breath. As soon as I thought of shifting to Wolf, the Change started, sensations coursing with my blood, waking those nerves and instincts that lay buried most of the time. Any time except full moon nights, I could hold it back. But if I wanted to shift, I just had to let that breath out, think of exhaling, and the next breath would belong to her.

My back bent, the first convulsion racking me. Think of water, let it slide, and fur sprouted in waves down my back and arms, needles piercing skin. I grunted, blocking the pain. Then claws, then teeth and bones and muscle—

She shakes, ruffling her fur and slipping into her muscles.

Her ears prick, and she raises her head to see the figure nearby. He stands on two legs and smells of danger, of mechanical pain. Her other self recognizes the weapons that can kill her.

Her other self also recognizes him, and keeps her hackles flat and buries the growls.

"Norville?"

Tension, anxiety, fear. She can take him, kill him if she has to. He's weak. But those weapons are stronger. They smell of fire.

"You in there? You know who I am?"

The tone is questioning, seeking reassurance. His anxiety isn't because of her, because there's another danger. The other one, the rogue, the outcast. She remembers.

Identifying him as friend, she wags her tail.

"Christ, I can't believe I'm doing this."

He says this to her back, because she's already running.

She seeks the one who has invaded her territory, caused havoc, broken the code. He's run far ahead, but the night is still, the ground is clear, and she can smell him, chase him, like she would a rabbit. With her nose close to the ground, her legs racing, her muscles flowing, close to flying, she will find him. Her mouth hangs open a little; her tongue tastes the air.

Closer, she gets closer. He's turned up ahead. She feels a thrill because he's trying to confuse her, to make her lose him, but she isn't fooled. Stretching full-out, running hard, she turns the corner.

He is waiting for her.

He strikes, tumbling into her from the side. She doesn't have time to stop or swerve. He lays his paws on her, clamps his teeth around her throat, and they roll in a tangle of legs. Snarls, driven from the belly and guttural, echo.

Her speed carries her away from him, sends her rolling out of his grasp and away from his teeth, but she is dazed. She shakes her head. He doesn't hesitate, springing to his feet and leaping at her again. She braces, her lips pulled tight from bared teeth. When he is about to reach her, she rears to meet him, their front legs locking around each other's shoulders, teeth snapping at whatever purchase they can find.

He is so much larger than she, though. He pushes her over without effort; she falls on her back, with him on top of her, her throat and belly exposed. She writhes, kicking, desperate to protect herself. He bites hard, catching her upper foreleg, and she yelps. The noise of pain spurs her to frenzy.

She arches forward, closes her teeth under his jaw, bites hard. Taste of blood. He cringes back, and she twists to her feet, is up and running.

Instinct, fear drive her away. She runs, wanting to escape, but he is faster. He jumps, catches her hind end, sends her sprawling. His claws dig into her fur, searching for flesh, scrabbling over her, pinning her to the ground. A memory of hate and wrongness surfaces.

He has no right to do this. He is outcast. But he is stronger. If she showed submission, if she whined and turned her belly to him, would he listen? Would he stop?

She doesn't think so. He would kill her.

She can't let him. She also thinks, He may be stronger. But I am better.

That other voice, the day self, the human, says: his eyes. Tear his face.

He climbs her, gnawing her fur and the tough skin of her shoulder, looking for the soft parts, for the chance to rip into her. His weight presses down on her, pinning her no matter how she struggles. She waits until he comes close, until his face is at her neck. Then she attacks.

Jaws open, she lunges. His muzzle is turned down, buried in her hackles. She slams into the top of his face, as hard as she can. Surprised, he pulls back. Released from his weight, her sinewy body twists back on itself. She smashes her mouth into him, searching for purchase, chewing, doubling her effort when her teeth find soft targets, when she can feel his flesh popping, shredding.

He squeals, scrambling backward. She will not let go; he's dragging her with him by the grip she has on his face, her canines hooked into his eye sockets. Her snarls sound like a roar.

He bows, head low to the ground, and swats at her with his forelegs, like he is trying to scrape mud off his face. His claws slash her face; the pain barely registers. He has made himself lower than she, has exposed himself. Has shown fear.

Opening her mouth, she dives at his throat so fast he doesn't even flinch.

She gnaws, breaking skin. Blood erupts into her mouth, washes warm over her muzzle. When she finds a firm grasp, she shakes, worries, mauls, back and forth as much as she can. He's too large for her to toss around properly. But she has this piece of him, and it is hers, and the blood flows hot and fast. The thick taste of it makes her dizzy, ecstatic.

His struggles fade to a reflexive kicking, then nothing.

Blood covers his neck and chest, and her own face, neck, and chest. She licks her muzzle, then she licks him, burying her nose in the wound she made. She keeps growling as she digs into him. Bites, rips, gnaws, swallows.

The body under her is shifting as she feeds. The fur shrinks to naked skin, the muscles melt, the bones reform, until she is digging into the neck of a human body.

"Norville!"

Crack, a sound like thunder bursts, with a smell like fire. She recoils, springing to stand a foot away from where she was, to assess the danger. Her nostrils quiver.

The man, the dangerous one, the friend, stands there, arm pointing up, hand holding the source of the burning smell. The weapon.

"Kitty!" he shouts and stomps toward her, radiating a fierce challenge. She trots a couple of steps away and circles back, staring. Does he mean it?

Pounding human footsteps travel toward them. More of them arrive, smelling of weapons, anxiety, danger. They are pointing at her.

The man yells, "Hardin, hold your fire! It's Kitty!"

There are too many of them.

She runs.

She runs for a long distance, until the world is quiet and the smells are peaceful. She searches for trees, shelter, comfortable scents, finds none of these. She's far from home, doesn't know this place.

A patch of dry ground in the corner between two walls makes an uncomfortable but acceptable den. She is hurt—aches in her face, leg, and shoulders, a sharp pain in her back. She needs rest. She misses the others. There should be others. There should be pack, for her to feel safe.

All she can do is curl tight around herself, snugged in the corner of the den.

chapter **11**

Sirens woke me.

I tried to stretch and moved about an inch before pain froze me. I groaned. I felt totally hung over. It was still pitch dark out, middle of the night, which meant I hadn't slept very long. I needed more time to sleep and recover from shifting back from the Wolf before I'd feel decent.

I bent my elbow enough to pillow my head. I was curled up in the corner formed by a brick wall and a wooden fence. I had no idea where I was. But I heard sirens. Police, ambulance.

I remembered enough of the last hour or so to not be entirely confused. I licked my teeth and tasted the blood. Blood still coated my mouth. I curled up tighter, squeezing shut my eyes.

Footsteps crunched up the gravel alleyway.

"Norville. You awake?"

For all my earlier lack of modesty, I now felt thoroughly naked. I pulled my knees up to my chest and hugged myself, covering myself as much as I could.

The footsteps stopped. I looked. A few steps away, Cormac knelt. He offered a blanket. When I tried to reach for it, I felt a cut open across my back. Wincing, I hissed.

He put the blanket over my shoulders, and with his hands under my arms, helped me sit up. I wrapped the blanket tight around me.

"You found me," I said.

"You were trailing blood."

I nodded. I could feel it caked on my face and neck. I hadn't even looked at my injuries yet. The wounds I got as a wolf transferred. They hadn't had enough time to heal. They itched.

I tasted blood. Blood in my mouth, in the back of my throat. I could taste it on my breath, all the way down to my stomach.

I choked, unable to hold back a sob, and my stomach quailed. I pulled away from Cormac and vomited. It was purplish. It had chunks. After a couple of waves, and a couple more dry heaves, I could take a breath and start to think of what had happened. I rested my head against the brick, which was cool and rough.

"Heap big werewolf, eh?" Cormac said with a half-grin.

"That's me," I said weakly.

"I told you not to fight him."

"It was self-defense, Officer."

"Can you stand?"

I thought about it, taking a couple more deep breaths while I assessed myself. I thought I could stand. I tried. I got my legs under me, but when I put weight on them, they shook. When I tipped, starting to fall, Cormac caught me.

I cried. I pulled close into myself and cried, gritting my teeth to stop the sound, embarrassed that I couldn't stop the sobs shuddering through me. I hugged my arms around my head, all the hiding I was able to do.

Cormac held me. He didn't pet me or make silly comforting noises. He just held me, halfway on his lap, bracing me.

Eventually, the crying stopped. The trembling stilled. My eyes squinted, swollen. I hiccuped, trying to fill my exhausted lungs. I didn't feel any better after crying my heart out. But I did feel ready to fall asleep without having nightmares.

Sometimes I had dreams where I was covered with blood, running through the forest, killing things, happy to be doing it. Sometimes I couldn't remember if they were dreams or not.

"You okay?"

"I don't know," I said, my voice small. I rubbed my face, which was gritty with dirt and grime.

"Come on. I'll drive you home." He started to stand, and this time when I put weight on my legs, they held me. Cormac kept his hand under my arm, just in case.

The blanket went down to my knees. I walked gingerly; my feet were bare and the alley was covered with broken glass and metal bits. I watched my feet and wasn't paying attention to much else. When Cormac stopped, I looked up.

Detective Hardin stood there. She turned and said something to the half-dozen uniformed cops trailing behind her. Reluctantly, they backed away. All of them had their guns out.

Hardin tucked her gun into a belt holster. She crossed her arms, regarding us like she was a high school teacher who'd caught a couple of kids necking behind the bleachers. Or maybe it was just that I felt like one of the kids.

She said, "I've got a body back there with its face ripped off. Why do I get the feeling if I check the guy's DNA, I'll get a match with the suspect's evidence from my mauling victims?"

I swallowed. My throat was still raw from trying not to cry. "You will."

"What about the guy from outside your apartment?"

"No. But, I'm ready to talk about him. I think."

Her face took on a pained, annoyed expression. "Does this happen often? Werewolves slaughtering each other for no apparent reason?"

"Oh, there's always a reason," I said. Realizing how bad that sounded, I looked away. "No, it doesn't happen often." Only when the power struggles happened. When a junior wolf like me got too big for her britches.

"Huh. And I thought police internal affairs was tough."

I glanced at Cormac. His expression was a mask, inscrutable. I was sure he hadn't called the cops. I said, "How did you know where to go?"

"Your sound guy called me."

"Matt. Bastard," I muttered. I thought he knew better than to get mixed up in supernatural rumbles.

"Why didn't you call me?"

"I didn't want you to get hurt."

"I'm touched. Really, I am. Do you have any idea how I'm supposed to write this up? What am I supposed to do with *you*?"

I shrugged, wincing when the cut on my back split again. I was going to have to lie still for a good couple of hours if I wanted it to heal. "Should I call my lawyer?"

She stared hard at me, like she was trying to peel back my skin. My shoulders bunched. If she'd been a wolf, I'd have taken her stare as a challenge. I looked at my feet and tried to seem harmless, small, and inconsequential, metaphorical tail between my legs.

She tipped her chin up, a sort of decisive half-nod.

"I saw dogs fighting. That's all I saw. But for God's sake, *call* me next time."

She walked away.

Cormac had my clothes in the passenger seat of his Jeep. I put them on, but still kept the blanket around me. I was cold.

He stopped the Jeep in front of my apartment building and shut off the engine. I had to work up to moving, taking a deep breath because I knew how much it was going to hurt.

When I gripped the handle of the door, Cormac said, "You need me to come in with you?"

The question was laden with meaning and unspoken assumptions. We weren't exactly a couple on a first date, testing the waters to see if the evening was going to go on a little longer, him wondering if I would invite him, me wondering if I should. But there was a little of that. Maybe he wanted a second chance. Maybe I wanted him to have a second chance. I had to decide how hurt I was—but if I was hurt enough to need help, I was probably too hurt to give him that second chance. Maybe he was just trying to be nice. But why would he be trying to be nice if he didn't want a second chance?

Or most likely I was reading too much into it. My head hurt, and I needed a shower. And sleep. Which meant no second chance.

But he had stopped the engine, like he really wanted to come inside.

"I'll be okay." I opened the door and eased myself to the sidewalk. I left the blanket on the seat. "Thanks. Thanks for everything. I think I probably owe you a couple now."

He shrugged. "You saved me a bullet."

I looked down, hiding a smirk. "You're not angry at me for stealing your kill?"

"Just like a wolf to think that way when there's plenty to go around." He started the Jeep. The engine roared, then settled into its rhythm. "Watch your back."

"Yeah. You, too." I shut the door.

He drove away.

I spent the walk to the building still wondering if I should have asked Cormac to come with me. He had guns and wasn't injured. There was the spot where T.J. killed Zan. What else was waiting in the shadows to attack me? Not the rogue wolf. Not anymore.

I'd killed the rogue. All by myself, I'd killed him. That should have made me feel strong, like I could walk down any dark street without fear, like I'd never have to be afraid again. Wolf could stand tall, her tail straight, unafraid.

But all I felt was tired. Tired, sad, sick. Even the Wolf was quiet. Even she'd had enough.

Behind every shrub and corner was a monster waiting to challenge me. The hair on my arms and neck tingled. I kept looking over my shoulder.

James had said *she* could give him a pack. *She* had made him, and she wanted him to kill the alpha.

Meg. Had to be. I didn't know what to think. What had she been thinking, taking this guy under her wing? Had she really wanted him as head of the pack? He must have looked tough, tough enough to take on Carl. But James wouldn't have lasted. He didn't have the mind to lead—he'd groveled to *me*, after all. The pack would have torn him to shreds. Meg must have realized this, changed her mind, and left him hanging.

It was too much. I should have expected it. It still hurt. At the same time, the path before me seemed clearer.

She was still out there. Who would she send after me next? Or would she come herself? I might have killed James, but I wasn't in any condition to fight like that again tonight.

Maybe she was waiting in my apartment. I crept up the stairs, slinking close to the wall. My head throbbed, I was concentrating so hard on listening. The building was quiet. I took quick breaths, testing the air, hunting for a scent of danger. If a werewolf had been through here recently, I should have been able to smell it. If someone had carried a gun by here, I might have caught a trace of oil and steel.

Nothing but the old apartment smells of sweat and aged drywall.

I got to my apartment door. Still locked. By some miracle, the key was still in my jeans pocket. I tried to slide it in the lock and turn it without making a sound. No luck. The scrape of metal rattled my brain. I listened for noises within the apartment, wondering if someone had gotten inside somehow and was waiting for me. Still nothing.

My heart was pounding in my throat when I opened the door. The place was empty.

I searched everywhere, even in cupboards too small for a rat to hide in. But I looked anyway. I locked the door behind me and pulled the shade over the window. Then I sat on the floor and covered my face, holding back hysterical laughter on the one hand and helpless tears on the other. Caution had degenerated into paranoia, and I was exhausted.

Huddled on the floor, I spent ten minutes debating whether to take a nap or a shower. Nap, shower, nap, shower. The skin over my entire body itched, so I decided I needed a shower more than anything. I smelled like the bad part of town.

By the time I got to the bathroom, I'd changed my mind and decided what I really needed to do first was brush my teeth. I brushed my teeth five times. Flossed twice. Didn't look too closely at the bits I spat out.

I woke up. The sun glared around the edges of my window shade with late-afternoon light. I stretched, arching my back, reaching with my arms and legs, and smiled because while I was stiff, nothing hurt. No injuries cracked along my back.

For the moment, I didn't want to move any more than that, because then I'd have to figure out what to do next.

Meg had overstepped her bounds.

T.J. didn't answer his phone. He hadn't for the last few days. He was far away, running from the cops, and I couldn't call him for help.

Taking the bus to Meg's place was much less cool than riding T.J.'s bike.

It also took longer, which meant I had a lot of time to reconsider.

I didn't have any proof. I could tell Carl about what had happened last night, but I couldn't trust him to do anything about it. After all, he hadn't done anything about Meg's conspiring with Arturo to kill me, when he had concrete evidence. Then again, he had essentially asked me to fight her. To kill her, really. Take her place. But I didn't want to be Carl's alpha female.

Pack dynamics were predicated on a two-way relationship. I owed the alphas, Carl and Meg, total loyalty and devotion, and they owed me protection. I hadn't felt protected in a long time. Carl seemed to value supporting Meg more than protecting me. All that trust was gone. The center did not hold.

While I'd felt pretty cocky about facing Meg, I didn't think I could face both of them. Not by myself.

I had to tell them what had happened last night. Doing so would probably start a fight. Their patience with me had probably worn thin enough that it wouldn't be just a dominance, slap-her-around-a-little fight. Maybe Meg would be by herself.

I really, really missed T.J.

I got to the house. The front door was locked. Nobody home. Meg had a real job. She kept up a pretty good semblance of a normal life, working as a stock clerk in a warehouse. It paid for the house, the car, the extras. Carl didn't work. It looked like she wasn't home yet and Carl was away.

The back door was locked, too. I sat against the wall on the patio and looked out to the hills, to the scattered trees that grew more frequent until they became the woods of the national forest property. The sun was shining straight at me. A warm, lazy afternoon, a scent of pines on a faint breeze. I closed my eyes, wanting to nap. If I didn't think too hard, I could enjoy the moment.

I caught a scent, a trace on the breeze, a familiar taste of wolf, of pack. Shading my eyes, I looked. Someone was out there. Not close. I scanned the hills, but couldn't see anything, not a flicker of movement. Then the scent was gone. Probably an echo, a shadow. This place was covered with the smell of pack.

Carl came around the side of the house. He stopped when he saw me, closing his fists and hunching his shoulders, posturing. I glanced at him, then turned my face back to the sun, basking.

"Hi, Carl."

"What were you looking at?" He said this suspiciously, like he thought I was hiding something.

"I don't know. I thought I saw something. T.J., maybe."

Carl relaxed a little and continued toward me. He leaned against the wall, towering over me. "I haven't seen him in days. I know he likes to go roaming. I thought you might know where he went this time."

"He's hiding. The police are looking for him, for killing Zan."

After a pause he said, "Zan is dead?"

I looked at him. I assumed T.J. told him everything. "You didn't know?"

"Meg told me he left. Ran off. I thought maybe he and T.J. ran off together." He made a suggestive humph, adding meaning to 'together.' Geez, even if Zan had swung that way, T.J. had better taste.

"Meg's a liar."

"Why would T.J. kill him?"

"Zan attacked me. T.J. was protecting me."

"Why would Zan attack you?" he said.

"Are you serious? Are you really so clueless about what's happening in your own pack?"

His shoulders tightened, hackles rising. Then he blew out a breath in a sigh and let himself slouch. "What am I going to do with you?"

I hugged my knees and glared out at the hills, painted gold by the sun. Shadows of the trees lengthened, crawling toward me. "I'm going to have a talk with Meg. I don't know what you're going to do. You'll either stay out of the way, or you'll back Meg. I don't know which."

"Can you take down Meg?"

"I can try."

"Then you'll take her place."

"No. I don't want her place." I wanted my own place; how could I make him see that?

"I can't be head of this pack by myself." He sounded almost panicked.

"Maybe you could learn."

He said, his voice tight, "Why won't you even consider it?"

"Because I don't need the pack. I have my own life." Rogue wolf. I could do it. "So, are you going to back her up or stay out of my way?"

He hooked his hands in the pockets of his jeans and looked away. It occurred to me that Carl wasn't that old. Maybe thirty-four, thirty-five. I didn't know how much of that time he'd spent as a werewolf. He lacked the confidence of maturity. How much effort did it take him to put on the tough act, to maintain that dominant stance he needed to stay in control? I'd never noticed before, but the confidence didn't come naturally to him. Not like it did to, say, Cormac.

"You want to come inside to wait for her?"

"I think I'll stay here."

He went back around the corner of the house.

Not too much longer after that, he came out the back door. Meg was with him. They stood side by side, looking down at me. I should have been butt-sore from sitting on the concrete that long. But it really was a nice afternoon. The air was starting to get a hint of twilight chill. I was comfortable.

"Hey, Meg. Tell me about James," I said without turning.

The pause before she answered went on a little too long. "Who?"

"James. Rogue werewolf."

Carl said, "Kitty, what are you talking about?"

"I think Meg's been holding out on you. I think she found somebody who looked big and tough, made him one of us, and started grooming him to be your replacement. She didn't want to fight you herself. He would be an alpha male who owed everything to her. But the guy was nuts. Unstable. She couldn't control him. She abandoned him, and he started killing. She didn't like me talking to the cops about it; maybe she was afraid I'd figure it out, catch her scent and trace the rogue back to her. So she sent Zan to get rid of me. Too bad the whole teaming-up with Arturo to hire Cormac to kill me didn't work earlier. Would have made everyone's lives easier. I think she's had it in for me for a while, ever since she thought I might threaten her place."

"Where is this James now?" Carl looked at me, not Meg.

But I looked straight at Meg. "I killed him."

Meg said, "I don't believe you."

Bingo. I got her. "Which part? That this guy exists, or that I—little old me—was able to kill him?" I stood without using my hands. "I ripped his fucking throat out, Meg. You want me to tell you what it tasted like? Should I demonstrate?"

That was way too cocky. I was starting to sound like Carl. Too late to back down now.

Meg moved a step behind Carl.

A thrill warmed me, a static shock up my spine. I hadn't even touched her yet, but she was scared. *Of me.* I could breathe on her right now and she might scream. I narrowed my gaze and smiled.

This was why Carl got off on being a bully. This was how it felt to be strong.

"If you want me dead, Meg, why don't you just challenge me face-to-face? Don't you have the guts?" I circled Carl, moving toward her. She moved as well, keeping him between us.

"Kitty, that's enough," Carl said.

"No, it isn't. I'm calling her out. I want to challenge her. What do you say, Meg?"

She stared at me, her body still. "I think you're crazy."

"I'm pissed off is what I am! I mean, what the hell were you *thinking*, dealing with that guy?"

Still, she didn't deny it, didn't confirm it. Didn't say anything.

It was going to happen. I could feel it, a charge in the air, our glares colliding. My blood rushed; I could feel my pulse pounding in my brain. My throat was tight, holding back a growl. She closed her hands, preparing.

Then Carl stepped between us. "I won't let you do this. Stand down, Kitty. Now."

"And why should I listen to you? Where were you all those times people tried to kill me? You're useless, Carl! I don't owe you anything!"

Carl took a couple of steps toward me. His posture was stiff, arms slightly bent, ready to swing fists.

However much I wanted to back away, I held my ground. Even my Wolf didn't cringe at his approach. Even she was too angry.

"I don't want to fight you," I said, my voice tight. "Let me challenge her, Carl. I thought you wanted me to challenge her."

He paused, glancing over his shoulder.

With a calculating look and a thin smile, Meg turned her gaze away from me. She stepped toward Carl, touched his back, and put her face against his shoulder. She glanced at me from the shelter of his body, then closed her eyes and rubbed her cheek down his shoulder, holding his arm, clinging to him.

She showed herself submissive to him. She put herself in his power; then, it followed, he would protect her. She was asking him to fight her fight.

My jaw opened, disbelieving. "Were you always this much of a bitch?"

That was a stupid question.

"I know my place," she said. Slowly, she crouched, until she was kneeling at Carl's feet. She gripped his leg, pressing her face to his thigh.

And Carl, insecure dominant that he was, fell for it. He swelled, appearing to grow a few inches in all directions as he puffed out his chest and cocked his arms, preparing to fight.

Oh, please.

"Come on, Carl," I said. "She's putting on an act. She's scared that I might actually have a chance against her."

"You challenge my mate, you fight me."

"And what about everything she's done? Giving the photos to Arturo, sending Zan after me—and that doesn't even touch on what she did to James. She wanted to kill you! Why protect her after all that?"

"She hasn't said she was behind James."

"She hasn't denied it."

We both looked at her. I might get out of this yet.

Meg, contrite as a Catholic schoolgirl, bowing her head so her hair fell across her face, said, "James was a mistake. It'll never happen again. I'm sorry."

That was ultimately why I could never take Meg's place at Carl's side. I couldn't grovel like that. At least, not anymore. Carl needed someone who would grovel at his feet.

The sun finally dipped behind the hills. Everything turned to shadow. The sky was darkening to that rich, twilight blue of velvet, of dreams. This was the Elfland blue that Dunsany described. It made me feel like I could take a step and be in another world, a magic place where nothing hurt. Where no one hurt another. Or where the adventures someone had were symbolic and meaningful, leading to enlightenment, adulthood, or at the very least a nice treasure. Maybe a talking goose.

I'd seen plenty of magic in my world. None of it impressed me a whole lot.

I shrugged. "Well, Carl. You're free to stand by her. Just as long as you know what she really is."

I was ready for him when he sprang at me.

Carl jumped at me, hands out, fingers spread, ready to grab me around the neck. I ducked and rolled. Technically, I'd learned all these fancy moves that would topple a charging opponent, use the momentum of a larger assailant against him, allow me to swing him headfirst into the ground at my feet. Those moves worked a lot better in the gymnasium with floor mats and time to practice.

As it was, I only managed to roll out of the reach of his arms. I grabbed for him, snagging the cuffs of his jeans. He stumbled, but didn't fall. Scrambling on all fours, I put distance between us, turned and faced him, crouching, waiting.

Carl didn't seem to be in a hurry. Pulling his shirt off, baring his sculpted, powerful chest, he circled me, making a rumbling noise in his throat.

I would do a lot better as a wolf, with claws and teeth and fewer inhibitions. But if I took the time to shape-shift, he'd attack.

Maybe I didn't have to shift all the way. I could let a little bit of Wolf bleed over, gain enough advantage to hold my own. My growl started. I'd attack Carl first, then Meg.

Tensing, I acted like I was going to leap. I jerked forward and got a reaction from him. He rushed me like he thought we were going to crash together. He'd have won a head-on collision between us. But I ducked, again avoiding the force of his attack. He passed close by. I felt the heat of his blood, smelled the sweat beading on his body.

When I reached out to touch him, my claws were sprouting. I arched my fingers and brought my arm down hard, slashing him. I caught flesh and saw a splash of red.

He snarled, a sound like wood ripping, and writhed away from sudden pain. He wheeled, gained some distance, and clutched his side. I'd slashed the skin on his left side, under his rib cage. No telling how deep I'd cut. He looked more angry than hurt, his face grimacing in a snarl, his eyes blazing.

Then something grabbed my neck and hauled backward. Meg. She held me in a headlock, her left arm pulling back on her right arm, which was braced across my neck. I gagged, choking while she crushed my throat. She dragged me until I was flat on my back, lying almost on top of her. She used all her strength to strangle me.

I slashed at her arms, reached back and tried to cut her face. In a panic now, I was having trouble keeping my shape. Fear made me want to melt, because Wolf could run away faster than I could. I struggled, both against her and myself, to break free of her, and to keep anchored to my body.

Her sugarcoated voice spoke by my ear. "I think we're done now. Would you like to finish her off, or should I?" She looked up at Carl.

Carl's arms thickened, his claws growing. He came toward me. I had time to think about how stupid I'd been to not watch my back. To think I could face them both. That was what I got for winning a fight. Made me think I was some kind of fucking Caesar.

I kept clawing Meg's arms. Blood covered my hands; I was ripping her to shreds. But she didn't let go. She was going to hold me for as long as it took Carl to finish me off. I whined, however much I wanted not to.

My legs were still free. I'd kick him. I'd fight for as long as I could.

Then Carl froze, his head tipped back. A shadow had appeared, broken away from the growing darkness to stand at his side.

T.J. held Carl's neck. His nails—too thick to be nails, they were almost claws—dug into the larger man's neck. All T.J. had to do was squeeze, pull, and he'd rip out Carl's throat. He was naked, like he'd shifted back from wolf recently. He said he was going to the hills. He must not have gotten too far. He'd come back.

He said, "Let her go, Meg. Or we both lose."

She let up some of the pressure on my neck. Not enough for me to escape. But I could breathe a little easier.

"On the other hand," she said. "This could be an opportunity for both of us. We both finish our rivals here, and the pack is ours."

Did she really hate Carl so much? What did he see in her, that would make him defend her? I knew the answer to that. I remembered: The first time I saw her, she was this wild goddess whose presence flared around her in an aura of strength. She was beautiful.

T.J. chuckled, lips turning in a half-grin. "You're not my type."
Then he looked at Carl, and the smile disappeared. "You're not a
very good pack alpha, Carl. Bullying only gets you so far. Maybe
I can do something about that."

"This isn't a fair fight," Carl said, his voice stifled.

"Neither is that." T.J. nodded at me and Meg.

"If you really wanted to kill me, you'd have done it already."
For a minute, I thought T.J. was going to tear his neck out right
there. He waited for several agonizing heartbeats before he said,
"You're right. I want a deal. Let Kitty and me go. We'll get out.
We'll leave this territory for good and you'll never have to worry
about us again. You can have your little show here and run it however you want."

On one hand, that sounded like a great plan. Save my skin, not
have to fight anymore. Didn't want to think beyond getting to
safety. But I still had issues with Meg's being a traitorous bitch.
And I had a life here. KNOB, the show, friends even. The pack.
The pack that had gone to hell somewhere along the line. But I
didn't want to leave. I shouldn't have had to.

I deferred to T.J. He'd earned alpha status. Above everyone else
I knew in the world, I trusted him to protect me.

Carl was breathing heavily, but T.J.'s hand never let up its grip.
Finally, he said, "All right. Let her go, Meg."

Glaring at T.J., she did. As soon as the pressure left my neck, I
squirmed out of her grip and scrambled away. I stood and backed
up, getting ready to run. My arms and claws shifted back to human,
the Wolf fading. As soon as T.J. was with me, we'd run and never
look back.

T.J. let go of Carl. They each took a step back, putting space between them.

Then Carl attacked him. He was, in the end, cut from the same
cloth as Meg. They were made for each other.

Carl pivoted on one foot and drove up with his hand, a massive
undercutting punch, claws outstretched. T.J. backed away, but not
quickly enough. Carl didn't gut him as the move had intended, but
he caught T.J.'s chin, whipping his head back, throwing him backward. Blood sprayed from rows of cuts on his face.

I screamed, which came out almost like a howl.

When I started for T.J., to help him against Carl, Meg ran toward
me. Looked like I was going to get my catfight after all. In a manner of speaking.

I bent and charged, tackling her in the middle, catching her before she had anticipated reaching me. I drove with brute strength I didn't know I had, lifting her off her feet for a split second, long enough to knock her off balance and slam her to the ground. I got on top of her, pinning her.

No teasing, no playing, no mercy. I laid my forearm across her neck and leaned with all my weight. She choked, her breath wheezing, whining. I brought my face to within a couple of inches of hers. She snapped, snarling, a wolf's actions showing through her human body.

I slapped her. Claws raked her face, ripping open her cheek. My claws had come back; I hadn't even felt them. A noise, not quite a growl, of pain, anger, hopelessness welled up in my chest. I hated her. I hated this.

A keening squeal, part human cry, part wolf in pain, distracted me. I looked to the scrub-filled yard beyond the patio. Shadows, I saw only black shapes against the darkening sky. I lifted my nose to a breeze that had started licking through the trees. I smelled trees, rain, pack, territory, wolves, and blood. The tang of blood crawled down my throat. A lot of blood, and the stench of waste along with it.

Two figures huddled on the ground. One of them stood, rolled back his broad shoulders, turned his bearded face toward us. Carl. The other figure lay facedown, unmoving. I bit my lip and whined.

I'd never moved so fast. I forgot Meg and ran to T.J. Carl, his right arm bloody to the elbow, reached for me but I dodged, skirting around him and sliding to the ground near T.J.'s prone form. He lay half-curled, one arm crooked under him as if he'd tried to get back up, the other arm cradling his gut, which had been ripped open. He was holding in glistening mounds, strange lumps of tissue—organs—which were straining through the gashes cutting upward through his abdomen, to his rib cage, under his rib cage. His heart's blood poured out of the wound.

We healed quickly only if we survived the wounds in the first place.

Crying, gritting my teeth to keep from making noise, I lay on the ground beside him. I touched his face. "T.J., T.J.," I kept saying. I brought my face close to his, our foreheads touching. I wanted him to know I was here. "T.J."

He made a sound, a grunt ending in a sigh. His eyes were closed. His lips moved, and I leaned in close. If he tried to speak, I never heard what he wanted to say. I kept listening for the next sigh, the next breath, and it never came. I said his name, hoping he heard me. Hoping it gave him a little comfort. I tangled my fingers in his hair, holding him.

I kept . . . hoping.

Then Carl was there, looming over us. I wasn't scared; I wasn't even angry. I was hopeless. Despair had made my face flush with tears.

I looked up at him, and my voice ripped out of me. "He was your friend!"

Carl was shaking; it showed as a trembling in his arms. "He shouldn't have challenged me."

"He didn't challenge you! He was going to walk away!" I bared my teeth, a grimace of contempt. "He's worth a hundred of you. Killing him doesn't change that."

Glaring down at us, Meg joined Carl. She was a mess, her face and arms dripping blood. She wouldn't last in a fight. But standing behind Carl, she acted like it.

Almost spitting the words, she said, "Finish her. Leave her with him."

I met Carl's gaze. Held it for a long time. He looked hopeless as well. It was like we both wondered how it could have been different. That all of this should have been different. Starting with the night that I never should have been made one of them.

He shook his head slowly. "No. She won't fight now." When Meg looked like she was going to argue, hc took hold of the back of her neck, and she stilled. To me he said, "You have a day to leave town. I want you out of my territory."

He could have his territory.

Before standing, I buried my nose in T.J.'s hair and took a deep breath, to remember the smell of him. The oil and grease of his bike, the heat of his kitchen. His soap, his jacket, a faint touch of cigarette, a stronger scent of pine. His wolf, sweaty and wild. He smelled like wind at the edge of the city.

I straightened, looking away. Never look back.

His tone hateful and biting, Carl said, "T.J. paid for your life. Remember that."

I swallowed a sob and ran.

Epilogue

Okay, we're back with *The Midnight Hour.* We have time to take a couple more calls for my guest this evening, Senator Joseph Duke, Republican from Missouri. Evan from San Diego, you're on the air."

"Yeah, hi," Evan said. "Senator Duke, first off I want to thank you for being one of the few members of our government willing to stand up for his beliefs—"

Inwardly, I groaned. Calls that started this way always ended with Bible thumping.

Duke said, "Why, thank you, Evan. Of course it's my God-given duty to stand for the place of moral rectitude in the United States Congress."

"Uh, yeah. And for my question, what I really want to know: In your knowledgeable opinion, what is the best method for punishing the minions of Satan—burning at the stake or drowning in holy water? If the federal government were to institute a code of mandatory punishment, which would you advocate?"

Why did people like this even listen to my show? Probably to collect quotes they could take out of context. The answers I gave to vampire orgy questions always came back to haunt me later.

The senator had the good grace to look discomfited. He shifted in his seat and pursed his lips. "Well, Evan, I'm afraid I'm not the expert on punishing the unrighteous you think I am. In this day and age, I believe the current penal system addresses any crimes for which the minions of Satan might be convicted, and the just punishments for those crimes. And if they come up with new crimes, well, we'll cross that bridge when we get to it, won't we?"

That was what made guys like Duke so scary. They were so articulate in making the weirdest statements.

Senator Joseph Duke, a fifty-something nondescript picture of

Middle America, like the guy in the *American Gothic* painting but twenty pounds heavier, sat at the other end of the table, as far away from me as he possibly could and still reach the microphone. He had two suited bodyguards with him. One of them had his gun drawn, propped in the crook of his crossed arms. The senator refused to be in the same room with me without the bodyguards. I asked about the gun—silver bullets? Of course.

After all the people declaring that the show and my identity had to be hoaxes, part of some elaborate ratings scheme, or a sick joke played on my gullible fans, Duke's unquestioning belief in my nature was almost refreshing. He almost refused to come on the show at all—originally he'd been scheduled to appear the week after Cormac invaded. We'd had to postpone. I'd had to agree to the bodyguards.

"Next caller, please. Lucy, hello."

"Hello, Kitty. Senator, I want to know how after all your talk about smiting heathens and ridding the country of the nefarious influences of the unrighteous, which you have openly stated include werewolves, can you sit there in the same room with Kitty like nothing's wrong?" I couldn't judge Lucy's tone. It might have been the height of sarcasm, her trying to get a rise out of him; or she might have been in earnest.

"Lucy, the Lord Jesus taught us not to abandon the unrighteous. That even the gravest sinner might be saved if they only let the light of Christ into their hearts. I see my time on this show as the ultimate chance to reach out to the unrighteous."

In my experience, becoming a werewolf had more to do with bad luck than with being a sinner. I couldn't mock his belief, or his sentiment, though. He wasn't advocating mass werewolf slayings, which made him better than some people. My folder of death threats had gotten thick over the months.

Lucy said, "So, Kitty, has he reached out to you?"

A couple of impolite responses occurred to me, and for once I kept them on the inside. "Well, as I've said before, while I may not be the most righteous bitch on the airwaves, I certainly don't feel particularly unrighteous. But I'm probably using the word differently than the senator. Let's just say I'm listening attentively, as usual."

The sound engineer gestured through the window to the booth, giving me a count of time left. Not Matt. I was in Albuquerque this week, at a public radio station that carried the show. It wasn't my booth, or my microphone, and the chair was too new, not as squishy as my chair back at KNOB. I missed that chair. I missed Matt.

"All right, faithful listeners—and mind you, I'm probably using the word 'faithful' differently than Senator Duke would use it. We've got just a couple of minutes left for closing words. Senator, I have one more question for you, if you don't mind."

"Go right ahead."

"Earlier in the show we discussed the little-publicized report released by a branch of the NIH, a government-sponsored study that made an empirical examination of supernatural beings such as werewolves and vampires. I'd like to ask you, if I may: If the U.S. government is on the verge of labeling lycanthropy and vampirism as diseases—by that I mean identifiable physiological conditions— how does that reconcile with the stance taken by many religious doctrines that these conditions are marks of sin?"

"Well, Ms. Norville, like you, I've read that report. And rather than contradicting my stance on these *conditions* as you call them, I believe it supports me."

"How?"

"I said before that I want to reach out to people suffering from these terrible afflictions—just as we as a society must reach out to anyone suffering from illness. We must help them find their way to the righteous path of light."

And what did the vampires think of being led to the path of light?

"How would you do this, Senator?" I said, a tad more diplomatically.

He straightened, launching on a speech like he'd been waiting for this moment, for this exact question. "Many diseases, such as lycanthropy and vampirism in particular, are highly contagious. Folklore has taught us this for centuries, and now modern science confirms it."

"I'd argue with the *highly*, but go on."

"As with any contagious disease, the first step should be to isolate the victims. Prevent the spread of the disease. By taking firm steps, I believe we could wipe out these conditions forever, in just a few years."

A vague, squishy feeling settled on my stomach. "So you would . . . and please, correct me if I've misinterpreted . . . you would round up all the werewolves you could and force them into, what? Hospitals, housing projects—" Dare I say it? Oh, sure. "—ghettos?"

Duke missed the jab entirely. "I think hospitals in this case would be most appropriate. I'm confident that given the time and resources, science will find a way to eradicate the mark of the beast that has settled on these blighted souls."

If it wasn't so sad, I'd laugh. Trouble was, I'd talked to people like this enough to know I'd never argue them out of their beliefs. "Right. I think I and my blighted soul need a drink. That must mean we're near the end of our time. Once again, Senator Duke, thank you so much for being on the show."

"Thank you for having me. And I want you to know that I am praying for you. You can be saved."

"Thanks. I appreciate it." The other thing about people like this was how they completely lacked the ability to identify sarcasm.

"Right, I think we have a whole lot of food for thought after that. And just so everyone out there is clear about how I stand on the issue, and because I've never been shy about expressing my opinion: I think we need to look to the lessons of history when we discuss how the government should handle these issues. I for one don't want people with black armbands coming for me in the middle of the night." This was my show. I always got the last word.

"Thank you for listening. This is Kitty Norville, Voice of the Night." Cue the wolf howl. Another one in the can.

I sat back and sighed.

Senator Duke was staring at me. "It won't come to that."

I shrugged. "That's what they said in Berlin in the thirties."

"I would think people like you would *want* to be helped."

"The trouble is in how many definitions of 'help' there are. Everyone thinks they have the right answer. I did mean it, though—I appreciate your being on the show, Senator." I stood and offered my hand to shake. Frowning, he looked at it. "I can't hurt you with just a handshake. Honest."

Nodding crisply at his bodyguards, he turned his shoulder to me and left.

I blew out the breath I'd been holding. That was rough. But never let it be said my show was one-sided.

I went to the control booth, where the engineer handed me the phone. "Hey, Matt."

"Hey, Kitty. Sounded good." Matt still worked on the show remotely, coaching the local guys on how to run things, making sure the phone number got transferred, stuff like that.

"Cool. Thanks. It only sounds good 'cause you're the best."

"Yeah, I'll believe it when Ozzie gives me a raise. Hey, speak of the devil. Talk to you later, Kitty." There was a rustling as he handed the phone over.

Ozzie came on the line. "Great show, Kitty. Just great. You had that bozo sweating, I could tell."

"You think they're all great, Ozzie."

"That's 'cause they are. I'm your biggest fan. Are you going to be in Albuquerque next week, or someplace else?"

"Someplace else, I think. I haven't decided. I'll let you know."

"I wish you could tell me why you're doing the fugitive bit."

"You don't really want to know. Trust me."

"Just remember, if you need anything, anything at all, you call me."

"Thanks, Ozzie. Give Matt a raise."

He grumbled, and I laughed.

Who said a pack had to be all werewolves?

I bought a car, a little hatchback with enormous gas mileage. I doubled my salary when I stopped paying off Carl. Maybe I'd even buy myself some new clothes. With a car I could go anywhere. I'd be traveling at my own speed from now on. And traveling, and traveling.

I checked in with my parents before I left Albuquerque; I checked in with them every week. They bought me a cell phone so I could be sure to call, no matter where I was—and so they could always find me. They weren't happy about my situation. They kept inviting me to stay with them however long I needed to. I appreciated the thought. But I couldn't do that to them.

I kept a lookout for Elijah Smith and the Church of the Pure Faith. There was still a story there. My ultimate goal was to get Smith himself as a guest on the show. Not likely, but a girl could dream. Every now and then I found a flyer, or someone sent one to me, advertising his caravan. I always seemed to be a week behind him.

Detective Hardin got hold of me through Ben O'Farrell. God help me, I hired the lawyer on retainer. I had my mail forwarded to him, and he had my contact information. He'd been calm and straightforward the night Zan died. In daylight hours, outside the stress of the police station, he proved just as straightforward. He was never above giving advice on something as mundane as car insurance.

Best of all, Hardin had to talk to him before she could get to me. But even O'Farrell couldn't put her off forever. We talked on the phone the week I stayed in Albuquerque.

"We found your DNA on the first werewolf's body, in his mouth and under his fingernails. That makes you an assault victim. Then we found your DNA in the saliva on the wounds of the second body, which could get you in trouble. But we're willing to make a case for self-defense since he also had your blood under his fingernails." She made it sound so technical. This was my *blood* we were talking about.

If it hadn't been *my* blood involved, I would have laughed at how the whole thing sounded like some werewolf version of a Mexican standoff. I admired Hardin for trying to sort out who had attacked whom first.

"We found a fourth set of werewolf DNA in the saliva on the wounds of the body outside your apartment. It's the only link unaccounted for. All I need is a name."

The implication was that I could be charged with a crime in the middle of this mess. O'Farrell wanted me to fess up.

I didn't have anyone to protect anymore.

"T.J. Theodore Joseph Gurney. He lives in the cabin behind the garage at Ninety-fifth and South. I don't think he's there anymore." Present tense. If I told Hardin he was dead, she would just open another murder investigation. I could have pointed her to Carl in that case. But I didn't. This had to end somewhere.

"Then where did he go?"

"I don't know." That at least was true. I didn't know where he was now. "He didn't tell me."

"Can I believe you?"

"Yes."

"Why did you leave town?"

"I had to. It wasn't safe for me to stay, after what I did."

"You were afraid of ending up like that body outside your apartment."

"Yes."

She sighed. "You might be interested to know, the powers that be are actually listening to me."

"You mean you say 'werewolf' and they believe you?"

"Yeah. The alternative is the theory that some ritual slaying specialist came up with about a cult of cannibals to explain why they found shredded bodies with pieces missing. The idea is the cult im-

ploded when it turned on itself and the members started eating each
other. Werewolves sound downright rational compared to that."

Except there was a hint of truth to the cannibal theory as well.

She said, "If I think of anything else, I'll call you."

"Yeah. Sure."

We parted civilly.

Hardin was a good person. I felt grateful for her open-mindedness and her professionalism through all this. I just wished I hadn't
been the focus of her efforts.

I didn't even have a picture of T.J.

I was closing in on Austin when NPR aired a report. I cranked
up the volume when I heard a key phrase.

The reporter said, ". . . Paranatural Biology, releasing findings to
Congress in response to questions that have been raised regarding
unusual appropriation requests. Doctor Paul Flemming, an assistant director of the National Institutes of Health overseeing the
Center for the Study of Paranatural Biology, offered this statement
at a press conference held earlier today."

Then Doctor Flemming spoke:

"I am authorized at this time to announce the formation of the
Center for the Study of Paranatural Biology within the National Institutes of Health. In conjunction with the British Alternative Bi-
ologies Laboratory, we are prepared to release findings recognizing
the existence of alternate races of *Homo sapiens*, races that were
once considered only legend . . ." Blood rushed in my ears. This
was the government, a spokesperson for the government. They
were blowing my world wide open.

More than that, I recognized the voice. Deep Throat. My secret
government spook. I stifled a laugh as he went on to explain the report in terms of taxonomy and science.

"These conditions are mutations brought on by as yet unidenti-
fied infectious agents. The following conditions have been identified . . . *Homo sapiens sanguinis* . . . commonly known as vampire.
Homo sapiens lupus . . . commonly known as werewolf. *Homo sapiens pinnipedia* . . ."

I had his name. As soon as I stopped for the afternoon, I was going to find his phone number and give *him* a call.

At a gas station somewhere in West Texas, I went into the store to
stock up on road trip munchies. On my way to the cash register, I

passed a rack of newspapers and stopped cold. I stared. I smiled. I bought a paper, the latest issue of *Wide World of News*.

I would frame it, and as soon as I had a wall, it would go up. The headline read:

"Bat Boy to Appear as Guest on *The Midnight Hour.*"

Kitty
Goes to
Washington

To Robbie
The Force will be with us, always.

Acknowledgments

I'd like to thank my beta testers: Daniel Abraham, Brian Hiebert, and Jo Anne Vaughn (a.k.a. Mom). Thanks to Sandy Karpuk for an awesome day job and for letting me use the printer; to Professor Kelly Hurley for the fascinating and useful *Dracula* discussions; to Ian Hudek for coming up with V.L.A.D.; to Jaime Levine for helping make this a much better book; to Chris Dao and the crew at Warner who've made the whole process easier; and also to my family, Max, and all the usual suspects. And of course, thank you to everyone who was so darned excited about *Kitty and The Midnight Hour*. The confidence boost really helped.

My agent, Dan Hooker, sold this book for me but passed away before he could see the finished product. My gratitude for his work on my behalf, and sadness at his loss are immense.

The Playlist

The Watchmen, "Together"
Peter Gabriel, "Games Without Frontiers"
Oingo Boingo, "No Spill Blood"
The Clash, "Know Your Rights"
Suzanne Vega, "Tombstone"
Shriekback, "Nemesis"
Pet Shop Boys, "DJ Culture"
Pink Floyd, "Us and Them"
Aqua, "Doctor Jones"
Prince, "Kiss"
Too Much Joy, "You Will"
The Clash, "(White Man) In Hammersmith Palais"
The Beatles, "Across the Universe"
 (*Let It Be . . . Naked* version)
New Order, "True Faith-94"

chapter 1

We have Beth from Tampa on the line. Hello."

"Hi, Kitty, thanks for taking my call."

"You're welcome."

"I have a question I've been wanting to ask for a long time. Do you think Dracula is still out there?"

I leaned on the arm of my chair and stared at the microphone. "Dracula. As in, the book? The character?"

Beth from Tampa sounded cheerful and earnest. "Yeah. I mean, he's got to be the best-known vampire there is. He was so powerful, I can't really believe that Van Helsing and the rest of them just finished him off."

I tried to be polite. "Actually, they did. It's just a book, Beth. Fiction. They're characters."

"But you sit there week after week telling everyone that vampires and werewolves are real. Surely a book like this must have been based on something that really happened. Maybe his name wasn't actually Dracula, but Bram Stoker must have based him on a real vampire, don't you think? Don't you wonder who that vampire was?"

Stoker may have met a real vampire, may even have based Dracula on that vampire. But if that vampire was still around, I suspected he was in deep hiding out of embarrassment.

"Even if there is a real vampire who was Stoker's inspiration, the events of the book are sheer fabrication. I say this because *Dracula* isn't really about vampires, or vampire hunting, or the undead, or any of that. It's about a lot of *other* things: sexuality, religion, reverse imperialism, and xenophobia. But what it's *really* about is saving the world through superior office technology." I waited half a beat for that to sink in. I loved this stuff. "Think about it. They make such a big deal about their typewriters, phonographs, stenography—this was like the techno-thriller of its day. They end up solving everything because Mina is really great at data entry and collating. What do you think?"

"Um . . . I think that may be a stretch."

"Have you even read the book?"

"Um, no. But I've seen every movie version of it!" she ended brightly, as if that would save her.

I suppressed a growl. "All right. Which is your favorite?"

"The one with Keanu Reeves!"

"Why am I not surprised?" I clicked her off. "Moving on. Next caller, you're on the air."

"Kitty, hey! Longtime listener, first-time caller. I'm so glad you put me on."

"No problem. What's your story?"

"Well, I have sort of a question. Do you have any idea what kind of overlap there is between lycanthropes and the furry community?"

The monitor said this guy had a question about lycanthropes and alternative lifestyles. The producer screening calls was doing a good job of being vague.

I knew this topic would come up eventually. It seemed I'd avoided it for as long as I possibly could. Oh well. The folks in radioland expected honesty.

"You know, I've hosted this show for almost a year without anyone bringing up furries. Thank you for destroying that last little shred of dignity I possessed."

"You don't have to be so—"

"Look, seriously. I have absolutely no idea. They're two different things—lycanthropy is a disease. Furry-ness is a . . . a predilection. Which I suppose means it's possible to be both. And when you say furry, are you talking about the people who like cartoons with bipedal foxes, or are you talking about the people who dress up in animal suits to get it on? Maybe some of the people who call in wanting to know how to become werewolves happen to be furries and think that's the next logical step. How many of the lycanthropes that I know are furries? That's not something I generally ask people. Do you see how complicated this is?"

"Well, yeah. But I have to wonder, if someone *really* believes that they were meant to be, you know, a different species entirely—like the way some men really believe they were meant to be women and then go through a sex change operation—don't you think it's reasonable that—"

"No. No it isn't reasonable. Tell me, do *you* think that you were meant to be a different species entirely?"

He gave a deep sigh, the kind that usually preceded a dark confession, the kind of thing that was a big draw for most of my audience.

"I have this recurring dream where I'm an alpaca."

I did a little flinch, convinced I hadn't heard him correctly. "Excuse me?"

"An alpaca. I keep having these dreams where I'm an alpaca. I'm in the Andes, high in the mountains. In the next valley over are the ruins of a great Incan city. Everything is so green." He might have been describing the photos in an issue of *National Geographic*. "And the grass tastes so lovely."

Okay, that probably wasn't in *National Geographic*.

"Um . . . that's interesting."

"I'd love to travel there someday. To see the Andes for myself. Have—have you by any chance ever met any were-alpacas?"

If it weren't so sad I'd have to laugh. "No, I haven't. All the were-animals I've ever heard of are predators, so I really don't think you're likely to meet a were-alpaca."

"Oh," he said with a sigh. "Do you think maybe I was an alpaca in a past life?"

"Honestly, I don't know. I'm sorry I can't be more help. I genuinely hope you find some answers to your questions someday. I think traveling there is a great idea." Seeing the world never hurt, in my opinion. "Thanks for calling."

I had no idea where the show could possibly go after that. I hit a line at random. "Next caller, what do you want to talk about?"

"Hi, Kitty, yeah. Um, thanks. I—I think I have a problem." He was male, with a tired-sounding tenor voice. I always listened closely to the ones who seemed tired; their problems were usually doozies.

"Then let's see what we can do with it. What's wrong?"

"It all started when these two guys moved to town, a werewolf and a vampire. They're a couple, you know?"

"These are two guys. Men, right?"

"Right."

"And the problem is . . ."

"Well, nothing at this point. But then this vampire hunter started going after the vampire, I guess he'd been hired by the vampire's former human servant."

"The vampire's human servant didn't travel with him?"

"No, he dumped her to run off with the werewolf."

There couldn't possibly be more. Bracing, I said, "Then what?"

"*Another* werewolf, who used to be the alpha female mate of the werewolf before he hooked up with the vampire, showed up. She wanted to get back together with him, saying this stuff about wolves mating for life and all, but he didn't want anything to do with her, so he hired the same hunter to go after *her*—"

"This hunter, his name wasn't Cormac by any chance, was it?" I knew a vampire and werewolf hunting Cormac, and this sounded like something he might do.

"No."

Phew. "Just checking."

The story only went downhill from there. Just when I thought the last knot had been tied in the tangled web of this town's supernatural soap opera, the caller added a new one.

Finally, I was able to ask, "And what's your place in all this?"

He gave a massive sigh. "I'm the human servant of the local vampire Master. They make me deliver messages. 'Tell them they have to leave town.' 'Tell your Master we don't want to leave town!' 'Tell the hunter we'll pay him to call off the contract!' 'Tell him if he doesn't come back to me I'll kill myself!' It never ends! And all I want to know is—"

Maybe he just wanted to vent. That was what I was here for. Maybe he wouldn't ask me to sort out his drama for him. Fingers crossed. "Yes?"

"Why can't we all just get along?"

Oy. It was one of those nights. "That, my friend, is the million-dollar question. You know what? Screw 'em. They're all being self-ish and putting you in the middle. Make them deliver their own messages."

"I—I can't do *that.*"

"Yes you can. They've got to realize how ridiculous this all looks."

"Well, I mean, *yeah*, I've *told* them, but—"

"But what?"

"I guess I'm used to doing what I'm told."

"Then maybe you should learn to say no. When they act surprised that you've said no, tell them it's for their own good. You've basically been enabling all their snotty behavior, right?"

"Maybe . . ."

"Because if they had to start talking to each other they might actually solve some of their problems, right?"

"Or rip each other's throats out. They're not exactly human, re-member."

Taking a deep breath and trying not to sound chronically frus-trated, I said, "I may very well be the only person in the supernat-ural underworld who feels this way, but I don't think that should make a difference. Crappy behavior is still crappy behavior, and letting yourself succumb to unsavory monstrous instincts isn't a good excuse. So, stand up for yourself, okay?"

"O-okay," he said, not sounding convinced.

"Call me back and let me know how it goes."

"Thanks, Kitty."

The producer gave me a warning signal, waving from the other side of the booth window, pointing at his watch, and making a slic-ing motion across his throat. Um, maybe he was trying to tell me something.

I sighed, then leaned up to the mike. "I'm sorry, folks, but that looks like all the time we have this week. I want to thank you for spending the last couple of hours with me and invite you to come back next week, when I talk with the lead singer of the punk metal band Plague of Locusts, who says their bass player is possessed by a demon, and that's the secret of their success. This is *The Midnight Hour*, and I'm Kitty Norville, voice of the night."

The ON AIR sign dimmed, and the show's closing credits, which included a recording of a wolf howl—my wolf howl—as a back-drop, played. I pulled the headset off and ran my fingers through my blond hair, hoping it didn't look too squished.

The producer's name was Jim something. I forgot his last name. Rather, I didn't bother remembering. I'd be at a different radio sta-tion next week, working with a different set of people. For the bet-ter part of a year, most of the show's run, I'd broadcast out of Den-ver. But a month ago, I left town. Or was chased out. It depended on who you talked to.

Rather than find a new base of operations, I decided to travel. It kept me from getting into trouble with the locals, and it made me harder to find. The radio audience wouldn't know the difference. I was in Flagstaff this week.

I leaned on the doorway leading to the control booth and smiled a thanks to Jim. Like a lot of guys stuck manning the control board over the graveyard shift, he was impossibly young, college age, maybe even an intern, or at most a junior associate producer of some kind. He was sweating. He probably hadn't expected to han-dle this many calls on a talk show that ran at midnight.

Most of my audience stayed up late.

He handed me a phone handset. I said into it, "Hi, Matt."

Matt had worked the board for the show when I was in Denver. These days, he coached the local crew. I couldn't do this without him.

"Hey, Kitty. It's a wrap, looks like."

"Was it okay?"

"Sounded great."

"You always say that," I said with a little bit of a whine.

"What can I say? You're consistent."

"Thanks. I think."

"Tomorrow's full moon, right? You going to be okay?"

It was nice that he remembered, even nicer that he was worried about me, but I didn't like to talk about it. He was an outsider. "Yeah, I have a good place all checked out."

"Take care of yourself, Kitty."

"Thanks."

I wrapped things up at the station and went to my hotel to sleep off the rest of the night. Locked the door, hung out the DO NOT DIS-TURB sign. Couldn't sleep, of course. I'd become nocturnal, doing the show. I'd gotten used to not sleeping until dawn, then waking at noon. It was even easier now that I was on my own. No one checked up on me, no one was meeting me for lunch. It was just me, the road, the show once a week. An isolated forest somewhere once a month. A lonely life.

My next evening was spoken for. Full moon nights were always spoken for.

I found the place a couple of days ago: a remote trailhead at the end of a dirt road in the interior of a state park. I could leave the car parked in a secluded turn-out behind a tree. Real wolves didn't get this far south, so I only had to worry about intruding on any local werewolves who might have marked out this territory. I spent an afternoon walking around, watching, smelling. Giving the locals a chance to see me, let them know I was here. I didn't smell anything unexpected, just the usual forest scents of deer, fox, rabbits. Good hunting here. It looked like I'd have it all to myself.

A couple of hours from midnight, I parked the car at the far end of the trailhead, where it couldn't be seen from the road. I didn't want to give any hint that I was out here. I didn't want anyone, es-pecially not the police, to come snooping. I didn't want anyone I might hurt to come within miles of me.

I'd done this before. This was my second full moon night alone, as a rogue. The first time had been uneventful, except that I woke up hours before dawn, hours before I was ready, shivering in the cold and crying because I couldn't remember how I'd gotten to be naked in the middle of the woods. That never happened when I had other werewolves there to remind me.

My stomach felt like ice. This was never going to get easier. I used to have a pack of my own. I'd been surrounded by friends, people I could trust to protect me. A wolf wasn't meant to run on her own.

You'll be okay. You can take care of yourself.

I sat in the car, gripping the steering wheel, and squeezed shut my eyes to keep from crying. I had acquired a voice. It was an inner monologue, like a part of my conscience. It reassured me, told me I wasn't crazy, admonished me when I was being silly, convinced me I was going to be okay when I started to doubt myself. The voice sounded like my best friend, T.J. He died protecting me, six weeks ago today. The alpha male of our pack killed him, and I had to leave Denver to keep from getting killed, too. Whenever I started to doubt, I heard T.J.'s voice telling me I was going to be okay.

His death sat strangely with me. For the first week or two, I thought I was handling it pretty well. I was thinking straight and moving on. People call that stage denial. Then on the highway, I saw a couple on a motorcycle: neither of them wore helmets, her blond hair tangled in the wind, and she clung to his leather jacket. Just like I used to ride with T.J. The hole that he'd left behind gaped open, and I had to pull off at the next exit because I was crying so hard. After that, I felt like a zombie. I went through the motions of a life that wasn't mine. This new life I had acquired felt like it had been this way forever, and like it or not, I had to adapt. I used to have an apartment, a wolf pack, and a best friend. But that life had vanished.

I locked the car, put the keys in my jeans pocket, and walked away from the parking lot, away from the trail, and into the wild. The night was clear and sharp. Every touch of air, every scent, blazed clear. The moon, swollen, bursting with light, edged above the trees on the horizon. It touched me, I could feel the light brushing my skin. Gooseflesh rose on my arms. Inside, the creature thrashed. It made me feel both drunk and nauseous. I'd think I was throwing up, but the Wolf would burst out of me instead.

I kept my breathing slow and regular. I'd let her out when I wanted her out, and not a second earlier.

The forest was silver, the trees shadows. Fallen leaves rustled as nighttime animals foraged. I ignored the noises, the awareness of the life surrounding me. I pulled off my T-shirt, felt the moonlight touch my skin.

I put my clothes in the hollow formed by a fallen tree and a boulder. The space was big enough to sleep in when I was finished. I backed away, naked, every pore tingling.

I could do this alone. I'd be safe.

I counted down from five—

One came out as a wolf's howl.

The animal, rabbit, squeals once, falls still. Blood fills mouth, burns like fire. This is life, joy, ecstasy, feeding by the silver light—

If turning Wolf felt like being drunk, the next day definitely felt like being hungover.

I lay in the dirt and decayed leaves, naked, missing the other wolves terribly. We always woke up together in a dog pile, so to speak. I'd always woken up with T.J. at my back. At least I remembered how I got here this time. I whined, groaned, stretched, found my clothes, brushed myself off, and got dressed. The sky was gray; the sun would rise soon. I wanted to be out of here by then.

I got to my car just as the first hikers of the morning pulled into the trailhead parking area. I must have looked a mess: hair tangled, shirt untucked, carrying sneakers in my hand. They stared. I glared at them as I climbed into my own car and drove back to the hotel for a shower.

At noon, I was driving on I-40 heading west. It seemed like a good place to be, for a while. I'd end up in Los Angeles, and that sounded like an adventure.

The middle of the desert between Flagstaff and L.A. certainly wasn't anything resembling an adventure. I played just about every CD I'd brought with me while I traveled through the land of no radio reception.

Which made it all the more surreal when my cell phone rang.

Phone reception? Out here?

I put the hands-free earpiece in and pushed the talk button.

"Hello?"

"Kitty. It's Ben."

I groaned. Ben O'Farrell was my lawyer. Sharp as a tack and vaguely disreputable. He'd agreed to represent *me*, after all.

"Happy to hear you, too."

"Ben, it's not that I don't like you, but every time you call it's bad news."

"You've been subpoenaed by the Senate."

Not one to mince words was Ben.

"Excuse me?"

"A special oversight committee of the United States Senate requests the honor of your presence at upcoming hearings regarding the Center for the Study of Paranatural Biology. I guess they think you're some kind of expert on the subject."

"What?"

"You heard me."

Yeah, I'd heard him, and as a result my brain froze. Senate? Subpoena? Hearings? As in Joe McCarthy and the Hollywood blacklist? As in Iran-Contra?

"Kitty?"

"Is this bad? I mean, how bad is it?"

"Calm down. It isn't bad. Senate committees have hearings all the time. It's how they get information. Since they don't know anything about paranatural biology, they've called hearings."

It made sense. He even made it sound routine. I still couldn't keep the panic out of my voice. "What am I going to do?"

"You're going to go to Washington, D.C., and answer the nice senators' questions."

That was on the other side of the country. How much time did I have? Could I drive it? Fly? Did I have anything I could wear to Congress? Would they tell me the questions they wanted to ask ahead of time, as if I could study for it like it was some kind of test?

They didn't expect me to do this by myself, did they?

"Ben? You have to come with me."

Now *he* sounded panicked. "Oh, no. They're just going to ask you questions. You don't need a lawyer there."

"Come on. Please? Think of it as a vacation. It'll all go on the expense account."

"I don't have time—"

"Honestly, what do you think the odds are that I can keep out of trouble once I open my mouth? Isn't there this whole 'contempt of Congress' thing that happens when I say something that pisses them off? Would you rather be there from the start or have to fly in in the middle of things to get me out of jail for mouthing off at somebody important?"

His sigh was that of a martyr. "When you're right, you're right."

Victory! "Thanks, Ben. I really appreciate it. When do we need to be there?"

"We've got a couple weeks yet."

And here I was, going the wrong way.

"So I can drive there from Barstow in time."

"What the hell are you doing in Barstow?"

"Driving?"

Ben made an annoyed huff and hung up on me.

So. I was going to Washington, D.C.

I seemed to be living my life on the phone lately. I could go for days without having a real face-to-face conversation with anyone beyond "No, I don't want fries with that." I was turning into one of those jokers who walks around with a hands-free earpiece permanently attached to one ear. Sometimes, I just forgot it was there.

I went to L.A., did two shows, interviewed the band—no demon possessions happened in my presence, but they played a screechy death metal-sounding thing that made me wish I'd been out of my body for it. That left me a week or so to drive to the East Coast.

I was on the road when I called Dr. Paul Flemming. Flemming headed up the Center for the Study of Paranatural Biology, the focus of the Senate hearing in question. Until a month ago it had been a confidential research organization, a secret laboratory investigating a field that no one who wasn't involved believed even existed. Then Flemming held a press conference and blew the doors wide open. He thought the time was right to make the Center's work public, to officially recognize the existence of vampires, werewolves, and a dozen other things that go bump in the night. I was sure that part of why he did it was my show. People had already started to believe, and accept.

I'd been trying to talk to him. I had his phone number, but I only ever got through to voice mail. As long as I kept trying, he'd get so sick of my messages that he'd call me back eventually.

Or get a restraining order.

The phone rang. And rang. I mentally prepared another version of my message—please call back, we have to talk, I promise not to bite.

Then someone answered. "Hello?"

The car swerved; I was so surprised I almost let go of the steering wheel. "Hello? Dr. Flemming?"

There was a pause before he answered, "Kitty Norville. How nice to hear from you."

He sounded polite, like this was a friendly little chat, as if there wasn't any history between us. He wasn't going to get away with that.

"I *really* need to talk to you. You spent six months calling me anonymously, dropping mysterious hints about your work and suggesting that you want me to help you without ever giving any details, then without any warning you go public, and I have to recognize your voice off a radio broadcast of a press conference. Then silence. You don't want to talk to me. And now I've been subpoenaed to testify before a Senate committee about this can of worms you've opened. Don't get me wrong, I think it's a great can of worms. But what exactly are you trying to accomplish?"

He said, "I want the Center to keep its funding."

At last, a straight answer. I could imagine what had happened: as a secret research organization, the Center's funding was off the books, or disguised under some other innocuous category. An enterprising young congressman must have seen that there was a stream of money heading into some nebulous and possibly useless avenue and started an investigation.

Or maybe Flemming had wanted the Center to be discovered in this manner all along. Now the Senate was holding official hearings, and he'd get to show his work to the world. I just wished he'd warned me.

"So all you have to do is make sure the Center comes off looking good."

"Useful," he said. "It has to look useful. Good and useful aren't always the same thing. I'd heard that you'd been called to testify. For what it's worth, I'm sorry."

"Oh, don't be," I said lightly. "It'll be fun. I'm looking forward to it. But I'd really like to meet you beforehand and get your side of the story."

"There's nothing much to tell."

"Then humor me. I'm insanely curious." Wait for it, wait for it— "How about I interview you on the show? You could get the public behind you."

"I'm not sure that's a good idea."

Good thing I was driving across Texas—no turns and nothing to run into. Flemming had all my attention.

"This may be your only chance to tell your side of the story, why you're doing this research and why you need funding, outside of the hearings. Never underestimate the power of public opinion."

"You're persuasive."

"I try." Carry them along with sheer enthusiasm. That was the trick. I felt like a commercial.

He hesitated; I let him think about it. Then he said, "Call me again when you get to D.C."

At this point, anything that wasn't "no" was a victory. "You promise you'll actually answer the phone and not screen me with voice mail?"

"I'll answer."

"Thank you."

Mental calculation—the next show was Friday, in four days. I could reach D.C. by then. I could get Flemming on the show before the hearings started.

Time for another call, to Matt this time. "Matt? Can you see about setting up this week's show in Washington, D.C.?"

For years I hadn't left the town I lived in, much less driven across country. I didn't want to leave the place where I was comfortable and safe. It was easy to stay in one place and let my packmates, my alpha, take care of me. Easy to stagnate. Then the show started, and the boundaries became too narrow. What was supposed to happen—what happened among wild wolves, behavior that carried over to the lycanthropic variety—was that a young wolf moved up through the pecking order, testing boundaries until she challenged the leaders themselves, and if she won, she became the alpha.

I couldn't do it. I challenged and couldn't lead. I left town. I'd been essentially homeless since then. Wandering, a rogue wolf.

It wasn't so bad.

I drank coffee, which put me on edge but kept me awake and driving. Before I left Denver I'd never done this, driven for hours by myself, until the asphalt on the highway buzzed and the land whipped by in a blur. It made me feel powerful, in a way. I didn't have to listen to anyone, I could stop when I wanted, eat where I wanted, and no one second-guessed my directions.

I took the time to play tourist on the way. I stopped at random bronze historical markers, followed brown landmark highway signs down obscure two-lane highways, saw Civil War battlefields and giant plaster chickens. Maybe after the hearings I could set some kind of crazy goal and make it a publicity stunt: do the show from every state capital, a different city each week for a year. I could get the producers to pay for a trip to Hawaii. Oh, yeah.

Matt set me up at an Arlington, Virginia, radio station. I got there Friday around noon. I was cutting it close; the show aired live Friday night.

Lucky for me, Flemming had agreed to be a guest on the show.

The station's offices and broadcast center, a low brick fifties-era building with the call letters hung outside in modernist steel, were in a suburban office park overgrown with thick, leafy trees. Inside the swinging glass doors, the place was like a dozen other public and talk radio stations I'd been to: cluttered but respectable, run by sincere people who couldn't seem to find time to water the yellowing ficus plant in the corner.

A receptionist sat at a desk crowded with unsorted mail. She was on the phone. I approached, smiling in what I hoped was a friendly and unthreatening manner—at least I hoped that the dazed, vacuous smile I felt would pass for friendly. I could still feel the roar of the car tires in my tendons. She held her hand out in a "wait a minute" gesture.

"—I don't care what he told you, Grace. He's cheating on you. Yes . . . yes. See, you already know it. Who works past eleven every night? Insurance salesmen don't *have* night shifts, Grace . . . Fine, don't listen to me, but when you find someone else's black lace panties in his glove box don't come cryin' to me."

My life could be worse. I could be hosting a talk show on *normal* relationship problems.

After hanging up the phone she turned a sugary smile on me as if nothing had happened. "What can I do for you?"

Wadded up in my hand I had a piece of paper with the name of the station manager. "I'm here to see Liz Morgan."

"I think she may be out to lunch, let me check a minute." She played tag with the intercom phone system, buzzing room after room with no luck. I was about to tell her not to worry about it, that I'd go take a nap in my car until she got back.

"I don't know. I'll ask." She looked up from a rather involved conversation on one of the lines. "Can I pass along your name?"

"Kitty Norville. I should be scheduled to do a show tonight."

Raised brows told me she'd heard the name before. She didn't take her gaze off me when she passed along the answer.

"Says she's Kitty Norville . . . that's right . . . I think so. All right, I'll send her back." She put away the handset. "Wes is the assistant manager. He said to go on back and he'll talk to you. Last door on the right." She gestured down a hallway.

I felt her watching me the whole way. Some time ago I'd stated on the air, on live national radio, that I was a werewolf. Listeners generally took that to mean a couple different things: that I was a werewolf, or that I was crazy. Or possibly that I was involved in an outrageous publicity stunt pandering to the gullible and superstitious.

Any one of them was stare-worthy.

I arrived at the last door, which stood open. Two desks and two different work spaces occupied the room, which was large enough to establish an uneasy truce between them. The man at the messier of the two stood as soon as I appeared and made his way around the furniture. He left a half-played game of solitaire on his computer.

He came at me so quickly with his hand outstretched, ready to shake, that I almost backed out of the way. He was in his twenties, with floppy hair and a grin that probably never went away. Former college cheerleader, I'd bet.

"Kitty Norville? You're Kitty Norville? I'm a big fan! Hi, I'm Wes Brady, it's great to have you here!"

"Hi," I said, letting him pump my hand. "So, um. Thanks for letting me set up shop here on such short notice."

"No problem. Looking forward to it. Come in, have a seat."

What I really wanted was to have a look at their studio, meet the engineer who'd be running the board for me, then find a hotel, shower, and supper. Wes wanted to chat. He pointed me to a chair in the corner and pulled the one from his desk over.

He said, "So. I've always wanted to ask, and now that you're here, well—"

I prepared for the interrogation.

"Where do you come up with this stuff?"

"Excuse me?"

"On your show. I mean, do you coach callers? Are they actors? Do you have plants? How scripted is it? How many writers do you have? At first I thought it was a gag, we all did. But you've kept it up for a year now, and it's great! I gotta know how you do it."

I might as well hit my head against a brick wall.

Conspiratorially, I leaned forward over the plastic arm of the retro office chair. He bent toward me, his eyes wide. Because of course I'd give away trade secrets to anyone who asked.

"Why don't you stick around tonight and find out?"

"Come on, not even a little hint?"

"Now where's the fun in that?" I stood. "Hey, it's been great meeting you, but I really should get going."

"Oh—but you just got here. I could show you around. I could—"

"Is he bothering you?"

A woman in a rumpled navy-blue suit a few years out-of-date, her black hair short and moussed, stood in the doorway, her arms crossed.

"You must be Liz Morgan," I said, hoping I sounded enthusiastic rather than relieved. "I'm Kitty Norville. My colleague should have been in touch with you."

"Yes. Nice to meet you." Thankfully, her handshake was perfectly sedate and functional. "Wes, you have that marketing report for me yet?"

"Um, no. Not yet. Just getting to it now. Be ready in an hour. Yes, ma'am." Wes bounded to his desk and closed the solitaire game.

Liz gave me exactly the tour I wanted and answered all my questions. Even, "That Wes is a bit excitable, isn't he?"

"You should see him without his medication."

She saw me to the door and recommended a good hotel nearby.

"Thanks again," I said. "It's always kind of a crap shoot finding a station that'll even touch my show."

She shook her head, and her smile seemed long-suffering. "Kitty, we're five miles from Washington, D.C. There's nothing you can throw at us that'll compare with what I've seen come out of there."

I couldn't say I believed her. Because if she was right, I was about to get into things way over my head.

I returned to the station a couple of hours early and waited to meet Dr. Paul Flemming. I fidgeted. Ivy, the receptionist, told me all kinds of horror stories about traffic in the D.C. area, the Beltway, the unreliability of the Metro, all of it giving me hundreds of reasons to think that Flemming couldn't possibly arrive in time for the show. It was okay, I tried to convince myself. This sort of thing had happened before. I'd had guests miss their slot entirely. It was one of the joys of live radio. I just had to ad-lib. That was why the phone lines were so great. Somebody was always willing to make an ass out of themselves on the air.

Ivy went home for the evening, so at least the horror stories stopped. Liz and Wes stuck around to watch the show. I paced in the lobby, back and forth. A bad habit. The Wolf's bad habit. I let her have it—it gave her something to do and kept her quiet. Anxiety tended to make her antsy.

Me. Made *me* antsy.

Fifteen minutes before start time, a man opened the glass door a foot and peered inside. I stopped. "Dr. Flemming?"

Straightening, he entered the lobby and nodded.

A weight lifted. "I'm Kitty, thanks for coming."

Flemming wasn't what I expected. From his voice and the way he carried on, I expected someone cool and polished, slickly governmental, with a respectable suit and regulation haircut. A player. Instead, he looked like a squirrelly academic. He wore a corduroy jacket, brown slacks, and his light brown hair looked about a month overdue for a cut. His long face was pale, except for the shadows under his eyes. He was probably in his mid-forties.

In the same calm voice I recognized from a half-dozen phone calls, he said, "You're not what I expected."

I was taken aback. "What did you expect?"

"Someone older, I think. More experienced." I wasn't sure if he intended that as a compliment or a mere statement of fact.

"You don't have to be old to have experience, Doctor." And what did he know about it? "Come on back and I'll show you the studio."

I made introductions all around. I tried to put Flemming at ease; he seemed nervous, glancing over his shoulder, studying the station staff as if filing them away in some mental classification system for later reference. I wasn't sure if that was his academic nature or his government background at work. He moved stiffly, taking the seat I offered him like he expected it to slide out from under him. The guy was probably nervous in his own living room. Maybe he *was* relaxed, and this was how he always acted.

I showed him the headphones and mike, found my own headset, and leaned back in my chair, finally in my element.

The sound guy counted down through the booth window, and the first guitar chords of the show's theme song—Creedence Clearwater Revival's "Bad Moon Rising"—cued up. It didn't matter how many different stations I did the show from, this moment always felt the same: it was mine. I had the mike, I was in control, and as long as that ON AIR sign stayed lit, I called the shots. Until something went horribly wrong, of course. I could usually get through the introduction without having a crisis.

"Good evening. This is *The Midnight Hour*, the show that isn't afraid of the dark or the creatures who live there. I'm Kitty Norville, your charming hostess.

"I have as my very special guest this evening Dr. Paul Flemming. As you may or may not know, a little over a month ago Dr. Flemming held a press conference that announced scientific recognition of what used to be considered mythical, supernatural forms of human beings. Vampires, werewolves—you know, people like me. He has an M.D. from Columbia University, a Ph.D. in epidemiology from Johns Hopkins, and for the last five years has headed up the Center for the Study of Paranatural Biology. Welcome, Dr. Flemming."

"Thank you," he said, managing to sound calm despite the anxious way he perched at the edge of his seat, like he was getting ready to run when the mortars started dropping.

"Dr. Flemming. The Center for the Study of Paranatural Biology. Am I correct in stating that this is a government-funded organization dedicated to the study of what I believe you've called alternate forms of human beings? Vampires, werewolves, et cetera?"

"Only in the simplest terms. The nature of the research was not always explicitly stated."

"You couldn't exactly put down 'Give me money for werewolves,' could you?"

"Ah, no," he said, giving me the tiniest smile.

"So this was a *secret* government research program."

"I don't know that I'd go that far. I don't want to enter the realm of conspiracy theory. The Center's findings were always available."

"But in the most obscure outlets. No attention was drawn to a potentially explosive area of research. I would have thought, as part of this research team, you'd have wanted to announce your findings a lot sooner."

"It's not so simple. You can appreciate that we risked a great amount of criticism if we drew too much attention before we were ready. We needed to have data in hand, and a good potential of public support. Otherwise we would have been relegated to the back pages of the annals of bad science."

"In your mind, this is clearly a scientific endeavor."

"Of course. The best way to approach any line of inquiry is through the scientific method."

I was quite fond of postmodern literary analysis myself, as a line of inquiry. "What drew you to the scientific study of a subject that most people are all too happy to dismiss as folklore?"

"So many legends have a seed of truth. In many cases, that seed of truth persists, even in the face of great skepticism. The existence of a real-life King Arthur for example. How many legitimate historical and archaeological investigations have been inspired by Arthurian literature? Vampire and shape-shifter legends exist all over the world, and I've always been struck by the similarities. I simply pursued the seeds of truth at their core."

I said, "I read a book once about how many vampire mythologies might have grown out of primitive burial practices and superstitions—bloated corpses bursting out of shallow graves with drops of blood on their mouths, as if they'd been feeding. That sort of thing. By the same token, some scholars traced werewolf legends to actual medical conditions marked by excessive hair growth, or psychological disorders that caused periodic animalistic, berserker-type behavior. That's where scientific inquiry into these subjects usually leads: to rationalizations. What told you that there was something real behind it all?" I was fishing for a personal anecdote. He'd had a run-in with a were-dingo as a small child and it changed him forever, or something.

"I suppose I've always appreciated a good mystery," he said.

"But there are so many other mysteries for a medical doctor to unravel. Like a cure for cancer. Surefire weight loss on a diet of chocolate ice cream."

"Maybe I wanted to break new ground."

"Why now? Why last month's press conference? Why draw attention to your research at this point and not earlier?"

He shrugged and began obviously fidgeting—wringing his hands, adjusting his seat. I felt a little thrill—was I getting to him? Was I making him squirm? Maybe he was just shifting his position on the chair.

"Ideally, a complete report would have been published in a respected journal, making all our findings public. But this isn't always an ideal world. Members of Congress began taking an interest, and if Congress wants to ask questions, who am I to argue? I wanted everyone to be clear that this project isn't shrouded in secrecy."

Could have fooled me. In a rare show of restraint I didn't say that. I had to be nice; wouldn't do any good to totally alienate my only source of information.

"What do you ultimately hope to accomplish with the Center?"

"To expand the boundaries of knowledge. Why embark on any scientific endeavor?"

"The quest for truth."

"It's what we're all trying to accomplish, isn't it?"

"In my experience, this particular subject evokes a lot of strong emotion. People vehemently believe in the existence of vampires, or they don't. If they do, they firmly believe vampires are evil, or they're simply victims of a rare disease. Where does this emotion, these strong beliefs, fit into your investigations?"

"We approach this subject only from the standpoint of fact. What can be measured."

"So if I asked what you *believe*—"

"I think you know what I believe: I'm studying diseases that can be quantified."

This was starting to sound circular. And dull. I should have known that Flemming wouldn't be an ideal interviewee. Every time I'd ever talked to him, he'd been evasive. I'd really have to work to draw him out.

"Tell me how you felt the first time you looked a werewolf in the eyes."

Until that moment, he hadn't looked at me. That was pretty normal; there was a lot in a studio booth to distract a newcomer: dials, lights, and buttons. It was natural to look at what you spoke to. People tended to look at the foam head of the microphone.

But now he looked at me, and I looked back, brows raised, urging him on. His gaze was narrow, inquiring, studying me. Like he'd just seen me for the first time, or seen me in a new light. Like I was suddenly one of the subjects in his study, and he was holding me up against the statistics he'd collected.

It was a challenging stare. He smelled totally human, a little bit of sweat, a little bit of wool from his jacket, not a touch of supernatural about him. But I had a sudden urge to growl a warning.

"I don't see how that's relevant," he said.

"Of course it isn't relevant, but this show is supposed to be entertaining. I'm curious. How about a cold hard fact: *when* was the first time you looked a werewolf in the eyes?"

"I suppose it would have been about fifteen years ago."

"This was before you started working with the Center for the Study of Paranatural Biology?"

"Yes. I was in the middle of a pathology residency in New York. We'd gotten an anomalous blood sample from a victim of a car accident. The report from the emergency room was horrendous—crushed rib cage, collapsed lungs, ruptured organs. The man shouldn't have survived, but he did. Somehow they patched him up. I was supposed to be looking for drug intoxication, blood alcohol levels. I didn't find anything like that, but the white blood cell count was abnormal for a sample with no other sign of disease or infection. I went to see this patient in the ICU the next day, to draw another sample and check for any conditions that might have accounted for the anomaly. He wasn't there. He'd been moved out of the ICU, because two days after this terrible accident, he was sitting up, off the ventilator, off oxygen, like he'd just had a concussion or something. I remember looking at his chart, then looking up at him, my mouth open with shock. And he smiled. Almost like he wanted to burst out laughing. He seemed to be daring me to figure out what had happened. I didn't know what he was at the time, but I'll never forget that look in his eyes. He was the only one who wasn't shocked that he was still alive. I never forgot that look. It made me realize that for all my knowledge, for all my studies and abilities, there was a whole world out there that I knew nothing about."

"And the next time you saw that look"—the challenge, the call to prove one's dominance, like the one I'd just given him—"you recognized it."

"That's right."

"Did you ever find out more about him? Did he ever tell you what he was?"

"No. He checked himself out of the hospital the next day. He didn't have health insurance, so I couldn't track him. He probably didn't think he needed it."

I'd seen werewolves die. It took ripping their hearts out, tearing their heads off, or poisoning them with silver.

"You wanted to find out how he'd survived. How his wounds had healed so quickly."

"Of course."

"Is that as far as your research goes? You mentioned once the possibility of a cure."

"Every scientist who studies a disease wants to find the cure for it. But we don't even understand these diseases yet. Finding a cure may be some time off, and I don't want to raise any hopes."

"How close are you to understanding them? I've heard every kind of theory about what causes them, from viral DNA to unbalanced humors."

"That's just it, the most interesting feature of these diseases is that they don't act like diseases. Yes, they're infectious, they alter the body from its natural form. But far from causing damage or sickness, they actually make their victims stronger. In the case of vampirism, the disease grants near immortality, with relatively innocuous side effects."

He called the need to drink human blood an innocuous side effect?

He continued. "To learn the secret of how that happens would be a fantastic discovery."

"You're talking about medical applications."

He hesitated again, folding his hands on the table in front of him and visibly reining back his enthusiasm. "As I said, I don't want to raise any hopes. We've barely begun to scratch the surface of this field of study."

I had a feeling that was all I was going to get out of him.

"Okay, I'm going to open the lines for calls now. Do you have any questions for the good doctor—"

His eyes bugged out, like I'd pulled out a gun and pointed it at him. Surely he knew I'd be taking questions from listeners.

Shaking his head, he said, "I'd rather not answer questions from the public."

Um, problem? "I'm the public," I said. "You answered my questions."

"No, not like this," he said. He put down the headset and pushed his chair away from the table. "I'm sorry."

Liz, Wes, and the sound guy stared through the booth window, helpless to stop him as he set his shoulders and rushed out of the room.

"Wait, Doctor—" I stood to go after him. Who did that bastard think he was, walking out on me? The wire trailing from my headset tugged at me. The show, I couldn't leave the show. Damn.

I settled back into my seat. I had to talk quick to cover up the silence. "I'm sorry, it looks like Dr. Flemming has urgent business elsewhere and won't be able to answer your questions. But I'm still here, and ready for the first call of the evening. Hello, Brancy from Portland . . ."

The Senate hearings were scheduled to start Monday, but I drove into D.C. proper Saturday evening. I had reservations at a hotel close to the Capitol, and within walking distance of many of the tourist attractions. I'd never been to the city. I saw no reason not to make a vacation out of this. I wanted to see the Smithsonian, dammit.

It was hard to drive and keep my eyes on the road, not craning my neck to catch a glimpse of the Lincoln Memorial. I'd checked a map; it had to be close. I didn't even know if I was looking in the right place. The sun was setting, casting a smog-tinted orange glow over the city. Sightseeing would have to wait until tomorrow it seemed.

Traffic ahead slowed. One of Ivy's notorious jams, on a Saturday no less. I was impressed. Then I spotted the flashing red and blue lights. Accident, maybe. The cars ahead crept to a stop. The trick was not to be impatient. I wasn't in a hurry. I hit the scan button on the radio, hoping to find something catchy. I could play drums on the steering wheel while I waited.

Orange reflective cones squeezed three lanes of cars into one. Up ahead, barricades blocked the road. A pair of police cars were parked on the shoulder. Four cops, flashlights in hand, were checking cars and license plates, asking the drivers questions, looking over passengers. A security checkpoint. Not surprising in these parts, I supposed. I hadn't heard anything about a terror alert or heightened security. Trust the powers-that-be not to tell anyone about a *real* threat.

My turn came to get waved through the checkpoint. A couple of uniformed cops approached the car from each side, shining their lights on the license plates, the interior, and finally at me. I rolled down the window.

"Can I see some ID?"

I had to dig in my backpack for a minute, then I showed him my driver's license. I smiled politely.

"Ma'am, could you pull over to the side of the road here?" He pointed to a spot on the shoulder beyond the barricade. He didn't give me back my license.

My stomach lurched. I suppose everyone's does when they get pulled over by the cops, no matter how innocent they are. I was pretty sure I was innocent.

"Um. What seems to be the problem, Officer?" That may have been the most cliché thing to ever come out of my mouth. In the movies, only guilty people said that.

"Just pull over and we'll get to you in a minute."

While I watched, the cops removed the barricades, cleared the cones, and worked to get traffic flowing normally again. The road-block had served its purpose. Apparently, they'd gotten what they were looking for: me.

I refused to believe this was all for me. I really didn't consider myself a terrorist threat. There was something else going on.

I found my cell phone and brought up Ben's number. My finger poised on the call button, I watched.

A dark sedan, coming from the other direction, did a U-turn over the median, zipped across the three lanes to this side of the road, and pulled over in front of me. The driver was so smooth the move only took a minute, and the tires never squealed.

Two men climbed out, one on each side. They wore dark suits, conservative ties, and looked clean-cut and unremarkable. They seemed big, though, broad through the shoulders, and confident.

Holy cow. Genuine, honest-to-God Men In Black. This had to be a joke.

The cop handed the driver of the sedan my license and pointed at me. Unconsciously, I shrank down in my seat, like I could melt through the floorboards.

I should have called Ben, but I waited, wanting to see where this was going to go. Surely this was all a misunderstanding.

The two Men In Black stalked toward me. Actually, they proba-bly walked perfectly calmly and normally. To me, though, they stalked. The Wolf wanted to growl. And she wanted to get the hell out of here. I was still in the car, I could still drive—and so could the cops. I waited. Had to listen to the human half, this time.

Thinking before acting. *Good girl.* That was what T.J. would have said if he'd been here. Maybe he'd even have given me a scratch behind the ears. I felt a little better.

They stopped by my window, peered in, and looked me over. My nostrils widened; I took a breath. Human, they were normal human beings. Warm blood coursing through live veins, so they weren't vampires. No hint of lycanthropy about them, either. Lycanthropes had a sort of musky, wild scent that couldn't be covered up. They had fur just under the surface and it always showed, if you knew what to look for.

But there was something about them, something cold. They made my shoulders bunch up, and the hairs on my neck stand up—hackles rising. I gripped the steering wheel, white-knuckled. I met the driver's gaze. Couldn't show weakness.

His gaze dropped first.

He offered my license back to me. "Ms. Norville? Alette, the

Mistress of the City, wishes to extend her hospitality. If you'll step out of the car, please?"

I stared in disbelief, and a wave of spent adrenaline washed through me, making my muscles feel like rubber. The fear left with that wave, but now I was annoyed. *Severely* annoyed.

"Mistress of the City? As in vampire?" I said, and I realized what I'd sensed about them. They weren't vampires, but they had a little of the scent on them. Human servants, who spent far too much time with vampires than was healthy. They were too pale.

"Yes. She's pleased that you're visiting her city and is anxious to meet you."

"*Her* city? The U.S. capital and she's calling it *her* city?" But then, what did I expect from a vampire?

The MIB pursed his lips and took a deep breath, as if collecting himself. He was probably under orders to be polite. "Will you accept Alette's hospitality?"

"Why should I?"

"She fears for your safety. You don't know the situation among your kind here. You lack protection. She wants to keep you safe."

"How did she know I was coming?"

"It's her city."

I wondered what she thought she'd get out of keeping me safe, because she surely wouldn't offer me protection out of the kindness of her undead heart. I also wondered what exactly the situation was that would put a lone wolf like me in danger. It meant there was an alpha here who didn't like intruders on his territory.

Right now, an alpha werewolf out for blood scared me more than a vampire.

"All right," I said.

"If you'll please come with me, I'll drive you to meet her."

"What about my car?" I loved my car. We'd been across the country together. "And my hotel reservation?"

"We took the liberty of canceling your reservation. Tom will drive your car to the building. We'll keep it safe for you while you're here. Free parking in D.C., Ms. Norville. Not something to refuse lightly."

Actually, this sounded like one of those offers you weren't allowed to refuse at all.

I put my phone away and got out of the car.

The other MIB, Tom, slipped into the driver's seat as soon as I was out of the way. I looked longingly at my reliable little hatchback, like I was never going to see her again.

The first guy escorted me to the sedan.

I said, "Just so we're clear: the city's vampire Mistress has the D.C. cops in her pocket, or at least enough of them in her pocket that she can order a roadblock on one of the major arteries, just to find one person."

"It would appear so," he said.

"She could have just *called* me, you know."

He glanced sidelong at me, and I rolled my eyes. This was a vampire we were talking about. It was all about theatrics.

At least as a passenger I could look for recognizable landmarks a little more safely. After making sure Tom was following us with my car, I leaned over the dashboard and peered out the windshield, searching.

"The other guy's Tom. What's your name?" I asked.

After a pause he said, "Bradley."

Tom and Bradley. Didn't sound very sinister and Men In Black-ish.

"So, Bradley, where's the Washington Monument?"

"We're going the wrong way to see it."

I sat back and sighed, not bothering to contain my disappointment. How frustrating, to be so close to a major national landmark and not see anything.

Bradley glanced at me. Sounding amused, he said, "Give me a couple minutes and I'll swing back that way." He flicked on the blinker and made a sharp right turn.

Wait, was he being nice to me?

Back in Colorado, I could see. The sky was big, and I could look west and always see the mountains. I always knew where they were, where I was. I needed landmarks. Here, and pretty much everywhere I'd been back East, I felt vaguely claustrophobic. Thick trees grew everywhere and blocked the horizon. Even in autumn, with their leaves dried and falling, they formed walls and I could only see the sky by looking up, not out.

We turned a corner, and Bradley said amiably, in tour-guide fashion, "We now approach the famous Washington Mall. And on your right, the Washington Monument."

I pressed my face to the window. My gut gave a little jump, like it did when I saw someone famous. It was just like the pictures, but bigger. The towering obelisk was all lit up, and the lights gave it an orange cast. In the center of the vast swath of lawn that was the Mall, it stood alone in the dark.

"Wow." I watched it until we turned another corner and left it behind.

I kept track of our route. We ended up driving the opposite direction, back toward the freeway, but we veered off and continued farther west until we came to a quiet row of townhomes in the area Bradley said was Georgetown. Even in the dark I could tell it was nice, and old. Tree-lined streets held rows of brick houses, with slatted shutters and window planters, painted doors, and fancy wrought-iron fences out front. Georgetown University was nearby. Bradley turned into an alley, then into a cobbled driveway wide enough to hold several cars. My car was already there.

I didn't get much of a sense of what I'd gotten myself into until we entered the town house, up a set of steps and through a back door.

That surprised me. Most vampires, even the heads of Families and cities, made their homes underground. It reduced the chance of them or any of their retainers suffering sunshine-related accidents. But Bradley and Tom led me into the house, through a hall, and to a parlor. This vampire held court in a room with windows—covered with heavy brocade drapes, but windows nonetheless.

The place managed to look cluttered and opulent at the same time: crammed with furniture, chaise lounges and wingback chairs, mahogany sideboard tables, end tables, and coffee tables, some with lace runners, others with lamps, both electric and oil. Curio cabinets held china collections, and a silver tea service was on display on the mantel above the fireplace. Persian rugs softened the hardwood floor. All the lamps were lit, but softly, so the room had a warm, honey-like glow. Scattered among the other decorations were pictures, small portraits, a few black and white photographs. Faces stared out of them all. I wondered who they were.

The decor didn't surprise me. Vampires lived for hundreds of years; they tended to carry their valuable collections with them. If the room reminded me of a Victorian parlor, it was probably because it was the real deal. As was its occupant.

A woman set a book down on a table and stood from an armchair that sat nearly hidden toward the back of the parlor, near a set of bookshelves. She was pale, cold, dead. No heartbeat. I couldn't guess her actual age, of course. She looked about thirty, in her prime and haughty. Her brunette hair was drawn back into a knot at the nape of her neck; her face was round, the lines of her lips hard, her gaze dark and steady. She wore a wine-colored dress suit with a short, tailored jacket and a calf-length, flowing skirt—a feminine-looking outfit that brought to mind Ingrid Bergman or Grace Kelly.

I decided she wasn't Victorian. She was older, much older. She had a gaze that looked across centuries with disdain. The present was only ever a stepping-off point for the really old ones. The oldest vampire I'd ever met was probably around three hundred years old. I couldn't be sure—it was rude to ask—but I bet this woman was older.

I had planned on being brazen. If she could disrupt my life, I could be snotty about it. But for once, I kept my mouth shut.

"Katherine Norville?" she said, an inquiring tilt to her head. She had a wonderfully melodic British accent.

"Um, Kitty. Yeah."

"I am Alette. Welcome to my city."

I still wanted to argue the *my* thing, but this woman had me cowed into silence. I didn't like the feeling.

"Bradley, Tom, any problems?"

"None, ma'am," Bradley said.

"Thank you, that will be all."

The two men actually bowed—smartly, from the waist, like trained butlers or footmen in a fairy tale. I stared after them as they left through the doorway to another part of the house.

"I do hope they treated you well."

"Yeah. Well, except for the whole getting stopped at a police roadblock thing. That was a little nerve-wracking." And this wasn't? I didn't think I could escape from her even with my claws out. What did she want with me, *really*?

"I won't apologize for that. It was necessary."

"Why?" I said. "I host a call-in radio show—my phone number is public knowledge. You could have called."

"I couldn't let you say no."

I started pacing, which required maneuvering around an expensive-looking armchair to find a straight, clear path along the edge of a rug. Alette watched me. She was elegant and regal, and I couldn't help but feel like she was indulging me this little outburst.

"You know if you try to keep me here against my will, I've got people I can call, I don't have to put up with this."

"Katherine—Kitty. If you'll please have a seat, we might discuss this in a civilized manner. I fear you're currently in danger of reverting to your other nature."

Pacing was a wolf thing. I'd been stalking back and forth, my gaze locked on her, like an animal in a cage. Obediently, I stopped and took a place on the chair she indicated. I took a deep breath and settled down. She sat nearby, at the edge of the sofa.

"I have a little better control of myself than that," I said sullenly.

"No doubt. But I am aware that I've placed you in strange surroundings and a possibly dangerous situation. I'd best not aggravate you, hmm?"

Carefully maintaining a calm to match hers, I said, "Why did you bring me here?"

Sitting with her ankles crossed, one hand resting on the arm of the sofa, she was no less poised and dignified than standing. She might have been a duchess or something, one of those proud noblewomen in a Gainsborough portrait, draped in silk and diamonds, calmly superior.

She gave an annoyed frown. "The werewolves here are wild and ungoverned. They might see you as easy prey, or an easy target to challenge and dominate. There is no alpha to control them. You'll have enough on your mind while you're here, I didn't think you'd want to worry about that as well."

Got that right. But I was betting there was more to it. From what I gathered from stories, throughout history werewolves had either been vampires' servants or rivals. At best they came to uneasy truces when they lived near each other.

I had never seen what it looked like when there wasn't a truce. Sometimes I felt so ignorant. My old pack, my old alpha, hadn't taught me much about the wider world. With them, I'd learned how to cower. Then I'd learned how to take care of myself.

"What else?" I said. "What do you get out of it?"

She smiled for the first time, a thin and enigmatic expression. "My dear girl, this Senate hearing will be the first time in centuries that one of our kind—vampire or lycanthrope—has been summoned before a nation's government in any official capacity. You seem to have made yourself an authority on the subject."

I shook my head, wanting to laugh. "I've never claimed to be an authority—"

"Nevertheless, many people turn to you. And now, so is the government. And when you speak before the Senate you will, however indirectly, be speaking on my behalf as well."

I didn't want that kind of authority. I didn't want that responsibility. Before I could deny it, she continued.

"I've brought you here to take the measure of you. To learn whose interests you serve. Whose interests you will be serving when you speak before the Senate committee."

Which web of political entanglements was I caught up in, she meant. She wanted to know who was pulling my strings, because in her world, everybody had strings.

She wasn't going to believe me when I told her.

"I serve my own interests," I said. "I left my pack. I don't have any other associations. I'm not sure I have friends anymore. There's just me. And my show. Ratings and the bottom line. That's it."

I was sure she didn't believe me. She narrowed her gaze, maintaining a vaguely amused demeanor. Like she didn't care what I said, because she'd figure out the truth eventually. She had time.

"I suppose," she said finally, "that makes you less corruptible than many. True capitalists are extraordinarily predictable. But I've listened to your show, and there's more to you than that."

"If you've listened to my show, then you know me. Because that's all it is. I parlayed my big mouth into a career. That's all."

"You may very well be right."

I looked away, because her gaze was on me, searching, looking for the layers to peel back. Legends said vampires could entrance you with the power of their gazes. That was how they lured their prey to them, and why some people were all too happy to bare their necks and veins to them.

I wasn't tied to anyone. I wanted to keep it that way.

She said, "If you are right, and there is nothing more to you than what I see before me, then I would be honored if you would accept my hospitality, which is, if I may be so bold, some of the finest in the city."

I would. I knew I would, probably the whole time I'd be here. Maybe because the room was nice and comfortable, and as intimidating as she was, she didn't make my hairs stand on end. Her use of the word hospitality seemed to have an Old World meaning behind it: it was more than offering a meal and bed for the night. It was a mark of pride and honor. It was an insult to refuse.

"Thank you," I said, striving for politeness though I felt ragged beside her.

Alette stood. Automatically, I stood with her, smoothing out my jeans and wondering if I should buy some nicer clothes while I was here.

"Welcome to Washington," she said and offered her hand, which I shook, a normal gesture that I accepted gratefully, even if her skin was too cold. "I've set aside a room on the second floor for you. I do hope you like it. Emma will show you to it. The kitchen is also entirely at your disposal. Tell Emma anything you need and she'll take care of it." A young woman, Emma I presumed, had appeared, called by some signal known only to her and Alette. She was fully human, bright-eyed and eager. Old World hospitality indeed. Alette had *maids*. "My only request, Kitty, is that you tell me if you plan to leave the house for any reason. I have offered you my protection and I will see the offer through."

That almost sounded like a challenge: could I get out of here without her knowing? What would she do if I tried?

And what if there really were ravening werewolves waiting to find me alone? That was a tough call.

"All right," I said noncommittally, and Alette gave me a skeptical look.

"If you'll excuse me, I have other business. Good evening to you."

She left Emma and me at the foot of a set of narrow, curving stairs outside the parlor.

"This way," Emma said, smiling, and gestured up.

Sometimes human servants were vampires in training, waiting for their masters to initiate them into true undeadness. Sometimes they were simply servants, although their brand of service usually involved a bit more than dusting the furniture. I looked around the collar of her blouse for telltale scars, signs of old bite marks. I didn't see any, but that didn't mean they weren't there, somewhere.

We reached the top of the stairs and entered a narrow hallway. More framed photographs and portraits decorated the walls. They represented different times, different eras; the hair, clothing, and demeanors of the people changed from portrait to portrait as we continued. Did Alette have some kind of obsession with collecting these images?

"Can I ask you a question?"

"Sure," Emma said. She was probably about nineteen. Hell, she might have been working her way through college.

I had to ask. "Do you know what she is?"

She smiled wryly and ducked her gaze. "My family's worked for her for generations. We followed her here from England two hundred years ago. She's been good to us." She opened a door at the end of the hall, then looked at me. "You know better than anybody, they aren't all bad."

I couldn't argue.

My duffel bag had already been brought up to the bedroom. The suite included a full bathroom, with brass handles on the sink and shower. Maybe this wasn't such a bad idea. I might even get spoiled.

Emma showed me an intercom by the door, a modern amenity in the antique house. "Just ring if you need anything."

I asked for a sandwich. Then sleep. Sleep was good. Sleeping meant I wasn't wondering where the rest of Alette's vampire clan was hanging out, because human minions could only do so much and I was pretty sure she didn't rule her empire all by herself.

Alette wanted me to tell her if I planned on going out. Well, of *course* I planned on going out. But by the time I woke up, it was full daylight, which meant she probably wasn't around.

So I left a note. I scribbled it on a piece of notebook paper and laid it on the coffee table in the parlor.

It wasn't completely honest of me. Tom and Bradley were probably on call. Alette probably meant for me to tell one of them. I could have gotten a private chauffeured tour of the city—nice, protected, safe.

I'd put my hand on the knob of the front door when I heard footsteps trotting down the stairs behind me.

"Miss Norville!" It was Emma, her brown hair pinned up in a sloppy bun, wearing jeans and an oversized sweatshirt. The clothes made her look young. "Are you leaving?"

I took a guilty step away from the door. "Call me Kitty. I, ah, just wanted to look outside to see what the weather was like." She wasn't going to buy that. I had my backpack hitched over my shoulder. "Alette puts you to work on Sunday, does she?"

"Oh, no. She lets me use the library upstairs to study. It's my last day to catch up on homework before class tomorrow. I was just heading to the kitchen for a snack."

Wow, she really was working her way through college.

"You go to Georgetown?"

"George Washington," she said. She stayed there, leaning on the base of the banister, smiling helpfully. "Have you had breakfast? You want me to fix you something?"

"No, thanks, I'm fine." I wanted to leave. No offense or anything. I fidgeted.

The awkward pause continued. I wasn't fooling anyone. I'd even convinced myself that if I left my car in the driveway out back and used public transportation, they'd just think I was sleeping in late or something.

Finally, she sighed and said, "I can't stop you from leaving. But Alette won't be happy about it when she finds out you went out alone."

Now that didn't make me feel guilty at all. "Are you going to get in trouble if I run off?"

"No. Alette doesn't get angry, not like that. But she'll be disappointed."

And no one liked to disappoint Alette.

"It won't be long. I just want to look around. I'll be back before she even wakes up for the evening."

"Have a good time," Emma said. The statement was perfunctory rather than sincere. She swung around the corner, disappearing through the door to the kitchen in the back of the house.

I felt like a heel. I went out anyway.

D.C.'s famous Metro subway didn't run this far out, but a shuttle bus made stops between Georgetown and the nearest Metro stations. In half an hour I was in the middle of the Mall.

Then I totally, unabashedly played tourist. I couldn't see it all in a day. I probably couldn't see it all in a week, if I factored in museums. Fortunately, there were plenty of companies willing to take my money to drive me around on their tour buses and give me the spiel. The buses even dropped me off in front of just about every museum I could hope to visit. I saw the White House!

All morning and part of the afternoon, I ran around like a maniac seeing the highlights. As I did, I kept my eyes open, looking at the faces around me, wondering. But they were all tourists, round-eyed and cranky. I wasn't going to find any lycanthropes among them. Not that I could scent one across the Mall anyway. They had to be somewhere, though, and I would have liked to have spotted a friendly-looking one to buy a cup of coffee for and ask what was really going on.

I was leaving the American History Museum when my cell phone rang. I just about jumped out of my skin. I'd shoved the thing in my jeans pocket and forgotten about it.

I answered it.

"Kitty?"

"Ben? Where are you?"

"I'm at the hotel. Where are you?" The lawyer had flown into town this morning on a red-eye. We'd reserved rooms at the same hotel—the place I hadn't checked into yesterday.

"It's a long story. We should get together."

"I'm having a late lunch in my room. Can you get over here? I'll order you a steak."

"Make it rare. Thanks. See you in a few minutes."

After a few hours of walking, I fancied I knew my way around well enough that I could find the hotel by myself, and I was pleased to no end by proving myself right.

It pays to have all the escape routes mapped out ahead of time.

The hotel was a few blocks from the Capitol, within easy reach of the office complex where the committee hearing was scheduled to take place. Ben had given me his room number, so I went right up and knocked on the door. He opened it and went back to the table, where he had a room-service tray spread out, and sat to finish his own steak.

"I suppose that's going on the expense account," I said, closing the door behind me. He just smiled.

The thing about Ben was he didn't stand much on ceremony. He wore a dress shirt, untucked and unbuttoned to expose the white undershirt. He was in his thirties, rough around the edges, weathered maybe. His dirtyish blonde hair was ruffled, the hairline receding. On the bed, a briefcase sat open, a storm of papers and legal publications strewn around it. He didn't look like much, but he worked hard.

"Nice flight?" I said.

"Yeah. Great. You look like you've been running all over town."

I probably didn't look too fresh, blonde hair plastered to my face with sweat. It wasn't summer, but the city was having a balmy fall. A sticky humidity dampened the autumn air.

I hadn't even thought about the distances involved. Most tourists would probably think it was crazy, trying to cram as much as I had into that little time. But I wasn't even tired. It was one of those times when being a werewolf had its advantages. I could run for miles.

"This place is incredible," I said. "I ran to the Air and Space Museum to see the Wright Flyer, the Natural History Museum to see the Hope Diamond and the dinosaurs, and the American History Museum to see the Star Spangled Banner. They also have Mr. Rogers' sweater, did you know that? One of them, at least, the guy must have had like a hundred. This has got to be the most culturally valuable square mile in the U.S." I'd hit the highlights in the big museums, making a sprint out of it. I didn't know when I was going to get another chance to sightsee this week.

He stared at me, wearing a mocking smirk.

"What?" I said with a whine, a little put-out.

"You actually got teary-eyed when you saw the Star Spangled Banner, didn't you? You been to Arlington Cemetery yet? You see Kennedy's grave?"

I *had* teared up. I wasn't going to admit it. "Not yet. I was going to do that tomorrow after the hearings."

"That'll push you over the edge, I bet. Bring Kleenex."

I pouted. "You don't have to make fun of me."

"Why not? You're a sentimentalist. I didn't know that before."

"So I'm a sentimentalist. So what? What does that make you?"

"A lawyer." He didn't even have to think about it. He continued straight to business. "You know who's chairing this committee you're testifying for?"

I didn't. I'd been busy with the show, the chance to interview Flemming, and traveling. I had Ben to worry about the rest, right? "No."

"You aren't going to like it."

How bad could it be? "Who is it?"

"Joseph Duke."

I groaned. Senator Joseph Duke was a witch-hunting reactionary. Literally. As in, in a world when such things were still mostly considered myth and fairy tale, Duke ardently believed in witches, vampires, werewolves, all of it, and felt it was his God-given duty to warn the world of their dangers. An earnestly religious constituency kept him in office. I'd had him on the show a few weeks ago. He'd promised to pray for my soul. It shouldn't have surprised me. He probably saw these hearings as vindication, his chance to declare to the world that he was right.

"It could be worse," I said hopefully.

"Yeah. You could be a communist werewolf." He gestured to the opposite chair. In front of it, as requested, was a mostly red steak on a plate. I sat and didn't feel much like eating.

"What's your story?" he said.

I told him. I tried to make it sound not quite so dangerous. But he gave me that frowning, *are you crazy?* look anyway.

He huffed. "The Master vampire of the city decided to make you her personal houseguest? I don't have to tell you that's creepy, do I?"

"I know. But she isn't all that bad."

"Kitty. She's a vampire."

"Yeah, and I'm a slavering werewolf. I get it."

"Listen, they've cobbled these hearings together at the last minute. I couldn't get the staff to give me a schedule of when witnesses are testifying. They're probably not going to call you tomorrow. I'm thinking they'll spend a couple days grilling Flemming. We should go and sit in, to see what kind of tone they set. Get a feel for the room, that sort of thing."

And it wouldn't hurt hearing what Flemming had to say. See if his answers to the senators were any less evasive than the ones he gave me.

"What do we know about Flemming?" I asked Ben.

"Whatever's been in the news. He's a doctor, he's been on the fringes of some pretty whacked-out research. You probably know more than I do."

"I know about his research, about his work with the Center. But I don't know anything about him. He said he did a residency in New York. Think you could track down a little history on him?"

"I'll see what I can do." He reached over to one of the piles of paper on the bed, scooped it up, and handed it to me. "Here's your mail from the last couple weeks. There's a couple of local invitations you might look at. Word seems to have got out that you were coming. You apparently got put on some media-related mailing lists."

That was it. Everybody knew I was here. Even people I didn't know about knew I was here. I supposed I ought to enjoy the attention.

"Why would people send me invitations?"

"Apparently, you have cachet," he said dryly. "You're hip."

Gah. That was almost worse than being an authority.

The invitations he mentioned were three pieces of mail that came in thick, stationery-type envelopes, cream-colored and pearl-gray. I cracked them open while I ate. One was an invitation for a cocktail party at the Washington town house of the Colorado representative from my district. Vote-pandering. I set it aside. The second was for the next installment of a lecture series sponsored by the League of Women Voters. Latent college feminist tendencies almost got the better of me on that one.

The third was a reception for the opening of a new exhibit at the Hirshhorn, the museum of modern art that was part of the Smithsonian. Attire: formal. Cultural, flashy. *Swanky*. An interesting crowd showed up to these things, I bet. It would sure beat hanging out at Alette's for the evening. I couldn't remember the last time I'd been to a real party.

I was going to have to buy a dress. And shoes. And I only had a couple of hours to do it in.

"I gotta run." I stuffed the mail in my backpack and headed for the door. "I'll see you tomorrow."

"Kitty." He stopped me, caught my gaze. He'd looked mostly at his plate until then, finishing off the last of his meal. He startled me into staring back. "I don't have to tell you to be careful, do I?"

I was a little dumbstruck. "Wow. I might start to think you really care."

"Have to protect the revenue stream," he said, quirking a smile.

I rolled my eyes and got out of there, thinking, what could possibly go wrong?

I'd never owned a little black cocktail dress. But every girl should own a little black cocktail dress before she's thirty. Now I had mine.

I returned to Alette's place just after dark, with an hour to spare before the reception. Alette met me in the foyer, like she'd been watching for me. My assurances to Emma that Alette wouldn't know I'd been gone scattered like dust.

She crossed her hands before her. "I would have preferred that you take Bradley or Tom on your outing."

Despite my best efforts, I stood there like a guilty teenager out past curfew, my backpack over one shoulder and the plastic garment bag from the department store over the other.

I shrugged, trying to turn a wince into a smile. "I didn't want to bother anyone."

Her glare told me what a poor excuse that was for flouting her hospitality.

"You've been shopping?" she said, indicating the bag.

She wasn't going to want me to go to the museum reception. She'd want me to stay all tucked up and safe, with her. But I'd been all over town today. I hadn't sensed any lycanthropes. What was more, no super-territorial werewolves had found me. That whole explanation was becoming increasingly lame.

Sneaking out while she was up and about would be a lot harder than sneaking out during daylight hours.

I wasn't going to make excuses. "Yeah. I got a dress. I have an invitation for a reception at the Hirshhorn." Earnestly, I dug in my backpack, found the invitation, and handed it to her. As if I had to prove something like that. "It sounds like fun, and it starts in an hour, and I'd really like to go."

This was ridiculous. I hadn't had to beg to go out since high school. Well, that wasn't true. I'd had to beg Carl, the alpha male of my old pack, to go out. He liked keeping his cubs under his paw, and he especially didn't want me having any fun without him. I thought I'd finished with all that when I left. When he kicked me out. I squared my shoulders and tried to seem a little bit dignified.

She examined the invitation, then me. "This dress. May I see it?"

I peeled off the plastic and held the hanger up to my shoulders. It was black silk with spaghetti straps, clingy in all the right places. The skirt was short without being trashy. I had to be able to sit down and stand up without embarrassing myself. And I found these killer strappy high heels on sale.

Alette rubbed the fabric between her fingers, stepping back to take in the whole garment. "Hm. Understated. Good lines. It will do, I suppose."

Like I needed her permission. "I'm going to get changed," I said, creeping toward the stairs.

She didn't stop me. After the first couple of steps, I ran the rest of the way.

I'd just closed the door to my room when my cell phone rang. I dug it out of my pocket, read the display—it was my mother. I'd forgotten, today was Sunday. She called every Sunday.

"Hi, Mom."

"Hi, Kitty. Where are you this week?" Her tone was laden with unspoken reprimands. She'd asked me to call her when I stopped in a new place, to let her know where I was. Since I was someplace different nearly every week, and on the road most of the time in between, it seemed kind of, well, futile to try to keep her updated on my whereabouts. I forgot, usually.

"Washington, D.C."

Her tone changed to sounding genuinely interested. "Really? That's exciting. Have you done any sightseeing?"

Thankfully, I was able to tell her yes, and we could talk about that for a minute or two. She sounded put out when I told her I hadn't been taking pictures.

"I'll send you a postcard," I said. "Look, Mom? I'm really sorry to cut you off, but I don't have time to talk right now. I've got someplace I have to be."

"Oh?" That unmistakable *Mom* question.

I relented. I felt bad for ditching her so quickly. "There's a reception at one of the art museums here. It sounded like fun."

"Are you going by yourself?"

I had no idea how she managed it, how she could ask one question and convince me she meant something entirely different. It scared me a little that we knew each other well enough that I knew exactly what she was *really* asking.

"Yes, by myself," I said with a sigh. "I haven't been here long enough to get asked out on any dates."

"Well, you know so many people all over the place, I can't keep track of it unless I ask. I worry about you, traveling alone."

This wouldn't be a good time to tell her that I was staying with a vampire. "I'm doing fine, Mom. I promise."

"All right, I believe you. Call me before you leave town, okay?"

Mental note, mental note. "I'll try to remember."

"I love you."

"Love you, too, Mom."

Finally, I was showered and dressed. I spent five minutes practicing walking in the new shoes and was ready to head downstairs.

Alette waited in the foyer at the base of the stairs. She might not have moved since I last saw her, except someone was with her now. She finished saying something to him and turned to watch me.

The one she'd been talking to, a man in a dark gray suit, stood behind her, leaning against the doorway to the parlor, his arms crossed. Not Bradley or Tom. In his mid-twenties, he was shorter, cleft-jawed, with spiky brown hair and a wry expression. He studied me slowly, pointedly dragging his gaze up my body, starting at the ankles and lingering over the interesting bits. His smile got wryer when he caught my gaze.

He smelled cold-blooded and no heartbeat sounded in his chest. Not just a vampire, but a smarmy one.

When I reached the foyer, I asked in a low voice, "Who's he?"

Alette lifted a hand to introduce him. "This is Leo. He will accompany you to the reception."

A chaperone. Great. A *vampire* chaperone? Double great.

"You know, I'm sure I'll be fine."

She gave me an arched-eyebrow look, the parental *you stay in my house you abide by my rules* kind of look.

She reached for him. Smiling, he took her hand, raised it to his lips, and kissed it lightly. Their gazes met and exchanged some long-practiced message of conspiracy. She said, "He's one of mine. You can trust him."

But I didn't trust her. I was about to suggest that I pack my bags and get a room in the hotel after all, that this wasn't going to work out. She looked me over, stepping to one side and the other to take in several angles.

Finally she said, "You really can't go out looking like that. Wait here a moment." All business, her heels tapping on the hardwood floor, she marched out of the foyer, into the back of the house.

I tried to figure out what was wrong with me. Everything fit, everything was straight—I thought. I craned my head over my shoulder to try to see my backside. Did I have toilet paper stuck somewhere?

Leo regarded me, openly amused. "So *you're* the infamous Kitty Norville." Like Alette, he had a British accent, but his was lighter, a bit more drawling.

"Infamous? I don't know about that."

"You should be flattered. Alette doesn't bother with everyone who crosses into her territory."

"I am flattered, really," I said, scowling.

Alette returned, holding something in her hand. "It's typical," she said. "You lot spend so much time running about in the woods, you forget how to properly accessorize. Hold this."

She carried a velvet jewelry box, which she opened and handed to me. While I held it, she carefully removed the necklace within, a diamond teardrop on a gold chain. At least it looked like a diamond. Not that I knew anything about them, my trip to see the Hope Diamond that afternoon notwithstanding. It was as large as my fingernail.

I'd left my blonde hair loose. It lay in waves to my shoulders. It would start to look tangled and ratty as soon as I stepped outside, but I didn't know what else to do with it. Standing behind me, she took my hair in hand and laid it to the side, then clasped the necklace around my neck. The diamond lay an inch below the hollow of my throat, halfway between chin and neckline. Perfect.

"Now, you may be seen in public," she said, stepping around to survey me from the front.

"Not silver."

"I should think not."

I smoothed my hair back into place. "My hair, is my hair okay?"

She grasped my hands and smiled. "It looks fine, my dear."

Suddenly, I liked her. I worried a little that she was working some wily vampire trick on me. But this didn't seem like a vampire trick. This was about loaning someone a piece of jewelry. It was such an unexpectedly girly thing for a centuries-old vampire to do.

Leo offered his arm, and I stared at it like I didn't know what to do with it. I stood there long enough to feel impolite and embarrassed that I was impolite. By way of apology, I put my hand in the crook of his elbow. He smiled like a laugh was on the verge of bursting forth. I squared my shoulders and tried to muster some dignity. His arm was stiff, and I kept thinking there should have been a pulse under the skin.

Alette saw us off at the door like we were a couple of kids going to the prom. Bradley chauffeured us in the sedan, which was waiting at the curb. He stood by the open door to the backseat, and this was all getting ridiculous. Continuing with his formal actions like it was some kind of game, Leo assisted me to my seat and made a little bow before walking around to the other side of the car.

I was torn between feeling like an actress on her way to the Oscars, and the butt of someone's joke, so I kept quiet.

The Hirshhorn's main focus was modern art and sculpture. The gallery where the reception took place was stark, with white walls and a gleaming floor, lit by strategically placed track lighting. Sculptures and the odd multimedia installments stood here and there throughout the wide space, while paintings hung in scattered isolation.

The art was, for the most part, incomprehensible without referring to the notes. Whitewashed papier-mâché-looking objects projecting from the wall, spindly bits of found material built into the shape of a chair, that sort of thing. The reception was being held in honor of one of the artists, an unassuming middle-aged woman standing in a far corner of the room, surrounded by admirers. I hadn't figured out which pieces were hers, yet. Wasn't sure I wanted to, in case I was called upon to speak intelligently about them. I was more likely to say something monosyllabic like "Neat," or "Whoa," which probably wouldn't go over well.

I parked by a Jackson Pollack painting, because I recognized it. Or recognized that this particular set of splatters was by Jackson Pollack.

I looked at the art. Leo looked at everything else. His behavior was oppressively bodyguardish, though with his indifferently amused grin no one but me noticed. He appeared to be a laid-back guy whose girlfriend had dragged him along to see Culture.

"So, Leo," I said, "where you from?"

"To start? Leeds," he said. "Haven't been back in ages."

Which could have meant anything to a vampire. "A few decades? A century? Two?"

"I wouldn't want to deprive you of the mystery."

"How long have you been with Alette?"

"Isn't that the same question?"

Well, couldn't fool him, could I? "Do you miss it?"

"What? Why would I want to be there when I'm lucky enough to be here playing nanny to you?"

Sue me for trying. I turned back to the wall and pretended he wasn't there. I couldn't, very well. His presence was like a rock in a stream, a cold solid place that all the life and movement in the room flowed around, avoiding. Without any overt gesture, he managed to keep himself apart from the crowd. I caught him staring at a woman across the room. She was young, dressed in slacks and a green blouse with a plunging neckline. She held a wineglass and absentmindedly ran a finger around the rim. She laughed at something the woman next to her said; her chin tipped up, exposing a slim, clean throat.

Leo's stance was watchful, focused, and his gaze was hungry.

Vampires hunted by seduction. Youth and beauty attracted them; they in turn made themselves attractive to youth and beauty. Leo was handsome, in a rakish, English way, dressed conservatively but smartly, and more importantly richly, and he'd most likely had decades to practice his pickup lines. She'd think she was being swept off her feet, and wouldn't know what really hit her.

"You take a step in her direction, I'll run right over there and let her know that while they couldn't prove anything at the rape trial, she ought to keep her distance."

He tried to keep his smirk in place, but his glare wasn't at all amused. "No one ever accuses you of being the life of the party, do they?"

"You're never going to find out."

He stepped closer and spoke so his breath touched my bare shoulder. "Werewolf blood is quite the delicacy. You might think of giving me a try. The experience isn't as one-sided as you might imagine."

A shudder charged up my spine and my heart rate doubled. I took a step back, almost stumbling over my own feet. It was pure instinct, wolf backing into a corner and preparing for an attack, bracing for a chance to run.

Leo laughed. He'd known exactly what button to push. I closed my eyes and straightened, taking a deep breath and trying to relax. Embarrassing, certainly. This was also proof of just how close to the edge I really was, how fine the line was between the two parts of my being. A little nudge like that, and I slid right over. If he'd pushed it, I might have started Changing right there, in self-defense.

"Jerk," I muttered. "I need to use the ladies' room. I'll be back in a minute."

"Take your time, take your time," he said and pointedly turned to continue visually menacing the woman across the room. I marched away.

I didn't really have to use the bathroom. I leaned on the tile wall and pressed my hands to my cheeks, which were flushed and burning. I'd let him get to me, and I was more angry at myself than him for it. I liked to think I was better than that.

I waited until my heartbeat had slowed and I felt calm again. Checking myself in the mirror, I smoothed out my dress and nodded, satisfied. I'd just ignore him.

On the way out the door, I ran into a man exiting the men's room. I'd had my head down, not paying attention—not as calm and collected as I'd thought. I stumbled, and he grabbed my arm to steady me.

I started to pull away and apologize, but I caught his scent, and it was wild. Fur and wilderness, open country under a full moon—not quite human. My eyes widened and my back tightened, like hackles rising.

He stared back at me, eyes also wide, his nose flaring to take in my scent. He'd sensed me just as strongly as I'd sensed him. He was tall, with a strong face, brown eyes, and dark hair.

For a moment, I tensed, ready to run, to flee what might have been a challenge; our wary gazes locked on each other. I didn't want to fight. I took a step back, but then his lips grew into a wondering smile. The expression said welcome. He didn't want to fight either.

"I don't know you. Who are you?" He had an unidentifiable accent, though his English was crisp and clear.

"Kitty," I said. "I've been looking for you. I mean, not you specifically, but—" He was a lycanthrope, but not a wolf. I couldn't identify the odd edge to his scent. "You're not wolf. What are you?"

The smile turned playful. "Jaguar."

"Really?" Awe filled my voice. That was so cool. "I had no idea."

"That's clear. My name is Luis. I work at the Brazilian embassy. You—are you visiting Washington?"

"Yes." We were just around the corner from the party. From Leo. I glanced nervously in that direction, expecting the vampire to walk in on us at any moment. I pulled Luis closer to the wall, as if that would hide us. "Luis, I was given to understand that the lycanthrope situation here is sort of unstable. Dangerous for strangers just passing through."

His brow creased. "Who said this?"

My hands wanted to clench, I was so nervous. I had so many questions, and I didn't know him at all, didn't know how he'd react, didn't know what I was getting myself into. But I was desperate for another source of information.

"Alette," I told him.

He shook his head and chuckled, but the gesture was humorless. "Alette, yes. She thinks we are rabble. Why have you spoken with her?"

I winced. "It's a long story."

"You should meet others of your kind, hear their side. I will take you there. No matter what she has told you, you will be safe."

I'd just met him. I shouldn't have trusted him, but my curiosity quickly overcame any sense of caution. And I felt something else— a warm shiver that had nothing to do with our lycanthropy. I hadn't let go of his arm. His body was close to mine, and he was *cute*.

"There's a problem. Alette sent Leo along to look after me. I don't think he'd be happy about this."

He pursed his lips, serious for a moment, and glanced over his shoulder. "It isn't a problem. Come."

He held my hand—his was warm and dry—and guided me away from the exhibit, around another corner to the service door where the catering staff passed back and forth with their trays of food and drink.

Luis said, "Some vampires have lived like nobility for so long, they forget about the servants. He won't be watching this door."

Sure enough, we traveled down a plain concrete corridor to a fire door and emerged onto the nighttime street. No one followed us.

We walked along the Mall, which even at night hosted joggers, dog walkers, people strolling before or after a dinner out. After ten minutes or so I took off my heels and carried them. My feet tingled on the concrete sidewalk. Nighttime, and I felt like running. Full moon wasn't for another week, though. Luis glanced at me, gaze narrowed, lips in a wry smile, like he understood.

Next we rode the Metro for a few stops, ending up a mile or so north from where we started. Luis led me on for a couple more blocks before stopping.

"Here we are."

A subtle shopfront sign, silver lettering on a blue background, lit by a small exterior light, announced the Crescent. Tinted windows didn't offer much of a view of the interior.

"Upstairs is a Moroccan restaurant. Decent, a little pricey, but don't tell Ahmed I said that. We're going downstairs."

Sure enough, we bypassed the brick stairs leading up and took the set winding down to a garden-level door. "Ahmed?"

"He owns the place. You'll meet him if he's here tonight."

I heard the music before Luis opened the door. Once he did, the sound opened up with all its richness and rhythm. Live music, not a recording. A Middle Eastern drum, a string instrument of some kind, and a flute. They weren't playing an identifiable song, but rather jamming on a traditional-sounding riff. It was fast, joyous, danceable.

Once inside, I saw the trio of musicians seated on chairs near the bar: one was white, one black, the other Arabic-looking. The whole place had an international feel to it, and I heard conversations in a few different languages. Cloth hangings decorated the walls, and while the area inside the door looked like any other bar, farther inside there weren't any chairs, but large cushions and pillows surrounding low tables. Oil lamps and candles provided light. I smelled curry and wine in the air.

A guy who couldn't possibly have been old enough to serve drinks was behind the bar, drying glasses. A few patrons sat nearby on bar stools, tapping their feet or nodding along to the music. A woman in a full skirt and peasant blouse danced—I supposed it was belly dancing, but my image of belly dancing was totally different. She was all about grace and joy of movement, not the *I Dream of Jeannie* fantasy. Her dark hair trailed in a braid that swung as she turned, and she wore a distant smile.

Another dozen people sat at the tables, watching the dancer or the musicians, talking among themselves, reclining on cushions, eating, and drinking. It was a calm, leisurely party, a nightclub of sorts, drawing people for conversation and atmosphere.

All of them were lycanthropes.

I stopped, shocked into immobility. I hadn't sensed this many lycanthropes in one place since I was with the pack. I had never seen this many in one place without them glaring at each other, stalking, picking fights, jockeying for position within the pack hierarchy. At the very least, if they weren't fighting they were cowering before the leader who kept them in line, who made peace by force. There was no leader here, not that I could see.

"Is something wrong?" Luis said.

"No, it's just—I wasn't expecting this. All of them in one place. It's overwhelming."

"You have always been alone, then?"

"I used to have a pack. But it was nothing like this."

He said, "Can I get you a drink?"

I probably needed one. "Wine. White. I think."

Two filled wineglasses in hand, Luis led me to the back half of the club, where we could sit in relative quiet. His face lit when he came to a small group gathered in a corner.

"Ahmed! You are here."

"Luis!" A large man rose to his feet more gracefully than I would have given him credit for. He displaced his friends to one side, who amiably continued their conversation without him. He managed to clap Luis on the shoulders without making him spill a drop of wine. He had a faint accent, thoroughly Americanized. "Good to see you, I was beginning to think you'd abandoned us at last."

"I've been busy."

Ahmed turned to me. He had olive features, black hair and dark stubble, a good deal of paunch without the impression of softness. It made him seem round and jovial. Over his shirt and trousers, he wore a flowing, pale-colored robe, which made him fit perfectly with the atmosphere of the place.

He was wolf. I pictured a great, grizzled old hulk of a wolf standing in his place. The image made me want to whine in terror and be on my best behavior. I suppressed an urge to inch closer to Luis and take shelter behind him.

Ahmed's gaze flashed, as if he knew exactly the effect he had on other werewolves.

"Luis, you seem to have gotten lucky tonight. Welcome, welcome!"

He offered his hand. Gratefully, I took it. I clung to normalcy when I could. He covered my hand with both of his and smiled warmly.

"Who might you be?"

"Kitty."

"Kitty. Kitty Norville? *The Midnight Hour*?"

Heaven forbid there should be more than one werewolf named Kitty loose in the world. I grinned, stupidly pleased at the recognition. "That's right."

Luis stared at me. "You're *that* Kitty? You didn't say anything."

"It didn't come up. You guys listen to the show?"

Ahmed shrugged noncommittally and Luis ducked his gaze.

"Of course I've heard it," Ahmed said. "A couple of times. But I have friends who are great fans, trust me."

I wrapped my arm around Luis's and took a glass of wine from him. The evening was looking much less bleak than it had a couple of hours ago. In fact, it was looking positively glorious.

"It's okay. I'm used to people not admitting they listen to it. Let's sit, you guys have to tell me about all this." I looked around at the room, the musicians, and the lycanthropes gathered together.

"Excellent idea!" Ahmed said.

Becoming a lycanthrope usually happened by accident, and it often didn't change the ambitions a person may have had before. The need to travel for a career, the desire to see the world, these things didn't just vanish. Lycanthropy often made them problematic, but people learned to deal with it. It was easier for some than others. Many of the other lycanthrope varieties weren't tied to packs, like werewolves typically were. But even solitary beasts had the problem of territory. Our animal instincts sometimes got the better of us, and travel meant the possibility of infringing on someone else's space, especially during full moon nights, when those instincts were most powerful. As I had quickly learned myself, the one thing a traveling lycanthrope needed more than anything was a safe place to Change and run during the full moon.

As home to the federal government, a bunch of embassies, and a couple of major universities, Washington, D.C., had a vibrant international community, and the lycanthropes were part of it. The Crescent gave them a safe place to gather.

Ahmed explained all this. "We who travel know there is no time for fighting. Death comes to us all and it is a tragedy to hasten it. We have much better things to do than continually fight over who among us is strongest. So, here we are. There are places like this in many large cities: New York, San Francisco, London, Istanbul."

If T.J. had had a place like this, if Carl had been more like Ahmed, if we could have all acted a little more *civilized*—too many ifs. I needed too many ifs to keep T.J. alive.

Ahmed pointed out a few of the patrons: Marian, the dancer, was a were-jackal from Egypt who had immigrated and was working to bring her sister over. Yutaka, near the bar, was a history student from Japan and a were-fox. The musicians: two wolves and a tiger. Ahmed also mentioned a friend of his who wasn't here tonight, a professor who had defected from Russia in the seventies, who was a bear. I couldn't even picture what a were-bear would be like. The place was a zoo.

It was also a paradise, a utopia, at least to my admittedly inexperienced eyes. I heard a lot of stories from doing the show—but then, people only called me with their problems. I'd only ever heard, and lived, the worst of it. I never heard about how things worked when they were going well.

The wine made me weepy. I wiped my eyes before tears could fall. Luis handed me a clean napkin from the next table over.

"Are you all right?" he asked.

"Yeah. This is so different from anything I've known. I never thought it could be like this. Everybody's getting along. You're all so friendly."

"I'm happy we could make you welcome here."

Ahmed said, "Your experience. What's it like?"

I shook my head absently. I wasn't sure I could put it into words. "Power. Jealousy. There was an alpha, and he protected us. But he controlled us as well. I had to fight for any kind of respect, but I refused in the end. It was all fighting and death. I had to leave. Then I get here, and Alette feeds me this line about the local lycanthropes being chaotic and dangerous, that they'd try to hurt me, and it was so easy to believe her. But she lied to me."

Ahmed shook his head. "Perhaps not from her point of view. Alette mistrusts us all because there is no alpha, no one she can negotiate with or control. That is why she says we are dangerous."

"You'd give her the benefit of the doubt?"

"I've encountered many of her kind, and I think she means well, in her own way. Her worst fault is arrogance."

I had to chuckle at that, but the sound turned bitter. I wondered if it was too late to refuse Alette's hospitality. I could stay here the whole time.

The woman had stopped dancing. The musicians played slower songs now, gentle background music as they experimented with each other's sounds and harmonies. The evening seemed to be winding down; a few people were leaving, waving at friends as they left. I wasn't ready for the night to be over. I wasn't ready to leave this place.

Luis put his arm around my shoulders, a warm, comforting contact. I leaned back and nestled against him. With him on one side, and Ahmed on the other, gazing serenely over his domain, I felt like I'd rediscovered the very best part of having a pack of my own: the safety, the protection. Friends all around me who wanted to keep me warm and safe. It was how I'd felt before T.J. was killed. I didn't think I'd ever find that again.

Ahmed looked at me, his lips pursed studiously. "You know the story of Daniel, yes?"

I searched my groggy mind. I felt like a puppy napping in a friendly lap. I didn't want to have to think. "Daniel?"

"The story of Daniel and the lion's den."

"That Daniel? Sure," I said. It was a Bible story. In ancient Persia, Daniel was persecuted for his belief in God and tossed into a den of lions to be eaten. In the story, God sent angels to hold the lions' mouths closed, and he emerged from the den unscathed.

"Yes," Ahmed said. "Do you know why Daniel survived?"

"It's a story about faith. God was supposed to have protected him."

He shrugged, noncommittal. "Yes, in a way. But not how you think. You see, Daniel saved himself. He spoke to the lions and asked them to spare him. He knew their language because he was one of them—were-lion."

My eyes widened. "The Bible doesn't say anything about that."

"Of course not—not explicitly. But it's there, if you look. This was thousands of years ago, remember. Humankind and animalkind were closer then—our years in the Garden together were not so long ago. And our kind, the lycanthropes, we were the bridge between the two. Daniel was very wise, and what he learned was his purpose. That there was a reason for him to be part lion, that God had a reason to make him that way. This is what we learn from Daniel. That we have purpose for being who we are, and what we are, though we may not always know it. Daniel is a saint to us. It's one of our greatest stories."

"I've never heard it that way before."

Ahmed sighed. "It saddens me that the tribes in this country do not tell the old tales to one another. If we gathered to tell stories and drink more, there would not be so much fighting, yes?"

"Hear hear." I raised my near-empty glass in a toast, drained it, and said, "Tell another one."

I lost track of time, lounging there on satin cushions, in Luis's arms, while Ahmed spoke of stories I knew, but had never heard like this, through the filter of my own experience: a werewolf who looked at the world through two sets of eyes, human and animal, and constantly had to bridge the gap between them. Enkidu, from the *Epic of Gilgamesh*, was a wild man who lived like a beast until he was tamed by a woman's touch. And what if he didn't just live like a beast, but *was* one, and yet found a reason to embrace civilization? There were tales that sounded like Aesop's Fables, about the kindnesses shown between humans and animals, thorns plucked from the paws of lions and the like, and Greek and Roman myths about gods and goddesses who could change form at will.

The way Ahmed told it, this wasn't a curse or a disease I'd been suffering with for the last four years. It was a gift that made me part of a long tradition of saints and heroes who slipped easily between one shape and another and made it a strength.

I wasn't ready to go so far as to feel grateful about what had happened to me. It had been an accident, a violent, bloody accident, and I didn't feel blessed. Except if I wasn't a werewolf, I wouldn't have my show and all the success it had brought me.

I was confused.

"Wait, Marian, you can't leave without saying goodbye!" Ahmed called to the dancer, who had just reached the door. "Excuse me," he said to us, then leapt to his feet and rushed over to sweep her up in a bear hug. Wolf hug. Whatever.

Luis took the opportunity to move his hand to my hip, where he settled it in an unmistakable invitation. When I tipped my face up to look at him, he was right there, looking back at me. I could feel his breath on my cheek. I craned my neck, leaned forward just a little—his lips pressed mine lightly, then drew away.

I must have flushed from scalp to toe, the way a sudden heat rose around me.

"My apartment is nearby," he said, whispering in my ear.

I felt his body stretched out behind me, the solidity of it, his warm scent, and I wanted it. I wanted him.

I pressed his hand and smiled.

We met Ahmed by the door to say goodbye, though I was self-conscious because I felt like I was glowing. Luis stood very close to me.

"Thanks for the stories," I said. "For everything." I meant the place, this shelter, the company.

"Kitty, it's a pleasure. The doors here are never locked. You're welcome anytime."

The air outside was cool; Luis and I walked arm in arm.

He had a sexy studio apartment with hardwood floors and exposed brick walls, sparse furniture and floor-length drapes. The kitchen had an island counter and looked well stocked, against expectation of the usual bachelor pad. As if he wasn't attractive enough already, he probably knew how to cook as well.

Not that I had that good a look at the place, because just like in a movie we were kissing before the door closed. He pushed me against the wall, and I wrapped one leg around his, pulling myself close to him. We couldn't get into each other fast enough. My skin was tingling, inside and out.

I suddenly realized, it wasn't enough to think back to the last time I had sex, which was long enough ago. But when was the last time I had *good* sex? That was a pathetically long time ago.

As his hand was climbing up my thigh, under my skirt, I stopped its progress, pressed it against me. I made him slow down, tasting his lips, drawing the weight and solidity of him closer. He smelled spicy, excited, simmering with sweat and hormones. I pressed my face against his neck and took a deep breath of him. He pulled the strap of my dress off my shoulder, bent his head over my bare skin, and did the same, breathing in my scent. I giggled, because I wasn't even supporting myself anymore; I was leaning into him, he was holding me, and we were breathing together.

I was going to enjoy this.

Much later, we rested together in bed, naked and glowing.

I dozed in a happy, languid haze when I noticed the mattress was vibrating with a soft, rumbling noise. I didn't think Luis was snoring; the sound was constant. It felt like one of those coin-operated massage beds in a cheap hotel. I looked up, glanced around, befuddled. The sound was coming from behind me. *Right* behind me.

I rolled over without displacing Luis's arm draped over my hip. "Luis? Are you *purring*?"

The rumbling stopped and he sleepily mumbled, "Hmm?"

chapter 4

Don't move. I'll get it."

Luis was already out of bed before I realized someone was knocking on the front door. The noise had a steady rhythm and was getting louder. Luis put on a robe and went to the door. "Yes?"

The answer was muffled by the barrier, but perfectly comprehensible.

"It's time for Kitty to leave now. She's had enough fun for one night."

Leo. He must have tracked me down.

It had to be getting close to dawn. Maybe I'd thought I could wait him out. As it was, he had just enough time to drag me back.

Luis looked at me. I didn't want to say anything. Leo rattled the doorknob.

"You don't have to go," Luis said. "He can't come in. *I'm* not going to invite him."

Ah, the home turf advantage. If we could stand another hour of Leo nagging at us through the door, we'd be fine.

A click and drag rattled the door—the sound of a dead bolt sliding back. Luis moved back in time to avoid being hit as the door swung in.

Bradley stood in the doorway, holding a device that was most likely a lockpick.

Leo leaned on the wall outside, safely beyond the threshold, regarding us with an expression verging on laughter. "Fortunately, the mortal humans in Alette's employ aren't bound by that annoying little restriction."

"You're trespassing," Luis said.

"Hello, Luis. How is your band of miscreants at the Crescent these days?"

Luis stood with his hands clenched and back braced, giving the impression that he was about to pounce. Was he going to defend me in some gloriously violent manner? How romantic. It scared the daylights out of me.

"Luis, it's okay. I should probably get going."

"Why should you go with them?" He spoke over his shoulder, without shifting his gaze from the vampire.

"They're holding my car hostage," I said. Luis didn't look convinced, but he didn't say anything else. I was still in bed, holding the sheets over my chest. I glared at Leo and Bradley. "Could you close the door so I can get dressed?"

"No," Leo said. "I don't trust you. I'm not taking my eyes off you this time."

Luis started to close the door anyway, but Bradley put out his arm to block it. Bradley tried hard to brace it, leaning forward and putting his weight into it, but Luis was stronger, and slowly pushed him back. Bradley put his other hand against the door. They'd break it before Luis got it closed. They glared at each other.

"Never mind," I said. I didn't want to start a fight. Not that I didn't think Luis couldn't handle himself. But I hated to think that I was the one who dragged him into it.

I climbed out of bed and made a point of not shrinking under Leo's gaze. Bradley was polite enough to look away, and Luis was still guarding his territory. But Leo watched me walk naked across the room to where I'd abandoned my dress on the floor. He was trying to aggravate me, which made it a little easier to ignore him. I'd run with a wolf pack; they'd seen me naked. I turned my back to him to pull the dress over my head. I found my shoes and handbag and met Luis by the door.

"Very nice," Leo said.

I said to Luis, "I had a good time. Thanks."

"Be careful with them."

"I'll watch my back." I leaned forward for a kiss and he gave it to me, gently, warmly. I closed my eyes and sighed wistfully.

"I'll see you later," he said. A statement, not a question.

I smiled. "Yeah." I lingered, thinking he might kiss me again—hoping he would.

"Finished?" Leo said. Scowling, I stepped out and Luis closed the door.

Leo and Bradley flanked me on the way out, my own personal Secret Service.

The vampire sat in the front seat of the sedan while Bradley drove.

"You're a fucking loose cannon," Leo said cheerfully over his shoulder. He crossed his arms and smirked. The sky was graying; he was cutting it close. I couldn't tell if he was anxious about it. His blasé attitude might have been an act to cover up how annoyed he really was, for all I knew.

"Thanks," I said. He rolled his eyes.

If I'd felt like a teenager on the way to her prom on the way out, Alette waiting up for me when we arrived back at her place completed the image. Bradley and Leo guided me to the parlor, where she was waiting, seated regally in her wingback armchair. At a gesture from her, they left.

Frowning, she rose. "I begin to understand why you're a wolf without a pack. Have you always been this contrary?"

"No. It took me years to develop a backbone."

"Your last pack kicked you out, did it?"

"I left."

"Leo tells me you found your way to the Crescent. What did you think of it?"

The question put me off balance. I was all ready for her to chew me out, and I was all ready to be, well, catty about it.

"I really liked it," I said. "It's been a long time since I felt like I was with friends."

"I've tried to give you that here."

Then why did I feel like a teenager being dressed down by her mother? "Leo made it difficult."

"He must find you easy to provoke."

I wasn't going to start this argument.

"Before I forget." I reached back and undid the clasp on the necklace. I hadn't taken it off all night, lest I end up a pathetic character in a de Maupassant story. I gave it back to her. "Thanks. I think it was what made Luis finally hit on me."

She narrowed her gaze. "Do I even want to know?"

"Probably not."

"We'll have to continue this tomorrow evening. I trust you can find your way to your room? Everyone else is asleep."

I had a feeling that was a very subtle, guilt-inducing dig. "Um, yeah."

"Good morning, Kitty." She swept past me, down the corridor and away.

Morning. Sleep. Yeah. What a night.

I was bleary-eyed when I met Ben in front of the Dirksen Senate Office Building at noon.

"What the hell happened to you?" he said by way of greeting.

I peered at him through slitted, sleep-encrusted eyelids and smiled self-indulgently.

"I went out last night."

He shook his head and took a sip of coffee out of a paper cup. "I don't want to know."

I blinked, trying to focus and feeling like I was only now waking up. I *knew* this was Ben standing in front of me. The figure certainly looked like Ben, and sounded like Ben. But his suit was pressed. His shirt was buttoned. He wore a tie, and his hair lay neatly combed back from his face.

I should have known it would take the U.S. Senate to polish him up.

"What are you staring at?" he said. I could only grin sheepishly.

We went inside and managed to find the room the hearing was being held in with only a couple of wrong turns. We sat in the back of the room, which was nicer than I was expecting: blue carpet, wood-paneled walls, the desks and tables in the front made of an expensive-looking wood. The place had a formal, legal air. The chairs for the audience were padded, which was nice.

The space for observers wasn't huge, but it was filled. A lot of the people looked like reporters. They held tape recorders or notepads. A couple of TV cameras stood off to the side.

No one noticed us. I considered it one of the perks of radio that I could be well known and completely unrecognizable at the same time. The reporters focused all their attention on the front of the room: the row of senators, eight of them, each with an identifying nameplate, and Dr. Paul Flemming, sitting at a long table facing them.

Ben leaned over. "You met him. What's he like?"

"I don't know. He's kind of cagey. Nervous. Territorial."

"He looks kind of mousy."

"Yeah, that too."

C-SPAN live wasn't any more exciting than C-SPAN on TV. I paid attention anyway, waiting for McCarthy to burst out of some unassuming senator's skin and ravage the hearings with Cold War paranoia. No such luck. The proceedings were downright sedate, very Robert's Rules of Order.

Senator Duke opened the hearings after laying down the rules of how long each senator could speak and when. As Chair, he got to decide such matters.

"Because of the highly irregular nature of the subject which we have convened to discuss, and the secrecy under which the research on this subject has been conducted, the committee has opted to reserve the first two sessions for questioning the gentleman who supervised the research. Dr. Paul Flemming, welcome. You have a statement for us?"

Each witness could enter a prepared statement into the record. They tended to be dry and academic. I expected Flemming's to be doubly so.

"Five years ago, I received a grant of funds from the National Institutes of Health to conduct research into a number of previously neglected diseases. These are diseases which have for centuries been shrouded in superstition and misunderstanding—"

And so on. He might as well have been talking about cancer or eczema.

The senators' questions, when they finally started, were benign: what is the Center, where is it located, who authorized funding, from which department was funding derived, what are the goals of the Center. Flemming's answers were equally benign, repetitions of his opening statement, phrases like the ones he'd given me: the Center strives to further the boundaries of knowledge in theoretical biological research. He never even used the words vampire or lycanthrope. I squirmed, wondering when someone was going to mention the elephant in the room.

Senator Duke granted my wish.

"Dr. Flemming, I want to hear about your vampires."

Dead silence answered him. Not a pen scratched in the entire room. I leaned forward, waiting to hear what he'd say.

Finally, Flemming said, very straightforward, as if delivering a paper at a medical conference, "These are patients exhibiting certain physiological characteristics such as an amplified immune system, pronounced canines, a propensity for hemophagia, severe solar urticaria—"

"Doctor," Duke interrupted. "What are those? Hemophagia? What?"

"Consuming blood, Senator. Solar urticaria is an allergy to sunlight."

He made it sound so clinical, so mundane. But what kind of allergy caused someone to burn into a cinder?

"And what have you discovered about these so-called patients of yours, Doctor?"

Flemming hesitated a moment, then leaned closer to the microphone set before him. "I'm not sure I understand your question, Senator."

"Vampires. In your opinion, what are they?"

Flemming cleared his throat, nervousness slipping into the calm, and said cautiously, "I believe I explained previously, that vampirism is characterized by a set of physical characteristics—"

"Cut the bull, Doctor. We've all seen *Dracula*, we know the 'physical characteristics.' I want to hear about the moral characteristics, and I want to hear about why they exist."

I leaned forward, scooting to the edge of my seat, not because I would hear any better. The microphones worked great. I was waiting for the fight to break out.

"My studies don't involve the scope of your question, Senator."

"Why not?"

"Those points are irrelevant."

"With all due respect I disagree with you. Strongly."

"Senator, I'm not qualified to comment on the moral characteristics of my patients."

"Your test subjects, your patients—how do you feed them, Doctor? Whose blood do they suck out? How many of *them* turn into vampires?"

"Despite all the stories to the contrary, the condition is not transmitted by direct fluid contact—"

"And the blood?"

"Blood bank, Senator. We use pints of the most common types that the existing blood supply can spare."

"Thank you, Doctor." He said it like he'd gained some kind of victory.

"Doctor, I have some questions over the budgeting of your research—" One of the other senators on the committee, a woman named Mary Dreschler, quickly steered the discussion back to more mundane matters. A Democrat from a Midwestern state, Dreschler had run for the seat held by her late husband, who'd died suddenly in the middle of a reelection campaign. She was on her third term.

After two hours of this, the day's session was over. It was just as well it wasn't an all-day thing. If people in Congress did this sort of thing a lot, I was going to have to respect them a little more. Here I was, thinking the job was all glamour and state dinners.

When Duke called the session into recess for the day, a sense of relief passed through the room, and the group sigh of exhaustion changed the air pressure.

Ben, leaning back in his chair, smirked in amusement. "If this is the tone the whole hearings are going to take, we're in for a roller coaster. I can't wait to see what Duke does with you."

"I thought you were supposed to be on my side."

"I am. It's still going to be fun to watch."

I could hear it now: *Eaten any babies lately, Ms. Norville?*

Eggs for breakfast. Does that count?

Looking purposeful, Ben gathered up his briefcase and jacket.

"Where are you off to?" I asked.

"I have some research I want to do. You don't need me for anything, do you?"

"Nope." I had some research of my own I wanted to take care of.

"Then I'll see you tomorrow." Outside the hearing room, he took off down the hallway, away from the front doors of the building.

As I turned to leave, a man with a mini digital camcorder tucked in his hand stepped into my path. I balked, startled.

"You're Kitty Norville," he said. "Aren't you?"

I wondered how he knew. I didn't include my picture with any of the publicity for the show for exactly this reason. But he might have overheard Ben talking to me. He might have pulled my file off DMV records. It could have been anything.

He wasn't tall for a guy, only a couple inches taller than my five feet six. His build was average and he dressed preppy, a brown leather coat over a sweater and khakis. But his eyes shone with a barely suppressed zeal that was unnerving, because it was focused on me.

"Who are you?"

"Roger Stockton, I'm a reporter for *Uncharted World*. Do you have a couple minutes to answer some questions?" Without waiting for an answer he hefted the camera and turned an eye to the little screen, which was no doubt showing me glaring at him.

I had to be calm. CNN was watching from down the hall. I didn't want to do something that would get me a starring role on the six o'clock news.

"Wow. I didn't think *Uncharted World* had reporters. Aren't you guys more the urban legend and unverified amateur video footage kind of show?"

He didn't react to that, but he was probably used to getting that kind of crap from people. "What was your reaction to being subpoenaed by the oversight committee?"

"I'm sorry, I really don't have time for this." I dodged him and continued down the hallway. The guy was persistent, though. He ran after me and planted himself in front of me again, cutting me off when I tried to go around him. The hall wasn't wide enough to avoid him.

He spoke quickly. "What are your thoughts regarding the Center for the Study of Paranatural Biology and Flemming's work there?"

The shining little eye of the camera lens stayed trained on me. I had to get away from that thing. "No comment."

"Come on, you've got more of a right to an opinion on this stuff than anyone else in that room, and you can't take a minute to share your thoughts with the public? Are you going to leave it to other people to decide what tone this debate takes?"

I turned on him, my shoulders bunched, my jaw tight, my gaze burning. I only half raised my hands and took a step toward him, but his reaction was immediate and unambiguous. He stumbled back against the wall, pressing himself to it as if he could fall through it, and clutched the camera to his chest. His eyes went wide and the blood drained from his face.

He knew I was a werewolf. More importantly, he believed it, and everything it entailed. He thought I might actually maul him, right here and now. Idiot.

"I don't want my picture on TV, especially not on *Uncharted World*. Get rid of the camera and I'll think about talking to you. But right now I'm not inclined to be nice."

I stalked away from him. And half a second later, I heard footsteps hurrying behind me.

He could *not* take a hint.

"Look, we're both in the broadcast business. Why not do a colleague a favor? Just give me a couple of quotes and I'll give your show a plug. We both win."

It didn't even help that his voice had a nervous waver to it now. I tried to ignore him, but he was right alongside me again, holding up that damned camera.

He was looking back and forth between me and the camera, so he didn't see Bradley standing in front of us, blocking the corridor. But I did.

I stopped. Stockton didn't, until Bradley grabbed his wrist and took the camera out of his hand.

"Hey!" Stockton struggled, until he looked at Bradley. First his chest, then up to his face. They couldn't have played it better if they'd been making a movie. All I had to do was sit back and watch.

"This guy bothering you?" Bradley said.

Oh, how a girl loved to hear those words from someone with Bradley's build. "I think he was just leaving. After he erases the last five minutes of footage off his camera."

Bradley let go of him, then studied the camera's controls. He started pushing buttons, and I had no doubt that in moments my face would be wiped clean from the camera's memory.

Stockton pointed a finger at him. "This is harassment."

"No, *that's* harassment," I said, nodding at the camera.

He frowned. "I don't understand why you're turning down free publicity."

"I'd like to hold on to the last bit of anonymity I have," I said. I was going to lose it soon enough when I showed up on C-SPAN.

Bradley handed back the camera. His expression was smug, so I was confident the purge had been a success.

Stockton backed away. "We'll talk again. Tomorrow."

The bodyguard and I made it out of the building without any other interruptions.

I gave a tired sigh. "I think I owe you one."

"Not to worry," he said. "It was my pleasure."

Only after a couple minutes did I realize that he'd been on his way to meet me after the hearings finished, to escort me to the car, as if I couldn't be trusted to make it to the curb without getting into trouble. Maybe I couldn't. It still annoyed me.

"Shotgun," I called as we neared the sedan in the parking garage.

He glared. He'd been heading for the rear door, preparing to be all chauffeur-y.

"I can see better out the front," I explained. He sighed in what I thought was an overly dramatic manner, but he opened the front passenger door for me.

As he pulled out of the garage and into the bright sunshine of the daytime street, I asked, "Can we make a detour? Just a tiny little stop. You can even leave the motor running."

I faced him, eyes wide and pleading. Even in broad daylight, he managed to look as foreboding as he had the night I first saw him, with his dark, nondescript suit and stony features. As we emerged into daylight, he put on a pair of sunglasses, completing the Man In Black image.

"You are an awful lot of trouble, you know that?"

"It's not on purpose, honest." The trouble I caused was almost always a direct result of speaking without thinking first. This, for example: a rational person would do whatever she could to avoid annoying Bradley. Not me. "Please? Just a tiny little errand, I promise."

"Where?"

I cringed. "The Crescent?"

"No, absolutely not!"

"I just want to run in and leave a message for Luis, that's all, I promise."

"No. No way."

"*Please?*" I wasn't above begging. "We wouldn't have to tell Alette."

"Do you really think I wouldn't tell her?"

He would, he absolutely would. For a moment, his sincerity almost made me back off. This genuine, seemingly uncoerced loyalty Alette inspired in her people was daunting. I set my elbow on the door and leaned my head on my hand.

Bradley pursed his lips, his gaze flickering at me. "She has your best interests in mind. She's only looking out for your safety."

"She thinks a wolf needs an alpha, does she? Doesn't want me running around without a leash?"

He didn't answer. As altruistic as he made Alette out to be, there was a core of truth to what I'd said. I stared out the window as we passed yet another neoclassical building. I wondered what that one was.

"All right," he said. "A minute. That's all. If you duck out on me, Alette may never let you out of the house again."

I gave him a tight-lipped smile. "All right."

He waited at the curb, with the motor running. Just so I knew the clock was ticking. I ran.

Maybe Luis would be there, maybe not. Maybe I just wanted to make sure the place was real, that I hadn't dreamed last night.

It was real. In the light of day, the silver on the sign above the restaurant part of the building sparkled. A menu was taped inside the window. I went downstairs.

The door to the lower section was propped open, letting in the slight breeze. I peeked inside. Only a few people were there, before the after work and supper crowds. A man at one of the tables in back drank coffee and read a paper, a couple was talking at the bar, and an old man sat alone at a table and chair, where the musicians had played last night. Hunkering inside a tired, stained overcoat, he stared into a tumbler that he gripped with both hands. He was a werewolf; I could tell without scenting him or sensing anything about him. He was grizzled enough, he looked the part. Wiry, steel-gray hair bristled from his liver-spotted head into thick sideburns, down his wrinkled neck, and under his ears, which were slightly pointed. I caught a glimpse of elongated canine teeth sitting just over his lower lip. His fingers were thick, ending in sharp, narrow nails. He probably terrified small children he passed on the street.

Here was someone who'd been a werewolf for a long, long time, and had spent much of that time in his wolf form. I'd heard of this, but I'd never seen it: his body was forgetting how to be human. If I hadn't known anything about werewolves, I might have looked at him and thought he was arthritic and aging badly. As it was, I expected his eyes to be golden-amber if he happened to glance up.

I somehow found my way to the bar. Bumping into it, I realized I'd been staring. I shook my head to clear it of the image of the old man.

"You're Kitty, right?" the bartender said. He was the same guy from last night, the young one. Now that I had a good look at him, I could tell that he wasn't wolf, or jaguar like Luis. I couldn't tell what the hell he was.

"Yeah, hi."

"Jack." He stuck out his hand. I gripped it. He squeezed back a little too hard, giving me a half grin as he did. Trying to prove something. He was strong—stronger than I would have expected from someone his size. But then, so was I. I let go and leaned on the counter like I hadn't noticed.

"Can I get you something?"

"No, thanks, I just wanted to leave a note for Luis." I nodded toward the old man at the table. "Who's he?"

Jack put his elbows on the bar and raised a conspiratorial brow. He whispered, "People call him the Nazi."

I blinked at him, startled.

"I don't know if he really is or not," Jack continued. "But Ahmed says he did fight in World War II, and that he is German. Who knows? He comes here every day at four, drinks his schnapps, and leaves without saying a word."

"Whether he is or he isn't, he must have some amazing stories to tell. I wonder—" And that was all I did, because the old man tipped his glass to his mouth, drained the last bit of liquid, stood, and settled his coat more firmly on his shoulders as he stalked out of the place. That was that.

I turned to Jack. "What about you? You have any good stories?"

"Me? I'm just a cub," he said, grinning. "Give me a few years."

"May your life be so dull that you don't actually collect any."

"Where's the fun in that?"

Fun? I glared at him.

I left a note for Luis. Not like I had anything to say beyond, *Hi, it's me.* It felt like high school all over again, which was kind of fun in its own way. I hadn't crushed this hard over anyone—outside of a movie screen, at least—in a long time. I felt giddy, young, and silly—and completely distracted, which meant the timing was horrible. Senate hearings were supposed to be serious, and I kept picturing Luis in bed.

Bradley got me back to Alette's house without any further ado.

Before I'd left that morning, Emma brought me an envelope, thick stationery paper with my name written on it in fancy cursive. Inside was a square of cardstock bearing a handwritten note informing me that Alette requested the pleasure of my company for dinner that evening. It felt very old-school, like something out of Emily Post.

I'd never had dinner with a vampire, and part of me dreaded finding out what that involved. The imagination ran a little wild. But if I was going to have a chance to talk to her, this was it. Maybe I could draw her out a little.

I wondered if she expected me to dress for dinner, in the Victorian tradition, silk gowns and suits in your own parlor. I'd worn slacks and a blouse for my day at the hearings, so I didn't look particularly ratty. But around Alette, I'd feel downright drab. Then again, no matter what I wore, I'd feel drab next to Alette.

In the end, I didn't "dress for dinner." If slacks and a blouse were good enough for the U.S. Senate, they were good enough for the vampire.

I hoped Leo wouldn't be joining us.

I took a nap, washed up, and Emma brought me to a dining room in another part of the ground floor. Like the parlor, this was classically English, with wood paneling on the walls, which were hung with many paintings, rows and rows of them, landscapes and still lifes of dead birds and hunting rifles, and a few portraits of scowling old men and grim-looking ladies in opulent gowns decorated with flounces and lace. More portraits, like the ones in the parlor and the photos in the hallway upstairs. Were they old friends? Relatives?

A long table ran down the center of the room. Twenty people

could have sat there easily, and for a moment I thought this was going to be like one of those comedies where two people sat at either end and had to shout at each other for the salt. But no, Alette stood by the chair at one end, and there was a place setting to her right, one chair away along the side.

"Welcome," she said. "Thank you for coming."

"Thanks for the invitation." I glanced around nervously, but Alette was alone. No Leo. I relaxed a notch. "Not that you gave me much of a choice, with Bradley keeping tabs on me all day."

She ignored the dig and indicated the chair with a graceful turn of her hand. "Please, sit."

The table only had the one place setting. By her chair, the polished mahogany surface was empty.

I should have been relieved.

She said, "I took the liberty of asking the cook to prepare your filet rare. I assume this is acceptable."

There was a time I didn't much like steak, and I preferred any meat I ate ground up and well burned on a grill. The Wolf, however, liked meat to bleed. So I ate rare steaks.

"Yeah, thanks." I gestured at the empty place on the table in front of her. "So, what are you . . ."

"I've already dined this evening."

This was going to be awkward. When one of her staff brought out a plate with the steak and tastefully arranged vegetables and set it in front of me, I half expected she'd also bring out a goblet full of thick red stuff and give it to Alette. Though it was probably just as well she wasn't going to be . . . dining . . . in front of me.

I managed to overcome a lifetime of socialization about eating in front of people who weren't and started in on the meal, which was perfect, of course. Warm, bleeding, tender, tangy. Small bites with fork and knife; *not* messily devoured. The Wolf and I compromised on these points.

"Tell me how the hearings went today."

I was supposed to be her spy, then? "I think C-SPAN was broadcasting. At least they had cameras there. You could have watched it for yourself."

She narrowed her gaze. "I was indisposed."

I shrugged, nonplussed. "You could tape it. Heck, you could probably download it off the Web." I didn't know if the old vampires even used the Internet. She probably let her minions do that.

Resting her elegant chin on her hands, she said, "I want to hear what *you* think."

Did she really want to know what I thought, or was she testing my bias?

"Flemming testified today. He's the head of the Center, and the committee has put him in the position of having to defend his project, his baby. In that respect, this could be any government research project being put under the microscope. But then there's Duke. He wants to turn it into a witch hunt. Since this is a PC world, he can't get Flemming to make a judgment call like 'vampires are evil' or 'werewolves are hellspawn.' Flemming's being very clinical about the whole thing, and I think it's pissing Duke off. I'm wondering if this isn't all his idea in the first place. He's always been on the fringe. He may see these hearings as a way to gain validation for his ideas."

"Senator Duke knows very little of the matters on which he speaks so fanatically."

"Yeah, but he's a fanatic with political clout. That makes him scary."

"The werewolf, afraid of the politician?"

I smirked. "As werewolves go, I'm a total coward. Give me a good alpha to hide behind any day."

"You just haven't found a good one, is that it?"

It was kind of like finding a good boyfriend. You kept hoping the perfect one existed, but the trial and error in the meantime could be gut-wrenching. "You're very nosy."

"It's how I learn. You have some experience with that yourself, I believe."

"Can't argue."

"What have they scheduled for tomorrow?"

"More grilling of Flemming, I think. If it's anything like today they'll end up going around in circles. This is an oversight hearing, so they could go for days, until they've heard everything they want to. They haven't even announced the whole schedule of witnesses yet. It's like the whole thing was thrown together."

"When do you testify?"

"I don't know."

"Duke will postpone your testimony until next Monday, if he can."

I paused and considered. Monday was the next full moon. Alette must have known that. Did Duke? Did he know that I'd be at my worst, the day Wolf rose so close to the surface? I didn't want to give him that much credit. "I hope not," I said simply.

She said, "What do you hope will result from these hearings?"

"I guess I just want everyone to say, 'Yeah, okay, this stuff exists.' Then I want them to leave us alone."

"What is the likelihood of that happening?"

"I don't know. The trouble is, I don't think they can both happen at the same time. I keep thinking, if the government recognizes the existence of these things, it'll want to regulate them."

"That is my fear as well. Whatever happens, that must not be allowed to come to pass. The government—Flemming, Duke, all of them—must, as you say, leave us alone."

"We may not have a choice what happens."

"Oh, there are always choices. Above all, the conclusion of these hearings must be that we are not a threat—to the public or to the government. You know very well we are not. We have regulated ourselves for centuries to ensure our secrecy, to ensure that the mortals *don't* have a reason to fear us and take action. It may be up to you to preserve that balance."

And I was one of the reasons that secrecy was coming to an end. No pressure or anything. "I don't think I have that kind of authority—"

"I think you sell yourself short. People listen to you, Kitty. You simply don't see it because you stay sheltered behind your microphone."

She was implying that it was all make-believe to me. That I didn't believe I really had an audience.

Maybe it was true. Here, for the first time, I was meeting some of my audience. I had to face them and stand up to defend all the stuff I'd been talking about on the air for the last year.

So much easier to hide behind the microphone.

"I'm only worrying about telling them the truth. I'm not going to be able to dictate what action the committee takes."

"The implications may run far wider than you think. Have you ever seen someone burned at the stake? I have."

Why was I not surprised? "It won't come to that. We've gotten past that."

"Perhaps."

Even with all the conversation, I'd managed to finish eating. The steak was good, and I'd been hungry. I tapped my fork—stainless steel, not silver, another courteous gesture from the mistress of the house—on the plate, fine china in some antique pattern. I should have been afraid of breaking it.

"Flemming's the one who's going to swing this," I said. "He's the scientist, and he's the one who depends on the committee for his livelihood. They'll listen to him."

Alette reached over and took the fork out of my hand, setting it down out of my reach. I stared at my hand, startled. I hadn't seen her coming. I hadn't had time to flinch. She said, "Are you suggesting we should be more worried about Flemming than Duke?"

"Duke is predictable. We know exactly where he stands. But Flemming? I don't know anything about him. Look, Alette. I have to be able to get out and travel around without your people hanging around me. You're worried about me and I appreciate that, but I want to look around, find out more about Flemming and his research, see if I can't follow up on a few contacts. But I can't do that with Bradley or Leo looking over my shoulder. No one would talk to me. I'm not trying to be disrespectful of your hospitality. But I can take care of myself, at least a little, and I need some freedom."

I'd had precisely two days to earn her trust. I didn't know if it was enough, especially since I'd already run off once. Er, twice. But if she wanted me as an ally, she had to know she couldn't keep me on a leash and expect me to be effective.

"You aren't saying this just so you can run off with that were-jaguar from the Brazilian embassy, are you?"

I shrank back in my seat and tried to look innocent. "Maybe just a little."

She studied me, lips pursed in a wry smile. After a moment she said, "I don't suppose I could blame you for that. All right, then. But I want to hear what you learn on your investigations."

"It's a deal." The kitchen staff came to clear away the dishes, then brought dessert: chocolate mousse in a crystal goblet. My God, what had I done to deserve dessert? The maid was human. I'd only seen a small fraction of the house. I was getting nervous. "Alette, can I ask—where are the others?"

"Others?"

"I've met you and Leo. But you must have other . . ." Minions? Lackeys? ". . . companions. Vampire companions."

She suppressed a wry smile. "You're accustomed to Master vampires who surround themselves with followers, as reflections of their own importance."

Vast halls filled with pouty Eurotrash vampires—yeah, that was the image.

She said, "I'm extremely selective about who I bring into this life, this existence. It's not necessarily an easy way to be. I require pure motives. You've met no other vampires because there are none. Just the two of us. I would not tie someone to me for eternity lightly, Kitty."

Then she saw something in Leo that I didn't. She might have looked forward to spending eternity with him. I couldn't stand being in the same room with him for a minute.

The next day, I scoured newspapers and major news Web sites for mention of the hearings. I wanted to find out what the press was reporting. The only place that had any sort of major headline on the hearings was the Web site for *Wide World of News*: "Are Vampires Controlling the Senate?" That was so not useful. I stopped mentioning that rag entirely since they ran a "story" claiming that my show broadcast secret mind-control signals that caused teenagers to join satanic cults and run up huge debts on their parents' credit cards.

Unless they involved epic disasters or scandals surrounding major political figures, Senate committee hearings didn't normally make front page news. "Fact-Finding Hearing Gets Its Start," on page four of the *Washington Post*, was about the extent. They ran a black and white photo of Flemming at his microphone, gazing up at the committee with his sleepy eyes. They also ran a fun little sidebar titled "What Are the Facts?" defining the scientific terminology the doctor had bandied about. It all served to make the topics seem like exactly what Flemming insisted they were: diseases. Nothing more, nothing less. Nothing to be afraid of, as long as we understood it. Maybe this would turn out all right.

The next session of the hearings found me in the same place, sitting in the back of the room with Ben. Roger Stockton sat on the other side of the room from me, at the edge, where he could get a good shot of the participants with his camera. I caught him filming me a couple of times. I couldn't do anything about it without making a scene.

Flemming testified for another two hours, suffering through more questions.

Senator Deke Henderson, a Republican from Idaho, was one of those western politicians who played cowboy, to make themselves

seem folksy and in touch with their roots. He wore a button-up
rodeo shirt under a corduroy jacket and a big silver belt buckle.
Outside the building, he'd put on the cowboy hat. He really had
gotten his start in ranching, though, which gave him a hint of legit-
imacy. One couldn't be sure the outfit was a costume.

Henderson said, "Now that you've studied these diseases, Doctor, how close are you to finding a cure? What program would you
recommend for preventing the spread of these diseases?"

Perfectly natural questions when confronted with any strange
new disease. I listened closely to Flemming's answers.

He cleared his throat nervously. "As diseases go, these are quite
unusual, Senator. For one, while they're life-altering, they aren't
particularly destructive. In fact, they're just the opposite. They con-
fer on the patient extraordinary resilience, immunity, rapid healing.
I've studied such aspects of these conditions in detail."

"You haven't found a cure?"

"No, Senator."

"Have you even been looking?"

After a long silence, Flemming said, calmly, "I have been studying the unique characteristics of these conditions in the hopes of
understanding them. For instance, if we understood the mechanics
behind a vampire's longevity, or behind a werewolf's resistance to
disease and injury, think of the application to medicine. I have a
case history here of a patient who tested positive for the HIV virus,
became infected with lycanthropy, and then all subsequent HIV
tests had negative results."

Duke piped in. "You'd turn everyone into werewolves to keep
them from getting AIDS? Is that what you're saying?"

"No, of course not. But I think you'll agree, the more knowledge
we have about these conditions, the more power we have over them."

Duke leaned back and smiled. I couldn't see Flemming's face,
which frustrated me. The two of them looked like they'd exchanged
one of those all-knowing glances, like they'd just made a deal under
the table in full view of everyone.

I had only assumed that the scientist and religious reactionary
could never work together. I hadn't considered that they both
wanted the same thing: to prove that this was real, for good or ill.

Ben and I exited into the corridor after the hearing adjourned for
the day.

I leaned close, so I'd have less chance of being overheard. Especially by Stockton, who was busy cornering Flemming.

"Flemming's got to have an office somewhere in D.C. Can you find out where? I have his phone number if that helps."

He pulled a sheet of paper from the outside pocket of his briefcase and handed it to me. "Already done."

The sheet was blank letterhead with Flemming's name on it, and an address at the National Institutes of Health medical complex in Bethesda.

I beamed. "Thanks, Ben. You're the best."

"That's my job." I'd turned to leave when he said, "Wait. I found out a little more about him. He say anything to you about serving in the army?"

"Flemming was in the army?"

"Yeah. I've got a request in for a copy of his service record, I'll know more then. There's also a CIA connection."

I huffed. "You're kidding. That's just a little too outrageous to believe." I stared at the blank sheet of letterhead, like it would offer up the truth about the real Flemming.

Ben shrugged, unapologetic. "Just watch your back."

Too many questions and not enough time to look for answers. I tossed him a mock salute before jogging out of there.

I turned my cell phone back on when I left the building. Caller ID showed three missed calls, all from my mother. I thought the worst: there'd been an accident. Someone had died. Quickly, I dialed her back.

"Mom?"

"Kitty! Hi!"

"What's wrong?"

"Nothing."

I rolled my eyes and suppressed curses. "Did you call me earlier?"

"Yes, I had to ask you, your father says he saw you on C-SPAN this afternoon at those hearings they're doing on vampires. You were sitting in the audience. Now, I didn't think that could possibly be right. You weren't on C-SPAN, were you?"

I hesitated a beat. It wasn't that she was going to be angry that I was on television. No, she was going to be angry that I didn't tell her I was going to be on television so she could call all the relatives and set the timer on the VCR to record it.

"Dad watches C-SPAN?" I said.

"He was flipping channels," she said defensively.

I sighed. "Yes, he probably saw me on C-SPAN. I was in the audience."

"Well, isn't that exciting?"

"Not really. It's kind of nerve wracking. I'm supposed to testify at some point."

"You'll have to let us know when, so we can tape it."

This wasn't the school play. But I wasn't going to convince her of that. "That's cool, Mom. Look, I have someplace I need to be. I'll talk to you later, okay?"

"Okay—I'll have to call your father and tell him about this."

"Okay, Mom. Bye—"

"I love you, Kitty."

"You, too, Mom." I hung up. Why did I always feel guilty hanging up on her?

I didn't have time to track Flemming down that afternoon. I had an appointment.

At 3:55, I was at the Crescent, sitting at the table by the bar, with a soda in front of me and a glass of schnapps in front of an empty chair. Right on schedule, the old man entered the club. He'd walked another three steps before he stopped, frozen in place, and stared at me.

I hadn't asked how long he'd been coming here. Probably since long before Jack started working here. When was the last time someone had interrupted his routine? I could almost see his thoughts working themselves out on his furrowed, anxious face as he processed this new event, this wrinkle in his life.

I nodded at the empty chair in invitation, but I didn't smile, and I didn't look directly at him. Staring might have been a challenge; smiling might have showed teeth, also a challenge. I worked on being quiet and submissive, like a good younger wolf in the pack. If his body was sliding more to the wolf half, I had to assume his mind was as well, and that those were the cues he would read.

Slowly, watching me carefully the whole time, he came to the table and took the empty seat.

"What do you want?" he said in a pronounced German accent. His voice was gravelly.

"To talk. I collect stories, sort of. I'm guessing you have some pretty good ones."

"Bah." He took a swallow from the glass. "There is nothing to talk about."

"Nothing at all?"

"You think that a pretty young thing like you will soften an old man's heart, with drink and blushing? No."

"I'm new in town," I said, soldiering on. "I came here for the first time two nights ago, and I'm just trying to learn as much as I can before I have to leave. I've been pretty sheltered until now. I was in a pack for a while. It wasn't anything like this."

"You came from a pack?" His eyebrows bunched together in curiosity.

I knew if I kept rambling long enough he'd interrupt. I nodded earnestly.

He scowled and shook his head. "The pack. Is archaic. In the old days, we needed it for protection. To defend against hunters, against rivals, against the vampires. Now? Easier to buy each other off. All the packs will go away soon, trust me."

I thought about Carl, my former alpha, running his pack into the ground to maintain his own sense of importance, and hoped he was right.

"My name's Kitty," I said.

He arched that peculiar brow at me. "A joke?"

"'Fraid not." I'd never seen much reason to change my name just because it had become a hideous irony.

He stared at me long and hard, like he was deciding whether or not to give something valuable away. Finally, he said, "Fritz."

"Nice to meet you, Fritz."

"Bah. You'll go away and in a week I won't remember you." He regarded his glass thoughtfully for a moment, then shook his head. "On second thought, you I will remember. Kitty." He snorted a brief laugh.

I had to smile. It heartened me that he could be amused by something, anything, and the icy wall around him seemed to chip a little.

He drained his glass, as he'd done the day before.

"Can I get you another one?"

He shook his head as he pushed back his chair. "Only one. Then I go. Goodbye."

"Where?" I blurted. "I mean, you obviously live in D.C. But what do you do? Where do you go?"

I'd said too much, crossed a line before earning his trust. He'd never talk to me again. He threw a glare over his shoulder and strode out the door, shrugging deeper into his coat.

Jack came over to pick up the empty glass and wipe down the table. "Good work," he said. "I've been here for a year and never heard him say more than one word."

I needed more than one word if I was going to get him to tell me his story. If I was going to convince him to tell his story on my show . . . But I was getting ahead of myself.

Then Luis walked through the door, and all such thoughts left my brain entirely. My giddy smile grew even giddier when I saw the same smile on him. He took me out for seafood, then back to his place, and Leo didn't break down the door on us this time.

The next morning, I drove to Bethesda and looked for Dr. Flemming.

The letterhead located him at the Magnuson Clinical Center, a research hospital that dated back to the fifties. I had to check in at the front gate of the campus, show ID and everything. I told them up front that I was visiting Flemming. Since the campus included several working hospitals, security was used to visitors. They gave me a pass and let me in.

Flemming's office was in the basement. I made my way from elevator to corridor, unsure of what I'd find. Fluorescent lighting glared off scuffed tile floors and off-white walls. I passed one plain beige door after another, marked with plastic nameplates, white letters indented into black backgrounds. At the ends of corridors, safety notices advised passersby about what they should do in case of emergency, red lines moving through floor plans helpfully directing them to the nearest exit. Wherever our taxpayer dollars were going, it wasn't for interior decorating.

The place smelled like a hospital, antiseptic and sickly. The vigilant attempts at cleanliness were never able to completely hide the illness, the decay, the fact that people here were hurting and unhappy. I didn't want to breathe too deeply.

I found Flemming's nameplate at the end of a little-used hallway, after passing several unmarked doors. I hadn't seen another person in the last five minutes. It seemed like he'd been relegated to the place where he'd be most out of the way.

I knocked on the door and listened. Somebody was inside. Leaning close to the door, I tried to make out the noises. A mechanical whirring sound, almost constant. Crunching paper. A paper shredder, working overtime.

And if *that* wasn't enough to make me suspicious . . .

I knocked louder and tried the doorknob. It was locked, requiring a magnetic key card to open. No sneaking in and catching the good doctor unawares, alas. I rattled the knob insistently. The paper shredder whined down and stopped. I waited to hear footsteps, heavy breathing, the sound of a gun being cocked, anything. Had Flemming—or whoever was in there—snuck out the back? I wondered if Bradley had a lock pick that worked on card readers.

I considered: was I ready to stoop to going through Flemming's waste bin, piecing together strips of shredded documents, to find out what his research really involved and what he was hiding?

I wasn't any good at puzzles.

Then, the footsteps I'd been waiting to hear sounded, the slap of loafers on linoleum.

"Yes?" a voice said. It was Flemming.

I put on my happiest radio voice. "Hi! Is this where we sign up for tours of the lab?"

The lock clicked and the door opened a crack. Flemming stared back at me with a startled, wide-eyed expression. "You shouldn't be here."

He turned away, leaving the door open. I considered it an invitation and stepped inside.

The place was a mess. I wanted to say like a tornado had struck, but that wasn't right. The chaos had a settled look to it, as if it had accumulated over time, like sediment through the eons. Flemming must have been the kind of person who organized by piling. Papers, file folders, books, trade journals, clipboards—that was just what I saw on a cursory glance. The stacks crowded the floor around the pair of desks, lurked in corners, and blocked the bookshelves that lined the walls. Three computers, older models, hunched on the desks. If I had expected the gleaming inhumanity of a high-tech, secret government laboratory, I was disappointed. This was more like a faculty office at a poorly funded university department. A second door in the back led to who-knew-where. Probably a collection of coats and umbrellas. It had a frosted window inset into it, but the other side was dark.

The waist-high, high-volume paper shredder lurked against the back wall. Flemming returned to it, and the stack of paper on the table next to it.

"Is everything okay, Doctor?"

"I'm just cleaning up."

"In case you have to move out, is that what you're thinking?"

"Maybe."

"So, no tours of the lab today?" He'd started shredding again, and I had to speak louder to be heard over the noise.

"Ms. Norville, this isn't a good time."

"Can I come back tomorrow?"

"No."

"You don't have any hapless interns who could show me around?"

"No. There's only me."

The scene made me think Flemming wasn't just afraid of losing his funding; he was already at the end of it.

The computers were on, but the screen savers were running. I wondered if I could casually bump the desk, and get an image to flash on-screen, maybe a word-processing file with a title across the top saying, "Here's What's Really Going on in Flemming's Lab."

I took slow steps, craning my neck to read the papers on the tops of various stacks. There were graphs, charts, statistics, and articles with titles containing long, Latinate words. Without sitting down and plowing through the documents, I wasn't going to get anything out of the mess.

I really wanted to take a look at what he was shredding.

He was keeping an eye on me, watching me over his shoulder while continuing to feed pages into the shredder.

"So, um, do you think the committee would want to take a look at what you're destroying there?"

"I don't think that's any of your concern."

"Then I guess if I asked you straight up what the real purpose of your research is, you wouldn't be inclined to tell me?"

"Do you treat everyone like they're on your show?"

I hadn't really thought of it like that, but he had a point. I shrugged noncommittally.

"I've told you a dozen times, and I've told the committee: I'm doing pure science here, information-gathering research, nothing more."

"Then what was all that you told the committee about finding the secret of vampire immortality?"

He'd run out of pages to feed into the machine. The room became still, a contrast to the grinding noise of the shredder. After a pause he said, "Potential medical application. That's all. Government-funded programs like research that leads to practical applications. That's what the committee wants to hear. I had to tell them something."

"Have you done it? Found the secret of vampire immortality?"

He shook his head, and for a moment the constantly watchful tension in his face slipped. The scientist, inquisitive and talkative, overcame the paranoid government researcher. "It doesn't seem to be physiological. It's almost as if their bodies are held in stasis at a cellular level. Cellular decay simply stops. Like it's an atomic, a quantum effect, not a biological one. It seems to be outside my immediate expertise." He gave a wry smile.

"Like magic," I said.

"What?"

"Quantum physics has always seemed like magic to me. That's all."

"Ms. Norville, I'm really quite busy, and as pleasant as your company is, I don't have time to talk with you right now."

"Then when?"

He stared. "I don't know."

"Which means never."

He nodded slightly.

I stalked out of there. The door closed behind me, and I heard the sliding of a lock.

chapter 6

The committee staffers finally put me on the docket for that afternoon. I was beginning to suffer anticipation-induced, nail-biting anxiety. I just wanted to get it over with.

Ben and I walked down the hallway to the hearing room. Fifty feet or so away, I put my hand on his arm and stopped him.

I recognized the silhouette of the man leaning against the wall outside the door. I would have noticed him in any case. He was out of place here, wearing laid-back, Midwest casual—a black T-shirt, faded jeans, biker boots—at odds with the East Coast business fashions that predominated the capital. His leather jacket hung from one hand. The building security guards let him keep his belt holster—still holding his revolver.

I knew exactly what I'd see when the man turned to face us. He was in his early thirties, with brown hair, a trimmed mustache, and a lazy frown. When he was amused, the frown turned into a smirk, which it did now. Cormac.

Somebody let Cormac in here with a gun. What happened to security? How had he snuck by them? A moment of blind panic struck. I glanced around for the nearest exit, which was behind me—I could run there in no time.

A split second of reflection reminded me that the last time I saw Cormac, I'd almost invited him into my apartment for the night. Maybe the panic wasn't entirely fear-driven. I didn't want the confusion of having Cormac around.

"What the hell?" Ben murmured, catching sight of who I stared at.

Cormac shrugged himself away from the wall, crossed his arms, and blocked the hallway in front of us. Ben matched his pose, arms crossed and face a wry mask. Ben was a couple inches shorter and a bit slimmer than the hit man, but he matched him attitude for attitude, smirk for smirk.

"What the hell are you doing here?" Cormac said to him.

With a nonchalant shrug, Ben said, "Representing my client."

The weird part of it was, Cormac was the one who referred Ben to me. By all accounts, Ben was the reason Cormac wasn't in jail. Neither of them would tell me if Cormac *ought* to be in jail.

I butted in. "What are *you* doing here?"

His eyes lit up, like this genuinely amused him. "The committee wanted someone with experience to be on hand in case things get out of control. Duke called me, hired me on as extra security. Great, isn't it?"

Security had been around the entire week. Knowing Duke and his paranoia, I had assumed they were all armed with silver bullets. That was the thing about all the "special" methods used to kill supernatural beings: a stake through the heart or a silver bullet will kill *anyone*.

I might have been mistaken. Normal security might not have changed their routine at all. Rather than arming the regular guards with silver bullets, in case the werewolf called to testify went berserk, why not call in the expert? Cormac was a professional, as he was pleased to call himself. He was a bounty hunter/hit man who specialized in lycanthropes, and brought in a few vampires on the side for fun. We'd had some run-ins. We'd even helped each other out a couple of times, once I talked him out of trying to kill me. The man scared the daylights out of me. And now he was standing here with a gun, looking at me like hunting season had just been declared open.

It seemed that Duke's paranoia knew no bounds.

"You wouldn't really shoot me, would you?" I felt my eyes go large and liquid, puppy-dog eyes. After all we'd been through, I'd like to think he wouldn't be so happy about traveling across the country for a chance to kill me.

He rolled his eyes. "Norville, if I really thought you were going to get out of control, I wouldn't have taken the job. I've seen you in action, you're okay."

I looked at Ben for a cue. His wry expression hadn't changed.

"No, I'm not going to shoot you," Cormac said with a huff. "Unless you get out of control."

"If you shoot my client, I'll sue you," Ben said, but he was smiling, like it was a joke.

"Yeah? Really?" Cormac sounded only mildly offended.

Could Ben simultaneously sue Cormac for killing me while defending Cormac against criminal charges for killing me?

I was so screwed.

Also on the docket for the day were some folklorists from Princeton who gave prepared statements about how phenomena attributed to the supernatural by primitive societies had their roots in easily explained natural occurrences. When the floor opened to questions, I was almost relieved that Duke harried them as hard as he'd harried Flemming. The senator was after everyone, it seemed. He'd cornered Flemming on vampires. He cornered the folklorists on the Bible.

"Professor, are you telling me that the Holy Scripture that tens of millions of good people in this country swear by is nothing more than a collection of folklore and old wives' tales? Is that what you're telling me? Because my constituency would respectfully disagree with you on that score."

The academics just couldn't counter that kind of argument.

Duke called one of the committee staffers over and spoke for a few moments. Then he left. The remaining senators conferred, while the audience started grumbling.

Then Senator Henderson recessed the hearing for the day. I didn't testify after all.

Anticipation produced the worst kind of anxiety. It didn't matter how nervous about a show I was beforehand, how worried I was that a guest wouldn't show, or that I'd get a call I couldn't handle, or that I was presenting a topic that would get out of control, once the show started that all went away. I was only nervous when I sat there, doing nothing, inventing terrible stories of everything that could go wrong.

The longer I sat at the hearing without doing anything, the more nervous I got. I'd be shaking by the time I finally got up there to testify.

Cormac stayed in the back, leaning by the door, where he could keep an eye on the whole room. When the committee members left out the back and the audience was breaking up to leave, he came to our row and sat beside Ben.

"Has it been going like this the whole time?"

Ben crossed his arms and leaned back. "No. They've been totally businesslike until now. I wonder if they've lost interest."

I pouted. "That doesn't matter, they still have to let me talk. I drove all the way out here, I've been sitting here for three days— could they really not let me talk?"

"Theoretically, they can do anything they want," Ben said.

Case in point: one of Senator Duke's aides, a young man looking stiff and uncomfortable in his suit, came down the aisle toward us. I guessed he was Duke's aide—the senator had returned to the room and watched us closely from the side of the benches. The aide only glanced at Ben and me, then leaned in to whisper to Cormac.

"The senator would like a word with you, if you don't mind." He waited, then, like he expected to escort the bounty hunter that very moment.

Cormac deliberately picked himself up out of the chair, taking his time, then followed the aide to see Duke. The reason for the summons became clear at once. Duke didn't even need a microphone to be heard.

"You didn't tell me you were friendly with her!"

If Cormac answered, he kept his voice subdued, and I didn't hear him.

Duke replied, "Does conflict of interest mean anything to you?"

He apparently didn't know Cormac very well. Even I knew the answer to that one.

"You're fired! You're off security! I want you out of this building!"

With as little concern as he'd shown strolling up there, Cormac walked back, wearing a wry smile.

"So sue a guy for trying to make an easy buck," he said.

Ben asked, "Could we? Sue, I mean. Is there a breach of contract?"

"No," Cormac said, shaking his head. "I took a kill fee."

Ben hesitated, then said, "Kill fee. That's funny."

"No, it's not," I said, interrupting. "That's not funny at all."

Too bad they were both grinning. I gave a long-suffering sigh.

"Come on," Ben said. "We'd better get you out of here."

Flemming left just ahead of us. He'd tucked his briefcase under his arm, ducked his head, and strode out of the room like he was late for something. His gaze flickered over us as he passed; we were all staring at him.

"Who's that guy?" Cormac nodded after him.

"Dr. Paul Flemming," I said. "He heads the Center for the Study of Paranatural Biology. The committee spent the first two days grilling him."

"He a straight shooter?"

"Not in the least. I went to his office this morning and found him shredding a stack of documents. Just try to get a clear answer from him."

"Used to working under the radar. Going crazy now with the spotlight on him. He looks the type." Ben nodded in agreement.

I said, "What I want to know is: what's he hiding?"

Cormac pursed his lips thoughtfully. "You really want to know? We could find out."

"How? I've tried talking to him. I even had him on the show."

Ben said, "I've pulled everything on him I could—military record, academic record. He's got this scientific veneer over everything he does. Talks a lot, uses big words, doesn't say anything."

"We could break into his office."

I hushed Cormac. "Are you out of your mind?" He was talking like this in a government building. I looked around, but no one seemed to have heard.

"You know I can do it," he said. "Especially since it looks like I'm not busy for the next couple days after all."

He could do it. I didn't know where he learned how to do things like breaking into radio stations and government buildings, but he could do it.

Cormac could probably learn more in a couple of hours of breaking-and-entering than I had in months of wheedling. He grinned, because my hesitation was all the confirmation he needed to go ahead with the plan.

"Officially, I'm not hearing any of this," Ben said. "Unofficially, be sure to wear gloves."

Cormac huffed. "I think I've just been insulted."

"I'm only saying." Ben squeezed past us to the door. "You kids have fun."

Cormac turned to me. "Where's this guy's office?"

"Bethesda. At the Magnuson Clinical Center, in the basement."

"Show up there at about four. Go inside the building, I'll be watching for you."

"Four—in the morning?" I said.

"Four this afternoon," Cormac said.

"You want to do this in broad daylight?"

"Do you trust me or not?"

If he really wanted to shoot me, he'd had half a dozen chances. And I still couldn't answer that question. I swallowed a lump in my throat. "Do I really have to be there?"

"You're the one who knows what you want to find."

Ben said to me once that Cormac wasn't a crusader. He wasn't a werewolf hunter because he hated werewolves, or had a religious beef against them like Duke. Rather, he liked to see how close he could walk to the edge without falling off. He didn't have any loyalty to the government, the people who hired him, or anyone else.

Cormac was only planning this to see if he could. For him, it was a challenge.

"All right. Four o'clock this afternoon." I sighed, hoping to still my pounding heart.

"Bring gloves," he said, then stood and walked away.

This was a bad, bad idea. I knew it in my gut. You didn't just go breaking into government buildings in the best of times, and this wasn't the best of times. But if I didn't show, Cormac might break into Flemming's office without me. If he learned anything juicy, he'd keep the information from me out of spite.

I had to go.

I drove my car from the alley around the corner and found Luis waiting outside Alette's town house. He casually leaned on the wrought-iron fence that divided the property from the sidewalk. By all appearances he looked like he was out enjoying the unseasonable sunshine, pausing during a stroll. I pulled up to the curb in front of him, parked, and got out.

He beamed at me. He had a generous smile and sparkling eyes. My stomach fluttered.

"You're a hard person to track down," he said brightly. "I hoped to find you outside the Senate building, but you were already gone."

I winced in apology. I hated the idea of him running all over town after me—then again, it was awfully flattering. "I gave you my cell number, right? You should have called."

He shrugged. "Chasing you is more fun."

Spoken like a true predator. He stepped toward me, looking like he was getting ready to pin me against the car. Part of me wanted to dodge, to keep the chase going for a little longer. But I let him put his hands on my hips and lean forward for a kiss. I held his arms and pulled him close.

I glanced over his shoulder at the windows of Alette's townhome, hoping no one was watching.

Coming up for air, I said, "You shouldn't be here."

He followed my gaze back to the building. "I'm not afraid of them. Is it too early for me to take you to dinner?"

"I'd love that. But—" I wanted to pull my hair out. I couldn't *be-*

lieve I was going to turn down Luis to go play *Mission: Impossible*
with Cormac. "But I can't. I set up a meeting and I can't miss it."

"Something for your show?"

"Yeah, something like that." It wasn't an outright lie. Most
everything ended up on the show eventually. But Luis looked at me
sidelong, like he knew I wasn't being entirely truthful. He could
probably smell it on me, or sense the twitchy nervousness through
my body.

He said, "The full moon is coming soon, in just a few days. Do
you know where you'll be?"

I knew the full moon was coming soon. I couldn't forget. "No. I
usually scout out a place to run, but I haven't had time."

"Come with me. There's a park about an hour outside town, a
few of us drive there. It's safe."

Full moon night with friends. It had been a long time since I had
anyone watching my back.

"I'd really like that. Thanks."

He brought my hand to his lips and kissed it. "Then it's a date."

When one lycanthrope said to another, "run with me," it was
usually a euphemism. I certainly hoped so.

"I should let you get to your meeting."

"Yes."

"Then until I catch you again." He touched my cheek, kissed me
on the corner of my mouth, lingering for just a moment as if he'd
draw the breath from me, then pulled back. He stepped away, grinning, and it was all I could do to keep from following him, step by
hypnotized step.

He turned and continued down the street, hands tucked in his
trouser pockets.

So where were all the seductive Brazilian hunks when I had time
on my hands?

I picked up a visitor's badge, found my way to the Clinical Center
building, and kept walking, like I was going to Flemming's office
again: down the hall, around the corner to the elevators. At this
point, I had no idea what I was doing. Cormac said he'd be watching for me.

It was easy for *him* to talk about sneaking into government
buildings. *He* hadn't been accosted by Men In Black on his arrival
in town. *He* wasn't having paranoid delusions about the hallway in

the Senate building being bugged so that some security goon heard all our plans and was waiting for us to make the first move and catch us red-handed.

I clung to the wall, glancing around with wide eyes, convinced someone was following me.

I scented Cormac—his light aftershave and the faint touch of gun oil that never left him—just before he stepped around a corner and grabbed my arm. I still gasped and had to swallow back a moment of panic. *This isn't danger, I'm not in danger.* He put his hand against my back and guided me forward, so that we continued down the corridor, walking side by side, like we belonged here. He'd left his guns at home this afternoon.

We stopped by the elevators. Cormac pushed the button. No gloves, I noticed. Maybe that came later.

I leaned close and whispered, "I have to ask, aren't you worried that maybe somebody heard us? That maybe the FBI or something knows we're here and is watching us? I mean, we planned this inside a Senate office building. They probably read our lips off the video surveillance." I glanced over my shoulders. First one, then the other.

"Norville, the thing you have to understand is, the government is a big bureaucracy, and the left hand doesn't know what the right is doing most of the time. The fact that it gets anything done is a miracle. Nobody's paying attention to us. But they'll start if you keep acting like you're up to something. Stop looking around."

We didn't much look like we belonged here. Cormac was still wearing jeans and a T-shirt. I was only marginally better in slacks and a knit top. But he acted like we belonged here, and that was the key. Keep quiet, don't spend too much time looking around like you needed directions, and know where you're going.

The elevator opened, we stepped inside, after letting the few occupants exit: a couple of people in white lab coats, a woman holding a flower arrangement. She was dressed about like I was. Cormac was right. No one paid attention to us.

He pushed the button to send us to the basement, carrying on like we had an appointment with Flemming. By the time the doors opened to spit us out, my stomach was doing somersaults.

"We can't walk right into his office," I whispered at him, hoping I didn't sound as panicked as I felt. "What if he's there?"

"He won't be. I sent him on a wild goose chase."

"You *what*?"

He looked down his nose at me, the long-suffering stare that made me feel like an annoying younger sibling.

"I called him from a pay phone, said I knew him from the army and had information about his research, but I had to talk to him in person. I told him I was in Frederick." He pursed his lips in a wry smile. "He'll be gone for a couple of hours."

Frederick, Maryland. Some thirty-five miles away. Close enough for Flemming to think that following the lead was worthwhile, far enough away to keep him busy for a couple of hours. Flemming would be gone all afternoon, assuming he took the bait. Considering Flemming was more paranoid than I was, I could assume he had.

That was hilarious. I was beginning to think that Cormac hadn't just done this sort of thing before. I was sure he'd done it *often*.

Now, Cormac put on gloves, made of thin black leather. I followed suit, though mine were cheap knit ones I'd dug out of my car. Not nearly as cool as his. By the time we got to the door of Flemming's office, he'd pulled something out of his pocket: a card key.

"Where'd you get that?" I hissed.

"Janitor," he said. "Don't worry, I'll give it back."

Oh. My. God.

The lock clicked; the door slipped open.

I followed Cormac into the office. He closed the door smoothly behind me.

The office was dark. Cormac made no move to turn the lights on. Enough ambient light showed through the frosted window in the door to find our way around the room. My sight adjusted quickly. Quicker than Cormac's—I headed toward the paper shredder in the corner while he was still squinting.

The bin under the shredder was empty. So was the counter next to it. All those papers, gone. Of course they were, he'd spent the morning shredding them.

I started working my way through the remaining stacks of documents piled around the desk and bookshelves. They were all medical journals, published articles, photocopies of articles, dissertations, and the like. Some of them I'd dug up on my own. At first glance, none of them offered insight into Flemming's research. It was all background and supporting documentation. The bread, not the meat at the middle of the sandwich.

Cormac went to the desk to fire up the computers. After they'd booted up, the screens coming to life, he shook his head at me. "Password protected," he said. "Hacking isn't my strong suit."

No, he was a stolen key and .45 revolver kind of guy.

I wasn't prepared for serious digging. I'd assumed—wrongly—that in all this mess I'd find *something* just lying around, even with all the shredding going on. I studied the bookshelves, hoping for a spark of inspiration. The physiology reference books butted up against the folklore encyclopedias amused me.

I sighed, on the verge of defeat. "Let's see if we can get into the next room."

The second door also had a frosted window in it, but the other side was dark. I couldn't see anything through the glass. Cormac took out his trusty stolen card key, slid it through the reader, and popped the door open. The door swung away from him. He straightened and gestured me inside.

"After you."

I felt like I was stepping into an ancient Egyptian tomb. The place was so still, I could hear my blood in my ears, and it was cold with the kind of chill that seeped through stone underground. I could see well enough in the dark. The linoleum floor continued, and like the office this room had walls of shelves. It also had lab benches, sinks and faucets, and a large metallic refrigerator that hummed softly. Also, Flemming had here a good collection of the medical equipment I'd expected to find in his laboratory: racks of test tubes, beakers, Bunsen burners, and unidentifiable tabletop appliances plugged into walls. They might have been oscillators, autoclaves, the kind of things one saw on medical dramas on television, or in the dentist's office. Again, the place had more of the atmosphere of a college biology laboratory than a clandestine government research facility.

The far wall was made of glass, maybe Plexiglas. Behind it, the room continued, divided in two by a partition. I moved closer. Both extra rooms had a cot, a washbasin, and a simple toilet in the corner. The Plexiglas had doors cut into it, with handles only on the outside. The doors had narrow slots through which objects might be handed through. Like meal trays. They were cells.

Moving quietly, Cormac stepped beside me. "This is kind of fucked up."

Yeah. "Do you smell garlic?" One of the cell doors was open. I wasn't mistaken; inside, the scent of garlic grew strong. It wasn't like someone was cooking with it, or there was a chopped-up piece of it somewhere. It came from everywhere. I went to a wall, touched it, then smelled it. "Is it in the paint? Did they put garlic in the paint?"

"Check this one out," Cormac said from the next cell over. He shined a penlight over the wall, which glittered. Sparkling like silver—tiny shavings of silver, imbedded in the paint. I kept my distance.

Two cells. One for a vampire, one for a werewolf, designed to keep each of them under control using innate allergies. They looked like they'd been empty for a while. The sheets were fresh, unwrinkled. They didn't smell occupied.

"Hands-on research, looks like," Cormac said.

Involuntary test subjects was what it looked like to me. My stomach hurt.

Cormac left the cell. "You seen enough?"

"Just a minute." I scanned the room one more time. Most of the paperwork had been moved to the office and shredded, it looked like. Nothing here but empty tables and defunct equipment.

To the side of the silver-lined cell, a clipboard hung on a nail. It looked like the kind of setup someone would use to keep medical records handy. It seemed rather forlorn and forgotten. I picked it up.

Only three sheets of paper were clipped to the board. They were charts, with a list of names. Names—jackpot. Quickly, I scanned them. First names only, maybe two dozen in all.

Halfway down the second page I read: *Fritz, 6', 210 lbs., h.s. lupus. Homo sapiens lupus.* It couldn't *possibly* be the same Fritz.

I flipped back to the first page and caught another name, one I should have noticed right away: *Leo, 5'9", 150 lbs., h.s. sanguinis.* Vampire.

Riddle wrapped in an enigma . . . I wasn't sure I wanted to know how Flemming and Leo were tied together. I was about ready to buy into any conspiracy theory that came my way.

"This is it," I murmured. "This is what I need." I took it off the clipboard and started to fold it, to take it with me.

Cormac snatched the pages out of my hand. He stalked back to the next room and the tabletop photocopier parked near the shredder. The machine was so loud, and the scanning lights so bright, I thought surely security goons would find us. Quickly, in a perfectly businesslike manner, Cormac had the three pages copied. He handed the copies to me, clipped the originals back on the board, and returned it to its nail on the wall. He closed the door to the lab and made sure it was locked.

He shut down the computers and surveyed the room. Satisfied, he nodded. "Looks good. Let's get out of here."

After making sure the door to the hallway was locked, he stripped off his gloves and shoved them in a pocket. I followed his lead, then nervously curled the papers we'd liberated.

We took one detour before leaving the building. Cormac stopped at a closet in a side corridor on the main floor. True to his word, he slipped the key card into the front tray of the janitor's cart parked there. It only took a second.

We didn't speak until we were outside, walking down the sidewalk with a dozen other anonymous pedestrians. Daylight still shone, which seemed incongruous with the darkness of Flemming's offices and our clandestine activities there.

"And that is how you break into a government office," Cormac announced at last.

"Those Watergate boys could have learned something from you, eh?"

He made a disgusted huff. "What a bunch of posers."

Supper that evening was room service at Ben's hotel. Cormac sat on the bed, plate balanced on his lap, one eye on the news channel playing on the TV, volume turned way down. He and Ben drank beers, like a couple of college buddies. Maybe that was where they'd met.

We'd debriefed Ben on our field trip. The chart from the lab lay spread across the middle of the table.

Ben nodded at it. "Is this a copy or did you just take it out of his office?"

"It's a copy."

He pursed his lips and gave a quick nod, like he was happy with that answer. "Was it worth it?"

They both looked at me. I rubbed my forehead. My brain was full. "Yeah, I think so."

Ben said, "This doesn't prove anything, you know."

"I know people on that list. At least, I think I do. If I can track them down, they'll give me someone else to talk to." I hoped.

"Will they talk to you?" Cormac said.

"I don't know."

Ben leaned back in his chair. "Kitty, I know this Flemming character is suspicious as hell. But maybe he's exactly what he appears to be: an NIH doctor, ex-army researcher, nervous because he doesn't want his funding cut. What is it you think you're going to find?"

Fritz the Nazi. I wondered what kind of questions Flemming asked him, assuming he actually talked to his subjects. I wondered if Fritz told him the stories he wouldn't tell me. What would an ex-army medical researcher want to learn from a Nazi werewolf war veteran—

"Military application," I whispered. I swallowed, trying to clear my throat, because both men had set aside their forks and beers and were staring hard at me. "He told this story about a patient in a car accident, horrible injuries, but he walked out of the hospital a week later. Flemming seemed totally . . . entranced by it. By the possibilities. He talked about it in the hearing, remember? Curing diseases, using a lycanthrope's healing abilities. Imagine having an army of soldiers who are that hard to kill."

"If he had military backing he wouldn't need to be explaining himself to Congress," Ben said.

Cormac said, "Even if he's developing military applications, is there anything wrong with that?"

"There is if he's using people," I said. "He has jail cells in his lab."

"Look, I thought you liked what this guy was doing," Ben said. "That you wanted all this out in the open. You want him shut down now?"

"Yeah, I think I do."

"Why?"

I shrugged, because it was true. I'd loved seeing this stuff in the *Washington Post*. I was enjoying the respect. But I could still smell the garlic paint in the lab. "Because he's unethical."

I hadn't finished dinner, but I couldn't eat any more. It was dark now; time to see Alette. "I won't be able to track one of these guys down until tomorrow, but I think I can find the other one tonight. I'm going to go do that."

"Need company?" Cormac said. Read: need help?

"No thanks, I'll be fine. I think." I collected the pages from Flemming's lab.

"You might want to think about making a copy of those," Ben said. "Maybe put them in a safety deposit box. Just in case."

"Or mail 'em to someone," Cormac said. "With a note to open it if anything happens to you. If you get in trouble you can use it as a threat and not be lying."

"Or you could not do it, say you did, and use it as a threat anyway." Ben said this pointedly at Cormac, weighing the statement with significance.

Cormac gave his best shit-eating grin. "Would I do something like that?"

Ben rolled his eyes. "I'm taking the Fifth on that one."

I stared. "Uh, you two go way back, don't you?"

They exchanged a look, one of those familiar, it'd take too long to explain the inside joke looks.

"You're not going to tell me, are you?"

"You're better off not knowing," Ben said.

Now I wanted to run to the nearest Internet connection and dig up what nefarious plot these two had cooked up in the distant past. At least, I *assumed* it was the distant past.

Maybe I should get a different lawyer. Except it would take too long to explain everything to a new one.

I wanted to show the list to Alette, both to find out if she knew any of the *Homo sapiens sanguinis* represented, and to rat out Leo. Yeah, I was tattling, and it hadn't felt this good since I was eight and ratted out my twelve-year-old sister's stash of R-rated videos. If she'd only let me watch with her, she could have kept the TV in her room.

I rushed into the foyer, pausing a moment to debate whether to look in the parlor or the dining room, or find Emma or Bradley and ask them where'd she be. Think, if I were the head vampire, where would I be?

A touch brushed my shoulder. I gasped and turned, shock frying my nerves. Leo stood behind me, calmly, as if he'd been there all evening, watching the scenery. I could have sworn he hadn't been in the foyer when I entered the house. But I hadn't sensed him approach, I hadn't seen him, smelled him, or heard him.

"Hello, there," he said lightly. "Can I help you with something?"

I wanted to punch him. "What the hell is your problem?"

"You're so easy to rile up, can you blame a man for trying?"

"Yes, yes, I can."

"Ah. Well, then." He strolled, circling around me, blocking the exits.

He was teasing me. That was all. Provoking me, like he said. I took a deep breath, determined to calm down.

"I have a question for you," I said, trying to sound bright and unperturbed. "What do you know about Dr. Flemming?"

He shrugged. "Government researcher. What would you like me to know?"

"I've spoken with him. Your name came up." Both were true, in themselves.

"Really? What did he say about me?"

"Nothing. He's closemouthed. That's why I'm asking you."

"And I'm openmouthed, am I?" He smiled to show teeth and fang. Then his expression softened. "I might have spoken with him a time or two."

"About what?"

"This and that. About being a vampire. I was—how would you call it?—a native informant." He started pacing, hands in his trouser pockets, gaze downturned. "I'll give him this much, he knows his subject. At least, he knows enough to know where to find us, if he wants to. Then, would you believe he simply asks nicely? He proves how much he knows, and you don't feel bad about answering his questions. You become just another data point. There's nothing more to it."

I had a hard time picturing Flemming traveling the streets, finding his way to a place like the Crescent, notepad and tape recorder in hand, and asking nicely.

"What did you tell him? What's it like being a vampire?"

He looked away for a moment, his gaze distant and thoughtful. It seemed he did have another personality buried in there somewhere.

"Time almost stands still," he said. "The world seems to freeze for a moment. You're able to study every little piece of it. All the microscopic points become clear. And you move through this world like a lion on the veldt. You realize everything is yours for the taking. All you have to do is reach out and grab hold of anything you like. Anyone you like."

In the next beat of time he stood beside me. Brushing my hair aside, he breathed against my neck, a faint, warm sigh. No teeth, no threat, only a caress. I shivered, but didn't move away from him. For some reason, I didn't move away.

"Is that what you expected to hear?" he said.

I turned and glared. But he hadn't done anything. They were only words.

I knew better than anyone what a person could do with mere words.

"Is that what being a vampire is all about?" I said. "Is that why you're such an arrogant prick?"

He laughed. "An arrogant prick? Really? I suppose that's how it must appear to the rest of you. But to us, you're little more than a bit of hair floating on the breeze. We don't care what you think."

"Not all vampires are like that. I've met some who are reasonable human beings." One or two. Maybe. "That's all Flemming's doing? Collecting stories? Gathering true-life accounts?"

"I'm sure that's not *all* he's doing. He's a medical doctor, isn't he? He's probably doing some blood tests on the side. I know I would." He licked his lips.

"What if I told you Flemming has a lab with holding cells? One of them has garlic in the paint, like it was meant to subdue a vampire. What if it looked like he was holding test subjects against their wills?"

His gaze had been wandering, studying the room as if he were a fan of interior design, unconcerned. Now, he focused on me, suddenly interested. I almost took a step back. Though if I'd taken one step, I might have gone ahead and run all the way out of the room. Leo's interest was not something I wanted.

"That would be extremely dangerous and foolish of him if he had done so," he said. "Even if he could trap a vampire, he could never again release it—and survive." His lips parted and he showed his teeth, the sharp points of his fangs.

"Unless he's *really* good with a stake," I said.

"In-*deed*." That British accent could make one word take on a world of meaning.

"Ah, Kitty, you've returned." Alette, queen of her domain, strode into the foyer, smartly dressed and elegant as always, looking like she was on her way from one task to another. She acknowledged Leo with a nod and stopped before me to regard me with that prim nod that made me feel like I'd somehow fallen short of her standards, and that I would always fall short. "I expected you back some time ago. I hope your tardiness means you've had a productive afternoon?"

This was where I ponied up that information I promised her. The only question was, how much did I tell her? "I've learned that Flemming has holding cells for vampires and werewolves in his lab. I think he's been keeping test subjects against their wills."

"By test subjects you mean vampires and lycanthropes? Do you know how he could possibly hold such beings against their wills?" Her disbelief was plain in her tone.

"I don't know, but he's done it," I said, frustrated. "Here, look at this. He's been talking to people." I showed her the list, being sure to point out Leo's name on the first page.

Alette looked at him. "You've been speaking with Flemming?"

I wanted Leo to squirm like a kid who'd been caught lying. I wanted him to blush, look abashed, duck his gaze, something. He stood quietly and completely unruffled.

"Yes," he said. "I have. The good doctor's been going around collecting folktales. I talked to him on the assumption that such conversations work both ways. I've been a bit of a double agent, if you like." He flashed his devil-may-care smile.

"You didn't see fit to tell me of this?" Alette said.

"Because I didn't learn anything. Which leads me to think he isn't hiding anything." He said this pointedly to me. "He really is just an earnest scientist in danger of losing his funding."

Why didn't I buy that?

Alette did. She gave a satisfied nod and handed the pages back to me. "Have those cells been recently occupied?"

"I couldn't tell," I said. I hadn't smelled anything. "I don't think so."

"We'll continue to watch Flemming. Your vigilance should be commended, Kitty. But don't let it become paranoia."

Leo said to Alette, "My dear, you seem to be in the middle of some chore. Might I be of service to you?"

"Always, Leo." He offered her his arm, and she took the crook of his elbow. She gave me one last glance over her shoulder as they left the foyer.

I had no way of knowing who to believe. I wanted to think well of Alette, and if she trusted Leo I shouldn't question it. She'd known him longer than I had. Maybe Flemming really was harmless, and all the cloak-and-dagger shenanigans with Cormac had been a waste of time. I felt like I was working my way through a maze. I *hated* mazes.

This town was getting to me.

chapter 7

Thursday was exploitative celebrity day at the hearings.

There was me, of course. I'd been told I *might* testify today, *if* the committee had time. Ben told me not to hold my breath. I was thinking of starting a pool among the press corps to guess when I'd actually be called up.

The good senators had called in others who'd made themselves famous based on the stuff of magic and the supernatural, and the others arrived today.

Waiting in the hallway outside the hearing room, a swarm of people collected around a lone figure, a slick-looking man in his thirties who smiled amiably. At first I thought the people surrounding him were reporters, but then the man took one of the notepads, signed his name on it, and handed it back. I recognized him, then: that easygoing smile, the fashionably trimmed sandy hair, the clean features that made him instantly likable and trustworthy. Jeffrey Miles, professional psychic and channeler.

He was best known on the daytime talk show circuit, where he impressed the hosts and awed the audiences with his intimate knowledge of their friends and relatives who had "passed on." He claimed to be able to communicate with the "other side," to deliver messages and reassurances from the dead, and to reveal information that only the deceased or the audience member could have known. Classic cold readings. He appealed to the angels and Precious Moments crowd.

I leaned on the wall and smirked at the proceedings. Someone in my position—werewolf, witness to the supernatural—might have been inclined to believe in his awesome powers. Except I didn't. It was manipulative bunk, and it was people like him who made it difficult for the rest of the world to believe in people like me.

The session was set to begin, and it took security guards to clear out Miles's admirers. His geniality didn't disappear with the fans; it wasn't some mask he put on for them. He shook his head, amused, straightening his blazer as he headed toward the door.

He walked right by me without a second glance, and was through the doorway before he stopped, backed up, and turned to look at me.

"You must be Kitty Norville," he said.

"And you're Jeffrey Miles." I crossed my arms.

"You know—" He scratched his head and seemed suddenly uncomfortable. "I have a confession. I hate to admit it, but I was one of those people who thought it was all a gimmick. Your show, the werewolf thing. But you really are a werewolf, and I have this urge to apologize for doubting."

I stared, dumbfounded and speechless for maybe the third time in my entire life. The polite, socialized part of my brain scrambled to graciously accept his apology. The sarcastic part clamped down on that right away.

He was human, straight up as far as I could see, with nothing in the way of heightened senses that a lycanthrope had. I really had to know, "How can you tell?"

"Your aura is very wild. Very animal. I only see that with lycanthropes."

The sarcastic part of my brain started beating itself against a figurative brick wall to stifle the laughter.

"Well, thanks for the vote of confidence," I said. "I'm sorry I can't return it."

"Too many documented frauds?"

"Something like that."

He closed his eyes for a moment and visibly relaxed, his shoulders sagging a bit, his face going slack, like he had fallen asleep right there on his feet. I watched, intrigued. Looked like I was going to get a free show.

Then he said, "Theodore Joseph holds a strong place in your thoughts."

I grit my teeth to make sure my mouth stayed closed. He might as well have punched me in the gut. I looked away before my eyes had a chance to tear up, the way they always did when I was reminded of T.J. at an unexpected moment.

My mind raced. He could have done research. He'd have known in advance that I was going to be here, he could have looked at the police record, the one where I named T.J., there were records that Miles could have easily found—

He continued. "He says—there's nothing to forgive. Stop asking for forgiveness."

That wasn't recorded anywhere. The police didn't know T.J. was dead. I hadn't told them that part.

I hadn't ever asked T.J. for forgiveness. Not out loud—I mean, how could I? He was dead. And it was my fault he was dead. I was so, so sorry, and maybe all these weeks I'd just wanted to say that. I wished I'd had a chance to tell him that. I wished that he were here for me to tell him.

And there was Jeffrey Miles, watching me with a quiet, sympathetic look in his eyes, wearing a grim smile.

I scrubbed my eyes with the heels of my hands, but it didn't work. Tears fell.

"I'm sorry," he said, handing me a tissue. He had it ready, like people burst into tears in front of him all the time. "This isn't the time or place for this."

"No, it's okay. I asked for it, didn't I?" I chuckled halfheartedly. "I can almost hear him sometimes. You're saying it's real?" Jeffrey Miles was for real. I felt like a jackass.

"I think he's been watching out for you. Not a ghost, nothing so strong as that. But he's interested."

"Where—where is he?"

"Even I don't know that. They come to me. I can't find them. Who was he?"

"Don't you know? I thought you were psychic."

"He's not a forthcoming presence."

"Got that right. T.J. My best friend. I got him killed."

"I don't think he sees it that way."

And I knew he was right. Somehow, that nagging little voice that I had mistaken for my conscience told me that it wasn't my fault. It had been there the whole time, telling me I was okay, to stop being silly. I hadn't believed it. T.J. had wanted that last fight with Carl, not just to defend me, but because the fight between them had been brewing for months. He'd wanted to win, but that hadn't happened. *Stop asking for forgiveness.*

After that, I wasn't sure I was ready to sit in that room for two hours, but the security guards were about to close the doors, and Jeffrey urged me inside.

Ben was already in place in the back row, his laptop open on his lap, typing away at something that may or may not have had anything to do with the hearings. I sat with him, and Jeffrey joined us.

"You okay?" Ben whispered. I nodded, waving him off.

Everyone looked back at a commotion brewing by the doors. The security guy seemed to be talking to someone who wanted in. After a moment, he opened the door and let in something of an entourage: a middle-aged man with short-cropped, steely hair, wearing a dark turtleneck and slacks, flanked by a couple of hefty bodyguard types.

All my hair stood on end and a shiver passed along my spine. Those two were werewolves, big and scary, and there was something about the way they followed the first one that was unnatural. Or un-supernatural. It was like they walked too close to him, or watched him too closely. Like Labrador retrievers with separation anxiety. Not wolf-like at all.

"Who's he?" I murmured.

Jeffrey leaned over. "That's Elijah Smith. He's a self-styled faith healer to the supernatural."

My blood chilled and the gooseflesh thickened. My shoulders stiffened, and I swallowed back a wolf-inspired growl. "I know him. I know of him. We had an encounter, sort of."

"You didn't try to join his church, did you?"

"No. This was indirectly. I met someone who tried to leave his church. It didn't turn out well." In the end, she'd killed herself. The vampire had staked herself to get away from him.

As exploitative celebrities went, Smith was in a class by himself. Jeffrey and I were little more than entertainers, to some extent. Our hearts may have been in the right places, wanting to help people, but we were also sort of freak shows. Smith, on the other hand, professed to save people.

He called his organization the Church of the Pure Faith. Preaching the motto "Pure faith will set you free," he claimed to be able to cure vampires and lycanthropes of their conditions through his style of old-fashioned, laying-on of hands faith healing.

The so-called church had more in common with a cult. Once healed, his followers never left. They traveled with him in a caravan that crisscrossed the country, collecting true believers who were utterly loyal, like the two werewolves seemed to be. My informant had said he really could cure them: vampires could walk in sunlight, werewolves never suffered the Change. But only if they stayed with him forever. For some, the loss of freedom might not have been too high a price to pay. The trouble was, Smith didn't tell them what the price was before they signed up.

What could he tell the committee? What was the point of having *him* here?

"How the hell did they manage to get him to testify?" As far as I knew, the few police who'd tried to investigate the church hadn't been able to touch him. Nothing persuaded Smith to leave his compound, and his followers defended him like an army. Jeffrey shook his head.

Ben piped in. "Rumor has it Duke offered his church official recognition and tax-exempt status. Then he can start collecting monetary donations."

"Can Duke do that?"

Ben said, "It really only takes an application with the IRS, but Smith may not know that. Maybe Duke can expedite the application."

Didn't that just beat all?

Jeffrey watched Smith distantly, lips pursed. After a moment he said, "I don't like him. He's dark. I don't think he's human."

I looked sharply at him. "Vampire?"

"No, I don't think so. This is different. Thicker. Would it be too melodramatic to say he looks evil?"

I was right there with him. My favorite theory about Smith at the moment was that he was some kind of spiritual vampire. Rather than feeding on blood, he consumed people's devotion, awe, and worship. He didn't cure his followers; rather, he had the power to suppress their weaknesses, the vulnerability to sunlight, the need to shape-shift. My acquaintance, a vampire named Estelle, thought she was cured, but when she left Smith's caravan, the condition returned. She burned in sunlight again. He was powerful enough to control vampires and lycanthropes, and sinister enough to use them.

I didn't know enough to guess what he was, especially if Jeffrey was right and he wasn't human.

Jeffrey testified first. He flashed me a smile and a thumbs-up before he went to the table. If he had a lawyer with him, he kept the attorney hidden. He had a prepared statement, speaking carefully and nonthreateningly about being open to strangeness in the world, to mysteries we didn't understand and might possibly fear. He stated a belief that the universe was basically good, and if we approached each new encounter with the unknown with that attitude, we would be rewarded with knowledge and understanding. It sounded a little metaphysical and New-Agey for my tastes. He'd obviously never encountered a hungry werewolf in the middle of the night. Wasn't much knowledge and understanding at the end of that meeting.

Either the television celebrity garnered more respect from the panel of senators, or Jeffrey did a better job of winning them over with his charisma and amiability. He treated them like a talk show audience, engaging them, telling jokes.

He did what Duke probably brought him here to do, which was to testify to the existence of the supernatural, at least his own little branch of it. To think, a couple months ago anyone with a rational thought in his head would have written Jeffrey off as a New Age kook at best, or a manipulative charlatan at worst. But in this context, this new frame of reference, where vampires were real, the U.S. Congress had to take him seriously. I wondered if he felt at all smug or vindicated by the turn of events, the change in attitude. He just looked calm.

I leaned forward when Elijah Smith took the stand.

Smith never left his caravan. People who wanted to join him were screened before they were let inside to meet him. He'd never spoken publicly, until now. Finally, I got to see him in the flesh.

Whatever Jeffrey saw in him that indicated he wasn't human, I didn't see it. He moved with confidence, holding himself with a somber poise. His werewolf bodyguards stayed behind, seated in the first row among the audience. They kept their gazes focused on him, refusing to let him out of their sights.

"Heaven's Gate," Ben whispered to me. I looked at him, raising my eyebrow to invite him to explain. He said, "The suicide cult. He's got that suicidal calm thing going. Jim Jones, David Koresh, you know?"

That didn't reassure me.

He didn't have a statement, so the committee launched right in to basic questions: where did he reside, what was his profession. Smith claimed to be based in California. I'd never been able to trace him to any permanent place of residence. His caravan was nomadic. Maybe he kept a post office box somewhere.

As to profession, he answered, "Spiritual adviser."

Which was about as surreal as when Jeffrey had said "communications facilitator." For some reason no one felt they could come before the Senate and say he was a professional medium or a faith healer.

Duke said, "I understand that you serve as a spiritual adviser to a specific group of people. Could you describe them?"

"They're vampires and lycanthropes, Senator." He spoke coolly, with maybe a hint of amusement.

I'd heard him before, from a distance over a tenuous phone connection. Even then his voice had had a haunted quality, hypnotic. He drew listeners to him, like any good preacher could. There was something else, though, in the way his voice hinted at mysteries to be revealed, at the dark secrets he would tell.

In person, that sense was doubled, or more. I leaned forward, head cocked, determined to hear every word. I wished the room's ambient noises—papers rustling, people coughing—would stop.

"And how do you advise them, Reverend Smith?" Duke said. This was the most respectful Duke had been of any of the witnesses. Did he actually think Smith was a good Christian preacher?

"I help them find their way to the cure."

Henderson spoke next. "Earlier this week, Dr. Flemming testified that he'd had some difficulty discovering a cure. Are you saying you've had better luck than medical science?"

"Senator, these states of being cannot be fully explained by medical science. They have a spiritual dimension to them, and the cures lie in the spiritual realm."

That was what I'd always thought. I wondered if it would be rude of me to move chairs so I was sitting closer. I didn't want to miss anything Smith had to say.

"I'm not sure I understand you."

Senator Duke turned to his colleague. "He's saying what I've been telling you, these people are cursed, possessed, and they need to be exorcized."

"We're not living in the Dark Ages, Senator Duke." Henderson returned to his witness. "Reverend Smith?"

He said, "I believe that those afflicted may look within to purge themselves of the taint of their . . . diseases."

"Through prayer," Duke prompted.

"In a manner of speaking, yes."

Prayer, yeah. That was all I had to do, it sounded so simple. I wanted to talk to him, to learn from him, because I'd struggled all this time to find some kind of peace in this life but he made it sound so simple—

"Kitty!"

My brain rattled. I blinked, disoriented. Jeffrey was shaking my arm. He'd hissed into my ear loud enough that the people in front of us looked back.

"What? What's wrong? What happened?"

Ben was staring at me, too. "You looked like a cliché there for a minute. I think you were even drooling."

"I was *not*."

But both men watched me closely, worriedly. Despite his flippant remark, Ben's brow was furrowed. Had I fainted? Passed out? I'd just been listening to the testimony, to Smith—

That steady, haunting voice filled the room. I could feel it against my heart.

"Oh, my God," I murmured. "Is it just me? You guys don't feel it—"

Jeffrey shook his head. "Not like that, but I can see it. It's like he's on fire. It started when he spoke."

Something about his voice sounded so reasonable, so pure. It hardly mattered what he said, because what I heard was, *Here is someone I can trust.*

I put my hands against my temples, quelling the headache I suspected I was developing. "This is seriously twisted."

"I think I understand his church a little better," Jeffrey said.

"No doubt." The cure was only the start of his power, it seemed. He could draw vampires and werewolves to him just by speaking. He hardly needed to cure them, if all he wanted was a flock of devoted followers.

If he had that power over me across the room, how was I going to get close enough to learn more about him? Did I dare bring him onto the show for an interview, and broadcast his voice across the country?

Then we were done for another day. The hearing adjourned.

Smith immediately came down the aisle between the two sets of chairs, his escort trailing him devotedly. I watched him the way a wolf watches a hunter approaching with a rifle: head down, eyes glaring, lips ready to snarl a challenge if the intruder comes too close. If Jeffrey and Ben hadn't been there, I might have followed along after him, as eager and devoted as his pets.

I wasn't anybody's pet.

As he passed by, he caught my gaze. For a half a second, his lips twitched a smile—a cold smile—and his gaze held triumph.

He knew he'd gotten to me.

Some vampires and werewolves liked to say they were top of the food chain. Stronger than mortal humans, able to hunt mortal humans.

But we might have found the thing that could top us. I had to find out what he was. If I didn't risk getting closer to him, I'd never learn.

I scrambled past Jeffrey to get to the aisle. I was too late to intercept him, but maybe I could catch up.

Ben called after me, "Kitty, what are you—"

I'd only taken a couple steps toward Smith when the werewolves turned on me. Their lips pulled back in grimaces, their shoulders tensed, bunching up as if they were preparing to cock their arms for a punch. A couple of werewolves, getting ready to rumble. A shot of panic charged through me; I couldn't take these guys and my Wolf knew it. I had to work to stand there and not look away. Not cringe and cower. *Please don't beat me up . . .*

I looked past them to Smith, who had turned to see what the disturbance was.

"Hi, Reverend Smith? I'm Kitty Norville from the talk show *The Midnight Hour*. I was wondering, could I ask you a few questions? I think my audience would be very interested in learning more about you. Maybe you could come on the show."

He stared at me for a long time, and my heart beat faster and faster, in anticipation of what he might say, and what his words would do to me. Fight or flight. I should run. I should get out of here.

"If you come to me as a supplicant, I will answer all your questions." He smiled a thin, knowing smile.

They were true words; I knew they were. If I came to him, gave myself to him, I would have no more questions—at least, no will to ask them. But I couldn't. I couldn't go to him, I couldn't do it, because I'd lose myself, and I'd fought too hard to claim myself. My own two feet stood on the floor, and I was anchored to them, and I would not let his gaze swallow me.

I looked after him as he walked away, and the retreating bodyguards blocked my view of him.

Something touched my shoulder. I gasped and pulled back.

It was Jeffrey, forehead creased with concern. "That wasn't the smartest thing you could have done."

I'd been accused of a lot of things, but flights of genius wasn't one of them, so I couldn't argue.

We had to clear the room for the next set of hearings, a different committee, a different subject. The wheels of government rolled on, no matter what little paradigm shifts were going on in my head. I lingered outside in the hallway, arms crossed, shoulders hunched in and angry.

"Can we sue him?" I said to Ben. "There's got to be something we can sue him for."

He shrugged. "I don't know. I'll look into it. I'm always game for a frivolous lawsuit."

"It's not frivolous! There's something seriously creepy about that guy. We have to figure out what he's really doing with that church of his, because I know it's just horrible. It has to be."

"If he hasn't broken any laws, then there probably isn't anything we can do."

How could we know if he'd broken any laws if we didn't even know what he was really doing? Really, he was just inviting people to an old-fashioned revival meeting, and if they wanted to stay with him, well, that was their choice, right?

I had to find out what he was. "Jeffrey, if Smith isn't human, what is he?"

"I was hoping you'd have a guess," Jeffrey said.

I humphed. "Believe it or not, you probably have more experience with that kind of stuff than I do. I mean, you can *see* that he isn't right. If we find out where he's camped, take a look, maybe you'd see . . . I don't know. *Something.*"

"I'm not sure I'm willing to get close enough to try that. He's dangerous, Kitty. I can see that much about him."

"Ben?"

"Don't look at me. Somebody's got to stay behind to bail your ass out of jail when things go wrong."

That vote of confidence was staggering.

Ben said, "If you're about to do something prosecutable, I don't want to know about it until afterward. I'll see you tomorrow." He started off down the hallway, waving over his shoulder.

Jeffrey watched him go. "He's your lawyer, huh? He's . . ."

"Brusque?" I said.

"I was going to say honest. He's got a good aura."

Well, that was something, I supposed. I apparently had an honest lawyer.

I sighed. "Since I don't know where Smith's caravan is, the whole plan to go looking for him is moot anyway."

I couldn't really see me climbing into a cab, flashing a fifty at the driver, and saying, "Follow that man!" I started to ask Jeffrey if he would do an interview on the show, when Roger Stockton stepped around from behind us, where he'd been lurking, eavesdropping, and who knew what else. He still had the camera, but at least he held it down and not pointed at me.

"I know where Smith is camped," the reporter said. "And I know he isn't human."

"Then what is he?" I said, once I'd regained control of my jaw. "And how do you know?" I'd tried to catch a scent off him, but his bodyguards stayed close, and I couldn't get past their smells, the overpowering scent of werewolf that set my instincts on edge.

"I'll tell you when we get out there."

"So I just get in your car and let you drive me to God knows where?"

"Look, we all want the same thing here. We all know Smith isn't curing anyone, not for real anyway, and he's got some kind of funky voodoo—I saw what he did to you back there. We all want to expose him, and we all know that he's dangerous. This way none of us has to go it alone and we all get to break the story together."

"Are you sure you're not just after some prime Kitty Norville footage for sweeps week?"

"I wouldn't *mind* that—"

I turned away with a dismissive sigh.

"He's telling the truth, Kitty. He knows," Jeffrey said. Jeffrey, who claimed to see honesty radiating off a man.

I had a guy with second sight and a reporter from *Uncharted World* for backup. A girl could do worse, I supposed. I looked around to see if Cormac was lurking somewhere. Now *there* was backup, assuming he kept his guns pointed in someone else's direction. But wouldn't you know it, the one time I might want him around, he'd disappeared. He hadn't been near the hearings since Duke fired him.

I said to Roger, "We find the caravan, we check it out. Then what?"

"Then, we see. Sound good?"

"No. If you know what he is then you should know what he's doing, and what we should do about him."

"I can't do it alone," Roger said. "Are you in?"

Jeffrey nodded. He seemed eager, even, as if this were just another enlightening experience.

I had to be out of my mind.

Stockton's smugness at knowing something I didn't was stifling. I was glad Jeffrey had agreed to come along. He sat in the backseat, regarding both of us with an amused smile.

I had no idea what we were going to do when we got there. If anything I'd heard about the caravan was true, shutting it down would take the National Guard.

Maybe between Jeffrey's intuition and Stockton's camera, we could collect enough evidence to bring about some kind of criminal prosecution. It was a modest enough goal.

It was all I could hope for. We weren't exactly the Ghostbusters.

Around sunset, we left tract housing and suburbs and entered countryside, driving along a two-lane state highway. The light was failing, streaking the sky shades of orange and lighting up the clouds. The land seemed dark, shadowy. The fields around us might have been fallow farmland, or rolling pastures. Fences bounded them by the roadside, but beyond that, trees surrounded them. Trees everywhere, rows of old growth oak or elm, windbreaks planted a hundred or two hundred years ago. The road curved from one valley into the next, making it impossible to see what lay ahead.

I was surprised, then, when we rounded a turn skirting yet another gently rolling hill, and Stockton put on the brakes. The seat belt caught me. He pulled onto the shoulder, to where we could look over the rail fence.

Ahead, occupying the back half of a wide swath of pasture, was what looked like the back lot of a down-on-its-luck traveling circus. Maybe two-dozen old-fashioned campers hitched to beat-up pickup trucks, a few RVs, Airstreams and Winnebagos, converted vans and buses, parked in a rough circle, like pioneer wagons. Another dozen cars were scattered among them. In the center, like the hub of a wheel, the top of a large canvas tent was visible. Around the perimeter, a few figures, indistinct forms in the twilight, walked around wire fencing that enclosed the settlement. Lights flooded the area inside: lights from the campers, the trucks, floodlights inside the tent. Even a hundred yards away I could hear the generators. The place was an event, a carnival without a town to go with it, a circle of light in an otherwise shadowed world.

A dirt road, little more than two tracks worn into the soil, led from the highway, through an open gate, to Smith's caravan. A couple of other cars were parked near the gate, their motors still running.

Stockton rolled down his window and leaned out, aiming his camera at the encampment.

"How did you find out it was here?" I asked.

"One of the guys at *Uncharted World*'s been following it. Caught up with it in DeKalb, Illinois, a couple weeks ago and tracked it here."

"Then why isn't he out here filming?"

"Because two nights ago a car with no plates forced him off the road and into a dry creek bed. He's in the hospital with four broken ribs and a smashed shoulder."

"Shit." I shook my head. "Do you see anything?" I said to the backseat. "I mean, you know. *See* anything?"

"At this distance, the floodlights muddy everything up," Jeffrey said. Then he pointed to one of the other cars, that had just turned its headlights off and shut off its engine. "Although that guy's a lycanthrope."

A man—young by his gangly figure and the way he slouched—got out, closed the door softly, and started walking along the dirt track to the caravan site.

Quickly I undid the seat belt and scrambled out of the car.

"Kitty!" Jeffrey called after me, which I ignored.

I trotted after the guy and was about to call out to get him to stop, but he heard me, or smelled me, because he turned and backed away, shoulders tense, like a wolf with hackles.

"Who are you?" he said sharply.

"My name's Kitty." I stayed put, kept my gaze turned down, my shoulders relaxed. He could smell me; he knew what I was. "I'm just curious. Why are you here?"

He let his guard down the barest notch, shrugging. "I've heard there's a guy here who can help."

"Help what?" I said, like I was ignorant or something.

He glared, his eyes narrowing, suspicious. "Help *this*. Help me be normal again."

"Ah. I'd heard the same thing."

"Then you know why I'm here."

"I've also heard that he's a fraud. That his church is really a cult. That he brainwashes people so they'll stay with him. Nobody knows what goes on in there."

"Yeah, I'd heard that, too." He hugged himself like he'd suddenly become cold.

"And you're still willing to go there?"

"What choice do I have?"

"Is it really so bad? So bad that you'd give up your freedom, your identity? Assuming the rumors are true."

"I haven't been able to hold a job for more than two weeks since it happened. I keep losing my temper. I can't—I'm not very good at controlling it."

"I'm sorry. You don't have a pack, do you?" He shook his head. He hadn't had anyone teach him how to control it.

He looked over my shoulder suddenly. Jeffrey and Roger had come up behind me. The young man took a couple steps back, then turned and ran, through the gate and toward the caravan.

"Wait!" When he didn't stop, I wasn't surprised. "Damn."

"That kid's scared to death," Jeffrey said.

"But not of *me*."

"Yeah, a little. Also of his own shadow, I think. It's funny to think of a werewolf being scared of anything."

"Oh, you'd be surprised. A lot of us spend most of our time being afraid."

"Let's go," Stockton said, gesturing toward the trees at the edges of the field, around to the side of the caravan, closer to it but still in shadow. "Before his flunkies figure out we're not here for the show."

I tipped my face up, turning my nose to the air, half closing my eyes to keep out distractions. Then I shook my head. "Let's go to the other side. It's downwind."

We walked along the road to a place where we were mostly out of sight of the main entrance to the caravan, then climbed over the fence. Quickly we made our way to the trees, following them along the edge of the pasture down a gentle slope, toward the caravan. As we approached, the floodlights grew brighter, and the area around the encampment grew darker. For all it appeared like a carnival lot, the place was quiet. No talking, no voices, no sounds of life, like pots and pans clanking together while dinner was being prepared. By all accounts, dozens of people were living there, but I couldn't make out any obvious signs of life.

Except for the smell: I sensed a kind of ripe, college dorm-room smell, of too many people living in close proximity, and not enough housekeepers. I wrinkled my nose.

"There." Stockton pointed to a gap in the trailers. Temporary wire fencing still enclosed the area, but here was a place where we might catch a glimpse of something interesting. A spot where a corner of the main tent was staked to the ground was visible.

When a pair of burly-looking men—Smith's bodyguards from earlier today—walked past, we kept very still. They were patrolling, and they didn't stop.

His back against a tree, Stockton settled down to wait, focusing his camera on the gap looking into the caravan. Jeffrey took the next tree over as his prop. I stayed by Stockton, watching what he watched.

The ground was damp, and I was getting damp sitting on it. The air was cold, getting colder. My breath fogged. Jeffrey hugged his jacket tighter around him. I wondered how long we could possibly sit here. Something had to happen soon. The pilgrims, including that young guy, had gathered at Smith's gate. He wouldn't leave them waiting.

I moved next to Jeffrey and whispered, "Can you contact vampires who have, you know, moved on?" I was thinking of Estelle. I was thinking she might be here and could tell us something.

"I never have. That is—none of them have ever tried to contact me. I hate to ask it, but do they even have souls?"

This came up on the show all the time, and my gut reaction said yes. How could someone like Alette *not* have a soul? But what was a soul, really? I didn't know.

I didn't answer, and he shook his head. "I'm not sensing anything like that. This whole space feels numb. Asleep, almost."

Stockton sat forward suddenly and raised his camera. "Here he comes. There."

Jeffrey and I crept over to join him. Squinting, I looked through the gap.

Smith walked past it. I only saw him for a second. But Stockton muttered, with some satisfaction, "Ha, I got you. If only I could get that on film, damn you."

I hadn't seen him do anything. He looked just like he had at the hearing, conservatively dressed, his manner calm. He moved across my field of vision, that was all.

Stockton was insane, suffering from some kind of delusion. And I'd fallen for it.

Before I had a chance to call him on it, he pulled something over his head: a locket on a chain that he'd kept hidden under his shirt.

Handing it to me, he said, "Put that on. The next time he walks by, tell me what you see."

It seemed like a simple piece of jewelry, not particularly impressive. The metal wasn't silver. Pewter, maybe. It felt heavy. The locket was a square, an inch or so on both sides, and cast with patterns of Celtic knotwork, worn with age.

I fingered the latch. "What is it?"

"Don't open it," he said. "It's got a little bit of this and that in it. Four-leaf clover, a bit of rowan. Cold iron."

Some kind of folk magic, then. Now, was it the kind of folk magic that worked, or the kind that was little more than a placebo against the nameless fears of the dark?

I put the chain over my head.

I had to give Stockton credit for being more patient than I was. He was used to waiting for his stories, and he was good at it. We had no guarantee that Smith would pass within our view again. But he did.

And he *glowed*. His skin wasn't skin anymore. It looked almost white, shimmering like mother-of-pearl. At first I thought he'd gone bald as well, but his hair had turned pale, almost translucent. He looked completely different, but I knew it was him, because he wore the same clothes, and had that same meticulous bearing. For just a moment I saw his eyes, and they were far too large, and dark as night, dark enough to fall into and never climb out again.

I almost shrieked, but Stockton grabbed my arm and pinched me to keep me quiet. Then, Smith was out of sight again. My eyes remained frozen wide open.

"Holy shit, he's an alien!" I hissed.

"Um, no." Stockton donned a not very convincing Irish brogue. "In the Old Country they called them the Fair Folk, the Gentry, the Good People, the Hill Folk—"

"He's a *fairy*?" I couldn't decide which was more completely outrageous.

"Don't say that word, he'll hear you. Give that back." He held his hand out for the pendant. Reluctantly, I returned it. "Nobody was ever able to get close enough to confirm any suspicions until he came to testify. I'm lucky I was in the right place at the right time to see him."

I had to work to keep my voice a whisper. "You can't be serious. That's—it's all stories, folklore—"

"Pot calling the kettle black, anyone?"

Just when I thought I'd heard everything, just when I thought the last mystery had been revealed and that I couldn't be shocked anymore, something like this came along. I'd never be able to blow off another story as long as I lived. Flying monkeys? Oh, yeah, I could believe. Stockton was right. I should have known better.

Maybe I should chase a few more rainbows looking for pots of gold.

"How did you know?" I said to Stockton.

"I didn't," he said. "My grandmother gave me the locket. For protection, she said. And, well, I couldn't say no to Grandma. She sets out milk for the brownies, even in the Boston suburbs. What can I say, I believed her. But I didn't know Smith was one of them until he walked into the room this afternoon. I have to tell you, I didn't expect the charm to work like *that*."

Jeffrey said, "I didn't know what I was looking at. I can't see through the disguise, but I can see the disguise. Interesting." He sounded far too academic about it.

Theoretically, having an answer to one question—what was he?—should have brought us closer to answering other questions. Like, what was he doing with his church? Why was he drawing vampires and lycanthropes to him, and what was he doing with them? Why would an old-style Celtic folklore *elf* do these things?

Activity within the camp increased. Smith was out of sight again, but people were gathering and filing into the tent. Based on what details I could make out from here, the people looked ordinary, commonplace. Like any fringe church community going to a service. People walked with their heads bowed, their hands clasped. I normally wouldn't see this kind of patience, this kind of humility, from these groups of people.

They almost looked tired.

I expected the guards to circle back around any minute. They didn't right away, because they remained at the other side of the caravan, by the entrance, helping to escort in the new recruits.

They might be clever enough to count the number of people come to join them, versus the number of cars parked on the road, and realize there were too many cars. We couldn't stay here all night, twiddling our thumbs.

I wanted to break up the caravan. This was a cult and Smith was using people. He had some kind of ancient power, and he was dangerous.

"You know about this stuff," I said to Stockton. "How do we break his power?"

He looked panicked for a moment. "I don't know *that* much. I know what my grandmother told me. I know a few little charms, the four-leaf clover, the iron. Maybe if we threw iron filings at him."

"Would your grandmother know what to do?" I said. "She knew the locket would work, right?"

"I don't know that she ever thought I'd actually run into one of these guys."

"Could you ask her?"

"Right now?"

"You have your phone with you, right?" Hell, I had my phone with me. *I'd* call her.

"Well yeah, but—"

"So call her." And maybe after that I could talk to her and learn where her belief came from. Did she leave milk for the brownies because her family had always done so, or did she have a more immediate reason?

Stockton pulled one of those fancy little flip phones out of his front pants pocket. I was glad to see he'd had it turned off for our escapade.

The thing lit blue when he turned it on. He searched the menu, then pressed the dial button.

He sat there, listening to the ringing, while Jeffrey and I watched. It had been such a great idea, I'd thought. But she probably wasn't even home. I was getting ready to suggest that we call it a night, leave, do some research, and have a couple of beers while we came up with a plan to confront him tomorrow.

Then Stockton said, "Yes? Hello? Gramma, it's Roger . . . Yeah, I'm fine. Everything's fine . . . What do you mean I only call you when something's wrong? No, Gramma . . . Mom and Dad are fine, as far as I know . . . I don't really remember the last time I talked to them . . ."

I was used to being the goddess of phone conversations. I wanted to grab the phone out of his hand and make his grandmother get to the point. Ask her the *right* questions. Then I imagined trying to explain to her who I was.

"I'm sorry, Gramma, I can't really talk any louder . . . I said I

can't talk any louder . . . I'm sort of hiding . . . That's what I
wanted to talk to you about . . . You know those stories you're always telling? About the Fair Folk . . . Yes, Gramma, I crossed myself—" He quickly did so, in good Catholic fashion. "Some friends
and I seem to have come across one who's doing some not very
nice things . . . What kind is he? . . . I don't know . . . Seelie or Unseelie? I don't know that either . . . No, Gramma, I *do* pay attention
when you tell stories . . ."

"Unseelie are the bad guys, right?" I whispered at him. "I bet
he's Unseelie."

"Neither one is very good," he said, away from the phone for a
moment. "Yeah, Gramma? I'm pretty sure he's Unseelie . . . That's
right, it's pretty bad . . . What would you do? Pray?" He rolled his
eyes. "What about getting rid of him? Will he just go away? No . . .
okay . . . okay, just a minute." He took out a mini notepad and pen,
and started writing. A shopping list, it looked like. "Okay . . . Got
it. Then what? Really? Is that all?"

Patience, Kitty. Back in the caravan, people had entered the tent.
I couldn't see anything now, or sense anything, except that a large
group of people had gathered.

"Thanks a lot, Gramma. This is just what I need. I have to go
now . . . Yes, yes I'm coming for Thanksgiving this year. No, I'm
not bringing Jill . . . She broke up with me six months ago,
Gramma." He held the phone an inch away from his ear, closed his
eyes, and gave a deep sigh. I could hear the woman's voice, slow
and static-laden, but not the words.

This was ridiculous. I wanted to throttle him.

"I have to go now . . . goodbye, Gramma . . . I love you." He
clicked off.

"What did she say? What do we do?" I said, forcing my hands
to not grab his shirt and shake him.

"We go grocery shopping."

"What?"

"Bread, salt, some different herbs. Unless you brought any of
this stuff with you?" He showed me the list he'd written: verbena,
Saint-John's-wort, rowan.

"Can we even find some of this at the local supermarket?"

He shrugged. "Once we get the stuff it doesn't sound like it's
that hard of a spell. We just walk around the camp, sprinkle the
stuff on the ground, and poof."

"Poof?"

"Poof, he's banished back to underhill, or wherever the hell he came from."

Wherever the hell. Apt phrase, that.

"So we go to the store, get the supplies, come back, and that's that. Easy," Jeffrey said, grinning like we were planning a school prank.

Stockton put the list back in his pocket. "I think I remember seeing a convenience store a few miles back, at the last intersection. They'll have some of this stuff. She didn't say we need all of it, these are just the options. Why don't you two wait here and keep an eye on things while I go get the stuff."

"Sure," Jeffrey said without hesitation. Stockton was already turning to go.

"Wait!" I tried to keep my voice down and sound desperate at the same time.

"You have a better idea?"

"I go get the stuff and you wait here?"

"I'll be back in half an hour, I promise. Here, hang on to this." He gave me the locket charm, then ran along the shelter of the trees, back to the road.

I had a bad feeling about this. "Split up," I muttered. "We can take more damage that way. You know we're stranded here once he takes the car."

"Calm down, it'll be okay. Smith's wrapped up in whatever he's doing in there and the guards haven't spotted us. We'll stay here, keep our heads down, and be fine."

"You're entirely too pleased about all this."

"Of course I am! I've never done anything like this before. I'm usually cooped up in a TV studio or a book signing. But this—running around, investigating, *spying*. How cool is it?"

How did I get myself into these situations? "So, Jeffrey—you want to be a guest on my show?"

"Um—just what exactly would that involve?"

Inside the caravan, nothing happened. If this had been any other church's revival meeting, there would have been singing, shouting, praying. I wouldn't have minded hearing some speaking-in-tongues.

But there was nothing, except Jeffrey and me sitting in the dark and the cold, under a tree, waiting.

Enough time passed for me to think that Stockton had set us up.

Somewhere, hidden cameras recorded us, and any minute now actors dressed as bogeymen would leap out of the woods, screaming and carrying on. I'd freak out, adrenaline would push me over the edge, and I'd turn Wolf, because that was what happened when I panicked in a dangerous situation. Stockton would get it all on film and broadcast it in "A Very Special Episode of *Uncharted World*: Kitty, Unleashed." I didn't know what Jeffrey would do. Get out of the way, I hoped.

Except the caravan of the Church of the Pure Faith was parked in front of us, and I wasn't going to take my eyes off them. The bogeymen would have to wait.

Jeffrey tapped my shoulder and pointed at the road. A car pulled up—Stockton's. The headlights were off, to draw less attention to it. I hissed a sigh of relief.

A few minutes later, he rejoined us, carrying a plastic bag. "Hi. Anything happen while I was gone?"

"Nothing," I said. "They've been quiet."

"*Too* quiet," Jeffrey added happily.

Stockton pulled items out of the bag: a loaf of sliced sandwich bread, a shaker of salt, a bottle of Saint-John's-wort herbal remedy, and a pill crusher.

"I figured we'd crush the pills up and sprinkle the powder," he said. "I don't think you can get Saint-John's-wort any other way these days."

I deferred to his supposedly greater knowledge, because I didn't have any better ideas.

"Jeffrey, you take the salt. Kitty—" He handed Jeffrey the salt, and me the loaf of bread. While he took the pill crusher out of the package and dug into the Saint-John's-wort, he explained. "We start at the north end of the caravan. Just sprinkle this stuff as we go, and that's that. Which way's north?"

The moon, a little over three-quarters, was rising. That marked east. I pointed to the left. "There." It was just off from the entrance of the caravan.

Stockton exhaled a deep breath. "Right. Here we go, then."

The reporter led us. He had the bottle of pills in his jacket pocket. Two at a time, he grabbed pills from the bottle, put them in the crusher, turned the knob until it crunched, then emptied the powder out on the ground. Jeffrey followed behind him, sprinkling salt. I tore the bread into pieces and dropped them. Just call me Gretel.

Stockton was whispering. I had to listen closely to understand the words.

"Our Father, who art in Heaven, hallowed be Thy name . . ." Prayer. A bit of verbal magic to bind the spell.

We walked around the caravan, clockwise, far enough away from the wire boundary to avoid drawing attention. Even the guards had gone in to Smith's service. I crumbled bread, afraid to say anything. Jeffrey pursed his lips in a serious expression, watching Stockton and the ground ahead of us. Stockton developed a rhythm, pill-crunch-sprinkle, his lips moving constantly.

Completing the circle seemed to take forever. We moved methodically, and therefore slowly. We didn't even know if this was going to work.

Finally, we returned to the north side of the caravan. We passed the entrance, which was blocked off with chains secured with padlocks, making the place look more like a prison than a religious camp. Stockton reached the spot where the trail of bread crumbs began. I closed the circle.

". . . and deliver us from evil. Amen." He sighed and licked his lips.

Nothing happened.

"What's next?" I said, trying to keep the anxiety out of my voice.

"I don't know," Stockton said. "That was supposed to be it. I can't be sure I even did it right. I mean, who knows what other shit is in those pills."

That was it, then. We did what we could. Maybe we could go back to town, do some more research, and try again later.

"No, no. Something's happening. The light's gone all funny."

Jeffrey didn't elaborate. From my perspective, nothing had changed. Who knew what he could see?

Then, inside the caravan encampment, two figures approached the entrance. They were large, male, and stalked with long, smooth strides, predators in hunting mode—Smith's werewolf bodyguards.

"Guys?" I said, backing away. "We might want to get out of here."

The two bodyguards put their hands on the chains of the gate and hopped over, leaving the chains rattling. They continued on, right toward us.

Drawing together instinctively, we moved away quickly, stepping back, unwilling to turn away from the werewolves.

They crossed the line of the circle we'd made, then stopped.

For a moment, outside the circle marked by the bread crumbs, they stood frozen. Then one of them stumbled, as if he'd lost his balance. The other one put his hand to his head and squinted. They looked around, expressions confused, like they'd just come out of hibernation. They glanced at us, then at each other.

"Oh, my God," one of them murmured.

"Spell broken," Jeffrey said.

I moved toward them slowly—let them get a good look at me, get my scent, prove that I wasn't a danger. "Hi. Are you guys okay?"

"I don't know," said the one who'd spoken. "I—we were stuck. What happened? I'm not sure what happened."

They both looked back at the gate, their faces long and sad, nostalgic almost. The chain they'd jumped over a minute before was still swinging.

"Do you want to go back?" I said.

The other one, shorter, quieter, said, "It's not real, is it?"

"No," I said.

"Shit," he muttered, bowing his head.

Now all we had to do was get everyone else to leave the caravan and cross that line.

I wondered what would happen if Smith crossed that line.

A crowd had gathered, Smith's congregation leaving the tent and filling the space behind the gate. Dozens of them stared out with earnest, devout gazes.

At the head of the crowd stood Smith himself. Surrounded by his people, he seemed small, slight. I still had Stockton's charm in my pocket. I put it on. He appeared otherworldly, his gaze blank and inhuman. He frowned, burning. Lines seemed to form around him, tendrils that joined him to all the people around him, like tethers, leashes. Two broken lines stretched in front of him, wavering, unanchored.

One of the men, the one who'd spoken first, stepped toward Smith. I ran forward, slipping in front of him, blocking his way.

"No, don't go back. Please."

Smith called out from behind the gate. "You are keeping them from peace. I can give *you* peace."

"Kitty, don't listen to him!" Jeffrey called.

But his words hadn't affected me. I didn't have to listen to him. The charm protected me.

Jeffrey stood a few yards up the hill from me, his hands clenched, looking worried for the first time all evening. Stockton was nearby, his camera up and filming. At least we'd have a record of this, however it turned out.

I had to draw him out—without seeming like I was drawing him out. He was probably already suspicious. Of course he was.

I approached the gate. "Kitty!" Jeffrey's voice was tight with fear. I waved a hand, trying to tell him it was okay. I had a plan. I hoped.

At the line, I stopped walking and tried to look pathetic and indecisive.

One of his followers started unlocking the chain. Smith never touched the metal. Steel contained iron, which was poison to his kind.

Once the people around him had pulled the chains away, Smith moved forward. I couldn't look away; his gaze trapped mine. I tried to make it a challenge. Wolves stared when they wanted to make a challenge.

"You're curious, aren't you?" he said.

I nodded. I had to keep him moving forward.

"But you hesitate. You're afraid."

He came closer. God, I wanted to run away. Wolf wanted to run away.

He was in front of me, holding out his hand, like he wanted me to take it, so he could draw me into his world. His goblin market.

Slowly, I took a step back—a hesitating step, to encourage him to follow. I was right on the edge, he could draw me to him if only he took another step toward me, over the line.

But he stopped. When he smiled, he showed teeth.

He said, "I see your spell. I'll not cross the line."

Screw it. Screw *him*. I grabbed his shirt and pulled, yanking him forward. Across the line.

I expected him to be heavier than he was. Hauling him felt like pulling on a pillow—he was light enough to fly out of my grip. Surprise at this made me lose my balance. I fell backward, but I kept hold of his shirt, determined to bring him down, literally if need be.

I hit the ground, expecting him to fall on top of me. But he didn't, because as soon as his body crossed the invisible barrier that we'd created he caught fire. He burst like a flare, yellow and red spewing with a shrill hiss that might have been a shriek. Ash and embers fell against me, onto my face, scalding. I screamed and put my arms over my face. My hands burned, throbbing and painful. I rolled, trying to get away.

Somebody stopped me and pulled me up until I was sitting. "Are you okay?" It was Jeffrey.

My hands were red, baked and itching, like a bad sunburn. My face burned and itched, too. I hated to think what it looked like.

I lurched out of his grip and twisted all the way around to look for Smith. "Where is he? Where'd he go?"

"He's gone," Jeffrey said, laughing a little, nervously. "He just burned up."

A few black cinders lay scattered on the grass. At the gate of the caravan, people were drifting out, stumbling, confused, shaking their heads.

"It's over," I said. I was too tired to feel any kind of victory. Yet, I couldn't help but feel like there should have been more. That had almost been easy—anticlimactic. I shouldn't have been able to finish off someone that badass all by myself.

Stockton was still filming, gripping the camera with both hands, white-knuckled. So how did you wrap up a story like this? Brush your hands off and go home?

Behind me, a groan sounded, deep, changing in tone. The tenor was familiar—a human voice, turning into a wolf's growl.

One of Smith's bodyguards was shape-shifting. And why not? How long had it been since any of these people had given in to the other side of their natures? And now the power that had controlled them was gone.

The shorter one doubled over, pulling off his shirt, ripping the sleeves as he did, and growling. As the other one watched, he backed away, but his muscles were rippling, his body melting, changing. All the lycanthropes would react to that; in moments, they'd all shift.

That didn't even begin to mention what the vampires would do, freed from Smith's control.

"Jeffrey, we have to get out of here."

He looked around, his eyes widening as he realized what was happening. "Yeah, I guess we do."

"Roger!" I shouted. "Get back to the car! Now!"

Sure enough, a woman who'd made her way out of the gate grabbed a man standing next to her, tripped him so he sprawled on the ground, straddled his back, and bared her teeth. She threw herself at his neck, biting into him. He thrashed, trying to roll and swipe at her. Claws sprouted from his hand.

Many of the others, realizing what was happening, ran flat-out into the woods, no looking back.

Helping each other, Jeffrey and I got to our feet and started running. Stockton stared out, his eyes wide and surprised. His camera was still up, still recording.

I grabbed his shirt as we passed him. "Come *on!*"

A furious snarl ripped the air behind me. A wolf could run faster on four legs than I could on two.

"Run. Just run," I said to Jeffrey, shoving him toward Stockton. I turned my back on them to face the wolf that was racing toward me.

He wanted the easiest prey in the area. I must have looked good. Small enough to be an easy target with enough meat to make it worthwhile.

That described me in so many ways I didn't want to think about.

He was pale, almost white, which made him glow in the moonlight. He was also big, one of the stockier wolves I'd ever seen: massive through the chest and shoulders, legs working, head low, like a battering ram. He'd plow into me and knock me over like I was nothing, then rip into me without a second thought.

But I'd survive the first few cuts. I already had lycanthropy, unlike Jeffrey and Roger. I was tough; I could take it.

Holy crap.

I dodged. At the very last possible moment I dodged and grabbed the wolf's tail. I was stronger than I looked. I kept hold of it long enough to change his momentum, to make him hesitate and look back, to pause before he adjusted the vector of his attack to where his prey had slipped.

His jaws were open, aimed at my shoulder, once again to try to shove me to the ground and hold me with his teeth. Swinging my body, I deflected his face away. Instead of locking a firm grip on my shoulder, his canines scraped down my arm. A couple of deep gouges on the bicep was better than losing a shoulder, right?

I couldn't slow down to think about how much it hurt. Jeffrey and Roger should have had enough time to get back to the car. Time to run away. I kicked the wolf's face before he could gather himself for the next attack. I had to convince him I wasn't as easy a catch as he first thought. This was a time I had to let a little bit of the Wolf into my mind. She was better at fighting than I was. Kick him, snarl at him, scare him off.

Do all that, and stay anchored to my human body as well. I

didn't want to lose control of that part of myself. I didn't want to leave myself vulnerable while I shifted. And I wanted to be able to talk about this when it was finished. Assuming I was still conscious when it was finished.

The wolf hesitated. He was thinking about it. Probably because other, potentially easier prey attracted him.

"Kitty! Kitty!" A kid ran up the hill toward me—the young man I'd talked to before everything hit the fan, the one who'd just tried to join the church. "Help, I don't know what to do, you have to help me—"

"Come on." I grabbed the guy's shirt, shoved him so he was behind me, and shouted at the pale wolf. "Get out of here! Go on, get away!"

I backpedaled up the hill. "Run!" I said to the guy. "Get to the car."

I turned and followed him. I didn't dare look behind me.

We hopped the fence, first the kid, then me. Jeffrey stood by the car, holding open the passenger side door. He also held a Club—the attached to the steering wheel so the car doesn't get stolen kind of Club—in his right hand, ready to swing it like it was, well, a club. Just in case something was following.

I shoved the kid into the back and piled in immediately after him. Jeffrey jumped in the front seat and slammed shut the door.

The pale wolf crashed into the door, jaws open, slobbering on the window.

Stockton was filming it.

"Roger, would you put down that camera and drive?" I shouted.

The second time the wolf charged us, causing the whole car to rock on its wheels, Stockton put the camera down and started the engine. We pulled out onto the road a second later.

My straggler curled up in his seat. Hugging himself, he shook, sweat breaking out on his face. He mumbled, "Stop it . . . stop it . . ."

He was starting to Change. It began inside, a feeling like an animal clawing its way out. It hurt more when you tried to keep it from happening. When you couldn't stop the Change from happening.

I grabbed him, taking hold of his face and making him look at me. "Keep it together, okay? Take a deep breath. Slow breath. Good, that's good. Nice and easy, keep it together." His breathing slowed; he stopped trembling. After another moment, he even relaxed a little. Some of the tension left his arms.

He closed his eyes. He wouldn't look at me.

"What's your name?"

He needed a moment to catch his breath. "Ty. It's Ty."

"Nice to meet you, Ty." He nodded quickly, nervously, keeping his head down. I moved a hand to his shoulder—a light touch to keep him anchored in his body—and sat back.

Now maybe I could catch *my* breath.

I didn't want to think about the can of worms we'd opened. In the long run, Smith being gone could only be a good thing. But all those people were homeless now, and confused. And monsters. At least we were in the middle of nowhere. They could only hurt each other. Which was bad enough.

"Kitty, you're bleeding." Jeffrey stared at me between the two front seats.

Blood covered my right arm. Just looking at it sent waves of pain riding through my shoulder.

"It's okay," I said, gritting my teeth. "It'll be fine by morning."

"The rapid healing, that's true?" Stockton said. The reporter turned his camera onto me, holding it between the front seats with one hand while steering with the other and only half watching the road. "Can I watch?"

"No." I glared until he set the thing down. I took the charm off and handed it to the front seat. Roger accepted it, pulling the chain over his head. "Roger, your grandmother got you into this, didn't she? The fairy charms, the supernatural. Working for *Uncharted World*."

He smiled wryly. "Some people think I'm on that show because I'm a crappy reporter. I could be on CNN if I wanted. Except I believe. No, I don't believe. I *know*. The supernatural—it's like any other mystery. You find enough evidence, you can prove the truth. This gig gets me closer to that." Just like Flemming. The search for truth. Stockton was just traveling a different road. "So—you sure you won't let me film you next full moon?"

"No."

"How about you, kid?"

"What?" Ty looked woozy.

"No," I said.

Stockton chuckled, entirely too amused. "Hey—where are we going?"

I found my phone in my pocket, turned it on, and hesitated, because I didn't know who I could call for help. I hated to say that my first impulse was to call Cormac. *He'd* know what to do with a

couple dozen rogue vampires and werewolves rampaging the countryside. Unfortunately, his solution would involve lots of silver bullets and stakes, and we'd end up with a bunch of corpses. I was trying to avoid that.

My next idea was to call Ahmed. I didn't have a phone number
for the Crescent, so I called information. They were able to get me
through to the restaurant side. A cheery-sounding hostess whose
voice I didn't recognize answered the phone.

"Good evening, this is the Crescent. May I help you?"

"Hi, yeah—is Ahmed there?"

"Who?"

A sinking feeling attacked my stomach. "Ahmed. The guy who
owns the place."

"Oh! Just a moment. May I tell him who's calling?"

"It's Kitty."

She set the phone aside. I could hear the murmur of generic
restaurant noises—voice talking, tableware clinking— in the background. The moment stretched on. I started tapping my foot. I
didn't have a lot of time here.

A familiar, robust voice picked up the line. "Kitty! How are you?"

Situations like this made it so hard to answer that question. "I
need some help, Ahmed. What would you do with a couple dozen
vampires and lycanthropes who'd lost it and you wanted to get
them under control so they didn't get hurt?"

I grit my teeth. When I said it out loud like that, this mess
sounded ridiculous.

He hesitated for a long time, so that I had to listen to the restaurant white noise again. Then he said, "I would leave the area, and
wait until morning to return to see what was left."

"But the vampires will die without shelter."

"That would not be my concern."

No, it wouldn't, would it? "Then what about the lycanthropes? I
know you'd want to help the lycanthropes."

"If you can bring them here, to the club, I can shelter them."

"But I have no way of getting them there."

"Kitty, what have you gotten yourself into?"

I sighed. He wasn't going to be any help. He probably never
even left the Crescent, his little domain. "It's a long story. I'll have
to talk to you later. Bye."

"Goodbye?" He sounded confused. I hung up anyway.

That left one other option.

I called Alette to ask her if she could help. Bradley answered the phone, put me on hold, and returned to say that she could. She'd meet me at Smith's caravan in an hour.

An hour later, we drove back by the site. The police had already arrived in squad cars, along with a sedan I recognized as the one Bradley drove, and a large, windowless van.

Stockton pulled onto the shoulder. A cop came forward and tried to wave him away. I rolled down the back window.

"I'm with Alette," I called. The cop hesitated, then let Stockton park.

While a trio of cops moved alongside the road setting out flares and obviously standing guard, Alette and Leo stood at the edge of the grassy field. A group of people approached them from the caravan. Leo held something out to them, and they moved slowly, cautiously toward him.

"Stay here, lock the doors," I said as I climbed out of the car. I didn't stick around to see if they listened to me.

I didn't get too close. I had my limits. The people drawn to Leo were thin, wan, cold—vampires. Leo held a jar of blood, open to the air, so that the smell drew them.

The vampires in Smith's caravan hadn't eaten in months, some of them. As they approached, Leo spoke softly to them. He touched their chins, their hair, and they bowed their heads and followed docilely. He led them to the van and guided them inside. Tom waited by the back door.

Bradley approached me, clearly on an intercept course to keep me from interrupting Alette and Leo.

"What's happening?" I asked, before he could chastise me or start issuing orders. "It looks like some kind of vampire hypnotism."

He said, "The ones who joined Smith aren't very old, only a few decades. Easy to control. Older vampires aren't going to go looking for a cure. If they've made it to a hundred without getting killed, it usually means they like it. But these—they're looking for guidance."

"What'll happen to them?"

"They'll stay with Alette until she can find out where they're from and send them home." He glanced back at Stockton's car. Of course the reporter had his camera pressed against the windshield, glaring out. He even leaned half on top of Jeffrey to get a better angle. "Your friends should leave."

His tone didn't allow argument. Besides, I pretty much agreed with him. This was like an accident scene, and Stockton didn't need to be broadcasting it on his show.

"I'll ask them, but Stockton's got the keys. Good luck getting him out of here." Then I had a brilliant idea. Stockton reported on the paranormal. He'd absolutely love this. I told Bradley, "Let me get the kid out and back in his own car. Then could you maybe pull the Man In Black routine on Stockton? It might just scare the crap out of him." I couldn't help it—I grinned.

"Man In Black?" Bradley's brow furrowed with distaste.

"Just be yourself when you tell him to get the hell out of here. It'll be fun." I trotted off to check on Ty.

Jeffrey unlocked the car for me. I opened the back door. Ty was sitting up, looking around, aware of his surroundings.

"Hey, Ty, you ready to go home? Can you drive?" I said.

He ran a hand through his floppy hair and nodded. "But can't I stay with you?"

I absolutely did not need that kind of responsibility. I'd run away from that kind of responsibility. I tried to let him down gently. "Walk with me, 'kay?"

I held out my hand. He took it and let me pull him from the car. Staying close to him, I walked him to his car. "There's a club in D.C. for people like us. A guy named Ahmed runs it. He can help you, there's lots of people there who'd be happy to help you cope with this. You should go there."

He scrounged a pen and piece of paper from his glove box, and I wrote down directions to the Crescent for him. I also gave him my number.

"No more quack cures after this, right?"

"Right."

"You going to be okay?"

He nodded, a little more decisively than he had before. "Yeah. I'll check this place out. Thanks, Kitty. Thanks a lot."

I sent him on his way.

I turned around just in time to see Stockton's car back up a few feet in order to zoom a U-turn onto the road, engine revving. Arms crossed, a looming monolith of a man, Bradley stood at the edge of the pavement and watched him go.

When Stockton's car was out of sight, Bradley turned around. He wore a big grin. He said, "You're right. That was fun."

I was so sorry I'd missed it.

Leo, supervised by Alette, was still herding vampires. The scene was surreal and vaguely appalling.

"Does it bother you?" I said to Bradley. "Working for a vampire? Emma said her family has worked for her for centuries. What about yours? Or are you related to Emma?"

"Distant cousins." His smile was amused, wry. He nodded to the cops. "One of the officers there is another cousin. I never really thought about it, to tell you the truth. It's just how it's always been. If you don't grow up thinking any of this is weird, then it isn't weird. When I was a kid, my parents would take me to her place to visit. It was like having another aunt."

The lycanthropes wouldn't fry when the sun rose, but I was worried about what they might do in the meantime. Alette wasn't. She and Leo set out raw meat as bait and armed the police with silver bullets.

Wasn't exactly what I had in mind. But it turned out the silver bullets were weapons of last resort. The vampire mojo worked on the weres as well. The two vampires lulled them to sleep, let them slip back to human, then let the police take over. Many of the people had missing person files on them. Eventually, they'd make it back home.

The two vampires cleaned up the whole mess. That was why lycanthropes needed large numbers to defeat vampires in a head-to-head confrontation.

We explored the caravan while Alette's police friends put up yellow tape and marked the whole thing off as an investigation site. Under the tent, a temporary stage made of plywood and milk crates stood toward the rear, and a string of bare lightbulbs hung from tent poles, across the top. It looked harmless enough. The rest of the camp, though, was a disaster. None of the trailers had sewer hookups. The few available camp and chemical toilets were overused. Immortality and rapid healing didn't preclude the necessity of other bodily functions. Nothing had been cleaned, piles of trash lay discarded in the corners of RVs, in the beds of pickups. Some signs of food remained: empty cans of soup and beans, along with dirty dishes, were stacked in sinks and on counters. Mold and slime spotted them, and dozens of flies rose and scattered when we opened doors.

I could hardly breathe, the smell was so strong. I kept my hand in front of my face.

We found a few people, both lycanthropes and vampires, hiding in the closets of campers, on the floorboards in trucks and cars. They hugged themselves, shaking, crying—symptoms of withdrawal. They looked pale and thin, their hair was dull and limp. I didn't think anyone with lycanthropy could die of malnutrition, their bodies were so hardy and resistant to damage. But they didn't look good. The vampires—their bodies might not break down. But they might lose their minds. Smith was sustaining them, that was how they had survived.

I tried to draw them out, talking to them, reassuring them, but they didn't like me. My scent was unfamiliar, and they cowered, more animal than human. Some of them followed me into the open. Some of them, Leo had to come and whisper to them, work some of his vampire charm on them, until their eyelids drooped and they followed on command.

These people had been living a dozen to a trailer, no food, no showers. Smith had turned them into zombies.

Alette joined us as we finished our tour of the camp.

"This is a rather impressive coup you've accomplished, for someone who claims to have no authority," she said, frowning.

She asked me what happened, exactly what we had seen and what we had done to banish Smith. She nodded and seemed unsurprised, like she recognized what he was and had expected as much.

"I never thought it could be this bad," I said. "I thought Smith was duping people. But he was sucking them dry. Keeping them alive so he could continue using them."

"It's what his kind do," Alette said. "What they've done for centuries, in one guise or another. The *sidhe*, the fairies, have always fed on the lives of mortal human beings. In the old days they stole infants and replaced them with changelings; they seduced young men and women; they kept mortal servants for decades. It's as if they aren't really alive themselves, so they need life nearby to sustain them. Vampires and lycanthropes have something more. They started as mortal, and became something powerful. Whatever the *sidhe* draw from living humans, they draw more of it from us. Smith created a situation where he could surround himself with their power. Because the *sidhe* have power over perception, especially over perceptions of space and time, he could make his followers believe anything. He could show them the world he wanted them to see. The stories say that food of the fairies would appear to be a feast, but turn to dust in your mouth." She gazed over the abandoned caravan with a look of sadness.

We returned to Alette's townhome near dawn. Bradley gave some excuse about finishing arrangements during daylight hours— Alette needed to rent a whole separate townhome where the vampire refugees could stay—and left me facing her in the foyer alone.

She stood, arms crossed, wearing a rust-colored dress with a tai-

322   Long-Time Listener, First-Time Werewolf

lored, silk top and flowing skirt, not at all rumpled after the evening's outing. How did she do it?

"Well. You're rather a mess," she said, regarding my singed clothing, dirt-smeared face, wounded arm, and bloodstained shirt. The observation sounded even more depressing in her neat British accent.

"Yeah," I said weakly. What else could I say?

"I do wish you had told me what you had planned. We might have been more prepared."

I really wanted to sit down, but I didn't dare use any of the antique furniture in the room in my grubby state. "There wasn't really a plan involved. We just sort of seized the moment. Look, I know I had no right to ask for your help and no reason to think that you'd give it—"

"Oh? You're saying I haven't given you any reason to believe that I would give aid in a crisis? That you believe I have no interest in what happens outside the boundaries of my personal domain? That my resources are for my own selfish use and haven't been developed precisely so that I might lend assistance in any situation where it might be needed?"

Alette was the vampire Mistress of Washington, D.C., and that probably wasn't an accident. From here, she could oversee goings-on around the world. She could make worldwide contacts. And she'd been humble enough to offer hospitality to a wandering werewolf. Hospitality, and the loan of a diamond pendant.

"I'm sorry." I looked away, smiling tiredly and feeling like a heel. Any rebellion had been completely wrung out of me tonight, and my arm still hurt.

She continued, softer in tone, kinder. "I happen to believe that immortality ought to make one more sensitive to the plight of the downtrodden, and more apt to work toward the betterment of humanity. Not less. We have the luxury of taking the long view. I know the behavior of some of my kind leaves much to be desired, but please do not judge me by their example."

Never again. "All right. I just . . . I keep wondering, asking myself . . ."

"Did you do the right thing?" I nodded. Destroying the church so abruptly might have caused more problems than it had solved. We might have found another way, if we could have lured people away instead of removing Smith all at once . . .

Alette said, "Elijah Smith drew people to him under false pretenses, removed their wills to decide whether or not to stay with him, and forced them to live in conditions that I consider to be criminal. Human law could not have remedied the problem. You did. Perhaps someone else might have done the job a bit more neatly. But as you say, you seized the moment. You shouldn't worry."

Would there ever come a time when human law could handle situations like this? I couldn't imagine the local sheriff's office with a copy of procedures on how to arrest and hold in custody an Unseelie fairy. Or a rogue werewolf, or a rampaging vampire. We kept having to police ourselves. We had to be vigilantes, and I didn't like it. I kept claiming we could be a part of the "normal" world, of everyday society. Then shit like this happened to prove me wrong.

"Thanks. Again," I said.

"Ma'am? Shouldn't we be off?"

Leo spoke and I jumped, startled. He'd appeared in the doorway behind me, and I hadn't heard him. He grinned wickedly; he'd known exactly what he was doing.

"All right, Leo. Thank you." She passed me on her way to follow him, pausing a moment to look kindly on me. Like someone might look at a dog who'd had a run-in with a skunk. "Do try to get some sleep," she said.

She'd turned down the hall, out of my sight, when Leo took the opportunity to lean in and say, "Might also try a shower there, luv." He turned on his heel and followed his mistress.

The perfect end to the day, really.

So much for turning this trip into a working vacation. I wasn't getting any sleep. I'd need a week off to recover from all this. Preferably some place with a hot tub and room service. At least my arm had healed quickly.

I got to the Senate office building early, despite the lack of sleep. It meant I was able to catch Duke before the session started.

He was walking down the corridor, conferring with an aide, who was holding a folder open in front of him. I stood against the wall, waiting quietly and out of sight until they reached me. Then I hurried to keep pace with them. Both him and his aide looked over at me, startled.

"Senator Duke? Could I talk to you for just a minute?"

The aide turned to shield the senator, blocking my access to him.

He said, "I'm sorry, the senator is much too busy right now. If you'd like to make an appointment—"

"Really, just a couple of questions, we don't even have to stop walking." I hopped to try to catch sight of Duke around his aide. "Senator? How about it?"

He looked straight ahead and didn't slow. "One question, if we can keep walking."

"Of course. Thanks." The aide glared at me, but shifted so I could walk next to Duke. "Why did you bring Elijah Smith here?"

"Because he understands my mission: to see these . . . diseases . . . eradicated. I'm sure you understand. And he's a man of the cloth, which brings a respect that these hearings are sorely in need of, wouldn't you agree?"

"A man of the cloth? Really? Of what denomination? Have you seen any kind of identification for him?"

He frowned. "I'm sure he's a good Christian preacher who teaches that faith saves."

"He wasn't what you think. He wasn't helping anyone."

"Was?" he said. He stopped and looked at me. "What do you mean, was?"

"He, uh, had to leave town suddenly."

Glaring, I thought he might start a fight with me right there. His aide's eyes widened, like he was worried, too. "What have you done?"

I stood my ground. I wasn't going to let him cow me. I had *authority*, didn't I? Yeah, right.

"You believe, Senator. I know you believe: ghosts, devils, angels, good and evil, the whole nine yards. Elijah Smith was a demon, preying on the weak and helpless. I hope you'll believe me."

His expression was cold, but his eyes held a light—a kind of fevered intensity. "If he was preying on anything, it was *your* kind. Vampires and werewolves—monsters. Hardly the weak and helpless." He gave a short laugh.

"We're all just people at heart, Senator. I wish I could make you understand that."

"That'll be for the committee to decide." He gestured to his aide and stalked down the corridor. His aide scurried to keep up with him.

I met Ben outside the Senate office building. He seemed surprised to see me coming out the door instead of arriving via the sidewalk.

"You're up early," he said, raising an inquiring brow.

"Um, yeah. By the way, we don't have to do anything about Smith. You don't have to look into it."

He studied me closely. "What did you do?"

"Nothing," I said far too quickly. "Well, I mean, we did a spell."

"A spell?"

"We just threw some herbs and stuff around. That's all."

"It's not something you're going to end up in court over, is it?"

Not *human* court, at any rate. "No, I don't think so."

He sighed. "Just for you, I think I'm going to raise my rates. To pay for the hair loss treatments."

He was such a kidder.

We entered the meeting room and found our usual seats. Cormac hadn't shown up since Duke fired him, but Ben said he was still in town. Just in case, Ben said, but wouldn't say in case of what.

Today's session was late in starting. Time dragged. Reporters fidgeted, Senate aides hovered in the background, wringing their hands. The senators themselves shuffled papers and wouldn't raise their gazes. Testimony that should have taken just a few days had been dragged out to the end of the week. I quivered, waiting for something to break.

The audience was dwindling. Most of the reporters had drifted off to cover more interesting stories, and maybe a dozen general spectators remained. Even some of the senators on the committee hadn't bothered showing up.

As expected, Roger Stockton was there, ready to stick it out to the very end. He looked like *he'd* been able to sleep. He invited himself into the seat next to mine. After last night he must have thought we were some kind of buddies.

Maybe we were.

He leaned close and immediately launched into questions. "So where are the aliens and what do they have to do with the vampires? Are vampires aliens?"

"Aliens?" Ben, overhearing, asked.

"A couple of really bad movies have covered that plot," I said. "Where did *you* come up with it?"

"Last night, the Man In Black with the vampires, the one keeping people away like it was some kind of UFO cover-up. You seemed pretty tight with all them—what aren't you telling me?"

I tried to smile mysteriously, which was hard to do when I really wanted to laugh. "It's not really my place to give away secrets. Honestly, though. The 'Man In Black' was just a guy. There aren't any aliens."

"That's what they all say," he said, glaring. "'It was Venus,' my ass."

Ben gave me a look that said, *What the hell are you talking about?* I gave him one back that said, *Later.*

Finally, the session started. I *still* hadn't been called. We listened to half an hour of testimony from Robert Carr, a B-grade filmmaker who'd been praised for the frightening werewolf shape-shifting effects in his movies—had he used real werewolves, by any chance? He claimed no, he had a talented CGI artist who used a morphing technique to shift images of people into images of wolves, and if his effects were more successful this was because he pictured actual wolves, instead of the unlikely broad-chested, fake-fur-covered mutant grotesques that most werewolf movies used.

I'd seen a couple of his films, and I was sure he was telling the truth and didn't use real werewolves. Though his effects *were* impressive and awfully realistic. He might have *seen* a real werewolf shape-shift. I'd have to tackle—er, approach—him after the hearings and get him to come on the show. We could talk about werewolves as metaphor in film.

I was a little put-out, though, that the committee decided to talk to the werewolf filmmaker before the actual werewolf. Okay, we were still in the entertainment industry portion of the testimony, and maybe some of the committee members didn't believe I was a werewolf. But I'd been on the schedule for three days now. Impatient didn't begin to describe it. I hadn't been able to eat more than half an English muffin for breakfast, I was so anxious.

"Thank you, Mr. Carr, that will be all." Duke straightened the papers on the table in front of him with an air of finality. "I'm afraid that's all the time we have for testimony today. We'll recess for the weekend and resume on Monday to hear from those witnesses we haven't called yet. Thank you very much."

The place burst into activity, people talking among themselves, getting up to leave, aides rushing to attend to the committee members. The other senators looked as confused as I felt; they hadn't been expecting this, either. The tension that had been there from the start didn't dissipate.

"This is weird," Stockton said. "Weren't you supposed to be up there today?"

"Yeah." I crossed my arms and pouted.

"I don't believe it." Ben flopped back against his chair with a sigh. "You see somebody's name on the docket, you expect them to get called. This isn't just annoying, it's unprofessional. They expect us to be on time, the least they could do is run an extra hour to hear everybody."

Maybe there was a reason. Was there anyone else due to be called after me? Or did Duke just want to postpone *my* testimony?

I counted forward, checking off days on the calendar I kept in my mind, confirming the day with the inner tide that felt the pull of it even if I didn't know exactly what day the full moon fell on. I stared across the room to the table where the senators were cleaning up, heading out, conversing with each other or aides. Duke glanced up and caught my eye. He set his jaw and turned away.

Alette was right. She'd called it.

"The bastard," I said. "He planned it. He planned it this way all along. He needs to drag the hearings out until Monday."

"What's Monday?"

"Full moon. He wants to make me testify the day of the full moon."

Stockton gave a low whistle. "Sneaky," he said with something like admiration. I glared at him. He may have thought we were great friends after our adventure last night, but he was doing a lousy job staying in my good graces. He was less like a war buddy and more like an annoying younger brother.

Ben said, "You make it sound like that's not good."

I shook my head, trying to call up some reserve of righteous outrage. Mostly I felt tired. "I'll be at my worst, that's all. Edgy, nervous. Itchy. He knows enough to know this. Maybe he thinks I'll lose my temper and Change right in front of them all." This put me in a foul mood.

"Can you handle it?" Ben said. "Should we put in a request to delay testimony for a day?"

The day after would be even worse than the day before. It felt like having a hangover, and I seemed to spend too much energy mentally holding the door to the Wolf's cage shut. I'd be distracted and no good.

"No, no," I said. "I mean, yeah. I can handle it. I think." I hoped. No caffeine for me that day.

I had to talk to Fritz, but it was getting late; I didn't know if I'd get to the Crescent in time to see him.

I ran from the Metro station to the club, jumped down the stairs, and grabbed the doorway to stop myself as I looked around in a panic.

I wasn't too late. He sat at his usual table, hunched over his tumbler, staring at nothing and wrapped up in his own world.

Pulling up a chair, I sat near him, close enough to whisper but far enough away to dodge if he decided to take a swing at me. I had no idea how this would play out.

He blinked at me, startled.

"What can you tell me about Dr. Paul Flemming?" I asked.

He stared, his gaze narrowing. "I do not know this name."

He could say that, but his expression told me otherwise. His lip twitched, his eyes were accusing. He looked like someone who had decided to lie.

"I saw your name on a list in his laboratory."

"I know nothing," he said, shaking his head. Quickly he drained his glass, slammed it on the table, and pushed his chair away.

"Please don't go. I just want to talk." This strange, lurking figure raised so many questions. At this point I didn't even care what he told me, just as long as he said something. A flash from the past, a story, an anecdote. The sweeping words of advice and judgment the old often seemed to have ready for the young. I didn't care. I wanted to find a crack in that wall.

He turned to me, looming over my chair, his lips curling. "I don't talk to anyone."

I met his gaze, my own anger rising. "If you don't want to talk to anyone, why do you even come here? Why not drink yourself to death in private?"

He straightened, even taking a step back, as if I had snarled at him, or took a swipe at him. Then he closed his eyes and sighed.

"Here, it smells safe. For a little while each day, I feel safe."

I resisted an urge to grab his arm, to keep him here. To try to comfort him through touch, the way I would have if we'd been part of the same pack. But we weren't a pack. He was a stranger, behind this wall he'd built to keep the world out, and I didn't know why I thought he'd talk to me. Just because I was cute or something.

"Why would you be afraid of anything?"

Slowly, a smile grew on his ragged features, pursed and sardonic. "You are young and do not understand. But if you keep on like this, you might."

He brushed his fingers across the top of my head, a fleeting touch that was gone as soon as I'd felt it, as if a bird had landed on me and instantly taken flight again.

"You are young," he said, and walked away, settling his coat more firmly over his shoulders.

His touch tingled across my scalp long after he'd disappeared out the door.

I had a show to put on tonight, like I did every Friday. I asked Jack for a cup of coffee. Something to keep me awake for the next ten hours. I took out my notepad on the pretense of planning tonight's show—though really, the day of the show was far too late to be planning it. Good thing I'd been cornering hearing participants like Jeffrey Miles and Robert Carr and convincing them to appear on the show. The rest of it I'd have to wing. Not too different than usual, come to think of it.

"He's right, you know." Ahmed appeared. He slipped into the chair across from me. I hadn't heard him, and the whole place smelled like werewolf so my nose hadn't sensed him. He'd stalked quietly, like he was hunting. Today, he wore a woven vest over his shirt and trousers. The vest gave him that same man-of-two-worlds air that the robe had.

I didn't want to talk to him. He might not have had any obligation to help me with the mess at Smith's caravan, but he hadn't even made an effort, and I wasn't in the mood to be lectured by him now.

I just stared at him.

"There is much to fear in the world. Trouble finds you when you get too involved. That is why the Nazi keeps to himself."

"Fritz," I said. "His name's Fritz."

Ahmed had said that this was a safe place, a place with no alphas, no rivalries, and no need to fight among ourselves. But that didn't mean he wasn't in charge, watching. Or that he didn't have clear ideas of how things should be run. And according to him, you stayed safe by keeping to yourself and not getting involved.

I'd stuck my neck out too many times to take that attitude. I tried to keep from tensing up defensively. He wasn't challenging me. There was nothing wrong with what I was doing.

"He is little more than a crazy old man. He has his rituals, his drinking, because they fend off his memories. But everyone else remembers for him, and do not speak to him because of it. I tolerate him here because he is harmless. He is to be pitied for the ghosts he carries with him."

I was about ready to scream with all the double-talk and hints of what people *weren't* telling me. "What did he do? He won't tell me. You call him the Nazi, which implies so much. But I want to know, exactly what did he do?"

He shrugged. "The time and place he comes from say much, do they not?"

"You say you remember. That everyone remembers. Do you really, or have you just made something up and figured it's close enough?"

He was a German soldier from World War II. Everyone else just filled in the blanks. But did that really make him a war criminal? I'd probably never find out for sure.

Ahmed's brow furrowed in a way that was admonishing. Here it came, the *I'm older and wiser than you so sit down and shut up* speech. It was like having a pack alpha all over again.

"Kitty." He spread his hands in a gesture of offering. "I don't want to see you get in trouble."

"Neither do I! But I'm getting tired of everyone hiding things from me."

"Perhaps they do not hide things from you—they hide things out of habit. Many of us would prefer to keep this world hidden. We owe nothing to anyone. That is the secret to a contented life. Don't become indebted to anyone."

"So you build an oasis and lock out the world, is that it? It means you don't have to go out of your way to help anyone." I had to get out of here before I said something I would regret later. "I'm sorry, I'd really like to talk more, but I have to get going. I've got the show tonight."

"I'm sure I do not have to tell you to be careful." I'd been hearing that a lot lately. If it weren't for all the people telling me how much trouble I was potentially getting into, this trip would be a breeze.

"I'm being careful. There's some hell of a tale behind Fritz, and I'm just trying to find out what it is."

As I reached the door, he called out, "Hey, tonight, I'll listen to your show. I'll turn on the radio in the bar so everyone can listen."

No pressure or anything. "Thanks. That'd be cool."

Jack gave me a thumbs-up on my way out.

chapter 10

Welcome back. If you just tuned in you're listening to *The Midnight Hour*. I'm Kitty Norville. For the last hour I have a new topic of discussion, something I'd love to get a little perspective on. I want to learn something new, and I want to be surprised. I'm going to open the line for calls, and I hope someone will shock me. The subject: the military and the supernatural. Does the military have a use for vampires, lycanthropes, any of the usual haunted folk? Are you a werewolf in the army? I want to hear from you. Know the secret behind remote sensing? Give me a call."

Considering how little time I'd spent on it, the show came together nicely. I'd taken advantage of the collection of interesting folk who'd gathered for the Senate hearings and spent the first hour of the show doing interview after interview. The trio from the Crescent played music, and Robert Carr came in and chatted about werewolves.

But for the last hour I opened the floodgates. I was sure someone out in radioland had some good stories to tell.

"Ray from Baltimore, thanks for calling."

"I can think of *plenty* of military jobs that are just perfect for vampires. Like submarine duty. I mean, you stick somebody on a sub for three months, cooped up in a tiny space with no sun. That's, like, *perfect* for vampires, you know? Or those guys who are locked up in the missile silos, the ones who get to push the button and start World War III."

That "get to" was mildly worrying to say the least. "There's still that food supply to contend with," I said. "It's always been a big limitation on anything vampires accomplish in the real world. I can't picture any navy seaman being really anxious to volunteer for the duty of 'blood supply.' Though it may be a step up from latrine duty."

"Aw, freeze a few pints, they'll be fine."

"All right, next call, please. Peter, you're on the air."

"Hi. Uh, yeah. When I joined the army, I knew this guy who washed out of basic training. We were all surprised, 'cause he was doing really well. Aced all the physicals, obstacle courses, hand-to-hand, nothing held this guy down. The drill sergeant said 'drop and give me a hundred,' and he seemed happy to do it. Never broke a sweat. But he turned up missing on a surprise inspection of the barracks one night. Then it happened again. They kicked him out for going AWOL."

"Let me guess: these were nights of the full moon."

"I don't really remember. I didn't notice at the time. But they were about a month apart. So I'm thinking, yeah."

"Do you think he would have made a good soldier, if he'd been allowed to take a leave of absence for those nights? If the army had made concessions?"

"Yeah—yeah, I think so."

"What about in the field? If his unit happens to be deployed in the middle of nowhere, during a full moon, what's he going to do?"

"Well, I don't know."

"I think it would take some advanced planning. A 'don't ask don't tell' policy probably isn't going to work. Thanks for calling, Peter. Moving on."

I checked the monitor. Then I double-checked it. Line four: Fritz from D.C. It couldn't be. It just couldn't be.

I punched it. "Hello, Fritz?"

"Yes. Kitty? Am I speaking with Kitty?" He spoke with a German accent, tired and grizzled. It was him. My Fritz.

"Yes you are, Fritz. It's me."

"Good, good. I almost did not wait, when the boy put me on hold." His conversational tone made me wonder if he realized that he was on the radio. How refreshing, though, to talk to someone like we were just two people on the phone, rather than being subjected to an attention-seeking crackpot.

"I'm glad you did wait. What would you like to talk about?" I held my breath.

His sigh carried over the line. "I have been thinking of what you said. All day I think to myself, 'Finally, here is someone who wants to listen to you, and you run away from her like a frightened boy.' Now, I think that was a mistake. So I call you. I will die soon.

Think, to die of old age. Is rare for ones like us, eh? But someone should know. This story—someone should know of it."

"All right." I didn't dare say more. Let him talk, let him say what he wanted without leading him on.

"You must understand, it was war. People did things they would not have thought possible before. Terrible things. But we were patriots, so we did them. On both sides, all of us patriots. I was very young then, and it was easy to take orders.

"The S.S. found us, people like us. I also heard rumors, that they created more, throwing recruits into the cage so the wolves would bite them. This I do not know. I was already wolf when they took me. They made us intelligence gatherers. Spies. Assassins, sometimes. As beasts, we could go anywhere, cross enemy lines with no one the wiser. Then we change back to human, do what we were sent to do, and return again. They trained us, drilled us, so we would remember what to do when we were wolves. Like trained dogs. I carried a sack in my mouth, with papers, maps, photographic film. I still remember."

"Fritz, just so I'm clear, you're talking about World War II. The S.S., the Nazi Secret Service—"

"Bah. They call me the Nazi, though they think I do not know. I am no Nazi. We had no choice, don't you see? It was a madness that took all of Germany. Now days, you do not blame the madman who commits a crime. No, you say he was insane. That was Germany."

If I stopped to think about it, my throat would go dry. I would fall speechless. I let the momentum of his story carry me forward. "Something I don't understand: you say you had no choice. But werewolves are stronger than normal humans. Even in human form, they can overpower just about anyone they come up against. Why didn't you? Why didn't you and the others rebel? It sounds like they recruited you against your will, but why did you let them take you instead of fighting them?"

"Besides the fact that it was war? You do not question your countrymen in uniform in time of war. It isn't done. But more than that, they had silver bullets. The cages were made of silver."

My heart thudded. Flemming had a cage made of silver.

"Fritz, is there any documentation of this? I've been doing some research. The Nazi resistance to Allied occupation after World War II were called the Werewolves. Were you involved in that? You're not telling me the members of that group were literally werewolves, are you?"

"I do not remember. It was a long time ago."

It didn't matter. With the story in hand, I had to be able to find the evidence somewhere. There had to be someone else with stories like this. Flemming, for instance.

"Have you told Dr. Flemming this story? Did he ask you to tell him what you did in the war?"

"Yes, he did."

I closed my eyes and felt the air go out of me. "Did he tell you why?"

Fritz gave a snort. "He works for government, yes? It seems obvious."

"You know, I'd give quite a bit to get Flemming back on the show right about now. Fritz—how do you feel?"

"I'm not sure what you mean. I feel old. Tired. Shape-shifting with arthritis in the hands, the shoulders, it's very bad."

"I mean about what happened. What was it like? How old were you? You don't like talking about it, but do you feel better? Does it feel better to talk about it?"

"I think I should go now. I told the story you wanted. The only story anybody cares about."

"Fritz, no! What did you do after the war? Where did you go? When did you come to America? Fritz!"

"Goodbye, Kitty."

"Fritz!"

The line went dead.

Damn. Now what did I do with that? Tiredly, I spoke at the mike. "Dr. Flemming, if you're listening to this, I'd love it if you called in. I have a few questions for you."

Again, I checked the monitor, dreading what I'd find. I wasn't sure I really wanted Flemming to call. This wasn't likely to inspire him to a sudden bout of openness and sharing.

But Flemming didn't call in. None of the calls listed looked remotely interesting. Anything I said next would be the height of anticlimax.

"Right. It looks like we need to move on to the next call. Lisa from Philly, hello."

"Hi, Kitty. Do you know anything about rumors that there's a version of Gulf War Syndrome that causes vampirism? I'm asking because my brother, he's a veteran, and—"

Sometimes, I had absolutely no idea how I got myself into these discussions.

You have a lot on your mind," Luis said. He was driving me around Saturday morning in a cute, jet-black Miata convertible he'd rented for the occasion. He looked dashing, elbow propped on his door, driving one-handed, with his handsome Latin features and aviator sunglasses.

God, did he know how to romance a girl. How could I *possibly* be distracted with him sitting not a foot away from me? A hot Brazilian lycanthrope at my beck and call, looking like something out of a car commercial, and I was frowning. I shook my head, because I had no idea how to answer him.

He'd taken me to Arlington National Cemetery because I'd wanted to see it, but it had been depressing. It wasn't just the acres and acres of headstones, of graves, most of them belonging to people who had died too young, or the Kennedy graves, which were like temples, silent and beautiful. JFK's flickering eternal flame seemed a monument to crushed idealism. The graves were peaceful. But the ceremonies: the changing of the guard at the Tomb of the Unknown Soldier; a full military honors burial, with the horse-drawn caisson and twenty-one-gun salute. All these rituals of death. They seemed so desperate. Did honoring the dead comfort us, really? Did it really do anything to fill the holes our loved ones left behind?

T.J. didn't have a grave to visit. If he did, would I feel better? Less forlorn? If he had a grave, it would be in Denver, where I couldn't go, so it was all moot.

I'm sorry, T.J.

Stop it.

After the cemetery, we drove out of town to the state park where Luis spent full moon nights. He wanted me to be comfortable there. It was nice, getting out of town, leaving the smog and asphalt for a little while, smelling trees and fresh air instead.

We even had a picnic. Another car commercial moment: strawberries and white wine, types of cheeses I'd never heard of, French bread, undercooked roast beef, all spread on a checkerboard tablecloth laid on a grassy hillside.

Luis was trying to distract me. He was doing all this to take my mind off everything I was worried about. The least I could do was pretend like it was working.

"Thanks," I said. "This is wonderful."

"Good. I had hoped you'd smile at least once today."

"I bet you're sorry you found me at the museum."

"No, of course not. I'm glad to have met you. I might wish you were not quite so busy."

He wasn't the only one.

I moved to sit closer to him, inviting him to put his arm around me, which he did. "Can I ask you a personal question?"

He chuckled and shifted his arm lower, so his hand rested suggestively on my hip. "After this week, I should hope so."

I smiled, settling comfortably in his embrace. "How did you get it? The lycanthropy."

He hesitated. His gaze looked out over my head, over the hillside. "It's complicated."

I waited, thinking he'd continue. His expression pursed, like he was trying to figure out what to say, and not succeeding. I didn't know him well enough to know if he was the kind of person who'd wanted to become a lycanthrope, who'd wanted to be bitten and transformed, or if he'd been attacked. We'd had a week of lust and little else, which meant we might as well have just met.

"Too complicated to explain?" I said.

"No," he said. "But it isn't a story I tell often."

"It was bad?" I said. "Hard to talk about? Because if you don't want to—"

"No, it wasn't, really. But as I said—it's complicated."

Now I had to hear it. I squirmed until I could look at his eyes. "What happened?"

"I forgot how much you like stories," he said. "I caught it from my sister. I thought she was hurt, I was trying to help her. She shifted in my arms. I didn't know about her, until then. Even when she bit me, I hardly knew what was happening. It was an accident, she didn't mean it. But she panicked, and I was in the way."

"Wow. That's rough. She must have felt terrible."

"Actually, when she shifted back to human and woke up, she yelled at me. Wanted to know why I couldn't mind my own business and leave her alone. By then I was sick, so she yelled about making her take care of me."

"Let me guess, older sister?"

"Yes," he said with a laugh.

"It sounds familiar."

"She was angry, but she was sorry, too, I think. She took care of me and helped me learn to live with this. Now we help each other keep our parents from finding out about it."

At least I didn't have that problem anymore. I'd never have to come up with another excuse about why I was missing a family gathering on a full moon night. "Your sister's in Brazil?"

"Yes. You know what she does? She spies on companies doing illegal logging in the rain forest and reports to the environmental groups. Sometimes I think she's a bit of a terrorist. Frightened loggers come out of the forest with stories about giant jaguars with glowing green eyes."

"She sounds like an interesting person."

"She is."

We'd been there maybe an hour when I glanced at my watch. I shouldn't even have brought it. But I did.

"Could we get back to town by four, do you think?" I said.

He put his hand on my knee. "Is there nothing I can do to convince you to stay a little longer?"

Oh, the agony. I put my hand on his and shook my head. "I'm sorry. Here you are, doing everything you can to sweep me off my feet, and I'm refusing to cooperate. I'm lucky you're still trying."

He grinned. "I love a challenge."

He leaned over to me, putting his hands on either side of me, trapping me with his arms, and moving closer—slowly, giving me plenty of time to argue and escape before he kissed me.

I didn't argue. Or escape.

I barreled into the Crescent at a quarter after four, convinced I was too late to find Fritz. Not that he'd ever speak to me again. I should have been happy with what he'd revealed last night on the show, but enough never was, was it?

My vision adjusted to the dimness of indoors. I watched Fritz's usual table, expecting his hulking form to be there, once I'd differentiated it from the shadow. I focused, squinting hard, but the table was empty.

Jack stood, elbows propped on the bar, reading a magazine. I leaned on the bar in front of him, and he looked up and broke a wide smile. "Hey! I heard your show last night. That was *cool*."

"Thanks," I said, distracted and not sounding terribly sincere. "I missed him, didn't I? Fritz already left."

"He didn't show today."

"But it's past four. He's never late. Does he not do weekends?"

"He never misses a day."

A weight settled into my gut. "Do you think he's okay? Do you have a phone number for him? Should I go check on him?"

"I don't have a clue where he lives."

This was my fault. Fritz was in trouble and it was my fault. He'd talked, he'd spilled the beans, and someone didn't like it. "Are you even a little bit worried?"

He shrugged. "Wouldn't do any good if I was."

Great, another disinterested isolationist. "Is Ahmed here?"

"I don't think so. I can call upstairs if you want, maybe he's there."

"Sure."

He hit a line on the phone behind the bar, stood there with the handset to his ear for what must have been five minutes, then shook his head. "Nothing."

"Do you think he knows where Fritz lives?"

"He might."

I asked for a pen and wrote my cell phone number on a napkin. "If he does, have him call me."

Jack tucked the napkin by the cash register. "You're really worried about him."

I smiled wryly. "Remember, it's not paranoia if they really are out to get you."

I called Flemming. Please, no voice mail, no voice mail—

"Yes?"

"Dr. Flemming? It's Kitty."

The pause was loaded with frustration. "I really don't have time—"

"Where's Fritz?"

"Who?"

"Don't give me that. He's an old werewolf, German. He said you talked to him. Where is he?"

"How should I know—"

"He always comes to . . . to this one place to have a drink. Four o'clock, every day. He didn't show up today, and I don't think it's a coincidence. He talked on my show, and someone isn't happy—"

"Why should I be that someone?"

"I don't know. But you're my only lead. You must have some idea where he might be."

"Look—yes, I know Fritz. I've spoken with him. If he called your show that's his own business, and I don't know why anyone would have had a problem with it. Not enough of a problem to take drastic action."

I wasn't thinking straight. If I didn't get anywhere with Flemming, I had nowhere else to go, no one else to ask. "I'm worried about him."

"He's a tough old man, he can take care of himself." His voice had changed; it had stopped being flat. I was getting to him.

"He's old. He's falling apart. Werewolves don't get sick, but they do get old. He doesn't have anyone looking after him, does he?"

He sighed. "I have his home address. If you'd like, I'll check on him."

"Can I meet you there?"

"Fine." He gave me the address.

I got the "Thanks" out about the same time I clicked off and ran out to the curb.

Luis was still waiting in the Miata. "Now where are we going?"

I told him the address.

He raised his brows. "You want me to take this car into that neighborhood?"

I smiled brightly. "You paid for damage coverage, didn't you?"

Long-suffering Luis rolled his eyes and put the car into gear.

I bit my lip. I was really going to have to do something nice to thank him later on tonight.

The address turned out to be a tenement building, about forty years old, in dire need of a coat of paint. Or maybe a wrecking ball. Flemming was waiting by the front door, arms crossed, looking around nervously.

His frown turned surly when we pulled up.

"I'm sure there's no need for this," he said as I hopped out of the car. Luis left the engine running.

"You're worried, too, or you wouldn't be here," I said.

"He's on the third floor."

The elevator didn't work, of course. I ran, quickly getting a full flight of stairs ahead of Flemming.

"What room?" I shouted behind me.

"Three-oh-six."

The door was unlocked. I pushed it open.

The place smelled like it hadn't been cleaned in a long time: close, sweaty, dank. Too warm, like the heat was turned up too high. The door opened into a main room. Another door led to what must have been a bedroom; a kitchen counter was visible beyond that.

Stacks of newspapers lined all the walls, folded haphazardly, as if Fritz had read them all, front page to back, and had meant to throw them out but never gotten around to it. Some of the piles leaned precariously. In the middle of the room, an old sofa sat in front of a TV set that must have been thirty years old, complete with rabbit ears wrapped in tin foil. It sat in a corner, on a beat-up end table. A static-laden evening news program was playing.

Something was wrong. Something in the air smelled very wrong—coldness, illness.

Dr. Flemming entered the room behind me, then pushed past me. I'd stopped, unable to cross the last few feet to the sofa. Flemming rushed to it, knelt by it, and felt the pulse of the man lying there.

Fritz lay slumped against one arm of the sofa, staring at the television, perfectly relaxed. His face was expressionless, his eyes blank.

Flemming sat back on his heels and sighed. "If I had to make a guess, I'd say it was a heart attack."

"So he's—he's dead."

Flemming nodded. I closed my eyes and sighed. "It couldn't be something else, something someone did to him?"

"You said it yourself. He's old. Something like this was going to happen sooner or later."

"It's just when he called last night, he almost sounded like he knew something was going to happen to him."

The phone—a rotary, for crying out loud—sat on the table next to the TV. He'd hung up and put it back before this happened.

"Maybe he did." Flemming stared at Fritz's body, like he was trying to discover something, or memorize him. "I've seen stranger things happen in medicine."

I bet he had. He claimed he wanted his research to be public, but he sure wasn't sharing. My anger, the shock of finding Fritz, was too much. Words bubbled over.

"Which is it, Flemming? Medical applications or military applications? Do you have dreams of building a werewolf army like the Nazis did?"

"No—no. That isn't what I wanted, but—"

"But what? What are you doing in that lab?"

He turned away. "I'll call the coroner."

He went to the phone by the TV and made the call. That didn't mean he wasn't going to get a shot at his own autopsy as part of his research. I didn't like the idea of Fritz falling out of official channels into some classified research hole of Flemming's devising, embalmed and pickled in a jar. Fritz had spent most of his life outside official channels. It left him in this lonely apartment, surrounded by newspapers and television, with a glass of schnapps at four P.M. for entertainment. How long would it have taken someone to find him if we hadn't come?

We returned to the street. Flemming said he'd wait for the coroner's van. There wasn't anything left for me to do, and Luis convinced me to leave with him.

As the car pulled away, I started crying.

Sunday morning, I was at Luis's apartment. I'd woken up before him, and lay awake in bed, staring at the ceiling, trying to think. Had Fritz really known his heart was about to give out?

I'd run into a wall. I didn't know what else I could learn about Flemming's research. Maybe there was nothing to learn, nothing but what Flemming had already said in the hearings. I was all worked up over nothing.

My cell phone rang. Luis shifted and mumbled, "Is that mine?"

"No." I retrieved my jeans and pulled the phone out of the pocket.

Caller ID said MOM. Her weekly Sunday call, but hours early. I sat up and pulled the blanket around me. Couldn't be naked, talking to Mom.

I answered the phone. "Hi."

"Hi, Kitty. We're having lunch at Cheryl's, so I wanted to make sure we talked before then. Is this a good time?"

As good as any. As in, not really. "It's okay, Mom."

"How is Washington? Dad's been taping the hearings—C-SPAN's been showing the whole thing, I think. I still haven't seen you in the audience, but he said he did, and he said that's not why he's taping them anyway. He thought you might want to have copies."

I had to smile. "That's cool. Thanks. I'm supposed to testify tomorrow, so tell him to have the VCR ready."

"Oh—good luck! I'm sure you'll do great."

"I just have to answer questions. It'll be fine."

Luis had propped himself on his elbow and was smirking at me.

"Have you had time to do much sightseeing? I visited there when I was in college, we got to see a session of Congress, but it was the House, I think, not the Senate, and—"

Her conversation was so ordinary. It was kind of nice. I made encouraging noises, and avoided saying anything that might make me sound frustrated or depressed. I didn't want her to worry.

Then again, she always knew when I was frustrated and depressed because I didn't say anything.

She actually brought the call to a close herself, almost before I was ready to hear her go. "We should get going. I think Cheryl's nervous about having us over, they've got the new house and I don't think she's got drapes up yet, and Jeffy's teething."

"Tell everyone I said hello."

"I will. Take care, Kitty."

"You, too, Mom. Bye."

"That sounded very suburban. Very American," Luis said, grinning unapologetically.

And there but for the . . . something . . . of lycanthropy went I. "Heard the whole thing, did you?"

"I assume Cheryl is your sister? Which means you have a nephew named Jeffy?"

"And a three-year-old niece named Nicky." He was still smirking. As if I could help it that my sister had picked names straight out of a 1950s sitcom. "Are you making fun of my normal family?"

"Not at all. Not at all." He considered thoughtfully, then added, "*Jeffy?*"

I threw a pillow at him.

After spending all weekend with Luis, I found getting myself to the Senate office building Monday morning almost impossible. I called Ben.

"Hi, Ben? What would happen if I just didn't show up today?"

"When you're scheduled to testify?"

"Yeah."

"They might send federal marshals after you."

Oh. Well then.

I had to stop by Alette's for a change of clothes before heading to the hearings. I thought I might get there before dawn, in time to see Alette, but no such luck. The sun was up when I pulled into the driveway. Tom, the other driver/ MIB, was in the kitchen. He told me that she'd just retired for the day. Briefly, I wondered what exactly that meant. Coffins in the basement?

For once, I didn't ask.

Tom offered me a cup of coffee and said, "We spent the night checking on the vampires you saved from Smith."

"Saved? That's giving me too much credit," I said, muttering into my cup.

He shrugged the comment off. "Some of them want to stay with Alette. They've never had a real place of their own—either they were by themselves or they had abusive Masters. That's why they went with Smith. It must have seemed better."

It probably had seemed better. Some frying pans made the fire look good.

"Is she going to let them? Will she take care of them?"

"Oh, probably. She likes taking care of people." His smile turned wry.

Turned out today was Tom's day off, but he offered to give me a ride to the Senate building anyway. I accepted, finished the coffee, and went to get dressed.

At the Senate building, Ben had something for me—he'd performed some legal wizardry and gotten a copy of Fritz's autopsy report. Flemming was right: heart attack. They were still waiting on some lab tests, but they were calling it a natural death. No conspiracy involved. He was just an old man who'd sensed his own end approaching and wanted to tell his story.

Maybe he'd just given up.

On Ben's advice, I dressed well for the day's session—a suit even, dark blue, with a cream blouse, conservative. He said, don't give them a chance to label me, or classify me as something different or alien. I was an expert witness, nothing more or less.

Not a spokesperson for the entire subject the hearing had been skirting around for the last week.

I'd never advertised what I looked like. I'd never done any publicity stills. When my appearance at the hearings was made public—the panel of witnesses was always made public—at least part of the reason some people were here was to check me out, maybe snap a few pictures for their audiences. I had no idea if I matched their expectations. I was probably younger than they thought I was: mid-twenties, on the thin side, blonde hair done up in a prim bun. Wide-eyed and a little scared. Absolutely not what one would expect a werewolf to look like: some sultry, monstrous seductress, no doubt. Someone who exuded sex and danger. I'd never exuded either. More like, "Go ahead, bully me, I'm weak and vulnerable." I wasn't up to explaining to anyone, much less a Senate committee, the subtleties of werewolf pack dynamics, how for every scary dangerous werewolf that fit the stereotype, there were a dozen who would just as soon grovel on their bellies. People who imagined "monster" when they thought "werewolf" might be surprised to see me.

My problem was, I may have been a monster, but all the other monsters were so much bigger and scarier than I was.

I had a short prepared statement that Ben and I had worked on. I carried the folder with the typewritten page with me to the front of the room. The week's anxiety hadn't prepared me for this. I felt like I was walking to my execution.

Ben sat in the first row, right behind me, ready to bail me out if I needed it. I'd realized, over the last couple of months of being alone, that even though I didn't have a pack anymore, I didn't have to be alone. I *couldn't* be entirely alone. I'd built my own little pack: Ozzie and Matt at my old radio station, Ben, even my mom. I couldn't be afraid to rely on them.

Ben gave me his predator's smile, the one that I was sure made opposing attorneys cringe in the courtroom. A wolf in lawyer's clothing, if that wasn't redundant. I felt a little better.

I settled at the table facing the committee members. They were like vultures, perched behind their desks, staring down at me. I rested my hands on the table and willed them to remain still.

"Ms. Katherine Norville," Duke said. He didn't look at me, but at the papers in front of him, as if searching for an important piece of information. He took his time. "Welcome to this hearing. You have a statement you wish entered into the record?"

There was a microphone in front of me, which was comforting. Hell, it'd be no different than how I made my living week after week. I was just talking to an audience, no different than any other, laying out what I thought and not pulling punches.

"Yes, sir. Senator Duke, I'd like to thank you and the rest of the committee for inviting me here to testify. This is a rare opportunity, and a rare time, to have so much of what is held as scientific fact challenged and reevaluated. I'm privileged to be a part of the process.

"I am what Dr. Flemming would call *Homo sapiens lupus*. That is, I'm a werewolf. I'm allergic to silver, and once a month, during the night of the full moon, I suffer a temporary physical transformation. What this means for me personally: I make adjustments to my life, as anyone with a chronic, nonfatal illness must. And like most people with a chronic, nonfatal illness, I continue to live, to pursue a career, to gain emotional support from my family. It's a decent life, if I do say so myself.

"These phenomena merit discussion for the purpose of bringing them out of the shadows of folktales and nightmares, and into the light of day, so to speak. So that we might confront fear with knowledge."

And just like in an episode of the show, I waited for people to ask questions.

The first came not from Duke—I was bracing for one of the grillings he'd been giving everyone else all week—but from Senator Mary Dreschler.

"Ms. Norville, you'll pardon me for expressing a little skepticism. It's one thing to have so-called experts talk to me about this subject in the abstract. But to have someone sit here and claim to be a werewolf is a bit much to take. What proof can you give us?"

I could have shape-shifted right then and there, I supposed. But I didn't trust my other half to behave herself in this setting—cornered and surrounded by screaming would-be victims. No way.

She wore a flower pendant on a long chain over her cashmere sweater and tailored jacket.

"There's a blood test Dr. Flemming could probably perform. But for right now—Senator, is your necklace silver?"

She frowned quizzically. "Yes."

"May I see it?" I eyed the security goon off to the side. "May I approach?"

No one said anything, and Dreschler slipped the chain over her head, so I went to her place on the risers. She offered me the piece of jewelry.

I took it in my left hand, curling the chain around my fingers for maximum skin contact. My hand started itching immediately, and within seconds the itching turned into burning, like the metal was hot, right out of the furnace hot. I couldn't take it for much longer; my face bunched up into a wince, and I hissed a breath between clenched teeth.

"Here," I said, handing it back to her. I shook it away quickly, more inelegantly than I meant to, in my hurry to get it away from me. I stretched my hand, which still throbbed.

A red rash traced lines around my fingers and left a splotch on my palm, all the places where the necklace had made contact. I held it out, so all the committee members could see it.

"A silver allergy," Dreschler said. "It might happen to anyone. My sister can't wear earrings that don't have surgical steel posts."

"Trust me, this didn't happen before I was infected. I had to give up some killer jewelry because of this."

She showed a thin smile, almost in spite of herself. I went back to my seat; she didn't put the necklace back on.

Next to her, Senator Deke Henderson spoke. "What else? What other changes does this . . . condition bring on?"

"Dr. Flemming mentioned a lot of it in his testimony. It affects the senses. Smell becomes more sensitive, night vision is better. I'd have to say in my own experience it affects mood as well, things like temper and depression. I've heard some jokes about how women make better werewolves since they're used to turning into monsters once a month." That got a few nervous chuckles. "Although I can't say how much of any depression is caused by the condition, or stems from the frustration of dealing with it."

Henderson, the rancher who'd probably spoken out on the debate about reintroducing wild wolves to ranch country, said, "You just called yourself a monster, Ms. Norville. These conditions, as you call them: do they pose a threat to society?"

I had thought long and hard about how I would answer this question. I'd written out a dozen versions of my answer, practiced it, slept on it. Or didn't sleep on it. People on both sides of the issue might not be happy with what I wanted to say.

"No, sir. I don't believe they do. I could mention a dozen issues that better merit your attention if you're worried about dangers to society—highway safety and cancer research, for instance. If they—werewolves, vampires, all of it—*were* a danger, you'd have had to confront them long before now. For centuries, these groups have lived under a veil of secrecy. They haven't revealed themselves to the public, and they have taken great care to monitor themselves, to ensure that they don't become a danger to society at large, and thereby threaten that secrecy. Like any other citizen, it's in their best interests to live by society's laws. Individuals may pose a threat to other individuals—but no more so than any other person. Domestic violence, for example, poses a much greater danger to more people, I think."

The veil of secrecy was gone, now. The centuries of cultural conditioning that we lived by, as governed by the packs and the vampire Families, by gathering places like the Crescent and patriarchs like Ahmed, all of it swept away. A lot of people weren't going to like it. I didn't know what would happen next, what would come of all this. I felt like I was in the middle of the show, with no other choice but to plunge forward. I clung to the familiarity of that fatalism.

Senator Duke pointedly adjusted his microphone to draw attention to himself. My heartbeat quickened. He had not been kind to witnesses this week. I suspected he had saved the bulk of his ire for me.

He said, "Ms. Norville. As a werewolf, have you ever killed anyone?"

He'd done his research, I was sure. He had to know the answer to that.

The whole truth and nothing but the truth. "Yes, sir. I have."

The murmur of the audience sounded like the distant crash of waves. I heard pens scratching on paper. How nice, that some people still used pen and paper.

"Care to explain?" Duke drawled.

"The Denver police have a report of the incident. The situation was self-defense. He—the man I killed—was also a werewolf, and he had murdered several women. When he attacked me, I defended myself the best way I could." It may not have been the *whole* truth . . .

"Did you enjoy it? Killing him?"

"I hope I never have to do anything like that again."

"What about your other half? That demon inside of you? How did it feel?"

He was determined to turn this into a good ol' witch hunt, wasn't he? "There is no demon, sir. Just me."

"That's what you'd like us to think, with your fancy suit and lipstick—"

"Senator, I'm not wearing lipstick."

"—and the Good Book says, 'When he speaketh fair, believe him not for there is abomination in his heart'!"

"Does this mean we're moving away from the 'scientific discourse' part of the testimony?"

"Senator!" That was Henderson. Duke shut up, finally. I sighed.

Henderson continued. "May we please return to the subject at hand? You're in danger of harassing the witness."

"Well past, I'd think," Ben muttered behind me.

Duke glared at Henderson, and I caught a glimpse of a long-standing rivalry, acrimonious and far beyond compromise.

"Senator Duke, do you have any further questions?"

Duke meaninglessly shuffled the papers before him. "I do. Ms. Norville, you host a weekly radio show called *The Midnight Hour*, is this correct?"

Yay, an easy one. "Yes."

"What is the purpose of this show?"

"Entertainment, primarily. Also education. On good days."

"Not conversion?"

I could hear Ben fidgeting, straightening, crossing and uncrossing his arms. He whispered, "Objection . . ." This wasn't a courtroom. He couldn't stand up and yell it.

"I'm not sure I understand you. Conversion to what?"

"You don't use your show to recruit?"

My jaw opened and it took me a second to close it and formulate a coherent sentence. "On the contrary, sir. I want to shatter any romantic illusions about these conditions that people might have picked up from late-night movies. I mean, just listen to the show."

"Ms. Norville, how many werewolves do you think are living in the United States today?"

"I have no idea."

"None at all?"

"No. There isn't exactly a space for it on the census form."

"Maybe we'll change that. If you had to make a guess, what would you say?"

I took at least a couple calls every week from people claiming to be werewolves or some other variety of lycanthrope. Sometimes more, if the topic was werewolf-specific. I didn't believe all the claims. Assuming I was only getting a small percentage of the total—

"Really, sir, I hesitate to even make a guess," I said. I wasn't going to stick my neck out on a question like that.

"What about vampires?"

"Look at the numbers for any rare disease. They're probably comparable."

He made a show of holding one of his pages up, staring at it down his nose like he was trying to focus on something, like maybe he'd found the one question he'd almost forgotten to ask. He made a long buildup, which meant it was going to be the bombshell. Even worse than *are you recruiting*?

"On your show, you've met a lot of your kind, haven't you? You've said that most of you have packs, that you tend to congregate. So, let's say there's another werewolf in this room. You could tell us who it is?"

"I suppose."

"If, in the name of security, I needed you to tell me how to find other werewolves, could you do that?"

Um, I didn't like where this was going.

"How many werewolves do you personally know?"

I glared. "I couldn't say."

"Could you give us names? In the interests of security."

"Right now?"

He shrugged nonchalantly. "In the future, maybe."

I leaned toward the mike. "I think the next thing you're supposed to say is 'I have here a list of known werewolves working inside the U.S. government.' Isn't it?"

He frowned. "I was rather hoping you could help me make up that list."

"Oh, no. No way. You guys—I mean you, the Senate as an institution—you've been down this road before. I won't have anything to do with it."

"Ms. Norville, are you refusing to answer my question?"

"I don't think it's a reasonable question. It's an invasion of privacy, it's—"

"I could hold you in contempt of Congress."

The world had suddenly shifted to an old black and white newsreel. This sort of thing wasn't supposed to happen anymore.

Ben leaned forward to say in a low voice, "The phrase you want is 'Fifth Amendment.'"

Duke pointed at him. "Who are you? Are you influencing the witness?"

Ben stood. "I'm Benjamin O'Farrell, Your Honor. The witness's attorney. Under the Fifth Amendment to the Constitution my client refuses to answer your question on the grounds that it may be self-incriminating."

There. That showed him. I sat a little straighter.

"That's nonsense! It's not an unreasonable question! I can hold you in contempt, I can throw you in jail if I want. The moral and spiritual sanctity of this nation is at stake, and right here in the nation's capital we have the spawn of Satan himself lobbying for equal consideration! The Constitution does not apply to you!"

Everyone started talking at once. Well, not everyone. But it seemed like it. I was stunned, glaring bullets at Duke, and I managed to sputter something about showing him my birth certificate proving I was a natural-born citizen and the Constitution in fact did apply to me. Ben was on his feet, talking about suing in federal court for civil rights violations. Dreschler seemed to be in a mild panic, speaking with one of the committee staffers behind her. Henderson was yelling at Duke; Duke was still shouting quasi-religious bigoted inanities at me.

If I'd been a spectator it would have all been very exciting, I was sure.

Amid the chaos, that deeply buried part of myself was rising to the surface, clawing at the bars of the cage I kept her in, wanting to escape, wanting to *run*, on all her four legs. She knew that in a few hours she'd get to do just that, and she didn't want to wait.

I stayed seated and breathed very calmly, because that was the only way I'd keep her, the Wolf, locked away.

Dreschler reached over and unplugged Duke's microphone, right from the back. That didn't stop Duke from continuing to rant, but now his voice was faded and lost in the back of the room. At last, he realized he'd been had. It took him a surprisingly long time. He glared at Dreschler, eyes bugging and face turning scarlet.

"The committee withdraws the question," Dreschler said coolly into her own mike. "And with all due respect, Chairman, another outburst like that and the committee will vote to censure you."

Ben, moving in slow motion, returned to his seat. Someone in the back clapped a few beats that echoed in the chamber. I dared to look over my shoulder to see who it was. Roger Stockton, camera tucked under his arm.

Dreschler sighed, sounding as tired as I felt. "One last question, Ms. Norville. This committee was convened to determine if the work of the Center for the Study of Paranatural Biology warrants greater attention from the United States Congress, and if the information made public by Dr. Flemming and the Center requires action by the federal government, or poses a threat to the American public. You've been here all week, you've heard the testimony that we have, and you have an insight that none of us understand. If you were sitting up here, what would be your conclusions?"

Was she asking me to do their job for them? Was this my chance to steer policy for the whole government? I spent a moment wishing I would sink through the floor. I hosted a cult radio show, that was all. I wasn't an expert. And a U.S. senator was expecting me to give her advice? Was treating me like some kind of authority? Once again, Alette had called it.

If I blew them off, refused to give them some advice they could use, no one would ever take me seriously again. I'd come too far to deny what I'd become.

"I suppose if I were going to turn activist, this would be my chance. Rally members of the supernatural underworld into some kind of new minority that can lobby the government for recognition and protection. But typically, such people are more interested in anonymity than activism. They just want to be left alone. And oppression hasn't been much of an issue when most people don't believe that the supernatural exists. What Dr. Flemming has done is brought these conditions out of the realm of mysticism and into the area of scientific examination. This is good, presuming that it is done for the right purposes. I worry about the Center's research precisely because its motives are unclear. And I worry that with these conditions now brought into the public eye, such oppression will start.

"I think it's too early to make sweeping decisions. But I would ask the members of the committee to keep their minds open. I would hope that whatever publicity comes out of this, people remember that these are diseases, and the Americans who have them are still Americans."

"Thank you, Ms. Norville. That closes hearings for today. The committee has a long deliberation ahead of it. We'll hope to reconvene in the near future with our concluding statements."

Henderson and Dreschler stood and booked it out of there like they couldn't wait to be somewhere else. Duke took a moment to glare at me vindictively, like it was my fault he'd lost control of his own committee.

Whatever.

Ben put his hand on my shoulder. "You did okay. Let's get out of here."

"Norville! Kitty Norville! Can I ask you a few questions? How long have you had this condition? Tell us how it happened—did you survive an attack? Do you recommend people arm themselves with silver bullets?"

"We have no comment at this time. Thank you," Ben said.

Ben tried to hustle me out of there. We looked like a hundred scenes aired on news programs, of people leaving courtrooms or hearings. I kept my head up, trying to salvage some dignity, but my gaze was down, avoiding eye contact. Ben stayed close, partially shielding me from the cameras and reporters. He wasn't a were-wolf, but right now he was my pack, and I was grateful for the pro-tection.

"Kitty!"

I looked up at the familiar voice. Jeffrey Miles was trying to push toward me through the crowd. He must have been sitting in the back of the room. I paused to let him catch up to us.

He wasn't smiling. His normally easygoing demeanor was gone. He looked tense.

"What's wrong?" I asked.

"It's Roger. He left in a hurry right before the session ended. He seemed really anxious."

Sure enough, Roger Stockton wasn't among the throng that fol-lowed me. I'd have expected him to jump out in front of me with that damned camera.

I couldn't help it; his absence made me nervous. I shrugged to cover it up. "Maybe he had someplace to be."

"I think he's up to something," Jeffrey said. "Be careful, Kitty."

I nodded, uncertain. Why would Roger be up to something? We were buddies now, right? Someone shoved between us, and the crowd carried me away. Ben kept his hand on my elbow until we made it outside.

Bradley waited at the curb with Alette's car.

"You should let him give you a ride back to your hotel," I said.

Ben looked over his shoulder at the reporters and agreed.

The car doors finally shut out the chaos.

"You're off to go all furry now, I assume," Ben said.

I couldn't think of a snide reply. "Yup."

"Be careful. I'm sure that Miles guy is right. Stockton knows what night it is. He'll probably try to follow you."

"We won't let that happen, sir," Bradley said, glancing at us in the rearview mirror.

Ben scowled. "Pardon me if I don't entirely trust a minion of the dark."

I shushed him. Fortunately, the hotel wasn't far away. We arrived before the discussion could degenerate further.

Ben got out, then leaned in before closing the door. "Just be careful. Call me when you get back."

I nodded, bewildered at his vehemence. He didn't look at all happy. I couldn't do anything about that.

"Thanks, Ben."

He closed the door, and we returned to Alette's. I needed to change into something scruffy.

Just after dusk, Bradley and Leo prepared to drive me to the Crescent. I'd meet Luis there. I didn't know why Leo had to come along. He said he wanted the air. Alette said she wanted him to make sure we weren't followed and that Luis would take good care of me. Like they'd turned into my parents who insisted on vetting the boys I dated. I was an adult, for God's sake. I tried to ignore him.

I couldn't wait. Before we even left the driveway, my foot was tapping a rapid beat on the carpeted floorboard in the backseat of the sedan. In moments, I'd be at the Crescent, with Luis and the others, away from Leo and politics and all of it. I was back in jeans and a T-shirt, my hair loose, feeling a weird and not unpleasant charge in the air. On these nights, when I could feel the full moon rising, even though it wasn't visible yet, the Wolf leapt inside of me. She turned into a kid at Christmas, giddy with anticipation, knowing her big moment was close.

I had to stay human a little while longer. I had to keep her locked in, and that was the hard part, because slowly, bit by bit, sliver by sliver, I was losing control. By midnight, I wouldn't be able to hold her in any longer.

"Lovely evening," Leo said conversationally, over the backseat. "I have to admit, I'm a little jealous. The chance to run around with a bunch of animals. I get chills just thinking about it."

It was a perfect night for running. Clear and crisp, with a touch of a breeze. Scents and sounds would carry. Morning would be cool enough to make me grateful to have others nearby, bodies contributing warmth. I rolled my shoulders, stretching, knowing what would come soon.

"You know," Leo continued in his mock-amiable tone. "I imagine you make a lovely little wolf. I'd very much like to see that."

I couldn't bring myself to care enough to tell him to shut up.

Bradley glanced at me in the rearview mirror. "Are you sure you're going to be okay?"

Him, I smiled at. "I've done this before, you know."

"Yeah, but it's a new place. New people. I just thought I'd ask."

"Thanks." I was sick of people asking if I was going to be okay. I'd made it this far, hadn't I?

I was going to be a little late. Just a few minutes. I hoped Luis would wait for me. But really, I didn't doubt that he would wait for me. Just nerves.

Leo said, "Bradley, would you mind pulling over here for just a moment? I'd like to take a look at something."

"Here?" Bradley pursed his lips, looking confused, but came to a stop at the corner, as Leo requested. "What is it?"

I wondered as well. The Crescent was only a few blocks away. I could walk there at this point.

"Don't worry, it won't take long." Leo flashed his grin at me, then lunged at Bradley.

It happened so fast the driver didn't have a chance to flinch. Leo grabbed his head and wrenched, twisting it sharply until it crunched. As a man, Leo didn't look like much. Didn't look strong enough to break a man's neck. But he was a vampire, with a strength and speed that were blinding. Bradley probably didn't even know what was happening.

I didn't even have a chance to scream.

Leo didn't pause before launching over the backseat. It should have been awkward, but he seemed to fly, leaping at me arms outstretched, pinning me. He grabbed my hands, slipped something out of his pocket, wrenched my arms back, and a second later I was locked in handcuffs, my hands behind my back. The cuffs burned, searing against my wrists like they were hot from an oven. When I pulled against them, the pain flared.

Who the hell had silver alloy handcuffs?

Leo rolled me faceup and straddled me, pinning my legs with his body, squeezing his hand on my throat. "Be a good little kitten and this will all be over soon. If you start shape-shifting, I *will* kill you. Understand?"

He wasn't actually wanting to *rape* me, was he?

I squirmed, the handcuffs seared my skin, and I whimpered.

"Oh, you poor dear." He leaned close, breathing against my cheek. I shut my eyes and turned away. I could get through this. Whatever he planned, I could get through it.

His teeth rubbed against my jawline just before a fang dug in. It felt like a pinch.

I screamed, arching my back to thrash away, not caring about him or the silver, just wanting to get away.

He held me too well, pinned against the length of the backseat,

my arms immobile under me. I wasn't getting away. He licked the
wound he'd made. Then, laughing, he straightened.

"My, you are high-strung, aren't you? Don't worry, as much fun
as it might be, this isn't what the evening has in store for you."

Howl, claw, bite, Change, run away . . .

No. Couldn't let Wolf out, couldn't let her panic overwhelm me.
Keep it together, stay in my body, my human body. I didn't doubt
that Leo would kill me if I Changed.

That took all my strength. I didn't have enough left over to even
tell him to fuck off.

From his jacket pocket he took out a couple of handkerchiefs. I
was breathing hard, whining with every breath, frozen with panic.
Bradley's face leaned against the seat, toward me, dead eyes staring at me. Dead, blank, gone. I should have seen it coming, he
should have seen it coming, this shouldn't be happening—

Leo jammed one scarf into my mouth, tying it behind my head.
Another went around my eyes.

Breathe, steady, stay anchored. Keep it together, that was what
T.J. always said. *Good girl.*

T.J. wasn't around to rescue me this time.

The car door opened, closed. Then another one opened and closed. My nose and ears worked overtime, compensating for the lack of sight. Leo had left the backseat and returned to the front seat. A weight shifted. He was shoving Bradley's body out of the way.

The engine was still running. Bradley hadn't shut it off, only shifted to park. Leo put the sedan in gear, and we drove away.

I didn't count turns, knowing it wouldn't do any good because I couldn't judge the distance. We drove for what seemed a long time. We must have been leaving town. We could be going anywhere.

All I could do was keep breathing, and keep my hands still so the silver didn't burn as much.

Finally, we stopped. Car doors opened, first the front, then the back.

"Sit up," Leo said.

I couldn't. My muscles were frozen. He grabbed my shoulder and hauled me up.

"Out."

Again, I tried. Given enough time, I could have made the epic journey from the seat to outside the car on my own. But I was too slow for Leo. He dragged me out, and he was strong enough to keep me on my feet when all I wanted to do was collapse. He held me up with one hand on my arm. The other clamped on the back of my neck, guiding me.

"Walk," he said.

I stumbled. He moved too quickly, but somehow I got my feet under me. We were outdoors, out of D.C. The air was a little fresher. Where were we? Given another moment I might have figured it out by the smell of the air, but Leo was in a hurry.

A door opened, then closed behind us. We'd entered a building.

Here, the air smelled antiseptic, sickly, too much disinfectant and not enough life. The floor was tile.

I knew that smell. I'd been here before. This was the NIH Clinical Center.

We rode an elevator. I tried not to think, because thinking made me scared and angry. The more emotion I felt right now, the closer Wolf came to breaking free. The moon was so close right now.

I leaned away from Leo; his grip on my neck tightened. I had to breathe, calmly and coolly. My mouth was dry. I swallowed back screams.

The elevator opened into the basement. Leo pushed me forward again. I knew how many steps we'd go, I knew which door he guided me through. Without seeing, I could have made my way around the furniture in the office.

In the next room I smelled people. I sucked in air, trying to sense them, how many, who they were.

"My God, was this really necessary?"

I knew that voice. I knew that voice better than I knew the man it belonged to. Dr. Paul Flemming.

"Could you have done it any better, then?" Leo said, annoyed. "You wanted me to bring her, you didn't say how."

Leo rattled the handcuffs—turning a key. Unlocking them. All my muscles tensed. He said he'd kill me and I almost didn't care. I just wanted to hurt him.

The burning metal fell away, but before I could turn, he shoved me forward. I scrambled to keep my balance. I stayed on my feet, and in the same moment tore off the gag and blindfold.

I stood in the werewolf holding cell of Flemming's lab. The walls sparkled silver, pressing against me. The door was locked. Slowly, I stepped toward the Plexiglas wall. *Keep it together,* I told myself. I wanted to face them as a human, to tell them what I was thinking.

Flemming's lab was full of people. At least, it seemed like it. I had to stare, studying the scene before me for a long time, because it didn't seem real. I didn't believe it. Flemming stood near my window, arms crossed, looking hunched-in and miserable, lips pursed and gaze lowered. To my right, near the wall, stood Senator Duke and one of his aides, a man I recognized from the hearings. Beyond them were three hard-core army-looking types: they wore all black, down to the combat boots, had severe crew cuts, and toted machine guns. They glared at me. Leo stood directly in front of me, grinning like this was the funniest thing he'd seen all week.

To my left, occupying the largest space of floor that was free of lab benches and equipment, was a news crew. It looked like a full-on studio job, with a large television camera, a camera operator, and a sound guy with a mike on a boom and headphones. And Roger Stockton, sans handheld video camera. Someone had given him a promotion. An equipment bag on the floor nearby bore the logo of a local network affiliate.

He stared at me, wide-eyed, like a rabbit in a trap. He trembled like prey, like he knew that if I wasn't currently behind a locked door, I'd kill him.

I started to laugh, then stopped, because the nausea wracking my stomach was about to break loose. I swallowed, and my mouth tasted like copper.

"What's going on here?" My voice cracked.

No one said anything. They'd come here to see a monster. Monsters weren't supposed to talk back.

Finally, Roger said, "Live broadcast. I sold the story to the network. It's my big break. I can take my work to the mainstream. Hey, if you'd just given me an interview, I wouldn't have agreed to this." A smile flickered, then disappeared.

"Unreal," I muttered, not aware I'd spoken aloud until I heard my voice. But why stop myself? "Fucking unbelievable. You were supposed to be for real! Searching for the truth, looking for knowledge—not in it for the fame and money! But you really are scum, aren't you? Playing like you're my friend, then selling me out the first chance you get—" My first impressions weren't *always* faulty, apparently. "What the hell are you trying to accomplish with this? What the *hell* do you think is going to happen? And *you*." I pressed my hands to the glass in front of Leo. "What are *you* getting out of this? Does Alette know you're working for them? God, of course not—you wouldn't have killed Bradley then. You're moving against Alette, aren't you?" His expression of amusement didn't waver.

Duke said with a tone of disgust, "We don't have to explain ourselves."

"It's just for the night," Flemming said softly. "You'll be free to go in the morning."

Then, I did laugh. Bitter, hysterical laughter. I shut my mouth before it could become a howl. "Are you kidding me? Do you think that makes everything all right? You're supposed to be a scientist, Flemming. You call this *science*?"

"I think he calls it public relations," Leo said. "He's a bureaucrat. Well, gentlemen, it's been lovely working with you, but I have business elsewhere." The vampire wore a sly grin on his face, looking terribly amused. "Doctor, if you'll remember our agreement?"

If anything, Flemming became more pale and uncomfortable-looking, kneading the fabric of his jacket sleeves. He looked over at the soldiers and nodded. Two of them moved toward the door and waited.

Leo tossed me a salute. "Take care of yourself, Miss Norville."

He stalked out of the room without waiting for a response. The two soldiers followed him.

Soldiers. Flemming had given the bastard backup. I had to call Alette. Would someone let me call Alette?

Senator Duke marched over to the doctor and pointed an accusing finger at the door Leo had just left through. "Dr. Flemming, I have to protest you making deals with that monster. When I agreed to help you, you said nothing about working with the likes of *that*."

"I think there's some debate about who's helping whom here, Senator. I'm giving you the evidence you want. You said you didn't want to be involved in collecting that evidence."

"You'd do well to remember you wouldn't even have a chance to save your research if it weren't for me."

"I seriously wonder about that." He kept his gaze focused on me. I felt like a bug under a microscope.

I had to move. I had to get out of here. I saw the way out—through the door, past my enemies. Had to be a way out. If I kept moving, walking long enough, far enough, I'd find a way out. Had to turn before I got too close to the wall—it felt hot, the silver would burn me.

"Kitty!"

I flinched, startled out of my manic thoughts. Flemming had uncrossed his arms and was watching me, concerned.

"You're pacing," he said.

Like a caged wolf, back and forth across the front of the cell. I hadn't even noticed.

I couldn't see the moon. I didn't have to. A cramp wrenched my body. I doubled over, hugging my stomach, gritting my teeth, and unsuccessfully stifling a groan.

"Jesus, what's wrong with her?" the cameraman said.

Flemming frowned. "She's a werewolf."

Public relations. That was the game we were playing, was it? Flemming and Duke would both win support for their causes if they could prove, once and for all, that the monsters were real. The hearings hadn't been able to do that; that was all just talk. They needed videotape. Brightly lit, clinical videotape.

I didn't have to give up the fight that easily. There was a way out. If I could keep in control for a little while longer, I could beat them. I breathed, taking a moment to center myself, to convince my body to stay human. *You'll be out soon,* I told Wolf. *Just give me the next hour or so.*

She settled. We lived by compromise, my Wolf and I. She understood that the human half had to fight this battle.

"Roger, come here. I have to talk to you." I stood near the glass wall, by the dinner tray slot. I turned my back to the others.

"Why?" He laughed nervously. "You look like you want to kill me."

"That's because I do. But I won't. Come here."

I must have sounded serious, because he obeyed. Stockton crept forward slowly, like he thought I could break out of here. I couldn't; leaning on the Plexiglas told me it was solid. The hinges on the door were strong—and painted with silver. I might be able to break through, but I'd have to throw myself against it all night and probably wouldn't be in great shape afterward.

Let the human side deal with this.

"I have a counteroffer, Roger. How'd you like to produce the first live televised episode of *The Midnight Hour*?"

His brow furrowed, confused. "What, here?"

"Yup. Look, I know Duke and Flemming aren't going to let me out of here. But if I'm going to end up on TV, I want to do it on my terms. I get my show, I get to have my say, and you get your footage. That's what you want, isn't it? Real live film of a werewolf transformation, in a brightly lit lab, no shadowy forests and night-vision cameras, and you get a front-row seat. I just want a little credit. Duke and Flemming still get to prove their points. Everybody wins."

"What, you want me to put in a phone line, take calls—"

"No, there's no time for that. I just want a mike so I can talk to the audience. A few supplies, some music, I'll carry the whole thing by myself. That's all I'm asking for, some odds and ends and billing for the show. What do you say? You owe me, Stockton." That did come out as a growl. Just a little. I grit my teeth, glared—I couldn't imagine what I looked like to him. Like a werewolf. He stepped back.

"If all I want is werewolf footage, I'll get that one way or the other," he said.

And he was right, of course. I was in a very poor bargaining position. "Then tell me what you want."

He glanced at Flemming and Duke, who were their usual stolid and frowning selves. He hesitated, his face gone stony with thought. His jovial, animated facade had disappeared. Then, he said, "I still want that interview. I'll interview you, then you can do or say whatever you want for the rest of the broadcast."

Dammit, if he asked me any questions I was likely to swear a blue streak at him. I didn't know how much self-control I could manage for the next hour—surely not enough to produce a cohesive interview. All I wanted to do was scream. But I was in no position to negotiate. I wanted a microphone, and if this was what I had to do to get it, then so be it. "Fine, okay."

He pursed his lips and nodded. "Right. We'll do it."

I thought I was going to melt with relief. The night wasn't over yet, but I'd gotten the ball back in my court. Half a ball, anyway.

I said, "Call my home radio station and talk to the executive producer, Ozzie, he'll clear up all the legal stuff." I gave him Ozzie's phone number, and recited the list of gear I thought I'd need. CD player, Creedence Clearwater Revival and whatever other CDs he could scrounge up, a copy of London's *Call of the Wild*, and—

"A rump roast?" Stockton stared at me before writing it down.

"It'll make her much happier, trust me." Let him work out that bit of phrasing on his own.

Stockton conferred with his crew, then turned back to me. "I'll be back in twenty—no, fifteen minutes. Don't start without me."

"Wouldn't think of it."

Flemming looked worried. "What do you think this will accomplish?"

I shrugged, feeling giddy. "Don't know. Don't care. It's just nice to be doing something."

I wasn't supposed to be here. I *really* wasn't supposed to be here. As in, this wasn't the way my life was supposed to go. Even just a few years ago, as a child of yuppies my life had been pretty much laid out for me: a decent degree from a decent university, a decent job—maybe in radio, but probably something nine to five, like sales. Marriage, children, tract housing on the prairie and a golden retriever playing fetch in the backyard. What all the other girls were doing.

Then the attack, and the wolf came, and nothing could ever, ever be normal again. There'd never be a golden retriever in the back-yard—dogs hated me now. They could tell what I was.

Still, none of that explained how I got into these situations. Was I too young to retire? Get a nice, quiet job in accounting some-where?

On full moon nights, keeping human form became painful, then it became impossible. Wolf had to be free, she had to be released, and if she had to rip her way out, she would. So much easier to let it slide, let it happen.

I couldn't do that, not tonight. Had to stay human as long as I possibly could, had to be in control, know what was happening. I'd had practice at this. I sat still, kept still, breathed slowly. *Just a lit-tle while longer, girl.*

I had a couple of tricks I used to keep the Wolf at bay. Humming Bach while thinking of broccoli. My humming was becoming more frantic, and still my stomach churned. The thin line between human and beast was growing thinner. When it disappeared, I'd be gone.

I had to stay on my side of the line. I imagined the line growing thicker. I had to keep it in place.

"T.J., I wish you could help me."

I remembered him holding me, when I started to lose it. *Keep it together*, he'd whisper. *That's a girl.*

Keep it together.

The line remained drawn. I was still human. I took a deep breath, fitting into my skin a little more firmly.

Stockton returned in less than half an hour, more quickly than I expected despite his promise. He must really have been worried about missing something. He carried two big shopping bags. I pic-tured him running through the store, throwing things into a cart, and flinging his credit card at the poor checkout clerk.

"I talked to your producer. Ozzie, that's his name? He didn't be-lieve me, so he said to call him back and get you on the phone."

Of course Ozzie didn't believe him, and I didn't blame him. I'd avoided TV like the plague. I was so glad I had smart friends.

"Do it," I said.

Duke, still off to the side, showed me an ugly snarl. "You can't think this will help you. The world will still see you as you really are."

"That's what I'm hoping," I muttered.

Flemming turned to Stockton. "I'm having second thoughts. I'm not sure we should go through with it."

"Oh, no," the reporter said. "You were the one who called me, you were the one who arranged this whole thing. I want my story—it's out of your hands."

"Stand aside, Doctor," Duke said. "Let the man work. She can't possibly say anything that will save her from what's coming. Let her incriminate herself."

Stockton called Ozzie on the land line—no mobile reception in the basement. He managed to get the phone cord to stretch halfway across the room, and the handset barely fit through the tray slot.

Ozzie launched right in. "Kitty, what's going on, what's wrong?"

"You'll see it soon enough," I said with a sigh. "Did Stockton bring you up to date?"

"Yeah—he says you're televising the show. But it's not Friday, we haven't announced anything—"

"Just set it up, Ozzie. Make it legal. Secure the rights, grant the license to the network, whatever you have to do."

"Are you okay?"

"No. But don't worry about me. I'll get through it." I hoped. I really, really hoped. "Call Ben O'Farrell for me, will you? Use his cell number."

"Sure. Put that reporter back on."

I handed the phone back and immediately missed Ozzie. I wished he were here.

They talked for a couple minutes, then Stockton hung up.

"Roger. Can I have that phone back for just a minute? I just want to make a call." Two—I wanted to call Alette, and I should call Ben myself while I was at it. Ben and Cormac both. Three calls. No, make that four—Mom. I should call Mom.

Stockton glanced at Flemming, who shook his head.

That was it, then.

Stockton brought the bags to the cell. "If I open the door, will I regret it?"

How far did he think I'd get if I made a run for it? "That depends. Is Mr. Black Ops over there packing silver bullets?"

We looked at the remaining soldier, who didn't twitch a muscle.

"Silver bullets?" Stockton asked.

He nodded, once, curtly. I had no doubt he was a very good shot.

"I'll stand back," I said wryly. Of course, I could let him shoot me and spare myself the next few hours.

Stockton got Flemming to unlock the door and open it a crack—

just wide enough to shove in the shopping bags, before shutting and locking it again.

Well, I'd missed my chance to go out in a blaze of glory.

I went through the bags. It was a little like Christmas. He'd brought me a portable CD player with speakers and batteries, a stack of disks, a couple of books—London, Thoreau. And the meat, which I shoved in the corner for later. Couldn't think about that now, even though I could smell it through the plastic.

"You ready?" Stockton said, shoving a personal mike through the door slot.

I wasn't, but I'd have to be. I took the mike—still attached to a cord, which ran through the slot to the news team's broadcast equipment—and clipped it to my shirt. "How's that?" The sound tech gave me a thumbs-up.

I finished searching the CDs. One of them had a youthful and comparatively unaltered Michael Jackson on the cover.

I glared at Stockton. "*Thriller*? You brought me *Thriller*?"

"You know. *Thriller*." He clawed a hand at me and snarled like he was an extra in a certain music video.

The man had no tact. I tore the plastic off and put the disk on anyway. But I cued it up to "Billie Jean" and turned up the volume.

I watched out of the corner of my eye, and sure enough, by the second bar of music, the two news guys were tapping their feet. Stockton was bobbing his head a little; he probably didn't realize he was doing it. Hey, when the music said to dance, you had to dance.

Duke looked like he was fuming himself into a fit; his face was actually going red. But he couldn't do anything but stand there. His aide—who seemed old enough to remember freaking out over this album in grade school—shifted nervously. Like he *wanted* to tap his feet, but didn't dare.

Flemming's expression didn't change at all.

"Just tell me when we're on the air," I said to Stockton. He conferred with the crew's tech guy, then nodded quickly.

"We'll be in time for the ten o'clock news," he said. I could imagine it, the regular anchor interrupting the newscast with a very special report from Roger Stockton: Kitty Norville, Exposed.

It wouldn't quite work like that. I hoped. I had maybe an hour before the Wolf took over completely. Had to make it count.

I cut off Michael and put on John Fogerty. CCR's "Bad Moon Rising" was the show's theme song on regular nights. It wouldn't have felt right without it.

Wait for it . . . wait for it . . .

"Okay, Kitty, you're on in three . . . two . . . one . . ." He pointed at me. I punched the play button. I let the guitar strum a few chords before looking out the glass wall and facing the camera.

Think happy thoughts. No different than being behind the mike. Don't think about the fact that I can't hide, that I can't be anonymous anymore. This was about revenge, about turning the tables, and to do that I had to be on top.

I smiled. "Greetings! Welcome to the first televised edition of *The Midnight Hour*, the show that isn't afraid of the dark—or the creatures who live there. I'm Kitty Norville."

The inside of the cell was lit as brightly as the outside, and the camera was at an angle. They'd made sure there wouldn't be any glare. Everyone could see me. All of me.

"If you're not familiar with *The Midnight Hour*, let me tell you what this is all about. Every Friday night for a few hours, I talk to people on the radio. I take calls, I invite guests on for interviews— politicians, writers, musicians, anyone I can convince to talk to me. What do we talk about? Nightmares: werewolves, vampires, witches, ghosts, demons, and magic. All those stories you read under the blanket with a flashlight, that kept you awake on nights when the wind rattled your bedroom window? You may not be ready to believe it, but those stories are real. And if you don't believe it now, just stick around. Because in an hour or so, I'm betting you'll change your mind. I'm a werewolf, and tonight I put my money where my mouth is." Money shot? Hoo-boy.

I turned the music down but let it keep playing. It distracted the part of my brain that was starting to gibber. "If you *are* familiar with the show, you may notice something a little different about the format. You may also notice this isn't the usual time slot. And those of you who are very astute might notice that tonight's the full moon, and you might be asking yourself, what the hell am I doing locked in a room? Those are really good questions. Let me introduce you to the people who've made this possible. Can we get the camera pointed that way for a second? Great, thanks." The cameraman obliged, pivoting the camera toward the other side of the room.

Flemming backed away, shaking his head. But he didn't have anywhere to go. The camera lens pinned him against the wall. Duke, a little more used to appearing on camera, didn't flee. But he glared bullets.

"Let's see, to your right is Dr. Paul Flemming, director of the

3333

Center for the Study of Paranatural Biology, whose laboratory I'm currently locked up in. Across the room you might recognize Senator Joseph Duke, who's heading up hearings regarding the Center for the Study of Paranatural Biology. Camera back here, please. Thanks." Keep smiling. Beauty queen smile, frozen and glittering. Oh, yeah.

"I want to add at this point that I'm here completely against my will. You see, Flemming and Duke are both afraid that cheap talk in a special committee hearing isn't enough to convince the government or the American public that werewolves are real. They both really want to do this, because Flemming wants to keep his funding for the lab, and Duke wants to start a witch hunt. Wolf hunt. Whatever. So they arranged to tie me up with silver, lock me up, and broadcast the results live on national television. You know why they think they can get away with this? Because they don't believe I'm human."

"No, that isn't—" Flemming stepped forward, beginning some kind of protest. I glared him to silence.

"If you thought I was human you wouldn't have agreed to this. You wouldn't have this *jail*. So. I sort of made a deal to try to tell my side of the story before things get hairy. I mean, *really* hairy.

"A couple of things before we go much further. Mom, Dad, Cheryl?" If Cheryl was watching, she'd have called my parents by now. She was always telling on me. "I'd really appreciate it if you turned off the TV right now. You do not want to watch this. It'll upset you. You're probably not going to listen to me, but don't say I didn't warn you. I love you guys. And Ben, if you're watching? Just one word: lawsuit. No, make that two words: multiple lawsuits."

I rubbed my hands together. "Right. Let's get started then. Roger, come on over here."

The reporter slicked a hand over his mussed hair, smoothed the front of his shirt, and adjusted the mike he'd clipped to his collar before moving to stand by the door of the cell. We glared at each other through the Plexiglas, as if we could pretend it wasn't there.

"Also here tonight is Roger Stockton, a reporter for the supernatural exposé show *Uncharted World*. Hello, Roger. As I recall, you insisted on conducting an interview. Is now a good time for you?"

He smirked. "As long as you're not busy."

"I'm a captive audience. Do your worst."

As much as I hated to admit it, his interview was good. I wished it had been under more comfortable circumstances. He made it a conversation, letting one answer lead into the next question, rather than rattling off a rote list of prepared questions. He didn't jump on the ends of my answers, letting me finish before talking again. He began by asking about the show, how it started, what my policies were, behind the scenes insights. He might not have been entirely pleased with my answers: I didn't say anything that I hadn't already said at the Senate hearing or on the show at one point or another.

Stockton started the wrap-up. "One last question, Kitty. Tonight, those of us here along with the audience at home are going to witness the legendary transformation of a werewolf, with your help—"

"—my completely involuntary help, I want to make that clear."

"Um, yes. Of course. Can you tell us a little about what we can expect to see?"

"Sure. Out of all the movies I've seen, Robert Carr's werewolf films like *New Tricks* and *Bloody Moon* are the closest I've seen to depicting what it's really like. That's because at the end of the transformation you see something that looks like a real, wild wolf— *Canis lupus*. The only difference is the werewolf is usually bigger because of conservation of mass. The average full-grown person weighs more than a wild wolf. What happens in between—it's hard to explain. Bones re-form, skin grows fur, teeth change—all of it."

"Is it painful?"

"Usually. But most of the time it happens quickly. You try to make sure it goes quickly."

"How do these changes happen without killing the person? Without destroying the body completely?"

"People have been studying this, but no one has a good physical explanation for how the body changes shape without being destroyed. When all is said and done you still have to label this as the supernatural, because it goes beyond what we understand."

"Propaganda!" Fuming, Duke stormed into the camera's line of sight. His face was red and he was shouting, almost to the level of sounding incoherent. "This is a ploy by the left-wing radical media to undermine the truth of the Good Book, which tells us thou shalt not suffer a witch to live! This is what happens when you listen to the words spoken by an agent of Satan!"

Stockton stared at him, round-eyed and blinking.

"I'm not an agent of Satan," I said tiredly. Not that it would do any good.

"Time will tell! You're no more human than the beast inside of you!"

"Senator, for the last time, I have a birth certificate that proves I'm an American citizen, and you're currently violating my civil rights in a big way. Don't make me add slander to the charges I'm going to bring against you."

"Make your threats. I have great faith that the people will thank me for what I've done here tonight."

"Senator, look at this, look at this picture you're showing people: you've got me in a"—uh, probably shouldn't say that word on network TV—"a freaking cage! You're standing there slobbering like a madman, calling a reasonably cute blond an agent of Satan, and you think this makes you look like a good guy?"

"History will prove me right. When hordes of your kind overrun the homes and neighborhoods of God-fearing folk, people will know I'm right and my actions will be justified!"

Hordes? Huh? "Oh, you can just keep talking, because you're digging yourself a hell of a hole, monkey boy!"

"Kitty, maybe not so much yelling," Stockton said.

That stalled the tirade for the moment. I was breathing hard, like I'd just been in a fight. Duke and I glared at each other through the glass. Yeah, he could be a tough guy when I was locked in here. But put him in here with me . . .

I grunted as pain washed through me and ducked to hide my grimacing features. Too late. I'd run out of time. Pain burned through my nerves, down my limbs. I could feel every pore on my body. In moments, fur would sprout.

"Both of you, get away from the window," I said, my voice low and scratching. Surprised, they did so. I had to pull it together for just another minute.

I straightened and looked at the camera.

"Of all the authors I've read, Jack London gets my vote for most likely to have been a werewolf. Even if he wasn't, he spent a lot of time writing about the line between people and animals, civilization and the wild—how that line usually isn't much thicker than a hair, and how it gets blurred. He understood that space better than anyone. That's a lot of what being a werewolf is about: living in that blurred space and learning to reconcile the two sides. The other thing you learn is that a person doesn't have to look like a monster to be one. This is Kitty Norville, voice of the night. If you remember nothing else about this broadcast, please remember my voice. I'm not going to have it anymore."

T.J. had held me the very first time I shape-shifted. I imagined his arms around me now, his voice. *You'll be okay, you'll be okay—* The Change slammed into me, fast and brutal. A flood bursting the dam. My punishment for keeping it locked in too long. I bent double, trying to pull off my shirt. I couldn't help it—I screamed, and my sight disappeared.

Hate and fear. And all she could do was watch.

The next day I watched a recording of what Stockton's camera crew broadcast. The news station had framed the video with all sorts of nifty graphics, "Special Report!" and "Live!" logos and the like. It made the whole thing seem cheaper, somehow. As I shape-shifted, I ripped out of my shirt—I went bra-less on full moon nights—and squirmed half out of my jeans and panties. Half naked, tawny fur rippling down my back, I toppled to my side, writhing. My limbs melted and re-formed, my face warped—I'd seen this happen to other people, I'd been through it myself so many times. But watching it happen to me was strange, like what I saw didn't match what I knew I'd felt. The transformation looked fluid, one form morphing into the other in a change that rippled outward from the center of the body. What I'd felt was ripping: the human form ripping apart to let the Wolf out of her cage.

In a few seconds a large, adult wolf lay on the floor of the cell, kicking her hind legs to untangle herself from the jeans still pulled halfway up. She was sand-colored, darker fur trimming her ears, spreading down her back, and tipping her tail. On her chest and under her body the fur turned light, cream-colored. She was sleek, alert, her eyes gleamed a bright amber.

She was beautiful. She was me.

Immediately, she ran. Caged, frightened, she searched for the way out, which meant running along the window, whirling at the silver-painted wall, running back and forth. Unfortunately, she covered the length of the cell in a single stride. She pivoted back and forth, staring out at her captors, like the ultra-neurotic predators in a zoo who seem hypnotized by their own movements.

A domestic dog who's angry or afraid might bark itself hoarse— as they were bred to do in their role as watchdogs. In the wild, wolves rarely bark. My Wolf was silent. The whole lab was dead silent, except for the click of her claws on the linoleum. The personal mike still lay on the floor, clipped to my discarded shirt, picking up the sound of it.

Duke dropped to his knees before the window, laughing harshly. "You see? You see what we're dealing with? You can't ignore this!" He looked at the camera and pointed at Wolf.

She shied back, startled, head low and ears pricked forward, waiting for a challenge.

Evidently expecting a slavering, howling beast slamming herself against the window in an effort to attack him, Duke frowned.

"Don't give me that," he said. "Don't play coy. You won't get anyone's sympathy. You'll *show* them what you really are. I'll make you show them!"

He scrambled to his feet and lunged at Stockton, who stood on the other side of the cell. The reporter put up his arms in a startled defense.

Eyes wide, lips snarling, Duke grabbed Stockton's arm and pulled him off balance. Then he opened the tray slot in the door and shoved the reporter's hand into it.

Stockton shouted in a panic and struggled to pull away, but Duke kept him locked in place, bracing with his entire body. Spry old guy, wasn't he?

"Go on! Bite him!" Duke shouted. "Show us what you are, what you're like! Attack him!"

Wolf's tail dropped and she backed away, putting distance between herself and the raving madman in front of her. She knew how to keep out of trouble.

With a soft whine and an air of sadness, she settled in the far corner of the cell—as close to the corner as she could get without touching the walls—lying flat and resting her muzzle on her front paws.

Duke stared, mouth open, disbelieving. Stockton took the chance to break free and pull away from the door.

Everyone stared at the wolf huddled in the corner. Frightened, she just wanted to be left alone. She didn't even go for the meat.

The broadcast cut off there. Watching a miserable wolf wasn't that exciting, the network decided.

I woke up shivering. The linoleum was cold. I hugged myself, but I was naked, lying curled on the floor, unable to get warm. My jeans were all the way in the middle of the floor. My shirt was torn, I couldn't tell if it was salvageable.

The door to the cell stood open.

Sighing, I gathered myself for the effort of dressing. I had to get out of here.

I'd crawled halfway across the floor when I saw Flemming outside the cell, leaning against a lab table, arms crossed, watching me.

Nothing to do but carry on. Quickly I pulled on my jeans and retrieved my shirt. It had a rip up the side, along the seam, but it would have to do. I sat on the cot to lace up my sneakers.

"So. Did you get what you wanted? Besides getting to watch a naked woman sleep for half the night." I tried to sound angry, but my voice cracked, weary to the point of failing.

He scowled and looked away. "I don't know. The network aired the live footage for an hour. They sold the footage and the news channels have been replaying the pertinent clips all night."

The pertinent clips. That meant the thirty seconds of me shape-shifting, and nothing else. None of my words, nothing of what I'd said to explain those thirty seconds. What a farce.

"Is that what you wanted? Do you even know what you wanted?"

He took a shuddering breath and turned his lips in a pained smile. It might have been the first time I'd ever seen him smile. "I wanted to change the world. I wanted to single-handedly open a whole new discipline of study. I wanted to find the . . . the cure for everything. Superimmunity. Somewhere in your biology is the secret to that. If I could just convince the people with money that it's not fiction, that I'm not . . . crazy."

"And you think kidnapping me, locking me up, and putting me

on TV is the way to prove that?" I wanted to rip him to shreds. I could. Sprout a couple of claws, run a couple of strides, and be on his throat in a heartbeat. Inside, Wolf was growling. "The one thing you haven't learned is that you can't control this. No one can control this. People—werewolves, vampires, the church, the Senate, everybody—have been trying for centuries and it doesn't work. The Master vampires build their Families, take over cities, bully the lycanthropes, and play their little power games. Packs form and disintegrate, witches lay curses, charlatans make promises. The church holds its inquisitions, the Senate holds its hearings. And in the long run none of it works. This isn't nature, this isn't science, not like you think, because there's this . . . this *thing*, this ineffable part of it all, that takes it out of the realm of knowing. That's why it's called the supernatural, Flemming. It's magic."

He glared, quivering almost, like he wanted to argue but couldn't find the words. I glared back, challenging. Go ahead, start a fight.

His gaze dropped. "Primitive man thought the sun rising and setting was magic, but we know now that it isn't. It's science that they didn't understand. So is this. We *will* understand it."

"If you say so."

"Can—can I give you a ride somewhere?"

One of those moments, those noises that was laughter bubbling into despair, lodged in my throat. The nerve of him. The complete fucking nerve.

"You've done enough." I walked past him, concentrating so that I didn't launch into a run, keeping my head down. Clutching the torn edges of my shirt and hugging myself so I wouldn't be naked.

Part of my Wolf stayed with me. I could never be fully human because of it, despite all my high-toned rhetoric. But sometimes, her instincts were useful. It can be a strength, T.J. had always told me. I'd scoffed at him, because I hated that part of myself that I believed I had so little control over. Now, I used it. Wolf wouldn't collapse in a heap, sobbing, furious over what had happened and dreading what was to come. She'd stalk. Keep her head down and get out of there. If I could just keep moving I'd be okay.

I made it all the way out of the building. Someone had thoughtfully left the door unlocked for me. I kept walking. Kept moving.

I hadn't slept very long. The sky was still full dark, overcast. The air was cold and damp, like it was about to rain. I shivered. Keep moving. It'd keep me warm.

A ways down the sidewalk, where the building's drive intersected the main road, a midsized sedan parked by the curb turned on its headlights. My first thought was of Bradley. He couldn't be coming to pick me up. He was dead. I almost lost it, then. He was dead, and he shouldn't have been.

The two front doors opened and two men got out. It might have been Bradley and Tom, my Men In Black, the way I first saw them when I arrived in D.C. But no. I started to panic, backing up a couple of steps, ready to run. Then I breathed. I caught a familiar scent of gun oil and leather.

They moved to the driver's side of the car and leaned on the side of the hood, watching me. One had ruffled hair, wore a trenchcoat over slacks and a dress shirt unbuttoned at the collar. The other: biker boots, jeans, T-shirt and leather jacket, mustache over a frown. Ben and Cormac, with Ben's rental car.

Now, I wanted to start crying. I rubbed my face, and my hand was shaking.

Ben came forward, shrugged off his coat, and held it up for me, waiting to help put it on me like we were on some kind of date. Didn't say a word. He was mostly shadow, outside the reach of the headlights. I couldn't see his face.

Wolf wanted to run away, but I wanted to fall into his arms. While the two halves argued, I stayed rooted to the spot, unable to move.

He put the coat over my shoulders, adjusting it so it settled in place. The warmth from his body lingered and made me shiver harder for a moment, but I clutched the edges and held it tight around me. His hand stayed on my shoulder, and that made me shiver, too. I hated people, at that moment.

I was crying silent, frustrated tears and couldn't talk. Couldn't explain why I wanted him to go away, and why he couldn't, because I needed a friend.

"Let's get out of here," he said, pressing my shoulder to guide me to the car. I shuffled forward. He opened the back door and steered me inside, like I was a child or an invalid.

Cormac drove. He eyed me in the rearview mirror. "Anyone you want me to beat up?"

I laughed, a tight and painful sound. I gasped for a breath, thinking I might start hyperventilating. I said, "Can I get back to you on that?"

Ben sat with me in the back. "Personally, I like the sound of 'punitive damages' much better."

"That's because you get a percentage," Cormac said. Ben gave an unapologetic shrug.

I steadied my breathing. I was calming down a little. Maybe. "How bad is it?"

"How bad is what?" Ben said.

"Have the lynch mobs started? Torches and pitchforks? Repressive legislation?"

"Too early to tell," he said. "The talking heads are still mulling it over. They probably need to replay the broadcast for another twelve hours before people get really sick of it."

"Talking heads?"

"Every network. Every cable news network. I think the Sci Fi Channel is running a marathon of *The Howling*."

That wasn't going to help my cause. Wasn't anyone in the least bit offended that I'd been *kidnapped*?

"And your mother called. She wants you to call back."

"Are you *serious*?" My voice squealed. "What did she say?"

"She didn't say anything, she just called."

"Did she watch it?"

"I don't know. Call her back if you want to know."

I pressed my face to the cool glass of the window. Maybe if I slept, I'd wake up to find everything was all right. "Ben, what am I going to do?"

"I'd suggest heading to the hotel and getting some sleep."

"I mean big picture. My life, my job, the hearings—"

"Not much you can do about that right now. We'll see about pressing charges in the morning."

That would be up to Ben. I couldn't do anything. I didn't have control anymore, and I hated that. My attempt to turn their brutal exposé into my own show had been a flailing burst of desperation. Had it worked? Had it garnered any sympathy? And I wasn't talking about sympathy for the plight of soon-to-be oppressed werewolves and supernatural beings everywhere. I wanted sympathy for me personally—so that the public would skewer *them* instead of me. Selfish bitch.

This night wasn't even near over, and the ball was so far out of my court I couldn't see it anymore.

"Ben, let me borrow your phone." He handed it over.

Cormac turned a half smile. "Look at that, she really is calling her mom at four in the morning."

Except that I wasn't. I was calling Alette. I'd almost forgotten to include Leo in that skewering.

No one answered. I checked the flip phone's monitor for coverage, which was fine. It just kept ringing, and ringing.

I took a deep breath, shut the phone off, and gave it back to Ben. I said, "One of Alette's minions helped Flemming and Duke. He's the one who got me into the cell."

"How?" Cormac said. Not offended, like I was. More like with a tone of professional curiosity.

"Silver handcuffs." Cormac nodded thoughtfully. I almost growled at him.

Ben said, "I *told* you to stay away from her—"

"She didn't have anything to do with it. It's Leo, he's working with Flemming and Duke." Which meant Alette was in trouble. But she was several hundred years old and could easily take care of herself, right? They didn't get to be that old unless they could take care of themselves.

Leo had left the festivities in Flemming's lab in a hurry. And with backup, though why he needed backup was anyone's guess. She wouldn't be looking for danger from him.

I had to get to Alette's.

"I have a hard time believing Duke, Flemming, and some vampire minion are all in bed together," Ben said.

"Duke didn't know about Leo. Flemming's been talking to him. But Duke and Flemming, they both want government attention—just for different reasons. I think they both think they can one-up the other when the time comes. It's like they're all playing chess, but each of them only sees a third of the board—a different third."

"What does the vampire get out of this?" Cormac said.

"Contacts? Influence in the government?" Leo wasn't interested in those things, not like Alette was. He wanted pure, simple power. He wanted to play games with it. Maybe he wanted to start his own games. "He can go over Alette's head, for control of the city. Alette's got the cops, but if Leo got the military—"

We approached D.C. proper again. Cormac was taking us to the hotel. Get some sleep, Ben had said. Not likely. I'd be climbing up the walls.

"Stop the car. Let me out here."

Cormac kept driving, like I hadn't even said anything.

"Cormac, stop the car!"

He looked at Ben for a sign.

Ben said, "If he's got military backing, there's no way you can go up against him."

"Ben!" That *did* come out more like a growl. I'd shifted once tonight; didn't mean it couldn't happen again. I'd never done it twice this close together. It would hurt. I pressed the heels of my hands into my eyes. I had to keep human eyes. Keep it together.

"Kitty," Ben said, looking at me across the backseat. I had to hand it to him, standing up to a werewolf like this. I didn't know if he trusted me not to shape-shift. He only sounded a little anxious. "You can't do anything about it right now. Get some sleep, wait until morning. It's much safer going against vampires in daylight, trust me."

He was telling me what to do. Bossing me around. I might as well be in a pack again.

I wasn't going to put up with that.

We were at the hotel. Cormac slowed down to turn into the parking garage. I scooted closer to the door. Then, I pulled the handle, popped open the door, and rolled out. The car was still moving, jerking me over the pavement. I had to stumble to keep my feet, but I managed to stay standing. I launched into a run.

The tires screeched as Cormac braked, but I didn't look back. I didn't look to see if they followed me.

I must have run for three blocks before I got my bearings. By then, I was thinking I shouldn't have done it. They were only trying to help. Looking out for me, like friends should, no strings attached. Except I was paying Ben.

But what would I have done if they hadn't come to pick me up? Waited until morning and taken the Metro? Gone back for a ride from Flemming?

I had a couple of miles to get to Alette's. I could run that far, but I didn't want to go there, not right away. I put my head down, sucked in night air, and ran. A wolf on the open plains couldn't have gone much faster.

I arrived at the Crescent, pounded down the stairs and stopped at the door to catch my breath. It was closed. Hesitating, I tested it. Ahmed was true to his word. He kept the place unlocked, even on a full moon night. There probably wasn't anyone around, but I had to check.

No lights were on, but my eyesight worked fine in the dark. I saw the bar, moved quietly around tables, didn't see anyone. Let my nose work, taking in scents. The place wasn't empty. Someone was here. Something was here.

I continued on, and movement caught my eye. Past the front of the bar, where cushions on the floor replaced tables and chairs, a gliding shape drifted forward. Sleek, feline, huge. My heart pounded hard for a moment. I'd never seen a cat that big without a nice set of solid bars between us.

His face was stout, angular, more intimidating than any house cat's. His fur was tawny, and circular black smudges covered his coat.

He sat in front of me, blocking my progress, and for a disconcerting moment he *did* look like a house cat, straight and poised, his slim tail giving a nonchalant flick.

"Luis." I fell on my knees. It smelled like him, even now. More fur than skin this time, but it was him.

He licked my cheek, his rough jaguar's tongue scratching painfully. Laughing weakly, I hugged him. His fur was soft and warm. I buried my face in the scruff of his neck. He remained patiently still.

"He waited for you."

Ahmed appeared at the back of the club, tying closed a dressing gown over bare legs and bare chest. His hair was wild. He must have just woken up. He must have waited, too. I wondered if the two of them had gone running on the Mall, when their animals took over. They could have hunted pigeons.

"You didn't have to do that," I said to the jaguar. "Either of you."

Luis stood and rubbed the length of his body against me before flopping down on the floor and licking his paws, then using them to wash his face.

Ahmed shrugged. "He was worried. I said you could take care of yourself. Then, it seemed that you couldn't. By then it was too late to do anything."

"I was shanghaied."

"So it seems." He sat next to me, lowering himself, propping himself with his hand, as if he were an old man with creaking bones. I didn't hear any bones creak.

"Ahmed, I need help."

"What do you need? I can give you a safe place to stay, to hide you."

I shook my head. "Not for me. For Alette. Leo's the one who shanghaied me, and I think she's in trouble."

He frowned. His whole expression darkened, eyes narrowing, like how a dog looks when it growls. But I couldn't back down. Couldn't flinch.

"You don't owe her anything," he said. "She offered you hospitality, then failed to protect you."

A technicality. He harkened back to the old traditional ideals of hospitality, where people had to offer shelter to travelers who would otherwise fall prey to robbers or wolves on the wild, ungoverned roads. There was something else going on here. The wolves were the ones I was asking for help.

The jaguar had fallen asleep, his lean ribs rising and falling deeply and regularly. He'd curled up beside me, his back pressed to my legs, where I sat.

I said, "If something happens to Alette, Leo will be in charge of the city's vampires. Do you want that?"

"And what if Leo was acting on her orders?"

"I don't believe that."

"You are too trusting."

"Alette's been . . . kind to me."

"And I have not?"

"It's not that. But someone has to help her."

"Please take my warning as a friend, as an elder: don't involve yourself with them. It's not your concern."

He sounded so somber, so serious, using the tone of voice a favorite high school teacher might, when he put his hand on your shoulder and urged you to think twice before hanging out with "that crowd." Almost but not quite patronizing. Utterly convinced that I couldn't take care of myself.

Not that I had a real excellent track record in taking care of myself. But I couldn't ignore my instincts.

If I hadn't been watching him, absently stroking the fur across his ribs, I wouldn't have noticed Luis begin to shift back to human. It happened slowly, gradually, the way ice melts. His limbs stretched, his torso thickened, his fur thinned. Bit by bit, piece by piece, cell by cell.

"What are you doing here, Ahmed? This place, this little empire of yours—you say this isn't a pack, that you aren't an alpha. But everyone treats you like you are. You expect to be treated that way. Maybe you rule by politeness and respect instead of brute force. You promote this ideal of a safe haven so you don't have to fight to keep your place. And it works, I'll give you that. It's the best system I've seen. But you ignore everything that happens outside your domain. And I can't do that."

If I'd given that speech to any other alpha male I'd ever met, I'd have started a fight. I'd offered a challenge to his place—at least, as subtle a challenge as his claim to the place of alpha here was subtle.

He spread his hands and gave me a respectful nod. "Of course that is your choice."

Which meant he maybe hadn't deserved my speech in the first place.

"I'm sorry, Ahmed," I said, starting to get up. He didn't say anything.

I touched the shoulder of the man lying asleep beside me. I didn't do more; I didn't want to wake him.

I'd talk to Luis later. I hoped I'd be around later.

chapter 13

If I'd had any money with me I would have called a cab. I might have been able to borrow a couple bucks from Ahmed, but I was two blocks away from the Crescent before I thought of that. The shuttle to Georgetown didn't start for another hour. As it was, I jogged. I had to move fast, because dawn was near. I was so tired. I was numb, and barely felt my legs move.

I should have kept Ben's cell phone so I could call the cops. I should have had Ahmed call the cops. Should have, should have—this was why I sucked at politics. No planning ahead.

Leo would be there. I had no doubt Leo would be there, along with the two mortal soldiers. I didn't know what I was going to do about them.

I wondered who would tell Alette about Bradley. And where was Tom? Emma? Were they safe?

I arrived at the townhome; the inside was dark. Like all the other houses on the street, like any normal house should be at this hour.

Then I paused. I could see that the lights inside were dark, because the drapes over the front bay window, the window to the parlor, were open. They'd never been open before.

Now, what were the odds the front door was unlocked, letting me walk right in?

Slowly, I climbed the steps and tried the door handle. Not only was it unlocked, it hadn't been closed all the way. It stood open just a hair, as if whoever had passed through here had been in a hurry.

I opened the door a crack.

"Did you hear that?" a male voice called from inside.

Wouldn't have to lock the door if you'd posted guards. My heart in my throat, I scrambled off the steps, over the wrought-iron railing, and crouched in the shadow by the wall of the house. I held my breath, even though I thought my head was going to burst. I wanted to run so badly, hear the Wolf's claws scraping on the pavement as we put distance between me and danger.

Hold the line. Keep it together.

The door opened wide above me. Someone stepped out and looked around. Dressed all in black, his face seemed ghostly in the near-light of dawn. He must have been one of the black ops guys that went with Leo. He watched for a moment, carefully scanning the street, then went back inside, closing the door firmly this time.

Leo needed someone to guard the place during daylight hours, the way Bradley and Tom had done for Alette.

The sky was lightening. I shivered and pulled my coat closer. Ben's coat. I'd forgotten I was wearing it. Now, I was glad I had it.

I had to get in there. I had to find out if Alette was okay. My heart was sinking with the growing evidence that she probably wasn't okay at all. The soldiers had to be in the foyer or front room to hear the faint squeak of the door hinges. I had to get them out of there, distract them somehow. They were obviously twitchy. Some kind of noise, then.

I suddenly felt like I was in a bad spy movie.

Some debris lay on the concrete pad of the window well where I'd been hiding: a few stones, chipped plaster, a rusted piece of metal. I picked up a handful of these items and climbed the railing back to street level.

Backing onto the sidewalk, then to the deserted street, I looked up at the townhome's second-story windows. I hadn't played any sports in school. I hadn't been at all coordinated. I wasn't sure I could do this. Desperation convinced me, however. I *had* to do this.

All the strength my supernatural Wolf gave me, I poured into that throw. Pitch it hard, focus on the window right above the bay window of the parlor. I grunted as I let the stone fly.

It hit the brick wall and rattled back to the sidewalk.

I growled at myself and tried again, quickly. It wouldn't do any good to have the soldiers come out on the front porch. I hefted the piece of metal this time and threw.

With a spine-numbing crack, the window shattered. The tinkling glass was like music.

To be on the safe side, I turned to the window above the front door and tried again. My whole body was shaking with adrenaline, but I must have had the knack of it this time. I hit the window—this one didn't shatter, but it crunched and a network of cracks laced out like a spiderweb.

This whole plan depended on them going upstairs to see what

had broken the windows. I had to hope they wouldn't come out the front door.

Did all plans feel this stupid in the middle of the execution?

I ran to the front door and opened it. Leaning in over the threshold, I took a deep breath of air and listened close. I smelled Alette's house, but with an edge. People I didn't recognize had been moving around in here. But I didn't hear anything, no breathing, no footsteps. Except overhead—it sounded like someone was running on the floor above me.

I went inside and shut the door behind me.

The place was dark, empty feeling. I didn't hear any breathing—but vampires didn't breathe.

I moved through the foyer, attempting silence, but the rubber soles of my sneakers squeaked on the hardwood.

The parlor window faced east. The room was almost light, now. Gray and faded, but still light. In another half hour, the sun would pour in.

The furniture had been shoved away to make a clear space on the floor, in front of the window. In the middle of this space, far enough back that I couldn't have seen her from the sidewalk, Alette sat on a chair. She faced the window, like she waited for the sun to rise, like she planned on watching it. Like she planned to die.

"Alette?"

She didn't move. I stepped closer and saw her hands tied behind her back, to the legs of the chair. Rope or cord alone wouldn't have been enough to hold her; there were also chains with crosses on them. Her feet were secured to the chair legs in front. A gag bound her mouth.

Crosses. Leo needed mortal humans to tie Alette up with crosses, which he couldn't touch.

"Alette." I ran to her. Inside the room, the rug squished wetly. What had happened here?

I pulled down the gag, a strip of cotton fabric. It snagged on a fang, but I got it loose.

Her gaze was wild, desperate, rapidly searching me. "Kitty, are you well? What have they done to you?"

I worked on the rest of the bindings. I started to toss the crosses away, then decided I might need them. I shoved them in a coat pocket. "Forced my national television debut. Don't worry, I'm okay. I'm not hurt." Physically . . .

"And Bradley—where's Bradley?"

Dammit. I hadn't wanted to be the one to tell her. This was terrible to think, but I'd hoped Leo had gloated. So at least she'd know.

"I'm sorry, Alette. Leo moved so fast, and he wasn't expecting it."

"No, I imagine he wasn't. It was probably quick, painless?"

"Broken neck."

"Kitty." Her hands free now, she put them on my shoulders, gripping them. Free of the crosses, she was strong, very strong, and at the moment she forgot it. She squeezed, pinching, and all I could do was brace against it, so she wouldn't topple me over. "They're my children, do you understand? My children's children, I've looked after my family all these years. I've provided for them, watched them grow and prosper. That's all I wanted for them, to prosper. Do you understand?"

I started to. Bradley was her great—dozens of great—grandson. And Tom, and Emma, who said her family had been with Alette for decades. Her contacts in the police department, in the government—also descendants. That loyalty came from ties of blood. Would the distance in relationship have made any difference in Alette's mind? I thought of all those portraits in the dining room, the photographs in the hall, in the parlor, all of them were her children. She kept pictures of her family throughout the house, like any doting mother.

"Alette, we have to hurry, they'll be back downstairs any minute." Not to mention the sun was rising right in front of her. I held her hands and tried to pull her from the chair.

"Wait a moment, Kitty—"

"Geez, did a pipe break?" I'd been kneeling on the wet carpet. My jeans were damp.

"Holy water. I'm sitting in it. I can't walk."

Her feet were bare. Not only that, they were burned, the flesh red and shining, rashlike. The red crawled up from her soles, touching every place that had gotten wet. Even if she'd been able to break free, she couldn't walk anywhere. I scented a whiff of damaged flesh.

She looked at me matter-of-factly, though the acidlike touch of holy water must have tortured her.

"Well, that's just great." I looked around, trying to think. I hadn't come this far to be defeated by a damp rug. "If they had this much of it why didn't they just throw it on you?"

"It might not have killed me."

And whoever did this wanted Alette to watch the approach of her own death, through the window, to torture her.

Glancing back at the pale sky, her face was ashen. She set her expression in a stoic mask.

I couldn't just close the drapes. They weren't open; they were gone, completely removed. I had to get her out of here. The footsteps continued upstairs, but the soldiers would be back down in moments.

"I'll carry you," I said, kneeling by the chair. I thought she'd argue, muttering about dignity with her British accent and stiff upper lip. She didn't. Silently, she put her arms around my shoulders and held on as I lifted, cradling her. She was far lighter than I expected. She felt dried up and hollow.

I had no idea where to go with her. I couldn't take her outside, not with daylight so close and no shelter handy. Frantically, I looked around.

"There's a storage space under the stairs. The door is there, it's a hidden panel."

When she pointed to it, I saw the line that marked the door. Setting her down, I wrenched open the thin plywood door, wincing at how much noise I made. Quiet, had to be quiet.

Alette leaned on me, unable to stand by herself. Together, we fell into the storage space. I pulled the door closed just as footsteps sounded on the stairs over our heads.

We lay curled together against a pile of junk, holding our breaths. At least I held my breath. We stared at the door ahead of us as if we could see what was happening outside.

Footsteps crossed the floor of the foyer and stopped at the entrance to the parlor. Another set of footsteps followed.

"Shit," a male voice said.

"Maybe she's already gone," a second voice said. "Burned up."

"There's not any ash. There should be ash. A burning smell. Something."

"You ever see one of them go in sunlight?"

After a pause, the other said, "No."

"Look, even if she found a way to escape, it's too close to dawn. She won't get far—hell, she won't even leave the house. We'll look."

"You don't suppose she turned into a bat or something, do you?"

"Uh, no."

Footsteps crossed back and forth, moved to the back of the

house, returned to the stairs. They didn't come near the door to the storage space.

The closet ran the entire length of the flight of stairs, narrowing at the end. Despite this, we didn't have much room to move. In the faint light that seeped through the crack under the door, I could see that the place was crammed with boxes, cleaning equipment like brooms, mops, and buckets, old baby strollers, a high chair, a clothes rack stuffed with coats. Like any normal family's storage space. I got the feeling Alette had clung to the model of a normal family life after becoming a vampire.

I wondered how Leo fit into that.

"My hero." She looked at me and attempted a grim smile. Then, she slumped back, letting out a soft groan. If I didn't know better I'd have said she fainted.

I touched her, shook her shoulder. She was cold, stiff almost. Panicked, I almost shouted her name. I couldn't lose her now.

She touched her forehead, wincing, for all the world like a distraught lady in a Victorian novel. We needed a fainting couch.

I hissed, trying to keep my voice to a whisper, "What's wrong? What's the matter? It's the sun, isn't it? It's too close to dawn—"

"I haven't fed tonight," she said.

I stared at her, astounded. I was holding on to a starving vampire. Could I be any more stupid?

"Never mind that," she continued, trying to sit up. "Leo is still in the house. We've got to find him, I won't have him destroying what I've built here."

"You're not in any shape to go against Leo," I said, thinking of her injured feet as well as her lack of food.

"We can't stay locked up here, cowering, all day." She straightened, pulling herself out of my grip. She moved slowly, stiffly, like an arthritic old woman. "For good or ill, I must face him now. I don't expect you to come along. This is my fight. I'm the one who didn't see Leo's true colors. I don't believe it, almost two hundred years together and he picks now to stage a coup."

She wouldn't last, not in her condition. I'd seen him move against Bradley.

"Would it help?" I spoke quickly, before I lost my nerve. "If you took some of my blood, would it help you?"

"Kitty, if you're suggesting what I think you are, don't—"

"Because I'm not letting you go out there alone in your condition. And I can't take on Leo by myself. Will it help you?"

She hesitated a long, strained moment before saying, "Yes, it would."

"Then you have to."

God, my heart was pounding like a jackhammer. It overwhelmed thought. Lots of people, human servants, did this all the time. Nothing to it.

Except she was predator, and I was suddenly prey. I had an urge to defend myself. Or run. Fight or flight.

"Your wolf doesn't like the idea much, does she?" Alette said.

"No," I said, my voice wavering. "She—I—I mean, we don't much like feeling trapped. I'm sorry, it's under control, it's okay—"

She spoke, gently, soothingly. "I understand. You're being perfectly reasonable. You should be frightened of me."

"I'm not, not really." But I was. I knew what she was, intellectually I'd always known. But this was the reality, that she could devour me and I wouldn't be able to do anything about it.

But she wouldn't, she wasn't like that, she was kind. If only the last week hadn't completely eroded my faith in my ability to judge character.

"Just a little. I promise," she said. "A few seconds and it will be over. Is that all right?"

I nodded. She touched my face. She was a ghost in the pale light. "I will not betray your trust. Do you understand?"

"Yes."

"Are you left- or right-handed?"

"Right," I whispered.

She took my left hand and moved toward me, leaning so she spoke close to my ear. Her voice had a rhythm, lulling. It ran along my nerves, soothing them, coaxing them from taut panic to calm. More than calm—I felt yearning.

"Do not fear me. I would not have you come to me afraid."

She kissed my cheek, and I leaned into her. I let her hold me in her arms, let her do anything she wanted to me, because her touch reached deep inside me, into my gut. A warmth rose there; my body clenched in anticipation.

Her breath caressed my neck. I might have moaned a little, because I felt so warm, burning up. She held me close, pulling that warmth into her.

"Rest your head, my dear." She guided my head to her shoulder. I shut my eyes and pressed my face against her.

She pushed the coat sleeve up my left arm, past the elbow. She supported the arm—I couldn't have, at that point. I felt like I was melting; I wanted to melt into her. She kissed the inside of my arm, firing all the nerves. I bit my lip, overwhelmed.

She traced a line up my forearm with her tongue, tasting and kissing. My hand closed into a fist, which she braced. Her mouth closed over my wrist, but I didn't feel anything except her attention, her caresses, her love.

The skin pinched, the bite. By then, I wanted it.

When she drew away, I felt like a veil had fallen, or that I'd woken from a dream.

I needed a cold shower. Very cold.

"It's over," she said. And it was. She straightened, pulling away from me. I didn't know where I'd been, but suddenly I was back in the closet under Alette's stairs, in the dark, wrapped in a trenchcoat. "Are you all right?"

"Um, yeah. I mean, I think . . . wow." It made sense, really. All part of that vampire seduction gambit: lure the prey to you, give it a reason to open its veins. Sure cut down on that messy struggling. "Just so you know, I'm straight. Totally straight. As an arrow."

Her voice held a smile. "So am I."

I smelled a touch of blood on her breath. My blood.

She no longer sounded tired, defeated, like she had a moment ago. She sat straight without effort, and the glint in her eye had returned. She seemed ready for battle.

Two sets of footsteps pounded across the foyer, right outside our hiding place. Alette looked out at the sound, frowning. Then, she pushed at the door.

"No—" I grabbed for her but missed. She slipped through the opening before I could reach her.

What could I do but follow?

Outside, in the foyer, she stood tall on her injured feet—except they didn't seem quite as injured. The redness seemed to have faded, just as her face now seemed flushed and lively.

Before her, two black-clad soldiers held handguns pointed at her. They clutched the guns in two-handed grips, straight-armed, sighting down the barrels.

"You don't want to do that," Alette said, her voice like honey, music, seduction, passion, all together. "You'd like to put your weapons down now."

Calmly, she looked back and forth between them. I couldn't see Alette's eyes at this moment. I didn't want to—her gaze focused intently on the soldiers. The men didn't shoot, they didn't say anything. One of them—his arms were trembling, causing the gun to waver.

"I know you're both reasonable gentlemen. You deserve a rest. You're very calm. Very quiet. That's right."

They both lowered their arms slowly, hypnotically, until they were hanging loose at their sides. After that, they didn't twitch a muscle. They didn't shiver, they didn't blink. They stood like statues, caught in Alette's gaze. Their breathing was slow and rhythmic, as if they slept, but their eyes were open. One of the guys' jaw hung open a little. He wasn't quite drooling.

Alette pulled the guns out of their hands and gingerly put the weapons in the closet. She closed the door. She left the soldiers standing motionless in the foyer.

How did vampires *do* that?

I crept past them, hardly believing they wouldn't reach out to grab me.

She went to the back of the foyer, to the hallway that led to the kitchen. "Leo will be downstairs by this hour."

Her gaze narrowed. The hunter had found her trail.

She walked confidently down the hallway, which opened to a modern, impressively furnished kitchen—stainless-steel counters, pots hanging above an island workstation. It seemed to be equipped to prepare and serve state dinners. Who was I to say it hadn't? Alette passed it all by, heading for a door on the far side, by the fridge.

She paused, hand on the doorknob, tilting her head to listen. So, that was the door to the basement, where the vampires spent their days in darkness and safety. Leo might be stretching out for a nap, thinking he was safe.

Or he might have been waiting for us, armed with machine guns.

"Alette, this isn't—"

She opened the door.

Common sense didn't play any part in her current motivation. Revenge probably had a big part in it, along with a liberal dose of blind rage. She didn't wait to see if I'd follow or not.

I followed.

The glow of soft lighting cast an aura up the carpeted stairs. Soundlessly, Alette stepped down.

The basement room was as Victorian in decoration as the rest of the house. Brocade wallpaper, plush carpet, antique lamps. It was a bedroom. No coffins, but a king-sized four-poster bed sat in the back, along with dressers and wardrobes, and a vanity table without the mirror.

Leo sat on the edge of the bed, leaning over the body of a young woman. Her brown hair lay loose over her shoulders, and her hands were folded over her stomach. She wore a college logo sweatshirt and faded jeans.

"It's Emma," I whispered.

"He used her as a hostage. That was how he overcame me. He promised to keep her safe," she said, sharp as steel, biting off the words.

Emma seemed asleep. I hoped she was just asleep.

Leo looked up. He wiped his mouth with the back of his hand—an ominous gesture, though I didn't see what he wiped away. A snarl curled his lips. He stood, clenching his hands, and took a step toward us. He faced Alette across the room.

"You're supposed to be dead," Leo said, his voice low, tight with emotion.

"I've been dead for quite some time, my dear."

I left the stairs and moved from behind her, my back hunched like hackles rising, glaring warily.

His gaze met mine and narrowed. "Flemming set you loose, did he? He's too soft for the game he's playing."

I wondered, if I got a chance to wring Leo's neck, would he tell me what that game was? I could wring it with little crosses on chains.

"You could do what you liked with me if you kept Emma safe," Alette said. "What have you done to her?"

Leo laughed. "Wouldn't you like to know?" He rounded his shoulders like a prizefighter entering the ring. Alette seemed unaffected, standing poised and still as always.

"You sold me out, destroyed my home, my children. Why?"

Leo laughed, a sharp, bitter sound. "Why? That's simple. You are the worst waste of resources I have ever encountered. You command an empire, Alette. And what do you use it for? *Nesting*. You are an immortal goddess, and you can't seem to do anything but play the part of a stupid woman."

Wow. Not like he was from the nineteenth century or anything.

Alette didn't even flinch. In fact, a new resolve seemed to settle on her, like something inside her had hardened. "Is that so? If you felt that way, why stay with me for two centuries? That's a long time to have to cope with stupidity. I should know."

Leo's jaw dropped, like he was actually offended. I put my hand in my pocket, curling my fingers around the crosses there.

"He's only just now found allies with firepower," I said. "Tell us what Flemming gets by sending his men to work for you. You couldn't have taken over the place without their help."

He scowled. "I don't talk to animals."

"Oh, give me a break!"

"Answer the question, Leo," Alette said, cold and implacable. The "stupid woman" had commanded men for centuries with that voice. Even now, Leo couldn't break the habit.

"He gets a recruiting agent. Someone to help build his little army of the night. The Pentagon has already agreed to back his research when the NIH drops him. That's not what he wants, but he'll take what he can get. They've already given him a Special Forces unit to help run the operation."

Alette gave a sigh that managed to sound feminine and indignant at the same time. "You've sold one master and bought yourself another, do you realize that?"

"Oh, no," Leo said. "You're wrong about that. Flemming only thinks he's in charge. This goes far beyond him."

Flemming was too soft, Leo had said. The scientist looked the part of an academic, but played at military intelligence and black ops. Which was the real Flemming? And if Flemming was out of his league, as Leo suggested, then whose league were we playing in?

"How far?" I said, my voice falling to almost a whisper. "Who's calling the shots if not Flemming? Surely not you. You're a natural-born lackey."

Leo flashed his wicked, pretentious smile. "You'll never know, because you aren't leaving here alive."

He flew at us. In retrospect, he probably only launched himself, springing at us with the energy of frustration and determination. But he did it so fast, he might as well have flown.

Alette must have been expecting it, or she must have seen it, somehow able to slow the time frame down in a way that I wasn't. She was also moving at his speed. She dodged, stepping aside with efficient grace. The move might have been choreographed. They were like two fighters in a Hong Kong action flick, and I was the hapless bystander who was only trying to cross the street.

The move also left the path clear between Leo and me. I couldn't get out of his way fast enough. I could feel my feet backing up, as if I were looking at myself from outside. But my steps were slow, shaking. A whimper started in the back of my throat. Submissive, be submissive, lower than him—

He wouldn't listen to that.

I held the fist full of crosses in front of me and braced.

He didn't reach me, because Alette put her hand around his neck. She shouldn't have been able to stop him. He should have just tossed her aside and kept going. But who was I to decide what a multicentury-old vampire could and couldn't do? She didn't seem to strain, even, and Leo came up short, like he'd run into a clothesline. Her hand squeezed around his throat; her tendons flexing was the only sign of effort.

"I gave you everything," she said. "I'll take it all away."

"No." He gripped her wrist, scratching at it, trying to push her away. He was taller than she was, larger, rougher, yet she held him like he was made of cotton.

She couldn't kill him by suffocating him—vampires didn't breathe. She'd have to rip his whole head off. But she only stared at him, caught his gaze in hers, seeming to give him a chance to apologize, to beg forgiveness. To beg for his life. He began to thrash like an animal in a trap.

"No." He gasped, choking, his voice failing. "You're not my mistress, not anymore, you're not—"

From a reservoir of anger, he lashed out. Arms together, both hands making a fist, he swung around and hit her arm at the elbow. The joint bent, breaking her hold on him for a moment—long enough. He ripped away from her and punched her hard, once in the gut, once in the face. Something cracked, like bone breaking. Alette's expression didn't have time to register surprise.

She fell backward and hit the ground. Didn't move, and my belly turned cold. Leo turned on me, striking with an intent to do damage.

I still held the crosses as a shield, but Leo toppled into me anyway. He planted his hands on my shoulders and shoved, running me to the ground, pinning me to the floor. I clawed at him, the chains still laced around my fingers. The crosses pressed against his face.

He grimaced, his mouth opened wide as he hissed and shook himself to get free of them. The crosses left welts on his cheeks and neck, like allergy-driven hives, like silver did to me. Still, he didn't let up his pressure on me. I couldn't get away.

I didn't know if Alette was in any shape to help me. I was on my own.

Change, you can fight him—Pain burned through me, Wolf starting to claw her way out. The full moon still shone. I still had power. My hands were thickening. Wildly, I thrashed, arching my back, because I didn't want to do this, I didn't want to be trapped, I hated that he was making me Change. Human or Wolf, I wasn't strong enough to fight him.

He laughed, and in another quicksilver move, he grabbed my hand, the one holding the crosses, and jammed it to the floor. He managed to shift until both my hands were pinned, and his knee dug into my gut. He leaned in close, his fangs brushing my neck. Every breath I took was a growl, and he didn't care.

"I'll have you for dessert, my kitten," he said. He was in the perfect position to rip out my throat, and I couldn't do anything about it. I tried to work up enough spit to shoot at his face, since it seemed that was all I had left. My mouth had gone strangely dry, however.

"Leo." Someone new had arrived. I knew that voice.

Leo looked up, hissing in surprise. Then, something whistled. I felt the air whine above me. In the same moment, he fell back, as if jerked on a chain.

Freed, I rolled out of the way, away from Leo, and scrambled back on all fours.

Paul Flemming stood at the base of the stairs holding some kind of spear gun. He lowered it from the ready position and watched his target.

Leo crouched on his knees, staring at his own chest with blank astonishment. A foot-long wooden dowel, like an arrow, protruded from his heart. No blood poured from the wound, even though the spear must have gone all the way through his chest. It looked ludicrous somehow, like it was a stage prop glued to the front of his shirt. The fabric puckered in around it.

So, Flemming *was* good with a stake. It seemed the spot at the top of the food chain was still up for debate.

I gasped for breath, trying to pull myself back into myself, to stay human. Alette had recovered. She sat up, legs folded neatly under her, and watched Leo die. She frowned, her gaze showing sadness.

Leo gave a short laugh, or the sound might have been the start of a sob. He reached for her, then slumped onto his side, his eyes open and staring. The body turned waxen, then ashen, then began to collapse in on itself, turning to dust, the decay of the grave taking place in seconds instead of years. It took his clothes, the stake, everything with him. Everything touching him turned to dust, including a blackened oval shape on the carpet. He was gone.

I expected Alette to regain her feet gracefully, to resume her regal bearing and once again take charge. Instead, she remained on the floor, her eyes squeezed shut, gripping the fabric of her jacket over her heart, as if it hurt.

"How could I be so blind?" Her voice was thin, pained. "How could I be so . . . so *stupid*?"

Those words had been spoken by every woman who'd ever been screwed over by a boyfriend. Immortality didn't change some things, apparently.

She ran her fingers through her hair, and finally opened her eyes to stare at the pile of ash that had once been Leo. Her face puckered, like she might start crying. But she shook her head, and shook the mood away. "He fought at Waterloo, you know. When I met him, he was a shell, broken by what he'd seen there. But he could still laugh. I liked that. I gave him a reason to continue. I gave him a place in my household. Then—I gave him everything. I trusted him. I thought—"

She loved him. I wouldn't have thought it possible. Vampires seemed beyond love. What was more, she thought he'd loved her back.

A wave of fear crossed her expression. In a rush, she stood and went to the bed, sitting beside Emma. She touched the young woman's face, felt her neck, then held her hands. She stared at Emma's face for a long time, and my stomach turned into a lead weight.

"Alette, what—how is she?" I didn't want to know. If I didn't know, I didn't have to react.

"She's not dead," Alette said softly. She didn't sound pleased, though. She sounded resigned. "But—she's no longer precisely alive, either. On the third night she'll wake again as one of us."

Leo had turned her, made her a vampire. Had he seen the opportunity to possess something of Alette's and been unable to resist? I remembered his laugh when Alette asked him what he'd done to Emma. Maybe he'd done it as a joke.

"What are you going to do? What—what is she going to do?"

Alette smiled sadly. "I don't know." She leaned forward and kissed Emma's forehead. Emma didn't stir. Her face was white, bloodless.

Alette took a blanket from a trunk at the foot of the bed and spread it over Emma.

Flemming held the spear gun down by his side and slumped against the wall.

I swallowed, to make sure my throat was still human, that I still had a voice. "Why? Why are you here? Why did you do . . . that?"

"He was dangerous."

"Dangerous to whom? To you? To your research? Aren't you worried about losing your recruiting agent?"

"But would he recruit for me, or handpick the people he wanted on the inside of an elite military unit? I know he was spying on me." He glanced at Alette, then lowered his gaze. "I was being used. By everyone. Duke, Leo, the DOD—"

"Wait, what? The DOD?"

"Department of Defense. One door closes, another opens. Isn't that what people say? The military sees possibilities in my research. The NIH isn't going to continue my funding, not after this."

"Damn straight. Why did you ever go along with Duke? He's a nutcase."

"We both wanted government recognition. He wanted his control; I wanted funding that didn't come from the military. He was able to get my research a public hearing; I was able to give him his proof that the monsters are real. I thought—I believed that in the end, my science would trump his fanaticism. That Congress would take my proof and do some good with it."

Good defined as funding for his own project. That was the trouble with politics, everyone only believed their own personal idea of what was good and right. And science could become its own brand of fanaticism.

Flemming continued. "Duke misjudged public opinion. He really believes you aren't human, and that Congress could enact laws to set bounties on you, to let people hunt you to extinction, like they did with wild wolves a hundred years ago. He wanted to be a national Van Helsing, and he wanted my help to prove that he was right."

"I think you both came off looking like assholes," I said. "I think Jack London won. So the NIH cuts your funding, and the military welcomes you with open arms? You looked for military funding— Fritz gave you ideas. You don't care where the money comes from."

His voice turned harsh. "I got very good at telling the people with money exactly what they wanted to hear. Most researchers do. I told the DOD what I thought I could do, and by the time I decided that wasn't what I wanted . . . But I'm done, now. After this, I'll tell them all that I'm finished."

I wanted to wring his neck. "You can really just walk away? I don't believe you."

The expression he shot back at me was conflicted, full of hurt but also tinted with anger. His jaw clenched. The grip on his spear gun tightened, and with a pang I realized he was standing between me and the stairway.

"Kitty, that's enough." Alette rose from the bed and brushed off her skirt as if she'd just come in from a stroll. "Dr. Flemming, I suppose I ought to thank you for your timely arrival. Then again, I suppose it was the least you could do for helping to bring about this situation in the first place."

"I didn't do it for you," he said. "I'm tired of being a pawn."

"You very nearly decided that too late." She set her gaze on him, and for all that she was a slighter, slimmer figure than Leo, she radiated a menace that he hadn't been able to manage. Leo had been all about bravado.

Flemming reached to a long pouch strapped over his shoulder, which held more spears.

I thought I was going to have to break up a fight between them, but we were all startled by noises pounding on the floor above us, echoing over our heads. A door slammed open, several sets of footsteps ran, probably across the foyer.

Upstairs, in the kitchen, a male voice said, "Clear!" Another said, "The basement?"

I could fight. To the last breath, I could do it. Alette joined me in the center of the room; we stood side by side. Flemming remained at the base of the stairs, looking up.

The stairs creaked as someone made his way down, slowly and carefully. Another one followed. Two people. I took a deep breath, my nose flaring to catch a scent. Male sweat, leather jacket, an air of taut nerves and tired bodies, gun oil—

Cormac emerged from the shadow, gun raised and ready. Ben followed a step behind him, a stake in one hand and mallet in the other. Flemming pointed his spear gun at Cormac, and for a moment the two looked like they were going to face off.

My knees turned to pudding. I thought I was going to faint. "Hi, guys," I said weakly.

Cormac wasn't going to lower his weapon until Flemming did. The hit man stared at him, expressionless, steady as a rock. Flemming's hands shook.

"Doctor, it's okay. They're okay," I said. Finally, he lowered his arms. Cormac waited an extra beat before doing the same, holstering the gun.

More pounding footsteps sounded on the stairs, and a pair of police officers emerged into the room, which was becoming crowded.

Ben looked around the room, took note of me, Alette, and the pile of ash on the floor. "You mean we went through the trouble of finding this place, calling the cops, racing here in the nick of time, and after all that we missed the fun?"

"There's still one left," Cormac said, eyeing Alette.

I moved to stand in front of her. "This is Alette. She's a good guy."

One of the cops drew his gun on Cormac. Too many people in this room had guns, and it was starting to piss me off.

"Nathan, it's all right, we don't want to start anything," Alette said. The cop lowered his gun.

Cormac rolled his eyes, a *you've got to be kidding* look.

"It's all right, Kitty," Alette said, moving to the side, like she was amused that I'd tried to protect her.

"Alette? This is Ben, my lawyer, and Cormac, my—" My *what*? "And this is Cormac." She nodded politely. Ben and Cormac still looked ready for action: guns, stakes, crosses hanging from their belts.

"Uh, you guys do this a lot, don't you? Because you look like you do this a lot."

Ben and Cormac exchanged a look, and a curt, comradely nod. Ben sighed and finally lowered the mallet.

I had a vampire-hunting lawyer. Great.

Flemming said, "I'll leave. I don't want to cause any more trouble."

Alette crossed her arms. "No more recruiting, no more kidnapping. Yes?"

He nodded quickly, in a way that gave me no reassurance he'd even registered what she'd said. He turned to climb the stairs. Cormac blocked his way. The hit man glared at him in only the way that a man who carries guns that casually can. Just when I thought one of them might do something rash—they both still had loaded weapons—Cormac stepped aside. Flemming rushed up the stairs, pushing past the cops.

I wouldn't have minded asking him a few more questions.

"It's full day by now, isn't it? I can feel it my bones." Alette rubbed her forehead as if trying to erase the lines of weariness. She glanced at the bed in the back of the room. For a moment, she actually looked old. "Kitty, I don't know how to thank you. If you hadn't returned . . . well."

I gave a tired smile. "If there's anything else I can do to help—"

Ben interrupted. "Kitty, with all due respect, you pay me to give you advice, and right now I'm advising you to get the hell out of this house. I'll help you pack."

He'd wanted me to do that all along. I couldn't really argue anymore. But leaving felt like I was throwing all Alette's gestures of friendship back in her face. I wanted to stay—but I also wanted to feel safe. Alette's sanctum had been violated.

After the last twelve hours, I wanted to curl up into a hole and never come out again.

"It's all right," Alette said in response to my anguished frown. "You'll be safer away from here, now."

I nodded and forced a smile. When had safe stopped being the easy way out?

The pair of cops locked down the town house. Leo's two soldiers had been guided to a sofa in the parlor, where they now sprawled, sleeping it off. I sure didn't want to be around when they woke up. Flemming had disappeared utterly, and I couldn't blame him. He had no friends at that place.

Ben and I took my car to the hotel, while Cormac drove theirs. Ben carried my bags. I was still wearing my torn T-shirt and jeans. I needed a shower, badly. I needed to not remember the TV broadcast. I'd been able to forget, for the last few hours. When we got to the hotel, Ben handed me a homemade DVD and portable DVD player. Shit.

I showered first. I'd watch the video after. But the shower lasted a very long time. I had a lot of bad scents to wash off. Smells of antiseptic science, of calculated cruelty, of hate and violence. Of being beaten up, trapped in a jail cell, tied up with silver. My wrists had rashes from silver and puncture wounds from a vampire.

Eventually, I watched, mesmerized, my room-service breakfast abandoned.

Toward the end, Ben knocked at my door. I let him in.

"The committee's wrapping up this afternoon. You should go."

The Senate committee seemed incredibly far away at the moment.

"What's the press response to this?" I pointed at the screen,

where my Wolf had retreated to a corner to curl up in as tight a ball
as possible. "What's the media saying?" I hadn't looked at a newspaper yet. In a sudden nervous fit, I turned on the TV and flipped
channels until I found something resembling news.

". . . experts verify that the video is not a fake, that what you're
about to see is a real werewolf. We must warn you that the following images may be disturbing to some viewers . . ." The news show
aired a choice clip: me, my back arching, shirt ripping, fur shimmering where skin ought to be.

I turned the channel. I found a morning show where the familiar, perfectly saccharine hosts interviewed a man in a suit.

The woman said, "By now everyone's seen the film. We have to
ask, what does it mean? What's going to come out of this?"

"Well, we have to look at it in context of the hearings that have
been going on for the last week. This brings all that information out
of the realm of theory. For the first time we see the issue in stark
reality, and what it means is the Senate committee is not going to
be able to ignore it, or brush it off. I expect to see legislation—"

The next channel, a rather hyperbolic cable news show, had
Roger Stockton as a guest. Just the sight of him made my hackles
rise. He and the regular host were chatting.

"Is there a way to tell?" the host was saying. "If you didn't already know she was a werewolf, would you have been able to tell?"

Stockton had become an infinitely assured expert. "Well, Don, I
have to say, I think with experience you might be able to spot a
werewolf. They've got this *aura* about them, you know?"

"So that whole thing with the monobrow is bunk—"

Oh, give me a break.

And a fourth channel. "Who is Kitty Norville? She gained some
fame as the host of a cult radio talk show, and that put her in the
spotlight. A spotlight that got a little too bright last night. She has
been unavailable for comment, and investigators are looking into
the possibility that she may still be held captive—"

"I've been getting calls nonstop. I've been blowing them off, *no
comments at this time* sort of thing. Maybe you should hold a press
conference."

At least that would be organized. I might be able to claim a bit
of territory for myself.

"And your mom called again. You should probably call her back
soon."

I went back to the first news channel. They showed a new clip,
the Dirksen Senate Office Building where the hearings were being

held. A crowd had gathered: protesters, curiosity seekers. The reporter wasn't saying, just that the committee was convening for a final time. Some people were waving signs that I couldn't read because the camera refused to focus on them.

Did they hate me? What was happening?

"I can't do it," I said softly, shaking my head in slow denial. "I can't face them. Face *that*."

"Why not?" He sounded tired. He'd been awake for all of the time that I had, over the course of the night. He'd earned his retainer in spades.

Why not, indeed. I wanted that hole, that safe den shut away from the world, and I wanted it badly. I knew this feeling; I hadn't felt it so strongly in years. "It's all out. Everyone saw me. Saw everything. I have nothing left, that's what it is. I—I feel like I've been raped."

He gave a frustrated huff. "Now how would you know about that?"

I almost swung at him. I had to take a deep breath, to pull that anger back inside. We were both tired and speaking too bluntly. "You do *not* want me to answer that, Ben."

His expression fell. "Look, Kitty. We're going to sue. We're going to litigate the shit out of Duke, Flemming, Stockton, everyone we can over what happened. The whole goddamn Senate if we have to. And that's after the criminal charges are filed. But for all that to happen, you can't hide. Those crowds aren't going away anytime soon, and you're going to have to face them."

I'd started crying, tears quietly making tracks down my cheeks. Everything that had happened over the last twenty-four hours seemed to hit me at once, and the stress was suffocating. Like being in the cell again, silver walls pressing down on me. But he was right. I knew he was right. I'd survived too much to cave now. So I wiped the tears away and drank down the glass of orange juice.

This couldn't possibly be worse than wrestling with a vampire.

chapter **14**

I didn't want to bother with traffic and parking, so Ben and I took a taxi to the Senate office building. The crowd had grown until it clogged the street. Police directed traffic. They'd closed the street and weren't going to let us through until Ben rolled down the window and spoke a few words to one of the cops. The guy nodded, then called to one of his colleagues. The two of them cleared a path through the mass of people.

I hunched down, huddled inside my jacket, hiding. People outside were shouting. Most of it was incoherent, but I heard someone preaching, quoting the Bible in a clear, loud voice: *thou shalt not suffer a witch to live.*

A sign flashed, a placard someone waved above the crowd: a vertical acronym with the words spelled out horizontally. V.L.A.D.: Vampire League Against Discrimination.

That was a new one.

I closed my eyes. This was crazy. I should have just gone home. Mom wanted me to come home. I'd called her. I was right—she hadn't turned off the TV like I asked. But she seemed to have disassociated the images entirely. Like she'd decided that wasn't really me. All she knew, I was in trouble and she wanted me to come home, where I'd be safe. Where she assumed I'd be safe.

"Look," Ben said, pointing out the car window to the front door of the building. "The cops are watching the crowd. You'll be fine."

Fine. Right. Just dandy.

The taxi stopped, and my stomach coiled.

Ben paid the driver and said to me, "Stay there, I'll go around and get the door."

I waited. The driver stayed turned, looking at me over the back of the seat. Staring at me.

A lot of people were going to be staring at me in a minute. Better get used to it.

Then he said, "Hey—can I have your autograph?"

I gaped like a fish. "Really?"

"Yeah, sure. How else are the guys going to believe this?"

I bit my lip. Autopilot took over. "You got paper and pen?"

He pulled them off one of those notepads that stuck to the inside of the windshield. I wrote against the back of the seat. I had to think for a minute how to spell my own name.

"That show last night? That was something else. Hey, thanks a ton," he said as I handed back the paper. "And good luck out there."

"Thanks," I murmured.

Ben opened my door.

I looked up, and the crowd made a sound. Like an avalanche, it poured over me, cheering and cursing. I caught sight of two signs, quickly scribbled posterboard jobs their bearers shook wildly. One said, BURN THE HEATHENS!

The other said, WE ♥ KITTY!

God, this was going to be weird.

A barricaded path led from the curb to the front door. That didn't stop people from trying to lean over, hands stretched out, reaching for me. I forced myself not to cringe. Walk tall, chin up, eyes ahead. Ben had his arm across my back, keeping me moving, using his body as a shield. This was like something out of a movie, or a cop show, or Court TV.

"I love your show, Kitty!" someone screamed off to my right. I couldn't see who, but I flashed a smile in that direction. Cameras clicked—by the door, the press corps waited. TV cameras, photo cameras, a dozen microphones and handheld recorders reached out for me.

"Kitty! Kitty Norville! What action are you going to take against Senator Duke and Dr. Flemming? Have you spoken to the senator since last night? What are your plans? What do you think the Senate committee's response to this will be? Kitty!"

"My client has no comments at this time," Ben said. A couple of police officers stepped forward and cleared a path to the door.

If I thought it'd be calmer inside, I was wrong. People in suits packed the hallway. They looked official, carrying papers and briefcases, rushing around with purposeful expressions. Everyone who passed me stopped and did a double take.

"Where'd all the people come from?" I said.

"I think half of Congress is turning up for this. It's funny, the committee doesn't have any real power. They can just make recommendations, but it's like everyone's waiting for the word of God."

I thought people were just waiting for a clue, for an idea of which way to jump: if the authority figures decided I was dangerous, a threat to society, then people could react to that. They'd know to be afraid. But if they decided I wasn't dangerous—maybe people could let it go.

"Thanks for being here, Ben."

He smiled. "You're welcome."

The audience inside the hearing chamber was invitation only. They'd never have been able to fit everyone in, otherwise. Mostly, reporters and TV cameras crammed the place. We were late. The senators were already in place behind their authoritative tables. Senator Duke was absent, but I recognized his aide, the one from last night, standing in a corner. He refused to look in my direction.

I couldn't find Dr. Flemming among the audience, either. So, Duke, Flemming, and Stockton had all ditched. Did that make me the last one standing? Did that mean I won?

What, exactly, did I win?

Jeffrey Miles had made it into the audience. He smiled and gave me a thumbs-up. I wanted to hug him, but he was on the other side of the room.

Henderson leaned close to his microphone and cleared his throat. The general shuffling and murmuring in the room quieted as he drew attention to himself.

"I'd like to thank my esteemed colleagues in the Senate for taking an interest in this final day of oversight hearings regarding the Center for the Study of Paranatural Biology. I hope we can hold your interest. In the absence of Senator Duke, and with the consent of my fellow committee members, I'll be serving as the committee's acting Chair. This is mostly a formality, since the only activity on the day's schedule is our closing statement and recommendations. Without further ado, I'll now read those into the record.

"Due to recent events, and recent actions by a colleague, this committee decided to issue a statement regarding this hearing's subject matter as soon as possible, to reduce any confusion and to head off any speculation about what stance we will take. First off, I would like to thank all the panelists who testified for their time and their opinions. Without the testimony, formulating any response to the existence of the Center for the Study of Paranatural Biology and its research activities would have been impossible.

"This committee has already taken action in making recommendations to the full Senate about how that body should proceed. We have recommended that the Senate Committee on Ethics begin an investigation into the activities of our colleague Senator Joseph Duke, for suspicion of abusing his authority and conspiring to commit the crime of kidnapping. The full Senate may consider a censure against Senator Duke. We have recommended to the director of the National Institutes of Health that the Center for the Study of Paranatural Biology be dissolved, due to its questionable methodologies and possible unethical practices. Its research projects should continue, but under different supervision as part of the National Institute of Allergy and Infectious Diseases, according to all the regulations and guidelines set forth by the NIH. This committee sees no reason why, if the conditions under discussion really are the result of diseases, they should not be studied under the aegis of an existing disease research organization. It remains to be seen what, if any, criminal charges will result from the way in which the Center for the Study of Paranatural Biology conducted itself, especially in consequence of events leading to last night's television broadcast with which we are all no doubt familiar. I have received word that civil charges, at least, will soon be filed on behalf of Katherine Norville against the parties directly involved. At this point decisions and recommendations fall outside this committee's jurisdiction. We gladly leave such considerations to the judicial system.

"In closing, it is the committee's opinion that the victims of the diseases studied by Dr. Paul Flemming and his laboratory have lived in American society for years, unnoticed and without posing a threat. We see no reason why they should not continue to do so, and we urge all good people of reason not to fall into a state of hysteria. Thank you."

That was it. The whole thing was filed away, folded into the bureaucracy to be forgotten as quickly as possible. Which was what I'd wanted, wasn't it? It felt anticlimactic.

The exodus began, senators and their aides shuffling papers and closing briefcases, reporters sorting out their recorders, people massing toward the doors.

This was the first day Flemming had missed. I couldn't really blame him; he had a lot to answer for. And really, if I'd been able to corner him and talk to him, what would I have said? "Sucks to be you"? Maybe I just wanted to growl at him a little.

Maybe I should thank him for saving my life.

I hid away in a corner of the room and called his number. I expected it to ring a half-dozen times, then roll over to voice mail. But after the first ring, an electronic voice cut in. "The number you have dialed is no longer in service . . ."

I scanned the crowd and found the committee staffer who'd been herding witnesses all week. I maneuvered toward her as quickly as I could against the flow of the crowd, and managed to stop her before she left the room. She was in her thirties, businesslike, and her eyes bugged when she spotted me stalking toward her. I thought she was going to turn and run, like a rabbit. We all had the flight instinct, in the end.

"Hi, do you have a minute? I just have a question." I tried to sound reassuring and harmless.

She nodded and seemed to relax a little, though she still held her attaché case in front of her like a shield.

"Dr. Flemming wasn't here today," I said. "Do you know if he was supposed to be? Or where he might be if not here?" In jail, maybe? Was that too much to hope for?

Her gaze dropped to the floor, and the tension returned to her stance. She actually glanced over her shoulder, as if searching for eavesdroppers.

"He was supposed to be here," she said. "But right before the session started, I was informed that he'd be absent. That he had another commitment."

"Informed? By whom? What other commitment?"

"I know better than to ask questions about certain things, Ms. Norville. Flemming's out of your reach now." She hunched her shoulders and hurried away.

Conspiracy theory, anyone?

"Wait! Am I supposed to think that he's been sucked into some dark, clandestine project and no one's ever going to see him again? Is there a phone number for him? I've got court papers to serve, you know!"

She didn't even look back at me.

The senators arranged a press conference inside the hearing chamber. Henderson and Dreschler answered questions, many of them regarding Duke and what his future in the Senate, if any, might be. Listening between the lines, I felt like they were saying nothing much would happen to Duke. He'd be censured, and that was about it. A slap on the wrist. They expected the other people involved to take the fall for him. Stockton and Flemming. I didn't have enough energy left for righteous indignation.

Then came my turn. After the senators left, I agreed to spend a

few minutes at the podium, mainly because Ben convinced me that
facing all the reporters at once was easier than running the gaunt-
let. If I gave some comments now, it would be easier to ignore them
later on.

Ben was right. I had to face up to the reputation I'd built for myself. I had to face the consequences of that reputation.

I tried to think of it as being on the radio. The microphone
reached out in front of me, and that looked familiar. If I could ignore the lights, the cameras, the rows of faces in front of me, I
could pretend I was talking to my audience. As a voice on the radio, I could say anything I wanted.

I let Ben pick who would ask the questions. He was on hand to
jump in and save me if I stuck my foot in my mouth.

The first question came from a middle-aged man in a turtleneck.
"Ed Freeman, *New York Times*. It's been suggested that you were
complicit in arranging last night's broadcast. That it was a publicity stunt to garner sympathy and publicize your show. Any comment?"

My jaw dropped. "Who suggested that? The *National Enquirer*?"
Ben made an *erp*-sounding noise. Right, had to be serious. "Mr.
Freeman, it's well known that despite the success of my radio
show, I've never publicized my appearance. I never wanted to be
recognized on the street and that hasn't changed. I was forced into
that broadcast."

"Judy Lerma, the *Herald*. How much are you seeking in damages in your lawsuit against Duke and the others?"

I hadn't even thought of that. "I don't think it's been decided. I'll
leave that to my attorney."

"Ms. Norville, how and when did you become a werewolf?"

I was going to have to tell that story over and over again, wasn't
I? "It was about four years ago. I was a junior in college, and ended
up in the wrong place at the wrong time. I was attacked and survived."

"Does that sort of thing happen often?"

"I think you're more likely to get mugged in a small town in
Kansas than get attacked by a werewolf."

Then someone asked, "I hear that one of the networks has offered you your own TV show. Will you take the offer?"

I blinked. I looked at Ben. He wasn't so gauche as to shrug in
front of the cameras, but his expression was noncommittal enough.
He hadn't heard either. "This is the first I've heard of it," I said.

"Would you do a TV show? As the next step from radio?"

Good question. The little giddy show business side of me was jumping up and down. But another part of me still wanted that hole to hide in. Wolf was still scared, and so far she was doing a great job of keeping that fear locked down. But I had to get out of here soon, or we'd both blow up.

I offered a brave smile. "I don't know. I thought I might take a little time off to consider my options."

Ben stepped up and took hold of my arm. "That's all the time we have for questions today. Thank you."

Finally, we left, sneaking out a back door held open by a police officer. At last, I could breathe again.

Epilogue

I stayed in D.C. long enough to talk to Emma.

The third night, two days after the broadcast, I visited Alette's town house just after dusk. Tom answered the door. He looked grim and harried—he hadn't shaved, and his hair was tousled. The iron reserve of the Man In Black had slipped.

"How is everything?" I asked as he let me inside.

"A mess. We're all torn up over Bradley, Emma hasn't said a word. But Alette's holding everyone together. She's an anchor. I don't know how she does it."

"Tom? Is she here?" Striding briskly, Alette followed her voice in from the parlor. She wore a silk dress suit, and her hair was tied in a bun. I'd never have guessed the trauma her household had been through. "Kitty, I'm so glad you came."

Tom stepped out of the way, heading to the back of the house for some business of his own.

"How is she?" I said immediately, without even saying hello.

Alette smiled thinly. "I think she'll be all right. Eventually."

She led me to the parlor.

The rug had been replaced. This one had more blues than reds in it. Emma sat on an armchair, gripping a thick gray blanket tightly around herself. She stared, blank-eyed, at the curtains, which had been put back over the window. Her skin was sickly pale, and her hair limp. She smelled dead but not rotten—cold, static, unchanging, unliving. She smelled like a vampire.

Alette waited by the doorway while I pulled a chair closer to Emma. I put myself between her and the window, hoping she'd look at me.

"Hi," I said. Her gaze flickered. "How are you feeling?" Which was a stupid thing to ask. But what else could I say? I wanted to apologize.

"I'm cold," she said in a whisper. The words wavered, like she might start crying, but her expression remained blank. Numb. She pulled the blanket higher over her shoulders.

"Is there anything I can do?" I remembered what it was like, waking up and realizing that the world smelled different, that your body had become strange, as if your heart had shifted inside your chest.

She closed her eyes. "Should I do it? Should I open the curtains when morning comes?" And let the sun in. And kill herself. "Alette doesn't want me to. But she said she wouldn't stop me."

"I don't want you to either," I said, a bit shrilly. "You had this done to you, you didn't want it, and it's terrible. But it's not the end of the world. You're still you. You have to hold on to that."

She looked at me, her eyes glittering, fierce and exhausted at the same time, like she was on the edge of losing her self-control. "I feel different, like there's an empty place in me. Like my heart's gone, but there's something else there—and it feels like being drunk, a little. If I open myself to that—" She laughed, a tight, desperate sound, and covered her mouth. "I'm afraid of it."

"That's good," I said. "If you're afraid of it you won't let it swallow you up."

"I just keep thinking of all the things I can't do now," she said, shaking her head. "I can't see the sun ever again. I can't get a tan. I can't finish my degree—"

"There's always night school," I said.

"But what would be the point?"

"You tell me."

Her gaze was becoming more focused. I felt like she actually saw me now. Alette was right—she was going to be okay. She didn't really want to open the curtains.

"I'm still me," she said. I nodded. She held the blanket in a death grip—probably for more comfort than from the cold.

I stood, getting ready to leave her alone. She was curled up, staring at the arm of the chair, looking like she needed to be left alone.

"Kitty?" she said, glancing up suddenly. "Can I call you? Your show, I mean. If I need to talk."

I smiled. "I'll give you the private number."

Alette brought me to the kitchen for tea. She already had a pot made up. The kitchen seemed too bright, after the shadows of the parlor. It seemed too real, too normal.

She talked as she poured. Only one cup—she didn't drink tea. I wondered if she missed it.

"She didn't say it, but she's also upset about Bradley. We all are. I'm so glad Tom had that night off. I don't know what I'd have done if I'd lost them both. All three of them, in some ways. Emma will never be the same. She was so full of life, and to see her like this—"

"But you still have her, and Leo doesn't, for which I'm very grateful." I couldn't imagine what he'd have done with her, what she'd have done with him lording himself over her. Actually, I could imagine it, that was the problem.

"Yes," Alette said wryly.

"Something's been nagging me," I said, after taking a sip of tea. "Leo was a lackey. He couldn't move against you without help. He said something about this plot going beyond Flemming. That Flemming only thought he was in control. I've been wondering— who was Leo really taking orders from? The DOD?"

Alette frowned, her lips tightening. "Flemming was the military's contact, not Leo. Leo needed Flemming to get his military support. If Leo had ulterior motives, they served another purpose entirely. I wish I knew for certain. I wish I could give you a name. But the answers lie in shadow. There are stories that vampires tell each other, late at night, just before dawn, to frighten each other. To frighten ourselves. If vampires are truly immortal, there could be some very, very old beings in this world. They may be so old, their motives are alien to us. Some say that even the Master vampires have their Masters, and you would not want to meet them, even in bright daylight. I have kept quiet, kept myself and mine away from those who would seek such power."

People scared themselves with vampire stories. So what scared the vampires? A thing I hoped I never met. A thing that this brief mention of would haunt my mind. My hand held the teacup frozen, midway to my mouth.

"Are these beings like Elijah Smith?" I said.

Like I was afraid she would, she shook her head. "Creatures like Smith, the *sidhe*, come from another world entirely that rarely crosses paths with ours. They are isolated dangers. This has always lurked in the shadows of our world."

"What? What's always lurked?"

"Evil."

That sounded too damn simple. And yet, it opened a range of sinister possibilities in my imagination. I wasn't sure I'd ever met evil: madness, illness, ambition, confusion, arrogance, rage, yes. But evil?

"Just when I thought I was starting to figure things out," I muttered.

Alette straightened and brightened her tone. "I am confident that with Leo's failure, and Flemming's failure, we will not need to concern ourselves with such possibilities. Agreed?"

"Agreed," I whispered. That left one more question. I continued awkwardly. "I know this is a personal question, and if you don't want to say anything that's okay. But how did this happen? You becoming a vampire—is it something you wanted?"

She smiled and lowered her gaze, giving a hint of amusement. "I'll tell you the short version. I was desperate. I was poor, I had two children, and lived in a world where no one blinked at poverty. An opportunity presented itself, and I took it. I vowed that I would never leave my children, like their father did. Not even death would take me from them."

After a pause I said, "I suppose it worked."

"I have never regretted it."

Alette had very much proven herself adaptable to circumstance. The centuries would stretch on and she would still be here with her parlor, her pictures, and her children.

I fidgeted with the cup and saucer. "I should get going. I sort of have a date."

"With that jaguar fellow, I presume?"

"Um, yeah."

"Wait just a moment." She left me to fidget with my tea. When she returned, she held a small jewelry box. She offered it to me. "I'd like you to have this."

I opened it and found the diamond teardrop pendant on its gold chain. "Oh, Alette, you shouldn't—"

"It's something to remember me by. Do come and visit sometime."

She clasped my hand, kissed my cheek, and we said goodbye.

Earlier that afternoon, I'd had one last room-service lunch with Ben. Cormac had already left town, without even saying goodbye. I was simultaneously offended and relieved.

As usual, Ben ate while he worked, shuffling through papers, turning away just long enough to open the door. He'd ordered a steak for me. Rare.

I sat at the table and nodded at the current folder. "What's this?"

"The FCC wants to investigate you for indecency."

"What?"

"Apparently, somewhere between fully clothed human and fur-covered wolf, you flashed breast on national broadcast television. They've gotten about a dozen complaints."

"You have *got* to be kidding me." Flashing the TV audience had been the last thing on my mind.

"Nope. I rewatched the video, and sure enough, it's there. You have to be pretty fast with the pause button to catch it."

I loved the idea of all the prudish reactionaries who must have taped the show, then sat there with their thumbs poised over the scan and pause buttons, searching for something to complain to the FCC about. And they're charging *me* with indecency?

"I'll tell you what—forward the complaint to Stockton. No, better—forward it to Duke."

"Already done. I think it'll be pretty easy to argue the complaint and prove you had no responsibility for the broadcast."

Damn straight. "I got a message from Stockton." He'd left it on my cell phone during the hearings, like he'd called specifically at a time he knew I'd have my phone turned off so he could leave a message without having to talk to me. He'd sounded downright obsequious: "Kitty. It's Roger. Look, I'm probably the last guy you want to hear from. You'll probably never speak to me again. But I really wish you'd call me back. I've been asked about a follow-up show. I see us laying down a commentary track on the coverage from last night, you know? It could be a big move for both of us, career-wise. I really think you have a future in television. I want to do right by you. Thanks."

That maniac. If I ever decided to make a go at television, it would be without his help. "You think you can sue him a lot?"

"Oh, yeah, about our good Mr. Stockton. Cormac did some digging on our behalf. Have a look at this." Ben handed me a manila folder out of his stack.

I opened it and started reading. There were a half-dozen pages of official-looking forms, spaces with names and dates filled in, and a few mug shots of the same person, a skinny kid with a doped-out gaze and wild hair.

It was Roger Stockton. A younger, crazier Roger Stockton.

"These are arrest reports," I said, awestruck.

"Mr. Stockton put himself through college by dealing hallucinogenic drugs. Not the usual weed, but exotic stuff: opium, peyote, frog-licking, that sort of thing. It seems he was into experimentation, looking for a higher power, saying it was all part of some religious ceremony that he and his friends were conducting. You know how it goes. The charges never stuck. He never served time. But it still makes for fascinating reading, don't you think?"

If this information was leaked, Stockton might be able to talk his way out of it and salvage his career. But until he did, his life would become very interesting.

"Revenge or blackmail?" I said.

"Blackmail? That's illegal. Persuasion, on the other hand—I'm betting Stockton would sure hate to see this stuff come out in a civil trial. He'll settle out of court, or his network will."

Politics. Playing each other to get what we wanted. Was there any way to avoid it? Couldn't we all just get along?

"This is never going to be over, is it?"

"I think your place in American pop culture is assured. You're going to end up as a question on a game show, you realize."

I might have groaned. Ben chuckled.

"Sure, go ahead and laugh. It just means job security for you."

He sat back in his chair, abandoning the paperwork for a moment. He wore a vague, amused grin. "I know what Cormac sees in you."

"What, a target?"

"Not at all. He's downright smitten."

"Huh?" Constantly making veiled threats constituted smitten? To an eight-year-old, maybe. And how many times had he come to my rescue now? Urgh . . .

"It's true. I've known him since we were kids."

"Kids? Really? How?"

"We're cousins. I probably shouldn't even be saying this—"

Cousins? Had to keep him talking. "No, please. Say this. What does Cormac see in me?"

"You're tough. Tough and whiny at the same time. It's kind of cute."

I couldn't tell if he was making fun of me or not. Time to change the subject.

"So you've always known Cormac. Was he always like that?"

"Like what?"

"Hard-nosed. Humorless."

"No, I suppose not. But you have to go back a long way to see him any different. He lost both his parents pretty young. I figure he deserves to be as humorless as he wants."

Even saying "I'm sorry" sounded lame at that point.

"You told me once that Cormac likes seeing how close to the edge he can get without falling off. What about you? Why do you hunt vampires?"

He shrugged. "I don't hunt anything, really. I just look out for my friends. That's all."

Which made him a good person to have at your back—all anyone could ask for, really. That, and an honest lawyer, all wrapped into one.

"When are you going back to Denver?"

"After I file suit in court. Though it may not come to that. I've gotten word from both Duke's office and the NIH that they're willing to settle. Duke won't want to settle, but if the Senate Ethics Committee gets involved, he may come around. There are still criminal charges pending, but this might not drag on so long."

"Thanks for doing all this. I don't even care about the money, you know. I just want a little old-fashioned revenge."

"That's the best part," he said, grinning his hawk's grin, the one that made me glad he was on my side.

Luis had tickets to a symphony concert at the Kennedy Center that night. It seemed a great way to spend my last night in town. We met up at the Crescent.

I wore a smoky gray skirt and jacket with a white camisole. Understated, until I put on the diamond Alette had given me. Then, it looked awfully mature. Sophisticated, even. Like something Alette might wear. I didn't feel like myself.

Ahmed met me at the door. He didn't say a word at first, just closed me in a big monstrous hug until I thought I might suffocate. I didn't have much hope of hugging back, so I leaned in and took a deep breath, of smoke and wine and wild. It smelled a little like a pack.

"Come back to visit, yes?" he said, gripping my shoulders. I nodded firmly. Looked like I was coming back to D.C. at some point. Jack waved at me from the bar.

I sensed Luis come in through the door behind me. I didn't even have to turn around. He stalked like a cat and his warmth reached out for me.

He touched my shoulders and kissed the back of my neck. Fire, warmth, happiness, I felt all that in his touch. Finally, Wolf's fear uncurled. Some light came into her burrow. I felt like running— from joy this time, not fear.

"Ready?"

I almost asked if we could blow off the symphony. But I nodded.

I was glad I went, glad I didn't miss seeing the Kennedy Center. The place was so beautiful, so momentous, walking into the four-story-high Hall of States with the marble walls, red carpeting, state flags hanging from the ceiling. I wanted to cry. Felt like I should have been wearing a sweeping ball gown and not a suit.

People stared at me. At us. The people who had tickets for the seat next to me in the concert hall moved. Everyone watched the news, I supposed. I wilted. I would have stuck my tail between my legs if I'd had it. I would have left, if Luis had let me. Bless him, he didn't flinch once. He walked past them all, holding my arm tucked in his, his back straight and chin up. Like a jaguar stalking through his jungle.

Staring at his shoulder, I leaned in and asked him, "How can you stand it? The way they look at us?"

He said, "I know that I could rip out their guts, and I choose not to."

We stood in the Grand Foyer at intermission. I looked down the hall, taking in the floor-to-ceiling mirrors, the windows framed with soft drapes, a thousand glittering lights in the chandeliers, the immense bust of Kennedy gazing out over what he'd inspired.

A couple walked by. The woman, young and elegant in a blue cocktail dress, brushed past me. Her hand caught mine, hanging loose at my side, and squeezed for just a moment. Then she walked away. She never looked at me.

She smelled like wolf. I stared after her, until Luis tugged at my arm.

After the concert we went up to the roof terrace. Looking southeast, I could see the Washington, Jefferson, and Lincoln Memorials lined up, lit and glowing like beacons in the night. Great men and their monuments. They weren't perfect. They made mistakes. But they changed the world. They were idealists.

Luis stood behind me, arms around me, and kissed the top of my head.

"Thank you for this," I said, my voice hushed. "For showing me this."

"You ever need to get away, take a vacation, call me. I'll show you Rio de Janeiro."

"It's a deal." Like, how about now?

"What will you do next?"

"Take time off. I don't know. Maybe I should write a book." I pictured myself going back to the show, back to the radio station. I sat in front of the microphone, opened my mouth—and nothing came out.

I had a place in mind, a small town where I'd spent a couple of weeks one summer in college. I could go rent a cabin, be philosophical, run wild in the woods.

And try to remember how to be an idealist.

Kitty Meets the Band

WELCOME BACK, LISTENERS. For those of you just joining us, I'm Kitty Norville and this is *The Midnight Hour*. I just got a call from my scheduled guests this evening, the band Plague of Locusts, and I'm afraid they're caught in traffic and are going to be a little late, another ten minutes or so. So I'm going to take a few more calls while we're waiting for them to arrive. Our topic this evening: music and the supernatural.

"In the nineteenth century, rumor had it that the great violinist Paganini sold his soul to the devil in exchange for his amazing virtuoso abilities. Many artists are said to be inspired by the Muses. And music soothes the savage beast. What exactly is the mystical nature of music? Are all these tales mere metaphor, or is something supernatural controlling our musical impulses? I want to hear from you. Eddy from Baltimore, you're on the air."

"Hi, Kitty! Whoa, thanks for taking my call."

"No problem, Eddy. What do you have for me?"

"I want to sell my soul to the devil. If I had the chance, I'd do it in a heartbeat. To play guitar like Hendrix—oh man, I'd do just about *anything*!"

"How about practice?"

"It's not enough. I've been practicing for *years*. All that time and I can do 'Stairway to Heaven,' and that's it. What Hendrix had? That's not natural."

"Do you think Hendrix sold his soul to the devil?"

"Wouldn't surprise me. So, Kitty—have any idea how I'd go about doing that?"

"What, selling your soul to the devil? Are you sure that's such a good idea?"

"Why not? It's not like I'm using my soul for anything else."

Oh man, talk about missing the point. "I get enough accusations from the religious Right that I'm damning people's souls, I'm not sure I want to put any more fuel on that fire. But the answer is no, I have no idea how you'd go about selling your soul to the devil. Sorry. Next call, please. Rebecca, hello."

"Kitty, hi." The woman's voice was low, vaguely desperate.

"Hello. You have a question or a story?"

"A question, I think. Like, you know when you get a song stuck in your head, and it drives you crazy, and no matter how much you try to think of something else you can't stop it from playing in your head? Right now I have 'Muskrat Love' stuck. It's been stuck there for days. It's . . . it's driving me crazy." Her voice turned ominous. If she told me she was holding a butcher knife just then, I wouldn't have been surprised.

I tried to sound as sympathetic as possible. "The Captain and Tennille version of the song, I assume?"

She hesitated for a long moment. "You mean there's more than one?"

"Never mind. It's called an earworm," I said. "Scientists have been studying this phenomenon, believe it or not. When they aren't busy with a cure for cancer. Statistically, it seems to affect women more than men, and especially affects people who are slightly neurotic anyway." I had my suspicions about Rebecca.

"So it's not, like . . . demonic possession?"

"In the case of 'Muskrat Love,' I'm not entirely sure it isn't."

"How do I make it stop?"

"Have you tried listening to the song? Sometimes if you hear it all the way through, it goes away."

"I tried that. Five times in a row."

Well, if you asked me that was her problem right there. "How about a different song, completely different, like something by Ministry?"

"Will that pacify the demon horde?"

So we're possessed by a demon *horde*, now? "I'm not sure I'd guarantee that. Seriously, most people recommend listening to a different song, trying to get a different song stuck in your head. It's not a perfect solution, but with some songs, any alternative is better."

"What do you recommend?"

" 'I Think I Love You,' by the Partridge Family."

She hesitated a moment, then stammered, "Oh. Oh . . . God, no!"

Ah, success. "Did it work?" I asked brightly.

"Yes, but . . . are you sure this isn't worse than 'Muskrat Love'?"

"You tell me."

"I—I just don't know!"

"Right, while you think about it I'm going to move onto the next call. Hello, Ellen. What do you want to talk about?"

"Hi, Kitty. You know the Orpheus myth?"

I said, "Orpheus. The bard of Greek mythology who went into Hades, and his music was so powerful that he convinced the god of the underworld to release the soul of his dead wife. He was told that he could lead her to the surface, but if he looked back to make sure that she followed, he'd lose her forever. Of course, he looked back. It's a story about the power of music, but it's also a story about trust."

"Yeah," she said, and I caught a sadness in her voice, an uncertainty. "Kitty, you're always talking about myths and legends that have these roots in reality. That sometimes the stories are real, at least partly. Do you . . . do you think that's ever happened? That music—or anything—is so powerful it could bring back the dead?"

It amazed me sometimes, the stark emotion that people could expose with just their voices. The human voice is the most expressive musical instrument of all.

I closed my eyes to gather myself for the question I had to ask. If she didn't want to talk about it, she wouldn't have called in. "Who did you lose, Ellen?"

"My husband," she said, and her voice didn't even crack. She was just muted. Lost. "Eight months ago. It was cancer. We'd only been married three years. I know I can't bring him back, but . . . I'm a musician. I play the flute professionally, I'm in an orchestra and everything. Not as good as Orpheus must have been . . . but I wonder. Music was strong enough to bring us together the first time. Maybe it could bring him back. If I had the chance, if I thought I could, I'd try."

I rubbed my face and pinched my nose to stop tears. This happened every now and then. I didn't know what to say. Nothing I could say would be the right thing.

"Maybe not all the stories start out as true. A lot of them start out as wishes, I think. The Orpheus myth, it takes something powerful that people can do—make music—and turns it into something powerful we wish we could do. Like bring back our loved ones. Ellen, I know this sounds trite, but I'm betting there's a part of him, part of his spirit that comes through every time you play."

"I—I think so, too. But sometimes it isn't enough. Kitty—if it had been me, I wouldn't have looked back."

"I know."

With incredibly bad timing, the studio door opened and let in a swarm of noise from the outside. The producer in the sound booth waved manically and ran out to try to stop them.

I rolled with the punches. "Ellen, thank you for calling and sharing your story. I know I'm not alone in extending my thoughts and sympathies to you. We're going to break now for station ID." I signed Ellen off, then turned to the door.

There they were, crowding into the studio, lugging their instruments. I recognized the lead singer from the band's publicity photo: a skinny punk, twenty-two years old, wearing cut-off jeans, a ragged, oversize T-shirt, and combat boots.

I jumped out of my seat to intercept him. "Rudy? Hi."

Our introduction would determine how the rest of the evening went. Was he a stuck-up, self-absorbed musician type who barely deigned to speak to lesser mortals, or was he a regular guy who just happened to sing in a band?

He smiled at me. "You're Kitty? Hi!" He had a warm expression and easy-going manner at odds with his punked-out persona. He seemed more surfer dude than anti-social rebel. I relaxed; this was going to go well. "Let me introduce everyone. There's Bucky on drums, Len's our guitarist. And Tim there's on bass."

Tim stood out from the rest of the band. The other guys *looked* like they were in a band: Len had lightning bolts shaved into his crew cut, Bucky had tattoos crawling up both arms. Tim, however, was wearing a cardigan, like he'd been zapped through time from a '50s doo-wop group.

I considered for a moment, then said, "So, he's the one who's possessed by a demon?"

"Yup!" Rudy said proudly. "I don't know how it happened, but there it is."

Tim glanced at us as he was plugging his bass into an amp. His expression didn't change. He looked like a regular guy.

I contained my skepticism. "Rudy, do you mind if we have a few words on the air while the others set up? Then I'd love to hear you play."

"That's what we're here for!"

I brought him to the mikes. Right on schedule, the producer signaled that we were about ready to get back to the show. He counted down on his fingers, four, three, two—

"Welcome back, faithful listeners. This is *The Midnight Hour* and I'm Kitty Norville. I have as my guests this evening the L.A. band Plague of Locusts. They've just released their third album, and their single, 'Under a Dull Knife,' is climbing the charts. Next month they embark on their first national concert tour. We'll hear some music later on, but right now the band's lead singer, Rudy Jones, is here to chat with us. Welcome to the show, Rudy. Thanks for joining us."

"Are you kidding? This is so cool! We're big fans."

"Wow, that's sweet. Thanks." Here was someone who knew the way to a girl's heart. I beamed at him. "My first question for you: the band's name, Plague of Locusts, references an event in the Bible, in the book of Exodus. I was wondering why you chose the name, and what you might be implying with it."

"We just thought it sounded cool," Rudy said, totally deadpan.

I stared hopefully. "Nothing about raining destruction down on the world, or getting into wrath-of-God kind of stuff?"

He shook his head. "Well, I suppose a plague of locusts is like a swarm. We're like a swarm, you know?" He considered thoughtfully. "We want our music to swarm in and overwhelm people."

"Devouring them until nothing remains?"

"Yeah!"

"Now, your bass player, Tim Kane. Rumors say that he's possessed by a demon. You want to tell me how that happened?"

"It was the weirdest thing. We were in Bucky's mom's garage—that's where we got our start, you know. A real honest-to-God garage band. So there we were, practicing, only we weren't really practicing because we were fighting. We did a lot of that at first. Bucky wanted to know why we wouldn't play any of *his* songs, Len thought *he* should stand in front, we argued about who's more old school, Sid Vicious or Joe Strummer. So we're in the middle of all this, and then Tim, he goes into this, like, seizure or something. His eyes roll back into his head and everything. He was totally foaming at the mouth! Then he starts talking, and his voice. It's *different*. Totally deep. Kind of echoey, you know? And he says, 'Stop fighting.' I mean, what are you going to do in a situation like that? We stopped fighting. Then he tells us—only it's not Tim anymore, it's like this demonic muse or something. He tells us that if we want to be a great band, if we really want to follow our dream, we have to do what he says."

Fascinated, I asked, "This wasn't a 'sell your soul to the devil at the crossroads' kind of thing? This demon muse is giving you all this advice for free?"

"Yeah, totally! Isn't that cool?"

"Totally." I agreed. "Then what happened?"

"The demon tells us his name is Morgantix, and he's from another dimension, and he always wanted to play in a band. So he picked us, and I guess he picked Tim because he's, you know, so quiet. I mean, Tim started out as a really good bass player. But since Morgantix came along, the whole band just kind of jelled. It's been great. And I figure as long as Morgantix is having a good time, he'll keep helping us."

"Wow," I said. "That's almost heartwarming."

I glanced at Tim, who was standing by himself in the performance space, bass slung over his shoulder, fingering the strings. He was terribly unassuming. I wouldn't have looked twice at him on the street. He didn't *smell* like he was possessed by a demon. Not that I had any idea what someone possessed by a demon would smell like. Of course, anyone who dressed like a '50s preppy was possessed by something unnatural.

Then again, he *was* in a band.

Tim caught my gaze and quirked a sly grin at me. Not quite demonic, but still . . .

I said, "Do you suppose we might have a few words with Morgantix? I'd love to hear his side of the story."

Rudy looked over at Tim. "How about it?"

Slowly, Tim shook his head. In a deep, gravelly voice he said, "Morgantix play, not talk."

"How about Tim?" I said to the man himself. "Can we get a few words about what it's like being possessed by a musically inclined demon?"

Tim just glared.

Alrighty, then.

"It's kind of unpredictable," Rudy said. "He's there one minute, gone the next. We never really know who's in control when we talk to Tim."

I had to admit, I was a bit awestruck. The possibilities were intriguing. Tim certainly did have this manner about him. But was it just a typical, standoffish, artistic temperament, or really something supernatural?

"I have to confess to a bit of skepticism, Rudy. Where's your proof? Except for the voice thing, do you have any hard evidence proving the existence of Morgantix?" Really, though, who would make up a name like Morgantix? Score one in their favor.

"Believe me, Kitty, we wouldn't have gotten this far with the band without a lot of help from another plane of existence."

I had to take Rudy's word for that. I moved on. "I'm going to open the line for calls now. Do you have a question for Rudy? You know the number. Paula from Austin, you're on the air."

Paula let out a *squee!* of ear-shattering proportions. "Omigod, hi! Rudy, I'm *such* a big fan, you have no idea—"

The next ten minutes pretty much went exactly like that. Plague of Locusts seemed to have a bevy of screaming teenage fans across the country, and they all called in to gush. Rudy seemed impressed and chatted with them all.

I had fifteen minutes left to the show when I cut off the calls. "Rudy? How about you and the boys play something for us?"

His eyes lit up. "Yeah! Cool!" He was way too cheerful to be a real punk. He called over to the band, seated with their instruments. "Hey guys, what should we play?"

Bucky said, "We could play, you know, *that* one. The one with the *bum bum bum* part."

Len nodded quickly. "Yeah—the *new* version."

"I don't know," Rudy said, pursing his lips thoughtfully. "We haven't ever played that one live. How about the one with the cool bit in the middle?"

"We *could* do that one," Bucky said. "But what about the *other* one?"

"That one's okay too," Rudy said.

I had no clue what they were talking about. I stared, rapt.

Then Tim said, in his rough, demonic voice, "Play the fast one." Rudy perked up, his eyes going wide. "Dude, yeah! The fast one!"

Bucky jumped to his drums, Len stood with his guitar, and Rudy raced to his microphone. Tim watched them, calmly as ever.

All this carried over the studio mikes. I almost hated to interrupt the entertaining exchange, but the musicians had already turned their attention to their instruments.

I leaned in to my mike. "Okay, listeners, it looks like Plague of Locusts is going to play us some music. I have no idea what the name of the piece is, but they're calling it 'the fast one.' I, for one, am intrigued."

Rudy called over, "Are you ready, Kitty?"

Ready as I'd ever be. "Go for it!"

Bucky the drummer banged out a count and the band plunged in, full speed ahead. They went straight from zero to manic in half a second. The fast one, yeah. Still, their playing was strangely compelling. Len hunched over his guitar, legs spread, head bobbing in time to the music; I thought the poor guy was going to get whiplash. Bucky did the same, his long hair flying, the entire drum set rattling. Rudy clutched his microphone stand in both hands, pressed the mike to his face, and screamed.

Tim kept up with the song, fingers dancing on the frets, bass chords rumbling. The man himself, though, remained still, intensely focused, the eye of this particular hurricane.

I couldn't say I understood any of the lyrics, and there wasn't a melody of any kind to speak of. The rhythm resembled that of a massive downpour on a tin roof. That only made Plague of Locusts the latest in a long line of anti-establishment, anti-musicality musicians. Call it what you will, the fans loved it. My phone lines lit up, listeners calling in to beg for more.

The band played two more songs, we took a few more phone calls from eager fans, and then came the end of the show. I was almost sorry we were out of time. This had been a hoot.

Rudy and the others apparently had a great time, too. After the closing credits, Bucky and Len shook my hand enthusiastically. Rudy hugged me like we were long lost siblings. He promised we'd do this again sometime. I basked in a general feeling of success and well-being. It hardly mattered that Morgantix the demon hadn't agreed to speak to me through host body Tim. Though, I'd rather been looking forward to conducting the first live demon interview in radio.

Tim hung back as they left the studio, waiting until Rudy and the others were in the hallway, leaving the two of us alone. He had an air of calculating calm about him. I couldn't help it; he made me nervous. My heartbeat speeded up, and I eyed the exit.

"Can I tell you something?" he asked me in a regular tenor—an unassuming, undemonic voice. Morgantix has left the building . . .

"Okay."

He glanced at the floor a moment, suddenly looking sly, like he was about to tell a joke. "See, you're pretty cool, and I just have to tell somebody. Can you keep a secret?"

"Sure." Always say yes to that question. I learned the best stuff this way.

He said, "Okay, here it goes. I'm not really possessed by a demon named Morgantix."

Somehow, I was simultaneously surprised and not. "Are you possessed by any demon at all?"

"No," he said, shaking his head and smiling wryly.

It was almost disappointing.

"You could tell me anything and I'd have to believe you. I have absolutely no way of telling if you're possessed by a demon or not," I said.

"Fortunately, neither does anyone else."

"So why go around telling everyone you are? Is it some kind of publicity stunt?"

"Oh, it's not for the public. It's for them." He nodded out the hallway to his departing bandmates. "They're the most direction-less, indecisive bunch of people I've ever met. I realized the only way the band was going to get anywhere was with some kind of leadership. But they don't listen to me—I'm the *quiet* one. On the other hand, a being from an alternate plane of existence? They'll listen to that. It's the only way I could get them to agree on any-thing."

Enthralled, I considered him. It was the kind of story that if I hadn't seen it in action, I'd never have believed it. You can't make this stuff up.

"Aren't you afraid I'll blow your secret?"

He smirked. "What's easier to believe: that I'm actually pos-sessed by Morgantix the demon, or that I've spent the last three years fooling a trio of grown men into believing that I'm possessed by Morgantix the demon?"

"You know that's a toss up, don't you?"

He smiled a clean-cut, boyish smile and left the studio to follow the rest of the band.

Well, how about that? I chased down a story about the supernat-ural and found a completely mundane explanation. There's a switch from my usual prime-time drama sort of life. And it only re-inforced what I'd known for some time now:

I *love* my job.

Kitty
Takes a
Holiday

For Andrea, Denise, April, Melissa, Kevin, and Tim,
who were there at the start.

Acknowledgments

My first readers this time around were Paula Balafas and Jo Anne "Mom" Vaughn. Also, thank you to Paula for the ride-alongs, and to Mom for the road trip.

More thank yous: To Larry "Dad" Vaughn for looking after the dog, and to the rest of the family. To Andro Berkovic for bringing my computing power into the twenty-first century. To the Barony of Caer Galen for the overwhelming support. To Ashley Grayson and Co. for picking up the reins. And as always, to Jaime Levine and the crew at Warner, for believing in Kitty so very, very much.

The Playlist

Blondie, "Hanging on the Telephone"

Go Go's, "Head Over Heels"

The Killers, "Mr. Brightside"

Suicidal Tendencies, "Possessed"

Madness, "Animal Farm"

Pretenders, "I Go to Sleep"

VNV Nation, "Kingdom"

Noel Gallagher, "Teotihuacan"

The Dead Milkmen "Surfin' Cow"

Andy Kirk & His Twelve Clouds of Joy, "Until the Real Thing Comes Along"

Too Much Joy, "Crush Story"

Bach Collegiuim Stuttgart, "Sheep May Safely Graze"

Supertramp, "It's Raining Again"

Eurythmics, "When Tomorrow Comes"

chapter 1

She runs for the joy of it, because she can, her strides stretching to cover a dozen feet every time she leaps. Her mouth is open to taste the air, which is sharp with cold. The month turns, and the swelling moon paints the night sky silver, lighting up patches of snow scattered throughout the woods. Not yet full moon, a rare moment to be set free before her time, but the other half of her being has no reason to lock her away. She is alone, but she is free, and so she runs.

Catching a scent, she swerves from her path, slows to a trot, puts her nose to the ground. Prey, fresh and warm. Lots of it here in the wild. The smell burns in the winter air. She stalks, drawing breath with flaring nostrils, searching for the least flicker of movement. Her empty stomach clenches, driving her on. The smell makes her mouth water.

She has grown used to hunting alone. Must be careful, must not take chances. Her padded feet touch the ground lightly, ready to spring forward, to dart in one direction or another, making no sound on the forest floor. The scent—musky, hot fur and scat—grows strong, rocketing through her brain. All her nerves flare. Close now, closer, creeping on hunter's feet—

The rabbit springs from its cover, a rotted log grown over with shrubs. She's ready for it, without seeing it or hearing it she knows it is there, her hunter's sense filled by its presence. The moment it runs, she leaps, pins it to the ground with her claws and body, digs her teeth into its neck, clamping her jaw shut and ripping. It doesn't have time to scream. She drinks the blood pumping out of its torn and broken throat, devours its meat before the blood cools. The warmth and life of it fills her belly, lights her soul, and she pauses the slaughter to howl in victory—

My whole body flinched, like I'd been dreaming of falling and suddenly woken up. I gasped a breath—part of me was still in the dream, still falling, and I had to tell myself that I was safe, that I wasn't about to hit the ground. My hands clutched reflexively, but didn't grab sheets or pillow. A handful of last fall's dead leaves crumbled in my grip.

Slowly, I sat up, scratched my scalp, and smoothed back my tangled blonde hair. I felt the rough earth underneath me. I wasn't in bed, I wasn't in the house I'd been living in for the last two months. I lay in a hollow scooped into the earth, covered in forest detritus, sheltered by overhanging pine trees. Beyond the den, crusted snow lay in shadowed areas. The air was cold and biting. My breath fogged.

I was naked, and I could taste blood in the film covering my teeth.

Damn. I'd done it again.

Lots of people dream of having their picture on the cover of a national magazine. It's one of the emblems of fame, fortune, or at the very least fifteen minutes of notoriety. A lot of people actually do get their pictures on the covers of national magazines. The question is: Are you on the cover of a glamorous high-end fashion glossy, wearing a designer gown and looking fabulous? Or are you on the cover of *Time,* bedraggled and shell-shocked, with a caption reading, "Is This the Face of a Monster?" and "Are YOU in Danger?"

Guess which one I got.

The house I was renting—more like a cabin, a two-room vacation cottage connected to civilization by a dirt road and satellite TV—was far enough out from the town and road that I didn't bother getting dressed for the trek back. Not that I could have; I had forgotten to stash any clothes. Why would I, when I hadn't intended to Change and go running in the first place? Nothing to be done but walk back naked.

I felt better, walking with my skin exposed, the chill air raising goose bumps all over my flesh. I felt cleaner, somehow. Freer. I didn't worry—I followed no path, no hiking trails cut through these woods. No one would see me in this remote section of San

Isabel National Forest land in southern Colorado, tucked into the mountains.

That was exactly how I wanted it.

I'd wanted to get away from it all. The drawback was, by getting away from it all I had less holding me to the world. I didn't have as many reasons to stay in my human body. If I'd been worried about someone seeing me naked, I probably wouldn't have shifted in the first place. Nights of the full moon weren't the only time lycanthropes could shape-shift; we could Change anytime we chose. I'd heard of werewolves who turned wolf, ran into the woods, and never came back. I didn't want that to happen to me. At least, I used to think I didn't want that to happen to me.

But it was getting awfully easy to turn Wolf and run in the woods, full moon or no.

I was supposed to be writing a book. With everything that had happened to me in the last couple of years—starting my radio show, declaring my werewolf identity on the air and having people actually believe me, testifying before a Senate committee hearing, getting far more attention than I ever wanted, no matter how much I should have seen it all coming—I had enough material for a book, or so I thought. A memoir or something. At least, a big publishing company thought I had enough material and offered me enough money that I could take time off from my show to write it. I was the celebrity du jour, and we all wanted to cash in on my fame while it lasted. Selling out had sounded so dreamy.

I put together about a dozen "Best of *The Midnight Hour*" episodes that could be broadcast without me, so the show would keep going even while I took a break. It'd keep people interested, keep my name out there, and maybe even draw in some new fans. I planned to do the *Walden* thing, retreat from society in order to better reflect. Escape the pressures of life, freeing myself to contemplate the deeper philosophical questions I would no doubt ponder while composing my great masterpiece.

Trouble was, you could get away from society and learn to be self-reliant, like Thoreau advocated. Turn your nose up at the rat race. But you couldn't escape yourself, your own doubts, your own conscience.

I didn't even know how to *begin* writing a book. I had pages of scribbled notes and not a single finished page. It all looked so unreal on paper. Really, where did I start? "I was born . . ." then go into twenty years of a completely unremarkable life? Or start with the attack that made me a werewolf? That whole night was so complicated and seemed an abrupt way to start what I ultimately wanted to be an upbeat story. Did I start with the Senate hearings? Then how did I explain the whole mess that got me there in the first place?

So I stripped naked, turned Wolf, and ran in the woods to avoid the question. As hard as I'd struggled to hold on to my humanity, that was easier.

The closest town of any size to my cabin was Walsenburg, some thirty miles away, and that wasn't saying a whole lot. The place had pretty much stopped growing in the sixties. Main street was the state highway running through, just before it merged onto the interstate. The buildings along it were old-fashioned brick blocks. A lot of them had the original signs: family-owned businesses, hardware stores, and bars and the like. A lot of them were boarded up. A memorial across from the county courthouse paid tribute to the coal miners who had settled the region. To the southwest, the Spanish Peaks loomed, twin mountains rising some seven thousand feet above the plain. Lots of wild, lonely forest spread out around them.

The next afternoon, I drove into town to meet my lawyer, Ben O'Farrell, at a diner on the highway. He wouldn't drive any farther into the southern Colorado wilds than Walsenburg.

I spotted his car already parked on the street and pulled in behind it. Ben had staked out a booth close to the door. He was already eating, a hamburger and plate of fries. Not much on ceremony was Ben.

"Hi." I slipped into the seat across from him.

He reached for something next to him, then dropped it on the Formica table in front of me: a stack of mail addressed to me, delivered to his care. I tried to route as much of my communication through him as I could. I liked having a filter. Part of the Walden thing. The stack included a few magazines, nondescript envelopes, credit card applications. I started sorting through it.

"I'm fine, thanks, how are you?" I said wryly.

Ben was in his early thirties, rough around the edges. He seemed perpetually a day behind on his shaving, and his light brown hair was rumpled. He wore a gray suit jacket, but his shirt collar was open, the tie nowhere to be seen.

I could tell he was gritting his teeth behind his smile.

"Just because I drove all the way out here for you, don't ask me to be pleasant about it."

"Wouldn't dream of it."

I ordered a soda and hamburger from the waitress, while Ben set his briefcase on the table and pulled out packets of paper. He needed my signature in approximately a million different places. On the plus side, the documents meant I was the beneficiary of several generous out-of-court settlements relating to the fiasco my trip to Washington, D.C., last fall had turned into. Who knew getting kidnapped and paraded on live TV could be so lucrative? I also got to sign depositions in a couple of criminal cases. That felt *good*.

"You're getting twenty percent," I said. "You ought to be glowing."

"I'm still trying to decide if representing the world's first werewolf celebrity is worth it. You get the strangest phone calls, you know that?"

"Why do you think I give people your number and not mine?"

He collected the packets from me, double-checked them, stacked them together, and put them back in his briefcase. "You're lucky I'm such a nice guy."

"My hero." I rested my chin on my hands and batted my eyelashes at him. His snort of laughter told me how seriously he took me. That only made me grin wider.

"One other thing," he said, still shuffling pages in his briefcase, avoiding looking at me. "Your editor called. Wants to know how the book is going."

Technically, I had a contract. Technically, I had a deadline. I shouldn't have had to worry about that sort of thing when I was trying to prove my self-reliance by living simply and getting back to nature.

"Going, going, gone," I muttered.

He folded his hands in front of him. "Is it half done? A quarter done?"

I turned my gaze to a spot on the far wall and kept my mouth shut.

"Tell me it's at least started."

I heaved a sigh. "I'm thinking about it, honest I am."

"You know, it's perfectly reasonable for someone in your position to hire a ghostwriter. Or at least find a co-author. People do it all the time."

"No. I majored in English. I ought to be able to string a few sentences together."

"Kitty—"

I closed my eyes and made a "talk to the hand" gesture. He wasn't telling me anything I didn't already know.

"I'll work on it. I want to work on it. I'll put something together to show them to make them happy."

He pressed his lips together in an expression that wasn't quite a smile. "Okay."

I straightened and pretended like we hadn't just been talking about the book I wasn't writing. "Have you done anything about the sleazebag?"

He looked up from his food and glared. "There's no basis for a lawsuit. No copyright infringement, no trademark infringement, nothing."

"Come on, she stole my show!"

The sleazebag. She called herself "Ariel, Priestess of the Night," and starting about three months ago she hosted a radio talk show about the supernatural. Just like me. Well, just like I used to.

"She stole the idea," Ben said calmly. "That's it. It happens all the time. You know when one network has a hit medical drama, and the next season every other network rolls out a medical drama because they think that's what everyone wants? You can't sue for that sort of thing. It was going to happen sooner or later."

"But she's *awful*. Her show, it's a load of sensationalist *garbage!*"

"So do it better," he said. "Go back on the air. Beat her in the ratings. It's the only thing you can do."

"I can't. I need some time off." I slumped against the back of the booth.

He idly stirred the ketchup on his plate with a french fry. "From this end it looks like you're quitting."

I looked away. I'd been comparing myself to Thoreau because he made running away to the woods sound so noble. It was still running away.

He continued. "The longer you stay away, the more it looks like the people in D.C. who tried to bring you down won."

"You're right," I said, my voice soft. "I know you're right. I just can't think of anything to say."

"Then what makes you think you can write a book?"

This was too much of Ben being right for one day. I didn't answer, and he didn't push the subject.

He let me pay the bill. Together, we headed out to the street.

"Are you going straight back to Denver?" I asked.

"No. I'm going to Farmington to meet Cormac. He wants help with a job."

A job. With Cormac, that meant something nasty. He hunted werewolves—only ones who caused trouble, he'd assured me—and bagged a few vampires on the side. Just because he could.

Farmington, New Mexico, was another two hundred fifty miles west and south of here. "You'll only come as far as Walsenburg for me, but you'll go to Farmington for Cormac?"

"Cormac's family," he said.

I still didn't have that whole story, and I often asked myself how I'd gotten wrapped up with these two. I met Ben when Cormac referred him to me. And what was I doing taking advice about lawyers from a werewolf hunter? I couldn't complain; they'd both gotten me out of trouble on more than one occasion. Ben didn't seem to have any moral qualms about having both a werewolf and a werewolf hunter as clients. But then, were lawyers capable of having moral qualms?

"Be careful," I said.

"No worries," he said with a smile. "I just drive the car and bail him out of jail. He's the one who likes to live dangerously."

He opened the door of his dark blue sedan, threw his briefcase onto the front passenger seat, and climbed in. Waving, he pulled away from the curb and steered back onto the highway.

On the way back to my cabin, I stopped in the even smaller town of Clay, Population 320, Elevation 7400 feet. It boasted a gas station with an attached convenience store, a bed and breakfast, a backwoods outfitter, a hundred-year-old stone church—and that was it. The convenience store, the "Clay Country Store," sold the best home-baked chocolate chip cookies on this side of the Continental Divide. I couldn't resist their lure.

A string of bells hanging on the handle of the door rang as I entered. The man at the cash register looked up, frowned, and reached under the counter. He pulled out a rifle. Didn't say a word, just pointed it at me.

Yeah, the folks around here knew me. Thanks to the Internet and twenty-four-hour news networks, I couldn't be anonymous, even in the middle of nowhere.

I raised my hands and continued into the store. "Hi, Joe. I just need some milk and cookies, and I'll be on my way."

"Kitty? Is that you?" A woman's face popped up from behind a row of shelves filled with cans of motor oil and ice scrapers. She was about Joe's age, mid-fifties, her hair graying and pulled into a ponytail that danced. Where Joe's eyes frowned, hers lit up.

"Hi, Alice," I said, smiling.

"Joe, put that down, how many times do I have to tell you?"

"Can't take any chances," he said.

I ignored him. Some fights you couldn't win. The first time he'd done this, when I came into the store and he recognized me as "that werewolf on TV," I'd been so proud of myself for not freaking out. I'd just stood there with my hands up and asked, "You have silver bullets in there?" He'd looked at me, looked at the rifle, and frowned angrily. The next time I came in, he announced, "Got silver this time."

I went around the shelves to where Alice was, where Joe and his rifle couldn't see me as easily.

"I'm sorry," Alice said. She was stocking cans of soup. "One of these days I'm going to hide that thing. If you'd call ahead, I could make up some chore for him and get him out of here."

"Don't worry about it. As long as I don't do anything threatening, I'm fine, right?" Not that people generally looked at me—a perky blonde twenty-something—and thought "bloodthirsty werewolf."

She rolled her eyes. "Like you could do anything threatening. I swear, that man lives in his own little world."

Yeah, the kind of world where shop owners kept rifles under their counters, while their wives lined healing crystals along the top of the cash register. She also had a cross nailed over the shop door, and more crystals hanging from the windows.

They each had their own brand of protection, I supposed.

I hadn't decided yet if the werewolf thing really didn't bother some people, or if they still refused to believe it. I kind of suspected that was how it was with Alice. Like my mom—she treated it like it was some kind of club I'd joined. After full moon nights she'd say something like, *Did you have fun at your little outing, dear?*

A lifetime of believing that these things didn't exist was hard to overcome.

"How do you two stay married?"

She looked at me sideways, donned a wry smile, and didn't answer. Her eyes gleamed, though. Right, I wasn't going to press that question any further.

Alice rang up my groceries, while Joe looked on, glaring over his rifle. I had to think of myself as a goodwill ambassador—don't make any sudden moves, don't say anything snide. Try to show him that just because I was a monster didn't mean I was, well, a monster.

I paid, and Alice handed me the brown paper bag. "Thanks," I said.

"Anytime. Now you call if you need anything."

My nonchalance only went so far. I couldn't turn my back on Joe and his rifle, so I backed toward the door, reaching behind to pull it open, and slipped out, to the ringing of bells.

The door was closing behind me when I heard Alice say, "Joe, for God's sake put that thing away!"

Ah yes, life in a small mountain community. There's nothing like it.

chapter 2

The front half of my cabin held a living room and kitchen, while a bedroom and bathroom made up the back half. Only part of a wall separated the two halves, giving the whole place access to the cabin's only source of heat: a wood-burning stove in the living room. The hot-water heater ran on propane, electricity powered everything else. I kept the stove's fire burning to hold back the winter. At this altitude I wasn't snowbound, but it was still pretty darned cold, especially at night.

The living room also had my desk, or rather a small table, which held my laptop and a few books: a dictionary, a dog-eared copy of *Walden*. Shoved underneath were a couple of boxes holding more books and a bunch of CDs. I'd spent my whole adult life working in radio—I had to have something to ruin the quiet. The desk sat in front of the large window that looked out over the porch and the clearing where I parked my car. Beyond that, trees and brown earth climbed up the hill, to blue sky.

I'd spent a lot of hours sitting at that desk, staring out the window at that view. I should have at least made the effort to find some place with a nice mountain vista to occupy my long stretches of procrastination.

When twilight came, deepening the sky to a rich shade of royal blue, then fading to darkness, I knew I'd wasted another day and not written a single decent word.

But it was Saturday, and I had other entertainments. Very late, close to midnight, I turned on the radio. It was time for *Ariel, Priestess of the Night*. I snuggled up on the sofa with a fluffy pillow and a beer.

The front page of *Ariel, Priestess of the Night*'s Web site was all black with candy-apple-red lettering and a big picture of Ariel. She seemed fairly young, maybe my age—mid-twenties. She had pale

Ah, her. Standard dark lady of the night fare. She was exquisite, more intelligent and worldly than any woman he'd ever met. More brilliant, more attractive, more everything. She'd swept him off his feet, yadda yadda, and here he was, some six hundred years later, and all this time they'd played a game of seduction and mayhem that read like something out of a bodice-ripper.

It was quite the tale of danger and suspense. Out here, alone in a cabin in the woods, with a fire burning in the stove and wind shushing through the pine trees outside, I should have been shaking in my booties.

I'd sure love to give Ariel a *real* scare.

That gave me an idea. A really bad idea.

I retrieved my cell phone from my desk. I dialed the number that Ariel's aggravating voice had seared into my memory.

"You've reached Ariel, Priestess of the Night," said a man. A regular, nonmysterious-sounding man.

"Hi," I said. Oh my God, not a busy signal. I was talking to someone. Was I actually going to get on the show?

"Can you give me first your name and where you're calling from?"

Shit, I hadn't really thought this through. "Um, yeah, I'm . . . Sue. And I'm from . . . Albuquerque."

"And what do you want to talk about?"

What *did* I want to talk about? My brain froze. Was this what happened when people called my show? My big mouth took over. "I'd like to talk to Ariel about fear," I said.

"Are you afraid of vampires?" the screener asked.

"Sure."

"All right, if you could please turn off your radio and hold on for a minute."

Crap. Double crap. I turned off the radio.

Instead of hold music, the phone piped in Ariel's show, so I wouldn't miss anything.

Gustaf was talking about the inherent selfless nobility that vampirism conferred upon its victims. "One begins to feel a certain stewardship for humankind. We vampires are the more powerful beings, of course. But we depend on you humans for our survival. Just as humanity has learned it cannot wipe out the rain forests or destroy the oceans without consequence, we cannot rule over humankind with impunity. As we would certainly be capable of doing were we less conscientious."

So people were nothing more than a bunch of endangered monkeys? Was that it? No, vampires would never be able to take over the world because their heads were generally stuck too far up their own asses.

Finally, Ariel made the announcement I'd been waiting for: "All right, listeners, I'm going to open the line for calls now. Do you have a question or a comment for Gustaf? Now's your chance."

I desperately wanted Ariel to put me on the air so I could call bullshit on the guy. She took another call instead. A desperately awestruck woman spoke.

"Oh, Ariel, thank you, and Gustaf, thank you so much for speaking with us all. You don't know how much it means to hear such an old and wise being as yourself."

"There, there, my dear, it's my pleasure," Gustaf said graciously.

"I don't understand why you—I mean you as in all vampires—aren't more visible. You've seen so much, you have so much experience. We could learn so much from you. And I do think the world would be a better place if vampires were in a position to guide us—"

Ariel butted in. "Are you saying, then, that you think vampires would make good world leaders?"

"Of course—they've seen nations rise and fall. They know better than anybody what works and what doesn't. They're the ultimate monarchs."

Great. A freakin' royalist. Ooh, what I would say to this woman if this were my show . . .

Ariel was maddeningly diplomatic. "You're a woman with traditional values. I can see why the ageless vampires would appeal to you."

"Since the world would clearly be a better place if vampires were in charge—why aren't they? Why don't they take over?"

Gustaf chuckled, clearly amused in a detached, condescending manner. "Oh, we certainly could, if we wanted to. But I think you underestimate how shy most vampires are. We really don't like the harsh light of publicity."

Could have fooled me.

Ariel said, "I'd like to move on to the next call now. Hi, Sue, you're on the air," Ariel said.

Sue—that was me. Wow, I made it. Back on the air—in a manner of speaking. Ha. Here I go—

"Hi, Ariel. Thanks so much for taking my call." I knew the script. I knew how to sound like a fan. I'd heard it enough from the other side. "Gustaf, I don't think all vampires are quite as sensitive and charitable as you imply. Are they stewards watching over the rain forests, or shepherds fattening the sheep for market?"

Gustaf huffed a little. "Every vampire was once a human being. The best of us never forget our roots."

Even if they had to suck those roots dry . . . "But you give the worst human beings the power and immortality of a vampire, and what do you get? The Third Reich—forever. See, you know why I think vampires haven't taken over the world?"

God, I sounded snotty. I always hated it when people like this called into my show. Crabby know-it-alls.

"Why?" Ariel said.

"Theatrics."

"Theatrics?" Ariel repeated, sounding amused, which irritated me.

"Yeah, theatrics. The posing, the preening, the drawn-out stories of romance and seduction when the reality is Gustaf here was probably just some starry-eyed kid who got screwed over. You take all those petty, backstabbing, power trippy games that happen when you get any group together, multiply it by a few centuries, and you end up with people who are too busy stroking their own egos and polishing their own reputations to ever find the motivation to take over the world."

Aloof, Gustaf spoke. "Have you ever met a vampire?"

"I know a couple," I said. "And they're individuals, just like anyone else. Which is probably *really* why they haven't taken over the world. They couldn't agree on anything. Aren't I right, Gustaf?"

Ariel said, "Sue, you're sounding just a bit angry about all this. Why is that?"

I hadn't expected the question. In fact, I'd kind of expected her to move on to the next call by now. But no, she was *probing*. Which left me to decide: Was I going to answer her question? Or blow it off? What would make her sound like an idiot, without making me sound like an idiot?

I suddenly realized: I hated being on this end of a radio show. But I couldn't stop now.

"Angry? I'm not angry. This isn't angry. This is *sarcastic*."

"Seriously," Ariel said, not letting it go. "Our last caller practically worships vampires. Why are you so angry?"

Because I was stuck in the woods through nobody's fault but my own. Because somewhere along the way I'd lost control of my life.

"I'm tired of the stereotype," I said. "I'm tired of so many people buying into the stereotype."

"But you're not afraid of them. That anger doesn't come from fear."

"No, it doesn't," I said, hating the uncertainty in my own voice. I knew very well how dangerous vampires could be, especially when you came face-to-face with one in a dark room. I'd seen it firsthand. They *smelled* dangerous. And here she was promoting one like he was a damned philanthropist.

"Then what are you afraid of?"

Losing. I was afraid of losing. She had the show and I didn't. I was supposed to ask the difficult questions. What I said was, "I'm not afraid of anything."

Then I hung up.

I'd turned the radio off, so the cabin was silent. Part of me wanted to turn it back on and hear what Ariel said about my—or rather Sue's—abrupt departure, as well as what else Gustaf had to say about the inherent nobility of vampires. In a rare show of wisdom, I kept the radio off. Ariel and Gustaf could keep each other.

I started to throw the phone, and amazingly refrained. I was too tired to throw it.

Afraid. Who was she to accuse me of being afraid? The one with the radio show, that was who.

I couldn't sleep. Part of me was squirming with glee at the mighty blow I had struck against my competition. Er, mighty blow, or petty practical joke? I'd been like a kid throwing rocks at the old haunted house. I hadn't even broken Ariel's stride. I'd do better next time.

The truth was, I was reduced to crank calls, followed by bouts of insomnia.

Run. Let me go running.

Restlessness translated to need. Wolf was awake and wouldn't settle down. *Let's go, let's go—*

No.

This was what happened: I couldn't sleep, and the night forest beckoned. Running on four legs for a couple of hours would certainly wear me out to the point where I'd sleep like a rock. And wake up naked in the woods, kicking myself for letting it happen. I called the shots, not that other side of me.

I slept in sweatpants and a tank top. The air was dry with the heat and smell of ashes from the stove. I wasn't cold, but I huddled inside my blankets, pulling them firmly over my shoulders. I pulled a pillow over my head. I had to get to sleep.

I might even have managed it for a minute or two. I might have dreamed, but I couldn't remember about what. I did remember moving through cotton, trying to claw my way out of a maze of fibers, because something was wrong, a smell in the air, a noise that shouldn't have been there. When I should have only heard wind in the trees and an occasional snap of dry wood in the stove, I heard something else . . . rustling leaves, footsteps.

I dreamed of a wolf's footsteps as she trots through dead leaves on the forest floor. She is hunting, and she is very good. She is almost on top of the rabbit before it bolts. It only runs a stride before she pounces on it, bites it, and it screams in death—

The rabbit's scream was a horrible, high-pitched, gut-wrenching, teakettle whistlelike screech that should never come out of such an adorable fuzzy creature.

I jerked upright, my heart thudding fast, every nerve searing.

The noise had lasted only a second, then silence. It had come from right outside my door. I gasped for breath and listened: wind in the trees, a hiss of embers from the stove.

I pushed back the covers and stood from the bed.

Moving softly, barefoot on the wood floor, I went to the front room. My heartbeat wouldn't slow. *We may have to run, we may have to fight.* I curled my fingers, feeling the ghosts of claws. If I had to, I could shift to Wolf. I could fight.

I watched the window for movement outside, for shadows. I only saw the trees across the clearing, dark shapes edged with silver moonlight. I took a slow breath, hoping to smell danger, but the scent from the stove overpowered everything.

I touched the handle of the front door. I ought to wait until morning. I should wait until sunlight and safety. But something had screamed on my front porch. Maybe I'd dreamed it.

I opened the door.

There it was, lying stretched out in front of me. The scent of blood and bile hit me. The thing smelled like it had been gutted. The rabbit was stretched out, head thrown back, the fur of its throat and belly dark, matted, and ripped. The way it smelled, it ought to have been sitting in a pool of blood. It didn't even smell like rabbit—just guts and death.

My nose itched, nostrils quivering. I—the Wolf—could smell blood, the thick stuff from an animal that had died of deep wounds.

I *knew* what that smelled like because I'd inflicted that kind of damage on rabbits. The blood was here, just not with the rabbit.

I opened the door a little wider and looked over.

Someone had painted a cross in blood on the outside of my front door.

I didn't go back to bed. Instead, I put a couple of new logs in the stove, poked at the fire until it blazed hot, wrapped myself in a blanket, and curled up on the sofa. I didn't know what bothered me more: that someone had painted a cross in blood on my door, or that I had no clue who had done it. I hadn't seen anything, heard anything after the rabbit's death cry, or smelled so much as a whiff of a breath mint. What was more, I didn't remember if I had only dreamed the rabbit's scream, or if I had really heard it. If it had been real, and crossed into my dream, or if my subconscious had made it up. Either way, it was like someone killed the rabbit, smeared blood on the door, and then vanished.

At first light, I called the police.

Two hours later, I sat cross-legged on the porch—on the far side, as far away from the rabbit as I could get—and watched the county sheriff and one of his deputies examine the door, the porch, the dead rabbit, and the clearing. Sheriff Avery Marks was a tired-looking middle-aged man, with thinning brown hair and a fresh uniform with a big parka over it. His examination consisted of standing on the porch, looking at the door for about five minutes, then crouching by the rabbit and looking at it for about five minutes, then standing on the ground, hands on hips, looking at the whole ensemble for about ten minutes. His deputy, a bearded guy in his thirties, wandered all around the cabin and the clearing in front of it, staring at the ground, snapping pictures, and writing in a notepad.

"You didn't hear anything?" Marks asked for the third time.

"I thought I heard the rabbit scream," I said. "But I was still asleep. Or half asleep. I don't really remember."

"You're saying you don't remember if you heard anything?" He sounded frustrated at my answers, and I couldn't blame him.

"I thought I heard something."

"About what time was that?"

"I don't know. I didn't look at the clock."

He nodded sagely. I had no idea what that information could have told him.

"I'm thinking this looks like some kind of practical joke," he said.

A joke? It wasn't funny. Not at all. "Would anyone around here think something like this was funny?"

"Ms. Norville, I hate to say it, but you're well known enough that you may be a target for this sort of thing."

You think? "So what are you going to do about it?"

"Keep an eye out. You see anything suspicious, you see anyone walking around here, let me know."

"Are you going to do *anything?*"

He eyed me and gave the condescending frown that experts reserved for the unenlightened. "I'll ask around, do some checking. This is a small community. Something'll turn up." He turned to the earnest deputy. "Hey, Ted, make sure you get pictures of those tire tracks." He was pointing at the ones leading away from my car.

This man had not inspired my faith.

"How—how am I supposed to clean all this up?" I asked. I was grateful for winter. The smell hadn't become too overpowering, and there were no flies.

He shrugged. "Hose it down? Bury the thing?"

This was like talking to a brick wall.

My cell phone rang inside the house; I could hear it from the porch. "I'm sorry, I should pick that up."

"You do that. I'll let you know when I find something." Marks and his deputy moved toward their car, leaving me alone with the slaughter. I felt oddly relieved by their imminent departure.

I dodged the rabbit, made it through the door without touching blood, and grabbed the phone. Caller ID said Mom. Her weekly call. She could have picked a better time. Strangely, though, I realized I needed to hear her voice.

"Hi," I said, answering the phone. I sounded plaintive. Mom would know something was wrong.

"Hi, Kitty. It's your mother. How are you?"

If I told her exactly what had happened, she'd be appalled. Then she'd demand that I come stay with her and Dad, where it was safe, even though I couldn't. I'd had to explain it a million times when I told her last month that I wasn't coming home for Christmas. I didn't have a choice: the Denver pack had exiled me. If I came back and they found out about it, they might not let me leave again. Not without a fight. A *big* fight. Mom still gave me endless grief.

"We're in Aurora," she'd said. "Aurora isn't Denver, surely they'd understand." Technically she was right, Aurora was a suburb, but as far as the pack was concerned, Denver was everything within a hundred-mile radius.

I'd have to try to keep this short. Without lying outright. Damn.

"Oh, I've been better."

"What's wrong?"

"The book's not going as well as I'd like. I'm beginning to think coming here to get away from it all may have been a mistake."

"If you need a place, you can always stay here for as long as you need to."

Here we go again . . . "No, I'm okay. Maybe I'm just having a bad day." Bad week? Month?

"How are other things going? Have you been skiing?"

I had absolutely nothing to talk about. Nothing that I could talk about without getting hysterical, at least. "No, I haven't really thought about skiing. Everything's fine, it's fine. How are you doing? How is everyone?"

Mom launched in on the gossip. Everyone included Mom, Dad, my older sister Cheryl, her husband and two kids—a regular suburban poster family. Topics included office politics, tennis scores, first steps, first words, who went out to dinner where, which cousins were getting into what kind of trouble, and which of the great-aunts and -uncles were in the hospital. I could never keep any of it straight. But it sounded normal, Mom sounded happy, and my anxiety faded. She kept me in touch, kept me grounded. I may have exiled myself to the woods, but I still had a family, and Mom would call every Sunday like clockwork.

She brought the call to a close, making me promise to be careful, promise to call if I needed anything. I promised, like I did every week, no matter what kind of trouble I was in or what had been gutted on my front porch.

I left the conversation feeling a little better able to deal with the situation.

Hose it down, Sheriff Marks said. I went to get a bucket of water and a scrub brush. And a garbage sack.

The next few nights, I didn't sleep at all. I kept listening for footsteps, for the sound of another animal getting butchered on my front porch. The anxiety was killing me.

Human civilization was becoming less attractive every day. During daylight hours, I didn't even try to pound out a few pages of the memoir. I didn't even turn on the computer. I sat on the sofa and stared out the window. I could go out there and never come back. It would be so easy.

In the middle of another wakeful night, I heard something. I sat up, heart racing, wondering what was happening and what I was going to do about it. But it wasn't footsteps on the porch. Nothing screamed. I heard gravel crunching, the sound of a vehicle rolling up the drive to my cabin. My throat closed—I wanted to growl. Someone was invading my territory.

I got up and looked out the window.

A Jeep zoomed into the clearing, way too fast, swerving a little when the brakes slammed on.

Arms stiff, claws—fingers—curling, I went to the front door, opened it just enough to let me stand in the threshold, and glared out. If the invader challenged, I could face it.

But I knew that Jeep, and I knew the man climbing out of the driver's seat. Thirty-something, with light brown hair and a mustache, he wore a leather jacket, black T-shirt, and jeans, and carried a revolver in a holster on his belt. Cormac, the werewolf hunter. I'd never seen him panicked like this. Even from here I could tell he was breathing too fast, and he smelled like too much sweat.

Leaning on the hood, he came around to the front of the Jeep and shouted, "Norville!" He took a few steps away from the vehicle, glaring at me—challenging me, the Wolf couldn't help but think. His voice was rough. "Norville, get over here. I need your help." He pointed at the Jeep, as if that explained everything.

I didn't speak. I was too astonished. Too wary. He looked like someone getting ready to rush me, to attack, screaming. I knew he could kill me if he wanted to. I didn't move.

"Norville—Kitty, Jesus, what's wrong with you?"

I shook my head. I was caught up in some Wolf-fueled spell. I couldn't get over how weird this was. Suspicious, I said, "What's wrong with you?"

Anguish twisted his features. "It's Ben. He's been bitten."

"Bitten?" The word hit my gut and sent a tremor up my spine.

"Werewolf," he said, spitting the word. "He's been infected."

chapter 4

I ran to the Jeep. Cormac steered me to the passenger door, which he opened.

Ben sat there, relaxed, head slumped to the side—unconscious. Blood streaked the right half of his shirt. The fabric was torn at the shoulder, and the skin underneath was mauled. Individual tooth marks showed where the wolf had clamped its jaw over Ben's shoulder, and next to it a second wound—a messier, jagged chunk taken out of the flesh near his bicep—where the creature had found its grip and ripped. Ben's forearm also showed bite marks. He must have thrown his arm up to try to protect himself. All the wounds had stopped bleeding, were clotted, and beginning to form thick, black scabs. Cormac hadn't bandaged them, yet they were already healing.

They wouldn't have been, if it hadn't really been a werewolf that did this. If Ben hadn't really been infected with lycanthropy.

I covered my mouth with my hand and just stared, unwilling to believe the scene before me.

"I didn't know what else to do," Cormac said. "You have to help him."

Feeling—tingling, surreal, blood-pounding feeling—started to displace the numbness. "Let's get him inside."

I touched his neck—his pulse raced, like he'd been running and not slumped in the front seat for a five-hour car ride. Next, I brushed his cheek. The skin was burning, feverish. I expected that, because that was what had happened to me. He smelled sharp, salty, like illness and fear.

His head moved, his eyes crinkled. He made a sound, a half-awake grunt, turned toward my hand, and took a deep breath. His body went stiff, straightening suddenly, and as he pressed his head straight back his eyes opened.

"No," he gasped and started fighting, shoving me away, thrashing in a panic. He was starting to develop a fine sense of smell. I smelled different and his instincts told him *danger.*

I grabbed one arm, Cormac grabbed the other, and we pulled him out of the Jeep. Getting under his shoulder, I tried to support him, but he dropped his weight, yanking back to escape. I braced, holding him upright and managing to keep a grip on him. Cormac held on to him firmly, grimly dragging him toward the cabin.

Ben's eyes were open, and he stared in a wide-eyed panic at shadows, at the memory still fueling his nerves.

Then he looked right at Cormac. "Kill me," he said through gritted teeth. "You're supposed to kill me."

Cormac had Ben's arm over his shoulder and practically hauled him off his feet as we climbed the steps to the porch.

"Cormac!" Ben hissed, his voice a rough growl. "Kill me."

He just kept saying that.

I shoved through the open front door. "To the bedroom, in back."

Ben was struggling less, either growing tired or losing consciousness again. We went to the bedroom and hauled him onto the bed.

Ben writhed, then let out a noise that started as a whimper and rose to a full-blown scream. His body arced and thrashed, wracked with some kind of seizure. I held down his shoulders, leaning on him with all my weight, while Cormac pinned his legs.

I shifted my hands to hold on to his face, keeping his head still and making him look at me. His face was burning up, covered with sweat.

"Ben! Sh, quiet, quiet," I murmured, trying to be calm, trying to be soothing, but my own heart was in my throat.

Finally, I caught his gaze. He opened his eyes and looked at me, didn't look away. He quieted. "You're going to be okay, Ben. You're going to be fine, just fine."

I said the words by rote, without belief; I didn't know why I expected them to calm him down.

"Kitty." He grimaced, wincing, looking like he was going to scream again.

"Please, Ben, please calm down."

He closed his eyes, turned his face away—and then he relaxed, like a wave passing through his body. He stopped struggling.

"What happened?" Cormac said.

Ben was breathing, soft, quick breaths, and his heart still raced. I smoothed away the damp hair sticking to his forehead, turned his face toward me again. He didn't react to my touch.

"He passed out," I said, sighing.

Slowly, Cormac let up his grip on Ben's legs and sat back on the edge of the bed. Ben didn't move, didn't flinch. He looked sick, wrung out, too pale against the gray comforter, his hair damp and his shirt bloody. I was used to seeing him focused, driven, self-possessed. Not like this at all. I was always the one calling him for help.

How the hell had this happened?

I didn't ask Cormac that, not yet. The bounty hunter looked shell-shocked, his face slack, staring at Ben's prone form. He pressed his hands flat on his thighs. My God, were they shaking?

I unbuttoned Ben's shirt and wrangled it off him, carefully peeling the fabric away where the blood had dried, pasting it to his skin. The adrenaline was fading, leaving my limbs weak as tissue paper. My voice cracked when I said, "What was he saying? About you killing him? Cormac?"

Cormac spoke softly, in a strange, emotionless monotone. "We made a deal. When we were kids. It was stupid, the only reason we did it is because it was the kind of thing that would never happen. If either of us got bitten, got infected, the other was supposed to kill him. The thing is—" Cormac laughed, a harsh chuckle. "I knew if it happened to me Ben would never be able to go through with it. I wasn't worried, because I knew I could shoot myself just fine. But Ben—it was for him. Because he wouldn't have the guts to shoot himself, either. If it happened to him, I was supposed to take care of it. I'm the tough one. I'm the shooter. But I couldn't do it. I had my rifle right up against his skull and I couldn't do it. By that time he was screaming his head off and I had to knock him out to get him to stay in the Jeep."

I could picture it, too, Cormac's finger on the trigger, tensing, tensing again, then him turning away, a snarl on his lips. He was grimacing now.

Even at a whisper, my voice was shaking. "I'm glad you didn't shoot him."

"He's not."

"He will be."

"I brought him to you because I thought, you're a werewolf and you get along all right, and if he could be like you—he'd be okay. Maybe he'd be okay."

"He'll be okay, Cormac."

With his shirt off, Ben looked even more pale, more vulnerable. Half his arm was chewed up and scabbed over. His chest moved too rapidly, with short, gasping breaths.

"We should clean this up," I said. "He'll be out of it for a while. Maybe a couple of days."

"How do you know?" Cormac said.

"Because that's how it was with me. I was sick for days. Cormac . . ." I stood and moved next to him, reaching out, tentative because he looked like he might break, explode, or tear the room apart. He was the same kind of tense as a cat about to spring on a mouse. He still had the handgun in his belt holster. I had to make him look away from Ben. I touched his shoulder. When he didn't jump, flinch, or punch me, I lay my hand on his shoulder and squeezed.

He put his hand over mine, squeezed back, then stood and left the room, disappearing into the front of the house. I didn't hear the front door open, so he didn't leave. I didn't have time to worry about him right now.

Armed with a soaked washcloth and dry towel, I cleaned up the blood. The wounds, the bite marks and tears in his skin, had all closed over. They looked like week-old scabs, dried and ringed with pink. His skin was slick with sweat; I dried him off as well as I could. Within half an hour, Ben's breathing slowed, and he seemed to slip into a normal sleep. If he'd been in shock, the shock had faded. Nothing looked infected. The lycanthropy wouldn't let him sicken. It wouldn't let him die, at least not from a few bites.

I took off his shoes and covered him with a spare blanket. Smoothed his hair back one more time. For now, he was settled.

I found Cormac in the kitchen, leaning on the counter and staring out the window over the sink. The sun had risen since we'd brought Ben inside. The outline of the trees showed clear against a pale sky. I didn't think Cormac was really looking at any of that.

I started setting up the coffeemaker, being louder than I needed to be.

The strangeness was too much. Cormac gave me this image of him and Ben as kids, talking about werewolves—that wasn't exactly a kid thing to do. At least, not for real. Not meaning it. I'd always suspected Cormac was edging psychotic, but Ben was the levelheaded one, the lawyer. I'd always wondered how he took this world—lycanthropes, vampires, this B-grade horror film life I lived—in such stride, not even blinking. I'd been grateful for it, but I wondered. How long had *he* been living in it? Him and Cormac both?

I didn't know a damn thing about either of them.

I pushed the button, the light lit up, and the coffeemaker started burbling happily. I leaned back on the counter, watching Cormac, who hadn't moved. A minute later, the smell of fresh coffee hit with a jolt.

"Are you hungry?" I said finally. "I have some cereal, I think. A couple of eggs, bacon."

"No."

"Have you gotten any sleep?"

He shook his head.

"You think maybe you should?"

Again, he shook his head. Too bad. My day would be a lot easier if he'd just collapse on the sofa and sleep for the next twelve hours.

The coffee finished brewing. I poured two mugs and set one on the counter next to him. I held mine in both hands, feeling the warmth from it, not drinking. My stomach hurt too much to drink anything.

I had to say something. "How did it happen? How did you let him get—how did he get in a position to be bitten by a werewolf?"

He turned away from the window, crossed his arms, stared across the kitchen. I got my first good look at him since he arrived. He looked gaunt, caved in and exhausted, with shadows under his eyes. He hadn't shaved in days and was developing a beard to go along with his mustache. Dried blood flaked off his hands and spotted his shirt. He smelled of dirt, sweat, and blood. He needed a shower, though somehow I doubted that I could talk him into it.

"There were two of them," he said. "I knew there were two of them. That's why I called Ben, so he could watch my back. But the whole thing was messed up, right from the start. They were killing flocks of sheep, but nobody ever heard anything. I saw a whole field covered with dead sheep, all of them torn to pieces, and the herders sitting in their trailer a hundred feet away didn't hear a thing. Their dogs didn't hear a thing."

"How do you know werewolves did it?"

"Because the family hired me to kill the first one. They told me."

I shook my head. "Whoa, what?"

"The parents, the kid's parents."

"The wolf was a *kid?*"

"No, he was twenty years old! This is all coming out wrong."

"Then calm down. Start over." I held my coffee mug to my face and breathed in the steam. I had to calm down as well, if I expected Cormac to be civil. He was right on the edge.

"They knew he'd gone wolf, knew he was killing sheep, and

they were afraid he'd start in on people. Nobody could control him so they called me."

"They just gave up on him? Their own son and they wanted him dead?"

"It's a different world there. Out in the desert, on the edge of Navajo Country. Shit like this happens and they look at it as evil. Pure evil, and the only thing to do with it is kill it. You've seen this kind of thing, you know they're right."

I had, and I did. I just hated to admit it. "What happened?"

"I knew his territory, knew how to find him, because he was going after livestock. But I got out there and found two sets of tracks. Werewolves are tough, but one of them couldn't have done that much damage on his own. His family didn't know there were two of them."

"Him, and the wolf who turned him?"

"Maybe. I don't know. They had no idea who the second one was. Or they wouldn't tell me. That was when I called Ben. The whole job was a mess, I should have just walked away. Too many details didn't fit—like the noise. These two had slaughtered three flocks by the time I got out there. Somebody should have heard something."

"How did you find them?"

"I left Ben by the Jeep, with a gun. He was on the hood, keeping a look out while I went to set bait."

I almost interrupted again. Bait? Is that how he hunted werewolves, with *bait*? But I didn't want to stop him—he might not start the story again.

"I found them right away. One of them. I shouldn't have, it was too easy. And it still wasn't right—the wolf had red eyes. I've seen plenty of wolves, wild ones and lycanthropes, and none of them have red eyes. But this thing—if it wasn't a werewolf I don't know what it was. I sure as hell didn't like it. I aimed my rifle at it—and then I couldn't move. I tried to shout to Ben, and I couldn't move. I couldn't even breathe. I've stared down werewolves before. I've never frozen up like that.

"I'd be dead, I'm sure that thing would have ripped out my throat if Ben hadn't fired just then. Then it was like somebody flipped a switch and I could move. And there was Ben, on the hood of the Jeep, with a wolf on top of him. I don't know if he shot at the thing and missed, or if it was just too fast for him. But it got him. He didn't even scream."

Sunlight covered the clearing outside my house, but Cormac, turned away from the window, was still gray with shadows.

"What did you do?" I whispered. I almost didn't dare breathe.

"I shot the wolf. It was a lucky shot, one in a million. I could have hit Ben instead."

"Then what happened?"

"The other wolf—the one in front of me—screamed. Not howled, not barked. Screamed like a human. Like a woman. I turned back and was going to kill it next, but it was already running. I shot at the thing but it got away."

"And the wolf you did hit?"

"It was the kid, the one I'd been hired to get. The shot knocked him right off the Jeep. When I got to him he was dying. I put a bullet in his head. He turned back to human. Just like he was supposed to."

He was right to do it. A cold, rational part of myself knew that a werewolf who couldn't control himself, who killed indiscriminately, was too dangerous, impossible to control within the legal system. What are you going to do, call the cops and stick him in jail? Strangely enough, that rational part of myself included a little bit of the Wolf, who knew exactly what to do when one of our kind got out of line. Only one thing *to* do. To my human side, to my gut emotional level, it still looked like murder. I couldn't reconcile the two views.

"And Ben?"

"I brought him here. That's the whole story." He drew in a slow breath and let it out with a sigh. "He's not cut out for this shit. He never was."

"Then why did you drag him into it?" My voice was stiff with anger.

For the first time, Cormac looked at me. "He's the only one in the world I trust." He walked to the doorway to the bedroom, leaned on the frame, and stared in.

It wasn't true, that Ben was the only one he trusted. If that were true he wouldn't have brought Ben here. But I didn't say that.

Cormac straightened from the door. "You mind if I crash out on the sofa?"

"Be my guest," I said, trying to smile like a gracious hostess.

"I'll get my bedroll out of the Jeep." He went to the front door and opened it.

Then he stopped. He stared for a long time, holding the knob, not moving.

"What?" I set down my coffee and went to look out the door.

There on the porch lay another dead rabbit, gutted like the first. I wasn't surprised when I looked at the outside of the door and found a cross made of smeared blood, fresh blood covering the stained outlines of the old cross. It hadn't been there when Cormac got here with Ben. They hadn't been here that long, maybe an hour. So this had happened within the hour, and this time I hadn't heard a thing. Of course, I'd been a little preoccupied.

I groaned. "Not again."

Cormac glanced at me. "Again? How many times have you been animal sacrifice central?"

I went outside, smelling the air, staring at the ground, looking for footprints, for anything that showed someone had been here, how this had happened. But the blood and guts might have appeared out of thin air, for all the evidence I saw. I stood on the porch, circling, studying the clearing, the house, everything, which even in the morning light had taken on a sinister cast. The place didn't feel cozy anymore.

"I wanted *Walden* and got *Evil Dead*," I grumbled. I faced Cormac. "This is the second one. You have any idea what it means?"

The scene seemed to pull him out of his recent trauma. He sounded genuinely fascinated when he said, "I don't know. If I had to guess I'd say you've been cursed."

In more ways than I cared to count. I went back inside. "I'm going to call the sheriff."

He moved out to the porch, stepping carefully around the rabbit corpse, and said, "Let me hide my guns someplace first."

Cursed. Right. Cursed didn't begin to describe my life at the moment.

I had to explain Cormac to Sheriff Marks. "He's a friend. Just visiting," I said. Marks gave me that look, the judgmental *none of my business what folks do in the privacy of their own homes* look that left no doubt as to what he *thought* was going on in the privacy of my own home. For his part, Cormac stood on the porch, leaning against the wall of the house, watching the proceedings with an air of detached curiosity. He'd hidden his arsenal—three rifles, four handguns of various shapes and sizes, and a suitcase-sized lock box that held who knew what—under the bed. *My* bed.

Marks and Deputy Ted repeated their search and found just as little as they had the first time.

"Here's what I'll do. I'll post a deputy out here for a couple nights," Marks said, after he'd wrapped up. "I'll also put a call in to somebody I know in the Colorado Springs PD. He's a specialist in satanism and cult behavior. Maybe he'll know if any groups operate in this area."

"If it were satanists, wouldn't the cross be upside down or something?"

His expression of frowning disapproval turned even more disapproving.

"Sheriff, don't you think I'm being targeted because of who I am?" *What* I am, I should have said.

"That's a possibility. We'll have to take all the facts into account."

Suddenly I felt like the bad guy. It was that part of being a victim that made a person ask, what did I do to bring this on myself?

"We'll start our stakeout tonight. Have a better morning, ma'am." Marks and Ted headed back to their car and drove away, leaving me with another mess on my porch.

Cormac nodded toward the departing car. "Small-town cop like him don't know anything about this."

"Do you?"

"It's blood magic."

"Well, yeah. What kind? Who's doing it?"

"Who've you pissed off lately?" He had the gall to smile at me. I leaned on the porch railing and sighed. "I have no idea."

"We'll figure it out. You got a shovel and garden hose? I'll take care of this."

That was something, anyway. "Thanks."

When I looked in on Ben again, he'd rolled to his side and curled up, pulling the blankets tightly over his shoulder. Color was coming back into his skin, and the scabs on his wounds were healing. I touched his forehead; he still had a fever. He was still shivering.

The room smelled strange. It was filled with the scents of sweat and illness, with Ben's own particular smell that included hints of the clothes he wore, his aftershave and toothpaste. And something else. His smell was changing, something wild and musky creeping into the mundane smells of civilization. I'd always thought of it as fur under the skin—the scent of another lycanthrope. Right here in the room with me. My lycanthropic self, my own Wolf, perked up, shifted within my senses, curious. She wanted the measure of him: *friend, rival, enemy, alpha, same pack, different pack, who?*

Friend. I hoped he was still a friend when he woke up.

I made him drink some water. With Cormac's help I lifted his shoulders, held his head up, and tipped a glass to his mouth. As much spilled out as went in, but his throat moved, and he drank a little. He didn't wake up, but he stirred, squeezing his eyes shut and groaning a little. I shushed him, hoping he stayed asleep. He needed to rest while his body sorted itself out.

Then I made Cormac eat something. He wouldn't tell me when he'd last eaten, when he'd last slept. It might have been days. I made bacon and eggs. I hadn't yet met a meat eater who could resist bacon and eggs. Whatever else he was, Cormac was a meat eater.

After breakfast, he spread his sleeping bag on the sofa and lay down. Broad daylight outside, and he rolled over on his side and fell asleep instantly, his breathing turning deep and regular. I envied that ability to sleep anywhere, anytime.

I sat at my desk, because I didn't have anywhere else to sit, but I didn't turn on the computer. I rubbed my face, hugged my head, and leaned on the table.

I didn't think I could take it anymore. I'd reached my limit. If ever there was a time when turning wolf and running away sounded like a good idea, this was it.

"Norville?"

Startled, I straightened, looked. Cormac wasn't asleep after all. He'd propped himself on one elbow.

"Thank you," he said.

I stared back, meeting his gaze. I saw exhaustion there. Hopelessness. I'd told him Ben would be okay, but I wondered if he'd believed it.

"You're welcome." What else could I say?

He rolled over, putting his back to me, and went to sleep.

I turned on the computer and wrote. Typing whatever came into my head, I wrote about the random shocks of life, the events that brought friends to your doorstep begging for help, even when you felt that your own life had tumbled irrevocably out of control. You did what you had to do, somehow. You kept racing ahead and hoped for the best. I wrote about being at the end of my rope and made a list of the reasons I had to stay human. Chocolate, as always, was near the top of the list. I was in the kitchen eating chocolate chip cookies when Cormac woke up, after dark.

I was looking out the kitchen window, to where Deputy Ted's patrol car was parked at the end of the road, hidden in the trees. I spotted him when he turned on his dome light to eat a sandwich.

Cormac sat up, rubbed his face, then stretched, twisting his back, pulling his arms up. Something cracked. "What're you looking at?"

"Take a look," I said. "You'll like this."

He came to the kitchen area, and I moved aside to give him room to look out the window. The deputy still had his light on, making his car a glowing beacon among the trees.

Cormac made a derisive grunt. "They're not going to catch anyone if that's how they run a stakeout."

With the cop sitting there, nobody would come within a mile of my place to lay any sort of curse. Nobody smart, anyway. "At least I won't have rabbit guts all over my porch in the morning."

"You're a werewolf, I thought you'd like that sort of thing. Fresh meat, delivered right to your door. Maybe it's a secret admirer."

"I like picking out my own dead meat, thanks."

"I'll remember that."

He crossed his arms, leaned on the counter, and looked at me. I blinked back, trying to think of a clever response. Finally, I offered him the bag I was holding. "Cookie?"

He shook his head at it. "How's Ben?"

"Asleep. How are you?"

"Feeling stupid. I keep thinking of everything I should have done different."

"That's not like you. You're a head down, guns blazing, full steam ahead kind of guy. Not one to dwell in the past."

"You don't know anything about me."

I shrugged, conceding the point. "So what's the story? You know all about my dark past. I don't know anything about yours."

"You're fishing," he said and smirked.

"Can't blame a girl for trying."

"Save it for your show."

Ouch. If only I were doing the show. It occurred to me to consider how big a favor I would have to do for Cormac before I could talk him into coming on the show for an interview, if taking in him and Ben in their hour of need didn't do it.

Cormac pulled himself from the counter. "You have a bathroom in this place?"

"In the bedroom."

He stalked off to find it. A minute later, the shower started up. At least he'd be clean.

I found my cell phone, dialed the number I wanted, and went outside. The air was cool, energizing. The inside of the house had become stifling. I sat on the porch and put my back against the wall.

A woman answered, "Hello?"

"Hi, Mom."

"Kitty! What a nice surprise. Is everything all right?"

"Why wouldn't it be?"

"Because you never call unless something's happened."

I sighed. She had a point. "I've had kind of a rough couple of days."

"Oh, I'm sorry. What's wrong?"

Between the extracurricular shape-shifting, animal sacrifices on my front porch, my lawyer getting attacked by a werewolf, and a werewolf hunter camping out in my living room, I didn't know where to start. I didn't think I should start.

"A lot of stuff. It's complicated."

"I worry about you being out there all by yourself. Are you sure you don't want to come home for a little while? You've had such a busy year, I think it would be good for you to not have to worry about things like rent."

Strangely enough, rent was one of the few things I wasn't worried about. As much as going back to my parents' and having Mom take care of me for a little while sounded like a good idea, it wasn't an option. Not that Mom would have understood that.

"I'm actually not by myself at the moment," I said, trying to sound positive. "I have a couple of friends staying over."

"That should be fun."

If I would just break down and tell Mom the truth, be straight with her, these conversations would be much less surreal. I'd called her because I needed to hear a friendly voice; I didn't want to tell her all the gory details.

"Yeah, sure. So how are you? How are Dad and Cheryl?"

She relayed the doings of the family since her last call—more of the same, but at least somebody's world was normal—and finished by turning the questions back on me, "How is the writing going?"

"It's fine," I said brightly. If I sounded like everything was okay, maybe it would be, eventually. "I think I've gotten over the writer's block."

"Will you be starting your show again soon? People ask me about it all the time."

I winced. "Maybe. I haven't really thought about it."

"We're so proud of you, Kitty. So many people only ever dream of doing what you've done. It's been so much fun watching your success."

She couldn't have twisted the knife any harder if she'd tried. I was such a success, and here I was flushing it down the toilet. But she really did sound proud, and happy. To think at one point I'd been worried that she'd be scandalized by what I was doing.

I took a deep breath and kept my voice steady. Wouldn't do any good to break down now. "Thanks, Mom. That means a lot."

"When are you finally coming to visit?"

"I'm not sure . . . you know, Mom, it's been great talking to you, but I really need to get going."

"Oh, but you only just called—"

"I know, I'm really sorry. But I told you I have friends staying, right?"

"Then you'd better get back to it. It's good to hear from you."

"Say hi to Dad for me."

"I will. We love you."

"Love you, too."

I sat on the porch for a long time, the phone sitting in my lap. I was looking for someone to lean on. Cormac and Ben showed up with all this, and I wasn't sure I could handle it. Wolves were supposed to run in packs. I was supposed to have help for something like this. But I didn't have anyone. I went back inside, back to my milk and cookies.

From the bedroom, the shower shut off. Ten minutes or so later, Cormac, hair damp and slicked back, came into the front room. He'd shaved, leaving only his familiar, trademark mustache. He was cinching on his belt and gun holster.

"I'm going to help Rosco out there with his stakeout. Do a little hunting around on my own." The contempt in his voice was plain. He was restless; I hadn't really expected him to stay in bed for twelve hours.

"Be careful."

He gave me a funny look, brows raised. "Really?"

Exasperated, I sighed. "I wouldn't want him to shoot you because he thinks you're the bad guy."

"Who says I'm not?"

Wincing, I rubbed my forehead. "I'm too tired to argue with you about it."

"Get some sleep," he said. "Take the sofa."

"Where'll you sleep?"

"The floor, if I decide I need it. You looked after Ben all day, I'll keep an eye on him tonight. Take the sofa."

This cabin was *not* built for three people who weren't actually all sleeping together.

"Fine." I'd lost a lot of sleep over the last couple of days and was tired. Before I trudged over to the sofa, I faced Cormac. "If Ben wakes up, tell me, okay? He'll be confused, I'll need to talk to him."

"I'll wake you up. Don't worry."

"I can't stop worrying. Sorry."

"Go to sleep, Norville." He raised his hand, started to reach out—for a moment, he seemed about to touch me. I braced for it, my heartbeat speeding up—what was he doing? But he turned around and left the cabin before anything happened.

Slowly, I sat on the sofa, then wrapped myself in the blanket. The cushions were ancient, far too squishy to be comfortable. But it wasn't the floor, so I lay down.

This was a mistake, I thought as I fell asleep. Cormac and I staying in the same house—absolutely a mistake.

I woke up to find Cormac putting a log into the stove. I didn't feel cold. I probably would have let the fire burn out. Outside the window, the sky was pale. It was morning again already. He closed the door to the stove, then sat back on the rug and watched the flames through the tiny grill in front.

I hadn't moved, and he hadn't noticed that I was awake, watching him. Shadows still darkened his eyes, and his hair had dried ruffled. He'd taken off his jacket and boots—and the gun belt. He wore a black T-shirt and jeans. His arms were pale, muscular.

Suddenly he looked over and caught my gaze staring back.

I stilled the fluttering in my stomach and tried not to react. Just stay cool.

"Is 'Rosco' still out there?" I said.

"Yeah. He fell asleep around two A.M. I expect he'll wake up soon and get out of here."

"And no dead animal on my porch?"

"None."

I turned my face into the pillow and giggled. "If it weren't happening to me, this would be downright hilarious."

"I did find this." He held out his hand.

I looked at it first, then gingerly opened my hand to accept it. It was a cross made of barbed wire, a single strand twisted back on itself, about the length of my finger. The steel was smooth, the barbs sharp. Not worn or rusted, which meant this hadn't been sitting outside for very long.

"You think this is from my sacrificial fan club?"

"Could be. If so, the question is Did they leave it on purpose, or did they just drop it? If it's on purpose, then it means something. It's supposed to do something."

"What?"

"I don't know."

I could almost feel malevolence seeping out of the thing. Or maybe the barbs just looked scary. "What am I supposed to do with it?"

"I recommend finding somebody with a forge and have them melt the thing into slag. Just in case."

He thought it was cursed, and he brought the thing into my house? I groaned with frustration. I wanted to throw it, but I set it on the floor instead.

"Why a cross?"

"There's a dozen magic systems that borrow from Christianity. This part of the country, it might be an evangelical sect, or maybe some kind of *curandero*."

"*Curandero*. Mexican folk healer, right?"

"They do all kinds of stuff. Sometimes, they go bad."

"You know a lot about this sort of thing."

"It helps, knowing as much as I can. The people who hire me—they're believers. They have to believe in werewolves and magic to call me in the first place. The symbols may be different, the rituals are different, but they all have one thing in common: they believe in the unbelievable. You know what I'm talking about. You're one of them. One of the believers."

"I only believe because of what I am. I don't know anything about any of it."

"Hell, I don't know anything. This is just scratching the surface. There's a whole world of freaky shit out there."

He was being uncharacteristically chatty. I didn't know if it was stress or sleeplessness. Maybe something about sitting in a tiny cabin in front of a wood-burning stove on a cold morning made people personable.

"How did you find out about the freaky shit? I found out the morning after I was attacked—the whole pack stood there telling me, 'Welcome to the family, have fun.' But who told you?"

He smiled, but the expression was thin and cold. "I don't remember anyone telling me werewolves are real. I've always known. My family—we've been hunting lycanthropes for over a hundred years. My dad taught me."

"How old were you when he died?"

He looked sharply at me. "Who told you he died?"

"Ben."

"Bastard," Cormac muttered.

"That was all he said," I said quickly. "I asked how you two met and if you'd always been so humorless, and he said you had a right to be humorless. I asked why and he told me."

He was staring at me, and I didn't like it. Among wolves, a stare was a challenge. The thought of a challenge from Cormac made the wolf inside me cringe in terror. I couldn't fight Cormac. I looked away, hugging the blanket tightly around me.

"You still talk too much, you know that?" Cormac said.

"I know."

Finally, he said, "I was sixteen. I moved in with Ben and his folks after my dad died. His mother was my dad's sister."

"Then Ben knew, too. He was part of the family history."

"Hard to say. I think Aunt Ellen was just as happy to leave it all behind. Jesus, what am I going to tell her?"

"Nothing," I said wryly. "At least not until the full moon falls on Christmas and Ben has to explain why he's not coming home for the holidays."

"Spoken with the voice of experience."

"Yup. If Ben wasn't in on the werewolf hunting from the start, how did you drag him into it?"

"I didn't drag him—"

"Okay, how did you get him started in it?"

"Why do you want to know all this stuff about me?"

"You're interesting."

Cormac didn't say anything to that, just went back to staring at me with a little too much focus.

I said, "Could you not look at me like that? It's making me nervous."

"But you're interesting."

Oh, my. That clenching feeling in my gut wasn't fear—not this time.

I'd kissed Cormac once. It had been another situation like this. We were sitting and talking, and I let the urge overcome my better judgment. And he kissed back, for about a second, before he marched out of the room, calling me a monster.

Too many incidents like that could give a girl a complex.

He wasn't running away this time.

I swung my legs over the edge of the couch and slipped to the floor. I ended up kneeling in front of him, where he was sitting, close enough to grab. And he still didn't run. In fact, he didn't move at all, like he was waiting for me to come to him. How did wolves do this? Weren't the boys supposed to chase the girls? He wasn't a wolf, though. He wouldn't understand the signals.

Wolf was uncurling, overcoming her anxiety. Yeah, he was scary. Yeah, he was tough. That meant he could protect us. That was enough for her. That, and he smelled like he wanted me. He radiated warmth, and had a tang of sweat that wasn't even visible. A tension held him still as stone. All I had to do was touch him and break him out of his immobility. I raised my hand.

"I—I can smell you." The voice was low and painfully hoarse.

I must have jumped a foot. My heart raced like a jackhammer and I got ready to run.

Ben stood in the doorway to the bedroom, leaning against the wall. Still shirtless, his skin was pale, damp with sweat, and his hair was tangled. He only half opened his eyes, and he winced with what looked like confusion, like he didn't know where he was.

"I can smell everything," he said, sounding like he had bronchitis. He touched his forehead; his hand was shaking.

"Ben." I rushed to him, intending to take his arm and steer him back to bed. He wasn't well, he shouldn't have been up.

As soon as I touched him, though, he flinched back. He crashed against the wall, his face stiff with terror. "No, you smell—you smell wrong—"

His new instincts identified me as another werewolf—a potential threat.

I turned to call Cormac, but he was already beside Ben, holding his arm, trying to keep him still.

"No, Ben. I'm safe. It's all right. Take a deep breath. Everything's okay." I tried to hold his face still, to make him smell me, to make him recognize that scent as friendly, but he lurched away. He would have fallen if Cormac hadn't been holding him.

I put myself next to him again, intending to help drag him to the bed. This time, Ben leaned closer to me, squinting as if trying to focus. His eyesight was changing, too.

"Kitty?"

"Yeah, it's me," I said, relieved that he'd recognized me.

He slumped against me, resting his head on my shoulder, like he wanted to hug me. He found my hand and squeezed it tightly. "I don't remember what happened. I don't remember any of it," he murmured into my shirt.

Except that he remembered that something had happened, and that he should have remembered. A lot of his agitation was probably stress—the anxiety that came from blocking out the trauma.

I held him still for a moment, whispering nonsense comforts at his ear until he stopped shaking. Cormac, looking stiff and awkward, was still propping him upright.

"Come on, Ben. Back to bed." He nodded, and I pulled his arm over my shoulder. Between us, Cormac and I walked him back to the bed. He sank onto it and fell back to sleep almost immediately. He kept hold of my hand. I waited until I was sure he was asleep, his breathing deep and regular, before I coaxed back his fingers and extricated myself from his grip.

Cormac stood at the end of the bed, ran his hands through his hair, and blew out a frustrated sigh. "Is this normal?"

I smoothed back the damp hair from Ben's face. "I don't know,

I only know what I went through. I slept through the whole thing. At least, I only remember sleeping through the whole thing. I was hurt a lot worse than he is, though." I'd had my hip mauled and half my leg flayed. Not that I had any scars to prove it.

"Don't lie to me. Is he going to be okay?"

He kept asking me that. "What do I look like, some kind of fortune-teller? I don't know."

"What do you mean you don't know?"

I glared at him, and part of the Wolf stared out of my eyes. I made the challenge and I didn't care if he could read it or not. "His body will be fine. Physically, he's healing. Mentally—that's up to him. We won't know until he wakes up if this is going to drive him crazy or not."

Cormac scrubbed a hand down his face and started pacing. Tension quivered along his whole body; sheer willpower was keeping him from breaking something.

"Ben's tough," he said finally. "This won't drive him crazy. He'll be okay. He'll be fine." He said the words like they were a mantra. Like if he said them enough they'd have to be true.

My glare melted into a look of pity. I wished I could find the right thing to say to calm him down. To convince him that yes, he'd done all he could. Cormac had never been weak. He'd never been this helpless, I'd bet. I wondered if I'd have to worry about him going crazy, too.

Crazier than he already was.

Cormac left the room, and a moment later I heard the front door open and slam shut. I didn't run after him—I didn't dare leave Ben alone. I listened for the Jeep starting up, but it didn't. Cormac wasn't abandoning me to this mess. Maybe he just needed to take a walk.

I brought the laptop into the bedroom, pulled a chair next to the bed, kept watch over Ben, and wrote.

I wouldn't have wished lycanthropy on anyone, much less a friend. Life was hard enough without having something like this to deal with. I'd seen the whole range of how people handled it. In some people, the strength and near-invulnerability went to their heads. They became bullies, reveling in the violence they were capable of. People who were already close to psychosis tumbled over the edge. One more mental handicap to deal with was too much. Some people became passive, letting it swallow them. And some people adapted. They made adjustments, and they stayed themselves.

I regretted that I didn't know enough about Ben to guess which way he'd go.

My cell phone rang, and I fielded the call from Sheriff Marks.

"The deputy I had on the stakeout didn't see any sign of your perpetrator," he informed me.

"You know he had the interior light on in his car half the time he was out here?" I replied.

Marks was silent for a long time, and picturing the look on his face made me grin. "I'll have a talk with him," he said finally. "I'll try to have someone out there tonight, too. You let me know if you see anything."

"Absolutely, Sheriff," I said.

Hours passed, dusk fell, and Cormac still hadn't returned. I decided not to worry. He was a big boy, he could take care of himself. I certainly wasn't capable of babysitting both him and Ben.

Ben hadn't stirred since the last time he passed out. I had no idea how long he had to stay like this before I had to start worrying. When I did start worrying, who was I supposed to call for help? The werewolf pack that had kicked me out of Denver? The Center for the Study of Paranatural Biology, the government research office that was undergoing reorganization after its former director disappeared—not that I knew anything about that.

I stared at the laptop screen for so long I started to doze off. The words blurred, and even though the straight-backed kitchen chair I sat in wasn't particularly comfortable, I managed to curl up and let my head nod forward.

That was when Ben spoke. "Hi."

He didn't sound delirious or desperate. A little hoarse still, but it was the scratchy voice of someone getting over a cold. He lay on the bed and looked at me. One of his arms rested over the blanket that covered him, his fingers gripping the edge.

I slid out of the chair, set the laptop aside, and moved to the edge of the bed.

"Hey," I said. "How do you feel?"

"Like crap."

I smiled a little. "You should. You've had a crappy week."

He chuckled, then coughed. I almost jumped up and down and started dancing. It was Ben. Ben was back, he hadn't gone crazy.

"You seem awfully happy about my crappy week."

"I'm happy to see you awake. You've been out of it."

"Yeah." He looked away, studying the walls, the ceiling, the blanket covering him. Looking everywhere but at me.

"How much do you remember?" I asked.

He shook his head, meaning that he either didn't remember anything or he wasn't going to tell me. I watched him, feeling anxious and motherly, wanting simultaneously to tuck the blankets in tighter, pat his head, bring him a glass of water, and feed him. I wanted him to relax. I wanted to make everything better, and I didn't have the faintest idea how to do that. So I hovered, perched next to him, on the verge of wringing my hands.

Then he said, his voice flat, "Why did Cormac bring me here?"

"He thought I could help."

"Why didn't he just shoot me?"

As far as I knew, Cormac's guns were still under the bed. *This* bed. Ben didn't have to know that. What if Cormac was wrong, what if Ben did have the guts to shoot himself? What would I have to do to stop him? I couldn't let Ben die. I wouldn't let him—or Cormac—give up.

I spoke quietly, stiff with frustration. "You'll have to ask him."

"Where is he?"

"I don't know. He went out."

His gaze focused on me again, finally. A glimmer of the old Ben showed through. "How long have I been out of it?"

"A couple of days."

"And you two have been stuck here together the whole time?" His face pursed with thoughtfulness. "How's that working out?"

"He hasn't killed me yet."

"He's not going to kill you, Kitty. On the contrary, I think he'd rather—"

I stood suddenly. "Are you hungry? Of course you're hungry, you haven't eaten in two days."

Footsteps pounded up the porch then. Ben looked over to the next room at the same time I did, and his hand clenched on the blanket. Slowly, I went to the front room.

The door slammed open, and Cormac stood there. He carried a rifle.

"You have a freezer, right?" he said.

"Huh?" I blinked, trying to put his question into context. I failed. "Yeah. Why?"

He pointed his thumb over his shoulder to the outside. I went to the door and looked out. There, in the middle of the clearing in front of the cabin, lay a dead deer. Just flopped there, legs stiff and neck arced back. No antlers. I couldn't see blood, but I could smell it. Still cooling. Freshly killed. My stomach rumbled, and I fiercely ignored it.

"It's a deer," I said stupidly.

"I still have to dress it and put the meat up. Is there room in the freezer?"

"You killed it?"

He gave me a frustrated glare. "Yeah."

"Is it even hunting season?"

"Do you think I care?"

"You shot a deer and just . . . dragged it here? Carried it? Why?"

"I had to shoot something."

I stared at him. That sounded like me. Rather it sounded like me once a month, on the night of the full moon. "You had to shoot something."

"Yeah." He said the word as a challenge.

So which of us was the monster? At least I had an excuse for my bloodlust.

"Ben's awake," I said. "Awake and lucid, I mean."

In fact, Ben was standing in the doorway, holding a blanket wrapped around his shoulders. His hair was ruffled, stubble covered his jawline, and he appeared wrung-out, but he didn't seem likely to topple over. He and Cormac looked at each other for a moment, and the tension in the room spiked. I couldn't read what passed between them. I had an urge to get out of there. I imagined calling in to my own radio show: *Yeah hi, I'm a werewolf, and I'm stuck in a cabin in the woods with another werewolf and a werewolf hunter . . .*

"Hey," Cormac said finally. "How are you feeling?"

"I don't know," Ben said. "What's the gun for?"

"Went hunting."

"Any luck?"

"Yeah."

My voice came out bright with false cheerfulness. "Maybe you could cut us up a couple of steaks right now and we could have some dinner."

"That's the plan. If you can stoop to eating meat that someone else picked out," he said. "Oh, and I found another one of these." He tossed something at me.

Startled, I reached for it—then thought better of it and stepped out of the way. Good thing, too, because a piece of barbed wire clattered on the floor. It was bent into the shape of a cross, like the other, which was still lying on the floor by the stove. I kicked the new one in that direction.

Ben moved toward the front door, stepping slowly like he was learning to walk again.

Cormac could change his mind, I thought absently. He gripped the rifle, all he had to do was raise it and fire, and he could kill Ben. Ben didn't seem to notice this, or didn't think it was a danger. Or just didn't care. All his attention was on the front door, on the outside. Cormac let him pass, and Ben went out to the porch.

I went after him.

He stared at the deer. Just stared, clutching the blanket around him and shivering like he was cold, though I didn't think the chill in the air was that sharp.

"I can smell it," he said. "All the way in the bedroom, I could smell it. It smells good. It shouldn't, but it does."

Fresh blood spilled on the ground, hot and rich, seeping out of cooling meat and crunchy, marrow-filled bones—I knew exactly what he was talking about. My mouth would be watering, if I wasn't so nervous.

"It's because you're hungry," I said softly.

"I could eat it right now, couldn't I? If I wanted, I could eat it raw, skin and all—"

"Come inside, Ben. Please. Cormac'll take care of it."

Ben stood so tautly, his whole body rigid, I was afraid that if I touched him he'd snap at me, and I didn't know if his snapping would be figurative or literal. Something animal was waking in him; it lurked just under the surface.

Very gently, I touched his arm. "Come on."

Finally, he looked away from the deer. He turned, and let me guide him inside.

Hours later, Cormac stacked cuts of wrapped venison in the freezer, while I pulled steaks out of the broiler. Turned out everyone here liked them rare. Go figure.

Cormac came in from cleaning up outside and went to the kitchen sink to wash his hands. "Tomorrow I'll find someone to take care of the hide. The rest of it I buried—"

"I don't want to know what you did with the rest of it," I said, giving him a "stop" gesture while I took plates out of the cupboard.

"Come on, it's not like you haven't seen any of it before. In fact, you might have offered some help."

"I don't know anything about dressing a deer for real. I usually just rip into it with my teeth."

Ben sat at the kitchen table, staring blankly at the tabletop. Cormac had given him a change of clothes, but he still wrapped himself with the blanket. I tried not to be worried. He needed time to adjust. That was all. Not having him take part in the banter was weird, though.

The table, an antique made of varnished wood with a couple of matching straight-backed chairs, was small, barely big enough for two people, totally inadequate for three. After I arranged the steaks on plates, Cormac picked up his and stayed put, eating while standing by the counter. I brought the other two plates to the table. I set one, along with a set of utensils, in front of Ben. His gaze shifted, startled out of whatever reverie he'd been in, and tracked the food.

Determined not to hover, I sat down with my own meal. I couldn't help it, though; I watched him closely.

Meat looks different to a werewolf. I didn't used to be much of a meat eater at all. I used to be the kind of person who went to a steakhouse and ordered a salad. But after I was attacked, and I woke up and had a look at my first steak, so rare that it was bleeding all the way through—I could have swallowed the thing whole. I'd wanted to, and the thought had made me ill. It had been so strange, being hungry and nauseous at the same time. I'd almost burst into tears, because I'd realized that I was different, right through to the bones, and that my life would never be the same.

What would Ben do?

After a moment, he picked up the fork and knife and calmly sliced into the meat, and calmly put the bite into his mouth, and calmly chewed and swallowed. Like nothing was wrong.

We might have been having a calm, normal meal. Three normal people eating their normal food—except for the spine-freezing tension that made the silence painful. The scraping of knives on plates made my nerves twinge.

Ben had eaten half his steak when he stopped, resting the fork and knife at the edge of the plate. He remained staring down when he asked, "How long?"

"How long until what?" I said, being willfully stupid. I knew exactly what he was talking about.

He spoke in almost a whisper. "How long until the full moon?"

"Four days," I said, equally subdued.

"Not long."

"No."

"I can't do it," he said, without any emotion. Just an observation of fact.

He was making this hard. I didn't know what else I expected. He'd acquired a chronic disease, not won the lottery. Ben wasn't a stranger to the supernatural. He was coming into this with his eyes wide open. He'd seen a werewolf shape-shift—on video, at least. He knew exactly what would happen to him when the full moon rose.

"Everyone says that," I said, frustration creeping into my voice. "But you can. If I can do it, you can do it."

"Cormac?" Ben said, looking at his cousin.

"No," the hunter said. "I didn't do it then and I won't do it now. Norville's right, that isn't the way."

Ben stared at him a moment, then said, "I swear to God, I never thought I'd hear you say anything like that." Cormac looked away, but Ben continued. "Your father would have done it in a heartbeat. Hell, what if he'd survived? You know he'd have shot himself."

My mind tripped over that one entirely. My mouth, as usual, picked up where intelligent thought failed. "Whoa, wait a minute. Hold on a minute. Cormac—your father. Your father was killed by a werewolf? Is that what he's saying?"

We embarked on a three-way staring contest: Cormac glared at Ben, Ben glared back, and I glared back and forth between them. Nobody said anything until Cormac spoke, his voice cool as granite.

"You know where my guns are. You want it done, do it yourself."

He walked out of the kitchen, to the front door, then out into the night, slamming the door behind him.

Ben stared after him. I was about ready to scream, because he still wasn't saying anything.

"Ben?"

He started eating again, methodically cutting, chewing, swallowing, watching his plate the whole time.

I, on the other hand, had lost my appetite. I pushed my plate away and comforted myself with the knowledge that if Ben was eating, he probably wouldn't kill himself. At least not right this minute.

After supper, Ben went back to bed and passed out again. Still sick, still needing time to mend. Or maybe he was avoiding the situation. I didn't press the issue. In the continued absence of Cormac, I took the sofa. Dealing with Ben had exhausted me. I needed to get some sleep. Or maybe I was just avoiding the situation.

I fervently hoped Cormac wasn't out shooting another deer. My freezer couldn't handle it.

I dreamed of blood.

I stood in a clearing, on a rocky hill in the middle of the forest. I recognized the place; it was near the cabin. When I turned my face up, blood rained from the sky. It poured onto my face, ran across my cheeks, down my neck, matting my fur. I was covered in fur, but I couldn't tell if I was wolf or human. Both, neither. The forest smelled like slaughter. Red crosses marked the trunks of the trees closest to me. Painted in blood. Then the screaming started, like the trees themselves were crying at me: Get out, get out, get out. Leave. Run. But they hemmed me in, the trees moved to stop me, ringing me, blocking my way. I tried to scream back at them, but my voice died, and still the blood rained, and my heart raced.

It only lasted a second. At least, it only felt like a second. It felt like I had just closed my eyes when I woke up. But early sunlight filled the room. It was morning, and Cormac was kneeling by the sofa.

"Norville?"

Quickly I sat up. I looked around for danger—for blood seeping from the walls. I expected to hear screaming. My heart beat fast. But Cormac seemed calm. I didn't see anything unusual.

"How long have you been there?" I said, a bit breathlessly.

"I just got here. I found something, I think you should come take a look."

I nodded, pushed back the blankets, and followed him, after pulling on a coat and sneakers.

The air outside was freezing. I wasn't sure it was just the temperature. After that dream, I expected to find another gutted rabbit on the porch. I expected to see crosses on every tree. I hugged myself and trudged over the forest earth.

Cormac stopped about fifty paces out from the cabin. He pointed down, and it took me a minute to find what he wanted me to see: another barbed-wire cross, sunk in the dirt as if someone had dropped it there.

"And over here," Cormac said, and led me ten paces farther, along a track that paralleled the cabin.

Another cross lay on the ground here. Without prompting from him, I continued on, and after a moment of searching, I found the next one on my own.

I looked back at Cormac in something of a panic.

He said, "There's a circle of them all the way around the house."

The barbed wire had become more than a symbol. The talismans literally fenced me in. They created a barrier of fear.

"Who would do this?" I said. "Why—why would someone do this?"

"I don't know. Do you smell anything?" he asked.

I shook my head. I didn't smell anything unusual, at least. "That's weird, I ought to be able to smell some trace of whoever left these. But it's like the crosses just appeared out of thin air. Is that possible?"

"If these things are more than just a scare tactic, then I suppose anything's possible. I kept watch all night. I should have seen something."

"Were these here before last night?"

"I didn't see any."

I kicked the dirt, stubbing my toe on the ground. I let out a short growl at the pain. "This is driving me crazy," I muttered.

"That's probably the idea," Cormac said.

"Huh. As if I'm not perfectly capable of driving *myself* crazy."

"Is that what you've been doing stuck out here in the woods? Driving yourself crazy?"

It kind of looked that way. I didn't have to admit that, though. I started picking up the crosses, searching for the next one around the circle, intending to find every single one.

"Kitty—" His tone made him sound reprimanding, like he was about to burst forth with some great wisdom. We both knew it: picking up all the crosses was probably futile. Until we learned who was leaving these things, there'd always be more.

"You should look in on Ben," I said. "After his talk last night, he shouldn't be left alone. Or you could get some sleep. Or something."

He actually took the hint. After a moment's pause, he ambled back to the cabin.

When I finished, I had sixteen barbed-wire crosses pocketed in the corner of my coat. Eighteen when I added them to the two Cormac had brought into the house. I found a plastic grocery bag, put them all in, tied the bag closed, and left it out on the porch. I didn't want those things inside. Cormac's idea of melting them to slag sounded wise.

Inside, Cormac and Ben were sitting opposite each other at the kitchen table, dead quiet. Cormac looked at Ben, and Ben didn't look at anything in particular. I started fixing breakfast, pretending like nothing was wrong, trying not to throw glances at them over my shoulder. It felt like I had interrupted an argument.

"Eggs, anyone? Cereal? I think I've got some sausage that isn't too out-of-date. Frozen venison?" Silence. My own appetite wasn't what it should have been. I settled for a glass of orange juice. Finally, leaning back against the counter, I asked, "Who died?"

Then I wished I hadn't. Ben looked sharply at me, and Cormac crossed his arms with a frustrated sigh. I couldn't read the series of body language. Maybe if I could get them talking, then close my eyes and pretend I was doing the show, I could figure out what was wrong.

"No, really," I said, my voice flat. "Who died?"

Ben stood up. "I'm taking a shower." He stalked back to the bedroom.

That left me with Cormac, who wouldn't look at me. I said, "You going to tell me what I missed, or are we all going to go around not talking to each other for the rest of the day?"

"I'm inclined to say that it's none of your business."

"Yeah, that's why you brought Ben here in the first place, because it's none of my business. Real cute. What's wrong?"

"Ben and I worked it out."

"Worked what out?"

"A compromise."

I wanted to growl. "Will you just tell me why he won't talk to me and you won't look at me?"

Taking that as a challenge, he looked right at me. If I hadn't been against the counter I would have backed up a step, so much anger and frustration burned out of his gaze.

He said, "After the full moon, if he still wants me to do it, I'll do it."

I had to take a moment to parse that, to understand what it meant. And I did. I still had to spell it out. "You'll shoot him. Just like that. The only person in the world you trust, and you'll kill him."

"If he wants me to."

"That isn't fair. That isn't enough time for him to adjust to what's happened to him. He won't be any happier after the full moon than he is now."

"And how long did it take you to become the stable, well-adjusted werewolf you are today?" His tone dripped with sarcasm.

I crossed my arms and pouted. "Very funny."

"It's what we decided."

"Well, you're both a couple of macho dickheads!"

He stood. "Is it still okay if I sleep on the sofa?"

"I ought to make you sleep on the porch!"

He ignored me, just like I expected, and went to the sofa, wrenched off his boots, lay down, and pulled the blanket over his head.

So much for that.

I went to the desk and fired up the laptop. I started a new page and wrote a title at the top: "Ten Ways to Defeat Macho Dickheadism." Then I realized that most of the world's problems stemmed from macho dickheadism, and if I could defeat that I could save the world. It made for a pretty good rant, since Cormac and Ben were both refusing to get yelled at in person.

Ben came out of the bathroom an hour later, slightly damp and wearing jeans and a gray T-shirt that he must have borrowed from Cormac. It gave him this James Dean look. Or that might have been the only partially suppressed snarl he wore. I expected him to say something about me actually sitting at my desk and working. The old Ben would have said something snide and encouraging at the same time.

This new Ben just looked at me, then sank heavily into the kitchen chair.

I watched him. "Did you have breakfast while you and Cormac planned your suicide, or should I fix something?"

His voice was low. "I expected you of all people to have some sympathy."

"No way. I'm a sentimentalist, remember? You're the bitter, cynical one. I just can't believe you'd go down without a fight."

"I've already lost."

I moved to the kitchen table and sat across from him, where Cormac had been. I stared him down. He fidgeted, nervous, and looked away. Ah-ha, wolfish instincts were kicking in. He didn't try to challenge me back. Good.

"This is what I see: I have three days, plus a full moon night, to convince you that life as a werewolf is better than no life at all."

"Kitty, this isn't about you. It isn't any of your business."

"Tell that to Cormac. He's the one who dumped you in my lap."

"I told him off about that already."

skin, a porcelain smooth face, dyed black hair falling in luxurious ripples across her shoulders and down her back, and black eyeliner ringing bright blue eyes. That blue, they had to be contacts. She seemed to be in a radio studio, but for some reason the table in front of her was covered in red velvet. She draped herself suggestively across the velvet, her black satin gown exposing not a small amount of cleavage, and leaned toward a microphone as if preparing to lick it. She wore a pentacle on a chain around her neck, silver ankhs on each ear, and a rhinestone nose stud. Animated bat icons flapped in all four corners of the page.

And if all that weren't enough to drive me crazy, the show's theme song was Bauhaus's "Bela Lugosi's Dead."

After a few lines of the song, the woman herself came on the air. Her voice was low and sultry, as seductive as any film noir femme fatale could wish. "Greetings, fellow travelers in darkness. It's time to pull back the veil between worlds. Let me, Ariel, Priestess of the Night, be your guide as we explore the secrets, the mysteries, and the shadows of the unknown."

Oh, give me a break.

"Vampires," she continued, drawing out the word, pronouncing it with a fake British accent. "Are they victims of a disease, as some so-called experts would have us believe? Or have they been chosen, serving as undying ambassadors from the past? Is their immortality a mere quirk of biology—or is it a mystical calling?

"I have with me in the studio a very special guest. He has agreed to emerge from his sanctum to speak with us tonight. Gustaf is the vampire Master of a major U.S. city. He has asked me not to say which, to protect his safety."

Of *course* she wasn't going to say which.

I pouted a little. *I'd* never gotten a vampire Master to be a guest on *my* show. If this Gustaf really was a Master. If he really was a vampire.

"Gustaf, thank you for being here tonight."

"The pleasure is all mine." Gustaf had a low, melodious voice, giving a hint that he might burst out laughing at a joke he wasn't going to share. Very mysterious.

"Hm, I bet it is," Ariel purred. "Tell me, Gustaf, when did you become a vampire?"

"In the year 1438. It was in the Low Countries, what people call the Netherlands today. A very good time and place to be alive. So much trade, commerce, art, music—so much life. I was a young man, full of prospects, full of joy. Then I met . . . *her.*"

"You really think he made a mistake, bringing you here?"

He pursed his lips. "I do. He should have taken care of this back at Shiprock."

Ben had always been there for me. Now, when it was time for him to accept help, he was throwing it back in my face. Well, screw that.

"You know what, Ben? You're wrong. This is my business. You know why?" He gave the ceiling a long-suffering stare. That was okay, the question was rhetorical anyway. "Because I'm adopting you. You're part of my pack, now. That means you're under my protection and I refuse to let you go off and kill yourself."

He blinked at me. "What are you talking about?"

"Wolves run in packs. You're in my pack. And I'm the alpha female. That means you do what I say."

"Or what?"

"Or . . . or I'll get really pissed off at you."

He seemed to consider for a moment. In a mental panic, I wondered whether I could take him in a fight, if I had to back up my oh-so-brave words. He wasn't yet used to the strength he gained as a werewolf. He was still sick, still finding his feet. I had experience with this sort of thing. The thing was, I didn't want to have to assert my position by fighting him. I wanted to be able to just talk him into it.

Finally, he said, "Why do I have this urge to take you seriously?"

"Because the wolf inside you knows what's best. Trust me, Ben. Please."

"I thought you didn't have a pack."

I smiled. "I do now."

chapter 6

Come on, get your coat," I said, grabbing my own and my bag.

"Why?"

"We're going out. Quietly—don't wake up Cormac."

He went to the bedroom and came back with a jacket. He looked sullen, but didn't argue. That scared me a little. Was he really buying into the whole alpha female thing? I thought I'd been bluffing.

"Where are we going?" he finally asked when we were on the road.

"Into town to buy groceries. You guys are eating all my food." That wasn't all; I'd put the bag of barbed-wire crosses in the car. I planned on getting rid of them.

"Why do I have to come along?"

"Because part of being a werewolf is learning how to function in the real world. It's a little freaky at first. McDonald's will never smell the same."

He wrinkled his nose and made a grunt of disgust.

"Also, I'm not going to leave you alone and let you kill yourself just to spite me."

"I made a deal with Cormac. I'll stick it out through the full moon. I won't go back on that."

I sighed. "You're doing it again. You'll stick it out for Cormac, but not for me. I think you just don't like me."

He paused to consider. "You know you're crazy?"

"*I'm* not the one who wants my best friend to shoot me in the head!"

He turned away to stare out the window.

I'd been through what he was going through now. I'd awakened after being attacked by a werewolf, with my whole world turned upside down, and I hadn't wanted to die. I hadn't even thought about it beyond the vague, unserious half urges that came with depression. I had a life and I wanted to keep it, lycanthropy or no. What was wrong with Ben?

Nothing was wrong with Ben. He was right to be afraid, to want to avoid it. This was about me. I was the problem. Ben knew what was coming, because he'd seen what it did to me. I couldn't blame him at all.

I said, "I'm a werewolf—am I so terrible that you'd rather kill yourself than be that?"

"No." He glanced at me, and his look was sad. "You're not terrible at all. You're . . ." He turned back to the window without finishing.

I'm what? I almost yelled at him to make him finish. But what would that get me? An answer I wasn't sure I wanted to hear. *You're not terrible, you're* . . . confused.

I pulled into the driveway of Joe and Alice's store and parked. It was midday, but we were the only ones there. Small favors. I'd already gotten out of the car when Ben said, "I'll just wait here."

I put my hands on my hips. "That defeats the whole point of you coming along. And I need you to help carry groceries."

He lurched out of the car, slouching in his coat like a sullen teenager, his hands shoved in the pockets. I walked across the dirt parking lot, and Ben fell into step beside me. Halfway to the front door, though, he paused and looked up, turning his nose into the faint breeze. His brow furrowed, faintly worried, faintly curious.

I could filter it all out, the hundred smells that I encountered every day: spilled oil, gasoline, asphalt, the garbage Dumpster, drying paint from the shed around the corner, somebody's loose dog, a feral cat, the earth and trees from the edge of the woods. A normal human wouldn't be able to differentiate them at all. Ben was smelling it all for the first time.

"You okay?" I asked.

After a moment, he nodded. Then he said, "What do I smell like to you?"

I shrugged. I'd never tried to describe it before. "Now? You smell like a werewolf. Human with a little bit of fur and wild thrown in."

He nodded, like that sounded familiar—he could smell me now, after all. Then he said, "And before?"

"I always thought you smelled like your trenchcoat."

He made a sound that was almost a chuckle.

"What do I smell like to you?" I said.

He cocked his head for a moment, testing the air, tasting it. He seemed puzzled, like he was still trying to figure out the sensation. "Safe. You smell safe."

We went inside.

Ben hesitated at the door, once again looking around, nose flaring, wearing an expression of uncertainty and also curiosity. I looked, hoping to see Alice, bracing for Joe and his rifle.

Behind the counter, Alice looked up from the magazine she was reading. She smiled. "Hi, Kitty, how are you today?"

"Oh, fine. I have friends visiting. Alice, this is Ben. Ben, Alice."

Alice smiled warmly and extended her hand for shaking. Ben looked stricken for a moment—to the wolf side, it was not the most harmless of gestures. In fact, it looked a little like an attack. I waited to see how he'd react and let out a bit of a sigh when he recovered and took her hand.

"Good to meet you," he said. He wasn't smiling, but he behaved in a straightforward enough manner.

"Let me know if I can help you find anything," she said.

"Actually, I did want to ask you something. Do you know any blacksmiths around here? Someone with a forge who could melt down a bunch of metal for me?"

"Well, sure. Jake Torres is the local farrier, he's got a forge. What kind of metal?"

This was going to be hard to explain without sounding like a loon. But I *was* crazy, according to Ben anyway. Maybe I should just embrace it. "I've got a bunch of pieces of barbed wire that I'd love to see completely destroyed. You think he'd do that for me?"

She creased her brow. "Oh, probably. What kind of pieces?"

"They're in the car, I'll go get them. Ben"—I grabbed a plastic shopping basket from the pile by the door—"here. Find some food. Whatever looks good."

He took the basket, looked at me quizzically, then headed for the shelves.

Feeling like I was finally accomplishing something, I ran to the car, grabbed the bag of crosses, ran back to the store, and dropped the bag on the counter in front of Alice. It landed with a solid, steely *thunk*. She pulled out one of the crosses, studied it, and looked increasingly worried. That made *me* worried.

"Something's wrong," I said. "What is it? You look like you've seen one of these before."

Shaking her head, she dropped the cross back and quickly tied up the bag. "Oh, you know. Folklore, local superstition. Crosses are supposed to be for protection."

"Yeah, well, someone's been dumping them in a circle around my cabin and I don't feel very protected. Friend of mine thinks it's part of a curse. Like someone isn't happy with me being around."

Alice's eyes widened, startled. "That's certainly odd, isn't it?"

"I just want to get rid of them. Melting them down seems the way to go. You think your farrier will do it?"

"Jake stops in here once a week. He's due in a couple of days. I'll ask him myself," she said with a thin smile. She put the bag under the counter. It was out of my hands now.

That was easy. A weight lifted from me. "Thanks, Alice. That'd be great."

I went to check on Ben. He was standing with the still empty basket in front of a shelf full of canned soup, chili, and pasta sauce.

"Nothing sounds good," he said. "I just keep thinking about all that venison in your freezer. Is that normal?"

I patted his arm. "I know what you mean."

We stocked up on the basics—bacon and eggs, bread and milk. Ben gamely carried the basket for me, and Alice rang up the goods, her demeanor more cheerful than ever. We made it back to the car without incident.

"There," I said as I pulled the car back on the road, "that wasn't so hard."

After some long minutes of driving, Ben said, "I could hear her heartbeat. Smell her blood. It's strange."

I wet my lips, because my mouth had gone dry. Even smelling him, smelling him change into something not quite human, even seeing the bite wounds and knowing intellectually what was happening to him, it didn't really hit me until that moment. Ben was a werewolf. He may not have shape-shifted yet, he may have been infected for less than a week. But there it was.

"It makes them seem like prey," I said, aware that I was talking about people, normal people like Alice, in the third person. Like they were something different than Ben and I. "Like you could hunt them." Like you could almost taste the blood.

"Does that happen every time you meet somebody?" he said.

"Most of the time, yeah," I said softly.

He didn't say a word for the rest of the trip home.

When we entered the house, Cormac was awake, sitting at the kitchen table, cleaning a gun or three. As soon as the front door opened, he stood and turned to us. I'd have said he was in a panic, if I didn't know him better.

"Where'd you go?" he said.

"Shopping?" I said, uncertain. Both Ben and I hefted filled plastic grocery bags, which we brought to the kitchen. "You want to help unpack?"

He just stood there. "You couldn't have left a note?"

"I didn't think you'd wake up before we got back."

"Don't worry," Ben said. "She looked out for me."

"Should you even be out?" Cormac said accusingly, almost motherly.

I nearly snapped at him, something juvenile like *what's your problem?* Then I realized—I'd never seen Cormac worried before. At least, worried and actually showing it. He was downright stressed out. It was almost chilling.

Ben slumped into the other chair at the kitchen table. "I survived, didn't I?" Cormac scowled and looked away, which prompted Ben to add, "I'm okay, Cormac."

"At least for another three days," I muttered as I shoved food into the fridge. I put the groceries away loudly and angrily, as if that would make me feel better. The guys ignored me.

"You need help with that?" Ben indicated the spread of gun oil and gun parts on the kitchen table. Cormac had put paper towels down first, so I couldn't even get mad at him for messing up the table.

"I'm done." Cormac began cleaning up the mess, packing everything away into a metal toolbox.

Ben watched for a minute, then said, "If you'd just shot me, you wouldn't have to deal with this crap now."

"You are never going to let me live that down, are you?"

"We had a deal—"

Cormac slammed the toolbox on the table, making a wrenching crash. "We were sixteen years old when we made that deal! We were just kids! We didn't have a clue!"

Ben dropped his gaze.

I left the room.

Couldn't go far, of course. A whole five feet to the so-called living room. Still, the space made ignoring them marginally easier. The whole cabin became entrenched in a thick, obvious silence. A moment later, Cormac left out the front door, toolbox and rifles in hand. Then I heard him repacking his Jeep. I half expected the engine to start up, to hear him drive away forever, leaving me to deal with Ben all by myself. But he didn't. Maybe he planned on sleeping out there to avoid any more arguments, but he didn't drive away. Ben went to the bedroom. I sat at my desk, at my computer, pretending to write, and wanted to pull out my hair.

I'd spent a year on the radio telling people how to fix their supernaturally complicated relationship problems. And now I couldn't deal with the one right in front of me.

Ben emerged long enough for supper. More venison steaks. After, he pulled a chair into the living room and sat in front of the stove, just watching the embers burning through the grate, slipping into some kind of fugue state. I couldn't really argue. I'd done the same thing when this had happened to me. As the body changed, perceptions changed, and the world seemed to slow down. You blinked and a whole afternoon went by. The sense of disconnection had lasted for weeks. I'd almost flunked out that semester. If I hadn't been just a year away from finishing, I might have given into that urge to drop out and walk away. Walk into the woods, never to return.

Cormac stayed in the kitchen. They still weren't speaking.

Later, at the appropriate hour, I turned on the radio. Yes, it was that time of the week again. I curled up on the sofa, cell phone in hand.

Ben looked at the radio, brow furrowed. Then, he narrowed his eyes—an expression of dawning comprehension. "What day is it?"

"Saturday," I said.

Immediately he stood, shaking his head. "No, uh-uh, there is no way I am listening to this. I'm not watching you listen to this. I'm out of here. Good night." He went to the bedroom and flopped on the bed.

Cormac came from the kitchen, glancing at the bedroom, and sat on the other end of the sofa. "What's this?"

"The competition," I said.

The sultry voice announced herself.

"Good evening. I am Ariel, Priestess of the Night. Welcome to my show." And again, "Bela Lugosi's Dead." Of all the pretentious . . .

I muttered at the radio in a manic snit. "Tell us, Ariel, what shall we talk about *this* week?"

Ariel, via the radio, answered. "We've all heard of werewolves," she intoned. "We've seen countless movies. My little brother even dressed up as the Wolf Man for Halloween one year. All this attention has given short shrift to the *other* species. Lions and tigers and bears. And a dozen other documented lycanthropic varieties. *Oh, my.*"

Cormac crossed his arms and leaned back. "You have to wonder if she's got a body to go with that voice."

I *so* wasn't going to tell him about the Web site. I glared at him instead. Then, a niggling voice started scratching at the back of my mind. Scratching, gnawing, aggravating, until I had to ask, "What about my show? You know, before you saw me in person—did my voice ever, you know, make you wonder if I maybe had a body to go with it?"

He looked at me, stricken for a moment. "You're a little different," he said finally.

Oh, God, I'm a hack. An ugly, talentless hack and nobody ever liked me, not once, not ever. I hugged the pillow that was on the sofa and stewed. Cormac rolled his eyes.

Ariel was still talking. "Are you a lycanthrope who is something other than the standard lupine fare? Give me a call, let's chat."

I had the number on speed dial by this time. I punched the call button and waited.

Cormac watched thoughtfully. "What are you doing?"

I ignored him. I got a busy signal the first time, then tried again. And again, until finally, "Hello, you've reached Ariel, Priestess of the Night. What's your name and hometown?"

I had it all planned out this time. "I'm Irene from Tulsa," I said brightly.

"And what do you want to talk about?"

"I'm a were-jaguar. Very rare," I said. "I'm so glad that Ariel's talking about this. I've felt so alone, you know? I'd love a chance to talk."

"All right, Irene. Turn down your radio and hold, please."

I did so, pressing the phone to my ear and tapping my foot happily.

Cormac stared at me. "That's really pathetic."

"Shut up."

Then he had the nerve to take the radio to the next room, to the kitchen table. He hunched before it, listening with the volume turned down low. Couldn't he leave me alone?

I listened in on three calls: the callers claimed to be a were-leopard, a were-fox, and a werewolf who refused to believe that lycanthropes could be anything other than wolves, because, well, *he'd* never met any others *personally*. If he'd called into my show I would have told him off with a rant that would have left him dumbstruck. Something along the lines of: *Okay, you big jerk, let's try out a new word, shall we? Say it along with me: narcissistic . . .*

By comparison, Ariel was shockingly polite. "Marty, do you consider yourself to be an open-minded person?"

"Well, yeah, I suppose," said Marty the caller.

"Good, that's really good," Ariel purred. "I'd expect a werewolf to be open-minded. You're involved so deeply in the world behind the veil, after all. I'm sure there are lots of things you haven't had personal experience with, yet you believe—like the Pope, or the Queen of England. So exactly why is it that you can't accept the existence of other species of lycanthropes, just because you've never met one?"

Marty hadn't thought this one through. You could always spot the ones who spouted rhetoric with no thought behind it. "Well, you know. All the stories are about were*wolves*. And the movies— werewolves, all of them. It's the Wolf Man, not the Leopard Man!"

"And what about *Cat People?*"

Hey, that was what I'd have said.

"That's different," Marty said petulantly. "That was, you know, made-up."

Ariel continued. "Stories about shape-shifters are found all over the world, and they're about all kinds of animals. Whatever's common locally. You really have to accept that there might be something to all these stories, yes?"

"*I've* never heard of these stories."

Wow, I loved how some people were so good at digging their own holes.

"Your culture isn't the only one in the world, Marty. Moving on to the next call, we have Irene from Tulsa, hello."

My turn? Me? I was ready for this. I tried to sound more chipper and ditzy than I had the last time I called. "Hi, Ariel!"

"So, you're a were-jaguar. Can you tell me how exactly that happened? Jaguars aren't exactly native to Tulsa."

"When I was in college I spent a summer volunteering in Brazil for an environmental group, working in the jungle. One time I started back to camp a little late, and, well . . ." I took a deep, significant breath. "I was attacked."

How could you not sympathize with that story? Oh, yeah, somebody nominate me for an Oscar. I wondered how long it would take her to spot the fake.

"That's an amazing story," Ariel said, clearly impressed. "How have you coped since then?"

"I have good days, I have bad days. It's really hard not having anyone to talk to about it. As far as I know, all the other were-jaguars are in Brazil."

"You ever think about going back and finding someone who might be able to help you?"

"It just never worked out." *I'm so sad, pity me . . .*

"Well, Irene, if you really want something, there's always a way." Maybe that was why Ariel bothered me so much: that Pollyanna sunshine attitude. Sometimes, things just didn't work out.

"I want to get married under a full moon. Is there a way for me to get that?"

"Sometimes you have to adjust your wants to be a little more realistic."

"Easy for you to say."

She dodged, yanking control of the conversation back to her. "Tell me why you really haven't been back to Brazil."

I said breezily, "Well, you know, I had to come back home, finish school, then I met this guy, see, and then I broke up with this guy—and you know how it is, one thing then another, and I guess I got distracted."

Ariel wasn't having it. "Irene, are you pulling my leg?"

Damn, she got me. That didn't mean I had to admit it. "Oh, Ariel, why would I do something like that?"

"You tell me."

"Calling you with a fake story about being a were-jaguar would be—oh, I don't know—a delusion based in some psychiatric disorder? A desperate cry for attention?"

"That's what I'm thinking," Ariel said. "Moving on to the next call, Gerald—"

I hung up in disgust. I still hadn't gotten her to say anything stupid. *I* was feeling pretty stupid, but never mind that. My inner two-year-old was enjoying herself.

Cormac was watching me from the kitchen, which made me even more disgruntled. I didn't need an audience. At least not one that was sitting there staring at me.

He said, "You ever think that maybe she's really a vampire or a witch or something, the same way that you're really a werewolf? That she's keeping it under wraps like you did?"

"Right up until you blew my cover, you mean?"

He shrugged noncommittally, as if to say, *Who me?*

"She's a hack," I muttered.

"Then what the hell does that make you?"

"A has-been, evidently." I brushed back my hair and sighed.

He stood and grabbed his coat and gun off the kitchen counter. "You want a pity party, you can have it by yourself."

"I'm not . . . this isn't . . . I'm not looking for your pity."

"Good. 'Cause you're not getting any. If you're a has-been it's your own damn fault."

"Where are you going?"

"Guard duty. If I see any gutted rabbits I'll let you know."

Bang, he slammed the front door behind him and that was that.

I let out a frustrated growl, grabbed the blanket, and cocooned myself on the sofa.

I wasn't a has-been. I *wasn't.*

Yet.

I woke, startled, and sat up on the sofa. I hadn't heard anything, nothing specific had jolted me awake, but I felt like someone had slammed a door or fired a gun.

Cormac.

He was asleep in a chair, which he'd pulled over to the living-room window. He'd been keeping watch, just like he'd said. But I never thought he'd fall asleep on guard duty. It just wasn't like him.

Whatever had shocked me awake hadn't affected him. He even snored a little, his chin tipped forward so it almost touched his chest.

Outside, the sky was gray. Light, so it was past dawn, but still overcast, like it was about to snow. I had a queasy, stuffy-headed feeling that told me I hadn't gotten enough sleep.

"Cormac?" I said.

Immediately he sat up and put his hand on the revolver he'd left sitting on my desk. Only after looking around, tensed at the edge of the chair as if waiting for an attack, did he say, "What happened?" He didn't look at me; his attention focused on the window and the door.

"Something woke me up," I said.

"I hadn't meant to fall asleep," he said. "I shouldn't have fallen asleep." His hand clenched on his weapon like it was a security blanket. He didn't pick it up, but I had no doubt he could aim and shoot it in a heartbeat. Speaking of heartbeats, his had sped up. I could hear it, and smell his anxiety. He wasn't used to getting caught off guard. His fear fed mine.

"Something's out there," I whispered.

"You hear something?"

"I don't know." I concentrated, trying yet again to remember what my senses had told me, what exactly had fired my nerves awake.

I smelled blood. It wasn't new blood, fresh blood. It was old, rotten, stinking. And not just a little, but a slaughterhouse's worth. A massive amount, and it was everywhere, as if someone had painted the walls with it. No—no—

Get a grip. Keep it together.

"Do you smell something?" I said, my voice cracking. Of course he didn't. Not like this. How could he?

"I assume you mean something out of the ordinary."

"Blood."

"Are you okay?"

I went to the door. *Get out.*

My hand on the knob, I squeezed my eyes shut. There wasn't a voice. I hadn't heard anything. I cracked open the door.

The smell washed over me. I'd never sensed anything like it. The odor was hateful, oppressive, like it was attacking me. Could a smell be evil?

"There's something out there," I said. And it hated me. It had left all those signs that it hated me.

"Move over." Cormac, gun raised, displaced me from in front of the door. "Stay back."

I did, holding my clenched hands to my chest. He opened the door a little wider. His gun arm led the way as he stepped out, the weapon ready to face the lurking danger.

Sheltered behind the door, I watched his face. His expression never changed. It stayed cold, stony—his professional look. Then he froze.

"Jesus Christ," he said, his voice filled with something like awe. He didn't lower his weapon.

I slipped out the door to stand next to him on the porch and looked out.

All around the clearing in front of the house, carcasses hung from the lower branches of trees. Skinless—pink and bloody, wet with a sheen of fat and flesh, the dead animals were hung up by their hind legs, so that their front legs and heads dangled. Their teeth—the sharp teeth of carnivores—were bared, and lidless eyes stared. There must have been a dozen of them. They swayed a little on their ropes, ghosts in the dawn light.

I moved forward, like that would help me see better—like I even wanted to see them better—and leaned against the porch railing. They looked alien and terrible, so that I couldn't identify them at first. Four legs, straight naked tails, slim bodies with round rib cages and narrow hips. Heads with narrow snouts and triangular ears.

They were dogs. Some kind of dogs. Canines. Wolflike.

I made a noise like a sob.

I had to get out of here, but I couldn't, not yet, not until I'd gotten Ben through the full moon. But the walls were closing in. And there weren't even walls out here. The dead eyes all stared at me. *Get out.*

"Kitty?"

"Who hates me this much?" I started crying. Tension, exhaustion, uncertainty—in the space of a few days my whole life had fallen apart, and I didn't know what to do about it. It all just came out.

I stumbled back, away from the mess, and bumped into Cormac. Then I leaned into him. He was close, and I needed a shoulder, so I turned to his. Eyes leaking and nose dripping on his T-shirt, I let it all out, feeling profoundly embarrassed about it even as I did. I didn't care.

He put his arms around me. He held me firmly without squeezing, moving one hand to stroke my hair. For some reason this made me cry harder.

I didn't like being an alpha. For the last couple of days, I'd been pulling out alpha left and right. Now, though, Cormac was willing to take care of me, at least for a little while. I was profoundly grateful.

"We'll figure it out," he said softly. "After tomorrow, we'll work on figuring this out."

Tomorrow. After the full moon. After we got all that sorted out. I held on to him.

Arm around my shoulder, he guided me inside, shut the door, and set his gun on the desk. I stayed close to him. I didn't want him to pull away, and he took the hint. We stood there for a long time; I clung to him, and he kept his arms around me. I felt safer, believing he could actually protect me from the horrors outside.

"You're being very patient with me," I said, murmuring into his T-shirt.

"Hm. It's not every day a woman throws herself into my arms. I have to take advantage of it while I can."

I made a complaining noise. "I didn't throw myself into your arms."

"Whatever you say."

I chuckled in spite of myself. When I tilted my head back, I saw he was smiling.

"You'd better be careful," I said. "You're getting to be downright likable."

I could kiss him. Another two inches closer—standing on my toes—and I could kiss him. His hand shifted on my back, flattening like he was getting ready to hold me steady, like he wanted to kiss me, too. Then the hand moved away. He touched my cheek, smoothed away the tears. He pulled back.

"I'll start some coffee," he said, and went to the kitchen.

Part of me was relieved. All of me was confused. I covered up the confusion with my usual lame bravado. "There, you're doing it again. Being nice."

He ignored me. Cormac, back to normal.

We discussed the situation at the kitchen table over cups of fresh coffee.

"Whoever's doing this doesn't want to kill me," I said.

"But that's some pretty twisted stuff out there. It's all aimed at you, and it's escalating."

"What's next, if I don't listen to it now?"

"Listen to it? What's it saying?"

"Leave. Get out of here. Someone doesn't want me to be here. You'd think they could just write a note."

"Just because they haven't tried to kill you yet doesn't mean they won't. If you don't leave, and if they get desperate enough."

"Could it be that simple? They just want me to leave town?"

"That probably means it's somebody local," he said. "Shouldn't be too hard to track down somebody local who practices that sort of voodoo."

Ah, the charm of the small town. Everybody knew everybody. We just had to find out which ones were the squirrelly ones. Besides, you know, everybody.

I smiled grimly. "I think I'll give the sheriff a call. Have *him* clean up that mess."

Sheriff Marks was not happy. In a really big way, he was not happy. He only gave the hanging carcasses a cursory glance, wearing a stone-faced tough-guy expression to prove he wasn't grossed out or unduly disturbed.

I sat on the porch steps and watched him survey the clearing—

this involved standing in the middle of it, circling, and nodding sagely. He didn't even bring along Deputy Rosco—I mean Ted—to take pictures of my car this time.

Cormac stood nearby, leaning on the railing. Lurking.

I ventured to speak. "We think it might be somebody local trying to scare me off."

Marks turned to me, his frown quivering. "How do I know you didn't do this? That this isn't some practical joke you're playing on me?"

I glared back in shock. "Because I wouldn't do something like this."

"What about him?" He nodded at Cormac. "What did you say your name was?"

"I didn't," Cormac said, and didn't offer.

Marks moved toward him, hands on hips. "Can I see some ID, sir?"

"No," Cormac said. I groaned under my breath.

"Is that so?" Marks said, his attention entirely drawn away from the slaughter around us.

Cormac said, "Unless you're planning to write me a ticket or arrest me for something, I don't have to show you anything."

Marks was actually starting to turn red. I had no doubt he could come up with something—harassing a police officer, loitering with intent to insult—to pin on Cormac, just out of spite.

I stepped between them, distracting them. "Um, could we get back to the dead animals?"

Marks said, "If I'm right, I could have you up on a number of cruelty to animal charges."

"Should I call my lawyer?" My lawyer who was inside, asleep, recovering from a werewolf bite. "Recovering" was my optimism talking.

"I'm just giving you an out, Ms. Norville. A chance to 'fess up."

"I didn't do it."

"I'm still looking for the hidden cameras," he said, peering into the trees.

"Oh, give me a break!"

He jabbed his finger in my direction. "If you think being famous keeps you safe, lets you do whatever the hell you want, you're wrong."

If I'd thought this situation couldn't get any worse, I was obviously mistaken.

"Sheriff, I'm being harassed, and if you're not going to help me, just say it so I can find somebody who will."

"Good luck with that." He started back for his car.

"Hell, I could do a better job than this clown," Cormac said. "At least I can admit when I'm in over my head."

He didn't even try to say it softly, so Marks couldn't hear. No—he raised his voice, so Marks couldn't help but hear.

Marks turned around, glaring. "What did you say?"

Cormac scuffed his boot on the porch and pretended he hadn't heard.

"You'd better watch yourself," Marks said, pointing. "You so much as breathe wrong and I'll get you."

The hunter remained slouching against the railing, as unflappable as ever. He wasn't going to be the one to shoot first in a fight. I wasn't sure Marks knew that.

Marks started back to his car.

"Sheriff, what do I do about them?" I pointed at the dogs. Some of them were swaying gently, as the trees they were tied to creaked in a faint breeze. A garbage bag or a quickly dug hole wasn't going to clean this up.

"Call animal control," he said. The sound of his car door slamming echoed.

I fumed, unable to come up with a word angry enough for what I wanted to hurl after him.

Hearing steps in the house, I turned around. Ben emerged, standing just outside the doorway and staring out. "Holy shit, what's this?"

"Curse," I said.

"Yeah, I guess so."

"I don't suppose anyone's up for breakfast," Cormac said.

"Are you joking?" I said. He smiled. My God, he was joking.

"You two go inside. I'll take care of this."

"Sure you don't need help?" Ben said.

"I'm sure."

Ben hesitated, like he needed convincing. I pulled his arm, guided him inside. He said, "Does this sort of thing happen to you a lot?"

It was starting to seem like it. "I don't know."

"Is it because you're a werewolf or because you're you?"

Now that was an excellent question. I didn't really want to know the answer.

When my phone rang later that day, I almost screamed, because the noise was like claws on a chalkboard. Mom's call.

Cormac hadn't come back yet from taking care of the mess outside. Ben had gone back to bed. I didn't know if he was sleeping.

I curled up on the sofa. "Hi, Mom."

"Hi, Kitty. Are you okay? You sound a little off."

A little off. Ha. "I'm about the same as the last time we talked. Things could be better, but I'm hanging in there." Hanging. I shouldn't have said that. Didn't want to hear about anything having to do with hanging.

"What's wrong? I wish there was something I could do to help. You'll let me know if there's anything I can do—"

"Thanks, Mom. I can't really think of anything. Unless you know something about blood magic?"

She thought for a couple of beats, and I couldn't guess what kind of expression she had. "No, I really don't."

"That's okay."

"Kitty, tell me the truth, are you all right?"

My eyes teared up. I would *not* start crying at Mom. If I started I wouldn't stop, and then she'd really worry. And she was right to worry, I supposed. I took a deep breath and kept it together.

"I will be." Somehow . . . "Things are kind of a mess, but I'm working through it."

"You're *sure* there isn't anything I can do?"

"I'm sure."

"Are your friends still with you? Are they helping?"

"Yeah, they are." In fact, if Cormac hadn't been here to take care of the dog thing, I might very well have run screaming and never come back.

"Good. I'm glad. You know I worry about you."

"I know, Mom. I appreciate it, I really do." And I did. It was good to have people looking out for you.

"Well . . . please call me if you need anything, if there's anything I can do. And don't be afraid to come home if you need to. There's no shame in that."

"Thanks, Mom." Couldn't think of anything else to say. Just . . . thanks.

chapter 8

Then came the day.

According to the *Farmer's Almanac,* the full moon in January was known as the Wolf Moon. This was the time of year, the deepest part of winter, when people would huddle together in their homes, build up their fires against the cold, listen to the howling of hungry wolves outside, and pray that they were safe. The cold seeped into people's souls as well as their bodies, and their fears multiplied. Summer and safety seemed farthest away.

Maybe being cursed was really only a state of mind.

I decided that I wasn't going to let Ben die. If I had to tie him up with silver to keep him from hurting himself, I'd do it. If tomorrow came and he still wanted Cormac to kill him, I'd stop him. Somehow, I'd stop Cormac. Hide his guns, fight him, something.

Maybe I could knock Cormac out in a hand-to-hand fight—I was stronger than I looked, and maybe he'd forget that. If Cormac had a gun, though, I'd probably die. At least then they'd know how strongly I felt about the issue.

But I was getting ahead of myself. I had to get through today before I could worry about tomorrow.

I woke up at dawn—still on the sofa—but lay there for a long time, curled up and wishing it were all already over. Wolf knew what day it was; a coiling, wriggling feeling made itself known in my gut, and it would get stronger and stronger until nightfall, when it would turn to knives and claws, the creature trying to rip its way out of the weak human shell, until finally it burst forth and forced the Change. In the bedroom, Ben was feeling this for the first time. He wouldn't know what to do with it. He'd need help coping.

I'd meant to check on him, but he emerged first and went to the kitchen, where Cormac was already sitting. I wasn't sure Cormac

502 *Long-Time Listener, First-Time Werewolf*

had ever gone to bed. I stayed very still to try to hear what they said, but the cabin remained quiet.

Finally, I sat up and looked into the kitchen.

Ben sat on one chair, leaning forward to rest his elbows on his knees, and Cormac sat on the other chair, facing him across the table, arms crossed. They might have been like that for hours, staring at each other.

They'd been best friends since they were kids and now they were wondering if this was their last day together. Had Ben told Cormac about the monster waking up inside him?

I had to break this up. I marched into the kitchen and started making noise, pulling out pots and slamming cabinet doors.

"Who wants eggs?" I forced a Mrs. Cleaver smile, but my tone sounded more strained than cheerful.

They didn't even turn, didn't even flinch. At least it would all be over, after tonight. One way or another.

I cooked bacon and eggs, way more than I needed to, but it distracted me. This was going to be a long, long day.

I didn't notice when the anxiety-laden tableau between Ben and Cormac broke. I heard a noise, and turned to see Cormac getting up, going over to put a fresh log in the stove. Ben bowed his head and stared at the floor.

"Food's ready."

Cormac wandered back to the kitchen table and accepted a plate. The eggs had come out scrambled rather than over easy. I didn't much care. I wanted one of them to *say* something.

He smiled a thin, strained thanks. That was all.

"Ben?" Carefully, I prompted him.

He shook his head. "I can't eat. I hardly ate yesterday and I still feel like I'm going to throw up."

"Yeah. It's usually like that. You get used to it."

He glared at me, his lips almost curling into a snarl. "How? How do you *get used* to this?"

"You just do," I snapped back at him.

He started tapping his foot, a rapid, nervous patter.

So that was breakfast.

I don't know how I managed it, but I was thinking ahead today. I grabbed a change of clothes. I wanted to set up a den for tonight, a place to wake up in the morning.

I paused next to Ben, still camped on the kitchen chair, tense as a wire and frowning.

"I'm going to take a walk. You want to come with me?" I asked softly.

"Is that an order?" He spat the words. He was already in pain. He was already having to hold it in. I'd forgotten what it was like when it was all new; I'd had four years of practice holding it in, learning to ignore it. Getting used to it.

I wanted to grab his collar and shake him—growl at him. I grit my teeth and held my temper. "No. I just thought you might like to take a walk. Do you have a change of clothes I could take? Sweatpants and a T-shirt or something."

He looked at me, eyes narrowed, as he considered this—and then realized what I was really going to do on my walk. He grimaced, like he was holding back a scream, or a sob. I had a sudden urge to hug him, but I didn't. If I even tried to touch him, he might hit the ceiling, he was so tightly wound. That was what I'd have done.

Then, without a word he pulled out a duffel bag from next to the sofa, rummaged in it for a moment, and found the clothes.

I was at the front door when Cormac said, "If you're looking for company—"

"Actually, no offense, but I don't want you to know where I'm going. I don't want to wake up tomorrow morning staring down one of your guns."

"You think I'd shoot you in your sleep? Either one of you?" he said angrily. Clearly, I'd offended him.

I wanted to scream. I looked away. "I don't know. I just don't know."

"If I really wanted to do that, I'd track you. You know I could."

I left.

I was torn between wanting to hurry back in case Ben decided to do something rash while I was gone, and taking my time to avoid the situation at the house. I found my usual den and stashed the stuff. Then I sat there for a long time, tucked in the hollow, reveling in the peaceful scent of it. It smelled like me, like fur and warmth, and it felt safe. I wondered what it would feel like with two people in it.

Then I was ashamed to realize I was looking forward to finding out. I was looking forward to having a friend along for the run tonight.

God, I'd be lucky if either Ben or Cormac were still friends after tonight. I laced my fingers in my hair and made fists, as if trying to pull the craziness out of my head. Ben was going through hell; I was not going to look on it as a good thing.

I must have stayed there an hour before I decided to wander back to the house. I dreaded what I'd find when I got there. So help me God if Cormac was cleaning his guns—

He wasn't. He was in the kitchen reading my copy of *Walden*.

I must have stood there staring at him, because he glanced up and said, "What are you looking at?"

I shrugged. "I guess I'd halfway decided you didn't know how to read."

Ben, stretched out on the sofa pretending to sleep, snorted a chuckle.

Ah, the boy retained a sense of humor. Maybe there was hope.

"How are you doing?" I said to him, gently.

"Don't patronize me."

"I'm not—" But what I'd meant and what it sounded like to him could certainly be two different things. I wanted to kick the sofa, knock him out of it. "You're making this way more difficult than it needs to be."

He sat up suddenly; I thought he was going to lunge at me. I even took a step back.

He almost shouted. "You know how to make it easy? You want to tell me how to make it easier? 'Cause I'd sure love to hear about it. You keep talking about getting used to it, so if you know any tricks, now would be a great time to share!"

We glared at each other, eye to eye. My Wolf thought he was going to start a fight right here and wanted to growl. I closed my eyes and took a deep breath, to keep her in check. Let the human side deal with this. I just had to tell him to calm down. Had to be patronizing again.

Cormac interrupted. "Maybe I oughta shoot you both, put you both out of your misery."

Why did that make me want to laugh? Hysterical, psychotic laughter, yes. But still. If it wasn't so serious, it would have been funny.

I was looking at Ben when I said, "Who says we're miserable?"

Something sparked. He thought it was funny, too. At least part of him thought part of it was funny. He looked away, but not before I saw the smile flicker on his lips and disappear.

I pulled the chair from the desk and sat. I was in front of my laptop, not facing him. I'd planned on pretending I was working.

"Broccoli," I said after a moment. He looked at me. "I think about broccoli. And Bach. I think about things that are as far away from the Wolf as I can. Anything that keeps me human and makes the Wolf go away."

"Does it actually work?"

"Usually. Sometimes. You ought to make Cormac give you the book. To distract yourself."

"Don't tell me that's the only book you have in the house."

I huffed. "What kind of English major do you take me for?"

I dug through the box of books and CDs I'd brought and set him up with a copy of Jack London. Which probably wasn't the best choice, but oh well. The philistine had scoffed at Virginia Woolf. Maybe he'd thought I was trying to be funny.

I managed to write something that afternoon. I wasn't sure how coherent it was. I didn't have the patience to read back over it. Time enough for that tomorrow.

I wrote for so long that I didn't notice when darkness fell outside.

"Kitty." The word came out sharp and filled with pain.

Ben gripped the arm of the sofa; the fabric had started to rip under his hand. His fingers were growing claws. He was staring at his hands like they were alien to him.

I rushed over and knelt before him. I put my hands on his cheeks and turned his face, made him look away from the scene of horror to look at me instead. His eyes grew wide, filled with shock.

He said with a kind of rough laugh, "It really hurts."

"I know, I know." I hushed him, brushing his hair back from his face, which was starting to drip with sweat. "Ben, do you trust me? Please say you trust me."

He nodded. He squeezed his eyes shut and nodded. "I trust you."

"I'll take care of you," I said. "I'm not going to leave you. Okay? You'll be all right. Just get through this and you'll be all right. We're going to go outside now, okay?"

He slipped forward off the couch to fall into my arms, pressing his face to my shoulder and groaning. For a moment, I worried that he'd try to hold me with those hands turning into claws, but no, he'd pulled his arms in close and had gone almost fetal. Tears slipped from my eyes, stinging my cheeks. I hated this. I hated seeing him like this.

"What can I do?" Cormac stood by, hands clenched into fists, watching us with an expression I'd never seen on him before. Helplessness, maybe?

"Stay out of the way," I said. "Stay inside and lock the door."

"Cormac—" Ben's voice wasn't his own anymore. His jaw was clenched, his breath coming in gasps, and his words were thick. "Watch, I want you to see. Kitty, he has to watch."

I helped him stand, putting my arm around his back and hauling up. "Ben, I need you to walk outside with me. Stand up."

Somehow, he lurched to his feet, leaning hard against me.

Cormac started toward us. "Let me help—"

"No!" I said harshly. Growling, even. "He's got claws, he might scratch you. Just get out of the way."

Cormac stepped aside and opened the door for us.

Outside, the forest was silver and filled with crisp, deep shadows. Full moon night, bright and beckoning. The cold air sent a charge through my body.

I could feel Ben's body rippling under my arm, like slimy things moved under the skin. It would have been nausea-inducing, if I hadn't felt this happen to my own body. He was locked up with the pain; I half dragged him off the porch to the clearing in front of the cabin. We weren't going to get any farther than that. I let him drop to the ground, where he curled up on his side. Thick stubble covered his arms.

I took his moment of immobility to unfasten the button and zipper of his jeans. It took too long; my hands were shaking. But I had to get his clothes off before they tangled him up. That would only add to the pain and confusion. Taking both waistbands—jeans and underwear—at once, I pulled down as far as I could, then grabbed the hem of his T-shirt and pulled up, forcing it over his head.

"Come on, Ben, help me out here," I muttered. My own Wolf was bucking inside me—*It's time, it's time!*—she had a pack now, and we were all supposed to Change together to go running. I locked her away, clamped down on the writhing beast, and ignored it. I had to get Ben through this. His whole body was covered in fuzz—I could almost see the fur growing.

He groaned again, through grinding teeth and clenched jaw. He was doing his damnedest not to scream. I helped him straighten his arms to get the shirt off.

Once again, I took his face in my hands. The bones were stretching under my touch.

"Ben, don't fight it. I know you want to, but you can't stop it, and the more you fight it the worse it is. Look at me!" He'd squeezed his eyes shut, but they snapped open again and his gaze locked on mine. His eyes were amber. "Let it go. You have to let it go."

"It" was humanity. He had to let go of the body he'd had his whole life. It wasn't easy. It was all he'd ever known. And it was slipping away as sure as the sky turned above us and the full moon rose.

Finally, the scream that had been growing in him burst loose. The full-lunged note of agony echoed around us and into the sky. When the breath left him, he sounded a whine—a wolf's whine. He broke away from me and fell forward, hugging his belly, chest heaving with every gasp.

I stayed with him, got up behind him, hugged him from behind, my cheek pressed to his fur-covered back, and held him as tightly as I could so he would know I was here. He had to know he wasn't alone. My best friend T.J. had held me like this, my first time. The fear might have driven me crazy, otherwise.

He Changed.

His back arced with a powerful seizure, but I held on. Then his bones slipped, stretched, melted, re-formed. It happened slowly. Maybe it always did, the first time. I couldn't say I really remembered. I remembered the wide sweep of events and emotion from when it happened to me, not the details like this. It seemed to take forever, and I was too frightened to cry. What if he didn't come back together again?

Then the movement stopped, the groaning stopped. I was lying on the ground, my arms around a large, sleek wolf, who was stretched out and gasping for breath, whining with every heave of his chest as if he were dying. But he wasn't, only exhausted. I ran my fingers through his thick, luxurious fur. He was dark gray, flecked with a rust color that ran to cream on his nose and belly. Large ears lay flat against his head, and he had a long, thick snout. He was damp with sweat—human sweat matted into lupine fur.

I brushed my face along his neck and whispered by his ear, "You're all right, you're going to be fine. Just rest now. Just rest." Meaningless comforts, spoken through tears. He flicked his ears at the sound, shifted his head, looked at me. I swore I saw Ben in those eyes, looking at me as if saying, *Are you serious? You call this all right?*

I almost laughed, but the sound choked in my throat and came out as a whimper. He licked my chin—a wolfish gesture that said, *I won't make trouble, I trust you, I'm in your hands.*

Now, finally, it was time to join him. I could feel Wolf burning along every nerve. I pulled off my T-shirt.

"Kitty."

Startled, I looked behind me. Cormac leaned on the porch railing, backlit by the still open front door. He'd watched the whole thing. He saw what Ben was, now.

I couldn't see him well enough to read his expression, to guess what he was thinking. Not sure I wanted to.

"Look after him," Cormac said.

I answered him, my voice rough, thick with tears and failing. "I will. I promise. Now go inside and lock the door."

He went. Closed the door. Ben's wolf and I were left in shining moonlight. Quickly now, I peeled off my sweatpants. Let it come quickly, flowing like water, slipping from one form to the other. I kept an eye on Ben—he raised his wolf's head and watched me—until my vision blurred and I had to shut my eyes—

Opens her eyes to the moonlit world.

The scent of another fills her first breath. She recognizes him, knows him—she's claimed him as pack, which makes them family, and they'll run together, free this night.

He lies stretched out, unmoving, and gives a faint whine. He's weak, he's scared. She bows, stretches, yips at him—she has to show him that he's free, that this is good. Still he won't move, so she nips at him, snapping at his hind legs and haunches, telling him to get up, he has to get up. He flinches, then finally lurches to his feet, to get away from her teeth. He looks back at her, ears flat and tail between his legs.

He's just a pup, brand-new, and she'll have to teach him everything.

Bumping his flank with her shoulder, she urges him on, gets him to walk. His steps are hesitant—he's never walked on four legs before, he starts slowly. She runs ahead, circles back, bumps him again. As they pace into the woods of her territory, his steps become more sure. He starts to trot, his head low, his tail drooping. She can't contain her joy—she could run circles around him all night. She tries to get him to chase her. She tries to chase him, but he only looks at her in confusion. She has to teach him how to play, bowing and yipping—life isn't all about food and territory.

She shows him how to run. And how to hunt. She kills a rabbit and shares it with him, shows him the taste of blood. The eating comes naturally. She doesn't have to teach him how to devour the flesh and break the bones with his jaws. He does so eagerly, then licks the blood that has smeared on her muzzle.

He'll kill the next one, on another night.

They run, and she shows him the shape of their territory. He tires quickly though—his first night on four legs, she understands. She leads him home, to the place where they can bed down, curl up together, tails tucked close, and bury their noses in each other's fur so they fall asleep with the smell of pack and safety in their minds.

She hasn't felt so safe in a long, long time. She'll keep her pack-mate close, to preserve the safety. He is hers, and she'll look after him forever.

chapter 9

The thing was, Ben was part of my pack before this ever happened to him.

I might have been alone, a werewolf on my own, but I had people I could call. People who would help me if I showed up on their doorstep in the middle of the night. Ben was near the top of that list. Yes, he was my lawyer and I sort of paid him to be there for me. But he'd handled the supernatural craziness in my life without blinking, and as far as I was concerned that went above and beyond the call of duty. He could have dumped me as a client anytime he wanted, and he didn't. I could count on him, and that made him pack.

I didn't sleep well, waking before dawn. I was nervous—I wanted to make sure I woke up before Ben did. I had to look after him.

As the sun rose, I watched him. I curled on my side, pillowing my head on my bent arm, just a breath away from him—close enough to touch. Even in sleep, his face was lined, tense with worry. He'd had an exhausting night; the evidence of it remained etched in his expression. Shifted back to human, he lay on his back, one arm resting on his stomach, the other crooked up, the hand curled by his shoulder. One of his legs was bent, the foot tucked under the opposite knee.

His build was average. He didn't work out, but he wasn't soft; it was like he'd been thin as a wire when he was a kid, and was only just now filling out to a normal size. He had a stripe of hair running down his sternum. The hair on his head, still damp with sweat, stuck out, mussed and wild. I held back an urge to brush my fingers through it, smoothing it back. I didn't want to startle him.

The bite wounds on his arm and shoulder were completely healed, as if they'd never existed.

Almost, I dozed back to sleep myself, waiting for him to come around. Then, his slow, steady breathing changed. His lungs filled deep, like a bellows. His eyes flashed open, and his whole body jerked, as if every muscle flinched at once.

He gasped, a cutoff sound of terror, and tried to get up, tried to crawl back as if he could escape whatever it was that had scared him. His limbs gave out, and he didn't go anywhere.

I lunged over and grabbed his shoulders, pushing him to the ground. I had to lean my whole weight on him—that average build was powerful.

"Ben! Quiet, you're okay, you're okay, Ben. Please calm down."

He stilled quickly enough, but I kept hushing him until he lay flat again, his eyes closed, panting for breath. I knelt by him, keeping my hands on his chest, keeping him quiet, and watching his face for any reaction.

After a moment his breathing slowed. He brought a hand to his face, covered his eyes, then dragged it across his forehead. "I remember," he said in a tired, sticky voice. "I remember the smells. Running. Blood—" His voice strained, cracked.

"Shh." I lay next to him so I could bring my face close to his, brush his hair back, breathe in his scent, let him smell me, let him know that smell meant safety. "We're safe, Ben. It's okay."

"Kitty—" He said my name with a gasp of desperation, then clung to me, gripping my arm and shoulder, kneading the skin and muscle painfully. I bore it, hugging him back as well as I could. He was so warm in the freezing winter air; holding each other warmed us.

I kissed the hairline by his ear and said, "You're back. Two arms, two legs, human skin. You're back. You feel it?"

He nodded, which gave me hope because it meant he was listening.

"Wolf is gone, it's not going to come back for another month. You get to be yourself until then. It's okay, it's okay." I kept repeating it.

He relaxed. I could feel the tension leave him under my touch. He eased back against the ground instead of holding himself rigid from it. His death grip on me lessened until it was simple holding, and it was okay if he didn't let go. I didn't want him to. I didn't want him to withdraw, lock himself inside himself where I couldn't talk to him.

"Two arms, two legs," he said finally, wearily. Then he smoothed back my sweaty and tangled hair, the way I'd been brushing his. "Opposable thumbs."

I giggled, bowing my face to his shoulder. He was back.

"How do you feel?" I asked. He kept his arms around me, like he was still clinging for safety, and I snuggled into his embrace. Wolves touched for comfort. We both needed it.

After a long moment he said, "Strange. Broken. But coming back together. Like I can feel the pieces closing up." I tilted my head, trying to look at him. I saw his jaw, the slope of cheek, half an eye. "But I remember . . . it felt good. It felt free. Didn't it?" His face shifted into a wince. "I wasn't expecting that."

"Yeah," I said, and kissed his closest body part, his shoulder. Then I propped myself on my elbow, touched his face, and turned it to me, making him look at me. I held his gaze. "You're doing just fine, Ben. You believe me?" *You're going to live. You're not going to make Cormac shoot you.*

He nodded, and I kissed his forehead. I was trying to make him feel safe, to make him feel wanted, so he wouldn't leave.

"You're doing just fine," I repeated softly.

"That's because I have a determined teacher," he said, giving me a thin smile.

I kissed his lips. They were right there. It seemed so natural. His smile fell—then he kissed me back. And again, long enough this time that I lost my breath. Then we both froze for a moment.

My skin flushed, my whole body growing warm—*it* knew what it wanted to do, anyway. I stole a glance down Ben's torso—and yes, *his* body knew what it wanted to do, too.

Ben's hazel-colored eyes—green, mud, gold, all mixed together—flickered, trying to hold my gaze again. I looked away, human enough to be chagrined.

I said, "I should have mentioned, the lycanthropy thing, it sort of throws gasoline on the libido. You know—whoosh, fire, out of control."

He kept staring at me, until I couldn't keep looking away.

He said, with an unreadable curl on his lips, "I'm sure it has nothing to do with the fact that I'm lying here naked with a beautiful woman, who is also naked."

Blink. Double blink. My heart may have even stopped for a moment. "Did you just call me beautiful?"

He touched my cheek, my neck, sending an electric rush along my skin, then buried his hand in my hair. "Yeah."

That was it. I was gone.

I moved, sliding one leg over his stomach, slipping on top of him until I straddled him. I kept close, my chest against his, my breath on his cheek. His arms held me tight, hands sliding down my back, clenching, and we kissed, deeply, tasting each other, sharing our heat. We touched, nuzzled; I moved my lips along his jaw, to his ear. My eyes were closed, my mind gone. Mostly gone.

"I hadn't planned on this, honest," I murmured.

He said, his voice thick with sarcasm, "Gee, thanks."

"That's not what I meant," I said, smiling. "I feel like I'm taking advantage of you."

He made what sounded to my ears like a groan of contentment. "You just want me to like being a werewolf. That's what this is about."

I pulled away, just for a moment. "You don't have to like it. You just have to survive it."

His gaze focused, met mine. "All right."

I kissed him, and kissed, shivering to try to get closer to him— we already lay skin to skin along the length of our bodies. One of his hands clasped the back of my neck, the other worked its way to my backside, locking me close to him. His touch burned in the cold winter air.

He managed one more bit of commentary, his voice low and rough, "Kitty, just so you know, you can take advantage of me anytime you want."

So I did.

He lay curled in my arms, and I reveled in the scent of him— sweaty, warm, musky. All my mornings alone I had woken anxious and discontented. Now, here with him—I had a pack again, and all felt right with the world.

It was the lycanthropy, I told myself. I never would have slept with Ben if it hadn't been for the lycanthropy. Not that I regretted it.

But still.

The sun was almost above the trees. However much I wanted to stay here all day, we had to go back. Back to the world.

Ben was the one who said, "I guess we ought to get back before Cormac comes looking for us."

The bounty hunter would do it, too. Track us down. I wasn't entirely confident what he would do when he found us. I dug out the clothes I'd stashed and split them between us. We dressed, helped each other to our feet, and set off for the cabin.

In my pack back in Denver, the alpha male, Carl, had made

sleeping around a habit. If lycanthropy was to the libido what gasoline was to fire, Carl took full advantage of it. Shape-shifting was foreplay to him, and as head of the pack he had his own harem. At his call, every one of us would roll over on our backs, showing him our bellies like good submissive wolves. My Wolf had loved it: the attention, the affection, the sex. The abuse—verbal and occasionally otherwise—that he heaped along with the attention hardly mattered. At least until I couldn't take it anymore. Carl was still in Denver. That was why I couldn't go back.

I didn't want to be like that. If I had to be the alpha of our little pack of two, I didn't want to be that kind of alpha. I didn't want to screw around just because I could.

Or had it happened because I liked him? I did like him. But would I have ever slept with him, if we hadn't been naked in the woods and smelling like wolves? Would it have ever even been an issue?

Had that been Ben holding me tightly and kissing me eagerly, or his wolf?

Did it even matter?

These things were so much clearer to the Wolf side: You like him? He's naked? He's interested? Then go for it! Only the human side was worried about people's feelings getting hurt.

He walked a couple steps behind me—that submissive wolf thing again. His head was bent, and he looked tired, with shadows under his eyes. But he didn't seem angry, frightened, tense, or any of the other things I might have expected to see in a newly minted werewolf. He caught me watching him, and I smiled, trying to be encouraging. He smiled back.

"What are you going to tell Cormac?"

"Don't shoot?" He winced and shook his head. "You were right, I was wrong? I don't know. I'm confused. I don't want to die. I never did. You know that, right?"

I slowed my steps until we were walking side by side. A couple of barefooted nature freaks out for a morning stroll in the dead of winter. I wasn't cold; I could still feel his arms around me. "You were pretty determined there for a while."

"I was scared," he said. After a moment, he added, "Does it get easier? Less confusing? Less like there's an extra voice in your head telling you what to do?"

I had to shake my head. "No. It just gets confusing in different ways."

Then, almost suddenly, the trees thinned and the clearing in front of the cabin opened before us. The sun was shining full on the porch. Cormac stood there, leaning on the railing. A rifle was propped next to him. Ready and waiting.

I stopped; Ben stopped next to me. My instinct said to run, but Cormac had already seen us. He didn't move, he just looked out at us, waiting for us to do something.

Cormac had had plenty of chances to shoot me dead and hadn't yet. I didn't think he'd start now. I hoped he wouldn't start now. I walked toward the front door like nothing was wrong. Ben followed, slowly, falling behind. Cormac watched him, not me.

"Morning," I said, waving a little as I came within earshot. I tried to sound cheerful, but it came out wary.

"Well?"

Climbing the stairs, I crossed my arms and continued my campaign of strained brightness. "Well, it's a nice day. Lots of sun. Everything's fine."

By then Ben reached the porch stairs. Cormac's glare was challenging, but he wouldn't know that. Ben hesitated—I could almost see him start to wilt, growing defensive.

"Ben?" I said. He shifted his gaze to me, and the confrontation was broken.

"You okay?" Cormac said to him.

After a moment he said, "Yeah. Just fine." He sounded resigned rather than convinced.

"No more talk about shooting you, then."

"No."

I didn't know what Cormac expected. Maybe he'd spent all night working himself up to kill his cousin in cold blood, and now it seemed like he didn't quite believe that Ben had opted out. His expression was neutral, unreadable, as usual.

"What happened?" he said.

Ben bowed his head, hiding a smile. "It's hard to explain."

"You look like you had a pretty good time," Cormac said.

"Maybe I did." Ben stared at him. He actually did look pretty good, considering: tired, but relaxed. Not freaked out, like Cormac might have expected. Ben looked better than he had in days, since Cormac brought him here.

For my part, my face felt like I was blushing fire-engine-red. Yup, human Kitty was back. Wolf never blushed.

Cormac stared, like he could see through Ben, study him with x-ray vision. Cormac was the kind of guy who didn't like being out of control, who didn't like not knowing everything. Ben had traveled somewhere he couldn't go. He wanted to know what had happened to his cousin over the last twelve hours—that was all. But Ben couldn't tell him. He couldn't explain it—I couldn't explain it. That reality was part of the Wolf, inhuman and unspeakable.

Ben slumped under the pressure of his gaze. Shoulders hunched, he went into the cabin and slammed the door. Leaving Cormac and me on the porch.

I wanted to tell Cormac to leave Ben alone. He couldn't possibly understand, no matter how much he stared at Ben. Before I could think of a way to say this to him without him getting pissed off at me, he spoke.

"You were right about him changing his mind. I really wasn't sure he would. But you knew."

Actually, I'd hoped. I let Cormac think otherwise. "I've been through it myself. I knew he'd feel differently."

"You knew he'd like being a werewolf."

"That's not a good way to describe it."

"What happened out there?"

Surely he'd figured it out. Or his imagination had. I didn't know why he wanted me to spell it out for him. "That's not any of your business."

I turned to go inside.

"Kitty—" He grabbed my wrist.

I froze before I hit him. It was only instinct, my pulling back with fingers bent like outstretched claws. He saw it; we stood like that in a tableau. So many unasked questions played in his gaze.

He brought Ben here so I could help him, keep him alive. Not shack up with him. None of us had expected that. And now Cormac actually looked hurt, some pain-filled anguish touching his features. If Cormac had wanted things to happen differently between us, why couldn't he just come out and say it? He'd had his chance. I'd given him plenty of chances. I couldn't go backward.

"Cormac, I'm sorry." I brushed myself out of his grasp and went into the house.

My usual routine after a full moon: I came home, took a shower, and crawled into bed for a couple hours of more comfortable sleep. Then I woke up and had some coffee. No breakfast because I wasn't hungry. Wolf usually had had plenty to eat during the night.

Ben had already started the coffee. The scent filled the house, and I had to admit it smelled wonderful. Soothing, like I could curl up on the sofa and forget about the guys in my house. I didn't want to leave them alone long enough to take a shower. Like I still thought Cormac might draw a bead on Ben with that rifle. Easy to forget that Cormac was the one who'd brought Ben here because he *didn't* want to shoot him.

I was too wired to sleep. I'd already spent the extra time napping back in the woods with Ben. That man had screwed up my entire schedule. Though if I thought about it, what I really wanted to do was crawl back into bed with *him*—

I went to the kitchen and poured myself a cup of coffee. Ben, sitting at the table with his own cup, didn't say anything. Whatever he said, I was sure it would make me snap at him. I didn't want to do that. I gave him what I hoped was a reassuring smile.

Cormac joined us a minute later, after I heard the door to the Jeep open and close. He didn't have the rifle with him, so I assumed he put it away. Good. He sat across from Ben. I leaned back against the counter.

Here we were, back in the kitchen, glaring at tabletops and not saying anything.

I couldn't stand long silences. That probably came from working in radio. "So, kids. Any questions? We all squared away?"

"I don't know that I'd go that far," Ben said, chuckling softly. He shrugged his hands in a gesture of helplessness. "What do I do now? If I'm really going to live with this, what do I do?"

I said, "You're a lawyer. Go back and . . . lawyer. What would you be doing if this hadn't happened?"

"It's not that simple," he said. "It can't possibly be that simple."

He was right, of course.

"You take it one day at a time, Ben. Some days are easier than others. But you just have to work through it."

He scowled. "Don't talk to me like I'm one of the losers on your show."

That stung like a kick in the gut. My callers weren't losers—they were my audience. My *fans*. I wanted to defend them. But yeah, they had problems. A guy like Ben? He didn't have problems. He was a tough guy.

"Then stop acting like a loser," I said.

"That's rich, coming from someone who ran off to the woods with her tail between her legs—"

I took a step toward him, teeth bared in a silent growl, my hands clenched into fists. He flinched back in a sudden panic, jerking the chair off its front legs. We stared at each other for a moment—I dared him to take me. I dared him to say what he was thinking.

He looked down. Then he pulled his hands through his hair and leaned his elbows on the table. "What the hell's happening to me?" he muttered.

I turned away. I knew what was happening to him, but how did I explain it all? A whole new set of body language and emotions— I'd been living with them for years now. I took them for granted.

"Right, you two are even freaking me out," Cormac said, hands raised in a gesture of surrender. He stood. "I'm taking a walk."

"Cormac." Ben reached across the table, stopping him for a moment. The tableau held until Ben took a breath and said, "I'm sorry. I'm sorry for saddling you with this."

The hunter looked away, and his face tensed, pursing into an expression I couldn't read. Some emotion was there, that he was trying desperately to hide.

"No," he said. "I'm the one who got you into this mess. I'm sorry."

As he had so many times before during the past week, he walked out the door. Taking a walk. It was how he coped with the long, awkward silences.

Ben's arm still lay draped across the table, and he sighed, almost bowing his head to its surface. "I knew he was going to do that. I knew he was going to blame himself."

I went to Ben—slowly this time, nonthreateningly. He glanced sideways at me, warily, but didn't flinch. I touched his shoulder, held my hand there. Didn't say anything for once, but I smiled when he leaned into the touch.

Miracle of miracles, Ben listened to me. He went back to work. Borrowed my phone to check his voice mail, used my computer and Internet connection to check his e-mail, replied to a couple of panicked messages from clients. He had his own practice, small enough for one person to run but enough to make a living, fully in keeping with his independent character. Evidently, he'd decided that if he was going to live, he'd better get back to work. Werewolves still had to pay the rent. The human half did, anyway.

We had venison for dinner again. That stuff never got old. Though I was beginning to think I should invest in a grill, so we didn't have to keep sticking them under the broiler. Cormac ate leaning up against the counter, Ben and I sat at the table. The meal felt almost normal. Nobody was staring at anybody, nobody asked to get shot, and Cormac had put his guns away.

We talked about my evil stalker.

"How long's this been going on?" Ben asked.

"About ten days. The first one happened right before you got here," I said. "Okay, so whoever has it in for me knows what I am. Why didn't something happen last night? Why didn't they go after the wolf half?"

"They're scared," Ben said. "You're strongest at the full moon. They're not going to want to confront that."

Cormac said, "He's right. Full moon's the worst night to go after a werewolf. You wait until the morning after. Get 'em while they're sleeping it off." He smiled.

Even Ben shook his head at that one. "You just got a whole hell of a lot creepier."

"Me? I haven't changed a bit." He gave Ben a hard look.

I wasn't going to let that topic go any further than it already had. "They didn't come after me this morning. They were scared enough to stay inside last night, but didn't know to come looking for me this morning."

"They don't know what they're doing." Ben looked to Cormac for confirmation.

The hunter tapped the flat of his steak knife thoughtfully against his opposite hand. "If they'd wanted to kill you all it would take was a sniper sitting up on the road. Deputy Rosco could do it. They're just trying to scare you into leaving."

"So who is 'they'? Or he, or she, or it?" I said.

Ben continued the brainstorming. "Someone who doesn't want to kill you and doesn't know what they're doing."

"Amateurs," Cormac said. "Amateurs practicing some kind of fucked up blood magic. This is going to turn around and bite somebody on the ass."

"Hello?" I raised a hand. "I'm feeling pretty ass-bitten right here."

"But you're still here. Whatever spell it is your fan club thinks they're casting isn't working. You can't work the kind of magic that calls for hanging skinned dogs up in trees without paying some price. They've either got to give up soon, or escalate. I'd hate to see where that could go."

"You have any contacts who might know something about this?" Ben asked.

"I might. I'll make a call." He retrieved his cell phone from his duffel bag and went outside.

All I wanted was for the torture of small animals outside my house to stop, the book to be finished, and Ben to be okay.

I could check on at least one of those. "How are you doing?"
He thought for a moment, then shrugged. "All right, I think. I'm
not feeling much of anything. It's a whole lot better than yesterday,
though."

"Good," I said, inordinately pleased.

Ben and I were washing dishes when Cormac came back in. He
didn't say anything about how his call went, and we didn't ask. If
he didn't tell us, asking him wouldn't get him to talk.

It was strange, how I was getting used to having him around.
Maybe the three of us still had a chance of coming to some sort of
equilibrium. Some arrangement where Ben didn't lose his best
friend, I didn't lose my new wolf pack, and Cormac could hold on
to the only people who anchored him to the world. Or maybe that
was wishful thinking.

Later, I found Ben changing the sheets on the bed. He'd found
the clean set in the closet, and was stripping off the ones he'd
sweated, tossed, and turned on over the last week.

"I thought I'd get it ready for you," he explained as I leaned in
the doorway. "I've kept you out of it long enough."

This was going to be more awkward than I thought. We weren't
wolves tonight, and the lycanthropy wasn't lighting any fires. Any
acknowledged fires, at least.

"Where'll you sleep?" I asked.

Cormac answered, "The sofa. I'll take the floor."

"I can take the floor," Ben said. Cormac was already pulling out
his bedroll and spreading it out by the desk. "We can draw straws."

"Do I get to draw straws?" I said.

"No," they said, in unison.

My, what gentlemen. I smirked.

Ben ended up on the sofa. Cormac was very hard to argue with.
Eventually, the lights went out and the house fell quiet.

I hadn't gotten any sleep the night before. Being in my own bed
again, I should have been out for the count. But I lay there, staring
at the darkened ceiling, wondering why I couldn't sleep. I had too
much on my mind, I decided.

Then the floorboards leading into the bedroom creaked, very
faintly. I propped myself on an elbow. The figure edging inside the
room was in shadow, a silhouette only. I took a breath through my
nose, smelling—

It was Ben.

"I can't sleep," he whispered. He stepped toward the bed,
slouching a little—sheepish, if I didn't know him better. "I keep

fidgeting. It feels . . . weird. Being alone. I was wondering: could I . . . I mean with you—" He gestured toward the bed, shoulders tensed, and looked away.

He was a new wolf. A pup. A kid having nightmares. I'd been the same way.

I pushed back the covers and scooted to one side of the bed.

Letting out a sigh, he climbed in beside me, curling up on his side as I pulled the covers over us both. I put my arms around him, he settled close, and that was all. In moments, he was asleep, his chest rising and falling regularly. He was exhausted, but he'd needed to feel safe before he could sleep.

God help anybody who felt safer with me looking after him. I could barely take care of myself. But what else could I do? I held him and settled in to sleep. Tried not to worry.

As I faded, sinking into a half-asleep state, I glimpsed another shadow at the doorway. A figure looked in briefly, then moved away. Then I heard the front door open and close, and faintly, like a buzzing in a distant dream, the Jeep's engine started up, and tires crunched on the gravel drive.

He's gone, my dream self thought, and there wasn't anything I could do about it.

chapter **10**

He's gone," Ben said, leaning over the kitchen sink and looking out the window to the clearing where Cormac's Jeep was no longer parked.

Cormac had cleared out his bedroll, his duffel bag, his guns. After sharing the space with him for a week, the house seemed empty without him and his things. He'd packed everything up and driven off in the middle of the night. It was how he often made his exits.

This time, though, the bastard had left me to figure out this curse business on my own. I'd been counting on his help.

"Why?" Ben said.

"You know him better than I do. You know what he's like." I sat at the table, feet up on the seat of my chair, hugging my knees. "Did he have someplace he needed to be? Maybe he's following up on his contact, about the blood magic."

Ben shook his head. "Three's a crowd. That's what he was thinking. That's why he left."

"But . . ." And I couldn't think of anything more to say. If Cormac had felt that way, he should have said something. He should have told me. Why couldn't he ever just come out and say it? "Should we go after him? Should we call him?" I had his number stored on my cell phone. I'd entered it in when I first got the phone, a short time after I met him. He was the kind of person you could call in an emergency.

Again, Ben shook his head. "If he'd wanted us to contact him, he'd have left a note."

"It's not a matter of what he wants, it's a matter of what's good for him. He's not going to go do something crazy to get himself hurt, is he?"

Ben arched a brow wryly. "Any more so than he usually does?"

He had a point.

"What's the plan now?" I said. "Cormac left us with that curse. I'd just as soon let the curse win and get out of here."

Ben continued looking out into the forest. He seemed peaceful, if sad. The calm was holding. "One more day. Give me one more day to pull myself together. I don't think I'm ready for civilization yet."

I couldn't argue with that. I'd give him all the time I could. "You got it."

So. That started our first day without Cormac.

I worked at the computer. I'd tried to pull off a modern-day *Walden,* but I'd failed to live up to Thoreau's ideals. The real problem was that I didn't have a pond. It was Walden *Pond.* I needed a large body of water for effective contemplation.

But really, what would Thoreau have done if a friend had shown up with a werewolf bite and begged for his help? Which made me wonder if maybe there was a more sinister reason Thoreau went off to live by himself in the woods, and he dressed the whole experience up in all this rhetoric about simple living to cover it up. Werewolves were not exactly part of the accepted canon of American literature. What *would* Thoreau have done?

A WWTD? bumper sticker would take too much explaining. And really, he'd have probably lectured the poor guy about how his dissolute lifestyle had gotten him into the situation.

I wasn't Thoreau. Wasn't ever going to be Thoreau. Screw it. I wrote pages about the glories of mass consumerism offered by the height of modern civilization. All the reasons *not* to run off to the woods and deny yourself a few basic indulgences in life.

That night, without a word spoken about it, Ben and I slipped into bed together and snuggled under the covers for warmth. No making out, no sex, not so much as a kiss, and that was fine. We were pack, and we needed to be together.

We should have left town that day.

Something happened, woke me up. I could barely feel it as it pressed against the air, making its own little wind with its passage. A predator, stalking *me.*

No. This was my place, my territory. I didn't have to take this. I wasn't going to run and let it win. Just *no.*

I slipped out of bed and stomped out to the porch, in the dark of night, no visible moon or stars or anything.

"Kitty?" Ben said, from the bedroom.

Leaning on the railing, I smelled the air. Trees, hills, and *some-*

thing. Something wrong. Couldn't see anything in the forest, but it was here. Whatever hated me was here.

"Come out!" I screamed. I ran into the clearing, turned around, searched, and still didn't see anything. "I want to see you! Let me see you, you coward!"

This was stupid. Whoever laid that curse on this place wasn't going to come out in the open. If they'd wanted to face me, they'd never have snuck around gutting rabbits on my porch in the first place. All I'd do with my screaming and thrashing around was chase it off.

But that feeling was still there. That weight, that hint that something wasn't just watching me. It had trapped me. It had marked my territory as its own, and was now smothering me rather than letting me run.

Maybe this wasn't the curse. Maybe this was something else. Cormac said it might escalate, but escalate to what?

Something like eyes glowed, making a shape in the darkness.

My imagination. There wasn't really anything out there. But I went into the trees, stepping lightly. Think of wolf paws, pads barely touching earth, moving easily as air. My stride grew longer. I could jog like this for hours without losing my breath.

"Kitty!" Ben pounded down the porch steps, but I didn't turn around. If something was out there, if this thing was after me, I'd find it.

There, movement. That same shadow, large but low to the ground. Lurking. My pulse sped up, beating hot. This was what I should have been doing all along, turning the tables, hunting the hunter. Counterintuitively, I slowed, waiting to see what it would do, giving it a chance to leap this way or that. Once it moved, all I had to do was pounce and pin it with my claws.

Two red eyes, glaring, caught me. The gaze fixed on me, and I couldn't move.

I had good eyesight—a wolf's eyes. But I couldn't make out the form the eyes belonged to. Even when it moved closer, I only saw shadow. I heard a low noise, like a growl, so low it shook the ground under me.

All my instincts screamed for me to run. Get out. This wasn't right, this wasn't real. But I couldn't move.

Something grabbed my arm and yanked me from behind. I stayed on my feet, but I might as well have flipped head over heels, the way my vision swam and the world shifted.

"Kitty!"

My senses started working again, and I smelled friend. Pack. Ben.

"Did you see it?" I said, gasping for air, clinging to his arm.

"No, nothing. You ran out of the house like you were in some kind of trance."

And he followed, out of trust, out of loyalty. I pulled myself close to him. I kept looking out, scanning the trees, the spaces between them, looking for red eyes and a shadow. I saw skeletal branches against a sky made indistinct with clouds, earth rising up the hill, and patches of snow.

Both of our breaths fogged in the cold, releasing billowing clouds that quickly faded. Nothing else moved. We might have been the only living things out here. I shivered. Once I stopped running, the cold hit me like a wall, chilling my skin from toe to scalp. I was only wearing sweats and a T-shirt and went barefoot.

Ben blazed with warmth; I wrapped myself up with him. He was smart—he'd grabbed a coat. We stood, holding each other.

"What is it?" he asked. "What did you see?"

"Eyes," I said, my voice shaking. "I saw eyes."

"Something's here? What?"

"I don't know." My voice whined. Worse, I didn't know what would have happened if Ben hadn't come for me. If he hadn't shaken me loose from that thing's gaze. I made it a simple observation. "You came after me."

"I didn't want to be alone."

I hugged him tightly, still shaken, speechless. With my arm around him, I urged him forward, starting back for the cabin. "Let's go."

I'd traveled much farther than I thought. I couldn't have been following the shadow for more than a couple of minutes. But the cabin was over a mile away. I hadn't noticed the time passing. We followed the scent of smoke from the stove back home.

"It had red eyes," I said, but only when I could see the light in the windows.

"Like the thing Cormac saw," he said.

Yeah. Just like it.

That was it. This was war. I didn't need Cormac's help stopping this. I was a clever girl. I'd figure it out.

I hunted for it that day. Searched for tracks, smelled for a scent. I followed the tracks I'd made, the path I'd cut through the woods, ranging out from it on both sides. It had to be there, it had to have left some sign.

None of my enemies here had ever left a trail before. Why should they start now?

I walked for miles and lost track of time. Once again, Ben came for me, calling my name, following my scent, probably, whether he knew he was doing it or not.

When he finally caught up, he said, "Any luck?"

I had to say no, and it didn't make any sense. I should have found something.

He said, "I take it we're not leaving tomorrow."

"No. No, I have to figure this out. I can figure this out. It's not going to beat me." I was still searching the woods, my vision blurring I was staring so hard into the trees. Every one of them might have hidden something.

"It's after noon," Ben said. "At least come back and eat something. I fixed some lunch."

"Let me guess—venison."

He donned his familiar, half-smirking grin. How long had it been since I'd seen it?

"No. Sandwiches. Would you believe Cormac took most of the meat with him?"

Yes. Yes I would. "He uses it for bait, doesn't he?"

"You really want me to answer that?"

"No, I don't."

I worked while we ate, going online to search whatever relevant came to mind: barbed-wire cross, blood curses, animal sacrifice. Red eyes. Red-eyed monsters, to try to filter out all the medical pages and photography advice I got with that search. I found a lot of sites that skirted around the topics. A lot of people out there made jewelry that was supposed to look like barbed wire but wasn't nearly vicious enough to be the real thing. A lot of sites bragged, but few had any kind of authority.

As usual, the people who really knew about this stuff didn't talk about it, and certainly didn't blog about it.

I found one thing, though. A long shot, but an interesting one. The Walsenburg Public Library's electronic card catalog was online. Their three titles on the occult were checked out.

I called them up. A woman answered.

"Hi," I said cheerfully. "I'm interested in a couple of books you have, but the catalog says they're checked out."

"If they've been checked out for more than two weeks I can put a recall on them—"

"No, that's okay. I was actually wondering if you could tell me who checked them out."

Her demeanor instantly chilled. "I'm sorry, I really can't give you that information."

I clearly should have known better than to ask. In retrospect, her answer didn't surprise me. I tried again anyway. "Not even a hint?"

"I'm sorry. Do you want me to try that recall?"

"No, thanks. That's okay." I hung up. I wasn't interested in the books. I wanted to know who in the county was studying the occult. What amateur had maybe gotten a little too good at this sort of thing.

Again, we slept curled up together, looking for basic comfort. Rather, I tried to sleep, but spent more time staring at the ceiling, waiting for that moment of pressure, of fear, the sure knowledge that something unknown and terrifying was out there stalking me. The feeling had changed from when it was dead rabbits on my porch. This new force didn't just want me to leave—it wanted me dead. It made me think there was nothing I could do but freeze and wait for it to strike me.

Nothing had been slaughtered on my porch in days. The barbed-wire crosses had disappeared. Did that mean the curse was gone, or had it turned into something else?

I waited, but nothing happened that night. A breeze whispered through winter pines, and that was all. I thought I was going to break from listening, and waiting.

The next morning, Ben chopped wood for the stove. He was getting his strength back, looking for things to do. Normal, closer to normal. I watched him out the window, from my desk. He knew how to use an ax, swinging smoothly and easily, quickly splitting logs and building up the pile next to the porch. For some reason this surprised me, like I assumed that a lawyer couldn't also know anything about manual labor. It occurred to me that I knew as little about Ben's background as I knew about Cormac's. Ben had definitely spent some time in his past splitting logs.

He paused often to look around, turn his nose to the air, presumably smelling the whole range of scents he'd never known before. It took time sorting them out.

At one point he stopped and tensed. I could actually see his shoulders bunch up. He stared toward the road. Then he set the ax by the woodpile and backed toward the front door.

I went to meet him, my own nerves quivering. That thing that was hunting us . . .

"Someone's coming," he said, just as the sheriff's car came over the dirt road and into the clearing. Side by side, we watched the car creep to a stop.

Ben's whole body seemed to tremble with anxiety. He stared at Sheriff Marks getting out of the car.

I touched his arm. "Calm down."

Ben winced, tilting his head with a confused expression. "Why do I feel like growling at him?"

I smiled and patted him on the shoulder. "He's invading our territory. And he doesn't smell like a real nice person, either. Just try to act normal."

He shook his head. "This is crazy."

"How you doing, Sheriff Marks?" I called out nicely.

"Not so good, Ms. Norville. I've got a problem."

My stomach turned over. Why was the first thought that popped into my head, *What has Cormac done?*

"Sorry to hear that. Can I help?"

"I hope so." He stopped at the base of the porch and took a good, slow look at Ben. I could almost see his little mind ticking off the points on a formal police description: hair, height, build, race, and general suspiciousness. Ben crossed his arms and stared back. Finally Marks said, "Who's this?"

"This is Ben. He's a friend."

Marks smirked. "Another one? How many friends you shacking up with out here?"

Right, now I wanted to growl at him. "You said there was something I could help you with?"

Marks jerked his thumb over his shoulder to point at the car. "You mind taking a little ride with me?"

I did mind. I minded a lot. "Why? I'm not being arrested—"

"Oh, no," Marks said. "Not yet."

"How about I follow you in my car?" I said, admiring how steady my voice sounded. Something was very wrong. It was Cormac. It had to be Cormac. I wasn't going to say the name until Marks did, though.

But Marks was staring hard at me. Like it was me he was after.

He had no idea what his glare was doing to Wolf. I had to look away. That fight or flight thing was kicking at me.

"I don't know. I'd hate for you to run off," Marks said.

What in God's name had happened? "I'm not going to run off. All my stuff is here. And why are you worried about me running off?"

"You'll see. Let's get going. Take your car, but I'm keeping an eye on you."

"Of course." I went to find my keys and backpack.

"Can I come with you?" Ben said.

I relaxed a little. It would be good to have a friend at my back.

"Sure. You're my lawyer. I have this creepy feeling I might need my lawyer."

I drove behind Marks's car as close as I could without actually tailgating, so that I wouldn't give him the slightest idea that I was "running off." I watched him through his rear window as he checked his rearview mirror every five seconds.

Ben frowned. "It's a werewolf thing. Something happened, and he thinks a werewolf did it."

"Yeah. Maybe he's just trying to get back at me for all those times I called him about the dead rabbits. Maybe this is some practical joke. I'll end up on the first werewolf reality TV show. Wouldn't that be a hoot?" I muttered.

After a few miles we turned off the highway onto a wide dirt road, then after several more miles made another turn onto a narrow dirt road, then onto a driveway. A carved wood sign posted in front of a barbed-wire fence announced the Baker Ranch. A quarter of a mile along, Marks pulled off onto the verge behind a pickup truck, and I pulled in behind him. Dry, yellowed grass cracked under the tires.

An older man wearing a denim jacket, jeans, and cowboy boots leaned against a weathered fence post. Marks went to him, and they shook hands. The man looked over at us, still in the car. I expected to see the determined suspicion in him that I saw on Marks's face. But he looked at us with curiosity.

I got out of the car and went to join them. Ben followed.

Marks made introductions. "Ms. Norville, this is Chad Baker. Chad, Kitty Norville."

"Miss Norville." Baker offered his hand, and we shook.

"Call me Kitty. This is Ben O'Farrell." More handshaking all around. I looked at Marks and waited for him to tell me why we were all here.

"Why don't we all go take a look at the problem, shall we?" Marks said, smiling, and gestured across the field on the other side of the fence.

Baker slipped a loop of wire off the top of the nearest fence post, pulling back the top strand of barbed wire. The tension made it coil back on itself. We could all climb over the bottom part of the fence without too much effort.

We walked across the field, up a rise that overlooked a depression that was hidden from the road. Marks and Baker stood aside and let us look.

Six dead cows lay sprawled before me. They weren't just dead. They'd been gutted, torn to pieces, throats ripped out, guts spilled, tongues lolling. The grass and dirt around them had turned to sticky mud, so much blood had poured out of them. They hadn't even had time to run, it looked like. They'd all dropped where they stood. The air smelled of rotten meat, of blood and waste.

One werewolf couldn't have done this. It would have taken a whole pack.

Or something lurking in the dark, gazing out with red eyes.

"You want to tell me what happened here?" Marks said in a tone that suggested he already knew exactly what had happened.

I swallowed. What could I say? What did he want me to say? "Ah . . . it looks like some cows were killed."

"Massacred, more like," Marks said. Chad Baker's expression didn't change. I assumed they were his cows. He was taking this very calmly.

"What do you want me to tell you, Sheriff? What do you think I know?" I spoke softly, unable to muster any more righteous sarcasm.

"I think you know exactly what I think."

"What, you think I can read minds?" I was just being cagey. He was right, I knew: I was Kitty, the famous werewolf, who moved into his jurisdiction and then this happened. I told him, "You think I did this."

"Well?" he said.

"I assure you, I'm not in any way, shape, or form capable of this. No single wolf, lycanthropic or otherwise, is capable of this."

"That's what I told him," Baker said, flickering a smile. My heart instantly went out to him.

"Thank you," I said. "I don't think I could bring down one cow on my own, much less a whole herd."

"*Something* did this," Marks said unhelpfully.

"We couldn't find any prints," Baker said. "My dogs didn't hear a thing, and they'll set up a racket at the drop of a hat. It's like something dropped on them out of the sky."

"A werewolf isn't a normal wolf," Marks said, unable to let it go. "God knows what the hell you're capable of."

I took a deep breath, quelling the nausea brought on by the stench of death—not even Wolf could stomach this mess. I filtered out the smells I knew, looking for the one I was afraid I'd find: the musky human/lupine mix that meant werewolves had been here.

I didn't smell it.

"This wasn't werewolves," I murmured. What was weird, though: I didn't smell *anything* outside of what I expected. No predator, no intruder. Nothing that wasn't already here; no hint of what had *been* here. Just like around my cabin, when I chased after that intruder. Like Baker said, it was as if something dropped on them out of the sky.

"Kitty." Low and strained, Ben's voice grated like sandpaper.

He stared at the scene with unmistakable hunger. And revulsion, the two sides of him, wolf and human, battling over what emotion he should feel. His wolf might very well look on this as a feast and claw its way to the surface. The smell of blood—so thick on the air—was like an invitation, and he wasn't used to dealing with it. He clenched his hands. Sweat had broken out on his hairline. He was losing it.

I grabbed his arm and turned him away.

He squeezed his eyes shut, and his breaths came quick. I whispered, "Keep it together, okay? Don't think of the blood, think about something else. Keep it locked up inside, all curled up and harmless."

He started to turn around, to look back over his shoulder at the slaughter. Hand on his cheek, I made him look back at me. I held his face and pulled his head down closer to me. We touched foreheads, and I kept talking until I felt him nod, until I knew he heard me.

His breathing slowed, and some of the tension sagged out of him. Only then did I let go. "Take a walk if you need to," I said. "Walk back to the car and don't think about it, okay?"

"Okay," he said. Without looking up, he started back for the car, hunched in and unhappy looking.

"Weak stomach?" Baker asked.

"Something like that," I said. "Is there anything else I need to see here, or can we go back to the cars?"

We climbed back over the fence, and Baker replaced the top strand of wire. Ben was leaning on the hood of my car, arms crossed and head bowed. I wished Marks had given me some kind of warning, so I wouldn't have had to bring Ben into that. He wasn't ready to deal with that.

"We're having a hard time explaining what happened out there, Ms. Norville. Werewolves, though. That's a pretty interesting explanation," Marks said.

"Yeah, but it's wrong," I said. "I didn't do it. I don't know what did." I didn't tell him about the thing I saw outside my cabin. That thing I thought I saw. If I couldn't describe it, what was the point?

Marks clearly didn't believe me. He might as well have been holding a pair of handcuffs. Baker's expression was maddeningly neutral. Like he was happy to put it all in Marks's hands and get back to the business of ranching. Western reserve to the extreme.

"Look," I started, growing flustered. "It's easy enough to prove I didn't do it. Get somebody out here to take some samples, find the bite marks and get some saliva, test it. I'll give you a sample to compare—"

"You don't have to do that," Ben said, looking up. "Let him get a warrant first."

Marks glanced at him. "Who did you say you were?"

"Benjamin O'Farrell. Attorney-at-law."

The sheriff didn't like that answer. He frowned. "Well ain't that something."

Ben sticking up for me settled me down. He was right; I didn't have to defend myself here. They had no proof. I said, "You think about trying the UFO people? I hear they have a bead on this sort of thing." Anything could have done this.

"This isn't a joke. This is a man's livelihood." Marks gave Baker a nod.

"I'm not joking. Can we go now?"

Scowling, he went to the door of his car. "Don't think about leaving town. Either one of you."

Whatever. I opened my own car door and started to climb in.

Baker called out, "If you come up with any ideas about what happened here, you'll let me know?"

I nodded. My only idea at the moment was that this whole town was cursed.

As soon as I left the driveway leading out of Baker's ranch, Ben said, "Do you have your phone?"

"It's in my bag." I gestured to the floor of the backseat.

Ben found it, then dialed a number.

He must have gotten voice mail. "Cormac, it's me. There's been some cattle killed up here. Matches the MO of those flocks killed at Shiprock. Your rogue wolf may have found its way out here. I don't know where you've gone, but you might want to get back."

He lowered the phone and switched it off.

I glanced at him, though I wanted to stare. I still had to drive.

"Rogue wolf," I said. "The one he wasn't able to kill back in New Mexico?" I remembered he'd mentioned the sheep that had been killed. That there'd been two werewolves, and he'd only shot the one. "Why didn't you say anything back there?"

"Because I couldn't." Ben's voice was tight, almost angry. "Because that smell hit me and—and I wasn't in my head anymore. Something else was. I couldn't talk, I couldn't even think."

My own anger drained out of me. "It's the wolf. Certain smells, sometimes tastes, or if you're scared or angry, all of that makes it stronger. Calls it up. You have to work extra hard to keep it locked away. If I'd known what we were going to see I would have warned you. Or kept you away."

"I hate it," he said, glaring out the side window. "I hate losing control like that."

This was Ben, who stood in courtrooms telling off judges, who stared down cops, who didn't pull punches. Probably couldn't stand the idea of something else inside him running the show. I reached over, found his hand, and held it. I half expected him to pull away, but he didn't. He squeezed back and kept staring out the window.

We returned to the cabin, but I didn't go inside. I went out, into the trees, the direction I'd run the other night, chasing that thing. That nightmare. If I hadn't just seen that slaughtered herd, I might have been able to convince myself that shadow had been a figment of my imagination.

Ben followed reluctantly. "Where are you going?"

"I've got to figure out what did that."

"Clear your name?"

It wasn't that. Marks couldn't prove I'd done it, however much he wanted to. Rather, I'd gotten this feeling that things would only get worse until I stood up and did something. I was tired of waiting, cornered and shivering in the dark. That might have been okay for a lone wolf, but I had a pack to protect now.

Running away wasn't an option because what if this thing up and followed me?

Ben said, "You think this is the thing you saw the other night?"

"I'm still not sure I saw anything."

"And you think it's the same thing Cormac was hunting."

"What if it followed him here?" Whatever had been here, the signs were two days old now. Harder to find—and I hadn't found anything in the first place. But if it was the same thing, I had a second point of contact now. I headed overland, as the crow flies or wolf runs, in the direction of the Baker ranch. "I'll look around. I can cover this whole area between here and the ranch. You should stay here."

"No. You're not leaving me out of this. I'll come with you. I'll help."

"Ben—"

"I don't want to hear any more of that alpha wolf bullshit. Just let me help, please."

I could have gotten angry and stood my ground on principle. That would have been the alpha thing to do. Alphas didn't let new wolves argue with them. But it was just the two of us. I didn't have anything to prove. Maybe we'd be better off together.

"Look for anything out of place. Any sign, any feeling."

"Anything that smells like those cattle," he said, his voice low.

"Yeah."

Together, we hunted. I let a bit of that Wolf-sense bleed into my human self. Smell, sound, senses—the least movement of a squirrel became profound, I looked sharply at every rustling branch. Daylight wasn't the time to be doing this. Too many distractions. Whatever had made that carnage had done so at night. This was a nighttime kind of evil.

I watched Ben, worried that he might let too much of his wolf out, wondering if he might lose control and shift. Mostly, he seemed introspective, looking around like the world was new, or like he was waking up after a dream. He was right to want to come along, I realized. Being out here, learning to look at the world again, was better than him staying holed up at home.

We rounded the hill at the edge of the Baker ranch, overlooking his land. A backhoe was dumping the last of the carcasses onto a truck, to be hauled away.

We'd found no sign of the creature, and somehow I wasn't surprised. We turned around and went home.

That afternoon, I went online again, checking the usual weird Web sites and forums that might have the sort of data—or at worst, rumors and anecdotes—I wanted. I searched for livestock mutilations, particularly in the Southwest U.S. Sure enough, the hits I found included an inordinate number of UFOlogist sites. Kind of annoying. I tried to avoid knee-jerk skepticism, since lately I'd been forced to reassess a lot of my assumptions. About, like, the existence of werewolves for example. But I wasn't quite willing to believe that a vastly superior extraterrestrial intelligence would travel all the way to Earth just to turn a few cows inside out.

But I found something. It wasn't aliens, it wasn't werewolves. On a few sites people talked about a sort of haunting. Not by the dead, but by a kind of evil. It left death and destruction in its wake. It originated in the Native American tribes of the Southwest, particularly the Navajo and Zuni. They talked about witches laying curses that killed entire families, destroyed livelihoods, haunted entire communities. And about skinwalkers: witches who had the power to change themselves into animals. Like lycanthropes. They had red eyes.

Nobody seemed to want to talk about them in detail. Knowing too much about them drew suspicion onto oneself. In some places, a person could be excused for killing someone who was suspected of being a skinwalker. Like lycanthropes, again.

Again I avoided knee-jerk skepticism. In my experience, accusations of evilness often stemmed from the fears of the accuser rather than the real nature of the accused.

What attacked Ben in New Mexico was a werewolf, plain and simple. We had the proof of that in Ben himself. But there'd been two of them.

I grilled Ben about what he knew.

"Not much," he said. "Cormac picked up this contract for the werewolf, but he got down there and found signs that there were two of them. So he called me. I saw some of the sheep they'd killed. Completely ripped open, like the cattle today." He paused, closing his eyes and taking a deep breath. The memory had triggered a reaction, caused his wolf to prick his ears. Ben collected himself and continued. "I only caught a glimpse of it, right before I was attacked. It was a wolf, it looked like a wolf. Something was wrong, Cormac was letting it walk right up to him. He could have shot the thing from ten paces off. I started to shout, then . . ." He shook his head. Then he was attacked, and that was that. He'd been watching Cormac, and not what came after him.

"Cormac said you saved him. You got a shot off and that broke some kind of spell."

"I don't know. I don't remember it too clearly. Anything could have happened, I suppose. I do know there was something messed up going on."

"And now it's moved here. I really hate my life right now."

"Join the club," he said. Then, more thoughtfully, "I grew up on a cattle ranch. Dead cattle—it's serious. Every one of them is a piece of the rancher's income. It's a big business. Marks will go after it until he figures it out."

"Well, as long as he's after me, he isn't going to figure it out." Marks didn't know about Ben; I figured we'd keep it that way. Nobody had to know about Ben.

"You suppose there's a connection with what's been going on here, with your dead rabbits and dogs?"

I shook my head. "Those were organized. Ritual killings. That today—was just slaughter." Like we needed another curse around here.

I almost wished they were connected, so we'd only have one problem to solve.

That night, we lay sprawled in bed, like a couple of dogs in front of the fireplace. He pillowed his head on my stomach, nestling in the space formed by my bent legs. I held one of his hands, while resting the other on my increasingly shaggy head of hair. We didn't look at each other, but stared into space, not ready for sleep.

He was still shaken by the day's adventure. Not quite comfortable in his skin. I knew the feeling. I let him talk as much as he wanted.

He said, "It feels like a parasite. Like there's this thing inside me and all it wants to do is suck the life out of me then crawl out of my empty skin."

Now there was a lovely image. "I never looked at it that way. To me it's always kind of felt like this voice, it's looking at everything over my shoulder and it always has an opinion. It's like an evil Jiminy Cricket."

He chuckled. "Jiminy Cricket with claws. I like it."

"It digs into your skin like a kitten with those needley little things." I giggled. Silly was better than scary.

Ben winced. "Ugh, those things *are* evil. You ever want to see something fun, throw a kitten down somebody's shirt. Watch them squirm trying to avoid getting clawed while not hurting the kitten."

Now I winced. I could almost feel those little claws scratching on my stomach. "You sound like you've done it before."

"Or had it done."

I couldn't help it. I giggled again, because I could see it: him and Cormac as kids, cousins fooling around at the family reunion, and I just knew who would have thrown a kitten down whose shirt. Oh, the humanity.

Wearing a wry smile, he looked at me. His voice turned thoughtful. "I don't think I'd have made it this far without you. Cormac did the right thing, bringing me here."

"That's nice of you to finally admit it."

"When this happened to you, did you get through it alone or did someone help you?"

"Hmm, I had a whole pack. A dozen or so other werewolves, and half of them wanted to help and half of them were worried I'd be competition. But there was someone in the middle of all that. T.J. looked out for me. The first time I Changed, he held me. I tried to be there for you the same way. But T.J.—he was special. He was very Zen about the whole thing most of the time. He used to tell me not to look at the Wolf as the enemy, but to learn to use it as a strength. You take those strengths into yourself and become more than the sum of the parts." Always, this was easier said than done. But I could still hear T.J.'s voice telling me these things. Reminding me.

"Where is he now?"

To think, I had just been about to congratulate myself that I'd spent a whole minute talking about T.J. without crying. I spoke softly, to keep my voice from cracking, because I was supposed to be the strong one. "Dead. I called out the alpha male of our pack, and T.J. swooped in to back me up. We lost. He died protecting me. That's why I had to leave Denver."

"I hear that happens a lot, in werewolf packs."

"Maybe. I don't really know. There's a lot of different kinds of packs out there."

"I'd just as soon keep this one to you and me."

"Afraid of a little healthy competition?" I said wryly.

"Of course. I'd hate to have to share you with anyone."

"Or is it that you'd hate to have to fight to keep me to yourself?"

He shifted so he was looking at me. I looked back, down the length of my body. "You know, I think I would. If I had to." The playful tone went out of his voice.

My whole body flushed. Suddenly we weren't two friends snuggled together for comfort. He was male, I was female, and there were sparks. The weight of him leaning against me sent warm ripples through my gut.

"Is that you talking—you the human, I mean. Or is it the wolf?" I said.

He hesitated, then said, "It's all the same thing. Isn't it?"

Helplessly, I nodded.

He moved again, propping himself on an elbow so he leaned over me. Tentatively, he touched the waistband of my sweatpants. I didn't say anything. In fact, I pulled my arms away, tucking my hands under my head, so I wouldn't be tempted to stop him.

He pushed up the hem of my tank top, tugged down on my sweatpants, exposing a stretch of naked skin across my belly. He kissed this, working his way across, gently and carefully, like he wanted to be sure to touch every spot. Warmth flushed along my skin everywhere he touched. He eased the edge of my pants down farther, until he was kissing the curve of my hip, using his tongue, tasting me. My heart was beating hard, my breaths coming deep. I closed my eyes and squirmed with pleasure.

It was all I could do to keep from grabbing him, ripping off his clothes, and pulling him into me. He started this, so I let him work, reveling in the focused intensity of his attention. He kept at it until I gasped, a sudden jolt of sensation startling even me.

Then I grabbed him and ripped all his clothes off.

After that, we acted like we were on some kind of honeymoon. We'd start out washing dishes and end up making out over the sink, pawing each other with soapy hands. The bed got a workout. The sofa got a workout. The floor got a workout. The kitchen table—

after one attempt we decided it wasn't stable enough to withstand a workout.

I got a heck of a workout. I was *sore*.

It distracted us from our problems, from the curse, from the slaughter, from the threats that had taken up residence in my dreams. The reason Ben gave me for not sleeping was a much better one than lying awake waiting for doom to strike.

Then there was the nagging little voice that kept telling me it wasn't Ben, it was the wolf inside of him that had inspired this heroic passion. He wouldn't be here if he weren't a werewolf. Circumstance had brought us together, but I was enough of a romantic to want to be in love.

Neither one of us brought up the subject.

Over the next several days, two more herds of cattle were attacked. A dozen cows in all were slaughtered, torn to pieces. Each time, Marks called me up, wanting to know where I'd been the night before, what I'd been doing, and did I have witnesses who could verify that. Not really, seeing as how Ben and I were each other's alibi. Each time, Ben and I went out and searched the area, looking for something out of place, unnatural. Something that turned the world dark, and glared out with red eyes. But it must have been avoiding us.

I tried calling Cormac again, more than once. Voice mail picked up every time without ringing, so he was out of range or his phone was off. He didn't have a message, just let the automated voice carry on. I tried not to worry. Cormac was fine, he could take care of himself.

The second time Marks called I accused him of racial profiling—the only reason he suspected me was the fact that I was the only known lycanthrope in the region. He replied that he had applied for that warrant to collect a DNA sample from me.

I finished that phone conversation to see Ben sitting on the sofa holding his forehead like it ached and shaking his head slowly.

Ben and I were on the sofa, undressed, snuggled together under a blanket, basking in the warmth of the stove and drinking morning coffee. Didn't do much talking in favor of reveling in the simple animal comforts.

A tickling in the back of my mind disturbed the comfort. I lifted my head, felt myself tilting it—like a dog perking its ears up. And yes, I did hear something, very faint. Leaves rustling. Footsteps.

Ben tensed up against me. "What's wrong?"

"Somebody's outside. Wait here."

I slipped off the sofa and into the bedroom to find some jeans and a sweater to throw on.

It couldn't have been my mad dog-flaying curse meister, or the red-eyed thing. I'd never heard anybody actually moving around the house like this. Maybe it was some hiker who'd gotten lost. I could point them back to the road and be done with it.

Unfortunately, my life was never that simple, and dread gnawed at my chest.

I wished Cormac were here with a couple of his guns.

I went down the porch steps and looked around. Lifting my chin, I breathed deep. Didn't smell anything odd, but that didn't mean anything. Whoever it was could just be in the wrong place.

Something called through the trees, a low, echoing hoot. An owl, incongruous in the morning light. I couldn't see it, but it made me feel like something watched me.

Listening hard, looking into the trees, I started to walk around the house. Then I heard a crunching of dried leaves. Up the hill toward the road.

Knowing where to look now, I saw him. A short man, maybe forty, probably latino, his round face tanned to rust, wrinkles fanning from the corners of his eyes. His long black hair was tied in a ponytail. He wore a thick army-style canvas jacket, jeans, and cowboy boots. He wandered among the trees, hands on his hips like this was property he was planning on buying.

This was *my* territory. I walked toward him, stomping to make noise of my own, until he looked at me. He didn't seem surprised to see me standing in front of him.

I glared. "Can I help you with something?"

He glanced at me, not seeming at all startled or concerned.

"There was something here—" He pointed to the ground, drawing a line in the air that arced halfway around him. "In a circle all the way around the house. It's all kind of blurry now. But it's like someone was trying to build a fence or something."

He gestured right to where the ring of barbed-wire crosses had lain on the ground.

"There's been a lot of blood spilled here, too. All kinds. This place is pretty messed up, spiritually speaking."

I stared. My jaw might even have dropped open.

"Who are you?" I managed to demand without shrieking.

"Sorry. Name's Tony. Tony Rivera. Cormac asked me to come out and have a look. I haven't had the time until now."

Simultaneously, the situation became more clear and more confused. This guy knew Cormac *how?* "He said he called someone, but didn't say anything about you."

"That surprise you? Is he here?"

"No." Though he'd probably expected to still be here when he'd called.

"You must be Kitty." He approached me slowly, obliquely, swinging a bit to the side—not directly toward me—and keeping his gaze off center, looking out and around, to the ground and the trees, everywhere but directly at me.

He was speaking wolf. Using wolf body language, at least. Giving me space and letting me take a good look at him. The gesture startled me into thinking well of him. I tilted my chin, breathed deeply—he wasn't a lycanthrope. He smelled absolutely human, normal and a little earthy, like he spent a lot of time outside.

"Hi," I said, able to smile nicely while he stood in front of me. Before I realized I was speaking, I asked, "How'd you learn to do that?"

"I pay attention. So, what seems to be the problem out here?"

"You the witch doctor?"

"Something like that."

I gestured over my shoulder. "You want to come in for coffee while we talk?"

"Sure, thanks."

Ben, clever boy that he was, was dressed and waiting in the doorway when Tony and I reached the cabin.

Tony saw him and waved. "Hi, Ben. Cormac said you were here."

Ben's eyes widened. "Tony?" Tony just smiled, and Ben shook his head. "Should have known."

I said, "So, ah, I guess you two know each other."

"He's my lawyer," Tony said.

Small world and all that. I looked at Ben. He shrugged. "Guess I'm everybody's lawyer. Cormac didn't say it was you he'd called."

Tony glanced at me with a sparkle in his eyes. "Cormac likes his secrets, doesn't he?"

"I'm going to get some coffee." I went into the house.

I turned around with a fresh mug of coffee for Tony to find him and Ben studying each other. Ben wilted under the scrutiny, bowing his head and slouching, and I suppressed an urge to jump between them in an effort to protect him.

Tony said, "When did that happen?"

That. The lycanthropy. Tony could tell just by looking.

"Couple weeks ago, I guess. I was out on a job with Cormac."

"I'm sorry. That's rough." He pointed at me. "So you didn't—you're not the one who turned him, are you?"

"Do you think Cormac would have let me live if I'd done it?"

An uncomfortable silence fell. Tony took the mug I offered him, but didn't drink.

Tony wasn't here about werewolves, or about Ben. Cormac had called him here for the curse.

"Cormac thought you might know something about what's been going on. He thought it was some kind of curse."

"Yeah, he told me some of it. You still have any of the stuff? The crosses or the animals?"

I shook my head and tried not to feel guilty about getting rid of the bag of crosses.

He said, "That's too bad. I might have been able to lead you right to whoever's doing this."

"Yeah, well you try living with a dozen skinned dogs hanging outside your house."

"Fair enough. You know anything about who might be doing this?"

"We decided it has to be someone local, since they seem to want me to get out. Cormac thinks whoever it is doesn't know what they're doing. It's been pretty messy, and it isn't working." In a low, grumbly voice I added, "Much."

Ben said, "Can you really tell who's doing this just by looking at the mess?"

Tony shrugged. "Sometimes. Sometimes there's spiritual fingerprints. Even when two different people work the same spell, each of them leaves their own stamp on it. Their own personality. If the person is local, it might be as simple as driving around looking for that same stamp. If someone's trying to put a curse on you, you can bet they've cast spells around their own place for protection."

"Magic spells," I couldn't help but mutter. "Huh."

"You don't believe?" Tony said.

"Look at me, you can tell what I am. I have to believe in pretty much anything these days. It doesn't make believing easy. Magic sounds like so much fun when you're a kid, until you realize how complicated it makes everything. Because you know what? It makes no sense. It makes no sense that throwing a bunch of barbed-wire crosses around my house should scare the pants off me." My voice rose in volume. This whole situation had made me incredibly cranky.

"Except it does make sense, because finding a bunch of plastic Mickey Mouses around your house probably wouldn't have scared you so much, right?" Tony said, donning a half smile that creased his brown face.

My own smile answered his. "I don't know. That'd be pretty weird. I always thought Mickey Mouse was kind of creepy."

"Tony." Ben sat in the kitchen chair, leaning forward on his knees, an idea lighting his eyes. "You can spot the type of magic of something by looking at it. Sense it. Whatever. There's something else that's been happening around here. Probably not connected to what's been happening at the house, but who knows. You mind taking a look while you're out here?"

"What is it?" Tony asked.

"Messy," Ben said.

I tried to catch Ben's gaze, to silently ask him what he was doing. He was talking about the cattle mutilations, about the second werewolf that he and Cormac had tracked in New Mexico. What did he think Tony could tell about it?

Tony frowned thoughtfully. "What do you think it is?"

"I'd rather not say. Let you take a look at it without me giving you ideas."

"Sure. I'm game."

Ben looked at me. "How about it? Where was the last one, out by county line road?"

Marks wouldn't tell me exactly where it was. He'd sort of acted like he assumed I already knew. But he'd indicated that general direction.

"What do you think he's going to find?"

"Just curious," Ben said. "You keep saying this isn't a werewolf. I'd like to hear what Tony has to say about it."

With a complaining sigh, I went to find my car keys. "Ben, you're going to have to start trusting your nose." I looked at Tony. "It isn't a werewolf."

"Now I'm curious," he said.

"Whatever it is, I want to know so it doesn't blindside us like it did the last time," Ben said.

Which made it sound like there was going to be a next time. Why was I not surprised?

The county line road turned off from the state highway a few miles outside town. It was two narrow lanes, paved, no discernible shoulder. Barbed-wire fences lined yellowed pastures on both sides. We all kept our eyes open, peering out the windows for anything unusual, any break in the consistent rangeland.

Tony spotted it, pointing. "There."

I slowed down and pulled onto the grass on the side of the road. To the left, on the other side of a slope of grassland, someone had parked a backhoe. The ordinary piece of equipment seemed ominous somehow, lurking out here by itself. The operator didn't seem to be around. Gone to lunch, maybe.

The three of us crossed the road and picked our way over the barbed wire. Walking toward the backhoe—and whatever work it was here for—felt like the last time, when Marks had brought us to see the slaughtered herd. This marching inexorably toward some unnamed horror. I didn't want to see what lay over that slope. And yet I kept walking.

Finally, we crested the slope and looked down to what lay beyond.

The backhoe's work was done. A mound of newly turned earth lay over a recently covered ditch, a hole some twenty feet to a side. The evidence was buried, cleaned away.

I could see where the dead cattle had lain, though: the swathes of crushed grass, the dark stains of blood on the earth. Anybody could tell that *something* had happened here.

Tony stood with his arms crossed, regarding the scene, his brows furrowed. "Werewolves didn't do this."

"How do you even know what happened?" Ben said.

"Something died here," Tony said matter-of-factly. "Messy, like you said. But more. Evil. Can't you feel it?"

"I don't know. What am I supposed to be feeling?"

I knew what Tony was talking about. Werewolves weren't inherently evil. They came in all varieties. They were individuals, exhibiting a whole range of behaviors and individual intentions. But this—some miasma rose from the earth itself, seeping under my skin, raising the hair on my arms. It felt like something in the trees was watching me, but I looked and smelled the air, and couldn't find anything.

"Evil," I echoed. "It feels evil. All it wants to do is destroy."

Ben spoke with a clenched jaw. "I've been feeling that crawling under my skin ever since that son of a bitch bit me. How am I supposed to tell the difference?"

He could smell the blood, and the scent prodded his wolf, like poking a hornet's nest with a stick. But he didn't recognize it. Couldn't separate his own hunger from the wrongness that permeated the earth here. His shoulders and arms were tense, like he was bracing against something. His face held an expression of horror, but I couldn't tell if the expression was turned out to the scene before us, or inward, to himself.

I went to him. Didn't look at him, but gripped his hand and leaned my face against his shoulder.

"Practice, Ben. Patience."

He turned slightly, rubbing his cheek against my head, and I thought he might say something. I thought he might talk it out until this made some kind of sense. Instead, he abruptly broke away from me and stalked back to the road.

Tony watched him leave. "How's he doing really?"

"Oh, just fine," I answered lightly. "That's the scary part."

I couldn't imagine what Ben would be like if he were handling this *really* badly.

Side by side, Tony and I followed Ben back to the road. I tried to pin Tony down, studying him out of the corner of my eye. Despite the weirdness of the area, despite having spent most of the morning with a couple of werewolves, he didn't seem tense at all. He kept his head up, his gaze out, looking around at the trees, the top of the hills, the sky, watching everything just in case something interesting chanced by.

I didn't make him nervous, and that was refreshing.

"Did Ben tell you where he'd seen this before?" Tony asked.

"That job in New Mexico," I said. "The one that blindsided him and Cormac. They kept thinking there were two werewolves, but the evidence didn't add up."

"So one werewolf, and one something else? That narrows it down."

I couldn't help it; I laughed. Tony smiled in reply.

"One more question," he said. "Cormac said he'd meet me here. What happened?"

That one was a little harder to answer, because I wasn't sure myself. The tension had gotten thick. Then it had twisted, gone weird somehow. When we either couldn't stop glaring at each other, or couldn't look each other in the eye, something had to break.

I hadn't realized I'd let my hesitation stretch into a long silence until Tony answered for me.

"Ah—you and Cormac, and then you and Ben—"

"There was never a me and Cormac," I said.

"Oh. Okay."

He didn't sound convinced, and I declined to argue the point further. The lady doth protest too much, and all that.

Another car was parked on the shoulder, right behind mine. I recognized it; I'd seen it all too often the last week or so. Sheriff Marks's patrol car. His arms crossed, Marks leaned on the hood of his car, staring down Ben, who leaned on the back of mine, staring back.

"Who's that?" Tony asked as we made our way over the barbed-wire fence. Marks turned to watch our progress, his expression even more hooded and suspicious than ever.

"Sheriff Avery Marks. The local stalwart defender of truth, justice, and the American way."

"Hm, one of those."

"Norville," Marks called. He'd dropped the "Ms." I knew I was in trouble now. "May I ask what you're doing trespassing on Len Ford's land? Trying to clean up a little mess?"

I couldn't quite think of a response that wouldn't get me arrested on the spot. If he'd been five minutes later he wouldn't have seen us, and it wouldn't have been an issue. His timing was impeccable.

A bit too impeccable. "Have you been following me?" I said.

I didn't think it possible, but his frown deepened. "I have the right to keep a suspect under surveillance."

Ben straightened, pushing off from the car. "Your 'surveillance' is coming awfully close to harassment, Sheriff."

"You going to sue me?"

Ben only raised his brow. Marks didn't recognize the *try me* look, but I did.

Oh, this was going to get ugly.

Tony butted in, shouldering past me and in front of Marks like he really was breaking up a fight. "Hello, Sheriff Marks? I'm Tony Rivera. I'm afraid this is my fault, I asked Kitty to show me around. She said some weird stuff's been happening and I wanted to check it out."

He held out his hand, an obvious peacemaking gesture, but Marks took his time reaching out to it. Finally, though, they clasped hands. They held on for a long moment, locked in one of those macho *who's going to wince first* gripping matches.

Finally, they let go. Tony's face had gone funny, and it took me a moment to figure out what it was. He was frowning. He hadn't frowned once all morning.

He looked at me. "He's the one. One of them, anyway."

"One of them, what?" I said, perplexed, at nearly the same time Marks said, "One of who?"

Then my eyes widened as I realized what Tony was talking about: what he'd come here to look for, the curse, my house—Marks was the one.

"*You?*" I drew the word out into an accusation and glared at Marks. He didn't seem like the type to hang skinned dogs from trees. I'd have expected him to just shoot me. I'd never have pegged him as someone who knew *anything* about magic, even if what he knew was wrong. He was just so . . . boneheaded.

"What the hell are you people talking about?"

Tony said, "Anyone ever tell you that when you lay a curse, you better do it right or it's going to come back and smack you?"

If Tony was wrong and Marks didn't have anything to do with it, I'd have expected denials. I'd have expected more of the sheriff's blowhard posturing, maybe even threats. Instead, the fury left him for a moment, leaving his face slack and disbelieving.

His protest was too little, too late. "I don't know what you're talking about," he said in a low voice.

Tony ignored him, and glanced between Ben and me. "Remember what I said about spirits having fingerprints? Everybody's soul has its own little flavor. It follows them around, touches everything they do. This guy's stamp is all over your place."

"I called him out there a couple of times, to check things out. That could be why," I said.

"No. Too strong for that," Tony said. "This has malice in it."

Marks seemed to wake out of a daze. His defenses slammed into place, and the look of puckered rage returned. "You're accusing me of being the one who pinned those dead rabbits to her porch, and all that other garbage? What a load of crap. I don't believe this hocus-pocus nonsense."

I said, "But you believe I'm a werewolf—a monster that could do something like slaughter a herd of cattle. You can't have it both ways, Sheriff. Believe one and not the other." I'd learned that quickly enough.

"Okay, I won't say I don't believe it. Somebody's done something out at your place, I won't deny that. But I wouldn't know the first thing about *cursing* someone."

"Maybe you were just following directions," Tony said.

Again, that blank look while he organized his defense. "That doesn't even make sense."

I said, "Sheriff, you don't like me. You've made no secret of that. You don't like what I am, you don't like that I'm in your town. Maybe you're not the only one. And maybe you didn't do it, but I'm betting you backed whoever did."

The three of us—Tony, Ben, and me—surrounded him, pinning him against his car almost. If Marks had reached for his gun, I wouldn't have been surprised. To his credit, he didn't. He appeared stricken, though. Frozen almost, like he expected us to pounce.

I said, "I haven't hurt anyone. I didn't kill those cattle. I don't deserve what's been done to me, and I just want it to stop. That's all."

His lips pursed, his expression hardening. We weren't going to get anything out of him. In his mind, he'd drawn some kind of line in the dirt. I stood on one side, he stood on the other, and because of that we'd never come to an understanding. I might as well pack my bags and leave.

Tony reached out to him. He moved quickly. Marks and I held each other's gazes so strongly I didn't even notice it until Tony held Marks's collar. Marks only had time to flinch before Tony had pulled out a pendant on a hemp cord that had been tucked under the sheriff's shirt.

Tony held the pendant flat in his hand, displaying it: a flint arrowhead of gray stone, tied to the cord.

"Zuni charm," Tony said. "Defense against werewolves. He knows all about this magic."

Was *that* why I wanted to growl at Marks every time I saw him?

Marks snatched the arrowhead away from Tony, closing his hand around it. He took a step back, bumping against the hood of his car. His armor had slipped; now, he seemed uncertain.

"It wasn't my idea," he said finally.

The air seemed to lighten around us. At last, he'd said something that sounded like truth.

"Whose was it? I'm not out for revenge, Marks. I just want to know why."

"We wanted you to leave. We're a quiet community. We didn't want any trouble."

"I wasn't going to bring any trouble! I just wanted to be left alone."

"But you brought trouble. That's trouble." He pointed out to the backhoe across the pasture.

I shouted. I didn't mean to. It just came out. "You pinned rabbits to my porch before any of those cows died! You assumed I'd do something before anything even happened! You heard what he said about a curse coming back to smack you—you brought this on yourself! And then you had the gall to pretend to investigate, when you knew all along who was doing it—"

"Kitty, maybe a little more calm," Ben said softly. I must have been really worked up if Ben was having to settle me down. My whole back and shoulders felt tight as springs.

When Marks spoke, his voice had changed. He sounded suddenly tired, defeated. "We—we knew it wasn't working right. You should have just left. Quietly, without a word. We wanted it to be quiet."

"Well, you screwed up big time, didn't you?" I said.

"Can you blame us for trying?" he said roughly.

"Uh, yeah. Hello, I *am* blaming you."

"We all know what you are! A—a monster! We don't want that in our town! Nobody would!"

"You know, I don't think I'm the monster here, really."

Thankfully, Tony interceded. "Sheriff, I think I can help clean this all up. We can remove the curse, and remove the consequences of it." He pointed a thumb over his shoulder at the site of the slaughter. "But the person who planned it, who worked the spell, needs to agree to it."

He nodded. "All right. Okay. It's Alice. She planned it."

"Alice?" My jaw dropped, truly astonished. "But she's always been so nice to me. Why—"

"Because she's nice to everybody, at least in person," Marks said. "I don't think she could be mean to somebody to their face if you held a gun to her head."

Tony looked at me. "Should we go talk to Alice, then?"

I still couldn't believe it. Sweet, friendly Alice. Alice who kept healing crystals on her cash register and hung good luck charms on her front door.

Then again, maybe she did know something about planting curses.

"Right, then. Off we go." To Marks I said, "You want to come along? Back us up?"

"To break this thing right, everyone involved should be there," Tony said. He had an authority about him, from the gentle way he spoke to the way he'd grabbed Marks's arrowhead charm. Marks had let it go; it lay on top of his uniform shirt now, exposed.

The sheriff hesitated, then said, curtly, "I'll meet you there." He turned to yank open his car door. He revved the engine when he started it, and barely gave us time to get out of the way before he lurched the car into reverse, then spun in a U-turn, kicking up gravel all the way.

"I don't believe it," I said, on general principle.

"She didn't really seem the type," Ben said.

Tony said, "Those are the ones you really have to watch out for. The real mean *brujas?* Always the little old lady down the street. The one who feeds cats off her back porch."

"Every neighborhood has one of those," I said.

"Makes you wonder, don't it?" Tony grinned.

Sighing, I marched to the driver's side of my car. "Let's go and get this over with."

Marks was already at the convenience store when we pulled into the parking lot. That meant he'd had time to warn her, to prep and get their stories straight. That made me mad. The whole town was against me, and the worst part was I shouldn't have been surprised. I was the monster, they carried the torches and pitchforks, and nothing would change that. Human nature being what it was.

At least I had backup this time.

I didn't wait for Ben and Tony, though. I wanted to break up their little witches' coven, and I wanted to do it now. While they were still getting out of the car, I stalked to the door of the store. Slammed it open. Sure enough, Marks and Alice were in conference, leaning over the counter by the cash register. They looked at me, shocked, though they should have expected me. Joe, standing behind Alice, quickly ducked for his rifle. I should have kept my distance, but I wasn't thinking too straight.

I went right toward them, closing the gap in a few long strides, and I must have had murder in my eyes because they both flinched back. That inspired me; let them think I wanted to rip their throats out.

I slammed my hand on the counter, making them jump, at the moment Joe cocked and leveled his rifle, mere inches from my skull. I could smell it, cold and oily.

The bell on the door rang as it opened again. "Kitty!" Ben called, at the same time Tony said, "No, wait." I imagined Tony held him back from rushing to my rescue. I couldn't look away. I only had eyes for Alice.

"So," I said, filled with fake cheerfulness. "Did you really give those crosses to Jake to melt them down, or did you keep them so you could dump them back around my place?"

Bug-eyed and stricken, she stared back at me. Almost, she trembled, and a scent of fear-laden sweat broke out on her skin. She looked like prey. Like a rabbit caught in Wolf's sight.

What a great feeling. I had the power; I was the badass. If I so much as raised a finger, she'd probably scream.

Then, she knelt. Slowly, she disappeared behind the counter, and when she stood again, she held the bag of crosses I'd given her. They chimed when she set them on the counter.

This was one of those times when I hated being right.

"God*damn* it, Alice. I *liked* you! Why'd you have to turn out to be such a bitch?"

The overly polite woman, the one who couldn't be mean to anyone's face, took command. "You don't have to be so angry," she said, with a righteous tilt to her chin.

I wasn't finished. "If you hate me enough to kill small animals over it, don't turn around and pretend to be nice to me. Honestly, I prefer Joe here with his gun pointed at me. At least I know where I stand with him!"

Joe blinked at me over the stock of his rifle, like he was unable to process the rather backhanded compliment.

Marks said, "Joe, why don't you put that thing away." Joe obeyed and slowly lowered the weapon.

"I don't hate you," Alice said softly. "I just don't want you to live here." Her thin-lipped grimace was almost apologetic.

I didn't even know where to start. Maybe she wanted me to sympathize. Maybe she wanted me to feel sorry for her. Instead, the
rage flared even higher. I had to pause a moment, take a breath, and
think happy vegetarian thoughts before I growled for real. What
had I told Ben about holding it in taking practice? I was getting a
lot of practice right now.

Finally, I said, "Guess what? You don't get to tell me where to
live."

She looked away.

Tony stepped up then, sweeping away the tension with his presence. "You know what you did wrong, don't you?" He addressed
Alice.

"Who are you?" she asked.

"Tony. You know what you did wrong?"

She shook her head, hesitant, still full of that befuddled rabbit
look.

"The cross on the doorway," Tony said, gesturing back to where
Alice had hung a cross above the door. "The barrier of crosses.
They're supposed to prevent evil from crossing, yes? Keep evil
contained, keep it from intruding." He waited for her to nod, to ac-
knowledge what he said. "Kitty's not evil. I've only known her half
a day and I know that."

He said "evil" and I almost heard "dangerous." As in, "She's not
dangerous. She's harmless." I had an inexplicable urge to argue,
but Tony kept talking.

"She may have danger and darkness in her nature, but so do we
all. That isn't evil. Evil is seeking out the darkness, seeking out the
pain of others."

I glanced back at Ben, to make sure he'd heard. That was what
I'd been trying to tell him. He looked at me, gave a tiny smile. Yes,
he'd heard.

"Is it true what Sheriff Marks said, that our spell caused what's
been happening to the cattle?"

"Your spell called out to evil. You may have drawn it here, yes."

She rubbed her face—wiping away sudden tears, springing from
reddening eyes. "I'm so sorry. I thought I knew what I was doing,
I was sure I knew—I have to fix it. How do I fix it?"

"Apologizing is always a good start," Tony said.

Alice looked at me, and for a moment I did feel sorry for her.
She obviously felt so badly, and so tortured when the true consequences of what she'd done sunk in, I didn't want to be angry at

her anymore. The words—*Oh, it's all right, just as long as she never does it again*—were on the tip of my tongue.

But the Wolf in me shifted testily. And you know, she was right. Alice wasn't going to get off that easily. I waited for the apology.

"I'm sorry, Kitty," she said. "I'm sorry for all the trouble."

You'd better be . . . "Thank you," I said instead.

"I think I can help clean all this up," Tony said. "There's a ritual I know, it'll clear away the curse. Heal some of the bad feelings. Will you all help?"

He looked at each of us, and we all nodded. Even Joe.

"Good," he said. "Be at Kitty's cabin at twilight, about five o'clock. We'll get this taken care of. Oh—and I'll take those. Thanks." Smiling amiably, he grabbed the bag of crosses off the counter.

We left the store, Tony bringing up the rear, almost like he was herding us. Or keeping me from lingering and doing something stupid. Within minutes, we were in the car and back on the road.

"Cormac wanted me to have those melted down," I said, nodding at the bag of crosses in his lap.

"That'd work, but I was just going to hold them under running water."

"You mean that's all we had to do?" I shook my head. The more I learned . . .

He said, "I'm curious where Alice learned her magic. If she was raised in some kind of tradition—healer or witchcraft or something—or if she got those spells out of a book somewhere. That's the trouble with you white people, you read something out of a book, you think you understand it. This kind of magic, though— you really have to live with it to know it."

That reminded me of learning a language, how really learning it requires living it, speaking with native speakers, growing up with it—total immersion. Repeating vocabulary words in high school wasn't going to cut it.

I said, "I can assure you, everything I know about the supernatural I've lived with personally." That didn't mean I understood any of it.

Tony laughed. "I believe you."

From the backseat, Ben said, "You really think what they did caused what happened to the cattle? What about what we saw in New Mexico?"

"Maybe what Alice and them did drew it here," Tony said.

"Or did it follow Cormac?" I said.

That left us with an ominous silence. Because it made sense. There'd been two of them. Cormac killed one, and the other followed him, seeking revenge. Only Cormac wasn't here anymore. So it went wild, killing, like it had before.

If that was the case, Tony's cleansing spell wouldn't help. We needed Cormac back. If for no other reason than to warn him.

Twilight settled over the forest, clear and stark. The sky turned the beautiful deep blue of prize sapphires. The first star shone like a diamond against it. That clean, organic pine forest smell permeated everything.

Ben and I sat on the front porch and waited, watching Tony make preparations. He'd parked his truck at a national forest trailhead a few miles up the road, and moved it to my driveway during the afternoon. He pulled a box of supplies out of the back and got to work. First, he leaned a broom against the porch railing, then placed unlit white votive candles along the porch and around the clearing. Moving around the clearing to the four quarters of the compass, he drew something out of the leather pouch he carried and threw it into the air. A fine powder left his hands, and the smell of home cooking in a well-kept kitchen hit me. Dried herbs. Sage, oregano. I felt better.

"You think this'll work?" Ben said.

"I've learned to keep an open mind. I've seen something like this work before. So, yeah. I think it will."

"You look better already."

I felt a smile light my face. "What can I say? The man inspires confidence."

"Do you know in some regions it's traditional to pay a *curandero* in silver?"

I blinked, then frowned, suddenly worried. Would the ironies of my life never end? "Well, that's unfortunate. He knows I don't let silver get within miles of me if I can help it, right?"

Grinning, Ben leaned back against the wall. "Maybe he'll take a check."

I reveled in the moment of peace. Ben was getting his sense of humor back.

The sound of a driving car hummed up the road, then crunched onto the driveway that led to the clearing. Marks's patrol car, a pale ghost in the twilight, moved into sight, then pulled in behind Tony's pickup.

Wary, I stood. Ben stood with me. I felt that same sense of foreboding and invasion I had every time Marks had come here. I understood it, now: the spite he brought with him, his part in the curse that had been cast. Now, though, I felt something else: like a wall stood between us, a defensive barrier. This time, I had protection.

Sheriff Marks, Alice, and Joe got out of the car, and Tony walked out to meet them. They all shook hands, like they'd come for some kind of dinner party.

"Sheriff, Joe, I'm going to have to ask you to leave your guns in the car," Tony said.

"Like hell," Marks said, as expected.

"This is supposed to be a peacemaking. Kind of misses the point if you bring guns."

It was asking a lot, telling men like that they couldn't bring their guns. The whole thing might have come to a screeching halt right there.

Alice said, "Please. I really want this to work. I want to make this right."

They listened to her, and Tony led them into the clearing.

"Everyone ready to get started?" he said. No one gave a particularly enthusiastic affirmation, but no one said no, either. Tony went around and started lighting candles. Golden circles of light flared from them, warm spots in the night. They wrecked my night vision; I couldn't see anything past the clearing now.

"Gather in a circle. Blood has been spilled here, in malice. There must be atonement for that."

The others did so, then looked to me. I hesitated—they needed atonement, and as the wronged party here I had the power to forgive, or not. In Tony's ritual, as I saw it taking shape, that gave me control.

But it wouldn't do any of us any good if I withheld that forgiveness out of spite. This ritual seemed to be less about magic than it was a mechanism for reconciliation. Get us all in one place, make us willing to talk it out. The actions themselves were as important as the result.

I stepped off the porch and into the clearing. Ben followed me. Nervously, we looked at one another, because nobody but Tony knew what would happen next. Alice seemed sad but resigned, her face pulled into a deep frown, her eyes staring. Marks's frown was different, suspicious. He kept looking over his shoulder. Joe simply stood, stoic as ever.

Tony snuck up behind me. I flinched, startled, because I hadn't heard him. I'd been too distracted by the strange mood settling over the area—a kind of suspended, timeless feeling, like the air itself had frozen.

"Sorry," he said, smiling, and handed me something. A tightly bound bundle of some kind of dried plant. Sage, it smelled like, about as long as my hand and as thick as my thumb. He went to each of us in the circle, until everyone had a bundle.

I assumed he'd tell us what to do with it. I tried not to feel too silly just holding it. Alice clutched hers in both hands, held it to her chest, near to her heart, and closed her eyes.

Then Tony picked up the broom and began sweeping the dirt in front of the porch. Slowly, he made his way around the circle, clockwise.

An owl called. This wasn't a calm, random hooting, the low-pitched, hollow whisper I'd heard the first time Tony came to the cabin. This was rushed, urgent—a note of warning, rapid and increasing in pitch. Branches rustled—there was no sound of wings, but the owl's cry next sounded from the roof of the cabin, above where Tony stood. I still couldn't see the bird. It hid itself well in the shadows, or my eyes weren't working right.

Tony looked around, searching for something.

Something wasn't right. I'd have sworn I hadn't heard anything, hadn't noticed any scent on the air, but the smell of herbs and candles might have covered up anything else. Still, an all-too-familiar tingling wracked my spine. A sense of invasion. My sense of territory being violated.

It was out there. Tense to the point of shivering, I looked out, trying to see into the trees, beyond the light of the candles.

"What is it?" Ben breathed. He'd moved—we'd both moved, until we stood apart from the others, back to back, looking out, ready for danger. I hadn't noticed it because it had happened so smoothly, instinctively, unbidden. Even our little pack circled in the face of whatever danger lurked out there.

This was driving me crazy. It was like the mornings I'd found the rabbits and dogs all over again. If something was out to get me, why couldn't it just show itself, let me face it down?

Ben grabbed my hand and nodded over to a spot north of the circle. The sky had deepened almost to black now, and the trees were lost in darkness.

Red eyes stared back. Points of glowing embers, about the height of a tall wolf. I wasn't imagining it.

"Was that the thing you saw in New Mexico?" I whispered.

"I never got a good look at it." His voice trembled, just a little.

The others looked out to where we stared.

"Jesus—" I thought that was Joe.

"Nobody move," Tony said, his calm slipping a little.

"It's not a wolf," I said. "It doesn't smell like wolf."

"It smells like death," Ben said, and he was right. The embers went out for just a moment—blinking. The eyes blinked at us.

"Oh, God—" Alice said, her voice gone high, like a little girl's.

Tony said, "Alice, stay where you are, don't run!"

Too late. She backed up, her footsteps scraping clumsily on the ground. Then she turned, arms flailing, and raced. Not to the cars, not to the house, either of which offered safety. She ran blindly into the darkness, guided only by panic.

That was exactly what the monster wanted.

"No!" Tony called.

"Joe, get your rifle!" Marks shouted.

The wolf shot out of the darkness like a rocket.

My senses collided. It wasn't a wolf. It didn't smell right, it didn't look right, nothing about this was right. But it had four legs, a long snout, a sleek body with a tail stuck straight back like a rudder. Its coat shone coal-black, and its eyes glared red. Angrily red.

I intercepted it.

It raced straight for Alice, latching on to her terror and marking her as prey. Movement attracted notice. I knew the feeling. I didn't think about it—I just knew that I could stand up to the monster better than Alice could.

I crashed into it from the side, tackling its flank, wrapping my arms around it, pulling it down. I wasn't human—I had this thing inside me that let me move faster than I ever thought I could, that made me stronger than I should have been. My Wolf was a match for it.

But the wrongness of it was overwhelming. As soon as I touched it, a numbness wracked my limbs, poured into my body. It made me want to curl into a ball, fetal, and scream until the world turned right again. My vision went gray.

We rolled together in the dirt. The black wolf snarled and twisted back on itself, snapping at the sudden anchor that had brought it down. Teeth closed on my arm, jaws clamping down hard, ripping into my skin. Better me than Alice. I was already a lycanthrope. I could take it.

I gasped, and my Wolf writhed, growling in pain and anger. Again, a sense of wrongness—the attack didn't just happen on the surface of my body, but crawled inside it, trying to eat through me from the inside. I'd never felt anything like it. My body slipped a little—she wanted to Change, she could fight better as a wolf, she wanted out so she could protect herself.

Claws, I needed claws to tear. But I couldn't move. I expected my hands to thicken, my arms to melt. I wanted to feel my nails grow thick, hard as knives, and break through that monster's skin.

But I didn't.

I usually resisted the Wolf, kept her leashed tight. This time, now, when I wanted to feel her, wanted her to break free and save me—nothing happened. I froze with astonishment. With fear, while the monster grabbed hold of me.

"Kitty!" Ben shouted.

I prayed he stayed back. I wanted him out of this. I didn't want him to have to fight like this.

In something of a panic I slashed, as if I had claws. My fingers raked rough, oily, ugly fur, causing no damage. The thing slammed me onto my back—and made a noise that almost sounded like laughter. My head cracked against the ground, and I saw stars. It pinned me, thick paws on my chest, claws digging in. Its breath smelled of carrion, of sickness. Plague and death. I thrashed in pure animal panic, kicked, got my hands up, took hold of its throat, and pushed. *Get off . . . get the hell off me . . .*

Its jaws opened over my throat, and its sickly breath gusted over me. I melted, my strength ebbing.

"Kitty, get back!"

I kicked its ribs, and its hold broke. I twisted to slip from under its weight, obeying the voice instantly because I trusted it, because it belonged to a man who'd watched my back before. Cormac. As fast as I could, I rolled away from the black wolf.

In the same moment, a shot echoed, then another, and another. They were close, thunder in my ears, rattling my brain.

The wolf cried out—a human scream. Too human, a woman in pain.

The creature lay still before me. I swore I could see motes of dust settling around us, where we'd been fighting.

I couldn't think at all. I felt like I'd been locked in darkness and the prison door just blew open, and now my body floated through the opening. Now, Wolf wanted to run. On my knees, I bent over double, clutching my stomach, trying to pull my body back into myself. Trying to make myself human again. Skin, not fur. I wanted hands and fingers, not paws and claws. Keep it together, keep the line between us drawn. *Please, please . . .*

My Wolf crept back to her lair, growling low the whole time, not believing the danger was over, not believing I could take care of us. *Please . . .*

I took a deep breath, and my body stopped slipping. I flexed my hands, which were hands again.

"Stay back. Give her space. She might still shift." Cormac was speaking.

I kept my eyes closed, stayed crouched over for another moment, taking advantage of the moment of space and silence he made for me.

I want you to take care of me, I wanted to say to him. *I wish you were a wolf and could be my alpha.*

"I'm okay," I said, though my voice was weak and uncertain. I looked up. Cormac stood just a few feet away, looking the worse for wear, a few days' worth of beard covering his jaw. He held a rifle in both hands, ready to fire again if he had to. Briefly, his gaze shifted from the body of the monster to me. His look was searching, asking. *Are you all right?* I tried to pour gratitude back to him. *Yes, because of you.* I smiled. "You came back."

"I got your messages."

"Was this the second wolf you'd been tracking?"

"Yeah."

Ben stood beside me, close enough to touch, but he held back, his body fairly quivering with anxiety. He seemed to need reassurance as much as I did. I reached for him, and he grabbed my hand and knelt beside me.

"You okay?" he said.

"I'll heal." My whole body ached, pain stabbing along every limb. I wouldn't know how badly the wolf had torn me up until I got into some light and looked.

"The wolf," Cormac said. "It's not changing back."

When a werewolf died in its wolf form, the body shifted back to human—returned to its original state. Cormac had put at least three bullets in it, and I knew he used silver. The thing lay in a widening pool of blood. It had to be dead. It even looked dead, a pile of dull fur rather than a glowing, rippling creature.

But it wasn't changing back. It had never smelled like a were-wolf.

I crept forward. Wrong, this was all wrong, and my flesh crawled. I wanted to go inside and lock the door. But I had to know.

Cormac said, "Kitty, don't—"

I touched its neck. It felt cold and strangely pliant under my touch. Its chest was shattered, multiple flowering wounds on its back bleeding into one another. Cormac's bullets had found their marks. I ran my hand down its flank.

Fur. It was only fur.

I lifted back the head, and the fur and skin came off. Lifted right off, like it was a cloak. I pulled it all the way back and moved it aside. It was a tanned wolf hide, that was all.

A young woman lay before me, naked, sprawled on her side, exit wounds ripped in her chest. Her sleek black hair was long, tangled around her, matted with blood. Despite being marred by blood and destroyed flesh, her body seemed young, lean, and powerful.

"What the hell," Ben murmured, on behalf of us all, it seemed.

"*Dios,*" Tony said.

He was on the other side of the clearing, with Marks, Joe, and Alice. They'd grabbed her before she'd gone too far. Joe held her around the middle, supporting her, because she seemed about to fall to her knees. Marks had had time to retrieve his handgun from his car, and he stood over them protectively.

Tony moved toward us, in something of an astonished daze. When he reached the body, he knelt, put out his hand, and seemed about to touch the woman's hair. Instead, he drew back and crossed himself.

"*Dios,*" he said again. "I've heard of this but never thought to see it in my life."

"She's not a lycanthrope," I said.

"No. She's a skinwalker."

I'd read the stories, but wasn't sure I'd believed them. Everything started out as just stories. Even seeing the evidence lying before me, I didn't want to believe.

Then, as if belatedly responding to Tony's near-touch, she moved. Her head tilted a little, her lips pressed like she wanted to speak, and her eyes shifted under closed lids. Something in her still lived—something inside that ruined chest survived.

"Oh my God, she's not—" I only started to say it.

Cormac's rifle fired again, exploding close by like a crack of thunder in my ears.

At almost the same instant, the woman's face disappeared.

Instinctively, my arm went up to cover my face. I fell back, but not quickly enough to avoid the spray of blood and bits that fanned out from her head and over my jeans, my arm—everywhere. Across from me Tony sprawled away from her in much the same way, arm protecting his face, spatters of blood on his clothing. I looked back at the woman under the wolf skin. Half her head, where Cormac's bullet hit, was now a jagged, pulped mess.

Nothing moved now, except blood dripping from the wound.

Cormac looked down at her over his rifle, finger tight on the trigger, like he still expected her to leap up and attack. He was ready for her to move again. I couldn't tell what appalled and frightened me more: his lack of hesitation in finishing her off, or the lack of emotion in his eyes over doing it.

I gagged, pressed my face against my arm, and managed to not throw up.

Marks aimed his gun at Cormac and approached him warningly.

Cormac's finger remained on the trigger of his rifle. He could shoot back in a fraction of a second. Marks had to know that. He had to know better than to start a shoot-out with the hunter. But for some reason it wouldn't have surprised me if he did anyway.

"Would both of you put your guns down!" I shouted. My ears still rang from the shot. Everything sounded muffled.

Cormac did, slowly. Marks didn't. But he did relax enough to glance away from Cormac and to the woman's body.

The sheriff said, "Who is she?"

"How should I know?" Cormac answered roughly.

Ben said, "You might check missing person reports out of Shiprock." He'd taken my hand again, and I leaned into him.

"But you knew she was going to be here," Marks said to the bounty hunter.

"I've been tracking it, yeah."

Marks said, "I'm going to have to arrest you. A formality, you understand." But the look on his face said, *Got you.* He wore a thin smile.

Surely that was a joke. Cormac had saved my life. Then he'd . . . I didn't want to think about that. The look on his face, the woman's head vanishing in a spray of blood. But Marks didn't like either one of us. He didn't care about me—he had a dead woman and her killer standing there with the gun still smoking.

Cormac leveled that cold stare, unreadable and unsettling, at the sheriff. Beside me, Ben tensed. He didn't know what Cormac was going to do, either. The bounty hunter was going to spook Marks at this rate. Cormac was like some kind of animal himself, and Marks wasn't going to wait around to let him pounce.

Cormac put his left hand around the barrel of the rifle and dropped the gun to his side. "I kind of expected that."

Now, Marks approached him without hesitation. Still with his gun up and ready. I wanted to smack the guy. The sheriff held out his hand; Cormac handed him the rifle.

Marks holstered his handgun, tucked Cormac's rifle under his arm, and pulled out the handcuffs. Cormac handled it like he'd done this before.

"Don't talk until I get there," Ben said.

"Yeah, I know the drill." Handcuffed now, he went with Marks to his patrol car without argument.

"Joe, Alice, watch the body. Don't let anyone touch anything until the coroner gets here. Nobody leave until I get your statements," Marks said. The two were clinging to each other. Quick glances told that they'd heard him, but they didn't move.

I felt like I'd landed in a bad episode of some prime-time police show. Dead body, unlikely circumstances, too much drama.

"You want to go inside and get cleaned up?" Ben said.

I supposed I ought to. I felt like I'd been through a shredder. "Yeah. Should you go with Cormac?"

He looked after the pair, uncertain, his lips pressed together. "As soon as you're okay."

He helped me to my feet. My shoulders were stiff, and blood covered the front of my shirt. Another T-shirt ruined.

Tony had withdrawn, holding himself apart, hands folded in front of him. The candles had all gone out. I hadn't noticed how dark the clearing had become.

"That thing cut you," he said. "You're cursed. You're both cursed." He nodded after Cormac.

"Story of my life," I said. "Any recommendations?"

"A man can only meddle so much. Sometimes you just have to let things run their course."

That was the sort of thing people said when they had no idea what to do next. "Thanks," I muttered.

"I don't think you understand. That magic, the trade one must make to become a skinwalker—it's terrible. It's supposed to be too terrible to think about. But she did it, clearly. She sacrificed someone in her own family to work the blood magic." He held himself stiffly, the horror clear in his manner.

"I'm already a werewolf," I said. "So what are these cuts going to turn me into?"

Tony shrugged. "God knows. I tell you, though, this isn't over."

Well, no silver for him. I knew better than to ask how much worse this could get.

I started toward the cabin, wincing. I had to lean on Ben, because my whole body felt like glass on the verge of shattering.

Joe's words startled me because he spoke so seldom. "I can't believe you're all right. I thought you were dead. You ought to be dead after that."

"If I wasn't a werewolf, I would be dead." I still couldn't see how bad it was. My whole front was dark and shining with blood.

So much for the ritual of peacemaking. This situation had ramped up to a whole new level of surreal and frightening. I probably should have just left town. None of this would have happened.

I didn't want everyone to leave feeling like this.

"Do you guys want to come inside for some coffee? Or I might have some tea somewhere." Or a bottle of whiskey.

Joe and Alice exchanged a glance. Alice nodded, and the two of them approached.

"You, too," I said to Tony. "If you can stand being so close to someone who's as badly cursed as I am."

Tony hesitated for such a long time I thought he was going to refuse. That I was so tainted he really couldn't stand being near me, even though he'd declared me "not evil" earlier that day. I couldn't believe this was still the same day.

Then he said, "I have some tea. It should help. It helps to drink it when you've had a fright."

It certainly couldn't hurt. I hoped.

"Okay," I said, and he went to his truck.

The others gathered in the kitchen. Ben took me to the bathroom.

"Jesus, look at you," he said when he turned on the light.

I whimpered. I didn't want to look. I turned away from the mirror.

"Should we take you to a hospital or something?"

"No, it'll be okay. I've had worse." Brave words.

We had to cut away my shirt and bra. My chest and shoulders had a dozen puncture wounds where the skinwalker had dug in her claws again and again. My right arm was shredded. This was where she'd bitten and worried, and dozens of slashes and tooth marks streaked the flesh. I stood over the sink while Ben sponged me off. The blood had spattered on my face and hair as well. I'd have to stay in the shower for a week to get clean.

"I should have done something," Ben murmured. "I should have helped."

"I'm glad you didn't. We'd both have ended up like this. That thing—I was frozen. I couldn't move, I couldn't do anything. Just like Cormac said." Just like those cows. They couldn't run, they couldn't struggle. She'd slaughtered them at her leisure.

"When does this rapid healing start?"

"It should have started already." All the wounds still oozed and hurt like hell.

He shook his head absently, dabbing away fresh blood. "You have a first-aid kit? I think we're going to have to tape some of this up. You have something you can wear?"

"I think there's a button-up shirt in the closet. I ought to be able to get that on without crying." I was still propped up against the sink, afraid to move because I knew it would hurt.

Ben regarded me a moment, and then had the gall to smile. "For someone who says she doesn't like to get mixed up in the middle of things, you sure have a way of getting mixed up in the middle of things." He kissed my lips and left on his errand. That made me feel better. Heck, it was almost like I'd planned it: Ben was doing great now that he had someone else to worry about. I'd have to keep that in mind.

He came back with a flannel shirt, and I sent him back for something else. I didn't want to think about bits of flannel mixed with cuts scabbing over.

By the time we emerged back into the kitchen, Alice, Joe, and Tony were chatting. If not happily, at least cordially. Like they might actually come out of this as friends. Tony was pouring hot water from a kettle into mugs. His tea smelled rich, warm, soothing—just like he promised. I identified chamomile twined in with scents I didn't recognize.

Tony said, "You just don't seem like the kind of person who'd be into animal sacrifice."

"Well . . . I'm not. It was all roadkill Joe and Avery picked up.

We added blood from the butcher shop to make it look fresh. The only thing I did, really, was fix it so nobody saw or heard them placing the things."

Of all the . . . Before I could say something snotty, Tony continued. "That explains a lot. It didn't work, she didn't leave, because you weren't willing to make the sacrifice yourself, to spill the blood. You weren't willing to take that onto yourself to get what you wanted."

Softly, she said, "Not like that girl out there."

After a moment of silence, I took the opportunity to bust in on the group. "I spend all that money in your store, and you still didn't want me sticking around?"

Alice's face puckered like she was going to start crying and I regretted my cattiness. She really hadn't known what she was doing, had she?

"Oh, Kitty, I was just scared. We all were. We didn't know. You hear stories, and you think the worst. We were just trying to keep the town safe, surely you can understand that."

"So . . . the last couple full moons. Did you notice anything different? Could you tell that a werewolf was living in the neighborhood?" A law-abiding werewolf who made very, very sure that she didn't cause trouble.

"No, I didn't notice."

Joe said, "That's because we spent the night locked in the house with all the lights on."

"And the days I shape-shifted that *weren't* on the full moon—you didn't notice then, did you?"

They both looked at me. Alice said, "You turn into a wolf on other days, too?"

Even Ben looked at me sharply. I wasn't supposed to shape-shift on other nights. He knew I wasn't supposed to do that. Now what kind of role model was I?

"Whenever I want."

"I didn't know that," Alice said softly.

Tony straightened from where he'd parked by the counter. "Hey, Alice, you want to help me with something?"

"What?"

"That thing out there left a lot of bad feeling in the air. No reason we can't try to clean it up a little, even if things didn't go the way we planned."

"But the coroner, shouldn't we wait—"

"This won't bother them. We won't have to touch anything."

She brightened. Tony had offered a chance for redemption, and she seemed eager to take it. "All right."

The two left the cabin, and Tony flashed me a smile on the way out.

Joe busily rinsed out mugs.

I started toward him. "Don't worry about that, I can get it."

Ben interceded. "No, you sit down and start healing." He pointed at me until I sank into a kitchen chair. Funny—I hadn't noticed I was dizzy until I sat down and the room stopped trembling. Ben put a mug of something steaming in front of me, then went to help Joe.

Clutching the mug in both hands and sipping carefully, I watched Ben and Joe washing coffee and tea accoutrements at the sink, side by side. Joe, who wouldn't let me, the werewolf, into his store without holding a gun on me, stood next to another werewolf and didn't even know it.

Over the next half hour, Sheriff Marks's backup arrived, including a coroner's van and a few deputies to take statements. While they worked, Tony and Alice walked around the clearing, each waving a smoking bundle of plant matter—some kind of incense. Some kind of blessing, or cleansing. I didn't know if it would work. Alice seemed to feel better, at any rate. At least it worked for someone.

One of the deputies took Joe and Alice home. The cops had taken statements from everyone, and Tony was the next to leave. Before that, he found me, sitting on the porch steps to watch the proceedings.

He sat next to me.

"Here. Take this." He reached over his neck and pulled something from under his shirt: a small leather pouch on a long cord. Before I even had time to lean away in surprise, he put the cord over my head, so I was wearing the pouch around my neck. "It's protected me through the years. It may help protect you."

I put my hand over it. Small enough to fit inside my fist, the brown leather was soft. Stuffed inside was something crunchy and fibrous. Dried herbs, maybe.

"May?" I said.

He shrugged, like we were talking about the weather. "I do what I can."

"Well. Thanks for trying."

"If I had known that's what we were dealing with, I might have been able to do more." He nodded to where the coroner's people were loading the body onto a wheeled stretcher. Some forensics officers wrapped the wolf skin in a plastic bag and carried it away.

"Any advice for what to do next?" I said.

"Let it end here. Don't go asking any more questions. Don't look for any more trouble."

I hid a smile. Good advice, to be sure. Not sure it was the right advice. I had way too many questions, and this hadn't ended because Cormac was still sitting in the back of Marks's car, wearing handcuffs.

"Ben told me about the silver," I said. "I don't usually keep that sort of thing around, but we could probably pay you with some of Cormac's bullets." I'd pay Cormac back later. He'd understand.

"This one's on the house," he said. Then, as unobtrusively as he'd arrived, he disappeared into his truck and away.

Finally, after the coroner's crew and deputies were gone, the sheriff left with Cormac riding in the backseat, leaving the clearing suddenly empty and quiet. Ben and I stood on the porch, watching the chaos disperse. The night wasn't over for us; we had to get in my car and go spring Cormac.

"I don't know if I can do this," Ben said, watching the cars leave.

"Do what?"

"Sit there and argue with those clowns. Not without . . . something happening. Losing my temper. You know."

"You've done it before, haven't you?" They'd both acted like this was routine. Which was kind of scary.

"Lost my temper? Sure." He smiled a little. "Or do you mean representing Cormac? You keep saying you and I are a pack and we have to look out for each other. I feel like Cormac is part of my pack. I have to protect him. The wolf side would do anything to protect him." He flexed his hands, like he could already feel that anger, that determination, waking up inside him.

I touched his hand, to bring him back to himself. He let out a nervous breath.

"I'll go with you," I said.

Looking away, he nodded. "I was hoping you would."

I hadn't ever considered not going.

The truth was, the thought of him leaving me here, of being

alone after all that, made me ill. Between that and the queasy, injured feeling that still lingered after the fight, I wanted to throw up.
I wasn't okay at all, and I wasn't going to sit around waiting for the
next curse to arrive.

chapter 13

We took my car, and in forty minutes arrived at the sheriff's department and county jail in Walsenburg. Marks had booked Cormac by the time we got into the building, and the hunter was ensconced in a back room, out of sight.

Marks glared at us over the front desk. "He's already asking for his lawyer. You want to get back here so we can take his statement?"

Ben was tense. I knew him well enough by now that I could tell without touching him.

"You'll be fine," I said. "Just breathe slow and think about keeping it in. Stay calm."

"Easier said than done."

"Yup." I tried to make my smile encouraging.

He straightened his shoulders and stalked forward like a man preparing to go into battle.

I'd seen him talk down cops before. I'd seen him face a panel of senators and hold them off. In those cases he'd had this hawk's stare, the fierce-eyed glare of a hunter that had always instilled confidence in me, because he was always on my side.

The hawk was gone. I should have seen it, but it wasn't there. Instead, he looked like he'd been cornered.

I watched him go, wringing my hands on his behalf. Then all I could do was wait in the lobby on a hard plastic chair, leafing through copies of news magazines a month out of date. I wanted to climb the walls. The place was clean, not terribly old or worn out. But it smelled of sweat and fatigue. It was not a good place. People ended up here when they'd hit bottom, or were about to hit bottom.

My wounds still itched. They should have been almost healed. Cursed, Tony had said. I hadn't realized how much I took the quick healing for granted. Then again, if I didn't have rapid healing, I wouldn't go around intercepting attacking wolves.

I watched the clock. Hours later, after midnight, Ben came back to the lobby. He was pale, ill-looking, and sweat dampened his hair. He looked like he'd run a race, not talked with the cops. I stood and met him.

He smelled musky, animal, like his wolf was rising to the surface. I took hold of his hand. "Keep it together, Ben. Take a deep breath."

He did, and it shuddered when he let it out. "I don't know what Cormac did earlier, but Marks has it in for him. He already called the prosecutor. They want to file charges. Six eyewitnesses saw Cormac save your life, and they want to press charges. They won't set bail until the advisement hearing tomorrow. And I just sat there and *stared* at them."

"How does this usually work? You make it sound like this isn't the way things normally go for you guys."

"Usually I have plenty of evidence that Cormac had a good reason for doing whatever he did, and the charges don't even get filed. But we have a couple of problems this time. Somebody around here wants to make a reputation for themselves."

"Marks?"

"Marks and George Espinoza, a very earnest prosecutor who's probably never encountered anything more serious than trespassing." His tone was harsh.

"And?" There was an "and" in there.

"She was already dying when he killed her. It was excessive force, even for Cormac. That's the argument Espinoza's going to use."

This was going to be about splitting hairs. Cormac did what he had to—I could convince myself of that. A hundred horror movie climaxes said he did the right thing.

But how would a judge see it?

"How's Cormac?"

"Stoic. He's Cormac. There's something else. They've ID'd the body. The skinwalker. Miriam Wilson. She's the twin sister of John Wilson, the werewolf that Cormac shot. The one that got me. A missing person report on her was filed three months ago."

As if we needed the situation to be any more complicated. I tried to imagine a state of affairs where a brother and sister would become the things they were, and wreak the havoc they had.

"Brother and sister? One of them a werewolf and one of them a skinwalker. What's the story behind that?"

"I wish I knew."

"And her family reported her disappearance to the police, but they hired Cormac to hunt down the brother?"

He shrugged. "We don't know that it was her family that filed the report. I'm guessing they didn't send Cormac after her because she wasn't a werewolf. We don't know if they knew what she was. We don't know anything. Christ, I'm going to have to go buy a suit. I left all my clothes in my car back in Farmington. I can't go to court without a suit." He was currently wearing his coat over jeans and a T-shirt, like he'd been wearing for the last week.

"We'll go buy you a suit in the morning. Is there anything else you need to do? Can we get out of here?" I wanted to get him out of this place, with its unhappy smells and atmosphere of confrontation.

"Yeah, let's go."

That started a very long night. Ben used my laptop and spent hours looking through online legal libraries for precedents and arguments that would spring Cormac. He scratched out notes on a notepad. I watched, lying on the sofa, wondering how I could help. He grew more agitated by the minute.

"Ben, come to bed. Get some sleep."

"I can't. Too much to do. All my work is back in my car, I have too much to review, I have to catch up." He glared at the screen with a frantic intensity.

"How much are you going to be able to help him if you're falling asleep in the courtroom?"

He took his hands away from the keyboard and bowed his head. I could see the fatigue radiating off him. When he came to the sofa, I sat up, made room for him, and pulled him into an embrace. My body was healing, finally, but still sore. I didn't complain. He needed me to comfort him, however much I wanted someone to comfort me. We stayed like that a long time, his head pillowed on my shoulder, until the tension started to seep out of him. I got him out of his clothes, into bed, and held him close, curled up in my arms, until he finally fell asleep. He never fully relaxed.

The next morning, we went to buy a suit. We weren't going to find anything fancy in Walsenburg. This put Ben even further out of sorts. But we managed, somehow.

He changed clothes in the car on the way to the Huerfano County Courthouse, where Cormac's first hearing was scheduled to take place. The suit didn't fit quite right, it didn't make as slick a picture as he might have wanted. I brushed his hair back with my fingers, straightened his tie, smoothed his lapels. Like I was sending him to the prom or something.

Ben looked like I was sending him to an execution. He was still holding himself tense, shoulders stiff, like the raised hackles on a nervous wolf.

"You going to be okay?"

"Yeah. Yeah, sure. This is just a formality. The judge will look over his statement, the witness statements, and throw out the case. That's all there is to it."

He headed into the building alone to meet with Cormac before the hearing. I made my way to the courtroom. In other circumstances I might have admired the hundred-year-old building, made of functional gray stone and topped by a simple decorated tower. They built them to last in those days.

I didn't know what I expected—some kind of dramatic, busy scene like in a courtroom drama on TV. But the place was almost empty. Marks stood off to one side. A couple of people in business suits conversed quietly. Fluorescent lights glared. The whole place gave the impression of dull bureaucracy. I sat in the first row behind the defense side. I was sure this would be educational if I weren't so nervous on Ben and Cormac's behalf.

Without any preamble, a couple of bailiffs guided Cormac into the courtroom. He'd had a chance to shave, which made him look slightly less psychotic than he had last night. A point in his favor, and that was probably part of the strategy. It was a shock, though, to see him in an orange prison jumpsuit, short-sleeved, baggy, unflattering. It gave me a terrible sense of foreboding.

Ben followed, and both of them positioned themselves behind one of the podiums before the bench.

The whole procedure followed in a kind of haze. The judge, Heller, a middle-aged woman, brown hair pulled into a bun, wearing a no-nonsense expression, came into the room and took her place. Ben and Cormac remained standing before her. Across from them, one of the business suits, a surprisingly young man—no older than Ben and Cormac—shuffled papers on the desk in front of him. George Espinoza, the prosecutor. His suit was neat, his dark hair slicked back, his expression viperish. A crusader. No wonder Ben was worried.

The prosecutor read the facts—and just the facts, ma'am. The time and place of Cormac's arrest, the nature of the crime, the probable cause. The charge: murder. Not just murder, but first-degree murder. That was serious, way too serious.

Espinoza explained: "The accused was heard to say that he had tracked the victim, had in fact been focused on her for quite some time with the intent to kill her. He was seen in the area of Shiprock, New Mexico—the victim's hometown—on several dates over the last month. He was, in fact, lying in wait for the victim's appearance. This presents a clear display of deliberation, meeting the requirement for a charge of first-degree murder."

Cormac had been tracking her. He had meant to kill her. Which made the whole thing murky. I was glad I wasn't the lawyer.

This wasn't a TV show. Nobody shouted, nobody slammed their fists on the tables, nobody rushed in from the back with the crucial piece of information that would free the defendant, or pound the final nail in the prosecution's case.

They might have been lecturing on economic theory, as calmly and analytically as everyone spoke. It made it hard to concentrate on the words.

The judge spoke: "Mr. Espinoza has requested that Mr. Bennett—" Cormac Bennett. I'd never heard his last name before. Even such a small detail as that made the scene surreal. It was like Cormac should have been beyond something as mundane as a last name. "—be held without bail, on the basis of his past associations and the belief that he is a flight risk."

Ben argued: "Your Honor, my client has dealt with law enforcement agencies in several jurisdictions, and has always been cooperative. He's never once given the indication that he's a flight risk."

"Perhaps his past association with the Mountain Patriot Brigade hasn't been an issue until now. It is the experience and opinion of this court that members of such right-wing paramilitary organizations are, in fact, flight risks."

Again, the world shifted, becoming even more surreal, if that was possible. I'd heard of the Mountain Patriot Brigade: it was one of those militia groups, right-wing fanatics who ran around with guns and preached the downfall of the government. When they weren't actually blowing things up.

That didn't sound like Cormac at all. Not the Cormac I knew. Well, except for the running around with guns part. The number of backstories I didn't know was getting frustrating.

Ben's hesitation before responding was maddening. Hesitation meant uncertainty. Meant a weak position. Maybe even guilt. Which made me wonder: Where had Cormac learned about guns? Where had he become such a great shot?

Ben said, "Your Honor, Mr. Bennett's association with that group ended over a decade ago. It hasn't been an issue because it isn't relevant."

"Mr. O'Farrell, I've granted the prosecution's request that Mr. Bennett be held without bail."

"Your Honor, I'd like to lodge a protest. You've got his record—he's never jumped bail."

"And don't you think it's just a little odd how often your client has been arrested and had to post bail? Don't you ever get tired of standing with your client at these hearings?"

"Frankly, that's not your concern."

"Careful, Mr. O'Farrell."

"Your Honor, I'd like to move that the case against my client be dismissed. Miriam Wilson's attack was so brutal, lives were at risk. Katherine Norville's attempt to stop her without lethal force resulted in great injury to herself. My client was well within his right to use force against her under Title eighteen dash one dash seven-oh-four of the Colorado Criminal Code."

Espinoza countered: "The law protecting the right to use deadly force in cases of defense does not apply in this case. On the contrary, the accused was in fact lying in wait for the victim's appearance." That was wrong. I almost stood up and said something. I had to bite my tongue. The prosecutor continued. "Your Honor, the victim was a twenty-year-old woman weighing a hundred and twenty pounds. Her ability to inflict lethal damage with her bare hands is questionable. Moreover, the evidence suggests she was highly mentally disturbed during the incident." He consulted a page of notes. "She was wearing a wolf skin at the time and it has been suggested that she believed that she was a wolf. I find it hard to believe that in such a mental state, judging by her physical attributes, she was at all a danger to anyone. Especially when she already had three bullet wounds in her chest. The victim was already incapacitated when the defendant fired the final, killing shot. In that moment this stopped being a case of defense and became a murder."

And nothing about any of that was false. She had been wearing a wolf skin. That it actually turned her into a wolf—suggesting that would sound ludicrous in this setting. And maybe she'd been fatally wounded. Maybe she wouldn't have lashed out with her skinwalker magic. But Cormac hadn't known that.

Ben offered another volley. "Seeing that a psychological evaluation of the victim is impossible, I would like to offer evidence and precedent that such a mental illness would in fact make her a danger to those around her, even while injured."

Heller asked a question. "The witness who was involved in the physical confrontation with the victim—how extensive are her injuries?"

A moment of silence weighed heavily on the room. How extensive were my injuries? They weren't, not anymore. I had a few scabs, where the worst of the scratches had healed, a few pink marks. In a couple more days even those would disappear. But if I hadn't been a lycanthrope I'd be in the hospital. If I hadn't been a lycanthrope, we could say, *Look, this is what Cormac saved us from, this is why he shouldn't be in jail.* But we didn't have that.

In lieu of an answer, Heller continued. "Was Ms. Norville even examined by a doctor after the confrontation?"

"No, Your Honor," Ben said softly. I should have let him take me to a hospital. He'd wanted to take me to a hospital. We could have at least taken pictures of what the wounds looked like.

None of us thought we'd be here arguing it in court. That we'd need the evidence.

"Then the violence of the victim's attack has perhaps been exaggerated?"

I should have just let Miriam Wilson kill me. That would have gotten Cormac off the hook. Made everyone's lives a whole lot easier. Nice defeatist thinking there.

Ben's voice changed, falling in pitch, becoming tight with anger. "You have the witness statements, Your Honor. At the time, they all feared for Ms. Norville's life. That's the scene my client encountered, and that's what should be taken into account. The only reason there's even a question is because Sheriff Marks has a grudge against him. This court is biased." He landed his fist on the table. From behind him, I could see his breathing quicken, his ribs expanding under the cheap suit jacket.

Heller shook her head, preparing to close out the hearing. "I am not inclined to dismiss this case on the basis of the evidence you've presented, Mr. O'Farrell."

Hissing a breath, Ben bent double almost, leaning on the table in front of him, bowing his head. The pose was familiar—it's what I did when the Wolf fought inside me, when she was close to the surface and trying to break out.

I stood quickly; leaning forward as far as I could, I was able to touch Ben's back. It was stiff as a board, in pain. Cormac gripped

Ben's arm with his bound hands. *Please, not here,* I begged silently. *Feel my touch, stay human, keep it together.* I tried to see his hands—that was where it usually happened first. The claws—did he have claws or fingers?

"Mr. O'Farrell, are you all right?" Judge Heller frowned with concern.

Everyone in the courtroom stared at us. I didn't care. I kept my hand pressed against his back, hoping he'd respond. Cormac and I both watched him intently, waiting.

Finally, he straightened. Creaking almost, like he had to stack each vertebra into place. His face was pale, and his neck sweating.

"I'm fine," he said, though his voice was still rough, like a growl. "Sorry for the interruption. I'm fine." He smoothed his suit and shook himself out of the spell. Slowly, Cormac and I sat back in our places.

My heart was racing. I couldn't help but feel like we'd had a close call. He shouldn't have been doing this, he shouldn't have had to face the stress of a courtroom in his condition. He was still just a pup.

Heller resumed. "Both parties should consult in order to agree on a time for a preliminary hearing, at which time the defendant will enter his plea to the charges filed."

Then, almost abruptly, anticlimactically, it was over. And Cormac wasn't leaving with us. Held without bail.

The courtroom rustled with activity. Bailiffs approached to take charge of Cormac, who looked over his shoulder at me. "Keep an eye on him. Don't let him out of your sight," he said in a low voice. I nodded quickly and watched them lead him away. He knew how close it had been, too.

Marks glared at us across the room, but didn't stick around for a confrontation.

Espinoza approached Ben, who still looked like he was about to pass out. I could hear his heart racing. I was ready to jump up and leap to his side, if he showed the slightest indication that he needed help—if he was about to break down. He held it together, though. He didn't look good, but he stayed upright, kept breathing.

I didn't like George Espinoza, even though I knew that wasn't fair. I didn't know him, I'd never spoken to him. But I saw him as a threat. He was attacking my people. My pack. I kept wanting to slip in between him and Ben and growl at him. But I had to just step aside and let things happen.

They talked in low voices. Ben did a lot of nodding. The bailiff hustled them out of the room then to make way for the next hearing. I trailed behind, trying to eavesdrop. I heard a couple of phrases. "Give me a week," and "plea bargain."

I approached Ben only after Espinoza left the lobby outside the courtroom. He stood stiffly, hugging a file folder that stood in for his briefcase. He carried himself rigidly—angry, and trying to hold it in. He was used to being able to channel his anger in the courtroom. Using it to strengthen his arguments. Now, the wolf wouldn't let him do that.

I put my hand on his shoulder. "Let's get out of here."

He let me guide him out of the building, leaning on me until we were outside.

Out in the sun I was able to ask him, "How close did you get in there? How close to Changing?"

He shook his head absently. "I don't know. I felt like I could have breathed wrong and it all would have come loose. I felt it push against the inside of my skin. I just don't know." He closed his eyes and took a deep, trembling breath. "I'm losing it."

"No, you're not. You're fine, you kept it together."

"Not me," he said. "I don't care about me. I'm talking about the case."

"It can't be that bad. Can it?" He was the lawyer. Who was I to second-guess him?

"Any rational person looks at the evidence and comes to exactly the conclusion Espinoza presented. If I stand up there and say, no she wasn't just wearing a wolf skin, she'd actually become a wolf, I sound insane. When it comes to believing the eyewitness reports of a few people who were in the dark and scared out of their skulls, or the hard evidence of the coroner's report, it isn't much of a contest. And she was incapacitated when Cormac killed her. He wasn't defending anyone at that point."

"We didn't know that, not for sure. Marks was there—why doesn't he tell them? He's a cop, wouldn't his testimony hold any more weight?"

"He's signed off on Espinoza's version."

Of course he would. "That's not fair. You'd think after everything he did to me he could at least stand up for Cormac."

"Except he's decided that she wasn't that dangerous, and Cormac overreacted. The coroner's report makes more sense than skinwalkers, so that's what he's sticking to. That's what's going to hold up in court. Not the ghost stories."

I wanted to shake Ben. Tell him to snap out of it and get his confidence back. He had to save Cormac, and he wasn't going to do it talking like that.

Ben said, "He shouldn't have shot her there at the end. That was a mistake."

"I know."

And that was what we kept talking around. That Cormac had gone too far to save this time. Nothing we said or did would ever erase that moment.

We walked a few more paces, and I changed the subject. "Why wouldn't the judge set bail?"

He scowled. "Espinoza doesn't want to take a chance on him getting away. Heller's right, those militia wingnuts do have a history of jumping bail. It's a case of them looking at the facts they want to and not the ones that matter. There might be some past history there that's coloring her judgment."

That brought up a whole other set of questions. We'd reached the car by then. "So what is all that about Cormac and the Mountain Patriot Brigade?"

Ben kept on, almost like he hadn't heard, climbing into the car and not looking at me. I'd started the engine before he finally said, "I'm not going to answer that."

"Why not? You know those guys are practically neo-Nazis?"

"I won't argue with that."

I couldn't fit that and Cormac in my mind at the same time. "And?"

"And I don't think the group even exists anymore. It's some guy in a basement running a Web site."

"How do you know this? How are you two even involved?" My voice was becoming shrill.

"I don't owe you an explanation."

That just pissed me off. "Oh, really?"

He glared at me, and I bristled. That was just what we needed. A fight. Posturing. A pissing contest. I didn't want to rile up his wolf any more than it already was.

I put the car in gear and pulled out of the parking lot.

The movement of the car, driving down the highway back to the cabin, settled us down. Ben didn't want to tell me, and that was his right, I supposed. But I had other ways of finding information. We had a lot of other problems to deal with right now.

A few more miles of ranch land sped past us when he said, "I want to get a hotel room in Walsenburg, to be closer to the courthouse."

We packed that night, and in the morning found a place to make camp for the duration.

The next day saw Ben working on building his case. Mostly, this involved talking to people, legwork, phone calls. He went to Alice, Joe, Tony, and Sheriff Marks. They were Cormac's defense. I offered to come along, but Ben said no. Cormac's lawyer needed to handle this, he said. My being there would muddy the issue. Remind them of their biases. Maybe he was right. Cormac told me not to let Ben out of my sight. But I let him go.

Besides, I had a research project of my own.

The public library, a couple of blocks down from the courthouse, had several computer terminals. I went to one and started searching. After a half an hour, I took my notes to the reference desk.

"Do you have copies of the *Denver Post* from these dates?"

The nice lady at the desk set me up at a microfiche machine, and away I went. It took about three hours of hunting to find the whole story.

Starting about fifteen years ago, a group of Front Range ranchers began protesting new restrictions and higher fees for grazing their cattle on public lands. Millions of acres across the West were owned by the government, and ranchers had been given access to those lands. To a lot of people, federally owned was the same as public, and anything that barred their access to those lands impinged on their rights as citizens. Some of them did the sane thing: they lobbied Congress, lodged complaints, took the issue to court. Others, though, turned to militias. They stockpiled arms and began to prepare for the violent overthrow of the government they saw as inevitable.

A man named David O'Farrell showed up in a series of articles. This was Ben's father, who at the time owned a ranch near Loveland. He was arrested several times on illegal weapons charges and went straight to the top of the list of people suspected of being the head of the Mountain Patriot Brigade, one of a network of paramilitary groups that gathered and trained in the backcountry, with the ultimate goal of defending by force their right to use public lands. Through the early nineties they had almost constant confrontations with local law enforcement—except in a few cases where local law enforcement happened to be members.

Eight years ago, after lengthy FBI surveillance and a carefully prosecuted case, Ben's father had been convicted on various felony weapons violations and conspiracy charges. He was still in prison.

The name Cormac Bennett didn't show up in conjunction with the Mountain Patriot Brigade in any of the articles and references I found. He'd never been arrested or suspected of any wrongdoing as part of the group. Espinoza's information about him came from FBI and police reports about the group. Young Cormac didn't rate the attention that the group's leaders did. He hadn't been considered a threat. But the association was there, especially since he was David O'Farrell's nephew.

I found another newspaper article, from a couple of years earlier than all the Mountain Patriot Brigade business, that featured Cormac. It reported on the strange death of Douglas Bennett. The coroner reported that the forty-eight-year-old had been mauled by an animal, possibly a bear or a very large dog. The police, on the other hand, claimed that he'd been murdered by a deranged assailant. Douglas's sixteen-year-old son, Cormac, had witnessed the attack, and shot dead the assailant. The police had the all-too-human body, with Cormac's rifle bullet in its head and Douglas's flesh between its teeth. The shooting was deemed a case of self-defense. No charges were filed against Cormac, who went to live with his aunt's family, the O'Farrell clan. His mother had died in a car accident when he was five.

It was déjà vu, this disagreement between the witnesses and the coroner's report. And Cormac had been in this situation before. Cormac had killed his first werewolf when he was sixteen years old. I didn't even know what to think about that. Once, I asked Cormac how he'd become a werewolf and vampire hunter, where he'd learned the tricks of it. He said it ran in the family. Which might explain why Douglas was in a position to get mauled to death in the first place, and why Cormac was there to witness it: Douglas had been training him.

I wondered what his mother would have thought of that, if she'd been alive to see it.

I printed off that article and a dozen or so others. By then, it was dinnertime. I called the hotel room, but no one answered. That meant Ben was either off being lawyerly—I hoped—or he was moping. I took a chance and picked up a pizza and beer for dinner.

When I got back to the room, Ben was there. Doing a little of both, it seemed: my laptop was on, plugged into the phone jack, and papers were spread over the table and half the bed. But he sat in the chair, staring at the wall. I couldn't even say that he was thinking hard. He was back in that fugue state.

He jumped when the door opened, clutched the arms of his chair, his mouth open slightly, like he was about to growl. He calmed down almost immediately, slouching and looking away. Tense—just a little.

"Hungry?" I said, trying to be nonchalant.

"Not really."

"When was the last time you ate?" He only shook his head. "You ought to eat something."

"Sure, Mom." He gave me the briefest flickers of a glance—half accusing, half apologetic. I must have glared at him. I didn't appreciate the label. I didn't appreciate having to behave like that label.

He cleared a spot on the table where I deposited the pizza.

I pulled my stack of papers out of my bag and set them between us. I'd put the one about Cormac's father on top. A grainy, black and white picture of the man occupied the middle of the page. He'd been lean and weathered, with short-cropped, receding hair. In the picture, a candid snapshot, he was smiling at something to the left of the camera, and wearing sunglasses.

Ben stared at it a moment, his expression blank. I thought I knew him pretty well by now, but I couldn't read this. He was almost disbelieving. Then, his lips quirked a smile.

Finally, he said, "I'd forgotten about that picture. It's a good one of him. Uncle Doug." He shook his head, then looked at me. "You've been busy."

"Yeah. It's funny how much of your family's history is plastered all over the newspapers."

He started shuffling through the articles. "Real busy."

"Just remember that the next time you think you can keep a secret from me."

"Why go to the trouble?"

"I wanted to make sure that you and Cormac aren't bad guys. I have to say, you have kind of a creepy past. When you say this stuff doesn't matter, I really want to trust you."

"I'm not sure that's such a great idea. You might be better off on your own. Get out of Dodge while the getting's good."

We were pack. I'd see this through. "I'll stick around."

"I haven't seen my father in over ten years. We had a throw-down screaming match over this Patriot Brigade garbage. I was twenty, first one in my family to go to college and so full of my-self. I was educated." He gave the word sarcastic emphasis. "I knew it all, and there I was to throw it back in the face of my poor benighted father. And he was so full of that right-wing nut-job rhetoric . . . I left. Cormac was still there, helping him work the ranch. That's the only reason he got tangled up with that crowd, was because of my father. When I left, so did he. I still don't know if it was something I said that convinced him. Or if we'd just spent so much time looking out for each other—we were already kind of a team, then.

"Dad called me right before that last trial. I'd just passed the bar. He wanted me to represent him. I said no. I'd have said no even if we were on good terms. He really needed someone with experience. But all Dad heard was that his only son, his own flesh and blood, was turning his back on him. The funny thing about it all, I wanted to convince him he was wrong. There wasn't a government conspiracy out to get him, I wasn't trying to sell him down the river. But everything that happened, from the FBI wiretaps to me walking out on him, confirmed everything in his mind. He's too far gone to come back."

"You haven't been to see him. You haven't talked to him at all," I said. "Do you want to? Do you think you should?"

He shook his head. "I made a clean break. We're all better off if it stays that way. Cormac and I always kind of knew that something he'd done in the past would come back to haunt him. I didn't think it would be this." He tossed the printouts back on the table.

"Where's your mom?"

"She divorced my dad after thirty years of marriage, sold the ranch to pay his legal expenses, and is now working as a waitress in Longmont. And that's the whole story of my sordid, screwed up family." He shook his head absently. "You know what's always gotten to me? My dad and I aren't that different. It's where we came from, that whole independent rural culture. I remember telling him, yeah, sure, take back the government, put it back in the hands of the people. That's great. But you're not going to do it with a stockpile of dynamite and hate speech. Me—I went to law school. Thought I'd work the system from the inside, sticking it to the man." His smile turned sad. "Maybe we were both wrong."

I wanted to hug him and make silly cooing noises. That Mom thing again. He had this traumatized look to him. Instead, I hefted the grocery bag. "I brought beer."

"My hero," he said, smiling.

We settled down to beer and pizza. "What have you been working on?"

"Precedents," he said. "You'd think in a state where half the population totes around guns in their glove boxes this sort of thing would have come up before. We have a Make My Day law for crying out loud. But there isn't too much out there to cover if you shoot something thinking it's a wild animal, then it turns out to be a person."

"Except for the werewolf that killed Cormac's dad."

"Which isn't going to help Cormac's case at all if the prosecutor digs it up, so I'd really appreciate it if you didn't draw anyone's attention to it. Judges get nervous when weird things keep happening to the same person."

I turned an invisible key at the corner of my mouth. "My lips are sealed."

He gave me a highly skeptical look. I wanted to argue—then realized I couldn't, really. We fell into a moment of silence, eating and drinking. He stared at the computer screen as if it would offer up miracles.

"How did the rest of your day go?" I asked, not sure I wanted to know.

"Pretty well, I think," he said, but the tone was ambivalent, and he still looked exhausted instead of fired up. "Tony's going to stick around to give a statement, Alice is downright enthusiastic about testifying. She seems to think she owes you a favor. But you know what? I keep running into that same problem."

"What problem? I don't see a problem. Eyewitnesses, that's what you need, that's what you have. Isn't it?" I had the feeling he was about to tangle me up in some legal loophole.

"Why were we all there in the first place?" he said.

I wasn't sure I could explain it anymore. It seemed so long ago. "We were going to remove Alice's curse. Tony said he had a ritual."

"Magic. Witchcraft," he said curtly. "So how do you convince the legal system that this is real? That when Tony and Alice talk about casting their spells, they're serious, and it's real. That they're not crackpots. I'm afraid Espinoza's going to use that angle to discredit their testimony. He'll say, of course a couple of people who are out in the woods at dusk lighting candles and burning incense are going to think up some story about how this woman really turned into a wolf. Of course they'll say that even shot through the chest and dying she was a threat because she was a skinwalker. He'll say they're as deluded as Miriam was and therefore their testimony is suspect."

He was twisting the words, manipulating the story. Just like a lawyer. Just like Espinoza. Ben was thinking of all the angles, but none of them seemed to work in our favor.

"So you can't use their testimony."

"Oh, I'm going to use it and hope for the best. Maybe I'm wrong and Espinoza won't shoot them down."

This was looking grimmer and grimmer. Grasping at straws. "What about Marks? He had it in for me in the first place—*that's* why we were at the cabin when Miriam attacked. Can't you use that to discredit him as a witness?"

"If you want to sue Alice and Sheriff Marks for harassment, I'm all for it. I think you have a good case against them. You don't even have to bring up magic to prove that leaving dead dogs in someone's yard is harassment. But it's a different case. I'll certainly bring it up, but the judge might decide that a suit against Marks doesn't have any bearing in the case of Miriam Wilson's death."

The pizza had gotten cold and I'd lost my appetite. Ben wasn't eating either.

"The whole thing seems rigged," I said. "It's not fair."

"Welcome to the American justice system." He raised his bottle of beer, as if in a toast.

"Cynic." I pouted.

"Lawyer," he countered, grinning.

"Ben. Drink your beer."

I went to see Sheriff Marks the next morning. I told Ben I was taking a walk to the grocery store for donuts.

Carefully, I approached the front desk at the sheriff's department like it was a bomb. I asked the woman working there, a nonuniformed civilian, "Hi, is Sheriff Marks in? Could I speak to him?"

"Yes, I think he is. Do you have an appointment?"

"No," I said, wincing. I fully expected Marks to refuse to see me. But I had to try.

The receptionist frowned sadly, and I tried not to be mad at her. She was just doing her job. "Then I'm afraid he probably won't be available, he's very busy—"

"It's all right, Kelly." Marks stood in the hallway to the side, just within view. His expression was guarded, pointedly bland, like he'd expected me to be here all along and didn't mind. He knew his place in the world and I couldn't shake it. "I'll talk to her. Send her back."

He turned and went down the hall, presumably to his office.

"Go on back," Kelly the receptionist said. I did.

Marks disappeared through a doorway halfway down the hall, and I followed him into a perfectly average, perfectly normal cluttered office: a desk with a computer sat against the wall. There was an in-box overflowing with papers and files, bookshelves, also overflowing, certificates and plaques on the wall, along with a huge map labeled Huerfano County. Colored pins marked various spots; a red pin was stuck about where I guessed my cabin was.

Marks sat at the desk and gestured me toward a couple of straight-backed plastic chairs by the opposite wall.

"Thanks" I said, sitting. "I didn't think you'd even talk to me."

He gave an amiable shrug, donning the persona of a friendly small-town cop. "I figure the least I can do is hear you out."

"The least you can do is let Cormac go."

"Have you seen that guy's file? You know what he's done? He should have been locked up years ago."

"And if he had, I'd be dead, and so would you and four other people." I matched him, glare for glare. "He saved my life, Sheriff. That's all I'm paying attention to right now."

His glare set like stone, unrelenting. "That man's a killer."

Yes, but . . . "You can't deny he saved my life."

"That girl couldn't have really hurt anyone," he said, giving a huff that was almost laughter.

"Didn't you see what she did to me?"

"You had a few cuts," he said.

Then I realized, maybe he hadn't seen. It had been dark; I hadn't even known how bad it was until I got inside and saw all the blood. Marks simply might not have seen it. Once again, I kicked myself for not taking pictures.

I said, "Then you don't believe she really turned into a wolf. You're buying the 'insane woman in a wolf skin' version." He answered with a cold stare that said it all. "How can you believe in werewolves but not in skinwalkers? How can you believe in magic enough to curse my house, but not enough to believe what she was? You just want to put Cormac away because you can, without giving him the benefit of the doubt or anything!"

"Ms. Norville, I think we're done here."

"You're a hypocrite—you've broken the law yourself, in the name of protecting people, when you did those things to me. Well, Cormac was doing the same thing."

Marks leaned forward, hand on his desk, his glare still hard as stone. Nothing could touch this guy, not when he was like this. "He shot and killed an injured, dying woman in cold blood. *That's* what he's being charged with. Goodbye, Ms. Norville." He pointed at the door.

I glared at him, my throat on the edge of a growl, and he couldn't read the stance. All he saw was an angry, ineffectual woman standing before him. And maybe that was all I was.

I left, gratefully slipping out of his territory.

I went back to the hotel, where Ben greeted me with, "Where are the donuts?"

I'd forgotten. Crap. I shrugged and said, "Didn't get them. Got lost."

"In Walsenburg?" Clearly, he didn't believe me. I just smiled sweetly.

Later, we returned to the county jail to see Cormac. I hadn't had a chance to talk to him, not after the attack, not before or after the hearing. It had been frustrating, sitting five feet away in the courtroom and not being able to say anything to him.

I had hoped Marks would be there to meet us. That he'd have seen the error of his ways and come to make amends by releasing Cormac. That all this would just go away. Wishful thinking. He wasn't there, and Cormac was still locked up.

"Has Marks talked to you?" I asked Ben. "Maybe changed his mind about all this?"

"Are you kidding? He's not even returning my calls."

So much for my grand speech at him having any influence and giving us that Disney happy ending.

Still, Ben had a plan. "I have to go to New Mexico. Talk to people who knew Miriam Wilson. Find out if they knew what she was, and if she killed anyone there. Espinoza's not going to have to dig too much to prove that Cormac's a dangerous man. So I have to prove that he didn't have a choice but to kill her."

"He didn't," I said. "Did he?"

"That's what I have to prove."

A deputy ensconced us in a windowless conference room, like a thousand others in police stations and jails all across the country. I bet they all had the same smell, too: dust and old coffee. Strained nerves. Ben got me in by claiming I was his legal assistant. Then the deputy brought Cormac.

Ben and Cormac sat across from each other. I hid away in the corner. I both did and didn't want to be there. I hated seeing Cormac like this. I didn't know exactly what *this* meant. Objectively, he looked the same as he always did, half slouching, appearing unconcerned with what went on around him—moving through the world without being a part of it. That orange jumpsuit made him look *wrong,* though.

Ben had a pen and paper out, ready to take notes. "I need to know everything that happened while you were gone. Between the time you left the cabin in Clay and when you got back in time to shoot her."

"I told you before."

"Tell me again."

"I got in my Jeep, I drove all night to Shiprock. Stopped to get some sleep at a rest stop. Went back to the place where we'd gone to bait them." As in, the place where Ben was attacked. "I spent a lot of time just looking around. I honestly didn't think she'd leave the area. That was her territory."

"Except she wasn't a lycanthrope. She didn't have a territory."

"Sure, we know that *now.*"

"Go on."

"I talked to the werewolf's family. The people who hired me. The Wilsons. Trying to find out more about the second one. They wouldn't tell me anything. They wouldn't believe me when I said there was a second one running around. They thanked me for freeing their son from his curse, and that was it. End of story. I didn't know anything about Miriam. I didn't know they were related."

I hadn't intended on interrupting, but I did. "You shot this guy and nobody said anything. Nobody hauled you in on murder charges there."

"No one reported it. No one witnessed it. Bodies just vanish out there."

That was just weird. But I'd never understood Cormac's "profession."

"They didn't mention their daughter?" Ben asked. "Not once?"

"Not once. I spent a couple more days looking. Then I got your message."

"Not checking your phone?"

"I was in the backcountry most of the time. I didn't have reception. I came back as soon as I did get it. I don't think she followed us. How could she?"

"You heard what Tony said. She was a witch. It may have taken her a few days, but she found us."

Then Cormac asked, "What are the odds they can pin this on me, Ben?"

Ben shook his head. "I don't know. The primary witness has it in for you, Espinoza's a hot young prosecutor who'd love to land a Class One felony conviction. We don't have a whole lot in our favor."

"We have a bunch of witnesses," I said.

"And Espinoza will do everything he can to discredit them."

"You'll figure something out," Cormac said. "You always do."

Ben's shoulders bent under the weight of Cormac's trust. "Yeah, we'll see about that," he said softly.

After an awkward moment, Cormac said, "What happened back there, at the hearing—should I be worried? Are you up for this?"

They stared at each other, studying each other. "If you want to get someone else—"

"I trust you," he said. "Who else is going to understand this shit?"

Ben wouldn't look at him. "Yeah. I'll be fine. Somehow. Not getting bail was a setback, but you'll be okay."

He didn't sound confident, but Cormac nodded, like he was sure. Then he made a sour-faced grimace and muttered, "I can't believe they dug up that Brigade shit."

I jumped on him. "Yeah, what the heck is up with that? Those guys are insane. It just doesn't seem like your style."

"And what would you know about it?" Cormac said.

Before I could fire back, Ben said, "She spent yesterday in the library digging up every article the *Denver Post* ever printed on the Brigade. Got the whole story."

"Talk too much, and you're nosy as hell," he muttered.

"I also found the story about your father," I said, almost chagrined at the confession, because when he put it that way, it did seem like going behind their backs. But what else was I supposed to do when no one would tell me anything? "I'm really sorry, Cormac. About what happened to him."

He waved me away. "That was a long time ago."

"And now she knows everything about our dark, secret past," Ben said.

"Shit, I was having fun being all mysterious."

"Now you're just making fun of me," I said. "The Brigade. Start talking."

"So. You want to know why I spent a couple of years running around with a bunch of gun-toting wannabe skinhead maniacs?"

"Uh. Yeah. And you can't dodge, 'cause I'm going to sit here until . . . until—"

"Until what?"

Until you convince me you aren't crazy. I looked away.

Then, he spoke almost kindly. "I was working on my uncle's— Ben's dad's—ranch. He got caught up in it, and I tagged along. I was just a kid, must have been nineteen or so. I didn't know any better. Those guys—I was still getting over losing my dad, and I thought maybe I could learn something from them. But they were playing games. They weren't living in the real world. They hadn't seen the things I had. I left. Quit the ranch. Spent a couple years in the army. Never looked back."

Simple as that. I knew as well as anybody how a person could get caught up in things, when that pack mentality took over. He'd been a kid. Just made a mistake. I bought it.

"Why are you worried about it?" he said, after my long hesitation.

I didn't know, really. After seeing what Cormac was capable of, it seemed strange to find him involved, however tangentially, with such garden-variety creepiness. I said, "I keep finding out more things that make you scarier."

And I had trouble balancing both liking him and being scared of him.

He stared at me so hard, so searching, like it was my fault we'd never been able to work out anything between us. Which one of us hadn't been able to face that there was anything between us? Which one of the three of us? Because Ben had dropped all those hints. He'd known. And now it was Ben and me, with Cormac on the outside, and all three of us locked in a room together.

He'd run, and that wasn't my fault. He scared me, and maybe that was my fault.

Then the spell broke. Cormac dropped his gaze. "It still cracks me up, that you're a goddamned werewolf and you can talk about me being scary."

"It's like rock-paper-scissors," I said. "Silver bullet beats werewolf, and you've got the silver."

"And cop beats silver bullet. I get it," he said, and he was right. Almost, the whole thing made sense. Cormac turned to Ben. "What's the plan?"

"I'm going to go to Shiprock to learn what I can about Miriam

Wilson. There's got to be someone willing to testify that she was dangerous, that it was justifiable. We'll decide our strategy when I get back."

"Has Espinoza said anything about a plea bargain yet?"

"Yeah. I told him I didn't want to talk about it until I had all my cards in hand. Hearing's on Wednesday. We'll know then, one way or the other."

He nodded, so it must have sounded like a good plan to him. "Be careful."

"Yeah."

Ben knocked on the door, and the deputy came to take Cormac back to his cell.

"I hate this," Ben said when he was gone. "I really, really hate this. We've never gone as far as a preliminary hearing. I want to tear into something."

I took his arm, squeezing to offer comfort. "Let's get out of here."

We'd only just stepped outside, into the late-morning sunlight, when we were ambushed. Not really—it was only Alice, lurking across the parking lot and then heading straight for us on an intercept path. My heart raced anyway, because all I saw was someone half running, half trotting toward me. I stopped, my shoulders tensing, and only an act of will forced me to smile.

Ben grabbed my arm and bared his teeth.

"Hush," I whispered at him, touching his back to calm him. "It's okay. It's just Alice."

He froze, seemingly realizing what had just happened. His features shifted; he didn't relax much, but he didn't look like he was going to pounce anymore.

Strange how I was still getting used to this new Ben. He was a new Ben—strangely, subtly different, slightly less steady, slightly more paranoid. As if he were recovering from some sort of head injury. Which maybe he was. Maybe all of us who'd been infected with lycanthropy were.

"Kitty! Kitty, hello. I'm so glad I caught you." She smiled, but stiffly, as you do in awkward social situations.

"Hi, Alice."

"I just came to give another statement to the sheriff. I thought it might help your friend. Even Joe gave another statement, said that if he hadn't come along—well, I don't know what would have happened."

I did, or I could guess. It really wasn't worth describing to her. "Thanks, Alice. I'm sure it can't hurt."

I was about to say goodbye, to get out of there before I said something impolite, when Alice spoke.

"I wanted to give you this. I've been thinking about what Tony said, about how much we all might still be in danger. It's not much, but I want to help." She offered her hand, palm up. "Tony may be right, I may not know what I'm doing most of the time. But this came from the heart, and I can't help but think that means something."

She held a pendant to me, a clear, pointed crystal about as long as my thumb. The blunt end of it was wrapped with beads, tiny beads made of sparkling glass and polished wood, strung together in a pattern and bound tightly to the crystal. A loop of knotted cord woven into the beadwork had a string of leather through it, so it could be worn around the neck. It was a little piece of artwork. It glittered like sunlight through springtime woods when I turned it in the sun.

"I usually use silver wire to string the beads," she said. "But, well, I didn't this time. I used silk thread."

It was so thoughtful I could have cried. If only it hadn't been too little, too late.

Did I trust it to actually work? A talisman made by Alice, who'd cast that horrific curse against me—and cast it badly, gutlessly, so that it hadn't worked. Had that one come from her heart as well? Did I trust her?

At the moment, it didn't cost me anything to pretend that I did.

"It's beautiful," I said. "Thank you."

She stood there, beaming, and I hugged her, because I knew it would make her feel better. Then I put the pendant over my head, because that would make her feel better, too.

She went to her car, waving goodbye.

"It's hard to know where to draw the line isn't it?" Ben said. "About what to believe and what not to believe. What works and what doesn't."

I sighed in agreement. "She's right, though. If it comes from the heart, it has to count for something."

chapter **14**

We set off in the morning. We had five days until the hearing, when Cormac had to enter a plea. Ben had to find evidence on Cormac's behalf that would get the case thrown out.

The weather was on our side; it felt like a small advantage. I hadn't had to work very hard to talk Ben into letting me go with him. I didn't know how much help I'd be in hunting down the information he needed to shore up Cormac's defense, but that wasn't the argument I'd made.

I had to be there to keep Ben sane.

"*Wolf* Creek Pass," he said when we passed the highway marker over the mountain. We had a couple more hours until we reached New Mexico. "Am I the only one who thinks that's funny?"

"Yes," I said, not taking my eyes off the road ahead. Too many signs advertising local motels and gift shops had featured pictures of fuzzy, howling wolves. The Wolf Creek ski area was doing a booming business.

I let him drive the stretch that took us over the pass. Just over the mountain, cruising into the next valley and toward the junction that turned onto the highway that led to New Mexico, a zippy little sports car with skis in a rack on the back roared up behind us, gunned its engine, swerved around us, and nearly cut us off as it pulled back into the right line, obviously expressing great displeasure at our insistence at driving only five miles an hour over the speed limit.

Ben clenched the steering wheel with rigid fingers and bared his teeth in a silent growl. Something animal crawled into his eyes for a moment.

"Ben?" I spoke softly, not wanting to startle him. Not wanting to startle the wolf that adrenaline had brought to the surface for a moment.

"I'm okay," he said. His breaths were rough, and his body was still more tense than the stress of driving mountain roads warranted. "How many days?"

"How many days?"

"Full moon," he said.

"Sixteen," I said. Keeping track had become second nature.

"I thought it was sooner. It feels sooner."

I knew the feeling. The wolf wanted to break free, and it let you know. "It's better if you don't think about it."

"How do you not think about it?" His voice cracked.

"Do you want to pull over and let me drive?"

He shook his head quickly. "Driving gives me something else to think about."

"Just don't let the jerks get to you, okay?"

He pushed himself back in the seat, stretching his arms, making an effort to relax. After another ten miles or so he said, "I started smoking in law school. It was a crutch, a way to get through it. You feel like you're going crazy, so you step outside for a cigarette. Everything stops for a couple of minutes, and you can go back to it feeling a little bit calmer. Quitting, though—that's the bitch. 'Cause as much as you tell yourself you don't need the crutch anymore, your body isn't convinced. Took me two years to wean myself off them. That's what this feels like," he said. "I want to turn wolf like I wanted a cigarette. That doesn't make any sense."

"Like any of this makes sense," I muttered. "You don't have to wait until the full moon to Change. The wolf part knows that. It's always trying to get out."

Watching him, I could almost see the analytical part of him trying to figure it out—the lawyer part of him on the case. His eyes narrowed, his face puckered up with thought.

He said, harshly, "Where does the part about that side of it being a strength come in?"

I could have said something cutting, but our nerves were frayed as it was. He needed a serious answer. "Being decisive. Sometimes it helps seeing the world as black and white, where everyone's either a predator or prey. You don't let details muddy up your thinking."

"That's cynical."

"I know. That's what I hate about it."

"You know what the trouble is? We all see this case—what they're doing to Cormac—as black and white. But we're looking at white as white and Espinoza's looking at white as black. Does that make any sense?"

"When maybe if we all saw it as gray we'd be able to come to some sort of compromise."

"Yeah." He tapped the steering wheel as he lost himself in thought.

It started snowing as we left the mountains.

Northern New Mexico was bleak, windswept, and touched with scattered bits of blowing snow from the storm. Stands of cotton-woods by the river were gray and leafless. All the colors seemed washed out of the landscape, which was barren desert hemmed in by eroded cliffs and mesas.

We didn't have much to go on. The woman's name, the missing person report. We arrived in Shiprock in time to stop at the police department—Tribal law enforcement. Shiprock was on the Navajo Reservation. The town's namesake, a jagged volcanic monolith rising almost two thousand feet above the desert, was visible to the south, a kind of signpost.

Ben spoke to the sergeant on duty at the front desk, while I lurked in the back, peering at them with interest.

"I'm looking for information about Miriam Wilson." He showed them a picture from the coroner's office. A terrible, gruesome picture because half her face was pulped, but the other half still showed recognizable features. Her cheeks were round, her large eyes closed. "A missing person report was filed on her about three months ago. I don't know if the Huerfano County sheriff's department sent you the news that she was killed in Colorado."

"Yeah, we got word," said the man behind the counter, a Sergeant Tsosie according to his nameplate. He had short black hair, brown skin, dark eyes, and an angled profile.

"You don't seem concerned."

"She won't be missed."

Ben asked, "Has her family been notified? The coroner up there hasn't received any instructions about what to do with her body."

"He's not likely to, either. She's not going to have anyone ask-ing about her. Trust me."

"Then who filed the missing person report on her in the first place? Families who don't want to find out where their kids went don't normally do that."

"This isn't a normal family," Tsosie said, almost smiling.

"What if I went to talk to them?"

"Good luck with that. The Wilsons are impossible to deal with."

The officer looked nervous. He kept glancing around—over his shoulder, toward the door, like he expected someone to come reprimand him. "You want some advice? Stop asking about her. She was bad news. That whole family's bad news. You keep going on about this, you won't like what you find, I guarantee it."

"Bad news," Ben said. "Would you be willing to testify to that in court?"

The officer shook his head quickly—fearfully, I might have said. "I won't have anything to do with it."

Ben leaned forward and almost snarled. "I'm the defense attorney for the man who shot her. I need to show that it was justifiable, and you need to help me do that."

Tsosie's lips pressed together for a moment while he hesitated. Then he made a decision. I could see it settle on his features. "Hold on a minute."

He went to a filing cabinet off to the side of the room. He opened the top drawer and flipped through a few folders, drew one out, and studied the top sheet for a moment. Then he brought the whole folder over and lay it open in front of Ben. "Take it," he said. "Take all of it. And your client? You thank him for us."

"Yeah. I'll do that," Ben said, a little breathlessly. "Thanks. Look, it would really help him out if I could get a statement. Just a signed statement."

"I'm not sure a judge would look twice at anything I could say about her."

"Anything'll help."

He got the statement. One paragraph, vague, but it was on the department letterhead and had a signature. It was a start.

Tsosie watched us leave, an unsettling intensity in his eyes.

"What was that all about?" I said as we returned to the car. I drove this time, while Ben studied the folder's contents.

"We just witnessed what happens when a police force wants a person put away, either behind bars or with a bullet, but they don't have any right to do it themselves. Miriam pissed somebody here off real good, but for whatever reason—no evidence, no real crime committed—they couldn't touch her. Tsosie here has expressed his gratitude that somebody was able to do it."

"Then why won't he testify on Cormac's behalf?"

"If they don't have any evidence against her, then he's just a bitter cop bitching about some local nobody liked."

"What did she do?"

"That's the million-dollar question." He turned a page over, studied it. "Looks like she's got an arrest record. Drunk and disorderly, disturbing the peace, vandalism. Typical juvenile delinquent-type stuff. A bad kid heading for trouble. Nothing unusual. But here's something." He shuffled a couple of pages aside and studied a typed report. "A little family history. Her older sister Joan died about three months ago."

"How?"

"Pneumonia. Natural causes. She was only twenty-three."

"Then what's it doing in a police file?"

"Someone thought it was important. It happened right before the missing person report was filed. Maybe there's a connection. Maybe that's what caused her to snap. And here's her brother John's death certificate. Two gunshot wounds. No investigation conducted."

"Does that seem weird to you?"

"It seems like no one was too sorry to see him dead, either. They must have made quite a pair. Here it is: Lawrence Wilson, her grandfather. He's the one who filed the missing person report."

"Just her grandfather. What about her parents? What would they say?"

He studied the file for a moment. "There's an address. It might be worth dropping in on them. We can do that tomorrow. Let's find out if my car got towed."

Ben had left his car in the parking lot of the motel in Farmington, some thirty miles away from Shiprock, where he and Cormac had stayed during their ill-fated hunting expedition. After two weeks, the sedan still lurked in the parking lot, unnoticed. It was the kind of place that might slowly sink into the ground without anyone thinking to panic. The motel was part of a national chain, but that couldn't remove the veneer of age and fatigue that rested over it. Over this entire region.

"Now let's see if the windows are broken and the radio's gone," he said, wearing a thin smile.

They weren't. He'd locked his laptop and other belongings in the trunk. But the tires were slashed. All four wheels sat on their rims.

He stared at them for a long minute. "I'm not going to complain. I am absolutely not going to complain. This is fixable."

I had to agree. When something was fixable, you didn't complain.

He retrieved his belongings, then went to get us a room.

The walls of the building couldn't keep out the weird taint in the air. It was like I could hear howling, but it was in my head. No actual sound traveled through the air.

Ben stayed up late refamiliarizing himself with the contents of his briefcase and laptop. More online searches, more note-taking. I wanted him to come to bed. I wanted to be held.

Then I remembered it was Saturday, and I turned on the clock radio by the bed.

"You're listening to Ariel, Priestess of the Night."

Like I needed to make myself even more depressed. I lay on the bed, staring at the ceiling. Ben scowled at me.

"Do you have to listen to that?"

"Yes," I said bluntly. He didn't argue.

Ariel droned on. "Let's move on to the next call. I have Trish on the line. She's trying to decide whether or not to tell her mother that she was infected with lycanthropy and became a werewolf two years ago. The kicker: her mother has terminal cancer. Trish, hello."

Strangely, I suddenly understood the attraction of a show like this, and why people listened to my show. There was always somebody out there who had bigger problems. You could forget about your own for a while. Or secretly gloat, *At least it's not me.*

"Hi, Ariel." Trish had been crying. Her voice had a strained, worn-out quality.

"Let's talk about this, Trish. Tell me why you think you shouldn't tell your mother what happened."

"What's the point? It'll upset her. I don't want to upset her. If it's true—if she doesn't have much time left—I don't want her to spend that time being angry with me. Or being scared of me. And once she's gone . . . it won't matter. It doesn't matter."

"Now, why do you think you should tell her?"

Trish took a shaky breath. "She's my mother. I think . . . sometimes I think she already knows that something's wrong. That something happened to me. And what if it *does* matter? What if when she's gone, there is something after? Then she'll know. She'll die and her soul will be out there and know everything, and she'll be disappointed that I didn't tell her. That I kept it secret."

"Even if you know it'll upset her now."

"I can't win, either way."

"Is there anyone else in your family you can talk to? Someone who might be able to help you decide what's best for her?"

"No, no. There's not anyone. No siblings. My parents are divorced, she hasn't spoken to my father in years. I'm the only one taking care of her. I've never felt this alone." She was on the breaking point. I was amazed she could even speak coherently.

"What's your first impulse? Before you started second-guessing yourself, what were you going to do?"

"I was going to tell her. I'm thinking—it's like everyone talks about how you should work things out before it's too late. But she's so sick, Ariel. Telling her something like this wouldn't be working anything out, it would be torturing her. It's easier to keep quiet. I want to try to make this time as comfortable and happy for her as I can. My problems, my feelings—they're not important."

"But they are, or you wouldn't be calling me."

"I suppose. Yeah."

Ariel said, "It's commendable, your wanting to put your feelings aside for your mother's sake. But you're not convinced it's the right thing to do, are you?"

"No. No, I've always talked to Mom about these things. And I'm not going to have her anymore. I don't want to face that." Finally her voice broke. My heart went out to her. I was almost crying myself.

Ariel spoke gently, but firmly. "Trish, if you're looking for me to tell you what to do, or to give you permission to do one thing and not another, I'm not going to do that. This is a terrible situation. All I can tell you is, listen to your heart. You know your mom better than anyone. You should think about what she would want."

I hadn't intended to do it this time. I was too tired to be snarky. But I found myself digging out my cell phone.

Ben noticed. "What the hell are you doing?"

"Shh," I hissed at him.

I fought through the busy signal and got to the gatekeeper. I explained my reason for calling—that I could speak to Trish's situation. Then I found myself telling him my name. "Kitty."

The guy didn't say anything. Why should he? I wasn't the only person in the world named Kitty. He didn't have any reason to think that Ariel's radio rival would call in to her show.

I wasn't angry this time. I wasn't frustrated and lashing out. I really had something to say.

Ben watched me, kind of like he might watch a train wreck on TV. I had turned down the radio, but he'd moved it over by him and was listening with it up to his ear. I paced the room along the foot of the bed and ignored him.

The call with Trish had drawn to a close. Then Ariel spoke to me. "Hello. Why have you joined me this evening?"

"Hi. I just wanted to tell Trish that she should tell her mother."

"Why do you say that?"

I wished I were in charge here. I wished Trish had called into my show so I could have told her directly. So I knew she was listening. For the first time in weeks, I really wished I were doing my show.

I said, "Because I told my mother that I'm a werewolf, and it was the right thing to do. I didn't mean to. It just kind of slipped out. But once I did, she wanted to know why I hadn't told her sooner. And she was right, I should have. I didn't give her enough credit for being able to handle it. She was upset, sure. But she's still my mom. She still wants to be there for me, and the only way she can do that is if she knows what's going on in my life. In the long run it meant I could stop making stupid excuses about where I was on full moon nights."

"How long ago did you tell her?"

I had to think a minute. "It's been a year or so."

"And you have a good relationship with your mother?"

"Yeah, I think I do. We talk at least once a week, usually." In fact, I should probably give her a call. I should probably tell her what was really going on in my life. "This is going to sound trite, but if Trish doesn't tell her mom, she'll always regret it. If she tells her now they still have a chance to talk it out. If she waits, she'll be telling it to her mother's grave for the rest of her life, hoping for an answer that isn't going to come."

An uncharacteristically long pause followed. Radio people were trained to shun silence, to fill the silence at all costs. Yet Ariel let maybe five seconds of silence tick by.

Then she said, without her usual sultry, sugary tone, "Wait a minute. You said your name is Kitty. Is that right?"

Damn. Caught. Now would be the time to hang up. "Uh, yeah," I said instead.

"And you're a werewolf."

"Yes. Yes I am."

"That's not a coincidence, is it? There couldn't possibly be two werewolves named Kitty. That would be . . . ridiculous."

"Yes. Yes it would."

"You're Kitty Norville. What are you doing calling in to my show?"

"Oh, you know. Stuck at home on a Saturday night, feeling kind of bored—"

"But you listen to my show. That's so cool."

Huh? "It is?"

"Are you kidding? You're such an inspiration."

"I am?"

"Yeah! You're so down to earth, you make it so easy to talk about things. You've changed the way everyone talks about the supernatural. You inspired me to try to build on that. Why do you think I started this show?"

"Uh . . . to cut in on my market share?"

She said, horrified, "Oh, no! I want to expand what you've done. Add another voice, make it harder for the critics to gang up on us. And now you're calling me. I hardly know what to say."

Neither did I. To think, I'd wanted to sue her, and here she was sounding like one of my biggest fans. I could have cried. "Thanks, I guess."

"So why are you sitting at home bored and not doing *The Midnight Hour*?"

"Let's just say I've had a rough couple of months."

Again, she hesitated, just a moment this time. She came back, almost shy. "Do you want to talk about it?"

Did I? On the air? But I had to admit, she was good. She knew the trick of making the caller feel like it was just the two of you having a chat over a cup of tea. Maybe I could talk a little.

I glanced at Ben, still listening to the radio turned way low. He kind of looked like he was suppressing a grin.

"A friend of mine was attacked and infected with lycanthropy a couple weeks ago. I've been taking care of him, and it's been tough. Another friend just got arrested for something he did to save my life. He's being charged with a felony. It's complicated. It also feels like the last straw. No matter how much you try to do the right thing, you get screwed over. Makes it easy to just drop out. To give up."

"But not really. Life gets hard, but you don't just run away."

"Except there's this thing inside me, the wolf side of me, and all she wants to do is run away. I'm really having to fight that."

"But you've always won that fight. I listen to your show. That's one of the great things about it, how you always tell people to be strong, and they listen to you. You understand."

"I'm flying by the seat of my pants most of the time."

"And that's gotten you this far, hasn't it?"

Was sultry Ariel giving me a pep talk? Was it working? I was a
bit taken aback, that here was this person I didn't know, out on the
airwaves, rooting for me.

Maybe I'd forgotten that anyone was rooting for me.

I smiled in spite of myself. "So what you're saying is I just have
to keep going."

"Isn't that what you always tell people?"

"Yeah," I murmured. Nothing like having that mirror held up to
you, or your words thrown back at you. "I think you're right. I just
have to keep going. I never thought I'd say this, Ariel. But thanks.
Thanks for talking to me."

"I'm not sure I really said anything."

"Maybe I just needed someone to listen." Someone who wasn't
depending on me to keep it together. "I'll let you go back to your
show now."

Ariel said, "Kitty, I'm really worried about you."

"How about I give you a call in a couple of weeks and let you
know how it's going? Or you could give me a call."

"It's a date. Take care, Kitty."

I shut off the phone and sat on the edge of the bed.

I felt Ben staring at me, but I didn't want to look back. Didn't
want to face him and whatever snide thing he was about to say. But
the room was too small for us to avoid each other for long. I looked
at him.

He said, "You really need to get back to doing your show. The
sooner the better. You're too good at it not to."

I wanted to cry. What I couldn't say—not to Ariel, not to him,
not to anyone—was that I was too scared to go back. Scared that I
couldn't keep it going anymore. I felt like I'd rather quit than fail.

Slowly, I walked over to him, putting a slink in my step and a
heat in my gaze. I needed distracting. I sat on his lap, straddling
him, pinning him to the chair, and kissed him. Kissed him long and
slow, until he put his arms around me and held me tight. Until his
grip anchored me.

"Come to bed, Ben," I breathed, and he nodded, kissing me
again.

We went to visit the Wilsons in the morning.

The family lived west of Shiprock, on a flat expanse of desert
scrub and sagebrush. The police report left directions. We turned

off the highway onto a dusty track masquerading as a road. A couple of miles along, we found the house. Some run-down rail and post fencing marked corrals, but nothing lived in them. The house was one story, plank board, small and crouching. It didn't seem big enough to serve as a garage, much less house a family. A couple of ancient, rusting pickup trucks sat nearby.

We parked on the dirt road and walked the path—a track lined roughly with stones—to the front door.

"If it were anyone but Cormac I wouldn't be doing this. I'd write the whole case off," Ben said. "I have to go in there and ask these people to help me defend the man who killed their daughter. This kind of thing didn't used to bother me but now all I want to do is growl and rip something apart."

I started to say something vague and soothing, but I couldn't, because I felt the same way. Every hair on my body was standing on end. "There's something really weird about this place."

We'd reached the door, a flimsy-seeming thing made of wood. Ben stared at it. Finally, I knocked. Ben took a deep breath and closed his eyes, opening them as the door opened.

A young woman, maybe eighteen, looked back at us. "Who are you?" The question and her stance—the door was only open a few inches—spoke of suspicion. Maybe even paranoia.

"My name's Ben O'Farrell. I'm trying to find information about Miriam Wilson. Are you her sister?"

Of course the girl was. I'd only ever seen Miriam dying and dead, but they had the same round face, large eyes, and straight black hair.

The girl stole a look over her shoulder, into the house, then said, "She's gone. Been gone a long time. I don't have anything to say about it."

Ben and I glanced at each other. Did she know her sister was dead? Surely someone had come to tell her, when the police here found out.

"What's your name?" I said.

She shook her head. "I don't want to tell you my name."

Names had power, yadda yadda. Okay, then. We'd do this the blunt way.

"Miriam's dead," I said, "She was killed near Walsenburg, Colorado. We're trying to learn as much as we can about her so we can explain what happened."

Some expression passed over her. Not what I expected, which was grief or sadness, or resignation at learning the truth after months of uncertainty. No, the girl closed her eyes and the release of tension softened her features. It was like she was relieved.

She said, "You're better off letting it go. You're better off forgetting about it. Let it end here." That was the same thing Tony had said. And Tsosie.

"We can't do that," I said. "It's not over. Don't you want to know what happened?"

"No." She started to close the door.

"Is there anyone else who'd be willing to talk to us about her? Are your parents here?"

"They don't speak much English," she said. A convenient shield.

Ben spoke up. "Would you be willing to translate for us?"

"They won't talk. My sister—my oldest sister died before Miriam disappeared, my brother died a couple of weeks ago. We've had a hard time of it, and we're trying to move on. I have to go now."

Ben put his hand out to stop the door from closing. "How much of that did they bring on themselves? They hired my client to kill your brother. He did it, then Miriam came after him. He's in jail now, and you know as well as I do he doesn't deserve to be there. Where did this whole thing get started?"

She was lost, cornered, staring at us with a panicked expression, unable to close the door on us and unable to speak.

"Please," I said, "talk to us."

The words seemed to war inside her, like she both did and didn't want to speak. Finally, the words won. "Joan was murdered. No matter what anyone else says, she was murdered. But the more we talk of these things, the more likely we are to bring more curses upon ourselves."

You got to a point where one more curse wasn't going to make a difference.

"Louise, who are you talking to?" a male voice shouted from within. The father who didn't speak much English, I bet.

"Nobody!" she called over her shoulder.

The door opened wide, revealing a short man with desert-burnished skin aiming a rifle at us.

I wondered if he knew that he'd need the bullets to be silver.

"My daughter's right," he said in perfectly decent English. "We've had enough. Get out, now, before you bring more evil with you."

It seemed to me that we weren't the ones carrying evil around with us. We just kept finding it. I had the good sense not to say anything. Funny how a loaded gun can shut you up.

"Well. Thanks for your time," I said. I took Ben's arm and pulled him away from the door. Slowly, we backed along the path, until the door to the house slammed shut.

Ben's muscles were so tense they were almost rigid, like he wanted to pounce. "Keep it together, Ben," I whispered.

"What a pack of liars."

"Does this surprise you? This is the family that produced John and Miriam Wilson. Both confirmed monsters."

"Okay, but you're living proof—in fact you've based your whole career on the belief—that being a monster doesn't make someone a . . . a . . ."

"A monster," I finished, grinning wryly. "A fucked-up family's a fucked-up family, whether or not werewolves are involved."

"You think I'd have figured that out by now," he said.

"You know, I'm sick and tired of people pointing rifles at me."

"That was a shotgun, not a rifle."

For some reason, that didn't make a hell of a lot of difference to me.

We got back in the car and pulled out on the dirt track. We didn't speak. Another door had closed, figuratively speaking. One less chance to boost Cormac's defense.

"Kitty, wait, look." Ben pointed to a figure running toward us, from the Wilson house. Small against the landscape, it looked like it fled something terrible. It was Louise, her black hair tangling in the desert breeze.

I hit the brakes and waited for her to catch up. I didn't see anything chasing her, but I wondered.

I'd started to unbuckle and climb out, but Ben said, "Wait. We may have to drive out in a hurry."

He was probably right. I left the car running while Ben got out and waited for her. She reached us more quickly than I expected—she was fast, and we hadn't gone far. The house was still visible. I wondered if her father would show up in a minute with his shotgun.

Sliding to a stop, she leaned on the car's trunk. Her dark eyes were wide, wild. She seemed too flustered to speak, but she said in a rush, "Let me in. I'll talk to you, but we have to go."

Ben put the seat down so she could climb in the back, then he returned to the front.

"Go, now, hurry," Louise commanded. I was already driving, before Ben even closed the door.

I glanced at her in the rearview mirror. She perched at the edge of the seat, her hands pulling at the fabric of her jeans. Her gaze never rested. She looked around, out both side windows, over her shoulder to the back window, ducking to see out the front. Like she was worried something might follow us. She had the look of someone who was always afraid that something was following her.

I said, "Do you always jump into strange people's cars and tell them to drive? How do you know we're not murderous psychopaths?"

Her gaze settled on me, briefly. "I know a murderous psychopath when I see one."

"A murderous psychopath like Miriam?"

"Yes."

"Miriam was a skinwalker," Ben said.

"*Yee naaldlooshii.* Yes."

"What else can you tell us?"

"Not here. Someplace safe. We'll talk someplace safe."

"We're in a car driving forty miles an hour," I said, annoyed. "What could possibly get at us?"

She gave me a look that clearly pitied my ignorance. "You never know what could be listening. Waiting."

I wanted to laugh, but I couldn't. I said, "If we're not safe driving, where do you want to go?"

"There's a place close by. I'll tell you where to go. Turn right on the highway."

Her directions steered us farther away from Shiprock, then off the highway. I feared for the car's suspension. Many miles out, a dirt track led down a slope to a ravine—gullies and dry riverbeds like this cut across the desert. I never would have found this cleft in the hills if I hadn't been guided here. It was very well hidden.

Ahead of us, toward the end of the ravine, was a hut made of logs sealed with mud. It was octagonal—almost round—ancient-looking, with a low-sloping roof.

We all climbed out of the car, and Louise hurried ahead of us.

She said, "This hogan belonged to my family years ago, in the old days. Everyone's forgotten about it. But I found it again. It'll keep us safe."

"Safe from what?" It seemed like the obvious question.

She gave me a look over her shoulder.

Ben was the one who said, "If you have to ask, you haven't been paying attention."

"Just trying to make conversation."

He took my hand and squeezed it quickly before letting it go and walking on. A brief touch of comfort.

The scene we were walking into was from another world, something out of a tour book, or maybe an anthropology textbook: the desert, the cold wind, the round hut that might have been sitting there for decades. I looked up, expecting to see vultures. I only saw crisp blue sky.

Louise pushed aside a faded blanket that hung over the door and invited us in with her intent stare.

The hogan was dark, windowless, except for a hole in the ceiling, through which a shaft of sunlight came through. My lycanthropic sight adjusted quickly. The single room was almost bare. Toward the back, to the right, a blanket lay spread on the floor. A couple of wooden trunks sat by the wall nearby, along with a pile of firewood. Clearly, this wasn't a room for living in. It was a sanctuary. I could feel it, the way the walls curled around me, the way that I was sure that even though only a blanket hung over the doorway, nothing could get in. No curses, no hate. I felt a great sense of calm.

Even Louise seemed calm now, confident in the hogan's security. She knelt in the center of the room and struck a match to light the fire that was already built there. The kindling lit, glowed orange, and flames started tickling the firewood. The air smelled of soot and ash, of many previous fires that had burned themselves out. The smoke of this one rose up through the hole in the roof.

She showed us where to sit, on the ground to the right of the blanket.

She sat on the blanket. Before her, spread on the ground, was a sandpainting.

The pattern showed a complex and highly stylized scene. The colors were earth tones—brown, yellow, white, red, and black—yet vivid. In the firelight, the figures seemed to move.

Four birds, wings outstretched, marked the four quarters of the picture. Their clawed feet pointed inward, toward a circle at the center of the painting. In the middle of the circle stood a figure, a woman: black hair streamed from her square head, and she held arrows in both hands. Crooked white lines—lightning, maybe—rose up from her feet. Her eyes and mouth were tiny lines, hyphens, making the figure seem expressionless. Sleeping. The whole picture was bounded on three sides by rainbow stripes ending in bunches of what must have been feathers. The fourth, unbounded side faced the door. All of it was symbolic, but the symbols eluded me, except for one: the dark-haired woman at the center of great power, armed for battle.

Louise picked up a plastic dish, an old margarine tub. She took a pinch of something out of it: a white, powdery sand, or some other finely ground substance, which she sprinkled onto the image. I didn't know how she got the lines so straight. Her movements added bolts of lightning radiating out from the circle, between the soaring eagles.

"Tell me how Miriam died," she said.

Ben looked at me. I was the talker. But I didn't feel much like telling the story. "She attacked me. Our friend shot her."

"Friend. The same man who shot John."

"That's your brother. The werewolf."

She said, "John and Miriam were twins. They were destined to be killed by the same man. It all happened so quickly. I didn't expect it to happen so quickly."

"What happened, Louise? How did this all start?"

She continued adding to the painting as she spoke. "John went to work in Phoenix. When he came back—he was different. That must have been when it happened. When he became the monster. He wouldn't talk to anyone but Miriam. They'd go off together, for days at a time. Then Joan died. Then John. Then Miriam." Her voice never cracked, her expression never slipped. She'd lived this over and over in her mind for weeks now. "I knew," she said. "Somehow I knew what had happened, that Miriam took Joan. This magic, this evil has lived in the land since the beginning of the world. My family has been part of it, on both sides. I've learned what I can, but I've had no one to teach me the right way. The way of harmony. The old ways are gone.

"My father believed that because John brought a new evil from outside, an outsider should stop it. He knew someone who knew of a wolf hunter—your friend. The wolf hunter came and did his work. But it didn't stop the evil. It only made it stronger."

The flickering light from the fire made the figures in the painting waver and move. I blinked, flinching back, bidden by an animal instinct to escape. My eyes watered, and I shifted so my arm touched Ben's. He felt shaky, nervous. Like me. Louise caught the movement, understood the way Ben and I stared at the picture on the ground.

"This is for Joan. She didn't die; she was killed. There's no one to help her find her way to the next world. No one else cares. I don't know how, but I have to try to help her with what I know."

It came from the heart, Alice had said. That had to count for something.

"She's still here. She hasn't traveled on. Maybe she'll talk to you. Maybe she'll tell you what happened."

"How will we know?" I said. "How will we know if she's talking to us?"

Ben muttered, "If she can't testify or sign a statement, what's the point?"

I elbowed him in the side.

"Joan?" Louise sat at the head of her painting, hands on her knees, gazing unfocused at the painting, or the light, or phantoms of her own imagination. She had the voice of a little girl calling in the dark. "I'm here."

Then she spoke a phrase in another language—Navajo, each sound punctuated, melodic.

The fire dimmed suddenly to embers.

Ben tensed; I felt for his hand, gripped it. He squeezed back. I expected the sudden spike of fear to rouse the Wolf. Any sense of danger always woke her, sparked her instinct, made her want to fight. I expected that instinct to kick in, but it didn't. This space, this weird timeless feeling, soothed her somehow. She slept, even though my brain was firing. It gave me a strange, disembodied feeling, like I wasn't really here. Like I couldn't feel the ground under me anymore.

After a long silence, Louise said, "She is telling me the story to tell to you. I can tell you like she's telling me."

An aura of blue light glowed around Louise, like some kind of static charge danced around her. No—she was backlit. The light was coming from behind her. I wanted very much to move around her, to see what was behind her. I stayed put.

"I was outside, mending one of the fences after a wind knocked it down. Miriam came to me. She called my name. I looked, and she stood right behind me. She held a powder in her hand and blew it into my face. I knew what it was, anyone would know what it was: corpse powder. She cursed me. She killed me, but no one would ever know. I grew sick. The doctors had a name for it, called it a disease, tried to heal me—but they couldn't, because it was witchcraft. Miriam stood by my bed at night—my last night—and told me what she would do: she would cut my heart out, take the blood, and put it on the wolf's skin. Take my soul and use its power for herself. I could see it, see her cutting out my heart, holding up the dripping fist of muscle, and I thought, *This is my heart, why can I see it? It should be hidden. My heart should be hidden, safe, but she has taken it from me.*"

I choked on a gasp, feeling my own heart suddenly. It wasn't me, it was her. I told myself it was only a story.

Louise shook her head, and when she spoke next, her voice was hers again. "Joan died of pneumonia, that's what the doctors said. But Miriam killed her. Miriam took her heart. I found her spirit crying in the desert, searching for her heart. But I'll help her find it. I'll help you, Joan."

She reached out, like she would clasp someone's hand, but there was no one in front of her. The glow faded, and she was left holding a point of light in her hand. She closed her fist around it before I could see more. As it was, it might have been my imagination.

In fact, a second of dizziness and a slip of time changed the look of the whole room: the fire burned again, as it always had. Louise held her hand over the painting, as if she'd just finished dropping the last grain of color into place.

None of it had happened. I was sure that none of it had happened. Except Ben still held my hand in a death grip. His hand was cold, his face pale. He swallowed.

Louise looked at us, her dark eyes shining. "I'll sign your statement. She wants me to sign your statement, to tell you what I know. To tell her story."

She swiped her hand through the painting, smearing the image, blurring the colors, stirring the ground until it showed a galaxy swirl of dark sand, and nothing more. Odd grains of quartz sparkled in the light like stars.

She sat back, closed her eyes, and sighed. "Let's go."

We scooped sand over the fire to put it out. Louise put her things—matches, the little containers of colored sand—into the trunk against the back wall. She drew something out as well, but tucked it into her fist so I couldn't see.

Pulling back the blanket over the door, she ushered us out of the hogan. She paused, looking back to scan the interior, as if searching for something. Or waiting for something. Then she slipped out, letting the blanket fall back into place behind her.

Walking back into the sun was like being in another world, a too-bright sunlit world where birds chirped and a fresh breeze smelled of dust and sage. Surely a world where nobody killed anybody.

Ben said, "I'll put together that statement."

Louise nodded. Ben gave a thin smile in acknowledgment, then went to the car. His hands were buried deep in his pockets, his shoulders bent against a cold wind that wasn't blowing. I was shivering as well. I hugged myself against the cold that came from inside rather than outside.

Louise and I waited, standing halfway between hogan and car. Her tangled hair made her look tired, older than when we'd started out. She looked up and around, studying sky, ground, distant trees, eyes squinting against the sun. For a moment she reminded me of a wolf taking in the scents.

I finally said, "Did you know what would happen in there? Has she ever talked to you before?"

She shook her head. "I didn't know if it would work with outsiders watching. Most people, if I said that Joan talks to me, they'd laugh. Or they'd feel sorry for me. They wouldn't think it was real. But you believe. I think that's why she came."

"I've had my own conversations with the dead."

"Some people aren't ready to go when they die."

I choked on a lump in my throat. "Yeah."

"I'm afraid—I'm afraid Miriam might come back. She was angry all the time. I'm afraid that might hold her to this world."

That damned cabin was going to be haunted forever. I didn't want to go back there to find out if Miriam's ghost was hanging around or not. Let someone else deal with it.

I said, "When she died, a man was there, a *curandero*. He was afraid of the same thing. He did something—I don't know exactly what. I think it was to keep her from coming back."

"Then maybe it'll be okay." She gave a smile that seemed brave and hopeless all at once.

Ben called us over to the car. He used the hood as a desk and transcribed while Louise told a straightforward version of the story. She signed it where Ben indicated. It seemed like such a slim thing to pin any hopes on. We were grasping at straws. After she'd signed, Ben packed away his briefcase.

"Can we give you a ride back?" I said.

"No thanks. I'm not in too much of a hurry to get back. The walk'll do me good."

The walk was something like fifteen miles, but I didn't argue. I understood the urge to walk yourself to exhaustion.

She drew something out of her pocket, holding it in a tight fist. She kept her face lowered. "I have something for you. The questions about Miriam, the thing she was and what you're looking for—it's dangerous. You should leave, you should go back and forget about it all. But I know you won't, so you need these."

She opened her hand to show two arrowheads tied to leather cords lying on her palm.

I took them from her. They were warm from her clutching them tightly. She must have sensed my hesitation, because she pulled at a length of leather around her own neck. An arrowhead amulet had been hiding under the collar of her shirt.

"Why do you think that I, out of all my sisters and my brother, am still alive?"

She had a point there.

"Thank you," I said.

She smiled and seemed calmer. Less fearful. Sometimes rituals weren't about magic. They were about helping people deal with events. Deal with life. She walked away from the road, heading into the scrubland between here and the town. Didn't look back.

I gave one of the amulets to Ben. Back in the car, I opened the glove box and pulled out two items: the leather pouch Tony had given me, and Alice's crystal charm. I lined them up on the dashboard above the steering wheel, added Louise's arrowhead to the collection, and regarded them, mystified.

Ben looked at me looking at the amulets. "Does this make you super-protected? The safest person in the world?"

I frowned. "I'm thinking they might all cancel each other out. Like red, green, blue light making white."

"Which do you pick?"

"Local color. I'll bet Louise knows what she's talking about." I took the arrowhead, slipped the cord over my head, and put the others back in the glove box. Ben put on his arrowhead. There we were—protected.

We left. Ben sat with his briefcase on his lap, his head propped on his hand, looking frustrated.

"Will her statement help?" I said.

He made a vague shrug. "Maybe the court will believe it, maybe not. When you get right down to it, there's an official death certificate saying Joan Wilson died of pneumonia. Louise is the only one saying Miriam killed her. Hearsay and ghost stories. I don't know, I'll take whatever I can get at this point." We trundled along in silence for a few minutes, when he added, "As dysfunctional goes, this family's really got something going."

I snorted a laugh. "No joke. Where to next?"

"The grandfather. Lawrence Wilson. See what he has to say about Miriam, since he was the only one who cared to look for her."

"After the rest of the family, I'm afraid to see what he's like."

"Tell me about it."

The sun had dipped to the far west, and a cold wind bit from the desert. We were nearing the turn to the highway. We'd have to pick one direction or another. I had a thought.

"You want to wait to see him until tomorrow?"

"If small-town gossip works here the way it works everywhere else, he's probably gotten word that someone's wanting to talk to him. It'll give him a chance to go to ground."

"Yeah, okay. But it's almost sunset. Call me chicken, but I don't really want to be out after dark. Not around here."

He thought, lips pursed, watching the desert landscape slide by. "Then back to the hotel it is."

I turned east, back to Farmington.

chapter 15

No, Mom. I'm in New Mexico now."

I'd returned to the motel room to find a message from Mom on my phone. As usual, the timing was not the best.

"What are you doing in New Mexico?"

Trying to track a dead killer without any evidence or witnesses? "I'm looking for some information. We'll only be here for a couple of days."

"We?"

Crap. I wasn't going to be able to talk my way out of this. "Yeah. I'm with a friend."

"Oh. Anyone I know?" She spoke brightly. Trying to draw me out.

I thought of the white lies and half-truths I could tell her. Then I remembered the phone call to Ariel last night. Be straight. Tell the truth. "By reputation. It's Ben O'Farrell. I'm helping him with a case." This was going to worry her. This was going to make her pry further. No information was better than too little information. I shouldn't have told her anything.

"Well, be careful, okay?" She just let it go. Like she actually trusted me to take care of myself.

"I will."

The rest of the conversation went pretty much as usual. Except for the part where Ben was sitting there smirking at me.

"I hope you're not planning on taking me home to meet the family."

I smiled sweetly at him. "Do you want to meet the family?"

He didn't answer. Just shook his head, with an expression like he was close to laughter. "That just sounds so damn normal."

Yeah, it did. And we weren't. Muddied everything up.

The honeymoon was over. That night, Ben and I lay in bed, holding each other, but it was as two people shored up together against the fears of the dark. He twitched in his sleep, like he was fighting something in his dreams. I whispered to him, stroked his hair, trying to calm him. We were near the new moon, on the downhill slide toward the full moon, when the pressure built, when the Wolf started rattling the bars of the cage. I'd forgotten how hard it was to resist when it was all new. I'd had over four years of practice keeping it under control. This was new to him. He was looking to me for guidance, which was perfectly reasonable. But I felt out of my depth most of the time.

Take this place for example. This magic. A family that decided it was okay to hire a bounty hunter to kill their son and pretend like their daughter didn't exist. A family so steeped in magic that all its members were terrified of each other. I didn't understand it.

We thought out loud during the drive back to Shiprock the next day.

"What's the series of events?" I said. "John comes back from Phoenix and he's different. A werewolf. We know how that can mess with someone. Then their oldest daughter, Joan, dies. Then Miriam disappears. They hire Cormac to hunt John."

"It sounds like John coming back from Phoenix as a werewolf was the trigger. Everything else happened after that," he said.

"What was it Tony said? A witch has to make a sacrifice to become a skinwalker. So Miriam cursed Joan, killed her, became a skinwalker."

"But why? Why did she want to do that? And why at that moment?"

"She wanted John to have a pack," I said softly. She didn't want her brother to be alone. It actually made sense, from a twisted point of view. I knew how hard it was to be alone.

"Why didn't she just let him bite her?" Ben said.

I thought about it a moment. Some people wanted to become lycanthropes. They sought it out, got themselves bitten. Why wouldn't Miriam have been one of those?

"Control," I said. "She wanted to be able to control it. She probably saw how it affected John. He wasn't able to control it. She wanted the power without that weakness."

He winced thoughtfully, his face lined with thought. "Thus begins their reign of terror. God, it almost makes sense. But we still can't prove she was dangerous. We need proof that she killed her sister. No one's willing to pursue the connection. Maybe they're afraid she'd take revenge on them. Curse them, kill them—"

"But she's dead. She can't do anything now."

"I'm not sure that changes anything in some people's minds."

Spirits lingered. Evil spirits continued to spread evil. If they—Louise, her family, Tony, others—believed that, I couldn't argue.

Miriam's immediate family may not have lived on a beautiful estate, but at least they had a house, a bit of land, an aura of normality.

Lawrence, on the other hand, lived in an honest-to-God shack, with weathered planks tied together for walls and a corrugated tin roof that seemed to just sit on top, without anything holding it down. It looked like he'd been living this way for years, because the place was actually several shacks attached to each other, as if he'd been adding rooms over the years whenever the mood struck him. The desert scrub around his place was covered with junked equipment, including several cars, or objects that had once been cars. The place was isolated, out on a dirt road, behind a hill, invisible from the town.

The question remained, did he live like this because he had to, or by choice?

"I have a bad feeling about this," Ben said, staring at the desolate house.

"Let's get it over with." I left the car, and Ben slowly followed.

I was afraid to knock on the front door. It looked like a deep sigh would knock it in. I tried it, rapping gently. The walls around it shuddered, but nothing broke.

No one answered, which wasn't entirely surprising. This didn't seem like the kind of place where people threw open the door and welcomed you with hugs. In fact, I kind of expected to hear rattlesnakes or yipping coyotes in the distance.

I knocked again, and waited for another minute of silence. "Well?"

"Nobody's home?" Ben shrugged. "Maybe we can come back later."

We didn't have a whole lot of time to wait. We also didn't have a whole lot of choice. What could we do, drive all over town asking random people where to find Lawrence?

"What do you want?" A man spoke with an accent, as if English wasn't his first language.

We had turned to leave, when the man leaning against the farthest corner of the building spoke. He was shorter than me, thick without being heavyset. He was old, weathered like stone, rough and windblown. His hair hung in a long gray braid.

"What do you want?" he said again, the words clipped and careful.

Ben said, "Are you Lawrence Wilson? Miriam Wilson's grandfather?"

He didn't answer, but Ben stayed calm, and seemed ready to wait him out.

"Yes," the old man said finally. For some reason the word was earth-shattering.

"I don't know if the police have told you—Miriam's been killed."

He nodded, his expression unchanging. "I know."

"We're trying to find out what she did before then."

Did Lawrence smile, just a little? "What is it you think she did?"

"I think she killed her oldest sister."

He slipped past us and opened the front door. It wasn't latched, locked, or anything. It just opened.

"You have proof?" he said.

"Still looking for it."

"And you came here to find it?"

"You filed the missing person report. The rest of her family seems happy enough forgetting about her. But not you. Why?"

Lawrence stood in the doorway, gripping the edge of it. I thought maybe he'd slam the door shut, after a good hard scowl. But he stayed still, watching us with hard, dark eyes.

"If I'd found her first, I could have helped her. I could have stopped her. That's why I filed the report."

"But she never turned up. You didn't find her."

"She didn't want to be found."

He went inside, but he left the door open. Like an invitation.

Ben and I glanced at each other. He gave a little shrug. I followed Lawrence inside, into the cave of the house. I sensed Ben come through the door behind me.

I'd never seen anything like it. The floor was dirt. The place wasn't sturdy. The planks had weathered and warped so that sun showed through the cracks between them, and dust motes floated in the bars of light that came in. In this weird, faded haze, I could make out the room's decorations: bundles of dried plants hung by the stems. Sage, maybe, fronds of yucca, others I couldn't identify. Along the opposite wall hung furs. Animal skins. Eyeless heads and snarling, empty mouths looked at me: the pale hide of a coyote; a large, hulking hide that covered most of the wall—a bear; a sleek, tawny, feline hide of a mountain lion. And a large canine, covered with thick, black fur. Wolf. One of each. His own catalog.

I couldn't smell it. At least, I couldn't smell what I expected. I should have scented the fur, dried skin, herbs, the stuffy air. But all I smelled was death. The stench of it masked everything. And it didn't come from the skins, from the room. It came from Lawrence. I wanted to run screaming.

"You're one, too," I said. "A skinwalker. You taught her."

He stood at the far side of the room, which looked somewhat functional: a table held a camp stove and cooking implements. Lawrence lit a pair of candles, which did nothing to brighten the place.

"No," he said. "She learned. She watched. I was careless. I let her learn."

"You couldn't stop her?" Ben said.

"Couldn't you? You aren't the only one who's been hunting her."

"If you knew what she was, if you taught her—then you had the power to stop her, and you didn't." His voice rose, along with his anger.

"I don't owe you any answers." He went to a box on the floor, a wooden crate that might have held fruits or vegetables for shipping, and pulled out a can. He started cutting it open with an old-fashioned, clawlike can opener.

The wolf skin on the wall had dark, curved claws intact.

"Yes, you do," Ben said. "A man may go to jail unless I bring the court evidence of what she was and what she did."

Lawrence looked at us coldly. "The man who killed my grandson? The man who killed Miriam?"

The strangeness of this place smothered my own anger. I felt strangely calm. "He saved my life when he killed her."

Lawrence was busy lighting the stove and pouring the can of soup into a pot. "You're lucky to have a friend who will kill for you."

So. I once had a friend who died for me, and now one who killed for me. Why didn't I feel lucky?

Ben turned his back on Lawrence and hissed at me. "We're not getting anywhere. He's not going to tell us anything."

"What do you want me to tell?" Lawrence said, and Ben flinched—he thought he'd been whispering. "That she was evil? That I am evil? Do you expect me to tell everything I know as some kind of atonement? What's done is done. Nothing will change it. Nothing will make it better. The dead don't come back."

"Wouldn't bet on that," I muttered.

"I don't have any proof for you. I can tell you that Miriam killed Joan, but the police have no record of it. The doctors say it was natural, not witchcraft. Three of my grandchildren are dead, but you won't find anyone here who will admit that they were ever alive. That's what it is to be a witch here."

"Then why do it? If it makes you disappear." If it made you live in a place like this, isolated, other.

"It never starts out that way. But the line between medicine man and witch, *curandero* and *bruja,* is very thin. The magic comes from the same place. The danger comes with the spells that pull you one way or another. Miriam saw what her brother became, and she wanted it. Donning the coat of a wolf, tasting blood—it pulls you toward the darkness. You understand this. Both of you. You live in the dark because it's what you are."

I did understand, and hated that I did. Wolf seemed to prick her ears up at the very mention of the word blood. Beside me, Ben stood frozen, staring. His eyes weren't his own, not entirely. Something wolfish swam in them. I had to get him out of here. But I wanted more answers.

"Why did she kill Joan?"

"She had a sister to spare? I don't know. Didn't anyone warn you about asking too many questions around here?"

"Who did you kill in trade for your powers?"

He hid a smile with a bowed head. "It's a good thing for a witch to have a large family."

My stomach lurched into my throat; I wanted badly to throw up. I took hold of Ben's arm and squeezed too hard.

Lawrence continued. "Bodies disappear out here. You go out to the desert, a body gets dried up and covered with sand in a day. In a month it's nothing but bones. You tell anyone you were coming out here?"

"Let's go." I wrenched Ben's arm and steered him out of there. The door to Lawrence's shack slipped closed behind us.

Back in the open air, I felt light-headed, giddy—free. I almost ran to the car.

Ben was stewing. Fuming. His shoulders hunched, his fists closed. He kicked the dirt on our path.

"He knows, but we'll never get him into court. He knows Cormac did the world a favor putting a bullet in her. Hell—that guy probably needs a bullet put in him."

"Calm down. We'll figure something out. We still have leads."

But we were running out of them. I tried to stay positive.

I stopped a few paces from the car. Something wasn't right. A sound tickled my throat—the start of a growl.

"Kitty." Ben's voice was tight. He moved toward me, so our shoulders touched. Side by side, protected—but from what?

A mountain lion leapt onto the roof of my car.

It had dodged around us in a couple of strides and made the jump without effort, so quickly I hadn't sensed it coming. Or maybe it had simply been able to slip by without us noticing. The thing was huge, solid, with thick limbs and a wedge-shaped face. It sat tall, its tail wrapped around its paws, looking for all the world like a house cat surveying its domain. Its tan fur was flat and slick, and dark smudges marked its eyes. Red eyes, bright as garnets.

Like somebody in a slapstick comedy, I looked back to the shack, then back at the mountain lion. And yes, the shack's door stood open.

"Kitty . . ." Ben murmured, taking my hand.

"Me or it?"

"Not funny."

We backed away.

The lion jumped off the car and stalked toward us, head low, tail flicking like a whip. Red eyes flashed.

Had to think of a plan. Had to do something. Couldn't just let this thing hypnotize me with its terrible gaze. All I wanted to do was scream. But I recognized the freezing terror that was numbing my limbs. I'd felt this when Miriam attacked me. Had to break out of the witch's spell somehow.

I whispered, "Ben, I'm going to break left. Try to draw him off while you get to the car and call for help."

"I was going to say the same thing, but with me drawing him off and you calling for help."

"No, I can fight him if I have to. I can take him."

"Just like you took Miriam?"

Details . . .

Both of us spoke quickly, breathily, on the verge of panic. I wondered how he was doing with his wolf. I still held his hand, which strained with tension. But no claws had started growing.

The mountain lion took another set of steps and opened its mouth to show thick, yellowed teeth, sharp as nails. It made a sound that was half growl, half purr, grating and skull rattling. Ben and I kept backing, until I slipped on the gravel. His grip on me kept me upright.

The monster crouched, its muscles bunching, gathering itself to jump at us.

"It jumps, we break," I murmured. Ben nodded.

But instead of jumping, it paused, stared at us, blinking those red eyes. It bowed its head. Then, its whole body seemed to collapse. Like the air went out of it. The face crumpled, and the eyes went dead.

A human hand reached out from under the lion's body and pulled off the tawny skin, revealing a naked man crouching in the dirt. A long gray braid draped over his shoulder.

Lawrence Wilson looked up at us and smiled.

"Louise got to you first. Lucky. Very lucky."

I touched my chest, feeling the hard shape of the arrowhead under my shirt. It worked. The damn thing worked.

"Let's get the hell out of here," I muttered to Ben.

Carefully, cautiously, we circled around the old man. Watching us, he stood, but didn't make another move toward us. Quickly we slipped into the car.

The tires kicked up a rain of gravel in my hurry to drive us out of there. Lawrence watched us go, standing at the side of the dirt road. He seemed to hold my gaze in the rearview mirror until we were out of sight. The mountain lion's skin hung limp in his hand.

Around the hill and out of sight, I snuck a glance at Ben. He sat straight against the back of the seat, staring ahead, expressionless.

"You okay?"

After a pause he nodded. "Yeah. I think I am."

We made it off the dirt road and onto pavement. "Good."

Another dusk had fallen by the time we returned to the motel. The sky had turned deep blue, and a cold wind blew across the parking lot. It smelled dry, desiccated, and wild. Wrong. Like something out there was looking for us, and meant us harm. It might have been paranoia. Or not.

We had police reports, death certificates, coroner's reports. We had a couple of statements, a couple of newspaper articles. Tales of crimes that might have happened, of the bad reputation of a certain family, and people who wanted nothing more than the rumors and fear to go away. We didn't have hard evidence that Miriam was anything other than a highly disturbed young woman, or that Cormac had had no choice but to kill her.

We got out of the car. Ben slammed shut the door, lingered, then leaned on the hood and kicked the tire. And kicked it again.

"Would you stop kicking my car?" I said.

Hands on the hood, he leaned over, breathing hard. His anger was getting the better of him, which meant his wolf was getting the better of him.

"Are you okay?"

If he started shifting, I didn't know what I'd do. He didn't have experience keeping it together, when everything around you poked the creature awake. When all you wanted to do was run.

"Ben?"

He turned his head, glancing at me over his arm. He was sweating, despite the cool air. He was so tense he was shivering. I was afraid if I touched him, he'd jump out of his skin. "This place is getting to me. I hate it. I completely fucking hate it."

Sort of like I hated a certain hiking trail where I'd gotten stranded one full moon night, some four and a half years ago.

"Ben, keep it together."

"Will you stop telling me that? It's not helping."

Anything I said now would just be patronizing. "I know it's hard. It'll get easier. It gets easier."

"I don't believe you."

"Look at me. If I can hang on this long, so can you."

He straightened, left the car, and started pacing. Pacing was a wolf thing, a nervous thing, the movement of an animal trapped in a cage. I wanted to grab him, to make him stop.

He said, "No. I don't think so. You're stronger than me."

"How can you say that?" I almost laughed.

"Because you are. You're the one knocking on doors, you're the one keeping me moving. Me—I can't get my hands to stop shaking. I can't get my head on straight. If it weren't for you I'd have shot myself by now. Cormac wouldn't have had to do it."

He hadn't broken yet. I was so proud of him because he'd made

it through one full moon and hadn't broken. But he still could.
Years from now, he still might.

I said, "You didn't see me after I was attacked. I was the same
way you are now."

Looking out across the desert, away from me, he said, "You deserve better than to get stuck with a guy like me." He spoke so
softly I almost didn't hear him.

Pain filled the words. A gut-wrenching, heart-stabbing kind of
pain. Like his heart was breaking. We were pack; his pain became
my pain. I thought I knew what caused it: he wanted us to stay together, and he didn't think we could. Didn't trust that I would stay
with him.

I had to make a joke—I wanted to keep things light. To not face
what was happening. I couldn't even articulate what was happening, it was all gut. Gut and heart. If I didn't make a joke, I'd burst
into tears.

My voice caught. "Are you sure it isn't more like you deserve
better than to get stuck with a girl like me?"

"You could have anyone you want," he said. He turned back to
me. At least he looked at me.

I didn't feel like a good catch. I didn't feel like I had that much
power. "Yeah, that's why I've been way single since before I got
out of college."

"You're still young. Plenty of time."

"You're not exactly falling into your grave."

"Feels like it some days. After thirty you start looking back and
realizing you haven't done a damn thing with yourself."

I wanted to tell him that he was worth the world. That he
shouldn't have any regrets. But I'd really only known him for a
year. I was only beginning to understand the baggage he carried.

Before I could say another word, he was walking to the door of
the motel, leaving me behind.

Ben worked into the night, sitting at the room's tiny table, staring
into his laptop, typing in notes, shuffling through papers, writing
on them. His work spread out to the foot of the bed. I lay under the
covers, trying not to disturb him. Not even pretending to sleep. I let
him work instead of trying to get him to come to bed, like I wanted.
I wanted to jump him and *make* him relax. I wanted him to forget

about work, at least for a little while. I wanted him to believe he was worthwhile.

I flipped through some of the pages that had fallen within my reach. One of them was the coroner's photograph of Miriam's body. I studied it, trying to figure out who she had been. What had been going on in her mind, what had made her think that killing her sister and becoming a shape-shifter was a good idea. What had she been like as a girl. I tried to imagine the four siblings in better days: three sisters and a brother kicking a ball or playing tag in the dusty yard of that house we'd been to. I tried to imagine a young Louise before she'd become so frightened and desperate, laughing with a young Miriam who wasn't dead. Little girls in black pigtails. I could imagine it—but what I couldn't imagine was what had brought them to where they were today.

What brought any of us to where we ended up?

Ben sat back and blew out a heavy sigh. His hair was sticking out from him running his hands through it over and over again. His shirt was open, his sleeves rolled up, and the job didn't seem to be getting any easier.

He left the table and stalked across the room. At first I thought he was heading to the bathroom. But he went to the door.

I sat up. "Ben?"

The door opened and he left the room.

I lunged out of bed, yanked on a pair of sweatpants, and shoved on my sneakers.

"Ben!" I called down the hall at him.

He didn't turn around, so I followed him. He'd already disappeared outside. I trailed him to the parking lot in time to see him take off his shirt and drop it behind him. He continued past the parking lot, through a trashed vacant lot to the desert beyond.

He was going to Change. His wolf had taken over.

We were too close to town. I couldn't let this happen.

"Ben!" I ran.

He was so focused on the path before him, on what was happening inside him, he didn't see me pounding up behind him. He wasn't in tune with those instincts yet, the sounds and smells, the way they bend the air around you and tell you something's wrong.

I tackled him.

I wasn't sure I could take him in a fight. He was stronger than I, but he hadn't had much practice. I half hoped he'd panic and freeze up. I jumped, aimed at the top half of his back, and knocked him over.

Probably wasn't the smartest way I could have handled that.

On the ground now, I sat on top of him, pinning him down, and tried to talk reason. I didn't get a word out before he growled at me—a real, deep-lunged, wolfish growl, teeth bared. His bones slipped under his skin—he was shifting.

"Ben, please don't do this. Listen to me, listen to me—"

Had to keep him on the ground. This had turned into a wolf thing, and this was how the Wolf would handle it. Keep him on the ground, keep on top of him, show him who's in charge.

I much preferred talking things out with the human Ben. The real Ben. But I couldn't argue that this *was* Ben—him with all the frustrations of the last couple of weeks coming to the fore, finally gaining expression and taking over. Deep down I couldn't blame him.

Screaming a cry of pain and frustration, he struggled, his whole body bucking and writhing. I couldn't hold him. I almost did, but then his arm came free and he swiped. He struck, and wolf claws slashed my face. I gasped, more at the shock of it than the pain.

He broke away. In the same movement, the rest of the shift happened, his back arcing, fur rippling across his skin, thick hind legs kicking off his trousers.

"Ben!" My own scream edged into a growl.

This was only his second time as a wolf. He stood, and his legs trembled. He shook himself, as if the fur didn't sit quite right on his body. He looked back at me, and his body slumped, his tail clamping tight between his legs, his ears lying flat. A display of submission. I held the side of my face, which was slick with blood. His slap had cut deep. His wolf was sorry.

I was frozen. Wolf wanted to leap at him. His struggle called her out, and she wanted to run. Keep our pack together. But I was so angry. Anger burned through every nerve and radiated out. She was the alpha and she wanted to prove it.

He ran. The wolf knew better than to stick around to see what I'd do next, so he leapt around and ran, body stretched out, legs working hard.

I sighed, the anger draining out of me. I ought to just let him go. Except that I couldn't. Had to keep him out of trouble.

I wiped blood off my face, wiped my hands on my sweats, and ran after him.

chapter **16**

I could run faster and for longer than someone who wasn't a lycanthrope. But I couldn't hope to keep up with a lycanthrope in wolf
form. I could only track him, hope he knew I was following, and
that maybe he would think about slowing down. Fortunately, his
instincts led him true: away from town, into the open desert.

The night was clear, the air crisp, but the moon was absent. The
world was dark. *Let me go, let me come out, I can see better in the
dark.*

No.

I smelled prey here—jackrabbits, quail. Ben had smelled it, too,
and it slowed him down. I spotted him ahead, trotting now, his head
low, his mouth open, and his tongue hanging.

He must have been tired. Afraid. His movements weren't assured. A wolf's trot should have been graceful, swinging, able to
cover miles without effort. His feet were dragging, his tail hung
low. He wasn't used to this—lucky for me.

"Ben!"

He froze, lifted his head, his ears pricked forward. Then he turned
and ran again.

I leaned on my knees, gathered my breath, and set off after him.

We must have gone on like that for half the night. He wasn't going toward anything. If I hadn't been chasing him, he might have
stopped to try to hunt—I seriously doubted his ability to catch anything in his current state. But he was just running away, and I just
followed. My face bled for a long time; I kept wiping the blood
away and didn't think of it. I only noticed that I hadn't touched my
face in a while when it started itching—scabs had formed and the
healing had started. I could only concentrate on my lungs working
overtime.

I'd lost sight of him, but his scent—musk and fear—blazed a trail. As long as I kept breathing, I could find him.

He came into view again when he slowed to a walk. I stopped following him then. Instead, I cut over obliquely from his trail. Like I'd stopped paying attention. Like I was circling back. I made a wide loop, and watched him out of the corner of my eye.

As I'd hoped, my change in behavior caught his attention. Now, I just had to tell him I was a friend. I almost wish I'd Changed so I'd have the throat to vocalize it. But I did what I could. I moved slowly, relaxed as much as I could manage, my gaze down and limbs loose. Just out for a stroll.

He watched, ears forward, interested. I kept walking, not moving toward him, not doing anything threatening. He should have been able to smell me—I should have smelled familiar, safe. *Come home, Ben. Please.*

He started trotting, taking a path that was parallel to mine. I walked a few more steps, then crouched and watched him. He circled me, not looking at me, swinging along, pretending I wasn't there. But his circles grew smaller, and he came closer. I didn't move, not even to watch him over my back.

Then, he stopped. He was off to my right. We stared at each other. This wasn't a challenge. Both his head and his tail drooped. Our hackles were down. I made a conscious effort to keep my arms and shoulders relaxed. We were asking each other: *Well? What's next?*

He gave the smallest, tiniest whine. A lost and tired breath wheezing through his throat. I stepped forward, crawling on all fours, and I wished I had a tail to hold out to tell him it was okay, that I'd take care of him. "It's okay, Ben. It's going to be okay." I'd been telling him that for two weeks now. I didn't know why he should believe me now.

He reached forward, stretching his body low, and licked my chin. I let him, closing my eyes and touching his shoulder. His fur was hot, his ribs still heaving with the effort of his run. I pressed my face to his neck and breathed deep. He leaned into me, whining softly with each breath.

I just kept saying, *It's okay.*

The wolf lay down, curling up next to me right there in the dirt—I was going to have to teach him how to find a safe place to bed down. But I supposed he figured that settling in next to me was safe enough. He fell asleep quickly. He dreamed, his breaths whining, his legs kicking out a couple of times. Chasing rabbits. Still running.

I'd taken it upon myself to look after him. To take care of him. So I did, staying awake while billions of stars arced overhead, against a velvet-black sky. More black and more stars than I'd ever seen, with no city lights to wash them out. All the clichés you could think of about the humbling vastness of the universe, the awe-inspiring sweep of sky and stars, seemed true now. The two of us might have been alone in the world.

The night was freezing cold, but I had a warm bundle of fur lounging against me and didn't mind so much. I buried my hands in his coat and watched the stars. Enjoyed the moment of peace, and hoped it would extend past this night.

I hummed to pass the time, something slow and classical. Slowly, Ben shifted back to human. This was almost gentle compared to the shift in the other direction. There, the wolf tore out of its human skin. But this, the wolf seemed to slip away, fading, limbs growing, hair thinning until only skin showed. By then, dawn had come, the sky growing pale. A bird sang, a series of high, watery notes—an incongruous beauty in the middle of the cold desert. Even in this desolate place, something lived and thrived.

Ben's skin looked gray, stonelike in the early light. Sitting close to him, I kept my hand on his shoulder, sheltering him. I sensed the moment he awoke; his arm twitched. He snuggled, pillowing his head more comfortably into my lap, which made me smile. I played with a strand of his hair, brushing it back from his forehead. He was awfully cute like this.

He opened his eyes.

"Oh, God." He squeezed them tightly shut again.

"Morning, sunshine," I murmured.

He rubbed a hand over his face, shifted uncomfortably on the hard ground. "What happened?"

"What do you remember?"

He thought for a moment, his brow furrowing. "Getting up. I thought I was going to the bathroom—but I just kept going, didn't I?"

I smiled wryly, brushing damp hair out of his face. That he remembered so little surprised me. I could usually track to the moment I shifted, even though I might forget everything after that. But he hadn't been in control at all.

"Yeah. At least you made it out of the parking lot before you shifted."

He groaned again, sitting up. He touched my sweatpants and shirt, which were smeared with blood. So was my hair, which had gone all dried and crunchy. I didn't want to know how I looked.

He said, "You're bleeding. You're hurt."

"Not anymore. All healed up."

"Did I do it?" I nodded. "God, I'm sorry."

"You can make it up to me later. Take me out for a nice steak dinner."

He thought for a moment, pursing his lips. "We've never even been out on a real date, have we?"

I hadn't thought of it. We'd fallen together by chance. But I didn't believe that anymore, not really, because something pulled at me. Something that kept me from looking away. I couldn't turn away from him.

I shrugged. "No sense in being all traditional."

"Why did you even bother coming after me?" He tilted his head to look out at the horizon. "Why did you bother staying?"

I touched his face. I couldn't not touch him. I held him, made him look at me, made him see my smile. This was another one of those situations that as a human seemed too weird, too strange to even consider. Sitting in the middle of the desert at dawn, me in pajamas, him naked. But it didn't feel strange. Sitting beside him, pulling him into my arms, felt right.

"You're afraid it's just the lycanthropy. That I wouldn't be here if we weren't both werewolves. You should know, I wouldn't have come after just anyone. I wouldn't have taken care of just any new werewolf that showed up on my doorstep. I wouldn't have sat out in the desert all night with just anyone."

He leaned his head against mine. "You're not just saying that to make me feel better?"

"I don't know, do you feel better?" He made an indecisive grumble. "Ben, you're naked. I can't lie to a naked man."

He took my hand, where it rested on his thigh. He studied it, rubbing the back of it with his thumb. "If you can't lie, this is when I should ask you anything. Anything I want to know, now's my chance."

This was the kind of conversation new couples had the morning after sex. I was sure I had no secrets from him—he was my lawyer, for crying out loud. But conversations like this were also tests. Uneasy, I said, "Sure."

"Did you and Cormac ever get together?" He gave a little shrug.

"No. Got close a couple of times. He kept running away."

He nodded, like this didn't surprise him. Like it was the story of Cormac's life. Then he asked, "If I hadn't come along, would you two have eventually gotten together?"

These were questions I was afraid to ask myself.

"I don't know. Ben, why do you need to know this?"

"I'm afraid I've messed things up for him. Again. But it's all 'what ifs' now, isn't it? No way to tell what might have happened."

No. No way at all to tell. Those "what ifs" followed us our whole lives, didn't they? What if I hadn't been at that hiking trail on a full moon night. What if I hadn't met Cormac. What if he hadn't brought Ben to me but shot him instead. What if I'd invited him back to my apartment that one night . . .

I had Ben here with me, not "what ifs." Had to move on.

"You didn't mess anything up. Cormac never had the guts to say anything about it to me."

"Ironic. He's always been the tough one."

Ben had his own kind of toughness. I smiled. "What about you? Are you with me because you want to be, or because you're a victim of circumstance?"

He kissed me gently, a press of warm lips. Took my face in his hands, holding me for a moment. And I felt safe with him.

I stood, rubbing the pins and needles out of my legs, and tugged on his hand. "Come on. We've got a long walk back, and you have no clothes."

He covered his eyes and groaned. "It's just one damn thing after another, isn't it?"

Slowly, he got to his feet, and we walked back, side by side, arms around each other.

We found his clothes on the way back to the motel, which was good. Then we discovered that we'd both left our keys in the room.

Just one damn thing after another.

chapter 17

We spent the morning replacing the tires on Ben's car. Then, he wanted to run an errand. He asked me to come along, and I did. He drove, and I didn't bother to ask where we were going or what he was doing until we ended up on yet another dirt track that led us miles into the desert. We stopped at the bottom of an arroyo, covered with tall scrub, more vegetation than I was expecting to find. Lots of places to hide. This was the kind of area where ranchers grazed herds of sheep, and where wolves liked to run.

I'd never been here, but I recognized it. He didn't have to tell me where we were. He stopped the car, shut off the engine, and looked out, staring hard. He gripped the steering wheel like he was clinging to a lifesaving rope.

"Is this where it happened?" I said.

"Up past the curve there. Cormac drove the Jeep into the clearing. I don't really recognize it in the daylight."

I couldn't guess what he was thinking, why he'd wanted to come here. Wanting to come full circle, hoping to find closure. Something pop-psychological like that.

"You want to get out?" I said.

"No," he said, shaking his head slowly. "I just wanted to see it. See if I could see it."

"Without freaking out?"

"Yeah, something like that. I wondered if there'd be more to this place. If I'd feel something."

"Do you?"

He pursed his lips. "I think I just want to go home." He turned the ignition and put the car in gear.

On the way back to town I said, "I've never been back to the place where it happened to me," I said. "Just never saw much point in going back."

"That's because you've moved on."

"Have I? I guess it depends on what you call moving on. Sometimes I feel like I'm running in circles."

"Do you want to go back? I'll go with you if you want to see it."

I thought about it. I'd replayed that scene in my mind a hundred times, a thousand times, since that night. I realized I didn't want to see the place, and it wasn't because I was avoiding it, or because I was afraid.

Ben was right. I'd come so far since then.

"No, that's okay."

We had lunch at a local diner before heading back to Colorado. We'd be caravanning back in separate cars. I was half worried that Ben might take the opportunity to drive through a guardrail and over a cliff, or into oncoming traffic, like he was still regretting not making Cormac shoot him.

But he seemed okay. He was down, but not out. Some life had come back into his eyes over the last week or so. Even though we were leaving New Mexico with stories, but no hard evidence. Statements, but no witnesses. Nothing to keep Cormac out of court.

Ben slouched in his side of the booth, leaning on the table, his head propped on his hand. "Everybody he's killed—every *thing* he's killed—deserved it. I have to believe that. I have to convince the court of that."

With a sympathetic judge, a less gung-ho prosecutor, or just one person from Shiprock willing to come testify, this probably would all go away. Lawrence had called us lucky, and maybe we were, but only to a point.

What it all came down to in the end: Cormac had shot an injured woman dead in front of the local sheriff, and nothing we could say changed that. And my opinion of Cormac was definitely colored by the fact that the first time we met, he'd been coming to kill me.

"Cormac's not clean, Ben. We both know that."

"We've spent half our lives looking out for each other. I guess it blinds you. I know he's killed people. The thing is, you drop a body down a mine shaft far enough off the main drag, nobody'll ever find it. And nobody's looking for the people he's killed."

Like what Lawrence said about bodies in the desert. Every place had its black hole, where people disappeared and never came back again. It made the world a dark and foreboding place.

"That's how the pack took care of things," I said. "T.J. ended up dumped in a mine shaft somewhere. I hate it."

"Me, too." He stared at nothing, probably mentally reviewing everything we knew, everyone we'd talked to, every fact and scrap of evidence, looking for something he'd missed, waiting for that one piece to slide into place that would fix everything. The check arrived, and I took it—Ben seemed to not notice it. I was about to go pay it when he said, out of the blue, "I should just quit."

"Quit what?"

"The lawyer gig. Too complicated. I should go be a rancher like my dad. Cows and prairie."

"Would that make you happy?"

"I have no idea."

"Don't quit. It'll get better."

A slow smile grew on him. "I won't quit if you won't."

"Quit what?" Now I just sounded dumb.

"Your show."

I hadn't quit. I'd just taken a break, why didn't people understand that?

Because it looked like I quit. Because if I wasn't making plans to go back to it, it meant I'd quit.

"Why not?" I said, feeling contrary. "They have Ariel, Priestess of the Night, now. She can handle it."

"There's room for both of you. You love your show, Kitty. You're good at it."

We were both leaning on the table now, within reach of each other, our feet almost touching underneath. Proximity was doing strange things to me. Sending a pleasant warmth through my gut. Making me smile like an idiot.

It was getting very hard for me to imagine not having Ben around.

I bit my lip, thought for a moment. Grinning, I took a chance. "Better be careful. You keep saying nice things about me I might fall for you or something."

He didn't even hesitate. "And you're cute, smart, funny, great in bed—"

I kicked him under the table—gently. "Flatterer."

"Whatever it takes to keep you coming after me when I go around the bend."

I touched his hand, the one lying flat on the table. Curled my fingers around it. He squeezed back, almost desperately. He was still scared. Getting better at hiding it, at overcoming it. But still scared, at least a little.

"Of course I will. We're pack."

He nodded, picked up my hand, brought it to his lips. Kissed the fingers. Then without a word he grabbed the check, slid out of the booth, and went to the front counter to pay.

Bemused, I followed.

Back in Walsenburg the next day, Espinoza was late for our meeting. The last meeting before the hearing. The last chance to convince him to drop the charges against Cormac. Ben had shaved, gotten a haircut, and looked as polished as I'd ever seen him. He had on his best suit this time. Even I put on slacks and a blouse and put my hair up. He paced along the wall with the window, in a conference room in the courthouse. Slowly, with measured steps. Not an angry, desperate, wolfish pacing. Just nerves. He held a pen and tapped it against his opposite hand, glanced out the window as he passed it.

I sat in a chair by the wall and watched him. He was a handsome, competent, intelligent, determined man. And none of that was enough to help Cormac.

The door opened, and the young prosecutor blazed in, like a general in wartime.

"Mr. O'Farrell, sorry to keep you waiting." He glanced at me, his look questioning.

Ben was right on top of things. "No problem. This is Kitty Norville, she's helping me with the case."

Espinoza nodded, and his smile seemed more like a smirk. "The infamous uninjured Kitty Norville."

"I heal fast."

"Real fast, apparently."

"Yeah."

"Too bad for Mr. Bennett. If you'd ended up in the hospital he might have had a case."

Of all the low, blunt, arrogant, shitty things to say . . .

"That kind of talk isn't really appropriate," Ben said, the picture of calm professionalism.

"Of course. I'm sorry, Ms. Norville."

My smile felt wooden.

"If you don't mind, I'd like to get moving on this," Ben said, handing Espinoza a written report.

Ben explained the report, a formal, legalistic retelling of everything we'd found in Shiprock. Somehow, between then and now, between his abrupt shape-shifting and our night in the desert and the drive back, he'd compiled our adventures into a narrative that sounded dry, believable, and even logical. He said that according to the local police Miriam had had a reputation for violence, that her younger sister Louise believed that Miriam killed her older sister Joan, that we'd been threatened by her grandfather Lawrence—in short, that the family's history and Miriam's character suggested that she was prone to murderous violence and it was entirely reasonable to assume that her motives here—against me and the others who'd witnessed the encounter—were violent. That Cormac had had no choice but to stop her.

Espinoza seemed to consider all this. He studied the report, tapping a finger on his chin, and nodded seriously. Then he said, "And what of the fact that she had only her bare hands as a weapon? Was a naked woman dressed in a wolf skin really that threatening?"

That was where Ben's scenario fell apart. We had no way to prove that she wasn't just a woman in a wolf skin.

Ben said, "You have four signed statements from witnesses who swear she would have killed someone. Two more statements from Shiprock. All of them saying that she was more than a woman in a wolf costume."

"Four people at night whose perceptions were muddled by fear and the dark, rendering their testimony somewhat unreliable."

They were testing each other, I realized. Practicing the arguments they'd have to use against each other in court. This was a practice run, to see if each really had a chance of beating the other.

Espinoza tapped the pages. "You've got hearsay. You've got nothing."

"I have enough to raise a reasonable doubt in front of a jury. You'll never land a murder one conviction."

"None of this is verified. I'll have it all disallowed. As I said—you've got nothing, and I will land the conviction. Your client's use of excessive force removes any protection under the law he might have had."

Ben turned away and crossed his arms. He was through arguing. I waited for a growl, a snarl, a hint that the wolf was breaking through. His shoulders hunched a little, like hackles. That was it.

"Mr. O'Farrell, for what it's worth, I believe you," Espinoza said, his tone turning sympathetic. I couldn't help but feel it was false sympathy—he was getting ready to bargain, softening Ben up. "I believe *this*. The skinwalker story, all of it. I grew up in this area, I've seen things that make no sense in the light of day. But you know how it goes in court. No judge is going to let you stand there and say she was a skinwalker, and that's the only way you can justify why Mr. Bennett did what he did."

Ben turned back to him. "If you believe, then this doesn't have to go court. A judge never has to see it. Drop the charges. You know the truth, you know he was justified. Drop the charges."

Espinoza was already shaking his head, and my gut sank. "Sheriff Marks is standing by his testimony. If I won't prosecute, he'll find someone else to do the job."

Ben said, "Marks threatened my client. He's a biased witness."

"That's for the judge to decide," Espinoza said, giving no doubt how he thought the judge would decide. "If both sides' witnesses are discredited, it'll come down to the coroner's report." The coroner's report that said Cormac shot a woman in the back, then killed her when she was already dying.

"So I guess that's it," Ben said curtly.

"No." Espinoza produced a paper of his own and handed it across the table. Ben read it while the prosecutor explained. "I can offer a plea agreement. It's very generous, and I think based on the circumstances it's the best any of us will get out of the situation."

Espinoza didn't seem to be in a hurry. He sat back and gave Ben plenty of time to read the document. Ben must have read it half a dozen times. I could hear the electric hum of the clock on the wall.

"Any questions?" Espinoza said.

Ben lay the paper aside. "You're right. It's generous. I'll have to talk it over with my client."

"Of course. Mr. O'Farrell, Ms. Norville." He gathered up his things and took his leave.

I waited another minute. Ben still hadn't moved. "Ben? You okay?"

He tapped the tabletop, then pressed a fist into it. Seemed to grind his knuckles into the wood. "I'm trying to figure out what I did wrong. I keep trying to figure it out."

My guess was he hadn't done anything wrong. Sometimes you did everything right and you still lost.

We went to the jail to visit Cormac.

The three of us sat in a small, windowless room, on hard, plastic seats, around a hard, plastic table, saturated with fluorescent lights and the smells of old coffee and tired bodies. Ben had his briefcase open, papers spread in front of us, everything we'd found in New Mexico, everything Espinoza had laid out for us. Cormac read through them all.

"Espinoza will lower the charge to manslaughter in exchange for a guilty plea. Two to six years max. Otherwise, the charge stays first-degree murder and we go to trial. Mandatory life sentence if convicted." Ben explained it all, then finished, spreading his hands flat on the table, like he was offering himself as part of the evidence.

The silence stretched on forever. No one would look at anyone. We stared at the pages, but they all said the same thing.

Then Cormac said, "We'll take the plea bargain."

Immediately Ben countered. "No, we have to fight it. A jury will see it our way. You didn't do anything wrong. You saved everyone there. We're not going to let them hang you out to dry."

Cormac took a deep breath and shook his head. "Espinoza's right. We all know how this is going to look in court. Everyone may be willing to sit here and talk about skinwalkers and the rest of it, but it won't hold up in court. The law hasn't caught up with it yet."

"Then we'll make them catch up. *We'll* set the precedents—"

Still, he shook his head. "My past's caught up with me. We knew it would sooner or later. This way, they put me away for a couple years, I get out and keep my nose clean, I'll get over it. If this guy pins murder one on me, I'll be in for decades. I've taken too many risks. I've gambled too much to think I can win this time. Time to cut our losses."

"Think about it, a felony conviction on your record. Don't—"

"I can handle it, Ben."

"I won't let you do this."

"It's my choice. I'll fire you and make the deal myself."

Ben bowed his head until he was almost doubled over. His hands closed into fists. Anger—anger made the wolf come to the surface. I half expected claws to burst from his fingers. I didn't know what we'd do if Ben shifted here, how we'd explain it to the cops. How we'd get him under control.

Ben straightened, letting out a breath he'd been holding. "Don't think you have to do some kind of penance because of what happened to me."

"It's not about you. If I hadn't taken that last shot . . ." He shook his head. "This is about folding a bad hand. Let it go."

"I feel like I've failed."

"You did the best you could. We both did."

Ben collected his papers, shoving them into his briefcase, not caring if they bent or ripped. I didn't know what to do or say; I was almost bursting, wanting to say something that would hold everyone together. That would somehow make this easier. Fat, hairy chance.

Ben said, "The hearing's in an hour. We'll enter a guilty plea. The judge will review the case and pass sentence. We've got Espinoza's word, six years max. They try anything funny, we'll file a complaint, get this switched to another jurisdiction. They'll be coming to get you in a couple of minutes. Is there anything else? Anything I've forgotten? Anything you need?" He looked at his cousin, a desperate pleading in his eyes. He wanted to be able to do more.

"Thanks, Ben. For everything."

"I didn't do anything."

Cormac shrugged. "Yeah, you did. Can I talk to Kitty alone for a minute? Before the goons come back."

"Yeah. Sure." Gaze down, Ben gathered up his things, threw me a quick glance, and made a beeline out the door.

That left the two of us alone, him in his orange jumpsuit sitting at the table, arms crossed, frowning. His expression hadn't changed; he still looked emotionless, determined. Though toward what purpose now, I couldn't guess.

I hugged my knees, my heels propped on the edge of the chair, trying not to cry. And not succeeding.

"What's wrong?" Cormac said, and it was an odd question coming from him. Wasn't it obvious? But it was an acknowledgment of emotion. He'd noticed. He'd been watching me closely enough to notice, and that fact was somehow thrilling.

Thrilling, to no purpose.

"It's not fair," I said. "You don't deserve this."

He smiled. "Maybe I don't deserve it for this. But I'm no hero. You know that."

"I can't imagine not being able to call you for help." I wiped tears away with the heels of my hands. "Cormac, if things had been just a little different, if things had somehow worked out between us—"

But it didn't bear thinking on, so I didn't finish the thought.

"Will you look after Ben for me?" he said. "Keep him out of trouble."

I nodded quickly. Of course I would. He slowly pushed his chair back and stood. I stood as well, clumsily untangling my legs. We didn't have much time. The cops would open the door any second and take him away.

Face-to-face now, we regarded each other. Didn't say a word. He put his hands on either side of my face and kissed my forehead, lingering a moment. Taking a breath, I realized. The scent of my hair. Something to remember.

I couldn't stop tears from falling. I wanted to put my arms around him and cling to him. Hold him tight enough to save him.

He lightly brushed my cheeks with his thumbs, wiping away tears, and turned away just as the door opened, and the deputies came at him with handcuffs.

Ben and I waited in the hallway, side by side, watching them lead Cormac away, around the corner, and out of sight. Cormac never looked back. I held Ben's arm, and he curled his hand over mine.

We'd lost a member of our pack.

Epilogue

I had to admit, being back at a radio station felt like coming home again. Like meeting a long-lost friend. I thought I'd be scared. I thought I'd dread the moment when that ON AIR sign lit. I discovered, though, that I couldn't wait. I had so much to talk about.

We'd set up the show in Pueblo, as far north as I dared to go. I'd packed up the house in Clay and left for good. It was time to head back to civilization. I had a lot of work to catch up on. Even Thoreau hadn't stayed at Walden Pond forever.

I held the phone to my ear but had stopped paying attention to the voice on the line. I was too busy enjoying the dimly lit studio, taking it all in, the sights and smells, the hum of jazz playing on the current music program.

". . . don't take too many this time, let yourself get back into practice." Matt, the show's original sound guy from back in Denver, was talking at me over the phone. Giving me a pep talk or something.

"Yeah, okay," I rambled.

"Are you even listening to me?"

"Yes." I was unconvincing.

Matt sighed dramatically. "I was saying you shouldn't take too many calls. Don't overwhelm yourself. You should spend most of the time on your interview."

For tonight's show I had scheduled a phone interview with Dr. Elizabeth Shumacher, the new head of the Center for the Study of Paranatural Biology, now organized under the auspices of the National Institute of Allergy and Infectious Diseases. I liked her a lot—she was smart, articulate, and much more forthcoming than the Center's previous director.

Next week was going to be even better: I'd convinced Tony and Alice to come in to talk about what had happened in Clay. They'd talk about where each of them learned their particular brands of spellcraft, and I'd get to tell my own personal ghost stories.

I hadn't yet found anyone willing to come on the air to talk about skinwalkers. I planned on running my mouth about it and hoped someone called in with a good story.

Yeah, *The Midnight Hour* was back, just like the old days.

Matt was *still* talking. I should have been more responsive.

I interrupted. "How about I take a lot of calls, but let Dr. Shumacher deal with them? I'll just referee."

He paused for a beat, then said, "I'm not sure that's such a great idea."

"Stop worrying, Matt. I'll be fine. You know if it gets really bad I'll break for station ID anyway."

"I just keep thinking that one of these days you'll break for station ID and not come back."

"Come on, I always come back."

"Then if you're all set, I'll hand it over to the local crew."

"We'll be fine."

Ben came into the room then. I beamed at him and waved. He smiled tiredly and sat in a chair by the wall.

"I can stay on the line to help out if you think—"

"Matt—we're fine. If we need you we'll call."

"Okay. If you're sure."

"I'm sure. Thank you, Matt."

"I'll talk to you later."

We hung up, and I turned my attention to Ben.

He'd just come from Cañon City where he'd checked on Cormac, who now and for the next four years resided at the Colorado Territorial Correctional Facility. The very thought of it was gutwrenching. But it could have been so much worse. That was what we'd all ended up telling each other. It could have been worse. This way, he'd be out in no time. We'd see him again soon.

I'd just have to make sure I kept out of trouble until then.

Ben looked exhausted. His hair had that sweaty, spiky look that meant he'd been messing it up for hours. A nervous habit. Then I noticed he carried a thick stack of paper, bound together by a rubber band, under his arm. It was the manuscript for a book. *My* book.

I'd finished it. I'd given it to him to read. Now, I wasn't sure I wanted to talk to him. I didn't want to know.

Yes, I did.

"Well?"

"Well, he's doing okay. Says the food stinks, but what do you expect? Says he's catching up on his reading." In fact, Cormac— the bastard—had asked me for a reading list, since I was always saying nobody read anymore. "I'm wondering if maybe the time off will do him some good. Does that sound weird?"

I felt bad that I'd really been asking about the book. I gave him a sympathetic smile. "No, it doesn't. You want him to find something else to do with himself. Give up the hunting."

"This all does seem kind of like a sign in that direction, doesn't it?"

"What would he do if he didn't do the bounty-hunting thing?"

"I don't know. He grew up on a ranch, like me. His dad was an outfitter, guided hunting expeditions and that sort of thing. Cormac used to work with him. Yeah, I guess I'm thinking that spending some time without a gun in his hand will give him the idea that he can do something else."

I was torn between agreeing with him, and writing the whole idea off as silver lining bullshit. I wanted Cormac out. I wanted him free.

Even with Ben here, even with everything that had happened to build the bond that now existed between us, part of me still asked, *What if.* What if Cormac hadn't run off, what if we'd managed to make a connection—

"I already miss him," Ben said. "My phone rings and I keep hoping it's his number on the caller ID. Even though I know better."

"Yeah," I said. "You know what he said, at the end of that last meeting in Walsenburg?" Ben raised a questioning brow, and I answered, "He asked me to take care of you. To keep you out of trouble."

"Did he, now?" Ben said, smiling. "He said the same thing to me about you."

I might have blushed. I did look away. It was almost like Cormac was giving us each a mission, to keep our minds off him.

I said, "Does he have so little faith in our ability to take care of ourselves?"

"Can you blame him?"

No, I couldn't. "Is he going to be the same when he gets out?"

"I don't know. He's been through worse than this. But who knows? Am I the same? Are you the same? I wonder sometimes what you were like before the lycanthropy, if we would have had the time of day for each other. I guess—some of him'll be the same, some'll be different. We'll just have to see what stays and what doesn't."

Like peeling back the bandages after surgery, hoping it worked. Praying it isn't worse. It made me feel so out of control.

"How did you do?" What I meant was: how did his wolf do.

"I kept it together. But I hate how that place smells."

I bet he did. I didn't want to think about how it smelled. "So. What did you think of it?" I gestured to the manuscript in his lap.

Idly, he flipped through the top half of the pages, around the rubber band, wearing a studious expression. He made some noncommittal noises that might have expressed a positive or negative opinion. My anxiety increased. If the whole thing was crap, I wasn't sure I could start over.

"I have to admit, I especially like the chapter called 'Ten Ways to Defeat Macho Dickheadism.' " I couldn't tell if he was joking or not. Or if the joke was at my expense.

I felt like I was eight years old and begging. "But what about the whole thing? Did you like it? Is it any good? Should I just give it all up and go into accounting?"

He chuckled and shook his head. Then, he set his joking manner aside. "It's good. It's not what I was expecting . . . but it's good. I think it'll go over like gangbusters."

It hadn't turned out the way I was expecting either. The publisher came to me wanting a memoir, a look back at my past experiences. It had ended up being more about the present, and a little about the future.

"Thanks—I mean, thanks for reading it. I really needed you to read it since you and Cormac ended up in it, at least a little bit."

"Yeah, that's what I wasn't expecting. But it's subtle. You don't use our names, but it's all there. I don't know how you got some kind of message, some kind of optimism out of that mess."

"Don't you know I'm an idealist?"

"God help us all."

The producer from the station, a young woman, the usual public radio night owl staff, leaned in the doorway and said, "Kitty, you've got one minute. We have Dr. Shumacher on the line."

"Thanks," I said to her, and she ducked back out. To Ben I said, "You going to stay and watch?"

"Sure, if you don't mind."

I didn't. I was glad to have him around. I found the headphones, adjusted the mike, checked the monitor, found my cue sheet. I didn't think I'd listen to Matt; I'd take as many calls as I wanted.

Because when I got right down to it, everybody was right: I loved this. I'd missed it.

The ON AIR sign lit, and the music cued up, guitar chords strumming the opening bars of CCR's "Bad Moon Rising." Sounded like angels. And there I was, just me and the microphone. Together again. Here we go—

"Good evening, one and all. I'm Kitty Norville, bringing you an all-new episode of *The Midnight Hour*, the show that isn't afraid of the dark or the creatures who live there . . ."

About the Author

CARRIE VAUGHN survived the nomadic childhood of the typical Air Force brat, with stops in California, Florida, North Dakota, Maryland, and Colorado. She holds a master's in English literature and collects hobbies—fencing and sewing are currently high on the list. She lives in Boulder, Colorado, and can be found on the Web at www.carrievaughn.com.

THE
Science Fiction
BOOK CLUB®

If you enjoyed this book...
Come visit our Web site at

www.sfbc.com

and find hundreds more:
- science fiction • fantasy
- the newest books
- the greatest classics

THE SCIENCE FICTION BOOK CLUB

has been bringing the best of science fiction and fantasy
to the doors of discriminating readers for over 50 years.
For a look at currently available books and details on how to join,
just visit us at the address above.